KU-309-487

READER'S DIGEST

CONDENSED BOOKS

FIRST EDITION

THE READER'S DIGEST ASSOCIATION LIMITED
25 Berkeley Square, London W1X 6AB

THE READER'S DIGEST ASSOCIATION
SOUTH AFRICA (PTY) LTD
Nedbank Centre, Strand Street, Cape Town

Printed in Great Britain by Petty & Sons Ltd, Leeds

Original cover design by Jeffery Matthews M.S.I.A.

ISBN 0 340 23152 1

Reader's Digest
CONDENSED BOOKS

HUNGRY AS THE SEA

Wilbur Smith

THE GOLD OF TROY

Robert Payne

THE SCOFIELD DIAGNOSIS

Henry Denker

THE LANTERN NETWORK

Ted Allbeury

COLLECTOR'S LIBRARY
EDITION

In this volume

HUNGRY AS THE SEA
by Wilbur Smith (p. 9)

Once Nick Berg was the chairman of a powerful shipping company. Now, a near bankrupt, he sets out with grim determination to make a new life for himself on the oceans he loves—and to revenge himself upon the man who ruined him. But the sea, as always, proves a fickle friend, a dangerous ally. . . .

THE GOLD OF TROY *by Robert Payne* (p. 185)

Heinrich Schliemann: penniless grocer's assistant; millionaire businessman; world-famous archaeologist—his career as amazing as his discoveries, numbering among them the fabled burial places of ancient kings, and priceless treasuries of ornate gold, exquisitely beautiful.

THE SCOFIELD DIAGNOSIS
by Henry Denker (p. 271)

Dr. Jean Scofield was worried. If only she were left alone to treat her young patient she was sure she could cure him. But she had enemies, both inside and outside the hospital. Even little Bobby's parents did not trust her. . . .

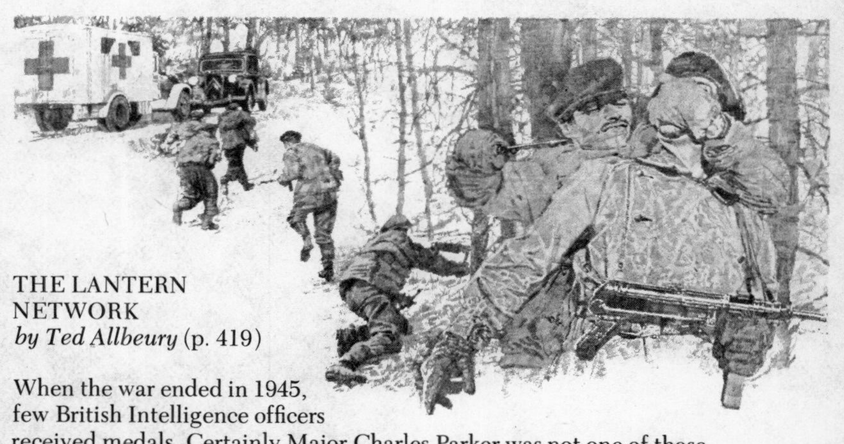

THE LANTERN NETWORK
by Ted Allbeury (p. 419)

When the war ended in 1945, few British Intelligence officers received medals. Certainly Major Charles Parker was not one of those favoured. His heroism unrewarded, he had died as secretly as he had lived—and as bravely. Or so his widow had always believed. For some, however, 1945 had marked not so much the end of one war as the beginning of another.

HUNGRY AS THE SEA

a condensation of the book by

Wilbur Smith

Illustrated by Michael Turner, John Rose
Published by Heinemann

Once Nick Berg had been riding high: happily married, the wealthy chairman of a successful shipping line. Now, robbed of both wife and livelihood by the suave Duncan Alexander, he is alone in the world, master only of the one small ship he sails in.

But *Warlock* is no ordinary ship, and Nick no ordinary master. Grimly determined to recover his lost fortune, he now captains the most modern and powerful salvage tug afloat. And, when a distress call comes from one of Duncan's luxury liners, drifting helplessly towards Antarctica, he knows that a vital prize is within his grasp.

But Nick has formidable adversaries: Duncan, poised now to complete his ruin; Levoisin, a rival salvage man racing to the same disabled vessel; and, above all, the savage fury of wind and sea. His mind set upon the success of his desperate enterprise, Nick scarcely sees the beautiful young survivor brought on board his ship. But Samantha Silver is a powerful, passionate woman, not one lightly to be ignored. . .

In this, his latest best-selling novel, the author of *Eagle in the Sky* now weaves a forceful story of the untameable oceans: an irresistible tale of high adventure—tumultuous, passionate, wholly absorbing.

PART ONE

Nick Berg stepped out of the taxi onto the floodlit Cape Town dock and paused to look up at *Warlock*.

Despite the exhaustion that fogged his mind, he felt a stir of the old pride. She looked like a warship, sleek and deadly, her superstructure was moulded steel and glittering armoured glass. Her high-flared bows and the swept-back wings of her main navigation bridge combined to make her safe in the cruellest weather and most murderous seas, while overlooking the wide stern deck was a second bridge, from which great winches and drums of cable could be operated to control a wallowing oil rig or a mortally wounded liner. High twin towers, between which was a miniature heliport, replaced the squat single funnel of the old-fashioned salvage tugs, and the illusion of a man-of-war was heightened by fire cannons on the upper platforms from which *Warlock*, fireproofed herself, could throw fifteen hundred tons of sea water an hour onto a burning vessel.

Nick felt a little of the despondency and spiritual exhaustion slough away, as he started towards the gangplank. "The hell with them all," he thought. "I built her and she is strong and good."

Although it was an hour before midnight, all of *Warlock*'s crew had turned out to see him arrive and they now filled every vantage point. David Allen, the young first officer, looking like a schoolboy under his shaggy bush of sun-bleached hair, stood with the chief engineer in the glassed wing of the main navigation bridge, and they watched the solitary figure pick his way across the shadowy dock.

"So that's him." David's voice was husky with awe.

"He's a bloody film star." Vinny Baker, the Australian chief engineer, hitched up his sagging trousers and his spectacles slid down the long thin nose as he snorted with scorn.

"He was first mate to our old rival, Jules Levoisin," David pointed out. "He's a tug man from way back."

"That was fifteen years ago." Vinny released his grip on his trousers and pushed his spectacles up on the bridge of his nose. "Since then he's become a master—and an owner. You'd better go down and kiss him." Vinny snorted again, and drifted off to the sanctuary of his control room, two decks down, where neither masters nor owners could touch him.

David was breathless and flushed when he reached the entry port. The new master was halfway up the gangway, and he lifted his head and looked steadily at the mate as he stepped aboard.

Though he was only a little above average stature, Nick Berg gave the impression of towering height, and the shoulders beneath the blue cashmere of his jacket were wide and powerful. He wore no hat and his hair was very dark, very thick and brushed back from a wide unlined forehead. The face was big-nosed and gaunt-boned, a heavy jaw blue now with new beard, and the eyes were set deep in the cages of their boney sockets, underlined with dark plum-coloured smears.

David was shocked by the face. Its pallor was that of exhaustion close to death. This was not the face of the legendary Golden Prince of Christy Marine that David had seen so often in newspapers and magazines. Surprise made him mute as Nick stopped and looked down at him.

"David Allen?" Nick's voice was low and resonant.

"Yes, sir. Welcome aboard."

Nick smiled and the edges of tiredness smoothed away at the corners of his mouth. His hand was cool but his grip was firm enough to make David blink.

"I'll show you your quarters, sir."

"I know the way," Nick said. "I designed her."

Minutes later he stood in the centre of the master's day cabin.

"Mac's funeral went off all right?" he asked.

"Yes, sir."

"The master was a good man," Nick said. "He and I were shipmates once."

"He told me. He used to boast about that."

Nick stood quietly for a moment, thinking about the late master, killed when a tow cable had parted and taken off his head like a bullwhip.

Exhaustion had softened Nick so that for a moment he was on the point of explaining why he had come to take command of *Warlock* himself rather than sending another hired man to replace Mac, but he forced aside the temptation. He had never whined for sympathy in his life.

"Please give my apologies to your officers," he said. "I have not had much sleep in the last two weeks, and the flight out from Heathrow was murder. I'll meet them in the morning."

He turned and staggered into his night cabin.

HE AWOKE with the anger on him. When he shaved, the mirrored face was grim, and in the early sunlight he noticed for the first time a flash of silver in his hair.

"Forty," he thought. "I'll be forty this January."

He had always believed that if a man never caught the big wave before he was forty he was doomed never to do so. So what were the rules for the man who caught the big one before he was thirty, and rode it fast and hard and high, then lost it again before he was forty and was wiped out into the trough of boiling white water? Was he doomed also?

Nick stepped into the shower and let the needles of hot water sting his chest. Through the tiredness he was aware, for the first time in months, of the underlying strength which he had begun to doubt was still there. He felt it rising to the surface—he had needed only a deck under him and the smell of the sea to arouse it. He realized that his decision not to replace Mac with a hired skipper had been the right one. He needed to be here himself.

He dried and dressed swiftly, then went up the master's private companionway to the upper deck.

Immediately the wind flew at him and flicked his dark wet hair into his face. It was force five from the southeast, and it came boiling over the great flat-topped mountain which crouched above the city and harbour. Nick looked up at it and saw the thick white cloud they called the "table cloth" spilling off the heights, and swirling along the grey rock cliffs.

This was the "Cape of Storms", where the tip of Africa thrust southwards into one of the most treacherous seas on all the globe. Here, where wind opposed current in eternal conflict, two oceans swept turbulently together. Here also was one of the world's busiest sea lanes, as a procession of giant oil tankers ploughed on its endless shuttle between the Western world and the Gulf of Persia. That was why Nick had stationed *Warlock* here at Cape Town on the southernmost tip of Africa; for despite their bulk those supertankers were perhaps the most vulnerable vessels yet designed by man.

Still feeling the strength and excitement surging upwards in him, Nick made his way down to the saloon for breakfast.

He stepped into the room and nobody realized he was there. There was an excited buzz of comment and speculation that absorbed them all. The chief engineer had an old copy of "Lloyd's List" folded at the front page and held above a plate of eggs as he read aloud. His spectacles had slid right to the end of his nose, and his Australian accent twanged like a guitar.

"—in a statement issued by the new chairman a tribute was paid to the fifteen years of loyal service that Mr. Nicholas Berg had given to Christy Marine—"

The five officers listened avidly, ignoring their breakfasts—until David Allen glanced up at the figure in the doorway.

"Captain, sir!" he shouted and leapt to his feet, while with the other hand he snatched the newspaper out of Vinny Baker's hands and bundled it under the table. "Sir, may I present the officers of *Warlock*."

Shuffling, embarrassed, the junior officers shook hands hurriedly and then applied themselves silently to their breakfasts. Nick took the master's seat at the head of the long table and David sat down on the crumpled sheets of newsprint.

The steward offered Nick a dish of stewed fruit.

"I'd like a boiled egg," said Nick mildly.

At that moment a huge man appeared from the galley, in a snowy apron and a theatrical chef's cap. He moved like a dancer, and wore his hair in a shiny, carefully coiffured bob that fell to his right shoulder. In the lobe of his left ear shone a small diamond earring. He gestured towards the stewed fruit with a hand as hairy as that of a gorilla, but his voice was as lyrical as a girl's.

"The sailor's curse is constipation, Skipper," he said. "I'm doing you your eggs now, dear, but eat your fruit first. It'll do you good." The diamond twinkled as he vanished.

Nick stared after him in the appalled silence.

"Fantastic cook," blurted David, his fair skin flushing pinkly. "Could get a job on any liner, could Angel. Also, he's almost a doctor. He did five years at medical school."

"It's useful to have a doctor aboard," said Vinny Baker.

Nick picked up his spoon, and lifted a little of the fruit to his mouth. Every officer watched intently. Nick took another spoonful.

"You should taste his jams, sir," David said.

"Thank you, gentlemen, for the advice," said Nick, the smile crinkling his eyes. "But would somebody convey a message to Angel that if he ever calls me 'dear' again I'll beat that ridiculous cap down about his ears."

In the relieved laughter that followed Nick turned to David and sent colour flying to his cheeks again by asking, "You seem to have finished with that old copy of 'The List', Number One. Do you mind if I glance at it again?"

Reluctantly David lifted himself and produced the newspaper and there was another tense silence as Nick rearranged the rumpled sheets and studied the year-old news story without any apparent emotion.

THE GOLDEN PRINCE OF CHRISTY MARINE DEPOSED

Nick hated that name. It had been old Arthur Christy's quirk to name all of his vessels with the prefix "golden" and twelve years ago, when Nick had rocketed to head of operations at Christy Marine, some wag had stuck that label on him.

> Managing director in charge of operations, Mr. Nicholas Berg helped to build Christy Marine from a small coasting and salvage

company into one of the five largest owners of cargo shipping operating anywhere in the world.

After the death of Mr. Arthur Christy in 1968, Mr. Nicholas Berg succeeded him as chairman, and continued the London-based company's spectacular expansion. Christy Marine is now building the 1,000,000-ton ultra-tanker *Golden Dawn*, which will be the largest vessel ever launched.

In 1965 Mr. Nicholas Berg married Miss Chantelle Christy, the only child of Mr. Arthur Christy. However, the marriage ended in divorce in September of last year and the former Mrs. Berg has subsequently married Mr. Duncan Alexander, the new chairman of Christy Marine.

Nick felt a hollow feeling in his stomach. He did not want to think of her now, but could not thrust the vivid image aside. She was bright and beautiful as a flame—and like a flame you could not hold her. When she went she took everything with her—the company, his life's work, and the child. When he thought of the child he nearly succeeded in hating her as he hated Duncan, and the newsprint shook in his hand. He became aware again that the five men were watching him—and hurriedly controlled himself. To be a player in one of the world's highest games of chance, inscrutability was a minimum requirement.

. . . the new chairman paid a tribute . . .

Duncan Alexander had paid the tribute for one reason, Nick thought grimly. He had wanted the 100,000 Christy Marine shares that Nick had owned. Those shares had been very far from a controlling interest. Chantelle had a million shares in her own name, and there were another million in the Christy Trust—but Duncan had realized that Nick's holding would strengthen his position in the company.

Using all Christy Marine's reserves to block and frustrate Nick, it had taken Duncan Alexander almost a year to get those shares —Nick's meagre reward for the labour with which he had built up a fortune of sixty million dollars for the Christy father and daughter. He and Duncan had bargained with cold loathing. They had hated each other from the first day that Duncan had walked into the Christy building in Leadenhall Street. He had come as old Arthur Christy's latest *Wunderkind*, the financial genius fresh from his triumphs in International Electronics. In the end, Nick had driven a dangerous bargain, taking as full payment the subsidiary of Christy Marine—Christy Towage and Salvage—all its assets and all its debts.

Nick lowered the news sheet, and immediately his officers attacked their breakfasts ravenously once again.

"There is an officer missing," he said.

"It's only the Trog, sir," David said. "The radio officer, Speirs. We call him the Troglodyte."

"He never comes out of his cave," Vinny Baker explained.

"All right." Nick nodded. "I will speak to him later."

They waited now, five eager men, and even Vinny could not completely hide his interest behind the tough Aussie veneer.

"I want to explain to you the new set-up. The chief has kindly read to you this article—presumably for the benefit of those who were unable to do so for themselves a year ago." Nobody said anything, but Vinny fiddled with his porridge spoon. "So you are aware that I am no longer connected in any way with Christy Marine. I have now acquired Christy Towage and Salvage. It becomes a completely independent company. The name has been changed to Ocean Towage and Salvage. We own two vessels—this one, formerly called *Golden Warlock*, and her sister ship, formerly called *Golden Sea Witch*, now almost ready for her sea trials."

He knew exactly how much the company owed on those two ships. He had agonized over the figures through long and sleepless nights, before he had given up his Christy shares, valued at three million dollars, for the company. On paper its assets were worth around four million dollars, but had debts for nearly four million more. If he missed just one month's interest payments on those debts—he dismissed the thought quickly, for on a forced sale his residue in the company would be worth nothing. He would be completely wiped out.

"It may interest you to know that the word 'Golden' has been dropped from the name not only of this ship but also from that of her sister. 'Golden' is a dirty word around Ocean Salvage. . . ."

They laughed then, a release of tension.

"I will be running this ship until *Sea Witch* is commissioned. It won't be long—and then there will be promotions." Nick superstitiously touched the mahogany mess table. A dockyard strike in France had been brewing since Christmas. *Sea Witch* was still on the way there, costing interest, and further delay could prove fatal. "I have tendered for an Esso oil-rig tow—Bight of Australia to South America. I will hear within forty-eight hours, but I don't have to tell you that when the big one comes up there will be no warning. I want *Warlock* ready for sea immediately." At the oblique reference to rescue work and prize money, they stirred eagerly. "Chief?" He turned to Vinny.

The engineer snorted as though the question was an insult. "In all respects ready for sea."

"Number One?" Nick looked at David. He had not yet become accustomed to David's boyishness, but he knew that the mate was over thirty and had held a master mariner's ticket for five years.

"I'm waiting on some stores, sir," David answered quickly. "But I could sail in an hour, if necessary."

"All right." Nick stood up. "I will inspect the ship at 0900 hours."

Nick stepped out of the saloon and Vinny's voice was pitched to reach him. It was a truly dreadful imitation of what the chief believed to be a Royal Naval accent. "0900, chaps. Jolly good show, what?"

Nick did not miss a step, and he grinned tightly to himself. It's an old Aussie custom: you needle and needle until something happens. It was so long since he had been in elemental contact with such tough physical men, and he found the novelty stimulating. With the anticipation of physical confrontation, he felt his step quicken and his spirits lift.

He went up the companionway to the navigation deck, taking the steps three at a time, and the door opposite his suite opened. From it emerged the stench of cheap Dutch cigars and a head that was pale grey and wrinkled like a turtle's with the same small dark glittery eyes.

The door was that of the radio room and, despite appearances, the head was human. Nick recalled clearly how Mac had once described his radio officer. "He is the most anti-social bastard I've ever sailed with, but he is probably the best radio man afloat. He can scan eight different frequencies simultaneously, in clear and morse, even while he is asleep."

"Captain?" inquired the Trog, in a reedy petulant voice. Nick paused. "Captain, I have an 'all ships signify'."

Nick felt heat at the base of his spine, and an electric prickle on the back of his neck. "Co-ordinates?" he snapped as he entered the radio room.

"72°16′ south. 32°12′ west." Nick felt the heat mount his spine. The co-ordinates fitted neatly in the chart that he carried in his mind. The ship was more than two thousand miles south and west of the Cape of Good Hope—down deep in the vast and lonely wastes of Antarctica, almost on the Weddell Sea. What could she be?

On this bright, sunny morning, the radio room was dark and gloomy as a cave, the thick green blinds drawn across the ports, the only source of light the glowing dials of the banked communication equipment. The Trog sat on a swivel seat, tending his dials, and there was a cacophony of static and electronic trash blurred with the sharp howl of morse.

"The copy?" Nick asked, and the Trog pushed a pad at him.

> CTMZ. 0603 GMT. 72°16′S. 32°12′W. All ships in a position to render assistance, please signify. CTMZ.

He did not need to consult the R/T Handbook to recognize that call sign. With an effort of will he controlled the pressure that caught him in the chest like a giant fist. Behind him he heard his officers' voices on the navigation bridge, quiet voices—but charged with tension. They were up from the saloon already. "Christ!" he thought. "How do they know so quickly?"

The door leading direct from the bridge slid aside and David stood in the opening with a copy of Lloyd's Register in his hands.

"CTMZ, sir, is the call sign of *Golden Adventurer*. Twenty-two thousand tons. Owners Christy Marine."

"Thank you, Number One." Nick nodded. He knew her well; he personally had ordered her construction and innovated for her the idea of adventure cruises. She carried rich passengers in search of the unusual. She was probably one of the very few cruise liners that was still profitable—and now she stood in need of assistance.

Nick turned back to the Trog. "Has she been transmitting prior to this signify request?"

"Twice since midnight—in company code. I was watching her."

"You recorded?" Nick demanded, and the Trog switched in the automatic playback of his tape monitor. With a clatter of keys, two jumbled blocks of code were promptly printed out on the strip.

Had Duncan Alexander changed the Christy Marine code? If so, they would never break it. Nick hurried out of the radio room with the print-out in his hands.

The navigation bridge of *Warlock* was gleaming chrome and glass—as bright and functional as a modern surgical theatre. The primary control console stretched the full width of the bridge, beneath the huge armoured windows. The old-fashioned wheel was replaced by a single steel lever. By means of a long extension cable for remote control, the helmsman could con the ship from any position on the bridge. In the rear was the navigational area, with the chart table and a battery of electronic aids, like a row of fruit machines in a Vegas gambling hall.

Nick switched the big Decca Satellite Navaid into its computer mode and the display lights flashed and faded and relit in scarlet. He fed it the block of garbled transmission and the six-figure control that he had himself devised for Christy Marine, then stared at the print-out.

> Christy Marine from master of *Adventurer*. 2216 GMT. 72°15′S. 32°05′W. Underwater ice damage sustained midships starboard. Precautionary shut down mains. Stand by.

So Duncan had let the code stand. Nick, feeling an intense desire to shout aloud, groped for his crocodile-skin case of cheroots. His hand was steady and firm as he held the flame to the tip of the thin black tube.

"Plotted," said David from behind him.

Nick glanced at the plot, saw the dotted ice line far above the liner's position, saw the outline of the forbidding continent of Antarctica below, groping for the ship with merciless fingers of ice and rock.

The second message and its reply had been despatched many hours later.

> Christy Marine from master of *Adventurer*. 0546 GMT. 72°16′S. 32°12′W. Explosion in flooded area. Emergency shut down all. Water gaining. Request your clearance to issue "all ships signify". Standing by.

> Master of *Adventurer* from Christy Marine. 0547 GMT. You are cleared to issue signify. You are expressly forbidden to contract tow or salvage without reference Christy Marine.

Duncan Alexander was not even putting in the old chestnut, "except in the event of danger to human life". The reason was too apparent. Christy Marine underwrote most of its own bottoms through another of its subsidiaries, the London and European Insurance and Finance Company. The self insurance scheme had been Duncan's brain child. Nick had opposed it bitterly.

"Are we going to signify?" David asked quietly.

"Radio silence," snapped Nick, and began to pace the bridge.

Was this his chance? Nick wondered. It would take *Warlock* five days and nights of hard running to reach *Golden Adventurer*, by which time she might have effected repairs and be under her own command again. Or, even if she were still helpless, she might have been taken in tow by another salvage tug.

Nick stopped his pacing at the door to the radio room and spoke quietly to the Trog. "Open the telex line and send to Bernard Wackie in Bermuda quote call the roll unquote."

Warlock's satellite telex system enabled Nick to communicate with his agent in Bermuda, or with any other selected telex station, without his message being broadcast over the open frequencies and monitored by a competitor. While he waited, Nick worried. The decision to go would mean abandoning the Esso oil-rig tow. The tow fee had been a vital consideration in his cash flow situation—two hundred and twenty thousand sterling, without which he could not meet the quarterly interest payment due in sixty days' time unless. . . .

"Bernard Wackie are replying," called the Trog above the chatter of the telex receiver, and Nick spun on his heel.

He glanced at his Rolex Oyster and calculated that it was two o'clock in the morning in Bermuda, and yet his request for information on the disposition of all his major competitors was now being answered by his agent within minutes of receipt.

> For master *Warlock* from Bernard Wackie latest reported positions *John Ross* drydock Durban. *Woltema Wolteraad* Esso tow Torres straits to Alaska Shelf. . . .

That took care of the two giant Safmarine tugs. The names and positions of the other big salvage tugs ran swiftly from the telex and Nick chewed his cheroot ragged as he watched, feeling the relief rise in him as each report put another of his competitors far beyond range of the stricken ship.

". . . *La Mouette*." Nick's hands balled into fists as the name sprang onto the white paper sheet. "*La Mouette* discharged Brazgas tow Golfo San Jorge on 14th reported en route Buenos Aires."

Nick grunted like a boxer taking a low blow, and walked out onto the open wing of the bridge and the wind tore at his hair.

La Mouette, the seagull, was a fanciful name for Jules Levoisin's black squat hull, with its old fashioned high box of superstructure and traditional single stack. From the days when he served aboard her, Nick could recall clearly how her captain's mind worked. If Jules Levoisin had discharged in the Southern Atlantic three days ago, he would have bunkered at Comodoro and now he would be running hard for the south; running like a hunting dog with the scent hot in its nostrils.

At the same time, Nick knew that Jules's nine thousand horsepower engines couldn't push that tubby hull at better than eighteen knots. *Warlock* had twenty-two thousand horsepower. With Jules Levoisin, however, that was not enough margin for complacency. Nick felt the sense of cheer and well-being with which he had buoyed himself that morning fall away from him like a cloak. He was afraid as he had never been before. His defeat by Duncan Alexander and rejection by the woman he loved had broken him. He realized that his wave had come, and would sweep by him unless he quickly found the strength to ride it. The choice was go now—or never go again. But how could he challenge Jules Levoisin, the old master? How could he reject the certainty of the Esso tow, and risk all that he had left on a single throw?

He turned back into the bridge. His officers watched him in a tense, electric silence.

His right hand went out and touched the engine telegraph, sliding the pointer from "off" to "stand by". "Engine room," he heard himself say in calm and level tones. "Start main engines."

Seemingly from a great distance he watched the faces of his deck officers bloom with joy.

"Number One," he continued. "Ask the harbour master for permission to clear harbour immediately. Pilot, a course to steer for the last reported position of *Golden Adventurer*, please."

From the corner of his eye he saw David punch Tim Graham, the third officer, gleefully on the shoulder before he hurried to the radio telephone.

Nick felt suddenly the urge to vomit. So he stood very still and erect at the navigation console, fighting back the waves of nausea, while his officers bustled to their sea-going stations.

"Bridge. This is the chief engineer," said a disembodied voice from the speaker above Nick's head. "Main engines running." A pause and then that word of special Aussie approbation. "Beauty!"—but the chief pronounced it in three distinct syllables, "Be-yew-dy!"

FOR THREE DAYS *Warlock* ran like an old bull otter, slick and wet and fast, for the south.

Uninterrupted by any land mass the cycle of great atmospheric depressions swept endlessly across these cold open seas, and the wave patterns built up into a succession of marching mountain ranges. *Warlock* was taking them on her starboard shoulder, bursting through each crest in a white explosion that leapt from her flared bows like a torpedo strike, the water coming aboard green and clear over her high foredeck, and sweeping her from stem to stern as she twisted and broke out, dropping sheer into the valley that opened ahead of her. Her twin propellers broke clear of the surface, their slamming vibration instantly controlled by the variable pitch gear, then bit deeply again as the thrust of the twin

Mirrlees diesels hurtled her down the slope. In the deep valleys between the crests the wind was blanketed, and an eerie silence enhanced the menace of that towering wall of water ahead. As *Warlock* climbed in a gut-swooping lift that buckled the knees of the watch, the angle of her bridge tilted back, and the sombre cheerless sky filled the forward bridge windows with a vista of low scudding cloud.

Nick was wedged into the canvas master's seat in the corner of the bridge. He swayed to the thrust of the sea and smoked his black cheroots quietly, his head turning every few minutes to the west—as though he expected at any moment to see *La Mouette* come up on top of the next swell—but he knew she must be many hundreds of miles away, racing silently down the far leg of the triangle which had at its apex the stricken liner.

Jules Levoisin had taught Nick the trick of silence. Jules would not use his radio until he had the liner on his radar scan. Then he would come through in clear: "I will be in a position to put a line aboard you in two hours. Do you accept 'Lloyd's Open Form'?" The master of the distressed vessel, believing himself abandoned without succour, would over-react to the promise of salvation—and when *La Mouette* came bustling up over the horizon, flying all her bunting and with every light blazing in as theatrical a display as Jules could put up, the relieved master usually leapt at the offer of Lloyd's Open Form—a decision often regretted by the ship's owners in the unemotional precincts of the arbitration court. For under Lloyd's Open Form "No Cure, No Pay", the pay would be a percentage of the value of the vessel.

The percentage depended upon the difficulties and dangers that the salvor had overcome, and a clever salvor such as Levoisin would paint a picture of such daring and ingenuity that the award could be in millions of dollars.

Nick could no longer sit inactive in his canvas seat. He judged the next towering swell and with half a dozen quick strides crossed the bridge deck and grabbed the chrome handrail above the Decca computer. On the keyboard he typed the function code that would set the machine in navigational mode, co-ordinating the transmissions it was receiving from the satellite stations high above the earth. From these, it calculated *Warlock*'s exact position over the earth's surface—accurate to within twenty-five yards.

Nick entered the ship's position and the computer compared this with the plot that Nick had requested four hours previously. It printed out quickly the distance run and the ship's speed made good. Nick frowned angrily. *Warlock* was not delivering the extra knots of speed that he had relied on when he had made the decision to race *La Mouette* for the prize. Abruptly, he crossed to the R/T microphone. "Engine room confirm we are top of the green."

"Top of the green, it is—Skipper." The chief's casual tones floated in above the crash of the next sea coming aboard.

"Top of the green" was the maximum safe power setting recommended by the manufacturers for the gigantic Mirrlees diesels. Nick was pushing her as high as he could without going into the "red" danger area above eighty per cent of full power, which at prolonged running might permanently damage her engines.

Nick stood there for a moment, trying to work out why *Warlock* was running slow. Suddenly he considered a possibility that brought a metallic gleam of anger into his eyes. Nodding to the third officer who had the deck, he ducked through the doorway in the back of the bridge into his day cabin. It was a ploy. He didn't want his visit below decks announced. From his own suite he darted down the companionway.

The engine control room was as modern and gleaming as *Warlock*'s navigation bridge. It was completely enclosed with double glass to cut down the thunder of the two enormous diesel engines which filled the white-painted cavern of the engine room beyond. It was only custom that made it necessary for any visitor, including the master, to announce his arrival in the control room to the chief engineer. Ignoring custom, Nick slipped in quietly through the glass sliding doors.

Vinny Baker was deep in conversation with one of the electricians. Nick had reached the control console before the chief engineer noticed him.

When Nick was very angry his lips compressed in a single thin white line.

"You pulled the override on me," he accused in a flat,

passionless voice that did not betray his fury. "You're governing her out at seventy per cent of power."

"That's top of the green—in my book," Vinny told him. "I'm not running my engines at eighty per cent in this sea. She'll shake the guts out of herself. . . ." He paused and the stern was flung up violently as *Warlock* crashed over the top of another sea. The control room shuddered with vibration. "Listen to her, man."

"I want the override out," said Nick flatly, indicating the chrome handle and pointer with which the engineer could cancel the power settings asked for by the bridge. "I don't care when you do it, just as long as it's any time within the next five seconds."

"You get out of my engine room—and go play with your toys."

"All right," Nick nodded. "I'll do it myself." And he reached for the override gear.

"You take your hands off my engines," howled the chief, picking up the iron locking handle off the deck. "You touch them and I'll break your teeth out of your head—you Pommy bastard."

"You stupid Bundaberg-swilling galah," Nick said quietly, as he reached for the override. "I don't care if I have to kill you first, but we're going to eighty per cent."

Vinny had not expected to be insulted in colloquial Australian. He dropped the steel handle to the deck, with a clang.

"I don't need it," he announced and tucked his spectacles into his back pocket and hoisted his trousers. "It will be more fun to take you to pieces by hand."

It was only then that Nick realized how tall the engineer was. His arms were ridged with lean taut muscle. His fists as he balled them were the size of a pair of nine-pound hammers. He went down into a fighter's crouch, and rode the plunging deck with an easy flexing of the long powerful legs.

As Nick touched the chrome override handle, the first punch came from the level of Vinny's knees, but it came so fast that Nick only just had time to sway away from it. He counter-punched instinctively, swaying back and slamming it in under the armpit. The chief's breath hissed, but he swung left handed and a bony fist crushed the pad of muscle on the point of Nick's shoulder, bounced off and caught him high on the temple.

Even though it was a glancing blow, it felt as though a door had slammed behind Nick's eyes. He fell forward into a clinch, clinging to the lean hard body as he tried to clear the singing darkness in his head. He felt the chief shift his weight, and was shocked at the power in that wiry frame.

Suddenly he knew what was going to happen next. There were little white ridges of scar tissue half hidden by the widow's peak of flopping sandy hair on the chief's forehead. Those scars from previous conflicts warned Nick.

Vinny reared back, like a cobra flaring for the strike, and then flung his head forward. It was the classic butt aimed for Nick's face and had it landed squarely it would have crushed his nose and broken his teeth off level to the gums, but Nick dropped his own chin, tucking it down hard, so that their foreheads met with a crack like a breaking oak branch. The impact broke Nick's grip and both of them reeled apart across the heaving deck.

"Fight fair, you Pommy bastard!" Vinny howled as he came up short against the far side of the control room. For a moment, he gathered his lanky frame, then as *Warlock* swung hard over, he used her momentum to hurl himself down the steeply tilting deck, dropping his head again like a battering ram to crush Nick's ribs.

Nick turned like a cattle man working an unruly steer. He whipped one arm around Vinny's neck and ran with him, holding Vinny's head down and building up speed across the full length of the control room. They reached the armoured glass wall at the far end, and the top of the chief's head was the point of impact with the weight of both their bodies behind it.

THE CHIEF ENGINEER came round at the prick of the needle that Angel forced through the flap of open flesh on top of his head. He came round fighting, but the cook held him down.

"Easy, love." Angel tied the stitch.

"Where is he, where is the bastard?" slurred the chief.

"It's all over, Chiefie," Angel told him gently. "And you are just lucky he bashed you on the head—otherwise he might have hurt you." He took another stitch.

The chief winced as Angel pulled the thread up and knotted it. "He tried to mess with my engines. I taught him a lesson."

"You've terrified him," Angel agreed sweetly. "Now you take a swig of this and lie still. I want you in this bunk for twelve hours —and I might come and tuck you in. Incidentally, the skipper said to tell you that, while you've been playing prima donna, Jules Levoisin has probably made up five hundred miles on us."

"Levoisin? I'm going back to my engines," announced the chief, and, promptly draining the medicine glass of brown spirit, lumbered off the bunk.

On the navigation deck, Nick settled into his canvas chair and fingered the big purple swelling on his forehead tenderly. His head felt as though a rope had been knotted around it and twisted up tight. He lit a cheroot, and it tasted like burned tarred rope. He dropped it into the sandbox as the telephone rang.

"Bridge, this is the engine room."

"Go ahead, Chief."

"Nobody told me *La Mouette* was running against us," Vinny announced. "There's no way that frog-eating bastard's going to get a line on her first. We are going up to eighty per cent *now*."

Nick found himself smiling, even through the blinding pain in his head. "Be-yew-dy!" he said, as he hung up the receiver.

DAVID'S VOICE was apologetic. "Sorry to wake you, sir, but *Golden Adventurer* is reporting."

"I'm coming," mumbled Nick and swung his legs off the bunk. He had been in that black death sleep of exhaustion, but it took him only seconds to pull back the dark curtains from his mind.

When he reached the bridge, the wind was rising force six. *Warlock*'s motion was more violent and abandoned.

The Trog was crouched over his machine, grey and wizened and sleepless. He hardly turned his head to hand Nick the message.

> Master of *Adventurer* to Christy Marine . . .

The Decca decoded swiftly, and Nick grunted as he saw the new position report—something had altered drastically in the liner's circumstances.

> Main engines still unserviceable. Current setting easterly and increasing to eight knots. Wind rising force six from northwest. Critical ice danger to the ship.

"The current and wind together are driving her down onto the land," David muttered as he worked quickly over the chart. He touched the ugly broken points of Coats Land's shoreline with the tip of one finger. "She's eighty miles offshore now. At the rate she is drifting, it will take only ten hours before she goes aground."

"If she doesn't hit an iceberg first," said Nick. "What's our time to reach her?"

"Another forty hours, sir." David hesitated and pushed the thick white-gold lock of hair off his forehead. "If we can make good this speed—but we may have to reduce when we reach the ice."

Nick turned away to his canvas chair. He thought about the terrible predicament of the liner's captain. His ship was at deadly risk, and the lives of six hundred souls with it.

"With respect, sir," said David, "if her captain knows that assistance is on the way, it may prevent him doing something crazy." David hesitated but Nick was silent. "The air temperature out there is minus five degrees, sir, and if the wind is at thirty miles an hour, that will make it a lethal chill factor. If they take to the boats in that. . . ." David looked at him expectantly. It was the humane thing to do: to tell them he was only eight hundred miles away, and closing swiftly.

On an impulse Nick left his chair and carefully crossed the heaving deck to the starboard wing of the bridge. He slid open the door and stepped into the gale. The shock of the freezing air took his breath away and he gasped like a drowning man. Frozen spray struck into his face like steel darts.

Carefully he filled his lungs, and his nostrils flared as he smelt the ice. It was that unmistakable dank smell, like the body smell of some gigantic reptilian sea monster—and it struck the mariner's chill into his soul.

When he stepped back into the green-lit warmth of the bridge his decision was made. "Number One, there is ice ahead."

"I have a watch on the radar, sir."

"Very good," Nick nodded. "But we'll reduce now to fifty per cent of power." He hesitated. "And maintain radio silence."

Nick saw the accusation in David's eyes before he turned away to give the orders for the reduction in power, and Nick had to steel himself against a sudden and uncharacteristic urge to explain the decision.' It had been a hard decision to make, but he was dealing with two hard men. He knew he could not afford to give an inch of sea room to Jules Levoisin. The other man, Duncan Alexander, was a hating and vindictive person who had already tried to destroy him. Nick must be in a position of utmost strength to deal with them both. The captain of *Golden Adventurer* would have to be left in the agonies of doubt a little longer, but Nick knew that any further drastic change in the liner's circumstances, such as a decision to abandon ship, would be announced on the open radio channels and would give him a chance to intervene.

Nick went to his chair and settled down to wait out the few remaining hours of the short Antarctic summer night.

THE HORIZON AHEAD of *Warlock* was cluttered with ice. Some of the fragments were the size of a billiard table and they bumped and scraped down *Warlock*'s side, then swung and bobbed in her wake as she passed. There were others the size of a city block, weird and fanciful structures of honeycombed riven white ice, that stood as tall as *Warlock*'s upper works as she passed.

She was running too fast, Nick knew it, but he was relying on the vigilance of his deck officers to carry her through. Above their horizon rose a great unbroken sweep of towering cliff which caught the low sun and glowed in emerald and amethyst—a drifting tableland of solid hard ice forty miles across and two hundred feet high. To windward the big sea piled in and crashed against the iceberg in explosive bursts of white spray.

"Look at the sheltered lee she is making." David pointed. "You could ride out a force twelve behind her."

Warlock made for the leeward side where the waters were protected, and in a ship's length passed from the plunging rearing action of a wild horse into the tranquillity of a mountain lake.

In the calm Angel brought trays piled with crisp brown baked Cornish pasties and steaming mugs of thick creamy cocoa—and they ate breakfast at three in the morning, marvelling at the fine pale sunlight and the ice towers of incredible beauty. The younger officers shouted and laughed when a school of five black killer whales passed so close that they could see the white cheek patterns and wide grinning mouths through the icy clear waters.

Nick did not join the spontaneous gaiety. He even found himself resenting the laughter, now when so much was at stake—six hundred human lives, a great ship, tens of millions of dollars, his whole future. . . .

Suddenly the radio crackled and hummed, and immediately the bridge was silent. Nick stood up abruptly as a voice came through in clear.

Mayday. Mayday. Mayday. This is *Golden Adventurer* . . .

Nick ran to the radio room as the calm masculine voice read out the co-ordinates of the ship's position.

We are in imminent danger of striking. We are preparing to abandon ship. Can any vessel render assistance? Repeat can any vessel render assistance?

"Good God—" David's voice was harsh with anxiety. "She's only fifty miles off Cape Alarm and we are still two hundred and twenty miles away."

"Where the hell is *La Mouette*?" growled Nick.

"We'll have to open contact now, sir." David looked up from the chart. "You cannot let them go down into the boats—not in this weather, sir. It would be murder."

"Thank you, Number One," said Nick quietly. "Your advice is always welcome." David flushed, but with anger, not embarrassment.

Nick knew that David was right. There was only one thing to consider now—the preservation of human life. He had to send now. *La Mouette* had won the contest of radio silence. Nick began composing a message urging the master to delay abandoning ship until *Warlock* could close the gap.

The silence on the bridge was heightened by the absence of wind. They were all watching him now, waiting for the decision. Then the radio hummed and throbbed, and Nick heard the rich Gallic accent that he remembered so clearly.

Master of *Adventurer* this is the master of salvage tug *La Mouette*. Am proceeding at best speed your assistance. Do you accept Lloyd's Open Form "No Cure, No Pay"? My position is . . .

Nick kept his face from showing any emotion, but his heart banged wildly against his ribs. Jules Levoisin had broken silence.

"God! She's inside us." David's face was stricken as he marked *La Mouette*'s reported position on the chart. "She's a hundred miles ahead of us."

"No." Nick shook his head. "He's lying. He always lies." He lit a cheroot and when it was drawing evenly he turned again to his radio officer. "Did you get a bearing?"

The Trog looked up from his radio direction-finding compass. "I have one," he said, "but you won't get a fix. . . ."

Nick interrupted. "We'll use his best course from Golfo San Jorge for a fix." And he turned back to David. "Plot that."

"There's a difference of over three hundred nautical miles."

"Yes," Nick nodded. "That old pirate wouldn't broadcast an accurate position to all the world. We are inside him and we'll put a line over *Golden Adventurer* before he's in radar contact."

"Are you going to open contact with Christy Marine now, sir?"

"No, Number One."

"But they will do a deal with *La Mouette*—unless we bid."

"I don't think so," Nick murmured, and almost went on to say, "Duncan Alexander won't settle for Lloyd's Open Form while he is the underwriter, and his ship is free and floating. He'll fight for daily hire and bonus, and Jules Levoisin won't buy that package. He'll hold out for the big plum." But he did not say it.

"Steady as she goes, Number One," was all he said.

CAPTAIN BASIL REILLY, the master of *Golden Adventurer*, was a tall and wiry man. His face was tanned and splotched with the dark patches of benign sun cancer. His heavy moustache was silvered like the pelt of a snow fox, and his eyes, set in webs of finely wrinkled skin, were bright and intelligent.

He stood on the windward wing of his navigation bridge and watched the huge black seas tumbling in to batter his helpless ship. He adjusted the lifejacket he wore, as he reviewed once more his position.

Golden Adventurer had taken the ice in that eight to midnight watch traditionally allotted to the most junior of the navigating officers. The ice had been a growler—one of the most deadly of all hazards. While most bergs stand high to catch the radar beams, or the eye of even the most inattentive deck watch, growlers lie awash with their great bulk and weight almost completely hidden. They show themselves only in the depths of each wave trough, or in the swirl of the current around it and, at night, even these indications pass unnoticed.

With the third officer on watch and steaming at cautionary speed of a mere twelve knots, *Golden Adventurer* had brushed against one of these monsters—and though the actual impact had gone almost unnoticed on board, the horizontal blade of ice that lay below the surface had opened her like the knife stroke which splits a herring for the smoking rack. It had made a fourteen foot rent through her side, twelve feet below the Plimsoll line, shearing two of her watertight compartments—and one of those was her main engine room section.

They had held the water easily until an electrical explosion, and since then the master had battled to keep her afloat. Slowly, step by step, fighting all the way he had yielded to the sea. Three days ago he had brought all his passengers up from below the main deck, and he had battened down all the watertight bulkheads. The crew and passengers were accommodated now in the lounges and smoking rooms.

The ship's luxury had been transformed into the crowded, unhygienic and deteriorating conditions of a city under siege. The sanitary arrangements were inadequate. There was no heating. The emergency generators delivered barely sufficient power to work the ship—to run the pumps, to supply minimal lighting, and to keep the communication and navigation equipment running. The outside air temperature had fallen to minus twenty degrees, and the passengers huddled in their coats and bulky lifejackets under mounds of blankets. There were limited cooking facilities on gas stoves usually reserved for adventure tours ashore; only soup and beverages were heated, and even these were rationed. Of the three hundred and twelve paying passengers, only forty-eight were below the age of fifty, and yet the morale was extraordinary. They had come to this outlandish corner of the globe in search of new experience and they seemed almost to welcome this danger as part of the entertainment provided by the tour.

Yet, standing on his bridge, the master was under no illusion as to the gravity of their situation. Peering through the streaming glass, he watched a work party, toiling heroically in the bows. Four men in glistening yellow plastic suits and hoods, drenched by the icy seas, were streaming a sea-anchor to bring the ship's head up into the sea so that she might ride more easily, and perhaps slow her precipitous rush towards the rocky coast. Twice in the preceding days the anchors they had rigged had been torn away by the sea and wind, and Reilly knew he must soon attempt to remove six hundred human beings from this helpless hulk to the hardly lesser dangers and hardships of Cape Alarm's barren, storm-rent shores unless the French salvage tug reached them first.

Cape Alarm was one of those few pinnacles of barren black rock which thrust out from beneath the thick white mantle of the Antarctic ice cap. It protruded almost fifty miles into the eastern extremity of the Weddell Sea, and terminated in a pair of bull's horns which formed a small protected bay named after the polar explorer Sir Ernest Shackleton.

Shackleton Bay with its steep purple-black beaches of round polished pebbles was the nesting ground of a huge colony of chinstrap penguin, and for this reason was one of *Golden Adventurer*'s regular ports of call. Only ten days earlier she had weighed anchor from the bay in a bright clear sun. Now, before a force seven gale, she was being carried back there.

Captain Reilly crossed from the windward wing of the bridge to the lee. Cape Alarm was already visible, black and menacing against the sow's-belly grey of the sky. Its ridges and valleys were picked out with gleaming ice and banked snow, and against the steep shore the sea creamed and leapt high in explosions of purest white.

"Only sixteen miles away, sir," said the first officer, coming to stand beside him. "And we've just received another message from head office."

"Very well." Captain Reilly glanced at the flimsy. "Send that to the tug master." The disdain for this haggling between owners and salvors was clear in his voice. He knew what he would do if the salvage tug made contact before *Golden Adventurer* struck the waiting fangs of rock—he would override his owners' express orders and exercise his rights as master by immediately accepting the offer of assistance under Lloyd's Open Form.

"But let the tug come," he murmured to himself. "Please God let it come."

SHE WAS NOT yet twenty-five years of age and even the layers of heavy clothing topped by a man's anorak three sizes too big could not disguise the coltish slimness of her body. Her mane of copper-golden hair was twisted into a rope almost as thick as a man's wrist and piled up on top of her head, yet loose strands tickled her nose so that she pursed her lips and puffed them away. Her hands were occupied with the heavy tray she carried.

"Come on, Mrs. Goldberg," she said. "It will warm you."

"I don't think so, my dear," the white-haired woman faltered. "But just for you . . ." The woman took one of the mugs and sipped it. "It's good," she said, and then quickly and furtively. "Samantha, has the tug come yet?"

"It will be here any minute now—and the captain is a dashing Frenchman. I'm going to introduce you—first thing."

The woman was a widow in her late fifties, a little overweight and more than a little afraid—but she smiled and sat up a little straighter. "You are a naughty thing," she said.

Samantha Silver was one of the ship's specialist guides, a brilliant girl on sabbatical leave from Miami University where she had a doctorate in biology and a research fellowship in marine ecology. Now, as she moved on, they welcomed her, each of them, men and women, competing for her attention, making up questions or little stories to detain her for a few extra moments.

Samantha paused at the entrance to the temporary galley they had set up in the cocktail room, and while a steward refilled her tray with mugs she looked back into the densely packed lounge.

The stink of unwashed humanity and tobacco smoke was almost a solid thing, but she felt a rush of affection for the passengers. They were behaving so very well, she thought. With a deliberate effort to control her own fear, she reset the smile brightly on her lips and picked up the heavy tray.

At that moment the public address speakers gave a preliminary squawk, and then filtered the captain's measured tones into the suddenly silent ship. "Ladies and gentlemen, this is the captain. I regret to inform you that we have not yet established radar contact with the salvage tug *La Mouette*, and that I now deem it necessary to transfer the ship's company to the lifeboats. . . ."

There was a sigh and stir in the crowded lounges. Samantha saw one of her favourite passengers reach for his wife and press her silvery grey head to his shoulder.

". . . You have all practised the lifeboat drill many times. I am sure I do not have to impress upon you the necessity to go to your stations in orderly fashion, and to obey all orders implicitly."

Samantha set down her tray and crossed quickly to Mrs. Goldberg. The woman was weeping, and Samantha slipped her arm around her shoulders.

"Come now," she whispered. "Don't let the others see you cry." She lifted the woman to her feet. "It will be all right—you'll see. Just think of the story you'll be able to tell your grandchildren when you get home."

CAPTAIN REILLY reviewed his preparations for leaving the ship, going over them item by item in his mind.

The most important consideration was that no person should be immersed, or even drenched by sea water during the transfer. Life expectation in these waters was four minutes. The second most important consideration was the psychological condition of his passengers, when they left the comparative security of the ship. They had been briefed, and mentally prepared as much as was possible. An officer had checked each passenger's clothing and survival equipment, and they had been fed high-sugar tablets to ward off the cold.

The motor lifeboats would go first—six of them, slung three on each side of the ship, each crewed by an officer and five seamen. While the great drogue of the sea-anchor held the ship's head on to the wind and the sea, they would be swung outboard and lowered swiftly to the surface of a sea temporarily smoothed by the oil sprayed from the pumps in the bows.

Although they were decked-in, they were not the warmest vehicles for survival in these conditions. For this reason the passengers would go into the thirty inflatable life rafts, which were self-righting even in the worst seas and enclosed with a double skin of insulation. Equipped with emergency rations and battery-powered locator beacons, each raft could provide shelter for twenty human beings, whose body warmth would keep the interior habitable. The motor boats would herd the rafts together and then tow them ashore. Even in these conditions the tow should not take more than twelve hours. The lifeboats were packed with fuel and food sufficient to keep the shipwrecked party until the French tug and other rescue ships could arrive.

Captain Reilly took one more look at the land. It was very close now, and even in the gloom of the onrushing night the peaks of ice and snow glittered like the fangs of some hungry monster.

"All right." He nodded to his first officer. "Begin."

The mate lifted the small two-way radio to his lips. "Foredeck. Bridge. Commence laying the oil now."

From each side of the bows hoses threw up silver dragonfly wings of oil, pumped directly from the ship's bunkers. It fell in a thick coating across the surface of the sea, broken by the floodlights into the colours of the rainbow. Immediately the sea was soothed, as the wind-riven surface was flattened by the weight of oil.

"Send the boats away," said the captain.

The hydraulic arms of the derricks lifted the six boats off their chocks and swung them out over the ship's side, suspending them high above the surface. In the floodlights the little boats shone wetly with spray, brilliant electric-yellow in colour, and decorated with garlands of ice and snow like Christmas toys. The officer of each lifeboat now had to judge the sea, and operate the winch so as to drop neatly onto the back slope of a passing swell.

At that moment the heavy nylon rope that held the cone-shaped drogue of the sea-anchor snapped with a report like a cannon shot. *Golden Adventurer* threw up her bows, slewed back across the scend of the sea, and was immediately pinned helplessly broadside—her starboard side to the wind, with its three lifeboats still suspended.

A huge wave reared up out of the darkness and as it rushed down on the ship one of the lifeboats sheared her cables and burst like a ripe melon against the steel side of the ship. From the bridge they saw the crew swirled helplessly away into the darkness.

The forward lifeboat was swung against the ship like a door-knocker, her bow cable jammed so she dangled stern first, and as each wave punched into her she was smashed against the hull. They could hear the men in her screaming, a thin pitiful sound on the wind, that went on for many minutes as the sea slowly beat the boat into a tangle of wreckage.

The third boat was also swung viciously against the hull. The releases on her clamps opened and she dropped twenty feet into the boil and surge of water, bobbed free for a moment like a yellow fishing float, then settled and submerged.

"Oh, my God," whispered Captain Reilly. In a single stroke he had lost half his boats.

"The other boats—" the first officer's voice was ragged with shock, "—the others got away safely, sir."

"Three boats," murmured the captain. "For thirty rafts." He knew that there were insufficient shepherds for his flock—and yet he had no alternative. "Send the rafts away," he said quietly, and then again under his breath. "And God have mercy on us all."

"COME ON, Number Sixteen," called Samantha. "Here we are, Number Sixteen." She stood at the heavy mahogany doors that opened onto the open forward deck, and gathered to her the eighteen passengers who made up the complement of her allotted life raft. "Be ready," she told them. "When we get the word we have to move fast."

The rafts were being inflated on the open deck, and the passengers hustled across to them between waves. The laden rafts were then lifted over the side by winches.

"Right!" The third officer burst in through the mahogany doors and held them wide. "Quickly! All together."

"Let's go!" sang out Samantha and there was an awkward rush onto the wet and slippery deck. It was only thirty paces to where the raft crouched like a monstrous yellow bullfrog, its ugly dark mouth gaping, but the wind struck like an axe and Samantha saw some of her passengers falter in the sudden merciless cold.

"Come on," she shouted, pushing those ahead of her, half

supporting Mrs. Goldberg's plump body that suddenly felt as heavy and unco-operative as a full sack of wheat. "Keep going."

"Let me have her," shouted the third officer, and he grabbed Mrs. Goldberg's other arm. Between them they tumbled her through the entrance of the raft.

"Good on you, Sam," the officer grinned at Samantha. His name was Ken, and his smile was attractive and warm, very masculine and likeable. "Now you get in." She crept into the crowded interior and looked back at the brightly lit deck that glistened in the arc lamps.

Ken had started back to where one of the women had slipped and fallen. Her husband was trying to lift her back to her feet. Ken reached them and lifted the woman easily.

The three of them were the only ones out on the open deck when Samantha saw the wave come aboard. She shrieked a warning.

"Go back, Ken! For God's sake go back!"

He looked over his shoulder an instant before it reached them, but they could reach neither the raft nor the shelter of the mahogany doors. She heard the clatter of the donkey-winch and the raft lifted swiftly off the deck. The operator could not let the wave crash into the helpless raft, for the frail plastic skin would rupture on the superstructure.

Samantha hurled herself to the entrance and peered down. She saw the sea take them, like the killing charge of a man-eating lion, swift and purposeful. For a moment Ken clung to the railing while the waters poured over him, then he disappeared and the ship's decks were empty of any human shape.

With the next roll of the ship the winch operator swung the raft outboard and lowered it to the surface of the sea where one of the lifeboats took them in tow.

Samantha secured the plastic door cover, then she groped her way through the press of terrified bodies until she found Mrs. Goldberg.

"Are you crying, dear?" the elderly woman quavered.

"No," said Samantha, and placed one arm around her shoulders. "No, I'm not crying." And with her free hand she wiped away the icy tears that streamed down her cheeks.

THE TROG lifted his headset and looked at Nick through reeking clouds of cigar smoke. "Their radio operator has screwed down the key of his set. He's sending a single unbroken homing beam."

Nick knew what that meant—they had abandoned *Golden Adventurer.* He nodded once and remained silent, standing restlessly in the doorway from the bridge. He was slowly facing up to the reality of disaster. It was now almost certain that *Golden Adventurer* would go aground and be beaten into a total wreck by this storm. He could expect no more than a charter from Christy Marine to assist *La Mouette* in ferrying the survivors back to Cape Town—the fee a small fraction of the Esso tow fee he had forsaken for this wild dash south. His gamble had failed and he was a broken man.

"We might still reach her before she goes aground," said David sturdily, and nobody else on the bridge spoke.

Nick frowned. "We are still ten hours away—and for Reilly to decide to abandon ship she must have been very close indeed to running ashore. Reilly is a good man." Nick had personally selected him. He stopped talking abruptly. He was becoming garrulous.

Behind him the Trog's voice crackled rustily with excitement. "I'm getting a voice—it's only weak and intermittent. One of the lifeboats is sending on a battery powered transmitter." He held his earphones pressed to his head with both hands as he listened. "They are towing a batch of life rafts with all survivors aboard to Shackleton Bay. They are asking *La Mouette* for assistance."

"Is *La Mouette* acknowledging?"

The Trog shook his head. "She's probably still out of range of their transmitter."

"Very well." Nick turned away. He had still not broken radio silence, and could sense his officers' disapproval, silent but strong. Feeling again the uncustomary need for human contact, he stopped beside the mate and said, "I have been studying the Admiralty sailing directions for Cape Alarm, David." Pretending not to notice that the use of his Christian name had brought a quick colour to the mate's features, he went on evenly, "The shore is very steep-to, but there are beaches of pebble and the glass is going up sharply again. Instead of vainly hoping that we reach her before she goes aground, I suggest you offer a prayer that she goes up on one of those beaches. There is still a chance we can put ground tackle on her before she starts breaking up."

"I'll say ten Hail Marys, sir," grinned David, clearly overwhelmed by this sudden friendliness from his captain.

"And say another ten that we hold our lead on *La Mouette*," said Nick and smiled. "Meanwhile, steady as she goes. Call me if anything changes." With that, he turned away to his cabin.

THEY HAD STEELED themselves for hardship, but not one of the survivors in life raft Number 16 had imagined what it would be like.

Now that Ken had gone, Samantha had naturally taken command. She immediately realized how the utter darkness would crush morale, and more dangerously would induce disorientation and vertigo, so she ordered two of them at a time to switch on the tiny locator bulbs on their lifejackets. These gave enough light for everybody to see each other's faces. Then she arranged the seating, making them form a circle around the sides with their legs pointed inwards, to give the raft better balance.

The motion of the light raft was a nightmare of uncoordinated movement. The wave crests were up to twenty feet high, and the raft swooped over them and dropped heavily into the troughs. It did not have the lateral stability of a keel, so it spun on its axis until the tow rope jerked it up and it spun the other way. The first of them to start vomiting was Mrs. Goldberg. Within minutes half a dozen of the others were vomiting also.

Meanwhile, the cold came up even through the flexible insulated double skin of the deck, and was transferred into their buttocks and legs. It came in through the plastic canopy and froze the condensation of their breaths.

"Sing!" Samantha told them. "Come on, let's do 'Yankee Doodle Dandy'. You start, Mr. Stewart. Clap hands with your neighbour." She hectored relentlessly, crawling among them, prodding them awake, and giving them barley sugar from the emergency rations.

Samantha's throat was now scratchy with singing and talking, and she was dizzy with fatigue and sick with cold, recognizing in herself the first symptoms of lethargy, the prelude to giving up. She roused herself,. and sang out brightly, "I'm going to light the stove and get us a hot drink. Who's for a mug of beef tea?"

She stopped abruptly, something had changed. It took her a long moment to realize what it was. The raft was riding more easily now—without the dreadful jerk of the tow rope snapping it back.

Frantically she crawled to the entrance of the raft, and with cold crippled fingers she tore at the fastenings. Outside the dawn had broken into a clear cold sky of palest ethereal pinks and mauves. Although the wind had dropped to a faint whisper, the seas were still big and unruly.

The tow rope had torn away at the connecting shackle. Number 16 had been the last raft in the line being towed by Number 3 lifeboat—but of the convoy Samantha could now see no sign. There was no sight even of the rocky, ice-capped shores of Cape Alarm. They had drifted away, during the night, into the vast and lonely reaches of the Weddell Sea.

Despair cramped her belly muscles, and she wanted to cry out in protest against this further cruelty of fate, but she controlled herself.

"I'm not going to die," she told herself firmly. "I refuse to just lie down and die."

She struggled back to the dark and stinking interior of the raft, and crawled to the central locker that held their emergency locator transmitter. It was packed in polyurethane and her fingers were clumsy with cold and the thick mittens, but at last she brought it out. It was the size of a cigar box. She switched it on.

Now, for forty-eight hours, until the battery ran out, it would transmit a homing signal on 121,5 Mega Hertz. It was just possible that the French tug might pick up the beam—and track it to its source.

Then, setting everything else out of her mind, Samantha devoted herself to the task of trying to heat a pannikin of water without scalding herself as she held the small solid fuel stove in her lap and balanced it against the raft's motion. While she worked she searched for the words to tell the others of their predicament.

GOLDEN ADVENTURER, deserted of all human beings, her engines dead, but with her deck lights still burning, drifted swiftly down on the black rock of Cape Alarm—rock so hard that, despite the onslaught of the sea, the cliffs still retained the vertical edges and the glossy polished planes of cleanly fractured faults. The cliffs ended in an abrupt and vertical headland, where it had calved three tall pillars of serpentine, as graceful as the sculptured columns of the temple of Olympian Zeus. Held off the cliffs by the returning swell, *Golden Adventurer* touched one of those pillars. The light bump, which scraped paint from her side and crushed in her rail, was just sufficient to push her stern around, and point her bows directly into the wide shallow bay beyond.

Here a softer, more malleable rock formation had been eroded by the weather, forming a wide beach of purple-black pebbles, each the size of a man's head, and water-worn as round as cannon balls. Each time the waves rushed up this stony beach the pebbles struck against each other with a rattling roar, and the brash of broken sea ice that filled the bay susurrated and clinked as it rose and fell with the sea.

Now *Golden Adventurer* was clear of the cliff, she was more fully in the grip of the wind, and took the ground ahead of her with a great metallic groan of straining plates. The pebble beach moulded itself quickly to her hull, giving gradually as the waves and wind thrust her higher and higher ashore. By noon she was held firmly by the bows on the beach, canted over at an angle of ten degrees. Only her after end was still floating, rising and falling on the swell, but the plummeting air temperature was rapidly freezing the ice around her stern into a solid sheet. Her upper works were festooned with snow and long rapier-like stalactites of shining translucent ice, while her lights burned gaily on and piped music played softly through deserted public rooms.

AFTER TWO HOURS of sleep Nick returned to the bridge. The Trog was still at his equipment. He looked up at Nick for a moment with his little dark eyes, and it was clear that he had not slept at all. Nick felt a prick of shame at his own indulgence.

"Captain Reilly has just reported the loss of one life raft during the night," said the Trog.

Nick thought gloomily of the hapless souls adrift in this cold, and decided that they would probably not last out the day.

"What of *Golden Adventurer*?" asked Nick.

"She's still sending—but her position has not altered in almost three hours."

"Then she's aground," Nick muttered. "And in one piece too." His early despair slipped away. At that moment David hurried onto the bridge still shrugging on his pea-jacket. "It looks like those Hail Marys worked, David."

Nick flashed a smile, and David slapped the polished teak top of the chart table. "Touch wood," he said.

Nick strode to the front windows and stared ahead. The sea had flattened dramatically and a yellow sun was low on the horizon.

"We should sight *Golden Adventurer* within three hours," David said, coming to stand beside him. "If this visibility holds."

"It won't," said Nick. "We'll have fog pretty soon." And he indicated the surface of the sea, which was beginning to steam, emitting ghostly tendrils and eddies of seafret as the difference between sea and air temperature widened.

While the air around them thickened and blotted out all visibility to a few hundred yards, Nick paced the bridge like a caged lion, his hands clasped behind his back. He broke his pacing every time the Trog intercepted a relevant transmission.

At mid-morning Reilly reported that he and his convoy had reached Shackleton Bay, that they were taking full advantage of the moderating weather to set up an encampment, and he ended by once again urging *La Mouette* to try and locate the missing life raft.

Transmissions between Christy Marine and *La Mouette* showed that the two parties had diametrically changed their bargaining standpoints. While *Golden Adventurer* had been adrift on the open sea, and any salvage efforts had meant that a tug would merely have to take her in tow, Jules Levoisin had pressed for Lloyd's Open Form "No Cure, No Pay" contract. Since the "cure" would have been almost certain, the "pay" would have followed as a matter of course. Under these circumstances, Christy Marine had been desperately trying to wheedle Levoisin into a daily hire and bonus contract instead.

Now that *Golden Adventurer* had gone aground, however, Jules Levoisin had immediately withdrawn his offer to go Lloyd's Open Form. The "cure" was suddenly far from certain, for the *Golden Adventurer* might already be a total wreck, beaten to death on the rocks of Cape Alarm, in which case there would be "no pay".

Now Levoisin was desperately eager to strike a daily hire contract, including the ferrying of survivors back to civilization. He was offering his services at $10,000 a day, plus a bonus of 2½% of any salved value of the vessel. They were fair terms. However, Christy Marine, who had previously been offering a princely sum for daily hire, had just as rapidly withdrawn that offer. "We will accept Lloyd's Open Form—including ferrying of survivors," they declared.

"Conditions on site have changed," Jules Levoisin sent back, and the Trog got another good fix on him.

"We are head-reaching on him handsomely," Trog announced with satisfaction, as Nick marked the new positions on the chart.

The bridge of *Warlock* was once again crowded with every officer who had an excuse to be there.

"Captain, sir," the Trog sang out suddenly. "I'm getting another transmission. It's only strength One—and it's on 121,5 Mega Hertz."

"Oh, damn!" David exclaimed "It's that bloody missing life raft."

"Relative bearing!" snapped Nick.

"She bears 045° magnetic," the Trog answered.

The life raft was somewhere out on their port beam, 80° off their direct course to *Golden Adventurer*. The consternation on the bridge was voiced by one of the other officers: "If we go to the raft, we'll be handing it to that bloody frog on a plate."

Nick's fists on the chart table bunched so fiercely that the knuckles were ivory white. He looked across at David and spoke levelly, without change of expression. "Number One, will you please instruct your junior officers in the rule of the sea."

David obeyed. "The preservation of human life at sea, gentlemen, takes precedent over all other considerations."

"Very well, Number One," Nick nodded. "Alter 80° to port and maintain a homing course on the emergency transmission."

He turned away to his cabin. He could control his anger until he was alone, and then he turned and crashed his fist into the panel above his desk.

SAMANTHA HELD the stove in her lap using the detachable fibreglass lid of the locker as a tray. She was heating yet another half pint of water in the aluminium pannikin.

The blue flames of the stove gave added light to the dim cavern of plastic but radiated insufficient warmth to sustain life. They were dying already. Mr. Stewart held his wife's head against his chest, and bowed his own silver head over it. She had been dead for nearly two hours now. Samantha could not bear to look across at them as she crouched over the stove and dropped a cube of beef into the water, stirring it slowly and blinking against the tears of penetrating cold. The beef tea was only a little above blood warmth, but she could not waste fuel on heating it further.

The metal pannikin passed slowly from mittened hand to numbed and clumsy hand. They slurped the warm liquid and passed it on reluctantly, though there were some who had neither the strength nor the interest to take it.

"Come on, Mrs. Goldberg," Samantha whispered. "You must drink."

Samantha touched the old woman's face, and cut herself off. The flesh had a puttylike texture and was cooling swiftly. It took long lingering moments for the shock to pass, then carefully Samantha pulled the hood of the old woman's parka down over her face. Nobody else seemed to have noticed.

"Here," whispered Samantha to the man beside her, and she pressed the pannikin into his hands, folding his stiff fingers around the metal to make certain he had hold of it. "Drink it before it cools."

The air around her seemed to tremble suddenly with a great burst of sound, like the bellow of a dying bull. At first, Samantha thought her mind was playing tricks with her, and only when it came again did she raise her head. "Oh God," she whispered. "They've come. It's going to be all right. They've come to save us."

She crawled to the locker, slowly and stiffly. There she lit the globe on her lifejacket and in its pale glow she found the packet of phosphorus flares.

"Come on now, everybody. Let's hear it for Number Sixteen." She tried to rouse them as she struggled with the fastenings of the canopy. "One big cheer," she hectored them, but they were still and unresponsive, and as she fumbled her way out into freezing fog the tears that ran down her cheeks were not from cold.

She looked up incomprehendingly. It seemed that from the sky around her tumbled gigantic cascades of translucent menacing green ice. It took her moments to realize that the raft had drifted in close beneath the precipitous lee of a tabular berg.

As the air resonated again with the deep gut-shaking bellow of the siren, she held aloft one of the phosphorus flares, and it required all the strength of her frozen arms to rip the igniter tab. The flare spluttered and streamed acrid white smoke, then burst into a dazzling crimson fire. She stood like a tiny figure of Liberty, holding the flare aloft in one hand and peering with streaming eyes into the sullen fog banks.

"THERE," CALLED NICK. "On the starboard beam." The distress flare lit the fog banks internally with a fiery cherry red and threw grotesque patterns of light against the belly of lurking cloud.

"New heading 150°," Nick told the helmsman and *Warlock* came around, bursting from the enveloping bank of fog into an area of open air.

Half a mile away the yellow life raft bobbed beneath a glassy green wall of ice, the tiny figure that held aloft the brilliant crimson flare an insignificant speck in the vast wilderness of fog and sea and ice. David blew one last triumphant blast on the siren.

"Prepare to pick up survivors, David," said Nick and, at that instant, he lifted his head in bewilderment. For a moment he thought it was gunfire, then the volume of sound mounted into a rumbling roar, the unmistakable roar of a mountain in avalanche.

The working of sea and wind, and the natural erosion of changing temperatures had set tremendous forces at work within the iceberg. Those forces had found a weak point, a vertical fault line, that ran like an axe stroke from the flattened tableland of the summit, five hundred feet down to the moulded bottom of the berg far below the surface. The booming sound waves of *Warlock*'s horn had found a sympathetic resonance within the body of the mountain that had set the ice on each side of the fault vibrating in different frequencies. Now the fault had sheared, and one hundred million tons of ice were breaking away from the berg.

"Good God!" whispered Nick as he saw the slab of solid ice, twice the size of Saint Paul's, swing out and twist free from the mother berg. As it did so, forces came into play within it, finding smaller faults and flaws so that ice burst within ice and tore itself apart as though dynamited with tons of high explosive. The air was filled with hurtling ice, some pieces the size of a locomotive and others as small and sharp and deadly as steel swords.

Faster and faster fell the slab. The hissing splinters of bursting ice formed a dense swirling cloud around it, until at last it collapsed into the green waters, sending out pressure waves that flung *Warlock*'s bows high in the air.

Since Nick's oath nobody had spoken on the bridge. They clutched for balance while the water churned and creamed. Of the yellow raft there was no longer any sign.

"Closer," urged Nick. "Get as close as you can." If by a miracle anybody had survived that avalanche, then there were four minutes in which to save them. Nick flung open the bridge doors beside him and stepped out into the freezing air of the open wing.

Red caught his eye, a flash of vivid red, seen through the green water, becoming brighter as it rose to the surface.

"Stop engines!" he screamed. "Both half back." And *Warlock* stopped dead as the twin propellers changed pitch and bit into the water, pulling her up in less than her own length.

Nick saw a body in a red anorak, supported by a thick inflated lifejacket. The head was thrown back, exposing the white face of a young boy.

"Get him" Nick yelled, and David, by his side, was already untying a life ring and line.

"Here!" called David. He threw the life ring with an expert round arm motion that sent it skimming to within two feet of where the hooded head bobbed on the agitated water.

"Grab it!" yelled Nick. "Grab hold!"

The boy made two inconclusive movements with a gloved hand, one actually bumped the ring but he could not hold it. Slowly it bobbed away from him.

"You bloody idiot," stormed Nick. "Grab it!" The boy looked up at him with two huge green eyes full of defeat, and with one stiff arm still raised—almost a farewell salute.

Nick did not realize what he was going to do until he had shrugged off his coat, and kicked away his shoes. He jumped feet first, throwing himself far out to miss the rail below him, and as the water closed over his head he experienced a terrified sense of disbelief at the cold.

It seized his chest in a vice that choked the air from his lungs, it drove needles of agony deep into his forehead, and blinded him with the pain as he rose to the surface again. The marrow in the bones of his legs and arms ached so that he found it difficult to force his limbs to respond—but he struck out for the floating figure.

It was only twenty feet, but halfway there he was seized by a panic that he was not going to make it. He clenched his teeth and fought the icy water as though it was a mortal enemy.

He struck the floating figure with one of his arms before he realized he had reached him, and he clung desperately to him, peering up at *Warlock*'s deck. David had retrieved the ring by its line and he threw it again. The cold had slowed Nick down so he could not avoid the ring and it struck him in the forehead, but he felt no pain.

The fleeting seconds counted out the life left to them as he struggled with the inert figure, slowly losing command of his own limbs as he tried to fit the ring over the boy's head. He did not accomplish it. He got the boy's head and one arm through, and he knew he could do no more.

"Pull!" he screamed in rising panic, and took a twist of line around his arm for his fingers could no longer hold, and he clung with the remains of his strength as they dragged them in. Jagged ice brushed and snatched at them, but he held the boy with his free arm.

Then they were bumping against *Warlock*'s steel side, were being lifted free of the water, the twist of line smearing the wet skin from his forearm, staining his sleeve with blood. With the other arm he hung on to the boy, holding him from slipping out of the ring. He did not feel the hands that grabbed at him. There was no feeling in his legs and he collapsed face forward. David caught him before he struck the deck.

Nick and the boy were carried into the steaming warmth of Angel's galley.

"Get their clothes off," said Angel.

While two seamen helped Nick, Angel himself lifted the boy's body onto the galley table and laid it out face upwards. With a single sweep of a butcher's knife he split the crimson anorak from neck to crutch and stripped it away.

Nick found his voice. It was ragged and broken by the convulsions of frozen muscles. "What the hell are you doing, David?" he grated. "Get this ship on course for *Golden Adventurer. . . .*" He would have added something a little more forceful but the next convulsion caught him, and anyway David had already left.

"You'll be all right." Angel did not even glance up at Nick as he worked with the knife, ripping away layer after layer of the boy's clothing. "A tough old dog like you, but I think we've got a ripe case of hypothermia here."

Suddenly Angel stopped and gave a gasp of amazement. Nick turned just as Angel spread a thick woollen blanket over the pale naked body on the table and began to massage it vigorously.

"You better leave us girls alone together, Skipper," said Angel with a sweet smile, and Nick was left with a single fleeting glimpse of the stunningly lovely body of a young woman below the pale face and the sodden head of copper gold hair.

NICK WAS SITTING in his canvas chair, swaddled in a grey woollen blanket, over a borrowed boiler suit and bulky jerseys. His feet were in thick Norwegian trawlerman's socks and heavy rubber working boots. He held a tin mug of almost boiling coffee in both hands, bending over it to savour the aroma of the steam. It was the third cup he had drunk in the last hour—and yet the shivering spasms still shook him every few minutes.

The morse beam squealed suddenly, a long sequence to which

every man on the bridge listened with complete attention, but it needed the Trog to say it for them. "*La Mouette* has reached the prize." He seemed to take a perverse relish in seeing their expressions. "She's beaten us to it, lads."

"I want it word for word," snapped Nick irritably, and the Trog grinned spitefully at him before bowing over his pad.

> *La Mouette* to Christy Marine. *Adventurer* is hard aground. Hull is flooded. Under no circumstances will Lloyd's Open Form be acceptable. Emphasize importance of beginning salvage work immediately. Worsening weather and sea conditions. My final hire offer of $8,000 *per diem* plus 2½% of salvaged value open until 1435 GMT. Standing by.

Nick lit one of his cheroots and irrelevantly decided he must conserve them in future. He had opened his last box that morning.

Probably Jules Levoisin felt safe that he was the only salvage tug within two thousand miles. Certainly he was playing it tough, dictating terms. Nick's own policy of silence was paying off.

Jules had seen *Golden Adventurer*'s hull. If there had been a fifty-fifty chance of a good salvage, Jules would have gone Open Form. So, it must be a tough one. *Golden Adventurer* was probably held fast by beach and ice, and *La Mouette* could build up a mere nine thousand horsepower. *Warlock*, on the other hand, had twenty-two thousand rated horsepower—and a dozen other high cards.

Nick glanced at his watch, and he saw that Jules had set a two-hour ultimatum. "Radio officer," he said quietly, and every man on the bridge stiffened and swayed closer, so as not to miss a word. "Open the telex line direct to Christy Marine, and send quote 'Personal for Duncan Alexander from Nicholas Berg master of *Warlock*. I will be alongside *Golden Adventurer* in one hour forty minutes. I make firm offer Lloyd's Open Form Contract Salvage. Offer closes 1300 GMT.'"

The Trog looked startled, and blinked his rheumy eyes.

"Send it," snapped Nick and rose to his feet. "Number One," he turned to David, "I want you and the chief engineer in my day cabin right away."

The buzz of excitement and speculation began before Nick had closed the door behind him.

David followed him three minutes later. "What are they saying?" Nick asked. "That I am crazy?"

"They're just kids." David shrugged. "What do they know?"

"They know plenty, and they're right. I am crazy to go Open Form on a site unseen! But it's the craziness of a man with no other option. Sit down, David."

Nick could no longer keep his steely silence. "When I turned down the Esso tow, that was when I did the crazy thing. The whole company depended on that cash. If I fail to pull *Golden Adventurer* out of there, I have lost nothing that is not already forfeit."

"We could have offered daily hire at a better rate than *La Mouette*," David suggested, and his colour was high, embarrassed by these confidences.

"No. Duncan Alexander is my enemy. The only way I can get the contract is to make it so attractive that he has no alternative. If he refuses my offer of Open Form, I will take him up before Lloyd's Committee and his own shareholders." Nick broke off at the heavy knock on the cabin door. "Come!"

Vinny Baker's overalls were pristine blue, but the bandage around his head was smeared with engine grease, and he had recovered all the bounce and swagger that Nick had banged out of him in the engine room.

"I hear you've just flipped," he said. "First you jump overboard and, when they fished you out, you went Open Form on a bomber that's beating herself to death on Cape Alarm."

"I'd explain it to you," offered Nick solemnly, "only I don't know enough words of one syllable." The chief engineer grinned wickedly at that and Nick went on quickly. "Just believe me when I tell you that I'm not risking anything I haven't lost already."

"That's good business," the Australian agreed handsomely, and helped himself to one of Nick's precious cheroots.

"Your share of twelve and a half per cent of daily hire is peanuts and apple jelly," Nick went on. "But if we can snatch *Golden Adventurer* and keep her afloat for three thousand miles, there will be a lot of big Gs. And that's beef and potatoes."

"You know something?" Vinny Baker grunted, "for a Pommy I'm beginning to like the sound of your voice."

"All I want from you now," Nick told him, "are your plans for getting power onto *Golden Adventurer*'s pumps and anchor winch. We will have to kedge her off the beach, and we won't have much time."

Kedging off was the technique of using a ship's own anchor and winch to assist the pull of a tug in dragging her off a stranding. Vinny waved the cheroot airily. "Don't worry about that. I'm here."

At that moment the Trog put his head through the doorway. "I have an urgent and personal for you, Skipper." He brandished the telex flimsy like a royal flush in spades.

Nick glanced through it once, then read it aloud:—

> Master of *Warlock* from Christy Marine. Your offer Lloyd's Open Form "No Cure, No Pay" accepted. You are hereby appointed Main Salvage Contractor for wreck of *Golden Adventurer*.

Nick grinned with that rare wide irresistible flash of very white teeth. "And so, gentlemen, we are still in business."

WARLOCK ROUNDED the headland, where the three black pillars of serpentine rock stood into a lazy green sea, and entered the ice-choked bay. The abandoned hulk of *Golden Adventurer* was so majestic that not even the savage mountains could belittle her.

"She's a beauty," whispered David, and his voice captured the sorrow they all felt for a great ship in mortal danger. For Nick, the bond was even more deeply felt. She was the child of his inspiration, and now his destiny depended upon her.

He looked away from her to where the squat and ugly *La Mouette* waited in the mouth of the bay. The headland would have blanketed *La Mouette*'s radar and this would be the first that Levoisin knew of *Warlock*'s presence. Nick could see the bustle of activity on her bridge and imagine the consternation there.

"Get *La Mouette* in clear," he instructed, and picked up the hand microphone as the Trog nodded to him.

"Jules, my dear pot-bellied little pirate, haven't they caught and hung you yet?" Nick asked kindly in French.

"James Bond, I think?" replied Jules with an unconvincing chuckle. "What kept you so long? I am arrived, you see."

"And I, old friend, am arrived also. But the difference is that I am Christy Marine's contractor."

"You are joking!"

"I am not joking," Nick told him. "My James Bond equipment lets me talk in private. But go ahead—call Christy Marine and ask them—and while you are doing it, move that dirty old greaser of yours out of the way. I've got work to do." Nick tossed the microphone back to the Trog. Then he spoke on the engine-room intercom. "I want you in full immersion with helmet as soon as possible, Chief. We are going on board her to take a look at her engine room." He turned to David. "Number One, tell Angel I want a hot meal for us before we go. And I want you to check all salvage gear immediately. All the diesel auxiliaries should be rigged to be swung out. I want to have power on *Golden Adventurer* by noon tomorrow."

"Sir."

But before he could go, Nick asked, "What is the barometric reading?"

"Reading is 1018." David checked hastily.

"It's too high," said Nick. "And it's too bloody calm. Watch it. We are going to have a pressure bounce. Watch it like an eagle, and inform me immediately of any variation over one millibar."

"Sir." David left the bridge.

The Trog called out, "Christy Marine has just called *La Mouette* and confirmed that we are the main contractor, but Levoisin has accepted daily hire to ferry a full load of survivors from Shackleton Bay to Cape Town. Now he wants to speak to you again."

Nick took the hand microphone. "Jules?"

"You don't play fair, Nick. You go behind the back of an old friend, a man who loves you like a brother."

"I'm a busy man. Did you truly call to tell me that?"

"I think you made a mistake going Lloyd's Open on this one, Nick. That ship is stuck fast—and the weather! Did you read the met. from Gough Island? You got yourself a screaming bastard of a job, Nick. You listen to an old man."

"*Au revoir*, Jules. Come and watch me in the arbitration court."

"I still think your boat's a whorehouse, not a tug. Send over a couple of blondes and a bottle of wine. Goodbye, Nick."

For a minute Nick looked after the departing tug as she waddled away over the swells, small and fat bottomed and cheeky, for all the world like its master—and yet there was something dejected and crestfallen about her going. He felt a prick of regret for the little Frenchman who had been a good friend as well as a teacher, but he crushed it ruthlessly. It had been a hard but fair fight—and Jules would bounce back, probably snatching the next job out from under Nick's nose. Anyway, Jules was right—this was going to be a screaming bastard of a job.

The high seas that had thrown *Golden Adventurer* ashore had been made even higher by the equinoctial spring tides—both had now abated and she was stuck fast. The liner's hull had swung also, so she was not aligned neatly at right angles to the beach. *Warlock* would have to drag her sideways.

Then he looked at the ice. A mass, like a monstrous octopus, was wrapping thick glistening tentacles around *Golden Adventurer*'s stern. The ice of the bay had not yet had sufficient time to become impenetrable, and *Warlock*'s bows were strengthened for just such an emergency, but Nick knew not to underestimate the problem.

Warlock bore down on the ice in the mouth of the bay at a full ten knots. Then, half a ship's length clear of it, Nick gave the order: "Both half back."

Warlock checked, her bows rose riding up over the ice as she decelerated, with a horrid rasping roar that echoed through the ship.

The ice gave with a rending crackle, huge slabs of it up-ending and tumbling together. Nick swung *Warlock*'s stern first starboard then port, deftly using the huge twin propellers to wash the broken ice free, then he pulled her out and lined her up again.

Butting, smashing and pivoting, *Warlock* worked her way deeper into the bay, opening a passage through the big chunks of floating ice.

David Allen was breathless as he burst onto the bridge. "All gear checked, sir."

"Take her," said Nick. "I'm going down now to kit up."

Vinny was in the aft salvage hold ahead of him. Angel hovered over them both with a tray of rich food.

"It's good," said Nick, although he could hardly force himself to swallow. The nerves in his stomach were bunched up too tightly.

"Samantha wants to talk to you, Skip."

"Who the hell is Samantha?"

"The girl. She wants to thank you."

"Use your head, Angel—can't you see I have other things on my mind?"

Nick was already pulling on the rubber immersion suit over a full length woollen undersuit. He called for a seaman to assist him to close the chest opening of the suit with a double ring seal. Then over the watertight bootees and mittens he put on another full suit, this one of polyurethane.

Nick and Vinny looked like a pair of fat Michelin men, as their dressers helped them into the full helmets, with wrap around visors and built in radio microphones.

"O.K., Chief?" Nick asked.

"Clear to roll," Vinny's voice squawked back too loudly.

Nick adjusted the volume, and then shrugged into the oxygen rebreathing set.

"Let's go," he said and waddled towards the ladder.

"GENTLEMEN, this is close as we can get," the seaman in charge of the Zodiac dingy told them. The sixteen foot inflatable craft coasted gently into a small open pool in the ice pack, fifty yards from *Golden Adventurer*'s stern.

A solid sheet of compacted ice separated them, and Nick studied it carefully. He had not taken the chance of working *Warlock* in closer until he could get a look at the bottom here. He wanted to know if there were hidden rocks to rip through *Warlock*'s hull. He also wanted to know the slope of the bottom, and if there was good holding for his ground tackle, but most of all he wanted to inspect the underwater damage to *Golden Adventurer*'s hull.

Nick worked swiftly checking out his gear, inflating his breathing bag, clipping his buddy line onto the Zodiac—a line to return along, like Theseus's in the Labyrinth of the Minotaur.

"Let's go," he said, and flipped backwards into the water. The cold struck through the multiple layers of clothing, and he waited only for Vinny to break through the surface beside him in a cloud of swirling silver bubbles. Paying out the line, Nick sank down into the hazy green depths, looking for bottom. It came up dimly, heavy shingle and pebble, and he checked his depth gauge. Almost six fathoms. He moved in towards the beach.

There was a current churning the sediment, and they had to fin hard to make headway. The light from the surface was filtered through thick ice, green and ghostly, and Nick felt claustrophobic panic stirring deep in him, ready to break into flame.

Suddenly *Golden Adventurer*'s hull loomed ahead of them, the twin propellers glinting like gigantic bronze wings in the gloom, her stern bumping heavily on the pebbly bottom, like a great hammer beating time to the ocean.

Nick realized that she was settling herself in. Every hour now was making his task more difficult. He drove harder with his swim fins. From Reilly's reports to Christy Marine, Nick knew exactly where to look for the damage, but he came across it without warning.

It looked as though a monstrous axe had been swung horizontally at the hull, a fourteen-foot slash the shape of an elongated teardrop. At its widest, the lips of the rent gaped open by three feet, and it breathed like a living mouth. The force of the ground swell pushing into the gap built up pressure within the hull, then as the swell subsided the trapped water was forcibly expelled.

"Let's penetrate," Nick told the chief. "I'll go first."

Nick hung four feet from the gash, finning to hold himself there against the current. He watched the swirl of water rushing into the opening, and then gushing out again in a rush of silver bubbles—then as it began to breathe again he darted forward.

The current caught him and he was hurled at the gap, with only time to duck his helmeted head and cover the fragile oxygen bag on his chest with both arms. Raw steel snagged at his leg; there was no pain, but almost instantly he felt the leak of sea water into his suit. The cold stung like a razor cut, but he was through into the total darkness of the cavernous hull. He was flung into a tangle of steel piping, and he anchored himself with one arm and groped for the underwater lantern on his belt. Seconds later, Vinny's lantern glowed eerily in the dark waters behind him.

"Work fast," instructed Nick. "I have a tear in my suit."

Though working in darkness, in a totally unfamiliar engine room, Vinny went unerringly to the pump system to check the valve settings, before finding his way to the main engines.

Nick was there ahead of him. The engine room was flooded almost to the deck above and the surface was covered with a scum of oil, in which floated a mass of loose articles—in the beam of his lantern Nick recognized a gumboot and a grease pot floating beside his head. The whole thick stinking soup rose and fell and agitated with the push of the current through the rent. Nick wiped the filth from his visor, checked the dark opening of the vertical ventilation shaft, then asked brusquely, "O.K., Chief?"

Vinny's voice squawked harshly. "Let's get the hell out."

Nick sank down to the glimmer of light through the gash. He had to judge his moment extra carefully for the return. The raw metal had been driven in by the ice, and was like the fangs in a shark's jaw. He used the suck of water and shot through without a touch, turning and finning to wait for the chief.

The Australian came through, in the next rush of water—but Nick saw him flicked sideways by the current, and he struck the jagged opening a touching blow. There was instantly a roaring rush of escaping oxygen from his breathing bag, as the steel split it wide, and for a moment the chief was obscured in the silver cloud of gas. The heavily leaded belt around his waist had been weighted to counter the flotation of the oxygen bag, and now he plummeted sharply into the green depths, the current dragging him down under the hull, where he would be crushed by twenty-two thousand tons of pounding steel.

Nick finned desperately to catch him. He had a fleeting glimpse of Vinny's face contorted with terror and lack of breath, the glass visor of his helmet already swamping with icy water. "Drop your belt," he yelled, but Vinny did not respond. The water had shorted out his headset.

Nick got a hand to him and threw back with all his strength on his fins to check their downward plunge, but still they went down and Nick's right hand was clumsy with cold as he groped for the quick release on the chief's belt.

Locked together like a couple of waltzing dancers they swung around and Nick saw the keel, like the blade of a guillotine rise up high above them. He could not reach Vinny's release toggle. Desperately he hit his own release and the thick belt with thirty-five pounds of lead fell away, and with it went the buddy line that would guide them back to the waiting Zodiac.

The abrupt loss of weight checked their downward plunge, and fighting with all the strength of his legs Nick was just able to hold them clear as the great keel came swinging downwards. The steel struck stone with a force that rang in Nick's eardrums like a bronze gong, but he had an armlock on the chief's struggling body, and now at last his right hand found the other man's release toggle.

He hit it, and another thirty-five pounds of lead dropped away. They began to rise, up along the steel hull, faster and faster as the oxygen in Nick's bag expanded with the release of pressure—and now their plight was every bit as desperate, for they were racing upwards to a roof of solid ice with enough speed to crack their skulls.

Nick emptied his lungs, exhaling on a single continuous breath, and at the same time opened the valve to vent his bag, blowing away the precious life-giving gas in an attempt to check their rise. Yet still they went into the ice with a force that would have stunned them had Nick not twisted over and caught it on his shoulder and outflung arm.

They were now pinned there under the ice by the buoyance of their rubber suits and the remaining gas in Nick's bag. With mild and detached surprise Nick saw that the lower side of the ice pack was not a smooth sheet, but was worked into ridges and pinnacles, like some abstract sculpture in pale green glass.

He only looked at it fleetingly, for beside him, Vinny was drowning. Inside the flooded helmet, his face was empurpled and his mouth contorted into a horrible rictus.

Holding Vinny to him, Nick cracked the valve on his steel oxygen bottle, reinflating his chest bag. With his right hand he began to unscrew the breathing pipe connection into the side of Vinny's helmet. While he worked he was pumping his lungs like bellows, hyperventilating, washing his blood with pure oxygen until he felt light-headed and dizzy. The connection came free. One last breath and then he unscrewed his own hose connection. Icy water flooded through the valve but he held his head at an angle to trap oxygen in the top of his helmet, keeping his nose and eyes clear. He rescrewed his own hose into Vinny's helmet, cracking the last of the oxygen from his bottle.

There was just sufficient pressure of gas left to expunge the water from Vinny's helmet. The chief choked and coughed, gulped and gasped. Nick felt him breathing again—"Which is more than I am doing," Nick thought grimly.

Having lost the guide line with his weight belt, Nick did not know which way to swim to reach the Zodiac. A suicidal urge to tear at the green ice roof of this watery tomb almost overwhelmed him. Then just before panic completely obliterated his reason, he remembered the compass on his wrist. Even then his brain was sluggish, beginning to starve for oxygen, and it took precious seconds working out the reciprocal of his original bearing. Still holding Vinny to him, linked by the thick black umbilical cord of his oxygen hose, Nick began to swim.

Immediately his lungs began to pump, convulsing involuntarily in spasms, craving air. He began to realize how exquisitely beautiful was the ice roof; translucent, wonderously carved and sculptured—and suddenly he remembered standing hand in hand with his wife beneath the arched roof of Chartres Cathedral, staring up in awe. The pain in his chest subsided, the need to breathe passed. Chantelle's face was before him then, glowing hair soft and glossy as a butterfly's wing, huge dark eyes so full of delight and warmth. "I loved you," he thought. "I really loved you."

Nick knew then he was dying, but panic had passed, as the cold had passed also. He realized now that his own legs were no longer moving; he lay relaxed not breathing, not feeling. It was Vinny's body that was driving forward. It was Vinny who was gulping the pure sweet oxygen and gaining strength with each breath.

"You be-yew-dy," whispered Nick dreamily, and felt the water shoot into his throat, but there was no pain.

Another image formed before him, an arrowhead-class yacht

with spinnaker set, running free across a bright Mediterranean sea, and his son at the tiller, the dense tumble of curls that covered his small neat head fluttering in the wind.

"Don't let her run by the lee, Peter," Nick wanted to shout to his son, but the image faded into blackness. He thought for a moment that he had passed into unconsciousness, but then he realized suddenly that it was the black rubber bottom of the Zodiac only inches from his eyes, and that the rough hands that dragged him upwards were not part of the fantasy.

NICK WRAPPED a towel around his waist as he came out of the shower cabinet. The night cabin was thick with steam, and his body glowed dull angry red from the almost boiling water. Vinny slouched in the armchair at the foot of his bunk. He wore fresh overalls, his hair stood up in little damp spikes around the shaven spot where Angel's cat-gut stitches held the wound closed. He held two glasses in his left hand, and a big flat brown bottle in the other. He poured two heavy slugs into the glasses. He passed a glass to Nick, and then showed him the bottle's yellow label. "Bundaberg Rum," he announced. "The dinky die stuff, Sport."

Nick recognized both the offer of liquor and the salutation as probably the highest accolade the chief would ever give another human being. Nick sniffed the dark honey-brown liquor and then took it in a single toss, shuddered, exhaled harshly and dutifully said, "It's the finest rum in the world."

"The mate asked me to give you a message," Vinny said as he poured another shot for each of them. "Glass hit 1035 and now it's diving like a dingo into its hole. It's going to blow!" They regarded each other over the rims of the glasses. "How are you going to plug that hull?" Vinny asked.

"I've got ten men at work already. We are going to fother a sail into a collision mat."

Vinny blinked at him for five seconds while he examined the proposition. A sail was fothered by threading the canvas with thousands of strands of unravelled oakum until it resembled a huge shaggy doormat. When this was forced into an aperture below a ship's waterline, the water swelled the mass of fibre until it formed an almost watertight plug.

"You haven't got pressure to drive it home," Vinny said.

"I'm going to run a wire down the ventilation shaft and out through the gash. We'll winch it home."

"It might work." Vinny was noncommital.

Nick took the second rum at a gulp, and reached for his working gear laid out on the bunk. "Let's get power on her before the blow hits us," he said.

NOW THAT NICK was certain that the bottom of the bay was free of underwater snags, he handled *Warlock* boldly. Like a fighting cock *Warlock* attacked the thicker ice line along the shore, smashing free huge lumps, giving herself space to work.

Nick had two Yokohama fenders slung from *Warlock*'s side, and the bloated plastic balloons cushioned the contact of steel against steel as he laid his tug alongside the stranded liner's stern. Vinny and his working party, swaddled in heavy Antarctic gear, had been waiting on the catwalk of *Warlock*'s forward gantry, seventy feet above the bridge and overlooking *Golden Adventurer*'s sharply canted deck, and now they dropped the steel boarding ladder across the gap between the two ships. Vinny led them over.

Nick then drew *Warlock* gently away from the liner's stern, and held her fifty feet off. Only then did he flick his eyes up at the sky. The midnight sun had turned it to a malevolent jaundiced yellow. The sun itself was a ball of dark satanic red, and it seemed that the snowfields and peaks of Cape Alarm were washed with blood.

"It's beautiful." Hearing the voice, Nick suddenly realized that the girl was beside him. The top of her head was on a level with his shoulder, and in the ruddy light her thick roped hair glowed like newly minted sovereigns in red gold. "I've come to thank you," she said shyly. "It's the first chance I've had."

She wore baggy, borrowed men's clothing that made her look like a little girl dressing up. Her expression was solemn yet, looking into her eyes, Nick saw the sparkle of laughter near the surface.

Nick was shocked by the strength of his sudden physical desire for her. He had not experienced such direct and instant involvement with a woman since the good bright times with Chantelle.

Suddenly he was aware that he had been staring into her face for many long seconds, that she was meeting his gaze steadily and that something was beginning to happen for which he was not in the least ready.

"Young lady," he said, "you have an absolute genius for being in the wrong place at the wrong time." His tone was colder and more remote than even he had intended it. From the chagrin in the green eyes, he realized with dismay that he had alienated her and he wanted to say something gracious that might retrieve the position, but he could think of nothing. Instead he lifted the hand microphone to his lips and spoke to Vinny over the VHF radio. "How's it going, Chief?"

"Their emergency generator has burned out, so we'll have to take on the alternator."

"We are ready to give it to you," Nick told Vinny, and then called David on the foredeck. "Ready with the alternator, David?"

"All set."

Nick began edging *Warlock* back towards the liner's towering stern, and now at last he turned again to the girl, but she had gone, taking with her that special aura of brightness.

Nick's voice had a jagged edge to it as he told David, "Let's do this fast and right, Number One."

Warlock once again nuzzled *Golden Adventurer*'s stern, the big black Yokohama fenders gentling her touch, and on her foredeck the winch whined shrilly, the lines squealing in their blocks as the four-ton alternator swung out from the open salvage hatch. It was mounted on a sledge for easy handling. The diesel tanks were charged and the big motor primed and ready to start. Five minutes later, the huge dangling machine dropped with the control of a roosting seagull onto the liner's deck. It was followed shortly by two high-speed centrifugal pumps which would augment *Golden Adventurer*'s machinery. Finally pallets with eight tons of salvage gear were lifted onto the liner's deck. By the time David came onto the bridge, the sun had gone and a luminous sky filled with the marvellous pyrotechnics of the aurora australis turned the night eerie and mysterious.

Nick told him immediately, "Take command, David, I'm going on board *Golden Adventurer*."

THE CHIEF had the work in hand, and going ahead as fast as even Nick in his overwhelming impatience could expect. The alternator had been secured against a steel bulkhead on B deck.

"As soon as I have power we'll drill the deck and bolt her down," he explained to Nick.

On the upper deck Nick found one of Vinny's gangs was already opening access to the ventilation shaft. The gas cutter hissed viciously and red sparks showered from the steel plate of the tall dummy smoke stack, as the last few inches of plating fell away leaving a square opening six feet by six feet which gave direct access to the half-flooded engine room fifty feet below.

On the open foredeck, another gang—with two men working over the ship's side—secured collars of heavy chain to the crowns of the twin anchors. *Warlock* would drag these anchors out, and drop them, so the flukes could dig in and hold. This ground tackle should resist the efforts of even a force twelve wind to throw *Golden Adventurer* further ashore, and when the chief had power running on the ship the anchor winches would be used to kedge *Golden Adventurer* off the bank, and thus assist *Warlock*'s own engines.

By the time they had finished the work on the anchors, the wind was rising force six, and wailing. The men were chilled and tired, and tempers were flashing. Nick led the gang back to the shelter of the main superstructure. His boots seemed to be made of lead, and he realized that he had not slept for more than two hours in the last thirty-six.

As he stepped over the door-sill into the liner's cold but wind-protected main accommodation, the power came back on. Suddenly garish light blazed throughout the ship and soft music wafted incongruously from the loudspeakers.

"Power is on!" Nick let out a whoop.

On B deck Nick found Vinny standing beside his roaring alternator. "Howzat, Sport?" he demanded.

Nick punched his shoulder. "Right on. The only thing left is to get the collision mat into place. Somebody has to go down to pass the wire."

"That is your trick," Vinny told him flatly. "You're not getting me into the water again, ever. I've given up bathing."

LESS THAN AN HOUR later, Nick was in full immersion kit again. Before going down he paused on the open deck. The ground tackle David had just completed laying held *Golden Adventurer* handsomely, even in the aggravated swell which was now pouring in to the open mouth of the bay. A low scudding sky of dirty grey cloud had blotted out the rising sun and the peaks of Cape Alarm. It was a cold dark dawn, with the promise of a wilder day to follow.

Nick took one last glance across at *Warlock*. David was holding her nicely in position, and the chief's team was ready, grouped around that ugly, black, freshly burned opening in the stack. Nick checked the radio.

"*Warlock*, do you read me?"

David's voice came back immediately. "The glass just went through the floor, Skipper. She's 996 and going down. Wind's force six rising seven. It looks like we are fair in the dangerous quadrant of whatever is coming."

"Thank you, David," Nick replied. "You warm my heart."

He stepped forward, and they helped him into the canvas bosun's chair. Nick checked the tackle, and then he nodded.

The interior of the engine room was no longer dark, for Vinny had rigged floodlights high above in the ventilation shaft, but the water was still black with engine oil, and as Nick was lowered slowly down, with legs dangling from the bosun's chair, it surged furiously back and across like some panic stricken monster trying to break out of its steel cage. The wind-driven swell was crashing into *Golden Adventurer*'s side and boiling in through the opening, setting up its own wave action.

"Slower," Nick spoke into the microphone. "Stop!" His downwards progress halted. He was now waist-deep in the churning water.

"Send them down," he ordered, and the huge steel pulley blocks came down out of the shadows and dangled in the floodlights.

"Stop!" Nick began directing them into position. "Down two feet. Stop!"

Now he struggled to secure the blocks to the main frames of the hull. Every few minutes a stronger surge would hurl the water over his head, forcing him to cling helplessly, until it relinquished its grip, and his visor cleared sufficiently to allow him to continue.

It was an hour before he was ready to carry the messenger line out through the gap.

The line was of finely plaited Dacron, with enormous strength and elasticity and one end was secured on the deck high above. Nick threaded it into the sheave blocks carefully, so that it was free to run. He clamped the reel of line onto his belt.

He realized then how close to final exhaustion he was, and he considered breaking off the work to rest, but the heightened action of the sea into the hull warned him against further delay.

He swam down towards the light that came through the gash of steel, pale light further diffused by the filthy muck of mixed oil and water in the hull.

He clung to one of the engine-room stringers, his head seven feet from the opening, feeling the ebb and flow through the hull, and trying to find some pattern in the action of the water, but now it seemed entirely random—a hissing, bubbling ingestion followed by three vicious exhalations of such power that they would have windmilled a swimming man end over end into those daggers of splayed steel. He had to choose and ride a middling-sized swell.

Judging his moment, he released his grip and instantly the water caught him. The speed appalled him as he was flung head first at that murderous steel mouth. He could feel the nylon line streaming out against his leg, the reel on his belt racing frantically.

His head hit something with a numbing shock, so that his vision starred in flashing colour and light. Then he was swirling, end over end, completely disorientated so he did not know if he was still inside *Golden Adventurer*'s hull, and the nylon line was wrapping itself around his throat and chest, around the precious air tube and cutting off his air supply. He thought of a stillborn infant strangled by its own umbilical cord, and he screamed soundlessly into his mask. He flung out his arms and found the rough irregular shape of ice above him. Then suddenly he broke out into light and air. *Warlock*'s work boat was only twenty feet away and butting itself busily towards him through the brash of rotten, broken ice.

THE COLLISION MAT looked like a gigantic Airedale terrier curled up to sleep in the bows of the work boat—just as shaggy, wiry, and shapeless and of the same furry brown colour.

Nick had pulled an Arctic cloak and hood over his bare head and suited torso. He was balanced in the stern of the work boat which plunged and porpoised in the big swells as the helmsman brought her in close under *Golden Adventurer*'s tall stern.

The thin white nylon line was the only physical contact with the men on the liner's towering stack of decks, the messenger which would carry heavier tackle. Nick paid it out through his own numbed hands, feeling for the slightest check or jerk which could mean a snag and a break off.

With hand signals he kept the work boat positioned so that the line ran cleanly into the pierced hull, around the sheave blocks he had placed in the engine room, from there up the tall ventilation shaft, out of the opening in the stack and around the winch, beside which Vinny supervised its recovery.

Vinny's voice over the two-way radio was thin in the buffeting boom of wind. "Line running free."

"Right, we are running the wire now," Nick told him. The second line was as thick as a man's index finger, and it was of the finest Scandinavian steel cable. Nick checked the connection between nylon and steel cable himself, then let it go over the side. The white nylon disappeared into the green water and now the black steel cable ran out slowly from the revolving drum.

Nick felt the check as the connection hit the sheave block in the engine room. He felt his heart jump. If it caught now they would lose it all—no man could penetrate that hull again, for the sea was now too vicious.

Then, the drum halted, made a half turn and jammed. Somewhere the cable had snagged. Nick signalled to the helmsman to take the work boat in closer, to change the angle of the line into the hull.

As the winch took up the pull again, he could imagine the fibres of the nylon messenger stretching and creaking. "Please God, let it run," he prayed, and then suddenly he saw the drum begin to revolve again.

Nick felt almost dizzy with relief, as he heard Vinny's voice over the radio strident with triumph. "Wire secured."

"Stand by," Nick told him. "We are connecting the cable."

Again the whole laborious, touchy, nerve-scouring process as the massive two-inch steel cable was drawn out by its thinner, weaker forerunner—and it was a further forty vital minutes, with the wind and sea rising every moment of it, before Vinny shouted, "Main cable secured—we are ready to haul!"

Nick signalled to his crew and the five of them shambled up into the bows, bulky and clumsy in their electric-yellow oilskins. Nick positioned them around the shaggy head-high pile of the collision mat before he signalled to the helmsman to throw the gear in reverse and pull back from *Golden Adventurer*'s side.

The mass of oakum quivered as the cable came up taut and they struggled to heave the whole untidy mass overboard. Slowly they heaved it forward and outward, and the work boat took on a dangerous list under the transfer of weight. Then the mass snagged and stuck.

The boat went down at the bows, and was canting at an angle of twenty degrees, when some instinct of danger made Nick look up and out to sea. *Warlock* was lying a quarter of a mile farther out in the bay, and beyond her Nick saw the rearing shape of a big wave alter the line of the horizon. It would hit the work boat broadside in thirty seconds. With bows held down, anchored by mat and cable, she would be swamped.

"Vinny!" Nick's voice was a scream in the microphone. "Heave all! Pull, damn you, pull!"

Almost instantly the cable began to run, drawn in by the powerful winch on *Golden Adventurer*'s deck. The strain pulled the work boat down sharply and water cascaded over her gunwhale. Nick seized one of the oars and thrust it under the mat at the point where it was snagged, and using it as a lever he threw all his weight upon it. They were almost knee deep now as the wave raced down on them, carelessly tossing aside the mass of broken ice.

Suddenly the snag cleared and the whole massive weight of oakum slid overboard. The work boat bounded away, relieved of her burden, and the helmsman brought her bows round so they went up the wave with a gut-swooping rush that threw them down onto the floorboards. But the collision mat was floating hard against *Golden Adventurer*'s side, buoyant with trapped air amongst the mass of wiry fibre.

"She's looking good," Nick told Vinny on the radio. "Take her in slowly, fifty feet a minute on the winch."

"Fifty feet, it is," Vinny confirmed.

Slowly the bobbing mat was drawn down below the surface, and the two-inch cable plugged it deep into the gash.

"It's done," Nick said. "You can start to pump her dry."

NICK'S EYES were inflamed, angry with salt and wind and cold; the smears of exhaustion that underlined them were as lurid as the fresh bruises and abrasions that covered his body. His hands shook in a mild palsy with the need for rest and his legs could hardly carry him as he forced himself back to *Warlock*'s navigation bridge.

"Congratulations, sir," said David, and his admiration was transparent.

"How's the glass?" Nick asked.

"990 and dropping, sir."

Nick looked across at *Golden Adventurer.* Below the dingy low sky she stood like a pier, unmoved by the big swells that marched on her in endless ranks. She was still hard aground and heavy with the water in her. Vinny's big centrifugal pumps, however, were running at full power, and from both her port and starboard quarters water poured out.

"Chief," Nick radioed Vinny on the ship. "Call me as soon as she alters her trim." Then he turned to David. "It will be four hours before she will be light enough to make an attempt to haul her off, but I want you to put the main towing cable on board her so we will be ready when she is." He moved like a drunkard towards his quarters. "Call me when you've done it, or if the chief reports alteration of trim—or if anything else changes."

He made it to the cabin before his knees buckled and he toppled forward onto his bunk as though he had been slugged.

DAVID CALLED the captain's suite for three minutes without an answer, slapping his open palm on the mahogany chart table with impatience and staring through the navigation windows at the spectacle of a world gone mad.

For two hours the wind had blown steadily from the northwest at a little over thirty knots, and although the big seas still tumbled into the mouth of the bay, *Warlock* had ridden them easily. During that time, Vinny had connected emergency power to *Golden Adventurer*'s steering gear, and David had put a messenger over her stern, firing the nylon line from a rocket gun. Vinny's men had retrieved it and winched across first the carrier wire and then the main cable itself. They had made it fast to *Golden Adventurer*'s main deck bollards with a double yoke—one on her starboard and one on her port stern quarters. The yoke was Y shaped—drooping over the high stern to join at the white nylon spring, three times the thickness of a man's thigh and with the elasticity to absorb sudden shock which might have snapped rigid steel cable. From the yoke the single main cable looped back a thousand yards to the tug.

But now the wind, which had been veering slowly into the north, suddenly brought the storm upon them. It came roaring like a ravening beast, flinging *Warlock* up so harshly on her main cable that her stern was pulled down sharply, water pouring in through her stern scuppers.

At last the buzzer penetrated Nick's fatigue-drugged brain. He forced himself up on one elbow, his body aching in every joint, as he groped for the handset.

"Captain to the after bridge!" He could hear something in David Allen's voice that forced him to his feet.

When Nick staggered onto the after navigation bridge, David turned gratefully to him. "Thank God you've come, sir."

The wind was tearing each wave to a shrieking fog of white spray and mingling it with the sleet and snow that drove horizontally across the bay. Nick glanced at the dial of the wind anemometer, and then discounted the reading. The needle was stuck at the top of the scale. The instrument must have been damaged by the initial gusts of this wind—to believe it would be to admit disaster, for nobody could salvage an ocean-going liner in wind velocities right off the Beaufort scale.

Warlock stood on her tail, like a performing dolphin, as the cable brought her up short. Nick crashed into the control panel and clung for purchase to the foul-weather rail.

"We'll have to shear the cable and stand out to sea." David pitched his voice above the tumult of the storm.

Nick clung to the rail and looked across the thousand yards to where the hull of the liner was just visible, a denser area in the howling, swirling, white wilderness.

"Chief?" he asked into the hand microphone. "What is your position?"

"The wind's got her, she's slewing. You'll not be able to take us off in this. Shear the cable and stand-off. We'll try to get ashore as she breaks up." Then with a hangman's chuckle he went on, "Just don't forget to come and fetch us when the weather moderates—that is if there is anybody to fetch."

Abruptly Nick's anger came to the surface through the layers of fatigue—anger at the knowledge that all he had risked was now to be in vain. He was going to lose *Golden Adventurer,* and probably with his men on her. "Are you ready to heave on the anchor winches?" he asked. "We are going to pull her off."

"Goddammit!" said Vinny. "She's still half flooded. You'll lose *Warlock* as well—"

Nick cut Vinny short. "Listen, you stupid Queensland sheep, get onto those winches." As he said it *Golden Adventurer* momentarily disappeared, her bulk blotted out completely by the solid, white curtains of the blizzard. "Engine room," Nick spoke crisply to the second engineer. "Disengage the override, and give me direct control. David, you take the wheel."

"Control transferred to bridge, sir." The engineer confirmed, and Nick grasped the shining stainless steel levers.

"Anchor winches manned." Vinny's tone was almost casual.

"Stand by," said Nick. "Starboard ten, David."

Warlock's bows came up into that hideous wind.

"Chief," Nick spoke into the microphone. "Haul starboard winch, full power."

Nick slowly nudged open the throttles, bringing in twenty-two thousand horsepower. Held by her tail, *Warlock* went berserk. She corkscrewed and porpoised to her very limits, every frame in her hull shook with the vibration of her screws.

Then with a wild lurch of elation Nick saw the forward speed indicator flick into green. Its electronic digital read-out, changing swiftly—they were moving forward at one hundred and fifty feet a minute.

"We are moving her," Nick cried aloud, and he snatched up the microphone. "Full power both winches."

"Both full and holding," answered Vinny immediately.

Nick glanced back at the indicator. It was slowing, and he realized with a slide of dismay that it was merely the elasticity of the nylon spring that had given them the first reading.

Warlock was now standing still. Held down by cable and power, she could not rise to meet the seas that tumbled aboard her, so she burrowed deeper and more dangerously. Nick still kept both clenched fists on the control levers, pressing them to the limit, sending the great engines shrieking, driving the needles up around the dials, deep into the red "never exceed" sectors.

"For God's sake, sir." David was no longer able to contain himself. "You'll drive her clean under."

"Chief?" Nick ignored his mate. "Are you gaining?"

"She is not moving," Vinny told him.

Nick pulled back the stainless steel levers. The needles sank swiftly back around their dials, and *Warlock* reacted gratefully, shaking herself free of the piled waters.

"Shear the tow," Vinny's disembodied voice was muted by the clamour of the storm. "We'll take our chances, Sport."

David reached for the red-painted steel box that housed the shear button, protecting it from accidental usage.

"Belay that!" Nick snarled at him, and then to Vinny, "I'm shortening tow. Be ready to haul again when I am in position."

Nick turned to the main cable controls. He moved the green lever to reverse, and felt the vibration in the deck as below him in the main cable room the big drums began to revolve, drawing in the thick ice-encrusted cable, up over *Warlock*'s stern.

Fighting every inch of the way like a wild horse on a halter, *Warlock* was drawn in by her own winches, and the officers watched in mounting horror as out of the white terror of the blizzard emerged the mountainous ice-covered bulk of *Golden Adventurer*.

"Now we can see what we are doing," Nick told them grimly. He could see now that much of *Warlock*'s power had been wasted by pulling at an angle to *Golden Adventurer*'s keel. He had been disorientated in the blizzard. It would not happen now.

"Chief," he said. "Pull until she bursts her guts!" And again he slid the throttle handles fully home.

"She's not moving, sir," David cried.

Nick turned on him angrily. "Give me the wheel," he said.

With both engines boiling the sea to white foam, and roaring like dying bulls, Nick swung the wheel to full port lock.

Wildly *Warlock* dug her shoulder in, water pouring on board her as she rolled. Instantly Nick spun the wheel to full starboard lock and she lurched against the tow, throwing an extra ton of pressure onto it.

Even above the storm they heard *Golden Adventurer* groan. Then the groan became a crackling hiss as the pebble bottom gave and moved under her.

"Goddammit she's coming!" shrieked Vinny.

Nick swung *Warlock* to full port lock again. "Pull, my darling, pull," he pleaded with her.

With a slow reluctant rumble, *Golden Adventurer* began to slide over the holding, clinging bottom.

"Both winches recovering," Vinny shouted gleefully, and *Warlock*'s ground speed indicator flicked into the green. Its little angular figures changing in twinkling electronic progression as *Warlock* gathered way.

Golden Adventurer's stern swung to meet the next great ridge of water as it burst around her. She was floating.

For moments Nick was paralysed by the wonder of seeing that great ship come to life again. Then, "Chief, get those anchors up," he snapped into the microphone. It was a point of honour to retrieve even the anchors. "And rudder amidships."

"Amidships it is," Vinny repeated.

Nick pulled back the throttle controls taking the intolerable strain off *Warlock*'s engines before they tore themselves to pieces.

"We've done it!" shouted Vinny.

"Anchors and all," Nick replied.

THEY RODE OUT the storm in the open sea, eight days of unrelenting tension.

The first task was to move the tow cable to *Golden Adventurer*'s bows. In that sea the transfer took almost twenty-four hours and three abortive attempts before they had her head-on to the wind. Now she rode more easily, and *Warlock* had merely to hang on like a drogue. Then they pumped *Golden Adventurer*'s engine room full of Tannerax, an anti-corrosive chemical that would save her engines and much of her vital equipment from further sea-water damage, adding enormously to her salvaged value.

Nick spent most of those days on the bridge, nagged by the fear that the plug in the gashed hull would not hold. Then, one clear and windy morning under a cold yellow sun, *Warlock* was able to tow *Golden Adventurer* into the sheltered waters of Shackleton Bay. It was like a diminutive guide-dog leading a blinded colossus.

As the two ships came up into the sheltering arm of the bay, the survivors came down from the encampment to the water's edge, with cheers and shouts of welcome.

Even before the ship's anchors had splashed into the clear green water, Captain Reilly's boat was puttering out to *Warlock*. When he came aboard his eyes were haunted by the hardship and difficulties of these last days, but when he shook hands with Nick his grasp was firm. "My thanks and congratulations, sir!"

"It's good to see you again," Nick told him.

Nick led him to his day cabin, and began with tact to deal with the hundred details which had to be settled between them. It was a delicate situation, for Reilly was no longer master of his own ship. Command had passed to Nick as salvage master.

Within half an hour they had made all the necessary arrangements to transfer the survivors back aboard the liner. Levoisin on *La Mouette* had been able to take only one hundred and twenty of the oldest and weakest on board his little tug.

Nick now went aboard *Golden Adventurer.* The cavernous engine room was lit by the eye-scorching blue glare of the electric welding flames as the chief placed steel over the wound and welded it into place. Even then neither he nor Nick was satisfied until the new patches had been shored and stiffened with baulks of heavy timber. There was the hard passage through the Roaring Forties to Cape Town ahead.

They sat side by side amidst the greasy machinery, and drank steaming coffee laced with Bundaberg rum. "We get this beauty into Duncan Docks, and you're going to be a rich man," Nick said.

"I've been rich before. It never lasts long, and it's always a relief when I've spent the stuff." Vinny gargled the rum and coffee appreciatively, before he went on shrewdly. "So you don't have to worry about losing the best goddamned engineer afloat."

Nick laughed with delight. Vinny had read him accurately.

Four days later, Nick's senior officers came to his day cabin and reported that all the repairs and preparation were completed. *Warlock* was ready to drag her massive charge three thousand miles to Cape Town. When they rose to leave, David Allen lingered self-consciously. "The wardroom is arranging a little celebration tonight, sir, and we would like you to be our guest."

THE WARDROOM was the officers' club from which, traditionally, the master was excluded. He could enter the small panelled cabin only as an invited guest, but there was no doubt at all in the genuine warmth of the welcome they gave him. They stood and applauded him when he entered, and David made a brief speech. Then Angel brought in a cake, iced in the shape of *Golden Adventurer*—a minor work of art, with the figures 12½%, being the crew's share of any salvage award, picked out in gold on her hull. After they had applauded Angel, they called on Nick to speak, and his relaxed style soon had them hooting with glee.

The girl was wedged into a corner, almost swallowed in the knot of young officers who pressed around her. She laughed with a clear unaffected exuberance, her voice ringing high above the growl of masculine mirth so that Nick found it difficult not to keep looking across at her.

She wore a dress of green clinging material, and Nick wondered where it had come from until he remembered that earlier that morning he had noticed the girl standing beside David in the stern of the work boat as it returned from the liner. She had been to fetch her gear—and she probably should have stayed aboard the liner. Nick was pleased she had not.

Nick finished his little speech, having mentioned every one of his officers by name and given each the praise they deserved. David pressed another large whisky into his hand, and then left hurriedly to join the tight circle around the girl.

Nick watched with indulgence the open competition for her attention. Then the circle around her opened, and she looked across the wardroom and their eyes met. The laughter stilled on her lips, and she returned his gaze. It was a solemn enigmatic gaze, and he found himself once again regretting his previous rudeness to her. Then David hurried to her with another offering, and cut off the look that passed between them.

A few minutes later, Nick made his excuses and returned to his day cabin where he sat at the desk and tried to concentrate on some paperwork. The muted sounds of revelry from the deck below distracted him, however, and he found himself listening for the sound of her voice. They were dancing, or playing some raucous game which consisted of a great deal of bumping and thumping and shrieks of laughter.

Suddenly Nick realized he was lonely. He toyed with the idea of returning to the wardroom and grimaced as he imagined the dismay of his officers at the master's inhibiting intrusion. Instead, he went through onto the navigation bridge.

The night lights were so dim that he did not notice Graham, the third officer, until his eyes adjusted to the glow.

"Good evening, Mr. Graham." He moved to the chart table and checked the log. Graham hovered anxiously, and Nick searched for something to say. "Missing the party?" he asked at last.

"Sir."

It was not a promising conversational opening, and despite his loneliness of a few minutes previously, Nick suddenly wanted to be alone again. "I will stand the rest of your watch. Go off and enjoy yourself."

"That's jolly decent of you, sir," said Graham, and he fled.

Nick Berg once again bent over the chart table, so intently that he was not aware for many seconds that Samantha Silver had entered the bridge. She stood quietly, until he looked up.

"I'm sorry to disturb you," she said. "I brought some cake for Timmy Graham."

"I've just sent him below to join the party."

"Oh, I must have missed him." She made no move to leave. "Could I interest you in the slice? It's going begging."

"Share it?" he suggested, and she came to the chart table.

"I owe you an apology," he said, and was immediately aware of the harshness in his own voice. He hated to apologize.

"I picked bad moments," she said, and broke off a piece of the cake. "But thank you again. I understand now that rescuing me nearly cost you *Golden Adventurer*."

They both turned to look out of the big armoured glass windows to where she lay. "She is beautiful, isn't she?" said Nick, and his voice had lost its edge.

"Yes, she's beautiful," Samantha agreed, and suddenly they were very close in the intimate ruddy glow of the night lights.

He began to talk, stiffly and self-consciously at first, but she drew him on, and with secret joy she sensed him warming and relaxing. Then as she spoke about the university, explaining her research project, and the other work she had in mind, the difference in their ages was of no importance. It was an intrusion when the watch ended, bringing other human presence to the bridge, and denying them further reason for remaining together.

"Goodnight, Captain Berg," she said.

"Goodnight, Doctor Silver," he answered reluctantly.

During the long day of getting *Golden Adventurer* under tow,

Nick thought of the girl at unlikely moments. That night, when he changed his usual routine and dined in the saloon rather than his own cabin, she was surrounded by a solidly attentive phalanx of young men, and with a small shock of self-honesty Nick realized that he was actually jealous of them. Twice during the meal he had to suppress the sharp jibes that came to his lips. He ate no dessert and took coffee alone in his day cabin. He might have relished Vinny's company but the Australian was aboard *Golden Adventurer*, working on her main engines.

At eight o'clock, on impulse, he went through to the navigation bridge, and again relieved Tim Graham of the watch. He made a slow round of the bridge, checking every detail from the riding lights to the cable tensions of the tow.

It was only when Nick became aware of the waft of her perfume beside him that he was honest enough to admit to himself that he had relieved his third officer with the express intention of luring the girl up to the bridge.

"There are whales ahead," he told her and smiled one of his rare smiles. "I hoped you might come up."

"Where? Where are they?" she asked with unfeigned excitement, and then they saw the spouts, golden feathers of spray in the low night sunlight two miles ahead. Nick lifted his arm and would have placed it around her shoulders, but he caught himself at the last moment before he actually touched her. She had felt his movement and tensed for it, swaying slightly towards him in anticipation—but he let his arm fall and stepped away. She only realized then how much she had wanted him to touch her—but for the rest of that evening he stayed within the physical limits which he seemed to have set for himself.

The next evening she was with him only minutes after he had assumed the watch from Tim Graham, and they grinned at each other like school children in a successful piece of mischief.

She asked him to explain how the Lloyd's Open Form contract worked, and she followed his explanation swiftly.

"If they take into consideration the danger and difficulties involved," she mused, "you should be able to claim an enormous award."

"I'm going to ask for twenty per cent of the hull value—that's seven million dollars, give or take a few cents—but I won't get it. I'll walk away with three or four millions."

"But . . ." Samantha shook her head. "What would you do with that much money?"

"It's spent already. It will just about enable me to pay off my loans and launch my other tug."

"You owe three or four million dollars?" She stared at him now in open wonder. "I'd never be able to sleep . . ."

"Money to me is a game," he explained, "the biggest most exciting game in town. . . ."

She listened attentively to it all, happy because he was gay and excited with future plans, and because he shared them with her. "What we will do is this, we'll come down here with both tugs and catch an iceberg," he said.

She laughed. "Oh, come on!"

"I'm not joking," he assured her. Moving to the chart table, he beckoned her to join him. "We'll put tow lines on a big berg, and we'll swing it northwards, up into the Western Australian current." He traced the course with his finger. "We will cross to the east coast of Africa with the current pushing all the way, just in time to catch the southwesterly monsoon drift—right into the Persian Gulf." He straightened and smiled. "A hundred billion tons of fresh water delivered right into the dryest, richest corner of the globe."

"But, but. . . ." She shook her head. "It would melt."

"From a helicopter we spray it with a reflective polyurethane skin to lessen the effect of the sun, and we moor it in a dock where it will cool its own surrounds. Sure, it will melt, but not for a year or two and then we'll go out and catch another one. Meanwhile we cut it into manageable hunks with a laser lance and lift the hunks into a melting dam."

She thought about it. "It could work," she admitted.

"It will work," he told her. "I've almost sold the idea to the Saudis already. They are drawing up plans for the dock and the dams. We'll give them water at one-hundredth the cost of using nuclear condensers on sea water."

She was absorbed with his vision and as they talked deep into the long watches of every night, they drew closer in spirit.

Although each of them treasured those shared hours, however, neither could bridge the narrow gap between friendliness and intimacy. There was time—Nick told himself—plenty of time, but *Warlock* bore steadily north by northeast, dragging her crippled ward with her at a good six knots. Time was running out. Samantha too had closed her mind to it. Even when one morning Nick showed her the fuzzy luminescence of the African continent on the extreme range of the radar screen, she pretended to herself that it would go on like this—if not for ever, at least until something special happened.

That very night, during the ritual of the eight to midnight watch, they fell into a heated discussion about tanker pollution.

"We found oil-soaked penguins on Cape Alarm, dead and dying," Samantha said. "They had hit an oil slick within fifty miles of that isolated shore."

"I cannot believe. . . ." Nick started, but she cut across him.

"That's just it!" she said. "Nobody wants to believe it. That's what should really terrify us, Nick!"

She had used his given name for the first time, and they were both acutely aware of it. They were silent, staring out into the starlit night.

"The world has to use fossil fuels, and we sailors have to transport them," Nick said at last.

"But not with an eye only to the profits, not at the cost of turning the sea into a stinking festering cesspool."

"There are unscrupulous owners . . ." he began, and again she cut across him angrily.

"Sailing under flags of convenience, without control, ships built to dangerous standards, equipped with a single boiler—" She reeled out the charges, and he was silent. "When they waived the winter load line for tankers rounding the Cape of Good Hope in the southern winter, to enable them to carry that extra fifty thousand tons of crude. . . ."

"That was criminal," he agreed.

"Yet you were chairman of Christy Marine, you had a representative on the board of control. . . ."

She saw that she had made a mistake. His expression was suddenly ferocious. His anger seemed to crackle like electricity in the gloom of the bridge. She felt a flutter of fear, but he turned away and lit a cheroot.

When he turned back to her, she could see the anger had passed.

"Christy Marine seems like another existence to me now." He spoke softly, and she could sense the deep pain of unhealed wounds. "When I ran Christy Marine we opposed the Cape winter line decision, and none of my tankers loaded to their summer line on the Good Hope passage. The design and engineering of every Christy Marine vessel was of the same standard as that ship there." He pointed back at *Golden Adventurer*. "Or this one here," and he stamped once on the deck.

"Even *Golden Dawn*?" she asked.

"Especially *Golden Dawn*," he said softly. "The name sounds absurdly presumptuous, doesn't it? But I really thought of her as that when I conceived her. The first million-ton tanker, with every refinement and safety feature that man has so far tested and proved." He paused and drew deeply on the cheroot. When he spoke again, his voice was harsh and hollow. "Still, I am no longer chairman of Christy Marine. . . ."

It was all turning out so badly. She wished vainly that she had not disturbed him so, and her instinct warned her she should leave him now.

He nodded off-handedly at her sudden plea of tiredness. "Goodnight, Doctor Silver."

"My name is Sam," she told him, wishing that she could comfort him in some way. "Or Samantha, if you prefer it."

"I do prefer it," he said, without smiling. "Goodnight."

She was angry with herself and him, angry that the good feeling between them had been destroyed, so she flashed at him, "You really are old-fashioned, aren't you?" and hurried from the bridge.

DURING THE VOYAGE, Samantha had streamed a very fine-meshed net from *Warlock*'s stern, collecting krill, plankton and other microscopic marine life. Angel had given her a small corner of his scullery in return for her services as honorary assistant chef, and she spent many hours there each day identifying and preserving her specimens. She was there the next morning when the helicopter came out to *Warlock*. She heard the buffeting of the machine's rotors, and she was tempted to go up and look, but she was in the middle of staining a slide. She worked on, and heard the roar of the rotors as the helicopter rose from the deck again.

Angel came in from the deck, wiping his hands on his apron. "You didn't tell me he was going, dearie."

"What do you mean?" Samantha looked up at him, startled.

"Your boyfriend, darling." Angel watched her shrewdly. "Don't tell me he didn't even kiss you goodbye."

She dropped the glass slide into the stainless steel sink and it snapped in half.

She was panting when she reached the rail of the upper deck and stared after the cumbersome yellow machine as it dwindled swiftly towards the far blue line of mountains.

NICK SAT IN the jump seat between the two pilots of the big S-S&T Sikorsky and looked ahead towards the flat silhouette of Table Mountain, overlaid by a thick mattress of snowy cloud.

Far behind them *Warlock* was still visible. A backward glance at her invoked a pang of regret that he had been so stubbornly trying to ignore, and he had a vivid image of green eyes and hair of copper and gold.

His regret was spiced by the persistent notion that he had been cowardly. He had left *Warlock* without being able to bring himself to say goodbye to Samantha, and he knew why. He would not take the chance of making a fool of himself. He grimaced as he remembered her exact words. "You really are old-fashioned, aren't you?" There was something repulsive in a middle-aged man lusting after young flesh. . . .

Still, it had been cowardice. She had become a friend during those weeks, and he really had owed her the common courtesy of a handshake and an assurance of the pleasure he had taken from her company—but he had not been certain he could restrict it to that. He winced again as he imagined her horror as he blurted out some sort of declaration, her disenchantment when she realized that behind the façade of the mature and cultured man, he was just a grimy old lecher.

"Let it go," he had decided. At the worst she might be a little piqued by his lack of manners, but in a week she would have forgotten his name.

Resolutely he turned in the jump seat and looked ahead. Always look ahead, there are never regrets in that direction.

They clattered in to land on the harbour helipad of Table Bay. As Nick jumped down, ducking instinctively under the still-turning rotors, a big red-faced man with a scorched-looking bald head and the furry arms of a bear came forward to meet him.

"Larry Fry, Mr. Berg," he growled. "You remember me?"

"Hello, Larry." He was the local manager for Nick's agent, Bernard Wackie.

"I've booked you in at the Mount Nelson, Mr. Berg, and I've invited the Press to meet you there in two hours. Shall we go?"

As they drove up the palm-lined drive to the gracious old hotel, Nick felt the stir of memory—but he suppressed that and continued to listen intently to Larry Fry's arrangements for the berthing of *Golden Adventurer*.

The hotel manager himself met Nick at the entrance. "Good to see you again, Mr. Berg." He waived the registration procedures. "We have given you the same suite—"

Nick would have protested, but already they were ushering him into the sitting room, lavishly appointed with antique furniture, oil paintings and flowers. The memories were as fresh as the flowers but not as pleasing.

Nick walked through to the bedroom. He remembered that from the four poster bed you could look out over the lawns. He remembered also Chantelle sitting under the canopy, with a gossamer sheer bed robe over her creamy shoulders, eating thin strips of marmaladed toast and then delicately licking each slim tapered finger with her pink tongue.

That time, Nick had come out to negotiate the transportation of South African coal to Japan. Perhaps he had had the premonition of imminent loss, for he had insisted that Chantelle accompany him. He had been rewarded with four days of rare happiness—the last four days ever. For, though he did not then suspect it, he was already sharing her with Duncan Alexander. Then, suddenly, for no good reason, he imagined Samantha Silver there instead of Chantelle. . . .

"Mr. Berg—Christy Marine," Larry Fry called from the sitting room interrupting him, and with relief Nick picked up the telephone by the bed.

"Mr. Berg, good morning, will you speak to Mr. Duncan Alexander?"

"Yes," he said, and his voice was steady and cool. "Put him on."

"Nicholas, my dear fellow." The accent was as glossy as satin, as slow as honey, Eton and King's College. "It is impossible to hold a good man down. Please accept my congratulations."

"Accepted," Nicholas agreed. "Now what do we talk about?"

"I hoped that we might avoid going up before the arbitration committee. Let's keep it in the family, Nicholas."

"The family. I'm not in the family anymore. Ocean Salvage, as main contractor for the recovery of *Golden Adventurer*, is open to an offer."

"Nicholas. . . ."

"Make an offer. I'm waiting."

"Well, my Board has considered the whole operation in depth, and I am empowered to make you an outright settlement of three quarters of a million dollars. . . ."

Nick cut him off. "We are wasting each other's time."

"Nicholas, you know the company is underwriting its own losses. It's not some big insurance consortium. It's Christy Marine. . . ."

"Duncan, you're breaking my heart. I'll see you at the arbitration court."

Nick dropped the receiver onto its bracket. In the silence, he heard the journalists converging on the drinks in the room next door. He moved across to the mirror, swiftly combing his hair and composing his features, startled to see how hard and bleak his expression was, and how fierce his eyes.

However, when he went through to the sitting room he was relaxed and smiling.

GOLDEN ADVENTURER lay against the wharf of Cape Town harbour, waiting her turn to go into the dry dock for repairs.

Globe Engineering had legally taken over responsibility for her but David Allen, standing on *Warlock*'s navigation bridge, looked at her across the harbour basin and still felt an immense proprietary pride. He thrust his hands deeply into his pockets and whistled softly to himself.

The Trog thrust his wrinkled head from the radio room. "There's a call for you on the land-line."

David picked up the hand set.

"David?"

"Yes, sir." He recognized Nick's voice instantly.

"Are you ready for sea?"

"Twelve hours," David replied.

"It's an oil-rig tow. Rio to the North Sea. Bernard Wackie will telex you full details at sea, but I want you running at top economic power for Rio by dawn tomorrow."

"Yes, sir. When are you coming aboard, sir?"

"I'm not," said Nick. "You're the new master. I'm leaving for London on the five o'clock flight. She's all yours, David."

"Thank you, sir," David stuttered. "Thank you very much."

NICK SAT in the lounge of Cape Town's DF Malan Airport and thought how dramatically the balance had swung in the last forty days, since he had made the decision to rescue *Golden Adventurer*. He had caught his wave, and now he was riding high and fast. It seemed that the fates were intent on smothering him with largesse—the oil-rig tow for *Warlock*, and news that the French dockyard strike at Construction Atlantique had been smoothed over and the delivery date for the new tug had come forward by two months. Also, at midnight the night before, a telephone call from Bernard Wackie had awakened him to let him know Kuwait and Qatar, as well as the Saudis, were studying his iceberg project.

"All I need now is to hear that I have won the football pools," he thought. At that moment, he turned his head, and immediately caught his breath.

She stood by the automatic doors to the lounge, and the wind had caught her hair and torn it loose from its thick twisted knot so that fine gold tendrils floated down onto her cheeks—cheeks that were flushed as though she had run fast—and her chest heaved so that she held one hand upon it, fingers spread like a star between those fine pointed breasts.

She was poised like a forest animal that has scented the leopard, fearful, tremulous, but not yet certain in which direction to run. Her agitation was so apparent that he thrust aside his briefcase and stood up.

She saw him instantly, and her face lit with joy. She started to run, stopping only a few feet in front of him.

"I thought I'd missed you," she said. "David told me you were taking the five o'clock flight." Her eyes slid away from his. "You didn't say goodbye."

"I thought it was better that way." And now her eyes flew back to his face, sparking with green fire.

"Why?" she demanded, and he had no answer to give her.

"I didn't want to. . . ."

What could he say to her, without making the kind of statement that would embarrass them both?

Above them the public address system squawked into life. "South African Airways announce the departure of their flight 235 to London. Will passengers please board at Gate Number Two."

She said quickly. "Nick, tomorrow you'll be in London, in mid-winter. I'll be riding the surf at Cape St. Francis."

They had often spoken of the surfing at Cape St. Francis. It had been part of their shared experiences. Cape St. Francis was three hundred and fifty miles north of Cape Town. The young and the young-at-heart came there from all over the world to ride the long set, for there was no other wave quite like it.

At the departure gate the shuffling queue was shortening, and he moved towards it, but she reached out and laid her hand on his arm, and he froze. It was the first time she had deliberately touched him, and the shock of it spread through his body like ripples on a quiet lake.

"Come with me, Nick," she whispered, and his own throat closed so he could not answer. He stared at her, and already the ground hostesses at the gate were peering around irritably for their missing passenger.

She had to convince him and she shook his arm urgently. "Nick, I really want you to."

"Who is arguing?" he asked quietly, and suddenly like magic she was in his arms, trying to burrow deeper into his embrace.

PART TWO

Sunlight was made for Samantha. She wore it in her hair, sparkling like jewellery, she used it to paint her face and body in lustrous shades of burnt honey and polished amber.

She sprawled in the sunlight like a sleeping cat, offering her face and her naked belly to it. She ran in the sunlight, light as a gull in flight, along the hard wet sand at the water's edge, and he ran beside her, tirelessly, the two of them alone in a world of sea and sun and tall pale hot skies. Even in the presence of others they were alone; for them nobody else really existed.

When they sat astride their boards waiting far out beyond the three-mile reef for the set of the wave, she reached across to touch his shoulder, as if she needed constant physical assurance of his presence—the two of them close together in the loose assembly of thirty or forty surf riders strung out along the line of the long set.

Then the ripple of excitement and a voice calling: "A three set!" The surfers arranging themselves, spacing out for running room, peering back eagerly over their dark shoulders, laughing and kidding each other as the triple wave bumped up on the horizon, running towards them at fifty miles an hour.

"Ride three!" Nick called.

The third wave in the set was traditionally the big one, and they let the first one swing them high and drop them again into its trough. Half the other riders were up and away, only their heads still visible above the peak of the wave, the land obscured by the moving wall of water.

The second wave came through, bigger, more powerful, and most of the other riders went on it, two or three tumbling and losing their boards.

"Here we go!" exulted Samantha, and the third came rustling, green and peaking, a transparent wall of water. Frantically they sculled, weight high on the board, until the boards came suddenly alive and started to run, tipping steeply forward, the waxed fibre-glass hissing through the water.

Then they were both up and laughing in the sunlight, dancing the intricate steps that balanced and controlled the board, lifted high on the wave so they could see the sweep of the beach three miles ahead, and the ranks of other riders on the twin waves that had gone before them.

Now out on their right hand the wave was feeling the reef and starting to curl over on itself, the crest arching forward, holding that lovely shape for long moments, then slowly collapsing.

"Go left," Nick called urgently to her, and they kicked the boards around, bending at the knees to ride the hurtling craft, their speed rocketing as they cut across the face of the water. Behind them the arching wave spread rapidly towards them, faster than they could run before it.

Now at their left shoulders the water formed a steep vertical wall, "Nick!" screamed Samantha, as the wave fanned out over her head, arcing across the sky, cutting out the sunlight, and they flew down a long perfectly rounded tunnel of roaring water. The sides were smooth as blown glass, the light green and luminous. Ahead of them was the opening; behind them, close behind them, the tunnel was collapsing in a thunder of murderous white water. Samantha was as terrified and as exultant as she had ever been in her life.

"We must beat the curl," Nick yelled.

For long moments they held their own, then slowly they began to gain, and at last they shot out through the open mouth of the tunnel into the sunlight again, leaving the white water like lace on the surface far behind.

"Let's go right!" Samantha sang out, and they turned and went back, swinging across the steep face, until at last the wave felt the beach and ran berserk, tumbling wildly upon itself, and they kicked free, falling back over the crest and dropping into the sea beside their bobbing boards, laughing and panting at each other with the excitement of it.

Samantha was laughter, laughter in fifty different tones and intensities, from the sleepy morning murmur when she woke and found him beside her to this wild laughter in the backwash of a racing wave.

Samantha was loving. She was soft sleepy loving in the early slippery grey-pearl light of dawn. She was loving in the sunlight, spread like a beautiful starfish in the fierce reflected sunlight of the sculptured dunes. She was loving in the night, with her hair brushed out and spread over him, lustrous and fragrant, a canopy of gold in the lamplight.

But more than anything else Samantha was life and youth, vibrant, bursting. To walk beside her was to feel vital and strong—strong enough for the long days in the sea and sun, strong enough to dance to the loud wild music half the night, and then strong enough to lift her when she faltered and carry her down to their bungalow above the beach, she in his arms like a sleepy child.

"Oh Nick, Nick. I'm so happy, I want to cry."

THEN Larry Fry telephoned from Cape Town.

"Two weeks," he blared. "London and Bermuda and the St. Nazaire shipyard have been driving me mad for two weeks! I've had to check every hotel register in the country to find you."

Samantha decided. "We must go now, today, or we will spoil it," she said.

Within the hour Nick had chartered a twin-engined Beechcraft Baron. It picked them up at the little earth strip near the hotel and put them down at Johannesburg's Jan Smuts Airport an hour before the departure of the flight for Paris.

In Paris they stayed one night at the Georges V hotel, then caught the early morning flight down to Nantes, the nearest airfield to the shipyards at St. Nazaire. Jules Levoisin, who lived just outside St. Nazaire, *La Mouette*'s home port, was there to meet them.

He was wearing expensive cashmere and an Yves St. Laurent necktie; ashore Jules was always the dandy.

"Nick!" he shouted joyfully and stood on tiptoe to kiss both his cheeks, enveloping him in a fragrant cloud of eau de Cologne and pomade. "I warned you not to take the job, didn't I?"

"You did, Jules, you did."

"You stole that ship from under my nose. I hate you!" he said. At that moment he became aware that Nick was not alone.

He took one long look at Samantha, then bowed over her hand, at the same time declaring, "She is too good for you, Nick. I am going to take her away from you.

"The same way you did *Golden Adventurer*?" Nick asked.

"Come on, I want to see my new tug. Then I'll buy you lunch at the Bon Accueil."

Jules had his ancient Citroën in the car park. It was lovingly waxed and fitted with shiny geegaws and dangling mascots. He handed Samantha gallantly into the front seat. Since he could not devote attention to both the road ahead and to Samantha, he concentrated solely upon her, without deviating from the Citroën's top speed, only occasionally turning to shout "*Cochon!*" at other drivers.

"You will enjoy Bon Accueil," Jules told Samantha. "Sadly I only eat there when somebody rich wishes a favour of me."

"How do you know I want a favour?" Nick asked from the back seat, clinging to the door handle.

"Three telegrams, a telephone call from Johannesburg. . . ." Jules chuckled fruitily and winked at Samantha, "You think I believe Nicholas Berg just wants to discuss old times?" He glanced back at Nick. "Come, I am in a good mood. You can ask me."

"I need a master for my new tug," said Nick. "I want you to leave those crooks you're working for, and come to work for me."

"Those ships you build, Nicholas, are not tugs. They are no more than fancy toys, all gimmicks and gadgets. Twenty-two thousand horsepower, *c'est ridicule!*"

"I needed every one of those horses when I pulled *Golden Adventurer* off Cape Alarm—"

Thus they fenced all the way from Nantes to St. Nazaire. It was snowing when they drove through the narrow streets of that area of the docks just below the bridge which comprises the sprawling shipyards of Construction Atlantique, one of the three largest shipbuilding companies in Europe.

The slipways for the larger vessels, the bulk carriers and naval craft, faced directly onto the wide smooth reach of the river; but the ways for the small vessels backed onto the inner harbour. Jules parked the Citroën at the security gates nearest the inner harbour, and they walked through to where Charles Gras was waiting for them in his offices overlooking the inner basin.

"Nick, it is good to see you again." Gras, who spoke in heavily accented English, was Atlantique's top engineer, a tall stooped man with a pale face and lank black hair, but with the sharp foxy

Parisian features and quick bright eyes that belied the morose unsmiling manner. "You will want to go directly to see your tug?"

Sea Witch stood high on her ways, and although she was an identical twin to *Warlock,* she seemed almost twice her size with her underwater hull exposed. Jules muttered and made remarks about "Berg's battleship", but he could not hide the gleam in his eye as he strutted about the uncompleted bridge or listened intently as Charles Gras explained the electronic equipment.

Nick, realizing that the two experts should be left alone together, took Samantha's arm and led her through groups of workmen to the upper deck.

Sea Witch now gave them a sweeping view, through the forest of construction cranes, to the river slipways where the keels of the truly big hulls were laid down.

"We've talked about *Golden Dawn,*" Nick said. "There she is."

It took some moments for her to realize she was looking at a ship. "My God," she breathed. "It looks like a city!"

The structure of steel seemed endless. The hull was as tall as a five-storey building, while the navigation tower was another hundred feet higher than that.

"What you're seeing is merely the carrying platform, the accommodation and the main power source," Nick explained. "Onto that we attach the four pod tanks. They are being constructed in Japan. Each can carry a quarter of a million tons of crude oil."

He was still explaining the concept while they sat at lunch, and Charles and Jules listened as avidly as she did.

". . . . A single rigid hull of those dimensions would crack and break up in heavy seas. . . ." He took the cruet set and used it to demonstrate. "But the four individual pods have been designed so that they can move independently of each other. This gives them the ability to ride and absorb the movement of heavy seas. They hive onto the main hull, relying on its multiple boilers and quadruple screws to carry them across the oceans." He pushed the cruet set around the table and they all watched it with fascination. "Then, when it reaches the continental shelf opposite the discharge site fifty or even a hundred miles offshore, the main hull anchors and detaches its pod tanks. In protected water and chosen weather conditions they can make those last few miles under their own propulsion." Nick detached the salt cellar from the cruet and docked it against Samantha's plate.

"Nick," Charles interrupted him abruptly. "When last did you inspect the drawings of *Golden Dawn*?"

Nick paused, taken a little off balance. He frowned. "Some fourteen months ago."

Charles twisted the stem of his wine glass between his fingers, and thrust out his bottom lip. "The ship you have just described is very different from the one we are building."

"In what way, Charles?" Nick's concern was immediate.

Charles shrugged. "It would be easier to show it to you. Immediately after lunch."

"*D'accord.*" Jules nodded. "It must not interfere with the further enjoyment of this fine meal."

Later, standing beneath the bulk of *Golden Dawn*, Samantha thought the ship looked like a mighty alp of steel. The men working on the giddy heights of her scaffolding were small as insects, and almost unbelievably, as Samantha stared up at them, a little torn streamer of wet grey snow cloud blew over the ship, obscuring the top of her navigation bridge for a few moments.

"She reaches up to the clouds," said Nick. "She looks like the ship I planned. . . ."

"Come, Nick," said Charles.

The little party picked its way through the crowded yard, then suddenly Nicholas stopped so abruptly that Samantha collided with him and almost fell on the icy concrete, but he caught her arm and held her as he stared up past Jules at the bulbous stern.

"Yes," Charles nodded. "That is one difference from the ship you designed."

The propeller was in lustrous ferro-bronze, six-bladed, each blade shaped with the beauty and symmetry of a butterfly's wing, but so enormous as to make the comparison laughable.

"One!" whispered Nick. "One only."

"Yes," Charles Gras agreed. "Not four, but one propeller only. Also, Nick, it is fixed pitch."

They were all silent as they rode up in the cage of the hoist which ran up to the main deck. There they stood high on one of the overhead steel catwalks looking down fifty feet onto the boiler and condensers in the echoing cavern of the engine compartment. Nick asked no questions but stared down for almost five minutes.

"All right, Charles. I've seen enough," he said. Again they rode upwards. It was like being in a modern office block—the polished chrome and wood panelling of the elevator, the carpeted passageways high in the navigation tower along which Charles led them to the master's suite.

The suite occupied almost half the width of the navigation bridge, large enough to house a diplomatic reception. Jules shook his head wonderingly. "Ah, this is the way to live," he breathed. "Nicholas, I absolutely insist that the master's quarters of *Sea Witch* be decorated like this—".

Nick did not smile, or even register Jules's implicit agreement to join his company. Instead, he slowly crossed the thick green carpet, woven with the letters C and M for Christy Marine, and stopped before the marble fireplace. There he turned to face them and, making a gesture that embraced the whole ship, spoke directly to Charles Gras. "This is a vicious, murderous fraud." He spoke quietly, his anger controlled. "One propeller cannot manoeuvre a hull of these dimensions in heavy seas. With a single boiler there is no fail-safe—a few gallons of sea water in the system could disable this monster." He stopped suddenly as a new thought struck him. "Charles." His voice became sharp. "The pod tanks—they are still self-propelled, are they not?"

Charles drew a breath to tell it with a rush. "No. They must be docked and undocked by tugs."

Nick stared at him, his lips blanched to thin white lines. "No. I do not believe it. Not even Duncan. . . ."

"Duncan Alexander has saved forty-two million dollars by redesigning *Golden Dawn*." Charles shrugged. "Forty-two million dollars is a lot of money."

IT WAS FRIDAY afternoon in the school holidays, and Samantha, Nick and twelve-year-old Peter Berg sat in the Cockpit Teashop waiting for the best scones in Britain to be brought to the table. Samantha had launched into an account of *Warlock*'s salvage of *Golden Adventurer*—a tale with emphasis on the derring-do of

Warlock's master, not forgetting his rescue of Samantha Silver from the icy seas of Antarctica, and Peter's eyes grew enormous as he listened.

Later, he showed Samantha how to spread strawberry jam and cream on her scones, and chewing together heartily, the two of them became fast friends. Nick joined their chatter easily, but had to end it at last. "Listen, Peter, if we are to get you home by five . . . " and the boy sobered instantly.

"Dad, couldn't you telephone Mother? She just might let me spend the weekend in London with you."

"I already tried that." Nick shook his head. "It didn't work."

From the back of Nick's Mercedes, the boy leaned forward into the space between the two bucket seats, and the three of them were very close in the snug interior of the speeding car.

It was almost dark when Nick turned in through Lynwood's stone gates. The drive climbed the hill in a series of broad curves through carefully tended woods and then the three-storeyed Georgian country house, so crowded with memories for Nick, came in sight. It was ablaze with light in every window.

"I've finished the model Spitfire you sent me for Christmas, Dad," Peter said. "Won't you come up and see it?"

"I don't think. . . ." Nick began, but Peter blurted out before he could finish, "It's all right, Uncle Duncan won't be here. He always comes down late from London on Friday nights." Then in a tone that tore at Nick like thorns. "Please, Dad, I won't see you again until Easter."

"Go," said Samantha. "I'll wait here."

Peter promptly turned to her. "You come too, Samantha, please."

"O.K., Peter, I'll come."

Nick followed them up the broad steps to the oaken doors, feeling himself carried along on the tide of events. It was a sensation that he never relished.

In the entrance hall Samantha looked around her quickly. It was so grand. There was no other word to describe the house: the stairwell reached up the full height of the three storeys while, on each side of the hall, doors opened into long reception rooms. She did not have a chance to look further, for Peter seized her hand

and raced with her up the marble staircase, while Nick followed them to Peter's room at a more sedate pace.

The Spitfire had place of honour on the shelf above Peter's bed. He brought it down proudly, and they examined it with suitable expressions of admiration. Peter responded to their praise like a flower to the sun.

When at last they descended to the hall, they were stopped by a voice from the drawing room on the left. "Peter, darling."

Chantelle Alexander stood in the open doorway. Dutifully Peter crossed to her. "Good evening, Mother."

She kissed him tenderly, then held his hand so he was ranged at her side, a subtle drawing of boundaries. "Nicholas." She tilted her head. "You look so brown and fit."

Chantelle was only a few inches taller than her son, but she seemed to fill the room with a shimmering presence. Her hair was dark and soft and glowing, and her skin and the huge dark sloe eyes were a legacy from her beautiful mother. Now she turned her head on its long graceful neck, and her eyes took a slightly oriental slant as she looked at Samantha.

"May I present Doctor Silver. . . ." Nick began, but Peter cut in.

"I asked Samantha to see my model. She's a marine biologist, and she's a professor at Miami University. . . ."

"Not yet," Samantha corrected him. "But give me time."

"Good evening, Doctor Silver. It seems you've made a conquest . . . ." Chantelle let the statement hang ambiguously as she turned back to Nick. "I was waiting for you, Nicholas. I want to ask your help on a matter concerning Christy Marine. You won't refuse me, will you?"

"I always was a sucker, wasn't I?"

Now she touched his arm. "No, Nicholas, please don't be bitter." She held his gaze directly.

"How can I help you?"

Her touch on his arm disturbed him. She was enveloping him with her scent and heady beauty.

"You are meeting Duncan on Tuesday morning to discuss the arbitration of *Golden Adventurer*. Will you call me at Eaton Square when you finish? I'll wait by the telephone."

"Chantelle. . . ."

"Nicky, I have nobody else to turn to on this one."

He had never been able to refuse her—which was part of the reason he had lost her, he thought wryly. "Yes, of course," he said.

Later, as he and Samantha drove back to London, she whispered, "I want to be closer to you, Nick. I feel threatened. . . ." Her voice had a sudden panicky edge to it. "I have a terrible foreboding."

"That's nonsense. . . ."

"It's been too good, for too long."

And then they were both silent until they reached Nick's Queen's Gate flat.

JAMES TEACHER was the senior partner of Salmon, Peters and Teacher, the lawyers that Nick had retained for Ocean Salvage. He was a man with a formidable reputation in the city, a leading expert on maritime law. He was florid and bald and so short that, as Nick noticed, his feet did not touch the floorboards of his Bentley when he sat on the back seat. He and Nick were on their way to a preliminary meeting with Christy Marine.

Christy House was one of those conservative smoke-stained stone buildings in Leadenhall Street, the centre of Britain's shipping industry.

The doorman greeted Nick. "Good to see you again, sir."

A cab, containing James Teacher's two assistants and their bulky briefcases, pulled in behind the Bentley. They all assembled inside, and the doorman passed them on to a senior clerk who took them in the lift to the top floor.

The board room was large, panelled, and hung with a single portrait of old Arthur Christy—fighting jaw and sharp black eyes under beetling white eyebrows. A log fire burned in the open grate, and there was sherry and Madeira in crystal decanters on a side table, which James Teacher and Nick refused curtly.

They waited quietly, standing facing the door into the chairman's suite—and they waited for exactly four minutes before the door was thrown open and Duncan Alexander stepped through it.

His eyes instantly locked with Nick's like the horns of two great bull buffalo—and the room was very still.

Duncan was a strikingly good-looking man, very tall—two inches taller than Nick—and slim. His blond hair was fashionably long

over the ears. His skin was smooth and tanned, and now when he smiled his teeth were dazzling white—perfect large teeth in the wide friendly mouth, but the eyes did not smile. "Nicholas," he said, without moving forward.

"Duncan," said Nick quietly, not answering the smile. Nick stared at him steadily, trying to measure him dispassionately. Now for the first time he began to see how it might have happened. There was a sense of excitement about the man, the fascination of the serpent. He had done his cobra dance, and Chantelle had watched like a mesmerized bird of paradise—until she had toppled from the branch. . . .

"Let us begin." Nick knew that his self control was near to breaking point.

It soon became clear that there was no hope of conciliation. The meeting smouldered with the antagonism of the two leading characters, so that they seemed to be the only persons on the stage. Flanked by their respective legal advisers, they sat opposite each other, separated by the glossy surface of the rosewood table-top, and their gazes seldom disengaged.

It was half an hour before Nick was convinced that something other than personal antagonism was motivating the man before him. His new offer of two and a half million was still far too low to have any hope of being accepted—so low that it became clear that he did not want to settle. Duncan wanted to go to arbitration—and yet there was nothing he could gain by that. It must be obvious to everyone at the table that Nick's claim was worth four million dollars. Nick would have settled for four—knowing that an arbitration board would almost certainly award more, but also knowing that the delay and costs of going to litigation could amount to another million. Duncan must also know that you never, but never, go to arbitration if there is another way out. Litigation makes only lawyers fat. Then why did he not try with a low, but realistic, offer?

Nick crushed the temptation to walk out of the room in disgust. Instead he lit a cheroot and leaned forward again, staring into Duncan's steely grey eyes, trying to fathom him.

What had Duncan to gain from not settling now? Then quite suddenly Nick knew what it was. Chantelle's enigmatic appeal for help flashed back to him. Duncan Alexander wanted time. It was as simple as that.

"All right." Satisfied at last Nicholas leaned back in the deep leather padded chair. "We are still a hundred miles apart. There will be only one more meeting. That's in Lloyd's on the twenty-seventh. Are we at least agreed on that date?"

"Of course." Duncan leaned back also and Nick saw the shift of his eyes and the little jump of nerves in the point of his clenched jaws. Had Nick not known he would lie, he might have missed the little tell-tale signs. "Of course." Duncan repeated, and began to stand up. He lied beautifully.

In the lift James Teacher was jubilant, rubbing his little fat hands together. "We'll give him a go!"

Nick glanced at him sourly. Win, lose or draw James Teacher would still draw his fee. "They are going to duck," Nick told him grimly. "Before noon tomorrow Christy Marine will have lodged for postponement of the hearing."

"Yes, you could be right," James Teacher sobered slightly. "They had me puzzled. . . ."

"I'm not paying you to be puzzled." Nick's voice was low and hard. "I'm paying you to out-jump them. I want them at the hearing on the twenty-seventh. Get them there, Mr. Teacher."

THE DRAWING ROOM in Eaton Square was decorated in cream and pale gold, cleverly designed as a frame for the single exquisite work of art which it contained—a group of ballet dancers by Degas. Even the roses on the ivory grand piano were cream. The one flash of bright colour was Chantelle's flaming Pucci dress, and as she rose from the huge shaggy white sofa and came to Nick, he knew he would never be immune to her beauty.

"Dear Nicholas. I knew I could rely upon you." She took his hand and led him to the sofa, and then she settled beside him, like a bright, lovely bird alighting. She lifted the Wedgwood teapot. "Orange pekoe." She smiled at him. "No lemon and no sugar."

He had to smile back at her. "You never forget," he said.

"I told you that you looked well," she said, slowly and unselfconsciously studying him. "And you really do, Nicholas. You look absolutely marvellous."

"What did you want to talk to me about?" he asked quietly, and there was a passing shadow of hurt in her dark eyes.

"Nicholas," she started. "There is something dreadfully wrong with Christy Marine. As you and Daddy created the company and you are still deeply involved with it. . . ."

He made a gesture of impatience. "There are only two things I am involved with now, Ocean Salvage and Nicholas Berg."

"We both know that is not true," she whispered. "You are a special type of man. It took me so long to recognize that." She sighed. "I believed your strength and nobility of mind were common goods. Some people learn the hard way."

He said nothing for a moment, thinking of all that those words revealed, then he replied, "Tell me what is worrying you."

She turned her head away for a moment, and then looked back at him. Her eyes seemed to have grown darker and sadder. "It is so difficult not to be disloyal, so difficult to find expression for vague doubts and fears. . . ." She stopped and bit her lower lip softly. "Nicholas, I have transferred my shares in Christy Marine to Duncan as my nominee, with voting rights." Nick stared at her in shock, and she nodded. "I know it was madness, but a year ago, I was willing to give him anything he asked for."

He felt the premonition that she had not told him all and he waited while she rose and went to the window, looked out guiltily and then turned back to him. "I also resigned as executrix of the trust."

He did not answer. The trust, set up by old Arthur Christy, was the backbone of Christy Marine: one million voting shares administered by three executors—a banker, a lawyer and a member of the Christy family.

Chantelle returned to the sofa. "Did you hear what I said?" she asked.

He nodded. "The other executors? Still Pickstone of Barclays and Rollo?"

She shook her head and again bit her lip. "No, it's not Barclays anymore. It's Cyril Forbes, head of London and European."

"But that's Duncan's own bank," Nick protested. "And Rollo?"

"Rollo had a heart attack six months ago. He resigned, and Duncan put in another, younger man. You don't know him."

"My God. There is no check on him. . . ."

"I know," she whispered. "It was madness. I just can't explain it."

"All right, tell me everything else."

"I have tried to follow the new structuring of the company; it's all so complicated, Nicholas. London and European is the new holding company and . . . and . . ." Her voice trailed off. "It just goes round and round in circles." Suddenly she was smiling at him wistfully and weeping. There was no sobbing or sniffing, the tears merely welled up from her huge dark eyes, and rolled softly down her cheeks. "The madness is over, Nicholas. It didn't last very long, but it was a holocaust while it did."

Nick took the linen handkerchief from his inner pocket and handed it to her.

"Thank you." She dabbed away the tears, still smiling softly. "What must I do, Nicholas? I am afraid, terribly afraid."

"Call in a team of auditors . . ." he began, but she shook her head and cut him short.

"You don't know Duncan," she said.

"There is nothing he could do."

"He could do anything," she contradicted him.

Nick could no longer remain seated. He put down his cup, stood up and began to pace about the room, frowning heavily.

"All right," he said at last. "I will do what I can to find out just how much substance there is to your fears."

"How will you do that?"

"It's best you don't know, yet."

He stood before her, and she rose, quick with alarm. "You aren't going, are you?"

"There is nothing else to discuss."

"I'll see you down." In the hall she dismissed the West Indian maid with a shake of her head, and fetched Nick's coat herself. "Shall I send for the car? You'll not get a cab at five o'clock."

"I'll walk," he said.

"Nicholas, I cannot tell you how grateful I am. I had forgotten how safe and secure it is to be with you." Now she was standing very close to him, her head lifted and her lips were soft and ripe, her eyes still flooded and bright. He knew he should leave immediately. She placed one of her slender ivory hands on his lapel, adjusting it unnecessarily in a proprietary feminine gesture, and she moistened her lips. "We are all fools, Nicholas, every one of us. I wish with all my heart that it were possible to wipe it all out and begin again."

"Unfortunately, it doesn't work that way." With a major effort of will Nick broke the spell, and stepped back. In another moment he would have stooped to those soft red lips. "I'll call you if I learn anything," he said, as he stepped out into the cold.

THE TELEPHONE RANG in Nick's Queen's Gate flat at two minutes past nine the next morning. Samantha had already left to visit some colleagues at the Natural History Museum. Nick was smoking his first cheroot of the day.

"Mr. Berg." James Teacher's voice was sharp and businesslike. "You were right. Christy Marine petitioned for a ninety-day postponement of hearing early yesterday afternoon."

"The bastard," grunted Nick. "What grounds?"

"They wanted time to prepare their submission."

"Block them," Nick instructed.

"I have already done so. They'll be in court on the twenty-seventh."

"Well done," Nick told him.

Nick hesitated for a time before he called Monte Carlo, a call that would cost him at least fifty thousand dollars. Still, the best is always the cheapest in the end, he reminded himself.

While he waited for the connection he thought how his life was complicating itself once more. Very soon there would have to be a London branch of Ocean Salvage—offices, secretaries, files, accounts—and then a New York branch, a branch in Saudi, the whole cycle again. He thought suddenly of Samantha, uncluttered and simple happiness, life without the wearisome trappings. Then the connection was made and he gave a secretary his name.

"Mr. Berg? Claud Lazarus." He heard the thin high, almost feminine voice. No other greeting, no expressions of pleasure at the renewal of contact. Nick imagined him sitting at his desk in the suite high above the harbour, his under-developed body with its huge bald domed head, and features including a nose hardly large enough to support the thick spectacles.

"Mr. Lazarus. Are you in a position to undertake an in-depth study for me?" The euphemism was for industrial espionage.

"Of course," Lazarus piped.

"I want the financial structuring and inter-relationship of all the elements of the Christy Marine Group and London and European. Further, I want the country of registration, and the underwriters of all bottoms traceable to their holdings."

"This is being recorded, Mr. Berg."

"Of course. Also I want an accurate estimate of the reserves of London and European. I am particularly interested in the vessel *Golden Dawn* at present being built at the yards of Construction Atlantique. I want to know if she has contracted with any oil company and, if so, on what routes and at what rates."

"Yes?" Lazarus squeaked softly.

"Time is of the essence—and, as always, so is discretion. My contact when you are ready to pass information is Bernard Wackie."

"I will keep you informed of progress."

"Thank you, Mr. Lazarus."

NICK STEPPED from James Teacher's Bentley outside Lloyd's and took Samantha on his arm. Despite the fact that he had come to hear the verdict given on his future, he paused on the pavement a moment and looked up.

As a seaman this remarkable institution touched him with a feeling of reverence. Not that the building itself was particularly old. Nothing now remained of the original coffee house, except some of the traditions: the caller who intoned the brokers' names like the offertory in the temple of some exotic religion; the stalls in which the underwriters conducted their business; the name and uniform of the institution's servants—the "waiters" with brass buttons and red collar tabs. Mostly it was the tradition of concern that was enshrined here—the concern for ships and for the men who sailed in them.

"Come," he said to Samantha at last and led her up the short flight of steps into the lobby, where a waiter received them.

"We will be using the Committee Room today, sir."

The earlier submissions by both parties had been heard in one of the smaller offices, leading off the high gallery above the vast floor of the exchange with its rows of underwriters' stalls, but now the decision of the two arbitrators would be given in surroundings more in keeping with the importance of the occasion.

They walked in silence to the grand room designed by Adams for Bowood House, the country home of Lord Lansdowne. It had been taken to pieces, panel by panel, transported to London and re-erected in its entirety—with such care and attention that, when Lord Lansdowne inspected it, he found that the floor boards squeaked in exactly the same place as they had before.

At the long table, under the massive glittering pyramids of the three chandeliers the two arbitrators were already seated. Both of them were master mariners, their faces toughened and leathery from wind and salt water. They talked quietly together, without acknowledging in any way the rows of attentive faces in the rows of chairs facing them—until the minute hand of the antique clock on the Adams fireplace touched its zenith. Then the arbitrator who had been designated president of the court looked up and the waiter closed the double doors.

"This Arbitration Court has been set up under the Committee of Lloyd's and empowered to receive evidence in the matter between Christy Marine Ltd. and Ocean Salvage and Towage Co. Ltd. . . ."

The president let no dramatics intrude on his assembly of the facts. He took nearly an hour to recount them in the driest possible terms, succeeding in making *Golden Adventurer*'s plight, and the desperate endeavours of her rescuers sound boring. Indeed, his colleague seemed to descend into a condition of coma at the telling of it.

Then the president suddenly rocked back in his chair and hooked his thumbs into his waistcoat. His expression became decisive, and while he surveyed the crowded room, his colleague stirred, opened his eyes, took out a white handkerchief and blew two sharp blasts, like the herald angel sounding the crack of doom.

There was a stir of re-awakened interest. They all recognized the moment of decision, and for the first time Duncan and Nick looked directly at each other over the heads of the lawyers and company men. Neither of them changed expression, and they did not unlock their gaze, until the president began to speak again.

"Taking into consideration the foregoing, this Court is of the firm opinion that a good salvage of the vessel was effected, and that therefore the salvers are entitled to salvage awards commensurate with the services rendered to the owners. . . ."

Nick felt Samantha's hand groping for his. He took it, and it was slim and cold and dry.

"This Court, in arriving at the value of the salvor's services, has taken into consideration, firstly, the situation and conditions existing on the site of operations. . . ."

As the president continued his summing up, Nick steeled himself. Three million dollars was the minimum he needed to keep *Warlock* afloat and to launch his new tug *Sea Witch*.

"This Court has considered the reports of the Globe Engineering Co., the contractors charged with repairing *Golden Adventurer*. There was no loss of equipment, the salvors recovering even the main anchors and chains. . . ."

And so it went on and on. Why cannot he come to it now? I cannot wait much longer, Nick thought.

"This Court has heard expert opinion and readily accepts that the salvors are entitled to an award of twenty per cent of the residual hull value. . . ."

For long cold seconds Nick doubted his hearing, and then felt the flush of exultation burning on his cheeks.

It was six—six million dollars! He was clear and running free as an albatross sweeping across the oceans on wide pinions.

Nick turned his head and looked at Duncan, who was speaking with his counsel, a waxen cast to his skin now as though the blood had drained away beneath the tan. Nick himself had never felt so strong and vital and alive in his life before. He felt like a giant, and at his side was Samantha's vibrant young body pressing to him, endowing him with eternal youth.

"ANYWAY, ANOTHER few days and you'd probably have started to find me a boring dolly bird." Samantha smiled at him, a pathetic, lopsided little grin, nothing like her usual brilliant flashing smile.

They sat close on the couch in the Pan Am Clipper lounge at Heathrow. Nick was shocked by the extent of his own desolation.

"Samantha," he said. "Stay here with me."

"My darling," she whispered huskily, "the semester has already started. It's not for long but I have to go. It's my life."

"Make me your life."

She touched his cheek, as she countered his offer. "I have a better idea, give up *Warlock* and *Sea Witch.* Forget your icebergs and come with me."

"You know I cannot do that."

"No," Samantha agreed. "You could not, and I would not want you to. But, Nick my love, no more can I give up my life."

"Damn it." He shook his head. "I don't like to let you run around loose. Next thing you'll také off with some twenty-five-year old, bulging with muscles and. . . ."

"You have given me a taste for vintage wine," she laughed in denial. "As soon as you have done your work here, come to Florida and I'll show you my life."

The hostess crossed the lounge towards them, a pretty smiling girl in the neat blue Pan Am uniform. "Doctor Silver? They are calling Flight 432 now."

They stood and looked at each other, awkward as strangers.

"Come soon," she said, and then she stood on tiptoe and placed her arms around his shoulders. "Come as soon as you can."

CHANTELLE HAD chosen the San Lorenzo when Nick had refused to go again to Eaton Square. He had learned that it was dangerous to be alone with her, but the restaurant was also a bad choice of meeting ground. It carried too many memories from the golden days. It had been a family ritual, Sunday lunch whenever they were in town—Chantelle, Peter and Nick laughing together at the corner table. They had been given the corner table again.

"Will you have the *osso bucco*?" Chantelle asked, peeping at him over the top of her menu.

Nick always had the *osso bucco,* and Peter always had the *lasagne*—it was part of the ritual.

"I'm going to have a sole. And we'll drink the house white." Always the wine had been Sancerre. Nick was deliberately downgrading this occasion.

When the wine was brought, Chantelle sipped it. "It's good," she said, and then set the glass aside.

"I spoke to Peter," she went on. "He sent you his love."

They chatted casually until the main course had been served, when Nick asked bluntly, "What did you want to speak to me about?"

Chantelle leaned towards him and her perfume was light and subtle and evocative. "Did you find out anything, Nicholas?"

"I have learned nothing," he said. "If I had I would have called you." His eyes bored into hers. "That is not what you wanted," he told her flatly.

She smiled and dropped her eyes from his. "No," she admitted. "It wasn't." Then she looked up again, and the huge eyes slanted with a sly heart-stopping sexuality. "Duncan wants you to come back into Christy Marine," she said. "And so do I."

"Duncan sent you to me?" And when she nodded he asked, "Why does he want me back? God knows what pains the two of you took to get rid of me."

"He says that he needs your expertise." She shrugged. "But that isn't the true reason, I'm sure."

"Why do you think he wants me?"

"There are two possibilities that I can imagine." She sometimes surprised him with her almost masculine appraisals. "The first possibility is that Christy Marine owes you six million dollars, due on the tenth of next month, and he has thought up some scheme to avoid having to pay you out."

"Yes." Nick nodded. "And the other possibility?"

"There are strange and exciting rumours in the city about you and Ocean Salvage. They say that you are on the brink of something big in Saudi Arabia. Perhaps Duncan wants a share of that."

Nick blinked. "And you? What are your reasons?"

"I have several. I want control back from Duncan, and I want my rightful place on the trust. I want you to get them for me."

Nick smiled, a bitter wintry smile. "You're hiring yourself a gunman. Duncan and I alone on the deserted street, spurs clinking. . . ." He was thinking hard, watching her. Then he saw tears well in the depths of those huge eyes, and he stopped laughing. Were the tears genuine, or all part of the intrigue?

"You have another reason?"

She did not answer immediately, but he could sense her

agitation. At last she spoke so softly that he barely caught the words. "I want you back. That's the other reason, Nicholas. Sweet merciful God, you'll never know how much I've missed you—how I've suffered. . . ." She fluttered one small hand. "I'll make it up to you, Nicholas, I swear it to you. But Peter and I both need you desperately."

He could not answer for a moment. She had taken him by surprise and he felt his whole life shaken again.

"There is no road back, Chantelle. We can only go forward."

"I always get what I want, Nicholas, you know that."

"Not this time, Chantelle." He shook his head, but he knew her words would wear away at him.

NICK LAY BACK in the rather tatty old brown leather armchair which was one of James Teacher's few concessions to creature comfort, and stared at the prints on the faded wallpaper through a thin fog of cheroot smoke.

James Teacher replaced the telephone and stood up behind his desk. "Well, I think we have covered all the entrances to the warren," he announced cheerfully, and began to tick off the items on his fingers. "The sheriff of the South African supreme court will serve notice of attachment on the hull of *Golden Adventurer* at noon local time tomorrow. Our French correspondent will do the same on *Golden Dawn*. . . ." He spoke for three minutes more, and listening to him Nick reluctantly admitted to himself that he earned the greater proportion of his enormous fees.

"Well, there it is, Mr. Berg. If your hunch is correct—"

"It's not a hunch, Mr. Teacher. It's a certainty. For the last two weeks, Duncan Alexander has been rushing round the city like a demented man looking for money. My God, he even tried to stall me with an incredible offer of a partnership. No, Mr. Teacher, it's not a hunch. Christy Marine is going to default."

"I cannot understand that," said James Teacher. "Six million dollars is peanuts to a company like Christy Marine, one of the healthiest shipping owners."

"It was eighteen months ago," Nick agreed grimly. "But since then Alexander has had a clear run." He drew on his cheroot. "I'm going to use this default to force a full investigation of the company's affairs. I'm going to have Alexander under the microscope and we'll have a close look at all his pimples. Most important, I'm going to stop him running that monstrous *Golden Dawn*. . . ."

James Teacher grinned and picked up the telephone at the first ring. "Teacher," he said, and then laughed out loud nodding, "Yes" and "Yes!" again. He hung up and turned to Nicholas, his face bright red with mirth. "I have a disappointment for you, Mr. Berg. With twenty-four hours to spare a transfer has been made to the credit of Ocean Salvage in Bermuda by Christy Marine. Six million and some odd dollars in full and final payment."

Nick stared at him, uncertain as to which of his emotions prevailed—relief at having the money, or disappointment at being prevented from tearing Duncan to shreds.

"It never pays to underestimate a man like Alexander," said James Teacher.

Nick agreed silently. "I wonder if your secretary could find out when the first flight tomorrow leaves for Miami?"

"You are leaving so soon? Will it be in order to send my account direct to Bernard Wackie in Bermuda?" Teacher asked delicately.

BEFORE LEAVING for Heathrow, Nick had a long telephone conversation with Bernard Wackie. James Teacher's was but one of many payments to be discussed. Running costs of *Warlock*, interest and capital repayments on the debts of Ocean Salvage, and agents' fees were soon whittling away the six-million-dollar award. One of the few payments that gave Nicholas any pleasure was the $12\frac{1}{2}\%$ salvage money to the crew of *Warlock*. David Allen's share was almost thirty thousand dollars, Vinny Baker's another twenty-five thousand. Nick asked Bernard to include a note with that last cheque: "Have a Bundaberg on me!"

"Good news, next," Bernard said. "Mr. Lazarus says he can meet you in Paris this Monday the fourteenth. Seven a.m. in the Place de la Concorde, by the French Naval Headquarters."

"Dammit," swore Nick. "I was hoping to spend at least a week in Florida."

"My other good news will soften even that disappointment." The excitement was evident in Bernard's voice. "The sheikhs are fixing to make you an offer. They want to buy you out and take over the whole show. Of course, they'll want you to run it for them—two years, while you train one of their own men. A hell of a salary. . . ."

Nicholas, amazed by the news, broke in. "How much?"

"Two hundred grand plus two and a half per cent profits."

"Not the salary. How much for the company?"

"They are Arabs, the first offer is just to stir the pot a little. The sum of five was delicately mentioned."

"What do you think they'll go to?"

"Seven, seven and a half."

Nick suddenly saw the vision of a new life such as Samantha had shown him—a life uncluttered, uncomplicated. "Seven and a half million dollars clear?" His voice was husky.

"Maybe only seven and a half," Bernard demurred, "But I'd try for eight."

SAMANTHA WORE her hair in twin braids down her back, and hacked off denim pants which exposed her long brown legs. She had sandals on her feet and sunglasses pushed up on top of her head.

"I thought you were never coming," she challenged Nick as he stepped through the barrier at Miami International. He dropped his bag and fielded her rush against his chest. He breathed in the clean, sun-drenched smell of her hair. It was only when a small sob shook her shoulders that he realized she was weeping.

"Hey now!" He lifted her chin, and saw her eyes were flooded. "What's the trouble?"

"I'm just so happy," Samantha told him.

Even when they left the building into the Florida sunlight, she had both arms around his waist, hampering his stride, as she led him to her vehicle.

"Good God!" exclaimed Nick, and he pretended to shy away when he saw it. It was a Chevy van, but its paintwork had been rainbowed in layers of vibrant colour and panels of fantastic landscapes and seascapes. "You did that?" he asked.

"It's not that bad," she protested. "I was bored and depressed without you. I needed something to brighten my life."

One of the panels depicted the translucent green of a curling wave, and on the face of the wave a pair of human figures on Hawaii boards. Nick leaned closer. The male figure was a subtle combination of Clark Gable and Superman.

"It's you," she said proudly. "From memory."

"It's tremendous," he told her. "But I've got bigger biceps, and I'm more beautiful."

Before she started the engine she looked at him seriously out of those great shining green eyes.

"How long, Nick?" she asked. "How long have we got together this time?"

"Three days," he told her. "Sorry, but I must leave lunchtime Sunday to be in Paris early Monday. I'll tell you about it. . . ."

"No." She covered her ears. "I don't want to hear."

She drove the Chevy very fast and efficiently, taking the Rickenbacker causeway across the water to Virginia Key.

"That's the marine division of Miami University—and that's my lab at the top of the jetty—see it?"

With no diminution of speed the Chevy flew past the crowded buildings and across the long bridge to Key Biscayne. Three miles on Samantha turned off sharply left on a narrow rough track that twisted through a lush tropical forest of banyan and ended at a clapboard shack just above the water. She led him up onto the screened porch.

"This is yours?" Nick asked. He could just make out the tops of big luxury flats on each side, incompletely screened by the palms. "It must be worth a million."

"There is no price on it," she said firmly. "Pa left it to me and it's not for sale."

She had the door open now, and he followed her.

"Welcome to my house, Nick. Let me show you around. This is the living room." It had Spartan furniture, with Indian rugs and pottery. "And this, surprise! surprise! is the bedroom."

The tiny room overlooked the beach. The sea breeze fluffed out the curtains and the sound of the surf breathed like a sleeping giant, a deep regular hiss and sigh that filled the air around them.

"I don't think I could have lived another day without you," she said and slid her arms around his waist.

The bed was too big for the room, all antique brass and an old-fashioned patchwork quilt. Nick pulled her gently down onto it. Suddenly his life was uncluttered and simple again.

NEXT AFTERNOON Samantha showed him her laboratory. It was a square room, built on piles over the water, and the soft hum of the electric pumps blended with the slap of the wavelets below. There were almost a hundred tanks, and suspended over each of them was a complicated arrangement of coils and bottles and wiring.

Nick sauntered across to the nearest of the tanks and peered into it. It contained a single large salt-water clam, feeding with its double shells agape and the pink soft flesh and frilly gills undulating in the gentle flow of filtered water. Thin copper wires were attached to each half of the shell.

Samantha, wearing a white dust coat, came to stand beside him, and he asked her, "What's happening?"

She touched a switch and immediately the cylindrical scroll above the tank began to revolve slowly and a stylus began to trace out a regular pattern on the paper scroll.

She said. "I'm passing an electric impulse through his heart—each spasm changes the resistance and moves the stylus."

"What's so interesting about his heart?" Nick asked.

"It's the closest and cheapest thing to a pollution meter that we have discovered so far. Or rather," she corrected herself without false modesty, "that I have discovered."

She took his hand and led him down the long rows of tanks to her work bench. "Clams are incredibly sensitive to any contamination of their environment. Their heart beat will register almost immediately even the minutest foreign element."

"Here. . . ." She held up a test tube. "Mercury. Did you see the photographs of the Japanese children with the flesh falling off their bones at Kiojo? That was mercury." She picked up another tube. "PCB, a by-product of the electrical industry. The Hudson River is thick with it. And then, here is the real bastard daddy of them all—cadmium. Present in some types of crude oil."

She carried the tube of cadmium across to the tank. "Now, watch this." She began to drip the solution into the water system.

"There," she said, with grim satisfaction as the stylus on the recording drum made a slight double beat at its peak and then just detectably flattened the second peak. "That's cadmium in ten parts to the million. At one hundred parts it will kill all sea life, at five hundred it will kill man."

Nick felt the tickle of horror and revulsion as the moving stylus dispassionately recorded the clam's increasing distress. "It's macabre," he said.

"Yes." She stood back from the tanks. "Fortunately these organisms have such rudimentary nervous systems that they don't experience pain as we know it. However, imagine an entire ocean poisoned with a crude oil rich in cadmium; imagine the incredible agonies of tens of millions of sea birds, of the mammals. Then think of what would happen to man himself. . . ."

She worked on in the laboratory until it was dark. Then Samantha looked up at him. "The gang are eating shrimps tonight on the boat—but we don't *have* to go. We could just eat at home like last night."

But he could see she really wanted to go.

SHE WAS FIFTY-FIVE FOOT, an old purse-seiner, with the ungainly wheelhouse forward, looking like a sentry box. She was tied up at the end of the university jetty, and as they walked out to her so they could hear laughter coming up from below decks.

"*Tricky Dicky,*" Nick read her name on the stern.

"But we love her," Samantha said, and led him across the narrow gangplank. "She belongs to the university. She's our boat for short field trips—and she's also the faculty clubhouse."

The main cabin was monastically furnished, bare planking and hard benches, a single long table, packed solid with sunburned young people, all in faded jeans and chunky knit jerseys.

The air was thick with the rich smell of broiling gulf shrimps, and there were gallon jugs of California wine on the table.

"Hey!" Samantha shouted above the uproar of voices raised in heated dispute and jovial repartee. "This is Nick."

A comparative silence descended on the gathering, as they looked him over. Nick returned the scrutiny, calmly meeting each pair of eyes. At the head of the table sat a big impressive figure, the oldest man in the cabin—perhaps Nick's age or a little older, for there were silver strands in his beard and his face was lined and beaten by sun and wind.

"Hi, Nick!" he boomed. "I won't pretend we've never heard of you. Sam has bored us all silly. . . ."

"You cut that out, Tom Parker," Samantha stopped him sharply, and there was a ripple of laughter, a relaxation of tension and a round of greetings.

"Hi, Nick—I'm Sally Anne." A pretty girl with china blue eyes behind wire-framed spectacles put a tumbler of wine into his hand. "We are short of glasses; guess you and Sam will have to share."

She slid up along the bench and gave them a few inches of space. "Tom is prof. of Biology Department," Samantha whispered. "After you, he's my most favourite man in the world."

A tall woman with dark hair in braids came through from the galley and placed, in the centre of the table, a bowl of melted butter and a huge platter piled high with bright pink shrimps and they all fell upon the food with unashamed gusto, but it did not inhibit the lively contentious flow of discussion that swung swiftly from banter to deadly seriousness and back again.

Suddenly they were all discussing a rogue tanker captain who the week before had scrubbed his tanks in the middle of the Florida Straits and left a thirty-mile slick down the Gulf Stream.

"We finger-printed him. . . ." Tom Parker spoke indignantly, and Nick knew he was talking of the process by which samples of a slick could be broken down and compared with samples from a suspect's tanks. Identification was good enough to bear up in an international court of law.

"But the trick is getting the son-of-a-bitch into court. He's registered in Liberia."

"We tried to cover cases like that in the last set of proposals I put up to the Maritime Conference. . . ." Nick joined the conversation for the first time, telling them of the difficulties of legislating on an international scale.

He spoke quietly, succinctly—and Samantha noticed how everybody listened. The moment he stopped, however, they came at him from every direction, using their bright young minds like scalpels. He answered them in the same fashion, sharp and hard, armed with total knowledge of his subject, and he enjoyed every moment of it.

He saw that they possessed so many of the qualities he valued in his fellow humans. They were intelligent, motivated, dedicated and free of avarice.

At the head of the table Tom Parker sat and listened, nodding and frowning in judgement.

TOM PARKER'S office had shelves to the ceiling, and they were sagging with hundreds of bottled specimens and rows of scientific publications. He sat well back in his swivel chair with ankles crossed neatly in the centre of the cluttered desk.

"I heard so much about you from Sam that I ran a check on you, Nick. Damned nerve, wasn't it. You have my apology."

"Was it an interesting exercise?" Nick asked mildly.

"It wasn't difficult. It's an impressive track record."

"I've kept busy," Nick admitted.

"Beer?" Tom crossed to the refrigerator in the corner that was labelled, 'Zoological Specimens. DO NOT OPEN'.

"It's too early for me."

"Never too early," said Tom and pulled the tag on a dewy can of Millers and then went on. "Yes, you have kept busy. We need such a man as you around here who can transform thought and intention into action." Tom sucked at the can. "I know what you have done. I've heard you speak. Most important of all, I know you care deep down in your guts the way we do."

"It sounds as though you're offering me a job, Tom."

"I'm not going to horse around, Nick. I *am* offering you a job." He waved a huge paw. "Hell, I know you're a busy man, but I'd like to romance you into an associate professorship. We'd want a little of your time when it comes to hassling in Washington; when we need real muscle to put our case." Tom watched shrewdly for some reaction from Nick, and went on more persuasively. "What can we offer in return? I know you aren't short of cash, and it would be only twelve thousand a year, but we can offer you the warm good feeling in your guts that you're doing a tough job that has to be done."

"When do I start?" Nick asked, and as Tom's face split into a great beaming grin, Nick held out his hand. "I think I'll take that beer after all."

THE WATER was cool enough to be invigorating. Nick and Samantha swam so far out that the land was almost lost in the lowering loom of dusk, and then they turned and swam back side by side. The beach was deserted; the lights of the nearest flats were no more intrusive than the stars.

It was the right time to tell her, and he did it in detail, beginning with the offer by the sheikhs to buy out Ocean Salvage.

"But you won't, will you?" she said quickly. "I cannot imagine you playing bowls or golf for the rest of your life."

"Part of the deal is that I run Ocean Salvage for them for two years, and then I've been offered a part-time assignment which will fill any spare time I've got left over."

"What is it?"

"Associate Professor at Miami University."

She dragged him around to face her.

"You're having me on!" she exclaimed.

"Tom wants me to trouble-shoot with legislators and the Maritime Conference, to be a sort of hired gun for the Green-peacers—"

"Oh Nick, Nick!" She was still wet and gritty with beach sand but she clung to him, quivering with joy. "This means that we can do everything together—work and play and *live* together like a man and woman should!"

"The prospect daunts me not at all," he murmured gently, and lifted her chin.

Later, they went indoors, washed off the salt and the sand, then lay together on the patchwork quilt in the darkness with the sound of the sea as background music to the plans and dreams they wove.

"I've got to leave for Paris tomorrow afternoon, but we're launching *Sea Witch* on Friday week. Will you break the bottle of bubbly and bless her?"

"Nick, I mustn't spend my life commuting across the Atlantic, but I wouldn't miss it for all the world." She moved across the quilt and found his ear with her lips. "I am honoured."

"Both of you are sea witches," Nick told her.

"And you are my warlock."

"*Sea Witch* and *Warlock*," he chuckled. "Together we will work miracles."

NICK WAS EARLY, he saw as he walked across the Place de la Concorde and glanced at his Rolex. Six fifty. Lazarus, however, was at the morning rendezvous ahead of him, dressed in sombre blue with a hat pulled down so low as to conceal the pale smooth bulge of his forehead.

"Let's find a warm place," Nick suggested.

"No," piped Lazarus looking up at him through the thick lenses of his spectacles. "Let us walk."

He led the way through the underpass onto the promenade above the embankment of the Seine and set off in the direction of the Petit Palais. At such an early hour they were the only strollers.

"You know there will be nothing in writing?" Lazarus piped.

"I have a recorder in my pocket," Nick assured him.

"Very well." Lazarus paused, it was almost as though a reel was being fitted into the computer, for when he began talking again his voice had a different timbre, a monotonous almost electronic tone, as though he was indeed an automaton.

First there was a recital of share movements in the thirty-three companies which made up the Christy Marine complex, every movement in the previous eighteen months, even the transfer of Ocean Salvage to Nick himself, and the reciprocal transfer of Christy Marine stock. It was an impressive exhibition of knowledge and total recall, but too complicated for Nicholas to make immediate sense of it. He would have to study it later.

Lazarus then began a detailed breakdown of cash movements within the group, and Nick was again amazed at the man's penetration. He drew a verbal picture of how the assemblage of enormous sums of money was marshalled and channelled by Duncan into orderly flows. Then, suddenly the cash flow was not so steady. There were eddies and breaks, until on the eighth, the day before the six million dollars award had been paid to Ocean Salvage, Duncan had been able to raise a massive sixty-day loan for that amount, running the group out along a knife edge. How had he done it?

Lazarus stopped on the corner of the Champs Élysées and the rue de la Boetie, then they began to retrace their steps.

"Insurance and marine underwriting of vessels owned by the Christy Marine Group of companies—" Lazarus began again with names and figures and dates. Duncan was still using his own captive company—London and European Insurance and Banking —to lead the risk on all his vessels, including *Golden Dawn*.

"Christy Marine did not even apply for a Lloyd's survey of *Golden Dawn*," Lazarus said. "But she has been rated first class by the continental surveyors." This was a much easier rating to obtain and less prestigious than "A.1. at Lloyd's."

Lazarus went on, lowering his voice slightly as two bearded Algerian students in combat jackets overtook them. "On the seventh of this month, incidentally, Christy Marine concluded a contract of carriage with Orient Amex. The tenure is ten years. The rate is ten cents per hundred-ton miles with a minimum annual guaranteed usage of seventy-five thousand nautical miles. . . ."

Nick registered the date, the day before Duncan had arranged his massive loan, and then he began to assimilate it all. The price—ten cents per hundred-ton miles—would impress any lender, but it was wrong, ridiculously high in this depressed market. Then what was there about Orient Amex that jarred his memory?

He stopped dead, ransacking his mind for buried items of information. He laid a hand on the little man's shoulder. "Let's get a coffee," he said.

He drew him into a brasserie which was thick with the steam of the coffee machine and the smoke of Caporal and Disque Bleu, and sat him at a tiny table by the window overlooking the pavement. Primly Lazarus asked for a Vittel water, and sipped it with an air of virtue, while Nick poured cream into his coffee.

"Orient Amex," Nick asked as soon as the waiter had left. "Tell me about it."

"Orient Amex is an American-registered oil company, at present undertaking substantial dry-land and offshore exploration throughout the world. It has erected a refinery at Galveston in Texas to operate under the new atomic catalyst cracking process."

The process of cracking the low-value high-carbon molecules, then breaking up the carbon atoms and reassembling them in volatile low-carbon molecules of high value was vaguely familiar to Nick.

"The company operates producing wells in Texas, in the Santa Barbara offshore field, in Southern Nigeria, and has proven crude reserves in the El Barras field of Kuwait to be utilized by the new cracking plant in Galveston. . . ."

"Good God," Nick stared at him. "The El Barras field is cadmium contaminated. It's been condemned by—"

"The El Barras field is a high cadmium field, naturally enriched with the catalyst necessary for the new process."

"What are the cadmium elements?" Nick demanded.

"The western area of the El Barras field has sampled two thousand parts per million. The northern and eastern have sampled as high as forty-two thousand parts per million." Lazarus recited the figures pedantically.

As he listened, Nick had a vivid mental image of the stylus in Samantha's laboratory recording the death throes of a cadmium-poisoned clam. Suddenly he shook his head with disbelief. No wonder Duncan was being paid ten cents per hundred-ton miles! In that vulnerable jerry-built monster, he was going to do what no other ship-owner had ever dared to do—carry across two oceans the cadmium-rich crudes of El Barras from Kuwait.

BACK IN HIS SUITE in the Ritz, Nick did a quick calculation and realized that it would be only five o'clock in the morning on the eastern seaboard of North America. Nevertheless, he put through a call. At least he would find Samantha at home.

The telephone rang and he picked it up. There was a confused mumbling, then, "Who is it? What do you want at this hour?"

"Tell that other guy to put his pants on and go home."

"Nick!" There was a joyous squeal, followed immediately by a crash and clatter that made Nick wince and lift the receiver well away from his ear. "Oh, damn it to hell, I've knocked the table over. Nick, are you there? Speak to me, for God's sake!"

"I love you. Now, wake up. I've got something to ask you."

"I'm awake—well, almost anyway."

"Samantha, what would happen if somebody dumped a million tons of forty thousand parts concentration of cadmium sulphide in an emulsion of Arabian crude oil into the Gulf Stream, say thirty nautical miles off Key West?"

"That's a freaky question for five in the morning."

"What would happen?" he insisted.

"The crude would act as a transporting medium. . . ." She was struggling to project a scenario through her sleepiness. "It would spread out on the surface to a thickness of quarter of an inch or so, and you'd end with a slick of a few thousand miles long and four or five hundred wide, and it would keep going."

"What would be the results?"

"It would wipe out all marine life on the Bahamas and on the eastern seaboard of the States."

"Human life?" he asked.

"Yes, there would be heavy loss." She was coming fully awake now, and a stirring of horror altered her tone. "In that concentration it would be poisonous on contact to fishermen, vacationers, anybody who walked on a contaminated beach. It could account for hundreds of thousands of human beings, and if it were carried beyond America on the Gulf Stream. . . . What kind of crazy guessing game is this?"

"In a few weeks' time *Golden Dawn* will run down her ways at St. Nazaire. Christy Marine has signed a contract for her to carry one-million-ton loads of cadmium crude from the El Barras field on the South Arabian Gulf to the Orient Amex refinery in Galveston."

Now there was trembling outrage in Samantha's voice. "That's mass murder, Nick. There's never been a more deadly cargo in the history of seafaring. You can't let them do it, Nick. You just have to stop them."

"I'll be working hard on it here, but you have to take over on your side," he told her. "Get Tom Parker to hit Washington with the news, hit all the media. Force a confrontation with Orient Amex. . . ."

Samantha picked up the line he was taking. "We'll have every environmental agency in the country at work. We'll raise a stink, like that of a million corpses."

"Fine," he said. "I'll telephone tomorrow to find out how you're getting on. I love you."

Nick's next call was to the house in Eaton Square. "Mrs. Chantelle Alexander, please."

"I am sorry, sir. Mrs. Alexander is at Cap Ferrat. Do you want the number?"

"That's all right, I have it." He dialled again.

"*C'est Chantelle Alexander qui parle.*"

"It's Nicholas. I am in Paris."

"Oh, my dear. How good to hear your voice. How are you?"

"Are you alone? Is Duncan there?"

"No, he's in London. He won't be out until next week."

"I have news. Can you get up here?"

"It's impossible, Nicholas. I'm helping this week with the Charity Ball. Can't you come here? There is a flight at five."

He thought quickly, then, "All right, will you book me in at the Negresco?"

"Don't be silly, Nicholas. We've thirteen perfectly good bedrooms here; you know that."

CHANTELLE WAS in the terrace room. She was dressed in ivory silk, woven gossamer fine, so it floated about her body as she moved, and as she crossed the room to greet him the last ruddy glow of the dying day came in from the French windows and struck through the sheer material putting the outline of her legs into momentary silhouette.

"Nicholas," she said.

This magnificent house standing in its pine forest high above that darkening Mediterranean and the fairylights of the coast was Chantelle's natural setting. She filled the huge room with her own special glow and gaiety.

When they went through to the small informal dining room, they sat at the table as they had done so often before, but the chicken cooked in Creole style and the *petit* Chablis had no special associations from the past. This time laughter was easy and the warmth uncontrived.

After the meal, she brought him a cognac in the drawing room.

"Now," he said, "let's talk about Duncan. In what circumstances can you reclaim control of your shares?"

"Duncan only holds them as an agent. I could apply at any time to have that appointment set aside, but it might take a year or more—"

"Unless you could prove he deliberately betrayed the trust of agency," Nick cut in.

"Can I prove that, Nicholas?" She turned to him now, lifting her face to him, "Has he betrayed that trust?"

"I don't know yet," Nick said cautiously, and began to pace the thick forest-green carpet and, as he paced, he told her in carefully prepared sequence all that he had learned from Lazarus.

She sat like a bird on the point of flight, turning her head to watch him, those huge dark eyes seeming to swell larger as she listened.

"Duncan could destroy Christy Marine," she whispered at last. "Completely!" She looked around slowly at the room and its treasures, the symbols of her life. "He has risked everything that is mine and Peter's on this monstrous ship. What can I do, Nicholas? Please help me. What can I do?"

"You must send in a team of auditors. You can then stop Duncan launching *Golden Dawn* until the hull and propulsion have been modified, and the whole vessel has been properly surveyed and underwritten—and until you have taken full control of Christy Marine out of his hands again." His voice was gentle, filled with compassion. "That's enough for now, Chantelle. If we go on, we will begin chasing our tails. Have you a valium for yourself?"

She shook her head. "I've never used drugs to hide from things." It was true, he knew, that she had never lacked courage. "How much longer can you stay?"

"I have a seat on the eleven o'clock plane to London in the morning."

THE SECOND-FLOOR guest suite opened onto the balcony which ran along the entire front of the building overlooking the sea.

Nick went through to a bathroom decorated with green onyx panels and eighteen-carat-gold fittings. He showered, turning the setting high so that the stinging needles of water scalded away his fatigue.

There were half a dozen thick white terry towelling robes in the glass fronted warming cupboard. He selected one and went through into the bedroom belting it around his naked waist. In his briefcase there was a draft of the agreement of sale of Ocean Salvage and Towage to the sheikhs which Bernard Wackie had sent express to him in Paris with a copy to James Teacher in London.

Nick must study it before tomorrow afternoon when he was to meet Teacher, prior to a first confrontation with the Arabs.

He took the papers from his case and carried them through into the sitting room of the suite. There he poured himself a small whisky, sprawled into a deep leather armchair, and began to work.

He became aware of her perfume first, and felt his blood quicken uncontrollably at the fragrance. Slowly he lifted his head. She had come in utter silence on bare feet. She had removed all her jewellery and had let down her hair, brushing it out onto her shoulders. It made her seem younger, more vulnerable, and the gown she wore was cuffed and collared in fine soft lace.

She moved slowly towards him, uncertain for once, her eyes huge and dark and haunted. When he rose from the armchair she stopped and one hand went to her throat. "Nicholas," she whispered. "I'm so alone. Please don't send me away. Not tonight, not yet. I cannot go on. Please."

He knew then that this had been going to happen. He had hidden the certainty of it from himself all that evening, but now it was upon him, and he could do nothing to avoid it. It was as though his resolve was melting like wax in the candle flame of her beauty. His thoughts lost coherence, began to tumble and swirl like storm surf breaking on rock, as she moved into his arms.

NICK ROSE SLOWLY towards the surface of sleep, aware of a brooding sense of regret. Her perfume still lingered on his skin, but the bed beside him was empty, though warm and redolent with the memory of her body.

Across the room the early sun struck a long sliver of light through a narrow chink in the curtains. It looked like a golden blade. It reminded him instantly of Samantha—he saw her again wearing sunlight like a cloak, barefooted in the sand—and it seemed that the blade of sunlight was being driven up slowly under his ribs.

He swung his feet off the wide bed and padded softly across to the bathroom. As he ran hot water from a golden dolphin's mouth into the basin he looked at himself in the mirror. "You bastard," he whispered at the unshaven face. "You bastard."

Breakfast was waiting for him, in the sunlight on the terrace under a gaily coloured umbrella. So was Chantelle. She wore a long loose housegown, and her hair was still down on her shoulders, so soft that it stirred like spun silk in the whisper of breeze. It was all calculated. Chantelle did nothing by chance, the intimately elegant attire and the loose fall of her hair set the mood of domesticity—and Nick found himself resisting it fiercely. He deliberately refused the festive array of food, and asked only for coffee.

She poured it into his cup. "It's as simple as this, Nicholas," she said softly. "I love you; I have always loved you—God, ever since I was a gawky schoolgirl." She had never been that, but Nick let it pass. "Duncan was a stupid mistake, but it's unimportant—"

"No, it's not unimportant. It changed everything. We can never be the same again. Besides—"

"Besides, what?"

"Besides I am building myself another life now, with another, very different person."

"Oh God, Nicholas, you aren't serious." She laughed then, clapping her hands delightedly. "My dear, that American child is young enough to be your daughter. It's the forty syndrome, the Lolita complex. . . ." Then she saw his anger, and she was quick to retrieve the situation. "I'm sorry, Nicholas. I should never have said that. Still, when you are ready, as one day you will be, Peter and I and Christy Marine will be waiting for you. This is your world; you'll never really leave it."

CHANTELLE, with the telephone receiver in her hand, stared impatiently from the study windows. The weather had changed shortly after Nick's departure, and now icy rain battered at the panes.

"Chantelle, my dear." Duncan's rich and glossy voice at last came onto the line. "What is it?"

"I must speak to you urgently, Duncan. I want to see you right away."

"That's impossible." He laughed, lightly, confidently. "Tell me now."

"All right," she said deliberately. "I'll tell you. I want a divorce, and I want control of my shares in Christy Marine again."

There was a long silence on the line, and Chantelle waited, the way the cat waits for the first movement of the crippled mouse.

"This is very sudden." His voice had changed completely, it was bleak and flat, lacking any timbre or resonance.

"We both know it is not," she contradicted him.

"You have no grounds." There was a thin edge of fear now. "Divorce isn't quite as easy as that, Chantelle."

"How is this for grounds, Duncan?" she asked, and there was a spiteful sting in her voice now. "If you aren't here tomorrow, then my auditors will be in Leadenhall Street. . . ."

She did not have to go on. He spoke across her, and there was a note of panic in his voice. He said, "You're right. We do have to talk right away. I can be at Nice by four o'clock tomorrow."

"I'll have the car meet you," she said, and broke the connection with one finger. She held the bar down for a second, then lifted her finger. "I want to place an international call," she said in her fluent rippling French when the operator answered. "I do not know the number, but it is person to person. Doctor Samantha Silver at the University of Miami in Florida."

SINCE NICK'S call to her on the Monday, Samantha had been caught up in a whirl of activity.

After a series of meetings with the leaders of the Green-peacers, and other conservation bodies, she and Tom Parker had sought to provoke a confrontation with Orient Amex. The big oil company simply ignored their invitations to debate the charges on radio or television. The media themselves let the subject drop flat on its face. The energy crisis, oil tankers and oil pollution were apparently joyless subjects. Nobody had ever heard of cadmium pollution, the Cape of Good Hope was half a world away, a million tons was a meaningless figure—impossible to visualize—and it was all rather a bore.

Now, on Tuesday morning, she was back on the telephone in her laboratory, trying to contact a deputy director of the Environmental Protection Agency in Washington. Suddenly, a telephone operator interrupted her dialling. "An international call for you. Person to person."

Samantha's pulse raced, and she pressed one hand against her heart to stop it thumping.

"Go ahead, please," said the operator, and there was a click and pulse on the line as it came alive.

"Nick!" she exulted. "Darling Nick—is that you?"

"No." The voice was very clear and serene, and for no good reason Samantha felt a sensation of dread. "This is Chantelle Alexander. We have met briefly."

"Yes." Samantha's voice was now small.

"I thought it would be kind to tell you in person, before you hear from other sources. Nicholas and I have decided to remarry."

"I don't believe you," whispered Samantha. "Nick wouldn't . . . ." Her voice broke, and she could not go on.

"You must understand and forgive him, my dear," Chantelle explained gently. "After our divorce he was hurt and lonely. I'm sure he did not mean to take advantage of you."

"But, but . . . we had planned a whole life together." Samantha shook her head wildly, and a thick skein of golden hair came loose and flopped into her face, she pushed it back with a combing gesture. "I don't believe it. I won't believe it until he tells me."

Chantelle's voice was compassionate. "I so wanted not to make it ugly for you, my child, but now what can I do but tell you that Nicholas spent last night here with me? I have already made the arrangements for a divorce from my present husband, and Nicholas will resume his position at the head of Christy Marine. . . ."

Samantha knew that it was true. Slowly she replaced the receiver of the telephone. She did not cry. She felt as though she would never cry, nor laugh, again in her life.

CHANTELLE ALEXANDER studied her husband carefully, fully aware of his discomfort. He twisted sideways in his chair, crossing and uncrossing his long legs, and he rolled a cigarette between his fingers, studying the rising spiral of blue smoke to avoid the level, expressionless gaze of her dark fathomless eyes.

"Thank you for coming so promptly," she said.

"It did seem rather urgent." He smiled for the first time, glossy and urbane—but with fear betrayed by the clenched sinew in the point of his jaw. "From what you said about divorce. . . ."

She lifted her hand to stop him. "That can wait. I merely wanted to impress you with the seriousness of what is happening."

She sensed that, suddenly, his fear was gone, but she continued. "What is of prime importance to me is the trust. I want auditors sent in. . . ."

He shrugged. "All this will take time, and you have appointed me—"

"No court of law would uphold that agreement."

"Perhaps not, Chantelle, but you don't want to drag all this through the courts at a time like this."

"I'm not afraid, Duncan." She stood up quickly, light on her feet as a dancer, and pointed the accuser's finger, the nails tipped in scarlet, the colour of fresh arterial blood. "You should be the one to fear."

"And precisely what is it that I should fear?"

And she told him, reeling off swiftly all the financial machinations about which Nick had told her. "When my auditors have finished, Duncan darling, not only will the courts return control of Christy Marine to me, but they will probably sentence you to five years hard labour."

He smiled. He actually smiled! She felt her fury seething to the surface. "You dare to grin at me," she hissed. "Are you denying. . . ."

He cut her off with a raised hand. "I am denying nothing, my love. On the contrary, I am going to admit it—and more, much more." He stubbed out the cigarette and while she stared at him, struck speechless, he selected and lit another from the gold case. "For some time now I have been fully aware that somebody was prying very deeply into my affairs. It didn't take long to establish that it was a little man in Monte Carlo called Lazarus. He is good. I have used him myself. In fact it was I who introduced him to Nicholas Berg." He chuckled, shaking his head indulgently. "The silly things we do sometimes. The connection was immediate. Berg and Lazarus—I have run my own check on what they have come up with and I estimate that even Lazarus could not have uncovered more than twenty-five per cent of the answers."

"You are not denying then. . . ." Chantelle began again.

"Be quiet, you silly little woman—and listen to me. I am going to tell you why you will not send in your auditors, and why you will do exactly what I tell you to do." He paused and stared into her eyes, a direct trial of strength which she could not meet. She dropped her eyes, and he nodded with satisfaction. "Very well. I have put it all—everything that is Christy Marine—onto *Golden Dawn.*"

Giddily Chantelle felt the floor turn under her feet. She sat down heavily. "What are you talking about?" she whispered.

Then he told her, in substantial detail, from the beginning, how it had happened. "The original calculations for *Golden Dawn* were based on demand for tanker space two years ago, and on construction costs at that time. . . ."

The energy crisis and collapse in demand for tankers had come with the vicious rise in inflation, bloating the costs of construction by more than double. Duncan had countered by economizing on the design on the gigantic tanker, thus forfeiting the A.1. Lloyd's rating. Without the backing of that huge underwriting market he had been forced elsewhere to find the cover to satisfy his financiers. The premiums had been crippling. He had had to pledge Christy Marine stock—the trust stock. Then the spiralling cost of production had overtaken him again and he needed more money. He had taken it where he could find it, at rates of interest that were demanded, and used more Christy stock as collateral.

"Then," Duncan smiled, almost as though he was enjoying himself, "then, there was that awful fiasco when I had to find six million dollars to pay the salvage award for *Golden Adventurer.* That was the last of it, when I had to pledge not only the trust but also the whole of Christy Marine."

"I'll break you," she whispered. "I'll smash you."

"You don't understand, do you?" He shook his head sorrowfully, as though at an obtuse child. "You cannot break me, you cannot whistle up your auditors, without breaking Christy Marine and yourself. You are in it, Chantelle, as deep as I am. You have everything, every penny, this house, that emerald on your finger, the future of your brat riding on *Golden Dawn.*"

"No." She closed her eyes very tightly, and there was no colour in her cheeks now. "I'm going to be sick."

"No, you are not."

He stood up and crossed quickly to her. Coldly he slapped her face, two hard open-handed back and forth blows that snapped her head from side to side, leaving the livid marks of his fingers across her pale cheeks. She merely sat there and stared at him.

"Pull yourself together," he snarled. "I have told you the worst that can happen. Now, I will tell you the best. If we stand together now, I will pull off one of the greatest financial coups of the century for you. I have signed an agreement of charter with Orient Amex. A single voyage by *Golden Dawn* between the Gulf and Galveston roads and I will have doubled your fortune. After that, we can sell her. There will be a dozen buyers for her." He stepped back, and straightened the lapels of his jacket. "Men are going to remember my name. In future when they talk of tankers, they are going to talk of Duncan Alexander."

"I hate you," she said softly. "I truly hate you."

"That is not important." He waved it away. "When it is over, I can afford to walk away—and you can afford to let me go. But not a moment before. In fact, it will be necessary for you to come up to St. Nazaire next Tuesday for the launching of *Golden Dawn*. I have been able to save vital time on her construction. Her pod tanks are being towed direct to the Gulf from the Japanese yards. Meanwhile we will launch the hull with workmen still aboard her, and they will finish her off at sea during the passage around the Cape."

"If this succeeds you think you will be able to stand comparison with Nicholas Berg, is that it?" She was recovering, her voice firmed. "You will never be—could never be—the man Nicholas is."

"Damn you." Suddenly he was shaking with anger, and she was screaming at him.

"You're a cheat and a liar. You're cheap and shoddy. . . ."

"I've beaten Nicholas Berg every time."

"No, you haven't, Duncan. It was I who beat him for you."

"I took you."

"For a while," she sneered. "Just for a short fling, Duncan dear. But when he wanted me he took me right back again."

"What do you mean by that?" he demanded.

"Last night, Nicholas was here, and he loved me in a way you never could. I'm going back to him, and I'll tell the world why."

"You are a whore." He half turned away, and then paused. "Just be at St. Nazaire on Tuesday. I want you smiling at the creditors." He began to walk away.

"You are going to be the loser, Duncan Alexander," she screamed after him, her voice cracking shrilly. "I will see to that. I swear it to you."

THE BANK OF THE EAST was in Curzon Street. Nick had been there, with his lawyers, from ten o'clock in the morning until six in the evening, every day since Wednesday. It was now late on Friday afternoon. He was learning at first hand the leisurely age-old ritual of oriental bargaining.

The only constant among the would-be buyers of Ocean Salvage was the figure of the prince himself, seated on the low couch, in a Savile Row suit but with the fine white cotton and gold corded headdress framing his dark handsome features with theatrical dash. Beyond him moved a shadowy, ever-changing background of unctuous whispering figures. Every time that Nick believed a point had been definitely agreed, another three or four Arabs would arrive in rose-pink or acid-yellow Rolls Royces, and the hushed discussion would begin all over again.

James Teacher showed no impatience, sipping the little thimbles of treacly coffee and waiting for the interminable whisperings to be translated into English before making a measured counter proposal.

"We are doing fine, Mr. Berg," he assured Nick quietly. "You can leave it to me now."

Nick had a headache from the strong coffee and he found it difficult to concentrate. He kept worrying about Samantha. For four days he had tried to contact her. He excused himself to the prince, and went down to the inquiries desk in the bank's entrance hall and the girl told him, "I'm sorry, sir, there is no reply to either of those numbers."

"There must be," Nick told her. One number was Samantha's shack at Key Biscayne and the other was her private number in her laboratory.

She shook her head. "I've tried every hour."

"Can you send a cable for me?"

"Of course, sir."

She gave him a pad of forms and he wrote out the message.

"Am leaving tonight for France. Please phone me. Reverse

charge to. . . ." He gave the number of Construction Atlantique and Hotel Europe in St. Nazaire, then he paused, trying to find the words to express his concern, but there were none.

"I love you," he wrote. "I really do."

ON THE MONDAY MORNING, Nick stood staring out of the windows of the site office. The view across the inner harbour was completely blocked by the towering hull of his tug. It already wore its final coat of glistening white and the wide flaring bows bore the name *Sea Witch* and below that the port of registration, "Bermuda".

Looking upward, he could see Jules Levoisin on the wing of the bridge. Like a pugnacious rooster he stood arguing with the electronics engineer who was responsible for the installation of *Sea Witch*'s communications system, and the new master's cries of "*Sacré bleu!*" and "*Imbécile!*" carried clearly above the cacophony of shipyard noises.

Suddenly the telephone rang. The foreman answered, and signalled to Nick. "It's a lady."

Samantha, Nick thought and snatched up the receiver.

"Nicholas?" He felt the shock of quick guilt at the voice.

"Chantelle, where are you?"

"In La Baule." The fashionable resort town just up the Atlantic coast was a better setting for Chantelle Alexander than the grubby port with its sprawling dockyards. "Staying at the Castille. Come and have lunch. I must speak to you. It's important."

"I can't leave here." He would not walk into the trap again. "If it's important, then come here," he said brusquely.

She sighed at his intransigence. "All right, Nicholas. How will I find you?"

Half an hour later, her Rolls was parked opposite the dockyard gates and Nick stepped through the door that the chauffeur held open for him. Chantelle lifted her face to him, her lips moist and slightly parted. He ignored the invitation, and lightly kissed her cheek before settling into the corner opposite her.

She made a little move, and slanted her eyes at him in amusement. "How chaste we are, Nicholas."

Nick touched the button on the control console and the glass soundproof partition slid up between them and the chauffeur.

"Did you send in the auditors?" he asked.

"You look tired, darling, and harassed."

"Have you blown the whistle on Duncan?" He avoided the distraction. "I understand *Golden Dawn* is to be launched at noon tomorrow. What happened, Chantelle?"

"There is a little bistro at Minden—it's just across the bridge."

"Damn it, Chantelle. I haven't time to fool around."

The Rolls was already gliding swiftly through the narrow streets of the port, between the high warehouse buildings.

"It will take five minutes to get there, and the lobster *Armoricaine* —the local speciality—is superb." She chatted archly, until the chauffeur checked the Rolls at the toll barrier before accelerating out onto the ramp of the St. Nazaire bridge. The great span of the bridge rose in a regal curve, three hundred feet above the waters of the Loire. The river was almost three miles wide here, and from the highest point of the bridge there was an aerial view over the dockyards of the town, dwarfed beside the mountainous bulk of *Golden Dawn*.

"They are still working on her," he said. "They are still working." He repeated it as an accusation.

"Nicholas, nothing in this life is simple."

"You didn't confront Duncan, did you?" he accused bitterly.

"Let's wait until we have a glass of wine—"

"Now," he snapped. "Tell me right now. Chantelle, I haven't time for games."

"Yes, I spoke to him." She nodded. "I called him down to Cap Ferrat, and I accused him of all you suspected. He didn't deny a thing. He told me that I knew only the half of it." Her voice rose sharply, and suddenly the enormity of her predicament spilled out in a torrent of words. . . .

"We've got him now," Nicholas said, at last, jubilantly. "That's it. He's betrayed the trust. We'll be able to stop *Golden Dawn* just like that—" He hammered his fist into the palm of the other hand. "You can get an urgent order before the courts. . . ."

The Rolls had stopped now outside the tiny bistro. It was on the river front, with a view across the water to the dockyards. The chauffeur held open the door and Chantelle was gone with her swift birdlike grace. Nick followed her.

The proprietor came through from his kitchen and fussed over Chantelle, seating them at the window and lingering to discuss the menu.

"Here's to us, Nicholas darling," she said at last, raising her glass of Muscadet.

He drank silently and then set down the glass. "Chantelle, when are you going to stop Duncan?"

"Don't spoil the meal, darling."

"In about thirty seconds I'm going to become very angry. When are you going to stop him?"

"I'm not, darling."

He stared at her. "What did you say?"

"I'm going to do everything in my power to help him launch *Golden Dawn*."

"You don't understand, Chantelle. You're talking about risking a million tons of the most deadly poison. . . ."

"Don't be silly, Nicky. Keep that heroic talk for the newspapers."

"There is still time to make modifications."

"No, there isn't. You don't understand, darling. Duncan has put us so deeply into debt that a delay of even a few days would bring us down. There is no money for modifications, no time for anything—except to get *Golden Dawn* under way. I have never been so frightened in my life, Nicholas. I could lose everything." She shivered with the horror of it. "I would kill myself if that happened."

"I am still going to stop Duncan. . . ."

"No, Nicholas. Please just leave it, for my sake—for our son's sake. It's Peter's inheritance that we are talking about. Let *Golden Dawn* make one voyage, just one voyage. Then we'll sell her, and I can rid myself of Duncan. It will be you and I again, Nicky. A few short weeks, that's all."

Suddenly it came to him as clear as crystal, the explanation for the silence that had haunted him for almost a week. "Just one more question, Chantelle. When did you telephone Samantha Silver?"

She looked puzzled for a moment as though she was trying to put a face to a name. "Samantha—oh, your little friend. Why should I want to telephone her?" And then her expression changed.

"Oh, Nicholas, you don't really believe I'd do that? You don't really believe I would inflict unnecessary hurt?"

"No," Nick agreed quietly, knowing that she lied. "You'd not murder more than a million, or poison more than a single ocean at a time, would you?" He pushed back his chair.

"Sit down, Nicky. Eat your lobster."

"Suddenly I'm not hungry." He stripped two one-hundred franc notes from his money clip and dropped them beside his plate.

"I'll send your car back," he said and walked out.

"TOM? TOM PARKER?"

"That's right. Who is this, please?" His voice was so clear and strong, although the Atlantic Ocean separated them.

"It's Nick, Nick Berg."

"Nick, how are you?" The big voice boomed with pleasure. "I'm glad you called. I've got good news. The job went up before the Board of Governors of the University yesterday. You're on the biology faculty as an associate. Isn't that great?"

"I'm delighted."

"You don't sound it," Tom roared. "What's bugging you, boy?"

"Tom, where the hell is Samantha?"

Nick sensed the mood change. The silence lasted a beat too long, and then Tom's tone was guileless. "She requested leave to go off on a six-week field trip down the Keys."

"Six weeks?" Nick's voice rose with frustration. "Damn it, Tom. She promised to come over here next Friday for the launching of my new vessel. I've been trying to get in touch with her for a week."

"She left yesterday," said Tom. "She won't be back till Independence Day or thereabouts."

Nick was silent, while a coldness settled on his chest.

"Listen, Nick," said Tom at last. "A word to the wise. Get your ass across here, just as soon as she gets back. That girl needs talking to, badly. That is if you care about her."

"I care about her," Nick said quickly. "I shall have sea trials here for the next few weeks, but I'll be across the weekend of her return. I promise."

"I believe it."

"If you see her, tell her that for me—will you?"
"I'll tell her."
"Thanks, Tom."

NICK TRIED TO BEAR the indignity of it with stoicism, but the thick coating of pancake make-up seemed to clog the pores of his skin and he moved restlessly in the make-up chair.

"Please keep still, sir," the make-up girl snapped irritably as she administered the ultimate indignity of painting his lips.

In the chair beside him the anchorman of "The Today and Tomorrow Show" lolled graciously. He was tall and elegant with dyed and permanently waved hair and a carnation in his button hole. "I've given you the first slot. If it gets interesting, I'll run you four minutes forty seconds, otherwise I'll cut it off at two, so try and make it tight and hard."

Interviewed by a prominent London journalist just after the launchings of *Golden Dawn* and *Sea Witch* three days later, Nick had managed to turn the conversation to his fears about the tanker. The subsequent article in *The Sunday Times* had caused enough fuss to excite the interest of "The Today and Tomorrow Show". They had invited Christy Marine and Orient Amex to meet their accuser. They had fielded their first teams: Duncan Alexander, and an Orient Amex director with the craggy honest face of a Gary Cooper.

The television studio was the size of an aircraft hangar, the concrete floor strewn with thick black cables and the roof lost in the gloomy heights, but they had created the illusion of intimacy in the small shell of the stage around which the big mobile cameras clustered like mechanical crabs. The egg-shaped chairs made it impossible either to loll or to sit upright, and the merciless white glare of the arc lamps fried Nick's thick layers of greasy make-up. It was small consolation that across the table Duncan looked like a Japanese *Kabuki* dancer in make-up too white for his coppery hair.

An assistant director in a sweat shirt and jeans clipped a small microphone into Nick's lapel. Somebody else in the darkness beyond the lights was intoning solemnly, "Four, three, two, one—you're on!" and the red light lit on the middle camera.

"Welcome to The Today and Tomorrow Show." The anchorman's voice was suddenly warm and mellifluous. "Last week in the French ship-building port of St. Nazaire, the largest ship in the world was launched . . ." In a dozen sentences he sketched out the facts, while on the repeating screens beyond the cameras Nick saw that they were running newsreel footage of *Golden Dawn*'s launching. He was so fascinated by the views of the enormous vessel that when the cameras switched to him he was taken by surprise and saw himself start on the little screen as the interviewer began introducing him, swiftly running a thumbnail portrait and then going on, ". . . Mr. Berg has some very definite views on this ship . . ."

"In her present design and construction she is not safe to carry even regular crude petroleum oil," Nick said. "However, she will be carrying crude oil that has been contaminated by cadmium sulphide, one of the more toxic substances in nature."

"Your first statement, Mr. Berg. Does anyone else share your doubts as to the safety of her design?"

"She does not carry A.1. Lloyd's rating," said Nick.

"Now can you tell us about these so-called cad-rich crudes?"

Nick had perhaps fifteen seconds to explain. It was too short a time, and twice Duncan Alexander interjected, skillfully breaking up Nick's presentation. Before Nick had finished, the anchorman cut him short. "Thank you, Mr. Berg. Now Mr. Kemp is a director of the oil company . . ."

"My company, Orient Amex, last year allocated two million US dollars to assist in the scientific study of environmental problems. I can tell you folks, right now, that we at Orient Amex are very conscious of the problems of modern technology . . ."

"Your company's profit last year, after taxation, was four hundred and twenty-five million dollars," Nick cut in clearly. "That makes point four seven per cent on environmental research—all of it tax deductible. Congratulations, Mr. Kemp."

Mr. Kemp looked pained and went on, "Now we at Orient Amex are working towards a better quality of life for all peoples. We cannot allow ourselves to be blinded by the romanticism of amateur environmentalists who would have us discontinue research such as the revolutionary cadmium cracking process which could give the world's oil reserves an extended life of twenty years or more . . ."

The anchorman now cut the oil man off in mid-flow and switched his attention to Duncan Alexander. "Mr. Alexander, your so-called ultra-tanker will carry the cad-rich crudes. How would you reply to Mr. Berg?"

Duncan smiled. "When Mr. Berg had my job as head of Christy Marine, *Golden Dawn* was the best idea in the world. Since he was fired, it's suddenly the worst."

They laughed, and Nick felt a hot red rush of anger.

"Is *Golden Dawn* rated A.1. at Lloyd's?" asked the anchorman.

"Christy Marine has not applied for a Lloyd's listing. We arranged our insurance in other markets."

Even through his anger Nick had to concede how quick he was.

"How safe is your ship, Mr. Alexander?"

Now Duncan turned his head and looked directly across the table at Nick. "I believe she is as safe as the world's leading marine architects can make her." He paused, and there was a malevolent gleam in his eyes now. "So safe that I have decided to end this ridiculous controversy by a display of my personal confidence. On *Golden Dawn*'s maiden voyage, when she returns from the Persian Gulf in the middle of July fully laden with the El Barras crudes, I and my family—my wife and my stepson—will join her at Cape Town for the final six thousand miles of her voyage." As Nick gaped at him wordlessly, he went on evenly, "That's how convinced I am that *Golden Dawn* is capable of performing her task in perfect safety."

"Thank you." The anchorman recognized a good exit line, when he heard one. "Thank you, Mr. Alexander. You've convinced me—and I am sure you have convinced many of our viewers. We are now crossing to Washington via satellite where . . ."

The moment the red "in use" light flickered out on the television camera, Nick was on his feet and facing Duncan. His anger at being so adroitly grandstanded was fanned by the stabbing anxiety of having Peter taken aboard *Golden Dawn*.

"You're not taking Peter on that death trap of yours," he snapped.

"That's his mother's decision," said Duncan evenly. "Try to

prevent it and I'm sure your efforts will be as ineffectual as those to stop *Golden Dawn*." He turned his back on Nick and spoke to the oil man. "I do think that went off rather well," he said.

JAMES TEACHER had Nick's urgent application before a judge in chambers within seventy-two hours, petitioning for a writ to restrain Chantelle Alexander from allowing her son by her former marriage to accompany her on an intended voyage aboard *Golden Dawn*.

The judge turned down the petition on the grounds that it would be placing unreasonable restraint on the child's mother.

Later, in the back seat of his Bentley, James Teacher murmured apologetically, "He was right, of course, Mr. Berg. I would have done the same in his place. These domestic squabbles are always . . ."

Nick was not listening. "I want you to stall the deal with the sheikhs," he said.

James Teacher broke off in mid-sentence and stared at him. "Good God, man, it's taken me four hard weeks to get them ripe to sign."

"I need to have control of my tugs for a little longer."

"Mr. Berg, we are talking about seven million dollars . . ."

"We are talking about my son," said Nick quietly. "Can you stall them?"

"Yes, of course I can, if that's what you truly want. How long?"

"Eight weeks—long enough for *Golden Dawn* to finish this crazy voyage—one way or the other."

NICK SPENT the next four weeks in St. Nazaire, helping Jules Levoisin with the sea trials for *Sea Witch*. Before taking off for Miami, he telephoned Bernard Wackie in Bermuda to check on the plans that he had asked to be put into operation immediately after his decision to postpone the sale of Ocean Salvage.

"Where's *Golden Dawn*?" he asked, and lit a cheroot while he listened to Bernard's reply.

"She arrived at El Barras a week ago today, coupled up with her pod tanks and made her turn-around within three hours. If she makes good her twenty-two knots, she should double the Cape within the next few days. I will have a report on her then. She'll be taking on mail by helicopter as she passes."

"And passengers," said Nick grimly. He knew that Peter had been taken out of school and that he and Chantelle were off to Cape Town shortly. He had telephoned the boy the night before. Peter had been wildly elated at the prospect of the voyage on the ultra-tanker. "Where's *Warlock*?" he asked Bernard.

"*Warlock*'s still in Mauritius. I had to fly out a new armature for the main generator. It was just bad luck that she broke down in that God-forsaken part of the world but Allen promises she will be ready for sea tomorrow. He won't be able to catch *Golden Dawn* before she rounds the Cape, but he'll be only a day or two behind her. He'll shadow her all the way into Galveston roads."

"Right. Have you confirmed the standby contract for *Sea Witch*?" The contract was for Jules Levoisin and the new tug to stand by three offshore working rigs that were drilling in the Florida Bay, that elbow of shallow water formed by the sweep of the Florida Keys and the low swampy morass of the Everglades.

Bernard gave a gasp of frustration. "Nick, it's ridiculous to use a twenty-two thousand horsepower ocean-going tug as an oil-rig standby. The daily hire won't cover your direct costs . . ."

"She will be sitting exactly where I want her," said Nick.

"Listen to me," pleaded Bernard. "What are the chances of *Golden Dawn* suffering a crippling breakdown on her maiden voyage—a hundred to one against? You've already got one tug shadowing her halfway round the world. It's going to cost a quarter of a million dollars, if you take into consideration the loss of earnings on both vessels . . ."

"It's my money," Nick snapped. "And Peter is my son. Now get a telex off and confirm that contract."

NICK LOOKED down upon Miami Beach as the aircraft made its final approach, losing height over Biscayne Bay.

He felt the uncomfortable nagging of guilt and uncertainty. It was no help to tell himself that his night with Chantelle had been forced upon him in circumstances almost impossible to resist. To Samantha it had been betrayal. He was uncertain as to just how much he had destroyed, how much was left for him to build upon. All that he was certain of was that he needed her, more than he had needed anything in his life. He loved her with something close to desperation.

He had only a single overnight valise so he passed swiftly through Customs, and as he went into the telephone booth, he glanced at his watch. It was just six o'clock.

He had dialled the first four digits of her number before he checked himself. "What the hell am I phoning for?" he asked himself grimly. "To tell her I'm here, so she can have a flying start when she runs for the bushes?"

He dropped the receiver back on its cradle, went to the Hertz desk at the terminal doors, and rented a Cougar sports car.

The brightly painted Chevy van was in the lean-to shelter next to the shack, and he parked the Cougar's nose almost touching its bumper. There was no way she could escape now, unless she went through the far wall of the shed.

He knocked once on the screen door of the kitchen and went straight on in. There was a coffee pot beside the stove, and he touched it as he passed. It was still warm. He went through into the living room, and called, "Samantha!"

The bedroom door was open. There was a suit of denims, and some pale transparent wisps of underwear thrown carelessly over the patchwork quilt.

The shack was deserted. He went down to the beach. The tide had swept the sand smooth, and her prints were the only ones. She had dropped her towel above the high water mark. He had to shade his eyes against the ruddy glare of the lowering sun before he could make out her bobbing head—five hundred yards out.

He sat down beside her towel, lit a cheroot, and waited while the sun settled in a wild, fiery flood of light, and he lost the shape of her head against the darkening sea. He felt no urgency, and the darkness was almost complete when she rose, waist deep from the edge of the gentle surf, waded ashore and came up the beach.

Nick felt his heart flop over and he flicked the cheroot away and stood up. She halted abruptly, startled, and stood completely still. "What do you want?" she faltered.

"You," he said.

"Why? Are you starting a harem?" Her voice hardened and her shoulders took on a stubborn set.

He stepped forward and she was rigid and unyielding in his arms and her lips hard and tightly unresponsive under his. "Samantha, there are things I'll never be able to explain. I don't even understand them myself, but what I do know very clearly is that I love you, that without you my life is miserable . . ." There was no relaxation of rigid muscles. Her hands were still held stiffly at her sides and her body felt cold and wet and unyielding. "Samantha, I wish I were perfect—I'm not. All I am sure of is that I can't make it without you."

"I couldn't take it again. I couldn't live through this again," she said tightly.

"I need you. I am certain of that," he insisted.

"You'd better be. You cheat on me one time more and you won't have me around to cheat." Then she was clinging to him and saying, "Oh God, Nicholas, how I hated you, and how I missed you."

Her lips were soft and tasted of the sea. He picked her up and carried her over the soft sand. He didn't trust himself to speak; it would be so easy to say the wrong thing now.

PETER BERG had twisted around in his safety straps, so that he could press his face to the round perspex window in the fuselage of the big Sikorsky helicopter.

The night was completely, utterly black. Then the helicopter banked gently and Peter gasped with excitement as the ship came into view.

She was burning all her lights; tier upon tier, the brilliantly lit floors of her stern quarters rose above the altitude at which the Sikorsky was hovering. She was so huge that she looked like a city. There seemed to be no end to her, stretched to the horizon and towered into the sky.

The helicopter sank in a controlled sweep towards the white circular target on the heliport, and Peter could see that the cargo decks were almost level with the surface of the sea. Every few seconds one of the rollers that raced down her length would flip aboard and spread like spilled milk, white and frothy, before cascading back over the side.

The helicopter bumped gently onto the green deck, insulated with its thick coat of plasticized paint to prevent the striking of sparks. The ship's party swarmed forward, doubled under the swirling rotor, and Peter was swung down onto the deck. He stood blinking in the glare of the lamps and wrinkling his nose to the characteristic tanker stench of fumes from the tanks.

Chantelle was handed down next from the cabin of the helicopter, bringing an instant flash of elegance to the starkly lit scene of bleak steel and ugly functional machinery. She wore a cat-suit of dark green with a bright Jean Patou scarf on her head.

Duncan followed her down to the deck, shook hands quickly with the first officer.

"Captain Randle's compliments, sir. He is unable to leave the bridge while the ship is in the inshore channel."

"I understand." Duncan flashed a smile. The great ship drew almost twenty fathoms and she had come in as close as was prudent to the mountainous coastline of Good Hope with its notorious currents and wild winds.

As the helicopter rose and circled away towards the distant glow of Cape Town, an elevator bore the new arrivals swiftly and silently five storeys up to the spacious, gleaming navigation bridge.

Randle, the master, was a man of Duncan Alexander's own choosing. He was young for the responsibility, just a little over thirty years of age, but his training and his credentials were impeccable. He was an honours graduate of the tanker school in France, where top men received training in the specialized handling of these freakish giants, working thirty-foot scale models that had all the handling characteristics of the real ships.

A short stocky figure with a bull neck and thrusting jaw, he greeted his important visitors, with just the right mixture of warmth and respect.

"Can I see your engine room, Captain?" asked Peter, almost immediately.

"Well," said the captain. "We go on automatic during the night, and there's nobody down there now. But I am certain the chief would be delighted to have you as his guest directly after breakfast."

The chief engineer was a Scot with three sons of his own, and he was more than delighted. Within twenty-four hours Peter was known throughout the ship. He had a pair of blue company-issue overalls altered to fit him and his name stitched across the back of them by the Lascar steward. He also wore a bright yellow hard hat. Thus clad he would help the stokers clean the fuel filters, or join the first officer on his morning inspection. Together they would check each of the pod tanks, every valve, and every one of the heavy hydraulic docking clamps that held the pod tanks attached to the main frame of the hull. Most important of all they checked the gauges on each compartment which gave the precise indication of the gas mixture contained in the air spaces under the main deck of the crude tanks. *Golden Dawn* operated on the "inert" system to keep the trapped fumes in a safe condition. The exhaust fumes of the ship's engine were caught, passed through filters and scrubbers to remove the corrosive sulphur elements and then as almost pure carbon dioxide and carbon monoxide they were forced into the air spaces of the petroleum tanks. The evaporating fumes of the volatile elements of the crude mingled with the exhaust fumes to form an unexplosive gas.

In the pump room was a cupboard containing samples of the cargo. Somehow Peter had always expected the crude oil to be treacly and tarlike—but it was as thin as human blood and as dark red.

"Some of the crudes are black, some yellow and the Nigerians are green," the pump foreman told him. "This is the first red that I've seen."

"I suppose it's the cadmium in it," Peter told him.

"Guess it is," the foreman agreed. All on board had quickly learned not to talk down to Peter Berg.

Within days Peter knew his way unerringly through the labyrinthine and usually deserted passageways. It was characteristic of these tankers with their huge bulk and tiny crews that you might wander through them for hours without meeting another human being. The only place where there was always a human presence was the bridge, and here the ship was sometimes taken out of automatic to allow Peter to spell the automatic pilot for a while; or he would assist the junior deck officers while they made a sun shot as an exercise to check against the satellite navigational Decca.

The only unpleasant time for Peter was at nights when he heard raised voices from the master cabin, and by now he was well aware of new and disturbing tensions between his mother and the stepfather he so fiercely, though silently, resented. Except for an hour in the afternoon when the swimming pool was placed out of bounds to officers and crew so that she might swim and sunbathe, Chantelle herself never left the owner's suite. Eating all her meals there, withdrawn and silent, she sat listlessly at the panoramic windows of her cabin, coming to life only for the cocktail hour when she played the owner's wife to the ships' officers.

Duncan on the other hand was like a caged animal. He paced the open decks, composing long messages which were sent off regularly over the telex in company code to Christy Marine in Leadenhall Street. Then he would stand out on the open wing of the bridge, staring fixedly ahead at the northern horizon, awaiting their replies and goaded on by the devils of doubt, impatience and fear. Often it seemed as though he were trying to force the mighty vessel onwards, faster and faster, by the sheer force of his personality.

So *Golden Dawn* ploughed massively on through the sweltering air and silken calm of the doldrums, northwards across the equator. The treacherous channels and passages through the Caribbean islands were not for a vessel of her immense bulk, deep draught and limited manoeuvrability. She was to go high above the Tropic of Cancer, and just south of the island of Bermuda where she would make her westings and enter the wider and safer waters of the Florida Straits above the Grand Bahamas. On this course she would be constricted by narrow and shallow seaways for only a few hundred miles before she was out into the open waters of the Gulf of Mexico.

Then, forty-eight hours after crossing the equator, disaster struck. The main bearing of her single propeller shaft began to run hot.

Unfortunately it was at eleven o'clock at night and there was nobody to hear or see it. The system was not duplicated, so that when the temperature of the bearing began to rise there was no automatic shut-down of power.

The massive propeller shaft, as thick as a tree trunk and polished brilliant silver, spun on while the over-heated bearing closed its grip upon the area of rough metal. The whole assembly began to glow a sullen cherry red and then the oxide paint that was daubed on the outer surface of the bearing began to blister and blacken. Still the tremendous power of the engine forced the shaft around.

What oil was still being fed between the glowing surfaces of the spinning shaft reached its flash point and burst into flame. The shaft tunnel filled with thick billows of stinking chemical-tainted smoke, and only then did the fire sensors come to life and the alarms sound throughout the ship.

The great engine, however, still pounded along, and the shaft still turned in the disintegrating bearing, buckling and distorting under unbearable strains. The chief engineer was the first to reach the control room, and without orders from the bridge he began emergency shut-down of all systems.

It was another hour before the team under the direction of the first officer had the fire in the shaft tunnel under control. The chief then discovered that the bearing shells had disintegrated, and the shaft itself was brutally scored and pitted.

It was mid-morning by the time the chief had the spare bearing shells brought up from stores and unpacked; but it was only when they came to fit them that they realized that the cases had been incorrectly stencilled. The half shells that they contained were obsolete non-metric types, and they were five millimetres undersized for *Golden Dawn*'s shaft. This tiny variation in size made them utterly useless.

It was only then that Duncan's steely urbane control cracked. He raged about the bridge for twenty minutes, abusing Randle and his engineer in wild and extravagant terms.

Peter had sensed the excitement and slipped up unobtrusively to watch. He was fascinated by his stepfather's rage. He had never seen a display like it before.

At last Duncan recovered partial control. "Captain Randle," he said. "We have a deadline to meet in Galveston roads. This ship, this whole concept of carrying crude is on trial. I want to meet the deadline."

In the silence Peter Berg piped up, "You could have new shells sent from Bermuda. It's only three hundred miles away."

"How did you get in here?" Duncan swung round. "Get back to your mother. And you, Randle, get an immediate call for spare parts to Construction Atlantique—and have them flown out from Bermuda."

IN THE NORTHWESTERN corner of the Caribbean basin there is an area of shallow warm water and saturated tropical air, hemmed in on one side by the island chain of the Great Antilles, the bulwark of Cuba and Hispaniola, and on the other by the Yucatan peninsula. Usually it is gently cooled and moderated by the benign influence of the northeasterly trade winds. When these fail, however, the air heats further and sucks up the evaporating waters. A fat bubble of wind like a swelling blister begins to rise.

As *Golden Dawn* drifted helplessly some two thousand miles to the northwest, such a bubble was forming. When it was only a hundred miles across, the rotation of the earth began to twist it like a top, so that the satellite cameras, hundreds of miles above, recorded a creamy little spiral wisp. Their picture quickly reached the desk of the senior forecaster of the hurricane watch at the meteorological headquarters at Miami in southern Florida.

"Looks like a ripe one," he grunted to his assistant. "Ask Charlie for a hurricane code name."

And a minute later his assistant told him. "Charlie says to call the bitch 'Bertha'."

"NICK, I'VE NEWS on *Golden Dawn*." On the telephone in Miami Bernard Wackie's voice was sharp and alert. "I've got to hand it to you; you've got a nose for it. Three engineers from Construction Atlantique flew in here this evening with a large crate, apparently containing bearing shells for Golden Dawn. They shuttled aboard a Sikorsky so fast that it looked like a conjuring trick. The trouble is there is a hurricane warning out."

"Where are *Warlock* and *Sea Witch*?" snapped Nick.

"*Warlock* crossed the equator three days ago," said Bernard. "And *Sea Witch* will reach Charleston late tomorrow."

"Is there another chopper available on the island to get me out to *Warlock*?"

"It can be arranged," Bernard said.

"Very well. There is a direct flight from here at seven tomorrow morning. Please meet me."

Samantha was sitting up naked in the centre of the bed. She hugged her knees to her chest with both arms, and under the gorgeous tangle of her hair her face was desolate as that of a lost child and her green eyes haunted.

"You're going again," she said softly. "You only came a couple of weeks ago, and now you're going again. Oh God, Nick, loving you is the toughest job I've had in my life."

He reached for her quickly and she clung to him, pressing her face into the thick hair that covered his chest.

"I have to go," he said, and she listened quietly while he told her about the hurricane warning.

In the morning while it was still dark outside she insisted on cooking breakfast for him. Later, she gave him one last kiss through the open window of the Cougar. "You've got an hour. You'll just about make it." He started the engine and still she held onto the sill. "Nick, one day we'll be together—I mean all the time, like we planned—won't we?"

"It's a promise."

"Hurry back," she said and he gunned the Cougar up the sandy driveway without looking back.

SIX HUNDRED MILES southwest of Miami the storm began to move forward, slowly at first but every hour gathering power, spiralling upon itself at unbelievable velocities, its high dome extended upwards through fifty thousand feet. Now the centre of the storm opened like a flower, a calm tunnel that extended from the surrounding surface of the wind-tortured sea to the very summit of the dome.

The she-devil called "Bertha" was about to launch herself across the Caribbean Sea.

DUNCAN ALEXANDER stood in front of the fireplace in *Golden Dawn*'s state room. His brow was heavily furrowed with worry and his eyes darkly underscored with sleeplessness.

Seated on the long couch on one side of the fireplace were the senior officers of *Golden Dawn*—her captain, mate and chief engineer—and in the leather studded wing-back opposite sat Charles Gras, the engineer from Construction Atlantique. He spoke now in heavily accented English, falling back on the French word occasionally which Duncan translated quickly.

"My men will have completed the re-assembly of the main bearing by noon today. To the best of my ability I have examined and tested the main shaft. I can find no evidence of structural damage. But I must emphasize that this does not mean that no damage exists. At the very best the repairs must be considered to be temporary . . ." He paused and turned deliberately to Captain Randle. "I must urge you to seek proper repair in the nearest port open to you, and to proceed there at the lowest speed which will enable you to work the ship."

Randle twisted uncomfortably in his seat, and glanced across at Duncan, who intervened smoothly. "We draw twenty fathoms of water. There are no safe harbours on the eastern seaboard of America. Our nearest safe anchorage is Galveston roads, on the Texas coast of the Gulf of Mexico."

The tanker's first officer was a young man in his twenties, with a clear level eye. "With respect, sir," he said, and they all turned their heads towards him. "Miami's hurricane alert now includes the Straits and southern Florida. We would be on a directly converging course. Our nearest safe anchorage is in the lee of Bermuda Island—"

"Do you have any idea of the daily interest on this cargo?" Duncan's voice rasped. "It is in the region of twenty-five thousand dollars. Apart from that, Bermuda does not have the facilities for major repairs."

Charles Gras looked to Captain Randle, waiting for him to assert the authority vested in him by law. But when the young captain remained silent the Frenchman smiled sardonically and shrugged a world-weary dismissal of further interest. "Then, I must ask that arrangements be made for my two assistants and myself to leave this ship immediately we have completed the temporary repairs." Gras emphasized the word "temporary".

Duncan nodded. "The helicopter will fly you both to Bermuda the moment we get under way."

Duncan had not taken his eyes from *Golden Dawn*'s officers during this exchange, and now he went on, "I am quite prepared to accept the resignation of any of the officers of this ship who wish to join that flight."

He looked at each in turn, and, one by one, they dropped their eyes from his. Randle was the first to speak. "If you will excuse me, Mr. Alexander, I must make preparations to get this ship under way again."

THERE WERE EIGHT of them crowded into Tom Parker's office. Although there was only seating for three, the others found perches against the tiered shelves of biological specimens and reference books. Samantha sat on the corner of Tom's desk, swinging her long denim-clad legs and answered the questions that were fired at her.

"Assuming she gets up steam again, how do you know she will take the passage of the Florida Straits?"

"It's Nick's educated guess. She's just too big and clumsy to thread the needle of the islands."

"The Straits are a hundred miles wide . . ."

"I know what you're going to say." Samantha smiled, and turned to one of the other girls. "Sally Anne will answer that one."

"You all know my brother is in the Coast Guard at Fort Lauderdale. All traffic through the Straits reports to there, so we'll have an immediate fix on her. We've got the whole US Coast Guard rooting for us."

They argued and discussed for ten minutes more, before Tom Parker slapped an open palm on the desk in front of him and they subsided reluctantly into silence.

"O.K.," he said. "Do I understand the proposal to be that this chapter of Greenpeace stages a demonstration the moment the tanker enters American territorial waters?"

"That's exactly it," Samantha nodded, and looked about her for support. They were all nodding and murmuring agreement.

"All right," Tom nodded. "Now. How do we get out there in the Straits to confront this vessel? Do we put on our water wings and swim?"

Even Samantha looked sheepish now. The others were studying their fingernails or gazing with sudden fascination out of the windows. "Well . . ." Samantha began, and then hesitated.

"Go on," Tom encouraged her. "Of course, you weren't thinking of using University property, were you? There is a law in this country against taking other people's ships. It's called piracy."

"As a matter of fact . . ." Samantha gave a helpless shrug.

"And as a senior member of the faculty, you would not expect me to be party to a criminal act." They were all silent. "On the other hand, if a party of graduate researchers put in a requisition, I would be quite happy to authorize an extended field expedition across the Straits to Grand Bahama on board the *Tricky Dicky* . . ."

"Tom, you're a darling," said Samantha.

"That's a hell of a way to speak to your professor," said Tom and scowled happily at her.

IT WAS GOOD to have a deck under his feet again and Nick, standing on *Warlock*'s navigation bridge, exulted. He had been greeted aboard by David Allen and Vinny Baker with news that, according to intercepted communications between *Golden Dawn* and various Coast Guard aircraft, the big tanker was once again under way. For the last two days they had been following her reported positions at eighty per cent power.

"We will continue to do so," Nick had told them, "until she docks safely—hurricane or not."

He turned to David Allen. "Are any of the opposition inside us?"

David shook his head. "McCormick has one in New York and another halfway back to Rotterdam."

"We are in good shape," Nick decided as he balanced the triangles of relative speeds and distances between vessels.

Suddenly the Trog stuck his grey wrinkled tortoise head through from the radio room. "Captain, *Golden Dawn* is being called up again by the Coast Guard."

Nick, followed by David, rushed over to the doorway. The radio conversation was only just beginning.

"Good morning, *Golden Dawn*. This is Coast Guard aircraft November Charlie One Fife Niner overhead. Are you appraised of the hurricane alert in force at this time?"

"Affirmative."

The Trog dexterously made the fine tuning, scribbled the bearing on his pad, ripped off the page and handed it to Nick.

Over the loudspeaker the Coast Guard was being politely persistent. "I must further trouble you, sir, in view of your sensitive cargo and the special weather conditions, for your expected time of arrival abeam of the Dry Tortugas Bank marine beacon and when you anticipate clearing the Straits and shaping a northerly course away from the predicted hurricane track?"

"Stand by." There was a brief hum of static while the operator consulted the deck officer and then *Golden Dawn* came back. "Our ETA Dry Tortugas Bank beacon is 0130 tomorrow."

There was a long pause now as the Coast Guard consulted his headquarters ashore on one of the closed frequencies, and then:

"I am requested respectfully but officially to bring to your attention that, in view of the very heavy weather expected, your present ETA Dry Tortugas Bank leaves you very fine margins of safety, sir."

"Thank you, Coast Guard One Fife Niner. Your transmission will be entered in the ship's log. This is *Golden Dawn* over and out."

Nick handed David the Trog's note. "I'd be obliged if you would immediately put this ship on a course to close with her as soon as is possible," he snapped. David blinked at him once, then disappeared onto his bridge, calling for the change in course.

"BERTHA" WAS NOW nearing full development. Her crest was reared high above the freezing levels so she wore a splendid mane of frosted white ice particles that streamed out three hundred miles ahead of her on the jet stream of the upper troposphere.

From one side to the other she now measured one hundred and fifty miles across, and the power unleashed within her was of immeasurable savagery. The winds that blew around her centre tore the surface off the sea and bore it aloft at speeds in excess of a hundred and fifty miles an hour. There was no longer a clear line between sea and air. Like a blinded and berserk monster she blundered across the confined waters of the Caribbean, ripping the trees and buildings from the tiny islands which stood in her path.

Less than four hundred miles ahead of her, across those shallow reefs and banks named "Hurricane Flats" after the thousands of other such storms that had followed the same route during the memory of man, lay the Florida Straits. At twenty miles an hour the whole incredible heaven-high mass of crazed wind and churning clouds trundled towards it.

GOLDEN DAWN's deck officer scanned the sea ahead.

"What the hell are they playing at?" he exclaimed irritably. Two miles ahead on the starboard bow, a fishing boat was approaching, almost head-on.

"Damn them. We'll give them a buzz." He reached up for the handle of the fog horn and blew three long blasts that echoed out mournfully across the Straits. There was a general movement amongst the officers to get a better view ahead through the forward bridge window. "They must be half asleep out there."

The deck officer flinched from the responsibility of manoeuvring the ship in these confined waters. Even at their current speed, it would take *Golden Dawn* half an hour and seven nautical miles to come to a stop. A turn in either direction would swing through a wide arc of many miles before she was able to make a ninety degree change of course. He was about to call the captain to the bridge, when Randle came bounding up from his cabin.

"What was that blast on the horn?" he demanded.

"Small vessel holding to a near collision course, sir."

Randle seized the handle of the fog horn and hung onto it. "God, what's wrong with them?"

"The deck is crowded," exclaimed one of the officers without lowering his binoculars. "Looks as though they have a movie camera team on the wheelhouse roof. And they are streaming some sort of banner. Can anybody read it?"

TO SAMANTHA in the *Dicky*'s wheelhouse, the tanker's bows seemed to fill the horizon from one side to the other. She felt distinctly uneasy.

"Do you think they have seen us?" Sally Anne asked.

"Of course they have," Samantha announced. "That's why they blew their siren. Go up and see if the TV boys are getting their stuff."

A minute later Sally Anne reappeared. "They'd like to get a shot of us holding up the banners in front of her."

"Son of gun," remarked Hank Petersen, the helmsman. "I don't like playing chicken with somebody that size."

"Don't worry. We'll get out of their way at the last moment. Turn ninety degrees to starboard, Hank. I'm going to help them on the deck."

The TV producer was shouting confused stage directions from the top of the wheelhouse roof. The wind tore at the thin white canvas banner as the *Dicky* began to turn, so that only the last word of the slogan was readable. "POISONER", it accused in scarlet, crudely-painted letters followed by a grinning skull and crossbones.

Samantha, struggling with the flapping canvas, felt the change of the engine beat. *Tricky Dicky*'s diesel had been bellowing furiously as Hank opened the throttle to bring the little vessel as fast as possible across the menace of those massive bows.

The smoking splutter of the exhaust pipe that rose vertically up the side of the deckhouse had made all speech difficult—but now it died away, and suddenly there was only the sound of the wind. Even their own raised voices were silenced, and they froze, staring out at *Golden Dawn* as she bore down on them without the slightest check in her majestic approach.

FOR TEN SECONDS Randle stood rigid, both hands gripping the foul-weather rail below the sill of the bridge windows, as he watched the stern of the wallowing fishing boat for the renewed churning of its prop. He knew that he could not turn nor stop his own ship in time to avoid a collision. The only chance was for the small vessel itself to get under way immediately.

"Damn them to hell," he thought bitterly. They were a boat load of nutters as the scarlet painted banner with its ridiculously melodramatic Jolly Roger made clear, and they were in gross default of the law of the sea. They deserved to be run down. Nevertheless, he must make every effort to avoid collision, no matter how futile those efforts would be.

"Full port rudder!" he snapped at the helmsman beside him. And with two swift paces he had reached the engine-room telegraph. It rang shrilly as he pulled back the chromed handle to "Full Astern".

GOLDEN DAWN'S chief engineer and the on-duty stoker were, at that moment, carrying out a tour of inspection in the shaft tunnel. The spinning shaft in its deep bed generated a high pitched whine that seemed to resonate in the steel box of the tunnel, as though it were the body of a violin.

The chief was squatting down, his face only inches from the spinning steel. He closed one eye, and cocked his head, trying once again to decide if the faint blurring of the shaft's outline was real or merely his over-active imagination. Was he seeing distortion or his own fears?

Suddenly, startlingly, the shaft slammed into stillness. He rocked back onto his heels, and almost instantly the shaft began to spin again, but this time in reverse thrust. The whine built up swiftly into a rising shriek.

They were pulling emergency power from the bridge, and it was madness, suicidal madness. The chief seized the stoker by the shoulder and shouted into his ear. "Get back to control. Find out what the hell they are doing on the bridge."

The stoker scrambled away down the tunnel. The chief lowered his head again, and now he could clearly see the flickering of the outline of the shaft. It wasn't imagination at all.

"God! They are going to blow the whole thing!" he shouted, and jumped up. He started back along the shaft, but the entire tunnel was juddering so violently that he had to grab at the metal bulkhead to steady himself. Disbelievingly he saw the huge silver shaft beginning to rise and buckle in its bed, the bearing tearing loose from its mountings.

"Shut down!" he screamed. "For God's sake, shut down!" But his voice was lost in the shriek and scream of tortured metal.

The main bearing exploded. The shaft itself began to snake and whip. The chief cowered back, but the kicking shaft seized him like a mindless predator, pounding him and crushing him against the metal wall of the tunnel.

Then the shaft snapped like a twig at the point where it had been heated and weakened. The huge revolving bronze propeller, with the stump of the main shaft still attached, plummeted downwards through four hundred fathoms. The sea rushed in through the opening, flooding the tunnel instantly until it slammed into the watertight doors.

Freed of the intolerable goad of her damaged shaft, *Golden Dawn* was suddenly silent, as she trundled on, slowly losing way. On her bridge, every officer stood frozen, waiting for the impact of collision with the fishing vessel directly in their path.

SAMANTHA WAS THE FIRST to recover from the shock of realizing that the *Dicky*'s engine had failed. She ran across the plunging deck to the wheelhouse. "Why have we stopped?" she yelled.

"It's the throttle linkage," Hank Petersen called. "It's snapped."

Half a mile away the tanker was coming on without any check in her speed. Samantha could hear the silken rustling sound of the water under its hull, the sough of the bow wave curling upon itself.

The *Dicky*'s throttle linkage had broken once before, a year ago, and she had helped Tom Parker repair it. She knew that it was possible to control the revolutions of the engine by hand.

She turned and dived down the vertical ladder into the engine room. The diesel was running, burbling away quietly at idling speed, but it was not generating sufficient power to move the vessel.

She tripped and sprawled on the greasy deck, and pulled herself up, crying out with pain as her hand touched the scorching hot manifold of the engine exhaust. On the far side of the engine block, she groped desperately under the air filter for the lever. She found it, pushed it against the direction of its spring—and instantly the diesel engine bellowed in her ears. She felt the ship picking up speed under her.

She did not hear the screams from the deck above her. She did not know how close *Golden Dawn* was. She just held the throttle open and prayed.

The impact when it came was shattering. She was hurled against the hot steel of the engine, her forehead striking with such force that her vision starred into blinding white light.

She was not unconscious for more than a few seconds before a spray of icy cold water in the face aroused her. She pulled herself up onto her knees. Spurts of water were jetting through the planking beside her.

Dimly she was aware that the diesel engine was idling again and that the deck was splashing with water as the boat rolled wildly in some powerful turbulence. She wondered if the whole boat had been trodden under by the tanker. Then she realized it must be the wash of the giant hull which was throwing them about so mercilessly, but they were still afloat.

Painfully she crawled up the ladder and made her way to the wheelhouse, where she found a dazed-looking Hank Petersen.

"Are you all right, Sam?" he asked.

"Water's pouring in," she said. "You're going to need the bilge pump."

"You saved our lives," he told her.

"I just held the throttle open," she said, and then with feeling, "but I'll be damned if I'll do it again. Somebody else can go down there, I've had my turn."

"Show me how," Hank said. "And you can take the wheel. The sooner we get back to Key Biscayne the happier I'll be."

Samantha peered across at the receding bulk of *Golden Dawn*. "My God!" She shook her head with wonder. "My God! We were lucky!"

"*MACKEREL SKIES and mares' tails, make tall ships carry short sails.*"

Nick recited the old sailor's doggerel to himself, shading his eyes with one hand as he looked upwards from the open wing of the navigation bridge. The cloud was beautiful as fine lacework. Thirty thousand feet high against the tall blue of the heavens, it spread swiftly in long filmy scrolls, a measure of the speed with which the high winds were blowing. Below it the air was clear and crisp. Only out on the western horizon the billowing thunderheads were rising, generated by the land mass of Florida whose low silhouette was still out of sight.

Warlock was racing into the chop of the Gulf Stream and scattering the spray like startled white doves, but she was running too slowly for Nick. He turned away impatiently, strode into the navigation bridge and through to the radio room. It was not necessary for him to ask. The Trog looked up and shook his head. Since that long exchange with the Coast Guard early that morning, *Golden Dawn* had kept her silence.

Nick crossed to the radar scope and studied the circular field for a few minutes. This usually busy seaway was peculiarly empty—only a few small craft crossing the Straits, scuttling for protection from the coming storm.

He had left the door to the radio room open and the bridge was quiet, so that they all heard it clearly.

> Mayday! Mayday! Mayday! This is the bulk oil carrier *Golden Dawn*. Our position is 79°59′ W. 25°43′ N . . .

Before Nick reached the chart table he knew she was still a hundred miles ahead of them, and as he pored over the table he saw his estimate confirmed.

> We have lost our propeller and we are drifting out of control. This is *Golden Dawn* calling any ship in a position to afford assistance.

Nick dashed to the radio room, where the Trog handed him the microphone.

> *Golden Dawn*, this is the salvage tug *Warlock*. I will be in a position to render assistance within four hours. I am offering Lloyd's Open Form and I want immediate acceptance.

He dropped the microphone and stormed back onto the bridge. "Interception course and push her through the gate," he ordered David grimly. "Also telex Levoisin on *Sea Witch* for his time to reach *Golden Dawn* at best possible speed."

Jules replied almost immediately. Running hard he could reach *Golden Dawn*'s position by seven o'clock the following morning, which was exactly one hour after the forecast time for Hurricane Bertha to make her passage through the Straits.

"David, there is no precedent for this that I know of—but with my son on board *Golden Dawn* I just have to assume temporary command of this ship. If there is a good salvage, the master's share will, of course, be yours."

"I'd be honoured to act as your first officer again, sir."

Nick thanked him with a touch on the arm. "Would you check preparations to put a line aboard the tanker?"

As David left the bridge, there was a screech from the Trog. "*Golden Dawn* is replying to our offer."

Nick strode across to the radio room, and read the first few lines of message as it printed out. "Offer contract of daily hire for towage this vessel from present position to Galveston roads"

"The bastard," Nick snarled. "He's playing his fancy games with me, in the teeth of a hurricane and with my boy aboard." Furiously he punched his fist into the palm of his other hand. "Right!" he snapped. "We'll play just as rough! Get me Captain Ramsden of the US Coast Guard at Fort Lauderdale."

The Trog's face lit with malicious glee and he made the contact. "Captain Ramsden for you, sir."

"Captain," Nick said. "This is the master of *Warlock.* I'm the only salvage vessel that can reach *Golden Dawn* before the passage of Bertha. Unless the *Golden Dawn*'s master accepts Lloyd's Open Form within the next sixty minutes, I shall be obliged to see to the safety of my vessel by running for the nearest anchorage, and you're going to have a million tons of highly toxic crude oil drifting out into your territorial waters, in hurricane conditions."

The Coast Guard captain had a deep measured voice, and the calm tones of a man upon whom the mantle of authority was a familiar garment. "Standby *Warlock*, while I contact *Golden Dawn.*"

Ten minutes later the Trog copied a telex from Duncan Alexander personal to Nick Berg accepting Lloyd's Open Form and requesting him to exercise all despatch in taking *Golden Dawn* in tow.

DARKNESS CAME swiftly but with the last of the light Nick could just make out the mountainous shape of Bertha beginning to hump up above the southern horizon.

The night was utterly black. There were no stars, no moon. Then suddenly, the heavens began to burn like a bed of hot coals, and the sea shone with a sullen ruddy luminosity as though the doors of a furnace had been thrown wide.

Nobody spoke on *Warlock*'s bridge. They lifted their faces with the same awed expressions as worshippers in a lofty cathedral and they looked up at the clouds that raced above them, clouds that glowed and shone with their terrible ominous flare.

Slowly the light faded and changed, turning a pale sickly greenish hue. The phenomenon was that part of mariners lore—the Devil's Beacon that leads a doomed ship on to its fate, and although in fact it was merely the rays of the sun below the western horizon catching the cloud peaks of the storm, somehow Nick could find little comfort in this mundane explanation.

The weird light faded slowly away, leaving the night even more foreboding than it had been before. Wanting to break the superstitious mood that gripped them all, Nick walked over to the radarscope. The sweeping arm lit a swirling mass of sea clutter, and the strange ghost echoes thrown up by electrical discharges within the approaching storm. Then, amid this trash, his eye picked out a harder echo on the extreme limits of the set's range. He watched it carefully for half a dozen revolutions of the radar's sweep, and each time it was constant and clearer.

"Radar contact," he said. "Tell *Golden Dawn* we are within sixty-five nautical miles. We will take on tow before midnight." And then under his breath, he added the old sailors' qualification, "God willing and weather permitting."

GOLDEN DAWN now lay within the two-mile ring of the screen, but from the *Warlock*'s bridge she was invisible. In the two hours since first contact the barometer had fallen steeply, and was still plummeting. Even *Warlock*'s twin searchlights, set seventy feet above the main deck could not pierce the solid curtains of rain.

Nick groped through the rain fog like a blind man, giving his orders to the helm in a cool impersonal tone which was belied by the pale set of his features. Then, abruptly another squall struck *Warlock*, shredding the curtains of rain, and for a moment Nick saw the tanker.

The wind had caught her high navigation bridge like the mainsail of a tall ship, and she was going swiftly astern. All her deck lights were burning, and she carried the twin red riding lights at her stubby masthead that identified a vessel drifting out of control. The following sea driven on by the rising wind piled onto her tank decks smothering them with white foam and spray.

"Steer for her starboard side," Nick told the helmsman.

He closed quickly, so that even when the rain mists closed down again they could make out the ghostly shape of her. "What bottom?" he asked David, without taking his eyes from her.

"One hundred sixteen fathoms and shelving fast." They were being blown quickly out of the main channel, onto the shallow ledge of the Florida littoral.

"I'm going to tow her out stern first," said Nick and immediately David saw the wisdom of it. Nobody would be able to get up into her bows to secure a tow line with those seas breaking over them.

"I'll go aft . . ." David began, but Nick stopped him.

"No, David. I want you here, because I'm going to board her. This will be our last chance to get passengers off before the full hurricane hits us."

David saw that it was futile to protest. Nick was going to fetch his son.

PETER BERG, wearing a lifejacket, stood beside his mother on the tanker's towering navigation bridge. "It will be all right," he comforted her. "Dad is here. It will be just fine now."

Warlock staggered and reeled in the grip of the wind as she came up into the tanker's lee. In comparison, *Golden Dawn* wallowed heavily, her pods laden with the oppressive weight of a million tons of crude oil, and the seas beat upon her with increasing fury as if affronted by her indifference. *Warlock* edged in closer.

Duncan came through from the communications room. "Berg is coming on board," he burst out with anger. "He's wasting valuable time that should be used to tow us into deeper water."

Peter interrupted and pointed down at *Warlock*. "Look!" he cried. "There's Dad! That's him in front."

At the extremity of her roll *Warlock*'s boarding gantry touched the railing of the tanker's quarter deck, ten feet above the swamped tank deck. The leading figure on the tug's upperworks now ran out along the gantry, balanced for a moment high above the roaring, racing green water and then leapt across five feet of open space, and landed on *Golden Dawn*'s quarter deck. Immediately the tug sheered off and fell in fifty yards off the tanker's starboard side.

"Dad's carried a line across," Peter said, and Chantelle, looking down, saw that a delicate white nylon thread was being hove in by two seamen on the tanker's quarter deck. A canvas bosun's chair was being winched across.

The elevator doors slid open with a whine and Nick strode onto the tanker's bridge. His oilskins ran with water that splattered onto the deck at his feet.

"Dad!" Peter ran to meet him and Nick embraced him fiercely before confronting Chantelle and Duncan Alexander.

"I'm taking off everybody who is not needed on board to handle this vessel," he said quietly.

"Your tug . . ." burst out Duncan. "You've got twenty-two thousand horsepower and surely you can . . ."

"There is a hurricane on its way," Nick cut in. "This is just the overture." He turned to Randle. "You will act as helmsman. I will control the pump room, and I'll need three volunteer seamen. Send everybody else off."

"Sir . . ." Randle began to protest.

"May I remind you, Captain, that I am salvage master. My authority overrides yours." Nick did not wait for his reply. "Peter, take your mother down to the quarter deck. I'll see you there before you go across." He turned to Duncan. "You too."

"I'm staying on board this ship," said Duncan abruptly. "It's my responsibility. I'm going to make sure you do your job, Berg."

Nick studied him for a long moment, and then smiled mirthlessly. "Stay if you will. We might need an extra hand."

AT THE QUARTER-DECK RAIL Nick hugged the boy, then lifted him into the bosun's chair, stepped back and windmilled his right arm. Immediately the winch party in *Warlock*'s upper works swung Peter swiftly out into the gap between the two ships.

As the two ships rolled and dipped, so the line tightened and sagged, one moment dropping the white canvas bucket almost to the water and the next humming with tension, threatening to snap. At last the chair reached the tug where strong hands lifted the boy clear. He waved back at Nick and then he was hustled away and the empty bosun's chair was coming back.

Only then did Nick become aware that Chantelle was clinging to his arm and he looked down into her face. She seemed very small, but as beautiful as ever, under the bulky oilskins and life-jacket. Her existence was being blown away on the wind, and she was afraid.

"You and this ship are all I have left," she sobbed.

"No, only the ship," he told her brusquely, and he was amazed that the spell was broken. With a sudden surge of relief he realized he was free of her, for ever.

She sensed it, for suddenly there was real fear in her eyes. "Nicholas, you cannot desert me now. What will become of me?"

"I don't know," he told her quietly, and caught the bosun's chair as it came in over *Golden Dawn*'s rail. He lifted her into it. "I really don't know."

Then stepping back, he windmilled his right arm again. As the chair swooped out across the water, he turned away to where the three volunteers were waiting.

"We will use the bosun's tackle to bring across a messenger from the tug," he said. "Just as soon as this ferrying is over."

Working with men to whom the task was unfamiliar, and in rapidly deteriorating conditions of sea and weather, it took almost another hour before they had the main cable across from *Warlock* secured to the tanker's stern bollards.

When Nick staggered back to the bridge, Captain Randle was standing grim-faced at the helm, and Duncan snapped accusingly at him, "You've cut it damned fine."

A single glance at the digital print-out of the depth gauge on the tanker's control console bore him out. They had only eighteen fathoms of water beneath the *Golden Dawn*. Nevertheless, Nick showed no alarm as he unhooked the hand microphone. "David," he asked quietly. "Are you ready to haul us off?"

"Ready, sir."

"I'm going to give you full port rudder to help your turn across the wind," said Nick, and then nodded to Randle.

"Forty degrees of port rudder on," Randle reported.

They felt the tiny shock as the tow cable came up taut, and carefully *Warlock* began to turn the huge ship across the wind and drag her out tail first into the deeper water of the channel where she would have her best chance of riding out the hurricane.

THE STORM had now unleashed its full strength, and *Golden Dawn* lay directly in its track. Out there somewhere, the sun was rising, but here there was no dawn, for there was no horizon and no sky. There was only madness and wind and water. The tank deck had disappeared in the racing white emulsion of wind and water, even the railing of the bridge wings six feet from the windows was invisible.

There was of course no visual contact with *Warlock*, and radio contact was almost drowned with static. The entire superstructure groaned and popped and whimpered under the assault of the wind, while outside there were shattering cannonades of thunder and sudden brilliance of eye-searing lightning.

Randle had locked the tanker's helm amidships, and now he stood with Duncan and the three seamen by the chart table, all of them clinging to it for support. Only Nick moved restlessly about the bridge, from the stern windows where he peered down vainly, trying to get a glimpse of either the tow cable or of the tug's looming shape, to the control console where he studied the display of lights that monitored the pod tanks and the ship's navigational and mechanical functions.

The screen assured him that none of the petroleum tanks had lost any oil and in all of them the nature of the inert gas was constant. However, there was no means of telling their position. The satellite navigational system and the marine radio beacons on the American mainland were completely blanketed by the electrical storm. The only indication was the ship's electronic log which gave Nick the speed of the ship's hull and the depth finder which recorded the water under her keel.

For the first two hours of the tow *Warlock* had been able to pull the ship back towards the main channel at three and a half knots, and slowly the water had become deeper until they had a hundred and fifty fathoms under them. Now, as the wind velocity increased, both tug and tanker were being pushed once more back towards the hundred fathom line.

"Where is *Sea Witch*?" Nick wondered as he stared helplessly at the gauges. She might be the ace that took the trick.

Nick groped his way to the communications room, and, clinging to the bulkhead with one hand, thumbed the microphone. "*Sea Witch.* This is *Golden Dawn* calling *Sea Witch* . . ."

He listened then, trying to tune out the crackle of static. Suddenly, above his head, there was a screech of rending metal. He dropped the microphone and staggered through onto the bridge. There was another deafening banging and hammering and all of them stood staring up at the metal roof. There was a scraping, dragging rush and then a confused tangle of metal and cable tumbled over the forward edge of the bridge.

"The radar antennae!" Nick shouted. He recognized the elongated dish of the aerial, just as the wind tore it loose. The entire mass of equipment flapped away like a giant bat and was instantly lost in the teeming white curtains of the storm. The radar screen was dead. They had lost their eyes.

Then abruptly Duncan was screaming something at Nick, and pointing up at the master display of the control console. Nick looked and saw that their drift had changed drastically. It was now almost eight knots, and the depth was ninety-two fathoms.

Nick felt icy despair clutch and squeeze his guts. It seemed that the same gust that had torn away the radar mast had done even worse damage, but he had to be sure. He began to hand himself along the foul-weather rail towards the elevator doors.

One of the seamen watching him from across the bridge seemed suddenly to guess his intention. He left the chart table and groped his way along the bulkhead towards Nick.

"Good man!" Nick grabbed his arm to steady him, and they fell forward into the elevator as *Golden Dawn* began another ponderous wallowing roll.

"The tow cable," Nick yelled in the man's ear. "We've got to check the tow cable."

Down in the depths of the ship they went carefully aft along the central passageway. When they reached the storm door, Nick tried to push it open, but the pressure of the wind held it closed.

"Help me," he shouted at the seaman, and they threw their combined weight against it. The instant they forced the jamb open a crack, the wind took the three-inch thick mahogany door and ripped it effortlessly from its hinges, whisking it away as though it were a playing card. Nick and the seaman were exposed in the open doorway.

The wind flung itself upon them, and hurled them to the deck, smothering them in the icy deluge of water. Nick rolled down the deck and crashed into the stern rail with such jarring force that he thought his lungs had been crushed.

As he lay there, he heard the seaman screaming thinly. The sound steeled him, and he slowly dragged himself to his knees, desperately clutching at the rail to resist the wind.

Six feet ahead of him, at the extreme limit of his vision, the railing had been torn away. The seaman was clinging to a long section of it which was dangling over the ship's side. His weight, driven by the wind, must have hit the rail with sufficient force to tear it loose.

On his belly Nick reached for the man, and as he did so the wind came again. It took the damaged railing with the man still upon it and tore it bodily away.

Nick clung with all his strength to the remaining section of the rail. Then, on his knees still, he clawed himself away from the fatal beckoning gap, towards the port stern bollard. The wind struck him full in the face, blinding and choking him.

At last, he flung both arms about the bollard like a lover. Still blind he felt for the woven steel of *Warlock*'s main tow wire. He found it and he knew then that what he had dreaded had happened. The storm had snapped the steel cable like a thread of cotton. *Golden Dawn* was loose.

Slowly, painfully as a crippled insect, Nick dragged himself back to the elevator which seemed as silent and tranquil as the inner sanctum of a cathedral.

Back on the bridge, the group of men at the chart table seemed not to have moved. "I lost one of your men," Nick told them. "He went overboard. The wind got him." Still none of them moved or spoke, and Nick went on. "The tow cable has parted. *Warlock* will never be able to re-establish it in this."

All their heads turned now to the forward bridge windows, to that impenetrable racing whiteness beyond the glass.

Nick reached up to the signal locker above the chart table and brought down a cardboard packet of distress flares. He stuffed half a dozen of them into the inner pockets of his oilskins. "Listen." He had to shout, even though they were only feet away. "We are going to be aground within two hours. This ship is going to start breaking up immediately we strike."

He paused. Duncan had picked up a handful of the flares from the table and was looking inquiringly at him.

"I will give you the word. As soon as we reach the twenty-fathom line and she touches bottom you will go over the side. We will try and get a raft away. I will give you twenty minutes to get clear. By then the pod tanks will have begun breaking up . . ." He didn't want this to sound melodramatic and he searched for some way to make it sound less theatrical, but could think of none. "Once the first tank ruptures I will ignite the crude with a flare."

"Dammit!" Randle was white-faced and shaking. "A million tons of crude. None of us will have a chance. It will go up like an atom bomb."

"Better than a million-ton slick," Nick shouted back.

Randle lurched across to the forward windows, and clinging to the rail he bowed over the gauges that monitored the condition of the ship's cargo, checking for tank damage.

Just then the wind charged the ship, crashing into it like a monster. Nick felt the blow in his stomach. It was a solid, deafening boom of sound and the forward bridge window above the control console broke inwards.

It burst in a glittering explosion of glass shards that engulfed the figure of Randle standing directly before it. In a moment of horror Nick saw the captain's head half severed from his shoulders by a guillotine of flying glass, then his body crumpled to the deck. Charts and books were ripped from their shelves and fluttered like trapped birds as the wind blustered and swirled in the confines of glass and steel.

Nick reached the captain's body, but there was nothing he could do for him. He left Randle lying on the deck and shouted to the others, "Keep clear of the windows."

He gathered the three of them in the rear of the bridge, against the bulkhead, while the wind and rain continued to rage about the bridge. Next, some loose material, perhaps a length of piping ripped from the tank deck below, smashed into the top of the bridge like a cannon ball and then flipped away into the storm, leaving a jagged rent through which a solid deluge of rain poured in. Soon the bridge was ankle deep with water.

Randle's body slid back and forth in the wash and roll, until Nick left the dubious security of the after bulkhead, half lifted the corpse under the arms, dragged it into the radio room, and staggered back.

Dully he registered that the depth of water under the ship was now only fifty-seven fathoms, and the barometer was reading nine hundred and fifty-five millibars. Nick had never heard of a reading that low. Surely it could not go lower, they must be almost at the centre of the revolving hurricane. With an effort he lifted his arm and saw the time. It was still only half past eight in the morning; they had been in the hurricane for only two and a half hours. . . .

Then suddenly a great burning light struck through the torn roof, and Nick threw up his hands to protect his eyes. He could not understand what was happening. He thought his hearing had gone for suddenly the terrible tumult of the wind was muted, fading away. Then he understood. "The eye," he croaked. "We are into the eye of the hurricane."

He stumbled to the front of the bridge. Although *Golden Dawn* still rolled ponderously, she was free of the wind. Brilliant sunshine poured down upon her through a dark funnel of dense swirling cloud that reached to the very surface of the sea. Directly overhead, the sky was an angry purple.

The sea was subsiding by the minute into the total calm of the eye. Nick reckoned that they had an hour at the most before the storm would be on them again.

He looked down onto the tank deck and saw at a single glance that *Golden Dawn* had already sustained mortal damage. The forward starboard pod tank was half torn from its hydraulic coupling, holding only by the bows and lying at almost twenty degrees from the line of the other tanks. Even worse, the entire tank deck was twisted like the limb of an arthritic giant.

Golden Dawn's back was broken. It had broken where Duncan had weakened the hull to save steel. Only the buoyancy of the crude petroleum in her four tanks was holding her together now. When they went into the far side of the hurricane, Nick knew, the weakened spine would give completely; and when that happened the thin skins of the pods would be bound to tear.

At that very moment, however, the terrible burden of despair was lifted—for a mile away, from behind that wall of dreadful grey cloud, *Sea Witch* burst abruptly into the sunlight, tearing bravely along with the water bursting over her bows.

"Jules," Nick whispered.

Nick felt his throat constricting and suddenly scalding tears of relief and thankfulness half blinded him as, half a mile out on *Sea Witch*'s port side and barely a cable length astern of her, *Warlock* came crashing out of the storm bank. "David," Nick spoke aloud. "You too, David."

They must have been in radar contact with him through those wild tempestuous hours of storm passage, holding station on *Golden Dawn*'s crippled hulk and waiting for their opportunity.

Above the wail and crackle of static from the overhead loudspeaker, boomed Jules Levoisin's voice. "*Golden Dawn*, this is *Sea Witch*. Come in *Golden Dawn*."

Nick snatched up the microphone.

"Jules." He did not waste a moment in greeting or congratulations. "We are going to take the tanks off her, and let the hull go. Do you understand?"

"I understand to take off the tanks," Jules responded.

"*Warlock* takes off the port tanks first—in tandem. Then you will take off the starboard side. . . ."

"You must save the hull," Duncan interjected fiercely. "Goddamn you, Berg. I demand that you save the hull."

Nick ignored him until he had finished giving his orders to the two tug masters—then he dropped the microphone and grabbed Duncan by the shoulders.

"You bloody idiot," he shouted in Duncan's face. "Don't you understand the storm will resume again in minutes? Can't you see this monster you have built is finished?"

"But we've got to save the hull. Without it . . ." Duncan

wrenched himself out of Nick's grip. "I'll not let you destroy me!" So saying he swung a clumsy round-armed blow at Nick's face.

Nick side-stepped, coming up onto his toes and aiming for the point of Duncan's jaw—but Duncan rolled his head with the punch, and the blow glanced off his temple.

At that moment *Golden Dawn* rolled back the other way and Nick was unbalanced. He fell back against the control console, and Duncan drove at him, kicking for Nick's lower body.

"I'll kill you, Berg," he screamed, and Nick had only time to roll sideways and lift his leg to protect his crotch. Duncan's kick caught him in the upper thigh. An explosion of white pain shot up into his belly and numbed his leg to the thigh, but he used his good leg to launch himself into a counter-punch, hooking with his right under the ribs—and the wind went out of Duncan's lungs with a whoosh as he doubled. Nick transferred weight smoothly and swung his left fist up into Duncan's face.

As Duncan's legs buckled, Nick caught him by the throat with his left hand and held him upright—but there was no fight left in him.

Nick let him go, and went to the signal locker. He snatched three of the small walkie-talkie radios from the shelves and handed one to each of the two seamen. "You know the pod tank undocking procedures for a tandem tow?" he asked.

"We've practised it," one of them replied.

"Let's go," said Nick.

IT WAS A JOB that was scheduled for a dozen men, and there were three of them. Duncan was of no use, and Nick left him in the pump control room after he had closed down the inert gas pumps, sealed the gas vents, and armed the hydraulic releases of the pod tanks for undocking.

They worked sometimes neck deep in the bursts of green frothing water that poured over the tanker's foredeck. They took on board and secured *Warlock*'s main cable, unlocked the hydraulic clamps that held the forward pod tank to the hull and, as David eased it clear, they turned back along the twisted wind-torn catwalk, and repeated the whole laborious energy-sapping procedure for the after tank.

When at last *Warlock* sheered away from the wallowing hull, she had both port pod tanks in tow. They floated level with the surface of the sea, two great shiny black whales with just their backs showing.

"*Sea Witch*," Nick spoke into his walkie-talkie. "Are you ready to take on tow?"

Jules fired the rocket line across personally. Arching high over the tank deck, the thin nylon rocket line fell ten feet from where Nick was standing.

They worked with a kind of restrained frenzy, for the wall of cloud was very close now, ten miles, no more, and above them the sun had gone.

There was no hydraulic pressure on the clamps of the displaced forward starboard pod tank. Nick and one of the seamen had to work the emergency release, pumping it open slowly and laboriously by hand. Still it would not release.

"Pull," Nick commanded Jules in desperation. "Pull all together."

The sea boiled under *Sea Witch*'s counter. The tow cable came up hard and straight, for half a minute nothing gave, nothing moved. Then, with a resounding metallic clang, the clamps slipped and the tank slid ponderously out of its dock in *Golden Dawn*'s hull. And, as it came free, so the hull—held together until that moment by the tank's bulk and buoyancy—began to collapse.

The catwalk on which Nick stood began to twist and tilt so that he had to grab for a handhold, and he stood frozen in horrified fascination as he watched *Golden Dawn* begin the final break-up. The whole tank deck, stripped of all but one of her pods, began to hinge shut at the point where her back had broken like an enormous nutcracker—and caught between the jaws of the nutcracker was the starboard after pod tank.

Nick broke into a lurching, blundering run down the twisting, tilting catwalk. *Sea Witch* and the doomed *Golden Dawn* were coupled inexorably—unless they could cut the two tanks apart and let *Sea Witch* escape with the forward tank.

"Shear!" he shouted on his radio to the seaman who was nearest the control box. "Shear the tandem tow!"

Nick could see him staggering wildly back along the catwalk.

His haste was fatal, for as he jumped from the catwalk to the deck where the shear control box was situated, two deck plates gaped open like the jaws of a steel monster and the seaman fell through waist deep into the opening. Then as he squirmed feebly to extricate himself, the next lurch of the ship's hull closed the plates, sliding them across each other like the blades of a pair of scissors.

The man shrieked once and then a wave burst over the deck. When it poured back over the ship's side there was no sign of the man; the deck was washed glisteningly clean.

Nick reached the same point on the deck, judged the gaping and closing movement of the steel plates and leapt across the deadly gap. He reached the control box, and hit the shear button with the heel of his hand.

With a gross surge of power from the ship's generators and a flash of blue electric flame the thick steel links sheared as cleanly as cheese under cutting wire. Half a mile away *Sea Witch* felt the release and pounded ahead, taking with her the forward starboard tank.

Nick stared down at the single remaining tank, still caught inextricably in *Golden Dawn*'s twisting, contorting hull.

Suddenly there was a sharp chemical stink in the air—the stink of crude petroleum oil gushing from the ruptured tank.

"Nick! Nick!" The radio set slung over his shoulder squawked and he lifted it to his lips.

"Go ahead, Jules."

"Nick, I am turning back to pick you up."

"Jules, you can't turn with that tow. You are off your head!"

"I have been that way for fifty years," Jules agreed. "I will put my bows against the starboard quarter deck rail, directly under the forward wing of the bridge. Be ready to jump aboard."

"O.K., Jules, but number four tank has ruptured. I want you to shut down for fire. Once I am aboard we will put a rocket into her and burn off cargo."

"I hear you, Nick, but I wish I had not."

Nick jumped the gaping gap in the decking and scrambled up the steel ladder onto the central catwalk. Glancing over his shoulder he could see the endlessly slippery grey wall of racing cloud and wind, now so menacing that he faltered for a moment before pounding back along the catwalk towards the tanker's stern with the single remaining seaman.

The heavy fumes of escaping oil burned Nick's pumping lungs, and constricted his throat as he ran. Below the catwalk the bloated pod tank was now punctured in a hundred places, and the dark red oil oozed from it like the blood from a carcass.

Nick reached the stern tower, and rushed to the pump control room. Duncan turned to him as he entered, his face swollen and bruised where Nick had beaten him. "We are abandoning now," said Nick. "*Sea Witch* is taking us off."

"I hated you from the very first." Duncan was very calm, very controlled. "Did you know that?"

"There's no time for that now." Nick grabbed his arm, and Duncan followed him readily into the passageway.

"Power and wealth and women is the game we played. Isn't that right, Nicholas?"

Nick was barely listening. They were on the quarter deck, standing at its starboard rail, below the bridge. *Sea Witch* was turning in now, only five hundred yards out. She would be alongside in less than a minute.

"Power and wealth and women." Duncan was still talking calmly. "That was the game—and I won. I won every time . . ." He was groping in his pockets, but Nick was not watching him. He was looking down below to where *Golden Dawn* was bleeding her deadly poison into the sea.

Duncan took one of the signal flares from his pocket and held it against his chest with both hands, slipping his index finger through the metal ring of the igniter tab. "I win this one also, Nicholas," he said. "Game, set and match."

And he pulled the tab on the flare with a sharp jerk, and stepped back holding it aloft. It spluttered once and then burst into brilliant sparkling red flame, white phosphorescent smoke billowing from it.

Now at last Nick turned to face him, and for a moment he was too appalled to move, then he lunged for Duncan's raised hand that held the burning flare, but Duncan was too fast for him. He whirled and threw the flame in a high spluttering arc, out over the leaking, stinking tank deck.

It struck the steel tank and bounced once, and then rolled down the canted oil-coated plating. Nick stood paralysed at the rail staring down at its pretty red twinkling light.

"It's not even burning," Duncan cried. "Why doesn't it burn?" He had expected a violent explosion, but out in the open air the oil had a very low flash point. It needed heat before releasing its volatiles.

The flare spluttered and fizzed in a black pool of crude, until the crude eventually caught with a red, sulky flame that spread quickly but not explosively over the entire deck, releasing billows of dark smoke.

Below where Nick stood *Sea Witch* thrust her bows in and touched them against the tanker's side. The seaman beside Nick jumped and landed neatly on the tug's bows.

"Jump, Nick!" Jules's voice thundered over the loudhailer.

Nick poised himself for the leap, but Duncan caught him from behind, whipping one arm around his throat, and pulling him backwards away from the rail.

"No!" Duncan shouted. "You're staying, my friend."

A greasy wave of black choking smoke engulfed them, and Jules's voice roared in Nick's ears. "Jump, Nick, I cannot hold her here."

Duncan had him off balance, dragging him backwards, and suddenly Nick knew what he must do. Instead of resisting Duncan's arm, he hurled himself backwards and they crashed together into the superstructure.

Duncan gasped and, as his arm fell away, Nick bounded to the ship's side. Below him the gap between *Sea Witch*'s bows and the tanker's side was rapidly widening but he vaulted onto the rail, poised for an instant and then jumped. He struck the deck and his teeth cracked together with the impact. He rolled once, then he was on his feet again.

He looked up at *Golden Dawn*. She was completely enveloped in the boiling column of black smoke, which was now shot through with the satanic crimson of high, hot flame. As *Sea Witch* sheered desperately away, the first rush of the storm hit them, and for a moment it smeared the smoke away, exposing the tanker's high quarter-deck.

Duncan stood at the rail above the roaring holocaust. He stood with his arms extended, and he was burning—like a ritual cross outlined in fire. Then slowly he seemed to shrivel, and he toppled forward over the rail into the bubbling, burning cargo of the monstrous ship that he had built—and the black smoke closed over him like a funeral cloak.

"CAN'T YOU GET us farther away?" Nick shouted above the thunder of the hurricane. He was standing only inches from Jules, both of them hanging onto the bridge's overhead railing.

"If I open the taps I will part the tow," Jules shouted back.

Sea Witch was alternately standing on her nose and then her tail. There was no forward view from the bridge, only green washes of sea water and banks of spray. The full force of the hurricane was on them once more, and a glance at the radarscope showed the glowing image of *Golden Dawn*'s crippled and bleeding hull only half a mile astern.

Suddenly the glass of the windows was obscured by the impenetrable blackness of the smoke. There was no reek of the hydrocarbons in the bridge, for *Sea Witch* was shut down for fire drill—all her ports and ventilators sealed, as her closed circuit system scrubbed and recharged the air with oxygen.

A fiercer rush of the hurricane winds laid *Sea Witch* over on her side, the lee rail deep under the racing green sea. But the craft had been built to live in any sea, and the moment the wind hesitated she fought off the water and began to swing back.

Suddenly the boiling bank of smoke turned to fierce white light that blinded every man on the bridge as though a photograph flashlight had been fired in his face.

"Fireball!" Nick shouted, and, completely blinded, reached for the remote controls of *Sea Witch*'s water cannons. Minutes before he had aligned them to their maximum angle of depression, so now as he locked down the triggers *Sea Witch* deluged herself in a cascade of sea water. In that furnace of burning air, despite the torrents of water, *Sea Witch*'s paintwork was burned away in instantaneous combustion. The heat on the bare scorched metal of her exposed upperworks was so savage that it struck through the insulated hull, and through the double glazing of the two inch armoured glass of her bridge windows. Nick's eyelashes were scorched and his lips blistered as he lifted his face to it.

The glass of the bridge windows wavered and swam as they began to melt—and then abruptly there was no more oxygen. The fireball had extinguished itself, consumed everything in its twenty seconds of life, everything, from sea level to thirty thousand feet above it, a brief and devastating orgasm of destruction.

It left a vacuum, a weak spot in the earth's thin skin of air, it formed another low pressure system smaller, but much more intense, and more hungry to be filled than the eye of Hurricane Bertha itself.

It literally tore the guts out of that great revolving storm, setting up counter winds and a vortex within the established system that ripped it apart.

New gales blew from every point about the fireball's vacuum, swiftly beginning their own dervish spirals and twenty miles short of the mainland of Florida, Hurricane Bertha checked her mindless, blundering charge, fell in upon herself and disintegrated into fifty different willy-nilly squalls and whirlpools of air that collided and split again, slowly degenerating into nothingness.

ON A MORNING in late July in Galveston Bay, the salvage tug *Sea Witch* dropped off tow to four smaller harbour tugs who would take the *Golden Dawn* Number 3 pod tank up the narrows to the Orient Amex discharge installation below Houston.

Her sister ship *Warlock*, Captain David Allen commanding, had dropped off his tandem tow of Number 1 and Number 2 pod tanks to the same tugs forty-eight hours previously.

Between the two ships, they had made good salvage under Lloyd's Open Form of three-quarters of a million tons of crude petroleum valued at $85.50 US a ton. To the prize would be added the value of the three tanks themselves—not less than sixty-five million dollars all told, Nick calculated, and he owned both ships and the full share of the salvage award. He had not sold to the sheikhs yet, though for every day of the tow from the Florida Straits to Texas, there had been frantic telex messages from James Teacher in London. The sheikhs were desperate to sign now, but Nick would let them wait a little longer.

Nick stood on the open wing of *Sea Witch*'s bridge and watched the four smaller harbour tugs bustling importantly about their ungainly charge.

He lifted the cheroot to his lips carefully, for they were still blistered from the heat of the fireball—and he pondered the question of how much he had achieved, apart from spectacular riches.

He had reduced the spill from a million to a quarter of a million tons of cad-rich crude, and he had burned it in fireball. Nevertheless, there had been losses, toxins had been lifted high above the fireball. They had spread and settled across Florida as far as Tampa and Tallahassee, poisoning the pastures and killing thousands of head of domestic stock. But the American authorities had been quick to extend the emergency procedures. There had been no loss of human life. He had achieved that much.

Now he had delivered the salvaged pod tanks to Orient Amex. The new cracking process would benefit all mankind, and nothing that Nick could do would prevent men carrying the cad-rich crudes of El Barras across the oceans. But would they do so in the same blindly irresponsible manner that Duncan Alexander had attempted?

He knew then with utter certainty that it was his appointed life's work, from now on, to try and ensure that they did not. He knew how he was to embark upon that work. He had the wealth that was necessary, and Tom Parker had given him the other instruments to do the job.

He knew, with equal certainty, who would be his companion in that life's work—and standing on the fire-scorched deck of the gallant little vessel he had a vivid image of a golden girl who walked for ever beside him in sunlight and in laughter.

"Samantha."

He said her name aloud just once, and suddenly he was very eager to begin.

Wilbur Smith

For Wilbur Smith the sea has always held a particular fascination. It's hardly surprising, therefore, that he and his wife now live close by the ocean, on a narrow peninsula at the extreme southern tip of Africa where, in his own words, "the sea is an intimate part of our daily lives—something to be cherished and feared."

Something to be cherished . . . this is a significant phrase, for the ever-present risks of catastrophic oil pollution concern Wilbur Smith deeply. "My concern grows with each new tanker disaster, each time I tread an oil-scummed beach or find a dead, oil-smeared seabird, each time I revisit a remote area of the coast and find its reefs denuded of shellfish. . . ."

Something to be feared . . . this too is significant, since the basic idea for *Hungry as the Sea* was born of fear. Some ten years ago Wilbur Smith was fishing for tuna off the coast of South Africa. Caught in a sudden impenetrable fog, he stood helplessly at the wheel of his frail fishing boat, listening with dread to the approaching engines of a colossal oil tanker. "Suddenly she burst out of the fog bank, towering over us like a mountain of steel in avalanche. With full power and good fortune I managed to duck my tiny craft out of her path, but we were swamped and badly beaten by the turbulence thrown out by that immense hull." The terror of that moment stayed with him, and became the starting point for the book he was one day to write.

As the story took shape in his mind there was research to be undertaken: journeys by helicopter in all weather out to the decks of passing supertankers, detailed conversations with their captains and crews, and with the tug-men of Safmarine, who sail the two most powerful ocean-going salvage tugs afloat. There were visits also to the Universities of Cape Town and Miami, and to shipyards in many parts of the world. Everywhere Wilbur Smith received a friendly welcome, and he's profoundly grateful for the expert advice that was given him so unstintingly.

"Sometimes I marvel," he says, "that I should actually be paid for having so much fun. My principal hope now is that my readers will get as much enjoyment out of the book as I did."

PALADI
VOTVM

THE GOLD OF TROY

The story of the archaeologist, Heinrich Schliemann

a condensation of the book by

ROBERT PAYNE

Originally published by Hale

Fragment of the "Warrior Vase" depicting Greek soldiers.

Tales of the glories of Troy have fired men's imaginations for more than three thousand years. Always there has been magic in the belief that once there was indeed a Golden Age upon this earth. . . .

In the middle of the last century, however, most scholars were questioning whether ancient Troy was really more than a beautiful legend. After all, even by Roman times all that might have remained of the city had long since vanished. Had Troy in fact ever existed? And if so, where?

Heinrich Schliemann alone was convinced that he had the answers to these questions. And Heinrich Schliemann, wildly eccentric, unschooled in even the rudiments of archaeology, alone had money enough to back his conviction. Even as a child, fascinated by stories of the Greek heroes, Schliemann had vowed that one day he would find Troy's fabled towers. And this dream of discovery spurred him on. Starting as a penniless grocer's assistant, by the time he was forty-seven he had amassed a vast fortune. Now, at last, he could set out to prove that Troy had been a real city, and that he alone knew where its gold lay buried.

Now, at long last, the time had come for his greatest adventure.

1. An Enchanted Childhood

During the seventies and eighties of the last century an old grey-haired scholar, wearing a high collar and a sun helmet, was to be seen wandering over the ruins of obscure mounds in Asia Minor. He was short and wiry, with dark brown eyes, high cheekbones, a heavy nose, and a sensual mouth; there was something of the peasant about him, something too of the German merchants who were his ancestors. He spoke in a high-pitched voice, dressed shabbily, walked with a curious gliding motion, and always carried in his pocket a dog-eared paperbound Greek edition of the *Iliad* or the *Odyssey*.

To the friendly inquirer he would explain that he had uncovered the ancient city of Troy and found in its walls a secret treasure hoard of gold, which he kept securely locked in his house in Athens. He believed that the ashes of Odysseus, the crown jewels of the Trojan Empire, and the golden death masks of Agamemnon and many other Greek heroes were in his possession, and it is just possible that his claims were justified. Until he was long past middle age he never touched a spade, but during the last seventeen years of his life he excavated continually. The most unscientific of archaeologists, he was to become known as the most important practitioner of that science in his century.

Luck helped him—luck, and a hunger for gold. When Heinrich Schliemann was born, however, on January 6, 1822, in the parsonage of the obscure village of Neu Buckow in Mecklenburg, with its lakes and brooding mists, not far from the Polish frontier, there was no hint of the millionaire banker he was to become or the great treasures he was to unearth.

Two years later his father became pastor in the nearby village of Ankershagen. And in later years, whenever Heinrich Schliemann remembered his childhood, he remembered the parsonage at Ankershagen with the cherry blossoms in the garden, and the treasures reputed to be buried in the neighbourhood. At the centre of the village stood a medieval castle with secret underground passageways. Once the castle had been owned by a famous robber baron who was believed to have hidden his treasure near its tower.

The young Heinrich grew up among such legends. He visited the castle and penetrated its underground galleries. He thought he knew the entrances to the secret passageways. He was fed on stories of hidden treasure. In a sense, to the end of his life he never so much as stepped out of his father's parsonage, but resembled the child with his face glued to the window, shuddering with joy as he gazed through the mists at the mysterious and legendary world outside.

In the crowded parsonage there were four daughters and two sons. Heinrich's mother was a quiet woman, the daughter of a burgomaster, who seems to have found little joy in her marriage with the gruff, domineering pastor. She was thirteen years younger than her husband, having married him when she was sixteen. She wore lace cuffs and played the piano, and the villagers thought she gave herself airs. Her husband despised her, and had affairs with the kitchen maids. To the end of his long life the pastor was a centre of scandal.

The pastor taught his children their letters. He was a man of moods, with a sternness which would sometimes give way to lighthearted garrulity. He told stories well. He especially liked to take his children on long walks through the countryside, telling them the history of every field and hamlet, spinning out his stories until they became completely ludicrous; and then he would throw back his head and roar with laughter at the spectacle of his children openmouthed in wonder. And sometimes on winter evenings he would tell stories out of Homer until the little parsonage reeled with the thunder of the Trojan War.

There was nothing in the least surprising in the parson's deep interest in the *Iliad* and *Odyssey.* Goethe and Schiller and a host of other German poets celebrated Homer to the skies. The children in the parsonage listened breathless to the stories of the war between the Achaeans and the Trojans, and the lives of the heroes entered their own childish lives.

At Christmas 1829, when Heinrich was seven years old, he received as a gift from his father Ludwig Jerrer's *Illustrated History of the World.* He turned immediately to the page showing Troy in flames. In the foreground was the Trojan hero Aeneas, plumed and helmeted, wearing a corslet, striding through the smoke and flames of the doomed city while carrying his father on his back and holding his son by the hand. The picture fired Heinrich's imagination. Everything in it helped him to identify Troy with his own hometown of Ankershagen: the round towers, the huge castle walls, the great gateway.

When he grew older, Heinrich liked to say that this engraving was the turning point of his life. He remembered turning to his father: "Troy had walls like that—"

"Yes."

"And these walls are much too large to be destroyed by fire, so there must be something left?"

The pastor was fairly sure nothing remained, but the boy held fast to his opinion. Fifty years later Schliemann told this story in an autobiographical fragment. He said that hardly a day passed in his mature life when he was not dreaming and planning to excavate the buried city of Troy, and stand in triumph on the Trojan walls. It is unlikely that Schliemann was exaggerating, for the dreams of a seven-year-old child are so vast that they can encompass the whole future and dictate his journey through life.

The boy dreamed his way through school. He was seven when he fell in love with Minna Meincke, the daughter of a local farmer. Minna was his own age. She had yellow hair and blue eyes. They met at dancing class, and thereafter they were inseparable. He sat by her side at school, attended her at dancing class, and accompanied her on long rambles through the countryside. She enjoyed listening to him tell stories. They haunted the castle and together they examined the secret passageways, and interrogated everyone who could tell stories about the robber baron. There was Peter Huppert, "Hopping Peter", the village tailor, who had only one eye and one leg. He told stories well and had a prodigious memory, like many illiterate people. From listening to Hopping Peter the children would go to the church, to amuse themselves by turning over the pages of the ancient registers, in which the names of long-dead villagers were inscribed in heavy Gothic script.

So for nearly two years the children wandered hand in hand through a legendary landscape. They swore to marry and live the rest of their lives together. They would remain in Ankershagen, because it was the only world they knew—the high church steeple, the cherry blossoms in the garden, the graveyard, and the great castle on the hill. They promised faithfully they would never allow anything to interfere with their dream.

Quite suddenly their dream came to an end.

For a long time Heinrich's mother had been ailing. She had known for many years that her husband had been sleeping with the kitchen maid. She had watched in silence when he gave the girl expensive presents. She had borne his children and suffered his fierce temper. Now, a few weeks after giving birth to a third son, she died.

The villagers had long known about the kitchen maid. Now they turned against the parson in silent anger, watched him from behind their curtained windows, and hoped to make life intolerable for him. But they only succeeded in making life intolerable for his children, who were sent away to stay with relatives until the storm blew over. The kitchen maid was glad: at last she had the parson to herself.

Heinrich was sent off to stay with an uncle who was a parson at Kalkhorst, also in Mecklenburg. His mother's death made little impression on him. As he wrote later, "I forgot my mother in my overwhelming grief for the loss of Minna. I have since undergone many great troubles in different parts of the world, but none of them caused me a thousandth part of the grief I felt at the tender age of nine years for my separation from my bride."

For the rest of his life he dreamed despairingly of her. He told himself that in some mysterious way, after great hardships and many perilous journeys, he would find her again. Minna, Troy—these were the names of the landscape of his dreams.

But no one can live with his grief every moment of the day, and at Kalkhorst Heinrich settled down to school, and worked hard. His uncle was kindly and unobtrusive. His professor of Latin recognized the boy's brilliance, and saw to it that he wrote his Latin essays on subjects that interested him: the Trojan War, and the adventures of Odysseus and Agamemnon.

The next year, when Heinrich was eleven, it was decided to send him to the *Gymnasium*, or grammar school, at Neustrelitz, where he was placed in the third class, which meant that he was considerably above the other boys of his age in intelligence. A pale, brilliant, unhappy youth, possessed of driving ambition, he could look forward to years of quiet study and eventually to some post in a university.

Within three months these dreams, too, were shattered. The villagers of Ankershagen, determined to ruin his father, whispered that he had embezzled church funds. He was suspended from the ministry and threatened with expulsion from the Church.

Since he could no longer afford to pay Heinrich's fees at the school, the boy was forced to enter the *Realschule*, the ordinary common school, where he spent the next four years in a state of quiet misery. The greatest blow fell in the spring of 1836, when he learned that his father could no longer afford to pay even the relatively small sums necessary to keep him at the common school. At the age of fourteen he had to go out and earn a living by himself, without friends, with no hope of ever pursuing a career of letters or entering a university.

With his whole world shattered, Heinrich went blindly about the business of obtaining a menial job. In the end he decided to become an assistant in a grocer's shop in the neighbouring village of Fürstenberg, thinking perhaps that in a grocer's shop he would at least have enough to eat.

He was still staying at Neustrelitz when, visiting the house of Herr Laue, a musician, he unexpectedly came face-to-face with his beloved Minna.

Five years had passed since he had last seen her, but he recognized her instantly. She was dressed very simply in black, but the simplicity of her dress only enhanced her beauty. Like Heinrich, she was fourteen years old now, and carried herself like a grown woman. They gazed helplessly at each other, burst into tears, and fell into each other's arms. Several times they tried to speak, but no words came. Minna's parents entered the room and they were forced to separate. It was to be more than five years before he saw her again, and then only for a brief moment. To the end of his life he remembered her as she had stood in the musician's house, the tears streaming down her cheeks.

Long afterwards he wrote, "I was sure that Minna still loved me, and from that moment I felt within me a boundless energy, and I was filled with an unshakable confidence in my ability to progress in the world. And so I implored God to grant that she would not marry before I had obtained an independent position for myself."

A few days later the boy rode off to Fürstenberg to become a servant in Herr Holtz's grocer's shop, at the beck and call of everyone who wanted herrings or a bottle of potato whisky.

2. The Storm

He hated the shop and everything about it. He hated old Herr Holtz, and he hated waking up at five in the morning to open the shop, sweep the floors, dust the counters, and oil Herr Holtz's boots. Above all he hated losing Minna and being so weary at the end of the day that it was impossible to study. Outside in the sunlight boys went to school and played leapfrog and sauntered home in the afternoon with their satchels on their backs. In the grocer's shop it was always dark and cold, and there were no legends to feed his imagination and no pictures of the ancient world to remind him of burning Troy.

For the next five years of his life, ambition gnawed at him. The village was poor, and the wretched people who came to the shop nauseated him. He would become a scholar. He would grow rich. He would show himself to advantage in an unbelieving world. Inevitably his ambition became a monstrous growth.

The best hours of the day were in the early morning, when the boy was left to himself. At eight o'clock Herr Holtz came down and sent him to the distillery with a sack of potatoes—everyone here drank potato whisky. Then he would hurry back to be in the shop until eleven in the evening. He was always trundling heavy casks around and running errands. Sometimes he would read for a little while at night before going to bed under the counter, his brain weary with figures, his hands damp with herring oil, and his clothes sprinkled with wood shavings. He wore the same patched suit summer and winter.

There were occasional interludes of contentment. One night a drunken miller lurched into the shop, and declaimed Homer in the light of the oil lamps. Heinrich could not understand Greek, but the rhythm of the words struck a chord in his soul, and when the miller had recited a hundred lines he was asked to repeat them. Then, still not satisfied, Heinrich asked him to repeat them a third time. He was so pleased that he gave the miller three glasses of potato whisky, even though it cost him all the money he had.

In time Heinrich came to know the drunken miller well. He was the son of the Protestant pastor at Roebel, who had been expelled from school for some misconduct—not before he had learned those hundred lines, which he always repeated with the same flourishes and the same sweetness of tone. Heinrich wrote long afterwards that tears had flowed down his cheeks as he listened. "From that moment," he said, "I did not cease to pray to God that by His grace it might one day be permitted to me to learn Greek."

He was always dreaming of escape. In 1840 when he was eighteen, he applied to his father for a loan so that he could join the emigrants flocking in thousands to America. But his father was again engaged in a love affair and no money was forthcoming. With a heavy heart he returned to the grocer's shop, and he might have served behind the counter for the rest of his life if an accident had not happened.

It was a cask of chicory that altered the whole course of his life.

The cask was heavy. He strained himself and suddenly spat blood. Pale and weak-chested, he knew he was in danger of dying surrounded by packages of herrings and whale-oil candles.

There was nothing to attract him back to the pitiable little village of Ankershagen. His father had married a woman of the people, and they screamed at each other and fought like wildcats, with alternating bouts of hate and lust. He decided to go to Hamburg, which was on the sea, and therefore closer to America. He had saved thirty Prussian dollars, about seven pounds. With this money and the clothes he stood in, he set out for Hamburg by way of Rostock, where he paused long enough to learn double-entry bookkeeping, completing in a few days a course which normally kept a student busy for a year.

Then he hurried on to Hamburg. The five great towers of the city fascinated him—he was to be fascinated by towers for the rest of his life—and he stood outside the city spellbound by its silhouette against the September sky. All his life he had known only small towns and villages, but here was a city with great avenues bordered by the palaces of merchant princes, with huge mercantile houses, and with markets everywhere. Wagons rattled along the paved streets; clocks chimed; there were carillons from the high belfries of the churches. Excited beyond measure by the magnificence, deafened by the noise, he was like a sleepwalker. And thinking of how he would soon make his fortune, he wrote to one of his sisters, "Hamburg has raised me to the seventh heaven."

But who in Hamburg wanted to employ a youth with a weak chest? He got a job as a bookkeeper, but this lasted only a week. He was in desperate straits, and wrote to an uncle for a small loan to tide him over.

Now luck worked for him again, bringing a chance encounter with a Herr Wendt, a ship broker who had known his mother. Herr Wendt introduced him to the captain of the brig *Dorothea,* bound for La Guaira in Venezuela. Schliemann jumped at the opportunity of making the journey. He sold his silver wristwatch and went out on a spending spree. He bought in a secondhand market two shirts, a coat, a pair of trousers, a mattress, and a blanket.

The *Dorothea* sailed out of Hamburg on November 28, 1841, with a fair wind. There were three passengers: Schliemann, a joiner from Hamburg, and the joiner's son. The ship stopped over at Cuxhaven and then sailed out into the North Sea. Two days later they found themselves in the path of a hurricane. The ship took on water, the pumps were manned continually, and Schliemann roped himself to a bench and set himself to learning Spanish from a Spanish grammar. The other passengers suffered in silence in their bunks.

On December 10 the gale was still raging. Snow was falling, and sea gulls kept circling around them in great flocks—this was thought to be a bad sign. It was intensely cold, and on the afternoon of the next day the waves piled up like mountains and hurtled down on the ship. Schliemann was by this time too seasick to worry. At about seven o'clock the cabin boy came down to the cabin with tea and biscuits. The boy was weeping and saying he would never bring them anything any more.

Around midnight the cabin door blew open and the captain was shouting, "All passengers on deck! The ship's going down!" A moment later an enormous wave smashed all the portholes and the ship lurched violently to port. Schliemann sprang out of his bunk and rushed up on deck stark naked. Badly bruised, he somehow managed to crawl to the starboard gunwale, silently commending himself to God. The ship's bell was tolling continually. It was like a death knell.

Naked, with the snow falling around him, he awaited his fate. The captain ordered the crew to man the lifeboats. One boat fell perpendicularly into the water and vanished. The second was smashed against the side of the ship. There remained the small stern boat, which was thrown free. As the ship keeled over and sank, the first mate pulled Schliemann out of the water and into the boat. There were fourteen people in it and no oars. They drifted until dawn, to be thrown up on a sandbank off the island of Texel, near the Dutch coast. Three of Schliemann's teeth were broken and there were deep cuts on his face and body. All the survivors lay gasping in the sand until a friendly farmer came along with a cart and carried them to his house.

For three days they remained at the farmhouse, recuperating

from the ordeal. Schliemann was given some wooden shoes, a pair of torn trousers, a blanket, and a wool cap, but what pleased him most was that his sea box with his shirts and his pocketbook, were found on the sandbank. When he took the ferry to the mainland he refused to return to Hamburg with the others, announcing that he felt that his destiny lay in Holland.

In Amsterdam he wrote a detailed account of the shipwreck to Herr Wendt in Hamburg, and by a lucky accident the letter was delivered while the ship broker was entertaining guests at dinner. Herr Wendt read the letter aloud. Everyone sympathized, and they made a collection that amounted to two hundred and forty gulden, a very small fortune. In a few days Schliemann was at work in the countinghouse of F. C. Quien and Co. as a messenger boy. His job consisted of stamping bills of exchange and getting them cashed in the town. From that moment there was no turning back. He had set his foot on the path which would lead him to riches.

He saw that the only way to make a fortune was to dedicate his whole life to it. First, he would reduce his expenses to a minimum, take a cheerless room in a lodging house, and waste no money on entertainment or women. Second, he would acquire an education, and train his memory, so that nothing that ever happened to him, no book he read, no figures he encountered in ledgers, would ever pass completely from his mind. He learnt Dutch and English by reading aloud, writing essays, and having them corrected by a tutor.

That lonely, spartan life left ineradicable marks on him. He had the pride and single-mindedness of the self-taught. With these went quirks of behaviour, terrible rages, and titanic resolutions. Ruthlessly, dispassionately, he mounted the steps leading to the temple of success, and for long years the vision of Troy was to succumb to an all-consuming passion for wealth.

Now every moment he could spare from the office was devoted to study—not the study of the Greek and Roman empires, which had been the love of his youth, but the study of all the languages used in business. He became a kind of memory machine.

After learning English and Dutch, he spent the next six months learning French. At the end of the year his powers of concentration had improved so vastly that he claimed it took him no more than six weeks of concentrated study to speak and write fluent Spanish, Italian and Portuguese. Now he could draw up business reports in seven languages, and read foreign newspapers. He maintained a ruthless schedule, learning long lists of words even when he was running errands in the rain, or memorizing whole passages while waiting for stamps at a post office.

The reward came shortly after his twenty-second birthday, on March 1, 1844, when he stepped into the office of Herr Schröder, who headed a vast import and export business in Amsterdam. Schliemann explained his qualifications for a job—seven languages, a head for figures, and two years' experience as an errand boy. Within minutes he was appointed a bookkeeper at six hundred gulden, and within a few weeks the salary was increased to one thousand gulden. Herr Schröder seems to have been amazed by his new bookkeeper. Schliemann advanced rapidly and soon became attached to the small circle surrounding Herr Schröder. When letters from Russia came to the office, Heinrich announced that he would learn Russian.

At the end of six weeks he sent off his first letter in Russian to a certain Vassily Plotnikov, the London agent of a large firm of indigo merchants in Moscow. That letter was to shape the next twenty years of his life. In time he was to acquire a huge fortune, and perhaps the largest part of it was derived from selling indigo in Russia.

In those days Amsterdam was still one of the great centres of trade in indigo, which was imported from India and the Far East. Periodically indigo auctions were held there, and Schliemann would be sent to attend the auctions.

For a year and ten months Schliemann continued to live in a series of dingy lodgings, always saving his money, his only apparent vice being innumerable cups of sweetened tea—a vice which he permitted himself to the end of his life. Sugar gave him spurts of energy. And all the time he dreamed about marrying Minna.

Towards the end of December 1845 he was summoned to Herr Schröder's inner office and asked whether he would like to represent Schröder's wide-flung business interests in St. Petersburg.

Schliemann accepted, and spent his last weeks in Amsterdam interviewing the heads of other businesses and suggesting that he could act as their representative as well.

Just before setting out for St. Petersburg he thought of writing to his friend Herr Laue, the musician at Neustrelitz, to inquire about Minna and to suggest that the time had come to marry her. Then it occurred to him that it would be better to postpone the matter until he had established himself in St. Petersburg. He wrote instead to his father explaining his good fortune, the result of his own single-mindedness. "Such gifts," he said, "do not fall from heaven on those who are unworthy of them."

So in a mood of profound self-satisfaction, at the age of twenty-four, only four years after being shipwrecked off the coast of Holland, he set out from Amsterdam as the chief representative of one of the greatest trading firms on earth, and sixteen days later, February 1, 1846, after an arduous journey by coach and sleigh, he arrived in St. Petersburg.

3. The Search for Gold

St. Petersburg in the time of Nicholas I was a city of extremes: wide streets, a few factory buildings, innumerable palaces, the hovels of the poor. In winter the whole city was white, the only colour coming from the bright scarlet liveries of the royal coachmen. While the courtiers endured the endless frivolities of the court, and the serfs endured their slavery, already students, with the young Dostoevsky among them, were planning to overthrow the Tsar. Throughout Russia there was a gradual awakening of a social consciousness: the bitterness and despair of a people enslaved.

But in all the years he spent in St. Petersburg, Schliemann told himself continually he was living in the best of all possible worlds. He took notes of everything he saw, and every night wrote up his diary. He was representing the Schröder interests and six or seven other interests as well, and for him St. Petersburg was a good substantial city, eminently suitable for business. From the moment he arrived he acted the part of international merchant with resounding success. He achieved his success by meticulous attention to detail, standing at his desk from early morning to late in the evening, and following every clue that would lead him to a profit, however small.

By October 1846 things were going so well that he at last wrote to Herr Laue in Neustrelitz and asked for the hand of Minna Meincke, only to learn that she had married a local farmer a few weeks before. The shock nearly killed him. He told himself that through all those seventeen years since he first set eyes on her he had lived for her alone. What did it matter that he was slowly acquiring a fortune, when he had no one to share it with? So he grew sullen and embittered, nursing his grief. But while Minna still dominated his dreams, the search for a fortune dominated his life. He had opened his own business agency while continuing his connections with Schröder. Now Schröder permitted him to draw off one per cent of the value of the merchandise passing through his hands, and Schliemann knew that only a few years would pass before he acquired an immense fortune.

So matters progressed until the end of 1848, when he fell ill with influenza. For four months he remained in bed, and as soon as he was recovered he threw himself so violently into his work that by June he was in a state of collapse.

The doctors put him in a dark room and refused to let him continue with his business. He raged at the doctors, but he had learned his lesson. He worked a little less avidly. He gave dinner parties, served fine wines, and surrounded himself with merchants and their eligible daughters. He fell hopelessly in love with a certain Sophia, who possessed no fortune but was thrifty and spoke three languages. He wrote to his father that he had found the girl of his dreams, only to write in the next letter that he had taken her to a party, where she showed unpardonable interest in a young officer, and at the sight of "giddy, stupid Sophia" behaving in this lamentable fashion he had broken off the engagement.

Some time in the summer of 1850 he was introduced to a certain Ekaterina Lyschin, a tall statuesque beauty, the niece of another business acquaintance. She had a pale oval face, dark eyes, and carried herself like a princess. Schliemann admired her, but since she was extremely haughty in her manner and possessed no fortune of her own, he was a little wary of her. He still did not know what to do with his life or the small fortune he had already built up, largely in indigo. As he stood at his desk in St. Petersburg, sending hurried messages to agents all over Europe, he was always close to nervous prostration.

Early in 1850 he had received news that one of his younger brothers, Ludwig, had reached the California goldfields. For some time Ludwig had acted as Heinrich's agent in Amsterdam. Headstrong, nervous, with a talent for languages, Ludwig also possessed a burning desire to make a fortune. One day Ludwig, on an impulse, had decided to sail to America. In New York, he had entered business. When he had saved enough money he struck out for the California goldfields, where he became a banker, and progressed well.

Then, in the middle of August Heinrich received a clipping from a Sacramento newspaper announcing that "on May 25, 1850, Mr. Schliemann, of German nationality, died from typhus in Sacramento City, at the age of 25 years." Together with the clipping came a brief covering letter which said that Ludwig had left a large estate.

For the rest of the year Heinrich continued to supervise his business, uncertain what he should do. He had a profound horror of death, and his brother's death shook him. By the end of the year he had made his decision. Out of a sense of brotherly duty he would go to the goldfields and start business with the money left by his brother, build a proper gravestone for his brother's tomb, and remain in America for the rest of his life.

On December 10, 1850, he said farewell to St. Petersburg. The Neva was frozen over, and an icy wind blew across St. Isaac's Square. His friends accompanied him to the post office, where the sleighs set out for the long journey to Germany; and as he passed the gleaming white Winter Palace, the Admiralty, and the equestrian statue of Peter the Great, he saluted them as though he never expected to see them again.

In America, as always, he kept a diary. It is written in English and contains some of his best writing. He liked New York—a "nice, clean town"—but found little to admire in New York women, and noted that "at the age of 22 they look just as old and worn out as they are beautiful and symmetrical at 16 and 18." He complained of their tendency to amusement and frivolity.

In Washington he called on President Fillmore. "I made my introduction by stating my great desire to see this beautiful country of the West," he wrote in his journal, "and to make the acquaintance of the great men who govern it." Soon after attending a soirée at the White House, he hurried off by ship to the isthmus of Panama, at that time the most direct route to the Far West. There was as yet, of course, no Panama Railroad or Canal. Prospectors journeyed by mule train across the isthmus, where yellow fever was prevalent and there were bandits in the surrounding jungles. Schliemann went armed with a revolver and a long dagger. He saw alligators in the Chagres River and butterflies as large as pigeons:

> The isthmus of Panama is an immense Eden in which the descendants of Adam and Eve . . . live upon the fruit which the splendid tropical vegetation puts around them in magnificent abundance. Their chief characteristic is a horrible laziness. . . . They cannot find themselves happier than lying in their hammocks and eating and drinking.

When he reached Panama City he discovered that the Spanish inhabitants suffered from the same laziness, and, in addition, the women possessed the vices he had attributed to the young women of New York. "Characteristic," he wrote sententiously, "is a great laziness, and a great lightness of character."

Because he had to wait several days for a ship, he amused himself by visiting the old city of Panama, destroyed by Morgan and his pirates and now half overgrown with jungle. It was the first time he had paid any attention to ruins since leaving Ankershagen. This visit to the old city must be accounted his first archaeological exploration. He noted that the guide was stupid, and seemed to know nothing at all about the ruins.

He sailed for California on March 15, 1851, on the SS *Oregon*, and complained bitterly about the food: no ice, no fresh meat, only salt pork and corned beef. Hating his fellow passengers, he took to reading about astronomy. He might have exploded altogether with ill temper if they had not arrived quickly at the Golden Gate. San Francisco delighted him, but he had no time to waste. He was off to Sacramento, in search of his brother's grave.

Sacramento in 1851 was still in its infancy, and as he went about that strange clapboard town which owed it existence to the neighbouring goldfields, he had the same feeling which came to him with surprising force when he visited St. Petersburg for the first time: here was undreamed-of wealth for the asking. He found his brother's grave and gave fifty dollars to a local undertaker for "a beautiful marble tombstone". He learned that Ludwig's partner had absconded with the fortune his brother had left. Nothing would be gained by an attempt to pursue him. The fortune had vanished into thin air.

Schliemann liked Sacramento, but June found him once more in San Francisco in conferences with the agents of Messrs. Rothschild and other businessmen, while he prepared to set himself up as a buyer of gold dust, with headquarters back in Sacramento.

He was attending these conferences in June 1851, and had retired to his room after an exhausting day, when the whole city burst into flame. Schliemann in his downtown hotel was caught in the middle of a huge, quickly spreading fire. Awakened by the clanging of fire bells, he dressed hurriedly and ran into the street. For a few moments he watched the houses all around him melting in the flames, and then he hurried up Telegraph Hill. "The cracking of the gunpowder, the falling stone walls, the cries of the people and the wonderful spectacle of an immense city burning in a dark night all joined to make this catastrophe awful in the extreme." So he wrote the next day. He also reports casually that many foreigners, especially Frenchmen, were murdered by the people of San Francisco on suspicion of setting the fires. He was amazed by the coolness of the Americans, who went about rebuilding their city while the ashes were still hot. In the morning he set out for Sacramento.

Afraid of fire and theft, he leased an office in the only fireproof stone-and-iron building in Sacramento, and he bought a huge iron safe. He stood over the safe from six in the morning to ten at night, working himself and his two assistants to the bone. Prospectors were flocking to California from all over the world, and so in a single day he would find himself speaking all the languages he knew. During his rare moments of leisure, he studied the Californian Indians. They were a small people, extremely dirty. "They lived," he said, "like ants in their heaps of earth."

There were days when a hundred and eighty pounds of gold passed through his hands. His wealth increased from week to week, until he became almost afraid of it. He went about armed with a Colt revolver. He was worried beyond measure because his doctor had told him he had the same constitution as his brother and was likely to die in the same way.

Yet he possessed a driving compulsion to acquire a fortune before he left Sacramento. He rose at five in the morning, weighed gold dust, wrote out banker's drafts and talked to prospectors in eight languages—a stiff, unsmiling, punctilious man, with a curiously shrill voice and the air of a scholar resolved to solve the mystery of wealth. Sitting over his hoard of gold, he lived, indeed, a life of "quiet desperation", certain of only one thing: he must make his fortune or perish.

On April 7 1852 he made a resolution. He visited the Rothschild bank in San Francisco and arranged for the liquidation of his business. He had made his fortune. Others had made larger fortunes from the California gold mines, but few had made them so quickly. In the course of nine months he had amassed $400,000.

He admired the Americans but found them uncouth, their manners reprehensible, and their women unattractive. Accordingly, he now decided to spend the rest of his life among the Russians, whose social graces he respected and whose women showed the proper seriousness he demanded. His fortune would enable him to lead a life of baronial magnificence in Moscow or St. Petersburg. He decided to return in style, paying six hundred dollars for a stateroom in the steamer taking him to Panama.

In Panama City an attempt was made to steal his luggage—he sat over it grimly with a Colt revolver in one hand and a dagger in the other. A few miles of the Panama Railroad had been laid, but thereafter the journey across the isthmus was by mule trail.

He had chosen the worst season of the year for his journey. It rained continually. The guides abandoned the party. The travellers were attacked by scorpions and rattlesnakes. Schliemann suffered excruciating pain from a wound in his leg, which became gangrenous. For fourteen days they pushed forward along the forest trail. Some died of dysentery, others of yellow fever, and their bodies were left for animals to feed on. And still a bitter cold rain came down.

In a short paragraph Schliemann permitted himself to describe the agonies of the journey:

> We became so familiarized with death that it lost for us all its terror . . . we began to like it. . . . Thus we laughed and amused ourselves at the convulsions of the dying and crimes were perpetrated among us; *crimes so terrible!* that now at a later date I cannot think of it without cold and trembling horror.

He never revealed what crimes were committed, or whether he himself committed them. Rape, murder, cannibalism—there are no clues. He never again referred to his journey across the isthmus of Panama. He did everything he could to forget those terrible fourteen days, and became more merciless and demanding of himself and of others; he became harder, sterner, and more than ever in love with wealth.

So he made his way back to Europe, pausing only long enough in London to have the gangrene burned out, and then he was back in Mecklenburg for a few weeks, giving expensive presents to his uncle, his father, his brother, and his sisters. He was thirty, and as he rode back in the sleigh to St. Petersburg he counted himself most fortunate. He had only to lift his finger and everything he had ever dreamed of during his poverty-stricken days—books, wine, women, servants, houses—would be given to him. He could not guess that for seventeen long years his wealth was to taste like ashes in his mouth.

4. The Merchant Prince

Outwardly he was a man of the world, the very type of the successful business executive, with his gold-rimmed spectacles and long coat with an astrakhan collar. He was cultivated and well mannered. He carried an ebony cane, and possessed his own carriage. His apartment in St. Petersburg consisted of two salons, seven bedrooms, five other rooms, a kitchen, stables, cellars, and a coach house. The best wines were in the cellars and three expensive horses were in the coach house. Princes and merchants clamoured for invitations to the house of the adventurous businessman who was believed to have made a vast fortune in the California goldfields. Had he not spent a thousand rubles to furnish a single guest room?

The inward man, however, bore very little resemblance to the image he showed to the world. Above all he had wanted a wife and children, and with all the women in Russia to choose from, he had to choose Ekaterina Lyschin. He called on her the day after he reached St. Petersburg. He told himself he was in love with her. They were married on October 12, 1852.

No one ever entered upon a marriage with such high hopes, or regretted them so quickly. Ekaterina had turned out to be a cold virago who refused to share his bed. Within a few weeks he was writing to his sisters, begging for advice and consolation. "I know that intense desire and hopeless passion can drive a man to madness. . . ." His sisters wrote, pointing out without malice that his own forbidding coldness might be the cause of the coldness in his wife. He must learn to be human, to be warm. But there was no school where he could learn the art of being human, and so he plunged voraciously into the world of business, where he was master.

He put his entire fortune into indigo, eventually controlling the market. He still worked twelve or fourteen hours a day. He saw little of his wife. Work was his opium: he drugged himself compulsively. He wrote to his father that his cash turnover amounted to a million silver rubles a month. There was no end to it—fortune piled on fortune, gold on gold, yet he was no nearer the happiness he yearned for. Indeed he was close to madness, and knew it, a strange sallow-featured genius of finance who sometimes broke into screams of rage and whose letters to his agents all over the world were often written in tones of demoniac fury because his orders were not instantly obeyed. By the end of 1855 he was worth $1,000,000.

In other respects, too, fortune now smiled on him. For the first time he was enjoying happy relations at home. Greater wealth made Ekaterina amenable, and that year she presented him with a child, who was called Sergei. For a few brief months he was overwhelmed with gratitude towards his wife. He bought an estate near the summer residence of the Tsar at Peterhof and gave his wife jewellery. At odd moments during 1854 he had learned Polish and Swedish. And in 1855, the Greek language—which he had always hesitated to learn because he was afraid he would fall completely under its spell.

He had suffered agonies of misery when forced to leave the school at Neustrelitz just when he was about to enter the Greek class. Over the years he had acquired a library of books concerned with Homer and the Greek heroes in a multitude of languages, but none in Greek. Now at last he could afford to permit himself the supreme luxury of studying Greek itself until he could recite whole books of Homer by heart.

For six days a week he worked at his office, but on Sundays he shut himself up in his study. After six Sundays of prodigious mental activity he was able to compose long, complex sentences in ancient Greek, and soon he was writing in modern Greek as well. He was overwhelmed by the beauty and clarity of this language. He wrote to his former teacher at Neustrelitz, enclosing a résumé of his whole life in the language spoken by Homer. "I am intoxicated by this language," he wrote. "I must go to Greece, and live there! It surprises me that a language can be so noble!" All his most secret thoughts he wrote in Greek, a language so beautiful that he believed to the end of his life that it was spoken by the gods. His Greek notes, written in thirty-five notebooks over a period of two years, contain his most revealing comments on himself. He wrote, "I am, I know, mean and avaricious. I shall have to give up being so mercenary."

Increasingly, as time passed, he saw the world through Greek eyes. He searched for a Russian-speaking Greek and found a tutor named Theokletos Vimpos. Vimpos was a priest of the Greek Orthodox Church who was studying in St. Petersburg, a warm friendly man who spoke Greek with the purest of Athenian accents, one of the few who ever penetrated Schliemann's reserve.

THE TROJAN WAR

The heroic stories told by Pastor Schliemann that so fired the imagination of his young son Heinrich were of a long and bitter war, some 1200 years before the birth of Christ, between two powerful Mediterranean rulers: King Agamemnon of Mycenae (in south Greece) and King Priam of Troy (in Turkey). A war which ended in the defeat of King Priam and the sacking of Troy.

The causes of that war and the adventures of its heroes are the stuff of legend, collected together many years later by the blind poet Homer in his two great poems, *The Iliad* and *The Odyssey*. Homer told of how Paris, a prince of Troy, had stolen away Helen, wife of Menelaus, King of Sparta; of how Menelaus's brother Agamemnon had in revenge led a huge force of Greeks against the Trojans.

He told of the battles between the Greek and Trojan champions, Achilles and Hector; of how, after a siege lasting ten years, the Greeks defeated Troy by concealing soldiers within a huge wooden horse and then tricking the Trojans into taking it within their walls; and of how, at last, Odysseus—the inventor of the wooden horse—came home to his own island of Ithaca.

ADRIATIC SEA

GREECE

ITHACA

Thebes

MYCENAE

Athens

Tiryns

Kea

SPARTA

Melos

Kythera

MEDITERRANEAN SEA

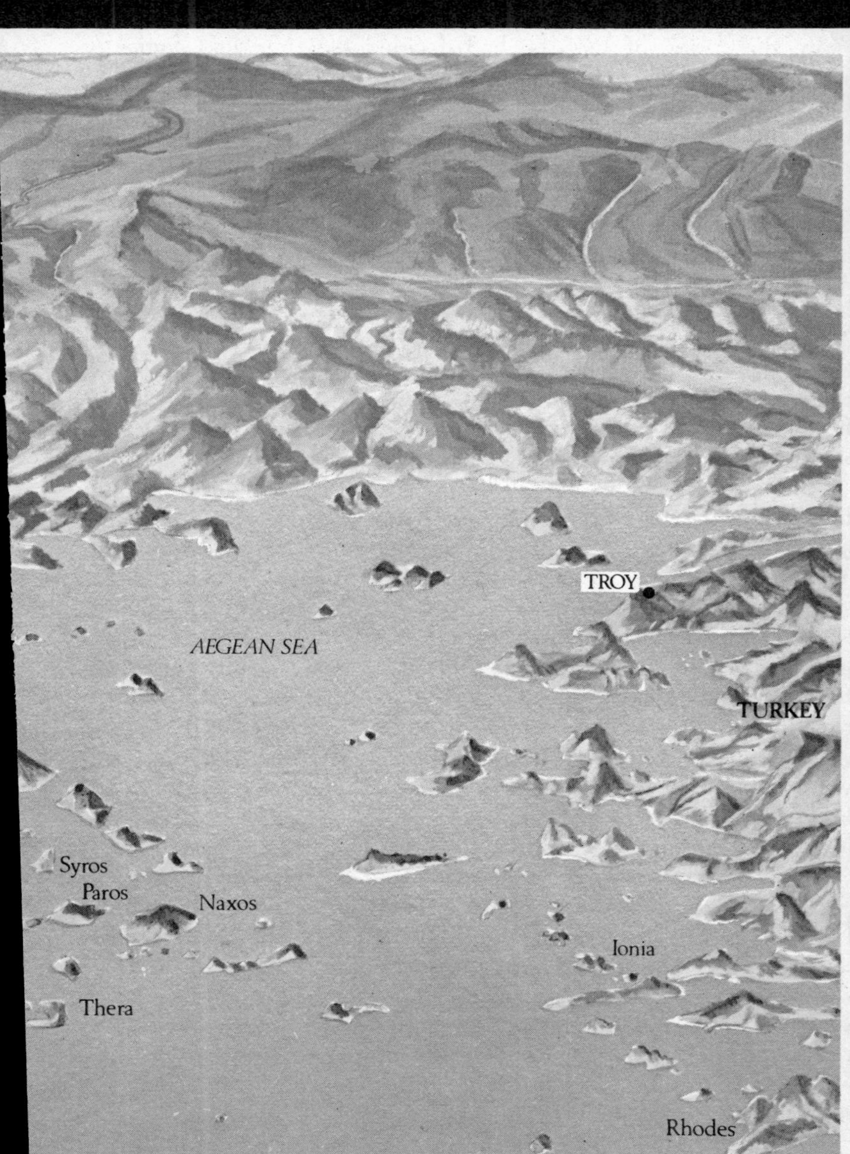

TROY
AEGEAN SEA
TURKEY
Syros
Paros
Naxos
Ionia
Thera
Rhodes

By the spring of 1858 he had decided the time had come to visit Greece. His relations with his wife had never been worse: they stared at one another coldly across the dining table and hardly exchanged ten words in a week. He had however begotten another child—"I stole it from her," he wrote brutally.

When summer came, he set out alone. He was a little afraid of going straight to Greece. He would see what Egypt had to offer him before throwing himself with heart and soul upon that land. As an ordinary tourist he sailed up the Nile on a large passenger boat called a *dahabeah* as far as the Second Cataract, learning Arabic during the journey. In later years he liked to remember that during his journey he disguised himself as a bedouin, had himself circumcised, and penetrated the holy city of Mecca. But he makes no mention of the visit to Mecca in his voluminous diaries, and seems to have imagined the entire journey.

Athens, that bright and glittering city, was everything he had hoped for. He put up at the best hotel, climbed the Acropolis, and was supremely content. Through letters of introduction from Theokletos Vimpos he was able to meet Greek scholars. Then suddenly he received a telegram from St. Petersburg announcing that he was being sued in the high court by a businessman on grounds of fraud. The court permitted no delay. Schliemann had to hurry back to St. Petersburg. For five more years he was to remain in Russia, safeguarding his fortune.

He won the trial; he won another child from Ekaterina; he won a third fortune; and he lost himself. He lost his interest in languages, and Greece frightened him. Now, when he spoke of journeying abroad, he never mentioned Greece—he would go to China or South America.

He was regarded as one of the greatest importers in the world. His son Sergei was turning into a bright boy, the apple of his father's eye. The second and third children were girls. Natalia was born in 1858, and Nadezhda—the word means hope—three years later. In 1862–63 his net annual profit on indigo alone was vast, and he decided he would settle down in Dresden with his wife and children, and live the life of a moneyed businessman in retirement.

He bought a house in Dresden and then sent an urgent message to his wife to join him. She refused. He wrote to a high government official in St. Petersburg. "With the aid of the police and my own arms, I shall take my darlings so that I can give them here in Dresden the German education which their mother denies them."

The official listened to his demands without sympathy. A greying millionaire with a high domed forehead, and watery brown eyes which lit up only when he was talking about money, he represented all that was most repugnant in Russian society.

In the winter of 1863 he sold his business, settled some money on his wife and children, and vowed he would never return to Russia. He had not the least idea what he would do. He seems to have gone travelling simply to drown his miseries. In April 1864 he was in Tunis, gazing openmouthed at the ruins of Carthage. He then went on to India. The heat and the noise frightened him, but he had high hopes for China. There at least were great scholars, and men held learning in high repute.

He reached Peking on April 30, 1865, after an uncomfortable journey by two-wheeled cart from Tientsin. There were no hotels. He found lodgings in a Buddhist monastery, where he was asked to pay twelve francs for a room, but after prolonged bargaining he succeeded in reducing the cost to six francs.

He spent only one day in Peking. It was raining, and he hated everything he saw. It never occurred to him to ask questions. He thought the shining palaces of the Forbidden City were in ruins, when they were merely invisible behind trees, and performed miracles of improvisation in his diary on the theme of a ruined city slowly sinking into the mud. A few years later, when engaged in excavating Troy, he would improvise theories in the same reckless way.

He was not thinking of Troy when he came to Peking. He was thinking of a far greater ruin stretching over hundreds of miles of mountain and desert—the Great Wall of China. Accordingly, the next day, he set out with a servant, reaching the wall two days later.

He had brought his measuring scale with him, and once he reached the wall he measured the size of the bricks and the height of the walls. He was sure the bricks dated from the earlier Han

Dynasty, about 200 B.C., although in fact they date from the Ming Dynasty, about A.D. 1400.

He remained in one of the towers most of the afternoon. It was not enough to have reached the wall: he wanted time to enjoy the spectacle and to remember everything he had read about the wall's heroic defenders. At last he carefully detached a brick from the wall. He was in good heart. This was the first serious work of excavation he had performed.

Some days later he wrote up his diary. Here, for the first time, the merchant prince surrenders to the ardent archaeologist:

> I have gazed on magnificent vistas, but never on one so magnificent as this. . . . I could not accustom myself to this miraculous wall, which had always excited me even in my earliest childhood. . . . The more I gazed at this immense wall with its formidable crenellated towers seeking always the crests of the highest mountains, the more it seemed to me to be the work of a fabulous race of antediluvian giants. . . .

When Schliemann wrote these words, the vision of the buried city of Troy was still remote, yet already he was announcing the theme which was to dominate the last years of his life—crumbling ruins, the endless pageant of the buried past.

Once he had stood on the Great Wall, China lost all interest for him, and he seems to have been glad when the time came to leave for Japan. In Japan he enjoyed himself greatly; he attended Kabuki plays, he admired the friendliness and silk kimonos of Japanese women, and he liked the little inns where he stayed. To him Japan was delightful and mysterious, like a fairy tale. Then in early September he set off across the Pacific for San Francisco. With time on his hands, he wrote an account of his travels through China and Japan, a small book but his first.

Still the wanderer, he stayed only a few days in San Francisco and then went on to Nicaragua and Mexico. At last, in the spring of 1866, he found himself in Paris with an apartment at the foot of the Place St. Michel, overlooking the Seine and the cathedral of Nôtre-Dame. He had made his fortune, visited half the countries in the world, sired three children, learned twelve or thirteen languages, collected a vast library, and grown grey and weary at the age of forty-four. But he had decided what he wanted to be: a philologist, a student of languages, going to classes at the Sorbonne; and in between lectures he would publish his book on China and Japan. It came out a year later, and seems, sadly, to have been of no particular value.

5. The Search for Troy

Schliemann was perfectly at home in Paris, studying at the Sorbonne. Wealthy, he could take a mistress, eat in the fashionable restaurants, and consort with the aristocracy. A linguist, he could seek the companionship of other linguists. A businessman, he could amuse himself by buying and selling property in Paris. He even bought some houses in the Bois de Boulogne and refurnished them for tenants. Why a multimillionaire should have troubled to become a house agent, spending his time in long discussions on wallpaper, is only one more of the insoluble problems presented by that lonely and embittered man.

As usual, he went about his life methodically: so many hours for study, so many for business, so many for amusement. He attended theatres and the races, and was welcomed in the salons of the great ladies. But he longed for his children. He wrote that if Ekaterina came to him he would provide her with every luxury she desired—carriages, jewellery, dresses. They would live chastely together, like brother and sister; he would make no demands on her.

Ekaterina remained unmoved. As for Schliemann, grey and balding, looking older than his years, he continued to wear the disguise of a middle-aged student at the Sorbonne. But when he read in the London *Times* that American politicians were clamouring to pay off certain bonds with paper money, he became afraid that his large American holdings would depreciate, and he decided to visit America. He sailed early in 1867, and as soon as he reached Washington he called upon the Secretary of the Treasury, and was gratified to learn that the bonds would not be repudiated.

All at once his consuming passion became the study of the American railway system. He rode on all the lines which reached out to the Great Lakes. He noted that they were all paying a ten per cent dividend, and invested huge sums in them.

Indianapolis pleased him. He came to know many of the businessmen and politicians there, and sometimes the talk would turn to the divorce laws of the state of Indiana, then undergoing revision. To divorce his wife according to the state law of Indiana, Schliemann would first have to become a citizen. With the help of his friends, who were not above stretching the law a little, he made arrangements for becoming a citizen the following year. He bought a house in Indianapolis and an interest in a starch business there, and he seemingly looked forward to the time when he would be free of Ekaterina for ever. But although he was outwardly debonair, he was seething with misery within. He did not want to divorce Ekaterina. He constantly sent her imploring letters, admitting his faults, promising to be more generous in future.

Then he was in Paris again. He resumed his study of philology, went to the theatre, bought more houses, and acted the part of landlord. But it was not long before it occurred to him that he was being bored to death.

Suddenly, in the middle of that restless spring of 1868, two things happened which changed the course of his life. He attended some lectures on archaeology at the Sorbonne, and his cousin Sophie Schliemann, daughter of his uncle, the pastor at Kalkhorst and a childhood playmate, died.

He flew into a passion of grief. The death of Sophie struck him where he was most vulnerable. She was one of the few who had ever been close to him. At long intervals in his life he had thought fondly about her. Suddenly at her death she returned from the grave to haunt him.

He was a man without faith in religion or any hope of an afterlife. He believed that man was the measure of all things: with industry and acumen any man could make a fortune and enjoy the good things of the earth. But now he found that the old shibboleths were wanting. Why was he living? There was nothing of any importance worth doing. Would he spend his life buying enamel baths and mirrors for his tenants? His grief over the death of Sophie was exaggerated and raw with self-pity; but there was a real despair in the hurried letters he wrote to Germany, asking for details of how she died, asking for a portrait of her.

Then there came to him, in that intolerable spring, the memory of Homer which had enchanted his childhood—not the *Iliad* with its tale of Troy besieged, but the *Odyssey*, the story of a wanderer who returns at last to his own home. He would go to Ithaca, where Odysseus found his Penelope in his own mountain stronghold. He would stand there, and somehow, by some miracle, he too would find his Penelope and there would be an end to his wandering.

Schliemann could add up sums at a prodigious pace and make decisions on financial matters quickly, suddenly, with an intuitive grasp of complex dealings in merchandise. But in all other matters he was slow, halting, unsure, and pathetically aware of his own weaknesses.

Nearly all the major turning points of his life came about as a result of forces over which he had no control. He went to Greece because he was haunted by the ghost of Sophie Schliemann and because his wife refused him. And in his distress he turned to Homer, who had reigned over his childhood.

When Schliemann made his way to Greece in the early summer of 1868 he had already decided to become an archaeologist. From the moment he stepped foot on Ithaca he was like a man enchanted. There were no hotels, but he found lodgings with two elderly spinsters. He met a miller with a donkey who offered to take him around the island, which was shaped like a figure eight with a thin craggy isthmus. On the isthmus was Mount Aetos where, according to legend, was Odysseus' home.

"Every hill, every stone, every stream, every olive grove reminded me of Homer," he wrote, "and so I found myself with a single leap hurled across a hundred generations into the glittering age of Greek knighthood."

After two days of exploration he organized an expedition up Mount Aetos. It was an inexpensive expedition, consisting of four workmen and a donkey. The first day he found nothing of any importance. The next day he set the workmen to digging in the northeast corner of the circuit wall. It flashed through his mind that here, on this very spot, Odysseus might have built his marriage chamber—that chamber of stone built around an olive tree that had served as a bedpost to his bed. Three hours later the workmen came upon the foundation stones of a building three metres wide by four and three-quarters metres long, and Schliemann was wild with excitement. He thought he had found the foundations of the marriage chamber. Then he discovered a semicircular stone covered with earth, carefully lifted it, and continued digging. Four inches below the surface his pickaxe struck a delicate vase and smashed it to fragments. A little while later he found twenty more vases, all containing ashes. He was sure they were human ashes. Then he found a sacrificial knife six inches long, a clay goddess holding two flutes to her mouth, and some animal bones.

There were no inscriptions, but his enthusiasm was boundless. He wrote in his diary, "It is quite possible that [one of these funerary urns] might contain the ashes of Odysseus and Penelope."

His appetite for archaeology was now whetted. He had stood on sacred soil and seen the mysterious past gazing up at him from the earth. This first easy success led him to believe in his innate ability as an archaeologist, and all his subsequent diggings followed the same plan. Intuitively, holding Homer in his hand, he would choose a spot where he thought there was some likelihood of treasure, and then he would order the workmen to dig. Only in rare cases could he explain why he had chosen the place. He worked by instinct and enthusiasm, and spent most of the remaining years of his life in fruitless digging. Twice he would discover great treasures of gold, but these were the exceptions.

After the excitement of that morning's digging, he found nothing more that day, and nothing the next. The following evening he recited for the villagers the last book of the *Odyssey*, translating the words into their own dialect. The peasants clustered around him, surprised and delighted to see a foreigner who knew their legends so well. Schliemann recounts the story:

> Their enthusiasm had no bounds, as they listened to the melodious language of Homer—the language spoken by their glorious ancestors 3000 years ago. . . . All eyes were bathed in tears, and

men, women and children came up to me and embraced me, saying: "You have given us a great pleasure! We thank you a thousand times over!" Then they bore me in triumph to their town.

A few days later, having made no more discoveries, he sailed for Corinth, and then on to Athens, where he renewed his acquaintance with Theokletos Vimpos, now Archbishop of Mantinea and a professor at the University of Athens. For a few days they were inseparable, and then in August Schliemann set out for Troy by way of Constantinople.

As he wandered over the plain of Troy he was in high spirits. It was soft rolling land; there were clumps of spruce and oak, and the air was like wine. At Bunarbashi, long believed to be the site of Troy, he found a huddle of small houses inhabited by Turks and Albanian Greeks. The walls were black with mosquitoes, and when he asked for milk to slake his thirst, it was given to him in a jug which had not, he thought, been cleaned out for ten years.

He had dreamed of a Troy of white marble, gleaming in an eternal noonday of the imagination. Homer speaks of the Achaeans making seven or eight journeys a day from the seashore to the site of Troy. Bunarbashi was ten miles from the sea and Schliemann felt sure that the hill of Hissarlik, at the western end of the plain, was a more likely site. Frank Calvert, an Englishman who lived in Constantinople and acted as American vice-consul at the Dardanelles, shared the same view. He owned half the hill and had done some preliminary digging. On the eastern slope he had discovered the remains of a palace or a temple formed of great blocks of hewn stone.

As Schliemann concentrated on the hill of Hissarlik, everything began to fall into place. The approaches, the shape, and size of the hill seemed to him to prove that Hissarlik was Troy. As he imagined it, the citadel was on the hill, while all around it stretched the wide-flung city, as Athens lies below the Acropolis. There would be ruins buried in the earth all around the hill, while the hill itself would contain Priam's palace, the treasures, and the bones of the heroes.

On August 21, less than two weeks later, he was back in Constantinople, busily discussing his theories with Frank Calvert. He was in a mood for quick action. Vast plans, furious onslaughts against the hill—he would enter into battle at once with the ghosts of the past. Calvert, whose mind moved more slowly, was a little amused. He suggested that it was already late in the season for digging. There would have to be careful preparations, and a *firman* from the Turkish government permitting the excavations. Calvert could have bargained with Schliemann—half the hill belonged to him—but it seems never to have occurred to him. He assisted Schliemann at every opportunity, and asked for nothing.

Troy had become Schliemann's obsession, but there was one other matter preying on his mind. Friends in Indianapolis had promised him a divorce from Ekaterina in the following spring. Accordingly he proposed to be in America in the spring, and as soon as the divorce papers were signed he would return to Troy. Meanwhile he decided to spend the autumn and winter in his apartment in the Place St. Michel, writing an account of his six-week tour through Greece, of which his Leipzig publisher was to print seven hundred and fifty copies at the author's expense.

The book, put together from his journals and scraps of philological learning, was to be his passport to fame. Setting himself up as the champion of Homer, he ascribes intolerable prejudice to anyone who would dare to find the least topographical inaccuracy in his cherished poet. His fundamental belief in the divinity of Homer emerges clearly, together with the fundamentalist's combative temper. How deeply he regarded his role as author can be seen from the letter he wrote at the beginning of November to his thirteen-year-old son, Sergei:

> If this book is successful, I will spend the rest of my life writing books. Writing, one is always so happy and content and at peace with oneself. . . . And everyone looks up to writers and welcomes them, and even though I am only an apprentice, I have ten times as many friends as I want. . . .

In fact he had almost no intimate friends.

Above all, Schliemann was driven by the desire to be honoured and respected. Nothing would please him more than to be addressed as Herr Doktor. Unfortunately, because of the Sorbonne's curriculum, he could only be an occasional student there. He applied to the University of Rostock for a doctorate. Asked what thesis he proposed to submit, he suggested an account of his career written in classical Greek. This extraordinary dissertation was accepted.

So November and December passed, while he wrote his dissertation. Towards the end of December 1868 he wrote to Frank Calvert, enclosing a list of questions about the arts of excavation. In these questions we see the tentative beginnings of the work which was to engross him for the remaining years of his life:

1. Is it not advisable to begin as early as possible in spring?
2. Have I to take a tent and iron bedstead and pillow with me from Marseille? For all the houses in the plain of Troy are infested with vermin.
3. Please give me an exact statement of all the *implements* of whatever kind and of *all the necessaries* which you advise me to take with me.
4. Do I require pistols, dagger and rifle?
5. Can I get labourers enough, where and at what wages?
6. You suggested to dig first a tunnel! But I am sure this is not practical, for if the hill really consists of ruins of ancient temples and walls, the cyclopean* stones will impede the tunnel being made.
7. What sort of a hat is best against scorching sun?

And so on.

Frank Calvert replied immediately. He had studied archaeology, and he explained exactly how the trenches should be dug and the best season for digging—between early spring and summer.

Contemplating this letter in early January, Schliemann went for a holiday in Germany, visiting Fürstenberg, where he had been a grocer's assistant, and Rostock, for the presentation of his doctorate; after that he was always annoyed if he was not addressed by his title. Then off he went to Indianapolis. He hoped to get the

*Cyclopean: applied to an ancient style of masonry in which the stones are immense and irregular in shape.

divorce immediately, but there were delays. On April 14 he wrote to Calvert, saying he feared he would be unable to obtain the divorce before June; consequently digging would have to be abandoned until the spring of the following year.

In his usual way Schliemann kept himself busy in Indianapolis. His starch factory was progressing well. He studied the money market, polished up his Arabic, and wrote long letters to acquaintances all over the world. He wrote enthusiastically on the subject of the Northwest Passage and the discovery of the North Pole. And while the divorce was still under consideration, he was preparing in the most extraordinary way to find a bride to replace Ekaterina.

He had decided upon a Greek bride, because he liked the sound of the language, especially when spoken by women. But how to find one? He could, of course, return to Greece and search for one, but an easier way occurred to him. Hesitantly he began a letter to Vimpos. Halfway through he made his supreme request—would Vimpos please choose a bride for him? Her qualifications? She should be poor, beautiful, an enthusiast for Homer, dark-haired, well educated, and the possessor of a good and loving heart.

Vimpos was not in the least outraged by the letter. He went about Athens, collected photographs of desirable Athenian girls, and sent them to Indianapolis. Among these photographs was one of Sophia Engastromenos, seventeen years old, a dark-haired girl of quite unusual beauty, with a delicate oval face, large eyes, and thick curving eyebrows. Schliemann sent a copy of her photograph to his father with a brief note saying he had decided to marry her if she was enthusiastic about learning.

At last, in late July, his divorce was granted. He took the first available ship across the Atlantic. He arrived in Greece at the end of August on the eve of the Feast of Saint Meletius, the patron saint of the little church near the country villa of the Engastromenos family at Colonus, slightly more than a mile northwest of Athens. Colonus was the birthplace of Sophocles. There was no place more auspicious.

The moment Schliemann reached the little town he found himself looking upon the celebration of an ancient rite, for the girls were carrying garlands to the church.

Sophia's family was not particularly poor. Her father was a draper, with a shop and town house in Athens, a solid, handsome man who had won a medal in the War of Independence. Sophia was in the church, standing on a stool and hanging up garlands, when Schliemann arrived at the house with Vimpos. In the church there was the cry, "The German has come!" He had not been expected so early in the day. Sophia jumped off her stool and hurried into the house to change her clothes.

At last Sophia came into the room, wearing a white dress, with ribbons in her hair, very demure. The whole family was there—father, mother, sisters, brothers, cousins—and they were all sitting around the table, gazing at the strange German with the sad smile and the gold-rimmed spectacles, nearly bald, with a heavy gold watch chain hanging over his waistcoat. Wine and cakes were served. Sophia sat down at the table with her eyes lowered.

Schliemann was talking about his travels in impeccable Greek. Suddenly he turned to Sophia and asked her three questions.

"Would you like to go on a long journey?" Sophia answered that she would.

The second question was, "When did the emperor Hadrian visit Athens?" Sophia gave the exact date.

The third question was, "Can you recite passages of Homer by heart?" Sophia could, and did. The examination had been passed with flying colours.

During the next three days Schliemann haunted the country villa, retiring to his hotel only in the evening. Sophia knew she was being watched closely, but she showed no nervousness. She played with her sisters and cousins, helped to prepare the table, and sometimes vanished into the cellar, where they kept their casks of oil and olives. There were so many relatives in the house that Schliemann had to slip a message into her hands to see her privately.

Once they were alone, he said abruptly, "Why do you want to marry me?"

"Because my parents told me you were a rich man," Sophia answered simply.

Schliemann was hurt to the quick and strode off in white-hot anger to his hotel. He wrote on his hotel notepaper:

> I am deeply pained, Miss Sophia, at the answer you have given me—one worthy of a slave. I myself am a simple, honourable, home-loving man. . . . If ever we were married, it would be so that we could excavate together and share our common love for Homer.
>
> The day after tomorrow I shall leave for Naples. But if you should ever need a friend, remember your devoted
>
> Heinrich Schliemann
> Doctor of Philosophy

This letter was dispatched by hotel messenger. Sophia was overwhelmed. While the whole family insisted that she compose a letter to allay the German's wrath, the letter she wrote shows no evidence of any assistance. She wrote on cheap notepaper hurriedly bought from a local shop:

> Dear Herr Heinrich: I am so sorry you are going away. You must not be angry with what I said this afternoon. I thought that was how young girls should speak. . . .

Schliemann was relieved, but determined to punish her. Six days passed before he relented, and then only because the seventeen-year-old girl wrote in her round careful handwriting a proposal of marriage. He had arrived in Athens late in August, and on September 24 they were married.

Schliemann wore a frock coat; Sophia wore a white dress and bridal veil wreathed with flowers from Colonus, and all her relatives attended in Greek national costume. Then there was a feast which lasted late into the evening, and that night the bride and groom drove to Piraeus, the port of Athens, and boarded the ship for Naples. Sophia insisted on bringing her dolls with her, and Schliemann was in no mood to argue. She had won her first victory, and she was to win all the others.

Childlike, moving with an easy grace which she never lost even in old age, Sophia loved him to distraction, with the violence of the young in love with the old, yet never completely understood him. Cold even with his intimate friends, he loved her passionately, delighting in her quick changes of mood, her laughter, and her profound seriousness, which was always like the seriousness of a child. During the honeymoon he wrote, "She has a kind of divine reverence for her husband."

It was true; but the words should not be allowed to stand alone, for he too possessed a kind of divine reverence for this wife. To the end of his life he worshipped her. In her company he was warm and gentle. The miracle had been accomplished; and sometimes he would find himself looking at her with the expression of a man bewildered by his own good fortune.

It was a strange honeymoon. Naples, Florence, Munich—always the hurried journeys through the museums, with Schliemann delivering in his high-pitched voice a running commentary, until Sophia could have cried out in agony. People stared at the elderly professor—he was forty-seven, but looked ten years older—and his young wife, both so intent upon the study of art. In the evenings he would ask her to recite two hundred lines of Homer, and often she would fall asleep before she finished.

He was determined to mould her closer to his heart's desire—she would learn German and French, one language a year; surely that was not demanding too much from her! He took her to Paris and installed her in the vast apartment overlooking the cathedral of Nôtre-Dame. He dressed her in the latest fashions and made her wear a chignon, but when some Greek girls came to visit her she tossed the chignon away, got down on her knees and showed them her dolls.

She hated Paris—the fog coming over the Seine, the knife-edge winds blowing up the Place St. Michel. She was bored by the visits to the Geographical Society, the continual talk about Troy, Mycenae, and the Greek islands, where unknown treasures might be buried. By the end of January Schliemann was planning to return to Troy. About this time he learned of the death of his daughter Nadezhda and was prostrated with grief. He thought of rushing to St. Petersburg to comfort his remaining children, and might have done so if Sophia had not fallen ill.

The doctors could find nothing wrong with her, but by the middle of February Sophia was no more than a ghost of herself, suffering from unaccountable fits of weeping. Perhaps it was no more than the fever of homesickness. Schliemann decided to take her to Athens and make his way to Troy. Calvert had promised to obtain a *firman* from the Turkish government to permit the excavations. When Schliemann reached Athens, however, there was no *firman* awaiting him. Impatient, he decided not to wait for it. There was nothing to prevent him from visiting the Troy area; nothing to prevent him from employing workmen. Alone, leaving Sophia behind in Athens, he decided to take Troy by storm.

6. The Gold of Troy

When Schliemann came to Troy, in 1870, there seem to have been only two people—Frank Calvert and Heinrich Schliemann—who believed firmly that Troy's walls and its palaces lay buried in the mound at Hissarlik. Charles Maclaren, the brilliant archaeologist, who wrote *A Dissertation on the Topography of the Plain of Troy*, had proved to his own satisfaction, as far back as 1822, that Troy was to be found at Hissarlik; but Charles Maclaren was dead, and in 1870 the consensus of scholars was that Troy was at Bunarbashi.

Frank Calvert had neither the money nor the inclination to make a complete excavation of the Hissarlik mound. The eastern part belonged to him; the western part belonged to two Turks living at Kum Kale. Schliemann was convinced that the more important discoveries would be made in the western part, overlooking the sea. Characteristically he decided to attack the part belonging to the Turks. He said later, "I was so sure of finding great buildings, and then too I hoped they would pardon my audacity when they saw the treasure."

On April 9 he dug the first trench with the help of ten Turkish labourers from the nearby village of Renkoi. Schliemann stood over them with a pistol in his belt, a riding whip in his hand. The first earth was dug on the northwest corner of the hill. After an hour's digging, two feet below the surface the workmen came upon the remains of a wall. Schliemann was excited. By sunset they had uncovered the foundations of a building sixty feet long and forty feet wide.

The next day, with eleven more workmen, he began digging at the southeast and southwest corners of the building which was slowly emerging before his eyes. At last the flagstones were revealed. They were covered with two feet of earth and detritus formed through the ages—sheep dung, the remains of plants, and atmospheric dust. Then he dug below the flagstones and found exactly what he had expected to find: cinders, calcined matter, evidence of fire. He came to the conclusion that altogether ten wooden houses had perished in the flames before the last stone house was built on their ruins. Among the cinders he found a coin, bearing on one side the image of the emperor Commodus and on the other the image of Hector, the son of Priam, the great general who commanded the Trojan forces. In Schliemann's eyes the coin, which bore the inscription *Hector Ilieon* (Hector of Troy), was the most auspicious of all.

On the third day he started on two long trenches, one from east to west, the other running due north. By slicing across the top of the mound he hoped to form a general picture of the buried city, just as a man drawing lines at right angles across a small village and examining all the objects encountered in the path of these lines might reasonably be able to form a rough sketch of the entire village. Somewhere these lines would cut through the main street, the mayor's office, the post office, the fire station.

Schliemann's plan was perfectly sound, but he had hardly begun these new excavations when the Turks arrived and ordered him to stop digging. That night, in a mood that curiously mingled resignation, despair, and vast hopes for the future, Schliemann wrote to a friend in Germany:

> I have uncovered . . . vast walls six feet thick and of most wonderful construction. 7½ feet lower down I found that these same walls rested upon other walls 8½ feet thick. These must be the walls of the Palace of Priam or the Temple of Athena.
>
> Unfortunately the two Turks who own the land will probably make me put an end to my work tomorrow. I intend to go to all possible lengths to buy the land, and shall not rest until I have uncovered the Palace of Priam.

Throughout his life as an excavator Schliemann had the habit of giving heroic names to his discoveries. He had found an immense wall, and instantly named it the Temple of Pallas Athena. A little later, while digging deeper in the north trench, he discovered below twenty-two layers of cinders the terracotta bust of a woman, and named it the bust of Helen of Troy. Never hesitating to make grandiose claims, he rarely permitted himself the annoyance of the slightest doubt.

For the moment, bowing to the inevitable, he paid off his workmen and returned to Athens. Sophia was still ill. Schliemann wrote an account of his adventure at Hissarlik for the *Kölnische Zeitung*, openly admitting that he had excavated the mound without the permission of the owners.

Weeks passed. In a misery of frustration, hating his inactivity, Schliemann wrote to Frank Calvert, begging him to intercede with the Turkish government. But there was little Calvert could do; the Turks were in no mood to offer assistance to a man who dug huge trenches across Turkish property.

Summer came. It was too hot for digging on the plain of Troy, and Schliemann set out for Paris. One day in the middle of June he received a letter from Sergei in St. Petersburg. The boy said he was not progressing well at school. Schliemann replied in a letter so filled with frigid boasting that he gives the impression of a man on the verge of insanity:

> Try to follow the example of your father who has always proved how much a man can accomplish provided he has a fierce energy. I performed miracles during my four years in Amsterdam. Then I became a merchant in St. Petersburg, and no merchant was ever so accomplished or prudent. . . . Today I am an archaeologist, and all Europe and America are dazzled by my discovery of the ancient city of Troy—that Troy which the archaeologists of all countries have searched for in vain for two thousand years. . . .

On July 19, 1870, Napoleon III declared war on Prussia, and Schliemann was still in Paris, burning with resentment against those two Turkish peasants who by this time had probably forgotten his existence. Shortly after the declaration of war he returned to Athens. At the end of August he wrote to Safvet Pasha, the Turkish minister of public instruction, a long, imploring letter saying that he had never hoped to find any treasures. On the contrary, he had acted out of "pure and disinterested love of science". Surely they would not blame him for having made, in the wild enthusiasm which overcame him when he found himself at Hissarlik, a few unimportant excavations which nevertheless proved the existence of Priam's palace and the great wall surrounding the city.

"I worked in rainstorms as though it were summer. I thought I had lunched and dined when I had eaten nothing all day, and every little piece of pottery which I brought to light was for me another page of history!" He begged His Excellency's pardon for having acted high-handedly. But his letter, with all its denials, only served to convince Safvet Pasha that Schliemann was indeed looking for buried treasure, and when Schliemann arrived in Constantinople at last, in December, the minister greeted him affably, promised him every assistance, and did everything he could to prevent the excavations from continuing.

While waiting in Constantinople, Schliemann's mind was also absorbed by the approaching fall of Paris. That winter of 1871 Paris was ringed around by the heavy guns of the army of the Crown Prince of Prussia. He received a letter from his wife in Athens, full of dejection and despair. But Schliemann was concerned about his apartment on the Place St. Michel, which contained his library and a small collection of treasures from the Far East and Ithaca, among them the vase containing the ashes of Odysseus. There was nothing for it but to return to Paris.

France and Prussia had at that point agreed that no one was to enter the French capital until peace was restored. Characteristically, Schliemann regarded all laws which impeded his progress as intolerable abuses of freedom. For five francs he bought a false passport, and with this he made his way through the German lines. He was detained for examination three times. He said later that he might have been put up against a wall and shot, but he remembered the German mania for titles, and by addressing every lieutenant as general and every simple soldier as colonel he passed through the lines unscathed. His apartment at 6 Place St. Michel and the house he owned next door were exactly as he had left them.

When the Communards were in possession of Paris, Schliemann was still there. He passed the time quietly in his study, contemplating the war from a distance. Sophia was pregnant. He imagined the child would be a boy and he had already settled the name he would give it—Odysseus. Again Schliemann simply walked through the German lines with his false passport. He reached Athens in May, in time for the birth of his child. It was a girl and he called her Andromache after the beautiful wife of Hector.

In June he presented a new offer to Safvet Pasha. This memorandum reveals the temper of the man—his Odysseus-like cunning, his highly developed sense of his own importance, and that quality which the Jews call *chutzpa*, which is neither nerve nor gall but the finest flower of these. He denied that he had any hope of finding treasure. All he had ever wanted to do was to prove that the Trojan War was no fable, that Troy had actually existed. If, however, any treasure was dug up, he offered solemnly to divided it between himself and the Turkish government. He made no claim on the two Turks' land—indeed by now the Turkish government itself had bought the land, and the title to it had been transferred to the ministry of public instruction. He stated that he would assume the entire financial burden for the venture; he asked for no financial assistance, but asked only that he be provided, in the name of the grand vizier, with a *firman* and with the protection which would be afforded to any foreigner in a remote part of Turkey.

On August 12, 1871 a sealed package arrived from the American Embassy in Constantinople. The package contained the *firman*. He had no intention of keeping to the agreement, but now at last there was a face-saving document which satisfied both parties. Anxious to start digging, Schliemann arrived with his wife in the Dardanelles on September 27. He established his headquarters in the village of Ciplak, chose his foreman, and hired the workmen. Wheelbarrows and baskets were assembled; spades, picks, and axes were unbundled. Still there were delays; despite the *firman* no permit had yet reached the local authorities. At last, on Wednesday, October 11, he was able to attack the hill at Hissarlik with the full protection of the Turkish government. Beside him as he worked was a Turkish official, Georgios Sarkis, "the eyes and ears of the government", to see that no treasure was taken from the earth without the Turkish government being aware of it.

Schliemann had brought only eight wheelbarrows from France, and accordingly he started work the first day with eight workmen. The next day, seeing that work was progressing rapidly, he employed thirty-five, and on the following day he employed seventy-four. He paid each workman nine piasters. The wages were paid out by Nicholas Zaphyros Jannakis, a colourful Greek who had entered Schliemann's service shortly after his marriage. Jannakis knew all the local dialects and acted as bodyguard, cook, cashier, and general factotum. Schliemann trusted him implicitly and always called him by his proper name, though it was his custom to give his other servants names out of Greek mythology.

The rains came, and they were still working. As usual, Schliemann was in a hurry; he hoped to uncover the whole of Priam's palace in six weeks. Even in the rain the workmen laboured from six in the morning to six at night. To speed matters, no one was allowed to smoke except during meals. Schliemann superintended the digging, cursing the rains and the interminable feast days which also held up operations.

Three weeks went by, and he wrote reports, but there was little to report: a few coins and calcined bones, huge walls, and some strange phallus-shaped objects which seemed to belong to a period long before the Homeric Age. Then on October 30, he began to dig up hundreds of lance heads of green stone, curious objects shaped like fiery mountains, and *phalloi* of hard black diorite, some striped with white. Among these were boars' tusks and boars' teeth. He thought of the heavy stone *phalloi* he had seen in the Indian temples, representing the male principle. Most puzzling of all were the terracotta shapes which resembled small spinning tops, sometimes with two holes bored into them, which he found at a depth of ten feet; and it occurred to him that the *carrousels* or tops represented the female principles.

It was the last thing he expected to find. Then he began to unearth little clay models which resembled owls, and it occurred to him that they might represent the owl sacred to Pallas Athena.

He had hoped to find treasure, the painted walls of a palace, perhaps a great funeral chamber; instead there were only these odd little objects. Fearing he had discovered nothing but relics from the Stone Age, too primitive to be of value, he wrote a discouraged letter to James Calvert, the brother of Frank Calvert, begging for advice. Calvert replied that the Greeks made no painted pottery until the seventh or sixth century B.C., and such abstract shapes had been found before. "You must not be discouraged by the supposition that you are working in a barbarous period," he wrote. "Go ahead!"

Schliemann continued to dig, and found obsidian knife blades so sharp they might have been used for razors, and small terracotta boatlike objects which reminded him of the canoes he had seen in India. Here and there he came upon clay tiles with swastikas cut into them. In the *Ramayana* the ships of King Rama bore the swastika on their prows. Perhaps all these objects derived from Vedic India. But there were also faint inscriptions which seemed to be Egyptian.

He went on working into November. The bitter north wind was by now sweeping across the plain of Troy. Huddled in his greatcoat and wearing a sun helmet, he superintended excavations until the last possible moment. But on November 24, after two days of violent storm, he abandoned all operations and returned to Athens, where he spent his enforced holiday rewriting his journal.

In spite of the *phalloi* and the *carrousels* he was still convinced that he had discovered the ancient city. In March 1872, just before setting out for his fourth expedition to Troy, he wrote, "I have an unshakable faith in Homer. If I succeed in bringing to light the palace of Priam, the Acropolis of ancient Troy, admirers of Homer will come in their hundreds of thousands to admire the sacred relics."

From his old firm, Schröder's, he received a present of sixty wheelbarrows and a large number of excellent spades and pickaxes. With his wife he returned to the Dardanelles at the end of March and resumed digging on April 5, employing around a hundred and twenty men every day. Three weeks after digging began, most of the workmen mutinied when he found them smoking and ordered them to stop. Worse still, the few who remained at work were stoned by the rest.

Schliemann spent the night rounding up replacements, so successfully that he had a hundred and twenty new workmen the next day. Work now started at five in the morning and ended at six in the evening. There were still no great discoveries. Occasionally Schliemann had moods of black despair, when he felt like a man committed to the task of honeycombing a mountain to no purpose.

In May there were more feast days. He attempted to bribe the workmen with higher wages, but they answered, "If we work, the saint will strike us." On those days he sometimes visited the workmen and prescribed remedies for their diseases. The local doctors were usually Greek priests, whose remedy was the bleeding cup. Schliemann especially detested the bleeding of children—one could always tell when children had been bled repeatedly because there were deep wrinkles around their lips. He thought the sovereign remedy was salt water, and wrote, "I prescribe sea bathing for almost all diseases."

One day a girl covered with ulcers was brought to him. Her left eye was ulcerated; she suffered from fits of coughing, and could hardly walk. His remedy was a dose of castor oil, frequent sea baths, and some simple exercises to expand her chest. Two weeks later, she made the three hours' journey from her village to Schliemann's camp at Hissarlik, threw herself at his feet, and kissed his shoes. She told him she had regained her appetite after her first bath in the sea. There was no hope for her left eye, but most of her ulcers were cured, and for years afterwards he liked to tell the story of the village girl who had been cured by sea water.

Summer came. The heat roared out of the sky, and the nights were thunderous with the croaking of frogs in the marshes. Small brown vipers, thin as whips and very dangerous, scuttled out of the ruins. Schliemann learned the villagers drank a concoction of snakeweed found on the Trojan plain, and for safety's sake followed their example.

But he was always taking risks. He cut deep trenches across the mound, and was surprised when the walls sometimes collapsed and his workmen were buried under the rubble—by a miracle no one was ever seriously injured. He climbed about the excavations like a monkey, laboured all day, and worked on his notes through the night.

Yet he knew nothing about scientific archaeology, a science which was then in its infancy. Émile Burnouf, the director of the French School of Archaeology at Athens, reprimanded him for carelessness. It was not enough to dig *phalloi* and *carrousels* and broken pieces of pottery out of the ground: the exact positions must be recorded, the date, the time, the circumstances, "or else you will never be able to come to definite conclusions on your wonderful discoveries". Schliemann obediently began to label everything, and came to realize at last that accurate records were almost the most important part of the excavation.

And still very little was coming to light. Huge walls, occasional marble slabs with long dedicatory texts, all very late, a few huge jars, and some delicate black pottery—this was almost the sum of his discoveries. Of King Priam, Hector, and of Paris there was no sign.

Suddenly on June 18, 1872, he discovered on a monument a relief of Apollo riding the four horses of the Sun. Though small, it was a brilliant work—the horses modelled lightly but with great skill and vigour, the god crowned with a spiked diadem with ten long rays and ten shorter ones, his hair flowing free. It was a late rendering, much later than Homer's Troy but Schliemann was immensely pleased with it and immediately set about smuggling it out of the country with the help of Frank Calvert, on whose part of the mound it was discovered. For years it graced the garden of Schliemann's house in Athens.

As summer advanced and still there was no sign of Homeric Troy, his moods of black despair returned. At enormous expense he had cleared a large terrace on the northern slope, and revealed a stone tower; but increasingly doubts entered his mind. For the first time he complained bitterly of sickness and the drain on his resources. There were dust storms for days on end, so that the workmen could hardly see, and in July came "the pestilential miasma", which in Schliemann's view arose from the decomposition of millions of dead frogs. He feared the snakes that fell from the rafters of the wooden house he had built for himself and Sophia on one of the cliffs of Hissarlik; he feared scorpions; he feared the workmen.

Sometimes he would wander off to a neighbouring village and forget his loneliness in conversation with a Greek shopkeeper, Constantine Colobos, who was born without feet, but who had learned Italian and French and could recite pages of the *Iliad* by heart. Then on August 4, when he was already suffering from marsh fever and was about to give up for the summer, he found his first treasure. It consisted of three gold earrings and a gold dress pin. Near by was a skeleton of a young woman. He was sure she had died during the burning of Troy. "The colour of the bones," he wrote, "leaves no doubt that the lady was burned alive."

Though he found some more *phalloi* and "a very pretty bird's egg made of fine marble", there were no more important discoveries. Suddenly there were thunderstorms and the whole mound seemed to turn to mud. He gave orders to abandon the excavations for the season, and with his wife he returned to Athens. He was a sick man. His three foremen, his bodyguard, and his wife were all suffering from fever.

In Athens he recovered his health. On January 31 he was back at Hissarlik with Sophia. The ice-cold north wind was blowing. He caught a cold. There were more thunderstorms and a plague of church festivals. By March, Schliemann was writing in his journal:

> March 15, 1873. The nights are cold, and the thermometer frequently falls to freezing point in the morning, but during the day the sun is beginning to be oppressively warm. The leaves are beginning to burst on the trees, and the Trojan plain is covered with spring flowers. For the last fortnight we have heard the croaking of millions of frogs in the surrounding marshes, and during the last eight days the storks have returned. The misery of life in this wilderness is increased by the innumerable owls who build their nests in the holes in the walls I have excavated: there is something mysterious and horrible in their screeching; it is unbearable, especially at night.

In April Schliemann was calmer. He seems to have had a premonition that he was close to a great discovery. On April 16 he found a paved street and nine enormous earthenware jars as tall as a man. Such jars had never come to light before, though similar jars would be found later in Knossos. In May he was hot on the trail. He uncovered two gates twenty feet apart, which he named the Scaean Gate, and the large building behind the gates he called Priam's Palace.

He was content. He had found what he had hoped to find. He announced that he was preparing to publish his discoveries—there would be two hundred plates and thirty-five hundred engravings. True, Hissarlik was a small mound, and people would say that Homer never envisaged a small city when he spoke of Troy; but the wide gate, the palace walls, the cyclopean breastworks, the innumerable pieces of black pottery, the great jars, and the thousands of artifacts proved that Schliemann had discovered the citadel of Troy.

Interrupting his joy, news came for Sophia that her father was dying. She hurried off to Athens, only to learn that he was already dead. From his house on the cliffs of Hissarlik, Schliemann wrote the gentlest of all his letters:

> Comfort yourself, my dearest, with the thought that after a short while we shall all join your wonderful father. . . .
>
> If you cannot master your grief, then come back to me by the first steamboat and I will do everything I can to assuage your grief. There can be no excavations without you.

He was lonely without her, and a few days later Sophia hurried back to him.

Summer was coming on, the spring flowers were dying, and soon the whole plain would have the burned-out black appearance which came with summer. Schliemann wrote to his son Sergei that he would bring the excavations to an end in the middle of June. He was pleased with his work; he had discovered the walls of Troy, excavated 250,000 metres of earth, and obtained enough antiquities to furnish a whole museum.

The letter to Sergei was written on May 30. On the same day

he wrote to Frank Calvert's brother Frederick, who had an estate at Thymbra near Bunarbashi, a letter of a different temper altogether. It was written in fear and trembling, and smuggled past the guards at night.

> I am closely watched, and expect that the Turkish watchman will search my house. I, therefore, take the liberty to deposit with you 6 baskets and a bag, begging you will kindly lock them up, and not allow by any means the Turks to touch them.

In the six baskets and the bag was the golden treasure of Troy.

In his published writings Schliemann never revealed the exact date on which the treasure was discovered. We know the hour and the place—it was about seven in the morning, and the place was a deep cut below the circuit wall close to Priam's Palace. He may have discovered the treasure on May 30, or a few days earlier. Certainly by May 31 they were out of his possession and safely in the hands of Frederick Calvert.

From three separate accounts written by him at different times it is possible to piece together the story. It was one of those hot May days, with the whole plain smoking with bright yellow dust. Eight days previously he had discovered a large silver vase with a small silver beaker inside it. Not far away he had found a copper helmet.

He was sure there must be more treasure near by. Accordingly, he divided his workmen into many groups, and by scattering them through long trenches and corridors which honeycombed the mound he felt sure that if he discovered any large cache he would be able to smuggle it unobserved to his own house. In particular, he was anxious that the Turkish representative now on the scene, a man called Amin Effendi, should not be present.

Schliemann, his wife, and a handful of workmen were digging along the circuit wall close to the Scaean Gate when Schliemann suddenly noticed at a depth of twenty-eight feet "a container or implement of copper of remarkable design." Peering through the dust and rubble, he was able to make out that the container was about three feet long and eighteen inches high, and that there were two helmet-shaped objects on top of it, and something which resembled a large candlestick. The container was broken, and he could see some silver vessels inside it. Above all this were some reddish and brown calcined ruins from four to five feet thick, as hard as stone, and above this again were the huge fortification walls, five feet broad and twenty feet high.

None of the workmen had noticed it. He turned to Sophia, beside him, and said, "You must go at once and shout '*Paidos!*'"

Paidos was a word meaning rest period. Sophia had not yet seen the treasure, and was amazed at the thought of ordering a rest period so early.

"Now, at seven o'clock?" she asked.

"Yes—now! Tell them it is my birthday, and I have only just remembered it! Tell them they will get their wages today without working. See that they go to their villages. Hurry!"

It was Sophia's task to call out the rest periods and so she climbed up a rickety ladder. Soon the workmen were drifting away, pleased at the unexpected holiday, and a little troubled, because there had been no such holidays before. Amin Effendi was especially puzzled, because he was usually well informed about holidays.

When Sophia returned, all the workmen had gone and Schliemann was attempting to dig the treasure out with a pocket knife. The fortification wall, composed of earth, rubble, and heavy stones, was threatening to fall. He turned again to Sophia and said, "Quick, bring me your big shawl!"

Once again Sophia had to make the journey up the stepladder to the upper platform and to the house. She returned with an enormous scarlet shawl, heavily embroidered, such as Greek women wear on feast days. The treasure was poured into the shawl, and together they carried it back to the house.

As soon as the door was locked, the treasure was spread out on the rough wooden table. Many of the pieces had been packed into one another. Such treasures gleam behind glass cases in museums, pale yellow, with a curious lifelessness, but when they were found they had a wonderful glowing reddish colour. The treasure consisted of a copper shield, a copper cauldron, a silver vase and another of copper, a gold bottle, two gold cups, a gold sauceboat, and a small cup of silver and gold alloy. There were three great

TROY

Troy as it looks today. Below right, Schliemann's house at the excavation site

Sophia Schliemann wearing the golden ornaments of Troy

Gold ornamental jewelry

Terra-cotta mask

Gold hanging ornaments

Earthenware vase

Earthenware container

Gold cup and two beakers found among "Priam's treasure"

Terra-cotta figure of a woman

Gold necklace

silver vases, a silver goblet, seven double-edged copper daggers, six silver knife blades, and thirteen copper lance heads. At the bottom of the largest silver vase there were two gold diadems, a fillet, four gold eardrops, fifty-six gold earrings and 8750 gold rings and buttons, most of them very small.

The most astonishing were the diadems, one of them consisting of ninety chains forming an elaborate gold headdress, with leaf and flower pendants and long tassels hanging down at the sides. Persian and Roman diadems were simply jewelled bands worn around the head; the Trojan diadems were formed of innumerable gold rings entirely covering the forehead. Nothing like them had been seen before and none has been discovered since.

Trembling with excitement, Schliemann placed them on Sophia's forehead. To the end of his life he seems to have thought they were the diadems of a queen, though they are more likely to have been those of a king. He heaped necklaces around her neck and put the gold rings on her fingers, until she shone with barbaric splendour. At last, after so many years, the obscure son of a Mecklenburg clergyman was standing in the place of kings before a woman arrayed like a queen.

He was sure he had found the treasure of King Priam, hidden secretly in the wall when Troy was in flames.

Much was, and remains mysterious about the finds. The gold vessels were of superb workmanship, but the tiaras, wonderfully impressive at first sight, proved to be of primitive workmanship, built up with coils of wire and thin gold sheeting. None of the rings was engraved. The beautifully modelled gold sauceboat was a masterpiece of design, but why should it have been found among knife blades and arrowheads? There were some crudely carved ivory and shaft-hole hammer axes of semiprecious stone, and also a little lead figurine of a woman. Idol worship and barbarism went hand in hand with artistic refinement. Was this the Troy of Homer or of some earlier, more barbaric age?

Schliemann had not completely succeeded in hiding his discovery. Rumours were flying across the Trojan plain. Amin Effendi called at his house, and said angrily he was sure something was being kept from him. The watchman ordered Schliemann in the name of the sultan to open all his chests, even the wardrobes. Schliemann's only reply was to throw him out.

That night the treasure was taken to Frederick Calvert's house at Thymbra and a few days later smuggled out of the country.

For a few more days Schliemann peered and probed at the foot of the wall, but no more treasure was discovered. On June 19 he was in Athens. He was on fire with enthusiasm and excitement. While he was writing to all the learned societies in Europe that he had discovered the treasure—the letters sometimes read like proclamations—he was busily arranging to bury the treasure in the earth. Sophia's relatives were brought into the conspiracy. All over Greece strange objects wrapped in straw were being concealed in barns and farmyards. A wickerwork basket was dispatched to an uncle living in Eleusis. Neither the Greek nor the Turkish governments would be able to lay hands on it. Some weeks later a trusted servant was sent to tell Sophia by word of mouth where each object had been buried.

Schliemann was caught on the horns of a dilemma. He wanted fame, which is impermanent, and the treasure, which was the most permanent of all things. He let it be known that he possessed the treasure and would give it to Greece, but they must give him full permission to excavate at Mycenae and Olympia. They refused his offer, apparently because they were afraid of trouble with Turkey.

Through the autumn and early winter Schliemann completed another book, consisting largely of his Trojan journals interspersed with photographs. With the book finished, he began to investigate Mycenae as his next project for digging. Then in April the Turks instituted proceedings against him for half of the treasure. He had to remain in Athens.

The trial lasted a year. By court order, policemen came to his house and searched for the treasure, and found no trace of it. He refused to say where it was hidden. During that strange year he quarrelled with everyone. He quarrelled with the police, who dogged his footsteps. He quarrelled with his own lawyers. He quarrelled with the Greek government and he quarrelled with his critics. Finally, to placate the government and to put himself in good standing with the Athenians, he offered to remove at his own expense the Venetian Tower, erected in the Middle Ages on the Acropolis. No one liked it. Built of marble, it was eighty feet high; it spoiled the view, and now the owls had nests in it. The Greek government accepted his offer. Then for many days he stood on the Acropolis, himself superintending the destruction of the old tower.

At last the long trial came to an end. Schliemann had played his cards skillfully. He had refused to say where the treasure was hidden, to answer the questions of the prosecutor, to make a settlement. The Greek judges found in favour of the Turks and ordered him to pay an indemnity of fifty thousand francs. Since he valued the treasure of Priam at a million francs, he had in effect won the trial. As a gesture of friendship he sent five times the amount to the Imperial Museum at Constantinople.

Having won his victory, he was in a mood to enjoy his growing fame. Gladstone had written him an affectionate letter of greeting, and his warmest admirers were in England. Accordingly he set out for England in the summer of 1875, taking Sophia and their daughter, Andromache, with him. In London he was lionized. All through July he was wined and dined in the best circles. Gladstone eulogized him. The Queen of Holland invited him to The Hague. There was a reception in his honour, attended by all the dignitaries of the kingdom. For long hours he pored over the Egyptian objects in the Leyden Museum in the Queen's company. The Queen spoke seven languages fluently. He wrote:

> Her Majesty is always inviting me for breakfast, lunch and dinner. I believe I could even persuade her to do some excavations in Asia Minor, the Greek Archipelago or in Italy.

By April 1876 he was engrossed in the thought of excavating Mycenae. Long ago he had stated his belief that there were royal graves there, dating from the heroic age, inside the citadel wall. He had discovered all he could reasonably hope to discover at Hissarlik. There remained Mycenae, to which the victorious Agamemnon returned after the sack of Troy, only to be murdered himself by his wife Clytemnestra and her lover Aegisthus. For the Greeks both Mycenae and Troy were equally sacred, haunted by the presence of great heroes. Having uncovered Troy, Schliemann was simply following the logical path when he turned his attention to Mycenae. Already he possessed the ashes of Odysseus and the treasure of Priam; the discovery of the royal graves at Mycenae would crown his career.

7. The Golden Masks

As soon as a favourable opportunity occurred, Schliemann sent a memorandum to the Greek government, offering to dig at Mycenae at his own expense, giving everything he found to the government, reserving for himself only the right to report and describe his finds. The minister of public instruction solemnly signed the agreement.

In Schliemann's day the traveller approaching Mycenae in summer saw the plain of Argos all yellow and white with stubble and dust, and the once great fortress city was no more than a rubble of stones on one of the foothills, guarding the pass between two mountains nearly twenty-five hundred feet high. These blue and barren mountains, ponderous, sharp-edged, had something threatening about them, with power in their heavy outcrops and huge shoulders. Today the mountains still threaten and wolves still howl in the foothills, but much has changed. There are good roads through the plain, orchards flower between tobacco and cotton fields, and there is barley in the foothills.

Mycenae commands all approaches and is an ideal site for a city dominating the plain of Argos. It appears to have been inhabited from prehistoric times. Here, about 1700 B.C., a powerful king built gigantic ramparts around an early Bronze Age city and erected a new palace. Homer knew of it as the city of Agamemnon, son of Atreus. No one knows the name of the king or where he came from. The entrance to the city was a paved highway flanked by two bastions. Deep within the bastions there stood, and still stands, a great Lion Gate, once closed by a double wooden door, with an enormous lintel crowned by a relief of two lionesses face-to-face. Once through the Lion Gate and beyond the walls, which are sixteen feet thick, the visitor comes upon a circular terrace. In Schliemann's day this was covered with the detritus of the ages, and beyond this lay the tumbled ruins of palaces and private houses. On the slopes of the ridges and in the surrounding valley lay the ruins of the lower city.

In Troy Schliemann had found the treasure near the main gate leading into the city. He had the feeling that at Mycenae, too, he would find the treasure near the main gate. He had few clues to work on. The most authoritative statement about the tombs of the heroes was made by the historian Pausanias in the second century A.D.

> In the ruins of Mycenae are the underground buildings of Atreus and his sons, where their treasure is buried. There is the tomb of Atreus and there are also tombs of those whom Aegisthus murdered on their return from Troy after entertaining them at a banquet. There is the tomb of Agamemnon. . . . Clytemnestra and Aegisthus were buried a little outside the wall, because they were thought unworthy of burial within it, where Agamemnon lies and those who were killed together with him.

Schliemann, who had read all the available books and plays about Mycenae, learned these words by heart. When Pausanias wrote, thirteen hundred years had passed since the fall of Troy, but the more Schliemann pondered Pausanias' words the more he became convinced that previous commentators were in error. According to them, the tomb of Clytemnestra lay outside the city walls, while the tombs and Agamemnon and those who died with him lay inside. But it occurred to Schliemann that even in the time of Pausanias the city walls had been reduced to rubble. He argued that Pausanias meant that the tomb of Agamemnon was to be found inside the walls of the Acropolis, not the city walls which could be traced across the surrounding countryside. With this belief, he set to work in August 1876 with sixty-three workmen in the neighbourhood of the Lion Gate. He was not allowed to work alone. Three officials from the Greek Archaeological Society watched every move.

Beyond the gate huge stones blocked the passageway. Schliemann set his workmen to removing the stones. As usual, he had divided the men into groups and hoped to confuse the officials by working on several projects at once. The heat was relentless and huge clouds of dust poured over the ruined city.

As the work went on, and Schliemann threatened to level more walls, the officials objected to his high-handed operations. Stamatakes, the chief representative of the Greek Archaeological Society on the spot, wrote to Athens, "He is eagerly demolishing everything Roman and Greek in sight." He spoke of the unbelievable rudeness of Schliemann, his obstinacy, his cunning, his devilish habit of making life insufferable for everyone.

There were brief reconciliations between Stamatakes and Schliemann, but in general they were at each other's throats. Whenever the air grew thick with threats and counterthreats, Sophia would watch her opportunity and then speak a few calming words. In the body of this girl there was the mind of a mature woman. Schliemann, who rarely gave credit to others, was unstinting in his admiration of her.

Nothing of great moment was being discovered. Curiously, they found no Roman or Byzantine coins like those found at Troy. But they did find splendid archaic vases painted with geometric patterns, and terracotta goblets bearing a strange resemblance to Bordeaux wineglasses. There were the usual clay figurines of goddesses painted bright red. There were knives, buttons, clay animals, arrowheads, combs, needles, and hundreds of *carrousels* made of a beautiful blue stone. There were millstones and hatchets, and pieces of bone which Schliemann believed to be parts of musical instruments.

At last in the fifth week the workmen digging within the great circular space south of the Lion Gate came upon two tombstones, each about four feet high, made of sandstone and bearing designs in relief in a technique resembling primitive wood carving. One showed a hunter in a chariot pursuing deer with a hunting dog running beside the chariot wheels. The other showed another chariot with the horse led by a naked soldier armed with a broadsword.

Schliemann thought he saw some resemblance between the style of carving on the tombstones and the style of the famous lions on the Lion Gate. The tails of the horses, dog, and deer were unusually thick and long. Though the chariots were only briefly sketched in, he came to the conclusion that they faithfully reflected the chariots used in the time of the Trojan War. Another important discovery was a solitary gold button. Schliemann felt he was hot on the scent.

As he continued to work there, all around the circle he discovered stone slabs arranged to form a nearly continuous ring of benches. This suggested that the circle represented the open-air meeting place where the nobility would be summoned by heralds to listen to proclamations; and perhaps too it served as a dance floor and a place where the poets celebrated their kings. Orators would stand there; prizes would be given; and the sacred symbols of power would be periodically shown to the people.

Such a place was called the *agora,* and though holy, was used as a marketplace. Euripedes in the *Electra* speaks of the people of Mycenae being called "to the agora to see the wonderful lamb with the golden fleece", the golden lamb being a symbol of royalty. Pausanias said that heroic tombs were within the agora of Megara. Pindar, too, speaks of heroes being buried in the agora on the island of Thera. Schliemann believed that the tombs of the heroes would be found within that ring of stone.

For some reason which he never made clear, he did not at once begin to excavate within the circle. South of the circle lay a gigantic house with seven large windowless rooms; and thinking this was the royal palace, he decided to excavate here. The great discovery in this place was a vase some twelve inches high, on which an ancient artist had depicted a lively procession of soldiers marching off to war. They are painted dark red on a yellow ground. Here for the first time we see the equipment of the soldiers who fought in the wars before Troy. They march out of an ancient past, but they have a curious air of modernity. They wear horned helmets with plumes fluttering from the crests, they carry long spears to which wine bottles are attached, and heavy semicircular shields. The Homeric heroes wore a garb similar to theirs. But Schliemann was puzzled by the horns on the helmets. "There is no word in Homer," he wrote, "to explain their existence on a Homeric helmet." For once he was caught napping: Homer refers to them in the third book of the *Iliad* in the description of the duel between Menelaus and Paris: "Menelaus drew his silver-mounted sword, swung it backward, brought it down on the horn of the enemy's helmet, and then the sword broke into pieces and dropped from his hand."

The soldiers on the vase march away from a slim-waisted woman waving to them from the left. Even their long noses, large eyes, and neat beards are what we might expect. These soldiers are related to those who fought hundreds of years later against the Persians, and they march with the same dancing step. In the most extraordinary way this broken vase illustrates the ancient history of Greece.

So the months passed, and with about a hundred and twenty-five workmen Schliemann continued to work from morning to dusk under the scorching sun. Clouds of hot dust roared across Mycenae. His eyes were inflamed, his temper was short. Visitors came. The Emperor of Brazil, Dom Pedro II, rode up from Corinth to examine the excavations. Schliemann was delighted to have so distinguished a visitor, and gave him a great dinner in the underground tomb called the Treasury of Atreus. Handsome, sceptical and unassuming, the emperor astonished Schliemann by his knowledge of archaeology, praised him highly, and spoke of "the invaluable contributions you are making to the understanding of ancient civilizations".

Summer came to an end and the rains came beating down on the agora, turning the rubble into mud. At last, about the middle of October, Schliemann started digging in the agora towards the centre of the circle. At a depth of fifteen feet he reached a layer of pebbles. Below this lay three bodies thickly covered with clay and what seemed to be the ashes of a funeral pyre. Through the clay came the glint of gold.

With the government officials peering over his shoulder, Schliemann was too nervous to uncover the bones himself. Sophia curled down in the hollow and stripped the clay off the bodies with a small pocketknife.

Five golden crosses with the arms shaped like laurel leaves lay on one body, five on the second, and four on the third. With each body also were five golden diadems. The diadems were made from thin sheets of gold hammered with decorative circles and bosses.

Where the diadems of Troy showed extreme sophistication, the Mycenaean diadems had a simplicity which suggested the raw nakedness of power.

Scattered about the shaft grave were small obsidian knives, fragments of painted vases, and a silver cup. Schliemann thought the pebbles at the bottom of the tomb somehow provided ventilation for the funeral pyres, and it was his belief that it was the Mycenaean custom to roast the flesh off the bones. The skeletons had suffered from moisture and soon crumbled. The treasure of Mycenae so far consisted of fifteen diadems and fourteen golden crosses.

Schliemann now decided to explore the side of the grave circle farthest away from the Lion Gate. At a depth of nine feet he found some skeletons, but there was no treasure. He went on digging. Only a little way below the skeletons, he came upon a third grave, a whole chamber crammed with objects which shone with a reddish lustre.

Most of the workmen were sent away and a ring of soldiers was placed on guard. Once more Sophia curled herself among the skeletons and the gold, carefully removing the soil which still covered the royal tombs. She worked slowly, afraid of destroying the delicately chased patterns on the thin sheets of gold. There were three bodies; one of them wore a gold crown with more than thirty gold leaves surmounting it. These leaves were lightly fixed to the crown, and they must have trembled and shimmered when the king wore it.

There were eight more diadems, and six more crosses of gold, some of them double crosses and very ornate. There were gold necklaces and goblets and vases and wine jars, some with golden lids attached by fine gold wires. There was a golden flower on a silver stalk. There were shining spheres of rock crystal which may have been the pommels of royal swords.

But the most surprising discovery was an enormous number of stamped golden discs—Schliemann counted more than seven hundred of them in this tomb chamber alone. Some were shaped like leaves, others like butterflies, octopuses, stars, and sunflowers, and there were some with purely geometrical designs. Schliemann came to the conclusion that they were miniature copies of shields, but it is more likely that they were symbols of the enduring life which the dead were expected to lead throughout their underground existence.

Together with the gold discs were a large number of gold plaques, rarely more than an inch across and not unlike the miniature gold plaques which have been found during excavations in Persia dating from the time of Cyrus and Xerxes. With extraordinary liveliness the artist had modelled a strip of gold foil into the shape of lions, griffins, cuttlefish, deer, eagles, and swans. These, too, were perhaps ornaments sewed onto the robes of the dead.

Schliemann thought he had found in this third grave three skeletons of women, and he pointed to the smallness of the bones and of the teeth, but it is just as likely that they were a king and two princes arrayed in their panoply. A dagger was found among the bones, and two sceptres of silver plated with gold.

With the third grave opened, Schliemann set about excavating the rest of the agora. He remembered being struck by the appearance of the soil to the west of the third grave. The soil was almost black, markedly different from the soil elsewhere in the agora. Twenty-four feet down he discovered what he thought to be a circular altar four feet high with a round opening, reminiscent of a well. He felt sure it was an altar raised in honour of the heroes who must be buried below, and perhaps gifts were poured through this altar for the dead. The royal graves of Sumeria have clay funnels through which offerings were poured, but they had not been excavated in Schliemann's time and as usual he was relying on his own guesses. His guess was right. Three feet below the altar he found five bodies smothered in gold and jewels. Three of them wore masks of gold, and near the head of the fourth lay a strange twisted mask in the shape of a lion's head.

Of these four masks one was so crumpled that it had almost lost the shape of human features. By gazing at it for some minutes, Schliemann thought he could make out a youthful face with a high forehead, a long Greek nose, and a small mouth with thin lips. This mask possesses no character. But two of these golden masks possess power and authority, and a terrible beauty.

Death is marked on them, but there is no hint of repose in those awesome features.

Schliemann thought they were portraits, representing the likenesses of the deceased. But if they are portraits they are reduced almost to abstractions. In one, the hollowness of death is conveyed by two bulbous eyes which appear to be bursting out of the face, and in the other the heavily ridged forehead and the tightness of the lips suggest the agony of death. Like the gold masks of Peru, which are extraordinarily similar, they represent portraits of death, moulded by an artist who has transferred to a thin sheet of gold his own terror before the sight of a decaying corpse. An unearthly beauty shines through the masks. It seems to have been the artist's intention to suggest the divinity in the dead rulers, who carried into the grave the mysterious power they exercised during their lives. These masks can be interpreted as portraits of kings at the moment of dissolution when they became gods.

One looks at these masks with awe and a sense of failure. All through Western history artists have grappled with death and attempted to depict it, but rarely with the success of these unknown artists at Mycenae. Here, at the very beginning of our civilization, death is depicted with power and simplicity.

Yet no one knows the precise purpose served by these masks. No Greek writer refers to death masks of any kind. We simply know that they were wrapped around the faces of the dead, and held in place with threads.

When Schliemann first discovered the lion mask, it was flat and broken. He made out the lion's eyes, ears, and muzzle, and pronounced that it was a mask and therefore worn over the face. It is possible that the lion mask was a helmet.

In the fourth grave the masks formed only a small part of the wealth of treasure. Two of the bodies wore golden breastplates, another wore a crown with dancing leaves, and there were eleven massive gold goblets. There were ornamental golden belts and ribbons, a gold garter, a gold tiara, golden brooches, and golden pins. There were minute double-headed battle-axes in gold less than an inch across. There were twelve enormous buttons covered with gold plate, and more than four hundred round pieces of gold which may have been coins, and more than a hundred and fifty gold discs. There was a lively cuttlefish in gold. There were ten golden plates which may have served as sword handles. There were copper cauldrons, and bronze swords like rapiers, very narrow. There was a cow's head of silver with flaring horns of gold which must have been a sacred emblem of the tribe.

The fourth shaft grave at Mycenae contained more treasure than he had discovered at Troy, but Schliemann was in no mood to stop. He began to dig directly north of it. Here he found the fifth and last grave, but it gave every evidence of having been rifled. After that he spent his last days at Mycenae carefully re-examining the first tomb. By digging farther he found three bodies within the inner walls. Two wore gold masks, and one of these still had flesh adhering to the skull. Squashed flat by the weight of debris, and without a nose, it still possessed recognizable features, and Schliemann was excited beyond measure because he thought he recognized the face of Agamemnon.

It was the round face of a man about thirty-five years old, who retained all his teeth in a perfect state of preservation. He wore a large gold breastplate, and golden leaves distributed over his forehead, chest, and thighs. A golden mask lay over the face. Schliemann raised the mask to his lips and kissed it.

From all over the plain of Argos people came to view the body of an ancient hero whose face was so miraculously preserved. For two days Schliemann watched over it in a fever of anxiety, afraid lest the face would crumble into powder before it could be embalmed. Then a druggist summoned from Argos arrived. He poured a solution over it which rendered it hard, and shortly afterwards the body was taken in triumph to Athens.

The masks in that tomb were almost the last thing Schliemann discovered at Mycenae, and one of them possesses a perfection lacking in the others. This mask shows the hero at the moment after he has become a god. There is no trace of earth's fevers, only of benignity. The large eyes are closed, the eyelids clearly marked, and the thin lips are pursed in a mysterious smile. There is a hint of a beard, and the eyebrows are heavily incised and curl upward in imitation of the flaring moustaches; the total effect of eyebrows and moustaches and smile is to give a curious depth to the face. It is a face to be compared with the great mosaics of Christ at Daphne, Cefalù, and Palermo, and belongs among the most superb achievements of ancient art.

Now the work was done and Schliemann gazed around the agora, which had come to resemble a crumbled honeycomb. Towards the end of November he sent off a telegram to the King of the Hellenes:

> With extreme joy I announce to Your Majesty that I have discovered the tombs which tradition, echoed by Pausanias, has designated as the sepulchres of Agamemnon and his companions. In the tombs I found immense treasures of the most ancient objects of pure gold. . . . I work only for the pure love of science. I give them intact to Greece. . . .
>
> I have gazed upon the face of Agamemnon.

For the first time Schliemann returned from his excavations empty-handed. He spent the winter in Athens. One day in January he sent one of the assistants he had employed at Mycenae to make a detailed drawing of the agora for his records. This assistant, a young engineer named Vasilios Drosinos, recognized near a partly excavated house south of the agora some roughly carved stones which resembled the stones in the tomb chamber. A workman with a pickaxe was brought to the spot. In less than half an hour he had dug up a small treasure consisting of four gold cups, all of them with delicate dog's-head handles, a number of rings fashioned out of gold wire, and two gold signets. One of these signets was a masterpiece. We know it now as the Signet of the Mother Goddess, and like the gold mask found in the first tomb it hints at an unexpected depth of religious feeling among the Mycenaeans. A ceremony is being performed. The goddess sits beneath the sacred tree, receiving a tribute of flowers from two women of noble aspect, who may be priestesses. All wear the flounced richly embroidered double skirts which were characteristic of Mycenaean culture during the heroic age. Like the Mother Goddess they are bare-breasted.

Between the first of the worshippers and the goddess stand two double axes, the smaller superimposed upon the other; these axes perhaps represent earthly and spiritual power. And

MYCENAE

A contemporary view of the royal tombs of Mycenae. Below left, archaeologists at the Lion Gate, 1890

Plan of the
OPOLIS OF MYCENAE
WITH THE EXCAVATIONS
made by
Dr HENRY SCHLIEMANN
by Vasilios Drosinos
Lieutenant of Engineers

Metres

English Feet

SUMMIT OF THE ACROPOLIS

Cyclopean Circuit Wall

Gold "Cup of Nestor"

Knife of silver, gold, and black enamel

Goid necklace

Stemmed cup with running lion

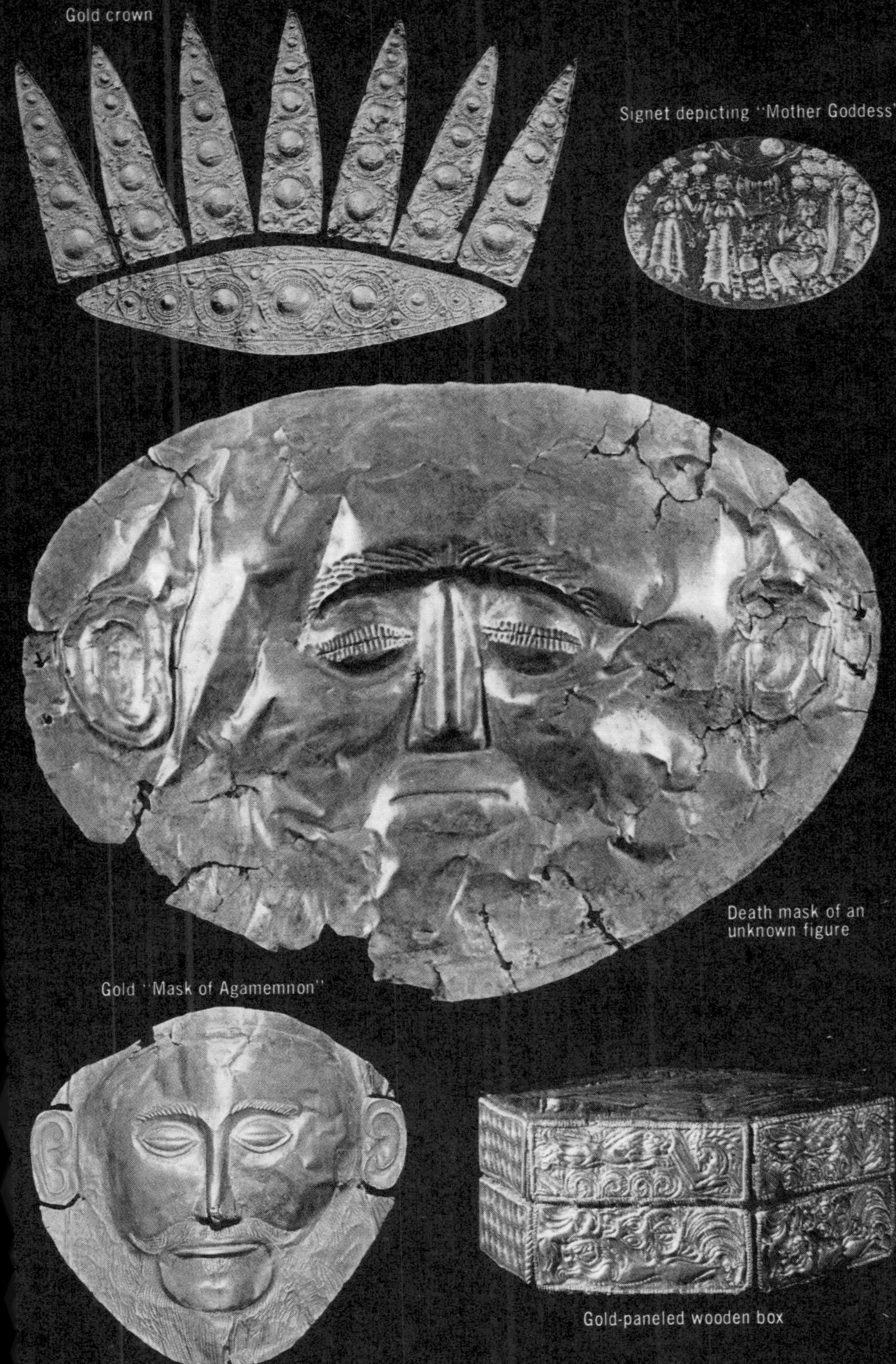

Gold crown

Signet depicting "Mother Goddess"

Death mask of an unknown figure

Gold "Mask of Agamemnon"

Gold-paneled wooden box

beyond this strange emblem there floats a presiding genius who is helmeted and holds a spear. Above this scene the sun shines in full splendour beside the crescent moon: it is at once noonday and the depth of night. But what is most remarkable about the signet is the serenity of these people. Such a signet could not have been carved except at a time of great self-assurance. Into the signet, hardly more than an inch across, the artist has poured the accumulated knowledge of centuries of religious meditation. The priestesses make their offerings out of affection for the goddess, with none of the servitude which can be seen in Egyptian paintings. Bathed in the light of the sun and moon, they stand and move according to their own volition.

In the *Iliad* Homer describes how Hephaestus made for Achilles a great shield with five panels, the first representing "the earth, the sky and the sea, the indefatigable sun, the moon at the full and all the constellations", and when Schliemann first saw the signet, he exclaimed to Sophia, "It must have been seen by Homer when he described all the wonders which Hephaestus wrought on the shield of Achilles."

Schliemann never returned to Mycenae, feeling that his work was done. He wrote a book about his finds in eight weeks. Gladstone, an excellent Homeric scholar, wrote an introduction to the work. During the summer Schliemann exhibited the treasure of Troy in the South Kensington Museum in London. When the members of the Royal Archaeological Society asked Sophia to address them, she came post-haste from Athens and stood beside her husband on the platform, telling how for twenty-five days she had knelt among the tombs, carefully scraping off thin layers of clay from the bodies of the ancient kings and queens of Mycenae. She spoke very simply in English, and received an ovation. Schliemann had written her speech, and was particularly delighted because she was carrying his child, a boy born later that year. Long ago he had chosen a name for his son—Agamemnon.

For eighteen months Schliemann basked in his growing fame, and it was not until July of 1878 that he put a spade into the earth again. Still looking for treasure, he thought he might find it in Ithaca in the great palace of Odysseus. He spent two weeks excavating among the walls at the top of Mount Aetos, but though he found the ruins of a hundred and ninety houses, he found little else of value and abandoned the excavations.

Troy summoned him again. It was his sixth journey there, and his luck held. On October 21, 1878, in the presence of some officers from a British warship, he discovered, northeast of the palace of Priam, not far from the place where he had found the first Trojan treasure, a small hoard of earrings, rings, bracelets, and beads. A few days later he found gold bars and pellets of gold, a gold bracelet, and a silver dagger. Schliemann was allowed to keep a third of the treasure; the rest went to the Imperial Museum in Constantinople.

Homer had mentioned that there were three towns rich in gold —Troy, Mycenae, and Orchomenus, once a great city in Boeotia. The following year Schliemann hoped to crown his achievements with the gold treasure of Orchomenus, but though he excavated the beehive tombs and mapped the walls of the ancient city, the results were disappointing. The years of luck were over. He had the eagerness of a child and the passion of an adolescent, but he was growing old. He must find roots somewhere, and so at last he decided to build a house in the heart of Athens.

Characteristically, he designed the house himself on the model of the palaces he had uncovered in Troy and Mycenae. He called it *Iliou Melathron,* or "the Palace of Troy". It stands on the Boulevard de l'Université at the foot of Mount Lycabettus. It is a huge house, cold and chilling, with marble steps and mosaic floors on which are depicted the gold cups and vases he discovered at Troy. Along the walls run friezes of Greek heroes.

On the lower floors he displayed his treasure. Upstairs was his study, with the notice on the door: ALL WHO DO NOT STUDY GEOMETRY, REMAIN OUTSIDE. The study was crammed with books. Here were some of the more precious objects he had gathered. On the walls were fading views of New York and Indianapolis, two cities which he especially admired. For whole days he would sit there in a heavily upholstered armchair studying the Greek classics, while the smaller chair beside him was piled high with the stock exchange lists which came every morning from Paris, London, and Berlin. Telegraph forms were always at hand for his financial dealings, for he was still a businessman.

In his house he behaved as tyrannically as any Homeric prince. His word was law. All messages were sent to him in classical Greek, and Greek was the language employed exclusively at table. He renamed all his servants. The porter was Bellerophon, the footman Telamon, his son Agamemnon's nurse was Polyxena, and the old gardener was called Calchas, after the soothsayer whose curses open the *Iliad.* Because the ancient Greeks employed little furniture, he did the same. He refused to have curtains, because it was unthinkable that Achilles would ever have stayed in a curtained house.

On the flat roof of the house, facing the four corners of the sky, were twenty-four marble gods. Zeus, Aphrodite, Apollo, Athena, and all the other gods stood there, protecting him during the declining years of his life.

8. The Last Years

During his last thirty-four years Schliemann read the *Iliad* avidly. It was his bible, the fountainhead of nearly all the thoughts that ever occurred to him. In his library were all the available editions, many in folio and bound in heavy morocco, but there were also cheap paperbound editions which he carried on his travels and annotated heavily. Both the *Iliad* and the *Odyssey* to him were holy texts, written with a nobility and elegance almost beyond the range of human accomplishment. In these books, he felt, a man could find all the fruitfulness and joy and all the tragedy of man displayed. In them was the perfect story told by the perfect poet.

Like nearly all the great epics, like the *Aeneid, Beowulf, The Song of Roland,* and *Paradise Lost,* the *Iliad* is the story of a defeat endured heroically in an evil time. To the gods, what is ultimate and significant is man's raw courage, the majesty he wraps around himself as he treads the path of danger. Homer, composing in old age some two hundred years after the events he described, wandered from town to town playing on his lyre, and the same stories were told by his disciples; and in time they were written down. Generations passed; the stories changed a little, but the unquenchable voice was so eloquent that the shapes and colours of an entire civilization were carried with it. Gradually the civilization that Homer portrayed, so rich, so beautiful, so filled with sensuous majesty, came to wear the aspect of a dream. Then Schliemann came along and staggered the world by showing that it was a waking dream: it had all happened in the sunlight of the Ionian seas.

AS THE YEARS PASSED Schliemann showed little sign of change. He still spoke in a gruff, clipped voice and carried himself like a man afraid of unbending. All his life he had maintained a vast correspondence, writing his letters and books while standing at a high desk; and he had never employed a secretary. He still saw no reason for employing a secretary, and he continued to write his letters in longhand, jumping from one language to another according to his mood.

His wealth increased. He kept a close watch on the stock market and the property he owned in Paris and Athens; he confessed that if a house stood empty, it cost him sleepless nights. He was recognizably the same man who had been washed ashore on the island of Texel with a burning ambition to make good. He was always in a hurry, always restless. In summer he would rise at three in the morning and ride to Phaleron Bay for a bathe, taking his wife with him. He still thought that salt water cured all the ills of the flesh. He did not know that his constant bathing was slowly killing him. In November 1877 he complained for the first time of deafness and illness. Sea water entering his ears caused inflammations and burning headaches. For the remaining thirteen years of his life he suffered intermittently from earaches and headaches, and sometimes he looked like a man frozen with horror at the thought of the pain he had to bear.

In *Ilios*, which he published in 1879, he presented a complete account of his excavations at Hissarlik, correcting some of his earlier theories. But there were problems which still troubled him. He calculated that this city on a mound could have held only five thousand inhabitants with an army of five hundred soldiers. Then where were the sixty-two vast and palatial rooms described by Homer? To the end of his life he was to return again and again to Hissarlik, continuing his excavations there in the hope that some fragment of ancient writing or another hoard of treasure would prove beyond doubt that Hissarlik was Homer's Troy.

But the problem which chiefly occupied his attention was the disposal of his Trojan treasure. At various times he had thought of offering it to Greece, Italy, France, and England. In the end it went to Berlin, and all because a friend plucked a sprig of blackthorn and presented it to him.

Schliemann had a friend, Rudolf Virchow, the famous German pathologist. Virchow was everything that Schliemann was not—calm, methodical, tactful. Schliemann cherished his friendship and often asked his advice on different matters.

In the spring of 1879, during a pause in digging at Hissarlik, Schliemann had suggested an excursion to the foothills of Mount Ida. Virchow was delighted to accept. Schliemann was unusually silent, and when the two men were resting in the shade of a blackthorn tree, Virchow asked him what was the matter. Schliemann mentioned that he was preoccupied with the thought of what would happen to the treasure of Troy after his death. Suddenly Virchow plucked a sprig of flowering blackthorn, handed it to Schliemann and said quietly, "A nosegay from Ankershagen!"

Virchow could never afterwards understand why he said these words. He observed the sudden change in his friend's features: it was as though a great weight had fallen from him at the mention of his childhood home.

"Yes, a nosegay from Ankershagen," Schliemann said, and they both knew that a decision had been made to give the treasure to Germany. Some hours later, when they were returning from the excursion, Virchow said casually, "With your permission, I shall speak to Prince Bismarck about it."

Schliemann nodded. The answer to the question which had plagued him was suddenly revealed.

All through the summer and autumn Virchow worked quietly at the task. Prince Bismarck, the German chancellor, was on fire with the idea of having the treasure on permanent exhibition in

Berlin and was prepared to go to extreme lengths to honour its discoverer. "What honour does Dr. Schliemann want?" Prince Bismarck asked. Privately, to Virchow, Schliemann suggested his terms. They were: a special letter of commendation from the Kaiser; the Order of Merit, the highest private order the Kaiser could bestow; the honorary citizenship of Berlin; membership in the Prussian Academy of Sciences, and the museum containing the treasure must bear his name in perpetuity. He did not receive the Order of Merit, but Virchow succeeded in arranging that all the other demands were met.

On July 7, 1881, Schliemann attended the royal reception in Berlin, where the treasure was solemnly handed over to the German nation. It was housed in a wing of the Völkerkundemuseum, and Schliemann's name was written in bright golden letters above the doors. Crown Prince Wilhelm escorted Sophia to the banquet. Sophia was twenty-eight, and her husband was six months short of his sixtieth birthday.

On that July day in Berlin Schliemann reached the pinnacle of his fame. The boy who had glued his face to the window of an obscure parsonage, viewing the legendary world outside, now had seen the world of legend come to life. Had he not summoned into his presence the most ancient kings, and a living king as well? Looking back on his life, he was content.

Still there was much to be done. He thought of doing excavations at several places, and then settled on Tiryns, the great citadel on the plain of Argos. Tiryns was old when Mycenae was young. Hercules was born there. Even the ancient Greeks regarded Tiryns with awe.

On March 14, 1884, Schliemann arrived in Nauplia to superintend the work at Tiryns. There, every morning, he rose before sunrise and was carried out to sea in a rowing boat just as the sun was coming up. He would jump overboard, swim for ten minutes, climb back in the boat, and shortly afterwards make the twenty-five minute journey to Tiryns on horseback.

The great fortress stood on a crag projecting over a swampy plain. The galleries were vaulted with huge blocks and had served for generations as sheepfolds, and in some places the stone had been rubbed smooth by the sheep. There they worked until June, and the workmen laid bare the floor plan of a Homeric palace.

Schliemann went to Tiryns again the next summer, and discovered a brilliant fresco showing a boy leaping over the back of a tawny bull, and portions of a geometric frieze. There were also many exquisitely fashioned vases; but it was the huge bull with the curving horns that astonished the world. Such bulls were to be found later in Knossos, and it is possible that the bull at Tiryns was painted by a Minoan artist.

Among the theories which Schliemann clung to throughout his life was the gradual decay of heroism. It seemed to him that heroism was concentrated in a quite extraordinary degree in the great heroes of archaic Greece. From that day to this the world had suffered at the hands of lesser men.

Physically he was changing. With his taut, weather-beaten skin, enormous forehead like an onion, and sad, wispy moustache, he was coming to resemble a mummy. Earaches drove him nearly mad, and sometimes his lips twitched. He made little jerking movements with his hands, and he stuttered. Suffering from insomnia, sometimes he read through the night. He began to pay particular attention to his dreams, analyzing them carefully; and he was profoundly worried if Sophia dreamed of crows, beanstalks, or visitors from abroad.

As the earaches grew worse and the cold winds of Europe made him shiver, he decided to spend his remaining winters in the south. Egypt attracted him. He had read most of the reports of the French and English archaeologists who had been excavating in Egypt for three generations. None of them possessed his genius, and he suspected that they knew very little about the science of excavation. As 1886 was coming to an end, he decided to spend three months in a leisurely progress along the Nile, alone except for a secretary and a heap of books in Greek and Arabic. He hired a magnificent *dahabeah,* at a cost of about £1,500. Sometimes as he sailed up the Nile, past Theban ruins and Ptolemaic temples, he would order a halt and come ashore and wander through a village. He liked talking in Arabic to the villagers, and he liked to offer them salves for their sores. He liked the Nubians, with their dark sculptured faces, the only people he had ever met who looked like heroes. He dug occasionally, thought a good deal about Cleopatra, took soundings of the depth of the Nile, studied cloud formations, and copied occasional inscriptions.

When he reached Aswan it was crowded with tourists. There was also a number of young dedicated archaeologists. Among them was E. A. Wallis Budge, then comparatively unknown, making his first mission to Egypt on behalf of the British Museum. Hearing of Schliemann's arrival, Budge rounded up two of his friends and got a boatman to row them over to the *dahabeah*. A butler led them to a large salon in the stern of the ship. Coffee was served, cigarettes were lit, and soon Schliemann was being invited by the three Englishmen to inspect the newly excavated Mohammedan tombs. And then an extraordinary thing happened. Schliemann drew himself up stiffly.

"I should like to place my archaeological science at your disposal and explain to you the tombs," he said, "but I have not the time as I am going to Wadi Halfa!"

Without another word Schliemann reached for the paper-bound copy of the *Iliad* in the Greek text which he had been reading.

The Englishmen were appalled, and asked permission to withdraw. Permission was granted, and they returned to Aswan.

Such conduct was unusual, and perhaps due to one of Schliemann's recurrent headaches. There were only three more years left to him now.

In 1888 he worked for a short while on the island of Cerigo—Cythera—where Aphrodite first appeared among men, and he dreamed of uncovering the royal city of Knossos in Crete. "I would like to end my life's labours with one great work—the prehistoric palace of the kings of Knossos," he wrote on January 1, 1889.

In the spring he visited Crete. The Turk who claimed to own the site at Knossos wanted a hundred thousand francs, but finally he agreed that Schliemann could purchase the land for fifty thousand francs. The price was to include twenty-five hundred olive trees that grew there. At the last moment before signing the contract Schliemann decided to count the olive trees. There were only eight hundred and eighty-eight. He flew into a temper, announcing that he could not sign a contract with a man who lied about the number of trees he possessed. Later he wrote to Virchow, "It was a terrible journey, with nothing gained."

As old age came to him, he went back to his first love. That year he held the First International Congress on the Trojan Antiquities, inviting scholars from all over the world to visit Troy. Accompanying them through the ruins, he told them about those long-distant days before the mound was carved up in trenches and great galleries. He was aging rapidly now.

He was at Troy again the next year, holding his Second International Congress. When the Congress was over, the work went on. He spoke lightheartedly of how all of Homeric Troy would be laid bare by the following spring. Meanwhile the hot winds roared across the plain and some of the workmen were struck with fever, but Schliemann continued to superintend the excavations, a small wizened man wearing a sun helmet. On August 1, 1890, he returned to Athens: to his great house with its marble steps, the children growing up, the table piled high with notes on the year's work, and the ever healing presence of Sophia to lighten his burdens. He did not know then that he would never see Troy again.

In Athens he was still pursuing dreams. He wrote to Virchow that he planned to visit the islands of Atlantis and to make a voyage to Mexico—perhaps there he would find the traces of Odysseus. He was sure he could find Atlantis in the Canary Islands; had not Homer himself proclaimed that these islands enjoyed perpetual spring? When Sophia went to Vienna, he wandered around the house like a ghost, remembering towards the end of September their wedding anniversary. He wrote to her a long chiding letter in classical Greek:

> I am proud of this day, so I am inviting your relatives . . . for we have lived together in health and happiness for twenty-one years. . . . I rejoice continually in your virtues, and by Zeus! I will marry you again in the next world!

About this time he decided to go to a clinic at Halle in Germany which had been recommended by Virchow. Sophia hurried back to Athens to help him pack. He seems to have had some premonition of his approaching death; once, when he was putting his clothes in a trunk, he was heard saying, "I wonder who will wear these clothes."

Sophia wanted to accompany him, but he said he would be gone for only six weeks and there were the children to be looked after. At the last moment, when he was leaving for the train, Sophia held him back by the watch chain. She seemed to know she would never see him again.

He arrived in Halle early in November. It was a cold winter, and snow was falling. The next day the doctors operated on both his ears. The operation lasted one and three-quarter hours. Though the doctors declared the operation successful, the pain returned, more terrible than ever. It seemed that the inflammation was spreading through the inner ear. Against the advice of the doctors he decided to leave the hospital. He went to Leipzig to visit his publishers, and to Berlin to visit Virchow, and then took the train for Paris.

He reached Paris on December 15, one of the coldest days of winter. He found six letters waiting for him from Sophia, who was beside herself with worry. He calculated that he had time to visit the museum at Naples, where the recent excavations at Pompeii were on display, and still reach Athens by Christmas. To his wife he admitted that he had forgotten to put cotton wadding in his ears in the drafty railway carriage when he was immersed in reading the *Arabian Nights* in Arabic. He wrote his last letter to Virchow: "Long live Pallas Athena! At last I can hear again with the right ear, and the left will get better."

He was already dying when he reached Naples. The pain was excruciating, and the two-day journey from Paris had weakened him. He summoned first one doctor, then another. A ship was waiting for him, but he was too ill to make the sea journey and telegraphed to Athens, asking Sophia to delay the Christmas celebrations, and then went to visit another doctor, who recognized him and suggested a drive to Pompeii. Bundled up in his greatcoat, Schliemann sat back in the carriage during the long journey around the bay in the shadow of Vesuvius. He saw Pompeii, the colonnades, the roads rutted by ancient Roman carts, the *tabernae* where the wine sellers stood two thousand years before. Then he returned to his hotel room and fought against the raging pain in his ears.

On Christmas Day he was crossing the Piazza della Santa Carità when he suddenly collapsed on the cobblestones, conscious, his eyes wide open. A crowd gathered. People asked him questions, but he could only nod: he had lost the power of speech.

Taken to the police station, he was searched for papers and money, but nothing was found. The police did find the address of his doctor, who was summoned and identified him. The police were perplexed. Judging by his clothes he was a poor man. Then why was the doctor so solicitous?

"No, he is rich," the doctor said. "I have seen him holding a wallet filled with gold coins!"

Then the doctor reached under the dying man's shirt and pulled out a heavy wallet full of gold.

Schliemann was carried back to his hotel, still in command of all his faculties except speech. At the hotel the ear was opened, but the malady had already attacked the brain. By the next day his right side was paralysed. Eight specialists were called in, and while they were in another room discussing trepanning, he died quietly in bed, conscious to the last.

On Sunday, January 4, 1891, nine days after his death, the coffin lay in the great hall of his palace in Athens. A bust of Homer was placed at its head. King George and Crown Prince Constantine came to lay wreaths beside the coffin, and messages of sympathy came from all over the world.

He had long ago chosen the place where he would be buried. He was buried among the Greeks he loved in their own cemetery south of the Ilissus, in a tomb fit for a hero. From there his unquiet spirit could look out upon the Acropolis, the blue waters of the Saronic Gulf, and the distant hills of Argolis beyond which lay the citadels of Tiryns and Mycenae.

He had been a legend while he lived; he was to become still more of a legend when he was dead. His rages, his arrogance were forgotten. People remembered his faith in Homer and the vastness of his determination to reveal the mysteries buried in the earth. His vices became virtues—his ruthless egoism no more than natural pride, his exaggerations the pardonable excesses of a man impatient for discovery.

So in the end he became one of the great forerunners, the man who opened the way, the first of modern archaeologists, because he was the enemy of the academic archaeology practised in his day. He was a pure romantic who threw the windows wide open and let the air in.

A few days after Schliemann's death Gladstone, who was then eighty-one, wrote in a failing hand a letter of consolation to Sophia. He described how deeply he had felt the force of Schliemann's particular genius, and in a single paragraph he described the nature of Schliemann's triumph:

> He had to encounter in the early stages of his work both frowns and indifference, yet the one and the other alike had to give way, as the force and value of his discoveries became clear, like mists upon the sun. The history of his boyhood and youth were not less remarkable than that of his later life. Indeed they cannot be separated, for one aim and purpose moved them from first to last.

DURING THE LAST FIVE YEARS of Schliemann's life, he gave the impression of being a man for whom only the Homeric heroes were real. He wrote and spoke in ancient Greek. He told a friend, "Only Homer interests me: I am increasingly indifferent to everything else." Schliemann was not mad, but close to madness. His mania was to believe that a bright and wonderfully pure civilization had once existed, and that it was worth while to enter that civilization even at the risk of lunacy.

Though Schliemann was brought up in a parsonage, he denied his Christian heritage, attended no church, and regarded the Bible as fiction. When Sophia's mother died, and he entered the death chamber where priests were intoning prayers for the dead, he was heard muttering, "Oh, it is all nonsense! There is no resurrection—there is only immortality!"

Many of Schliemann's assumptions were eventually proved wrong. "Priam's treasure" and "Agamemnon's tomb" in fact predated the Trojan War. Sadly the Trojan treasure itself has disappeared. When World War II broke out, the treasure was hidden in a secret bunker excavated deep below the Berlin Zoo. In the spring of 1945 Russian troops discovered it and sent it back through the lines. Today only the Russians know where it is.

Yet it was thanks to Schliemann that from all over Europe eager archaeologists came to Greece and the Near East to take part in the process of resurrecting an ancient heroic society. In the roll call of those who have brought the Homeric age to life there are the names of many people; but all of them have recognized the primacy of Schliemann. He stands above them all like a giant, because he was the boldest and saw farthest and never betrayed his faith in Homer.

The long toll of the brave
Is not lost in darkness . . .
Over the fruitful earth
And athwart the seas
Hath passed the light of noble deeds
Unquenchable for ever.

Robert Payne

Robert Payne is the author of over one hundred books, and these reflect the very wide range of his interests. But ancient Greece must be one of his earliest enthusiasms, stemming from his schooldays in London.

"I was a classical scholar at St. Paul's School," he says, "and therefore steeped in Greek culture. We all had lockers in the long corridors of the school, and my locker was surmounted by a bust of Plato. I became a Platonist, regarding Sophocles as only a little less magnificent than Plato.

"Then during the war I went to the Far East, and Greece faded away while I played with China and Japan, and even more voraciously with India. But I still had one foot in ancient Greece, and wrote three books about it."

Before becoming a full-time writer, Robert Payne had a varied career. After publishing his first novel in 1938, he went to Spain as a war correspondent. Then came World War II, and he found himself in Singapore as an armaments officer in the navy. Just before Singapore fell to the Japanese, he was appointed cultural officer to the British Embassy in Chungking, and spent the next five years teaching English literature at Chinese universities.

Robert Payne has written biographies of such world figures as Lenin, Hitler and Gandhi, and this year will see the publication of a biography of Trotsky and a book on Leonardo da Vinci. Meanwhile he is making films about India and finishing a biography of Shakespeare and a novel about China.

It was New York, where Robert Payne now lives, that indirectly inspired the writing of *The Gold of Troy*. He discovered that the main public library there has a very large collection of Heinrich Schliemann's writings, and the fact that so much material was available tempted him to write the book. Nowadays the complexities of Oriental art absorb a lot of his time, and his enthusiasm for Greece has been forced into the background. But he is still contemplating a biography of Friedrich Hoelderlin, a German poet famous for his passionate interest in Greece. This book, he says, could be a first step for him back into the Greek countryside he knows and loves.

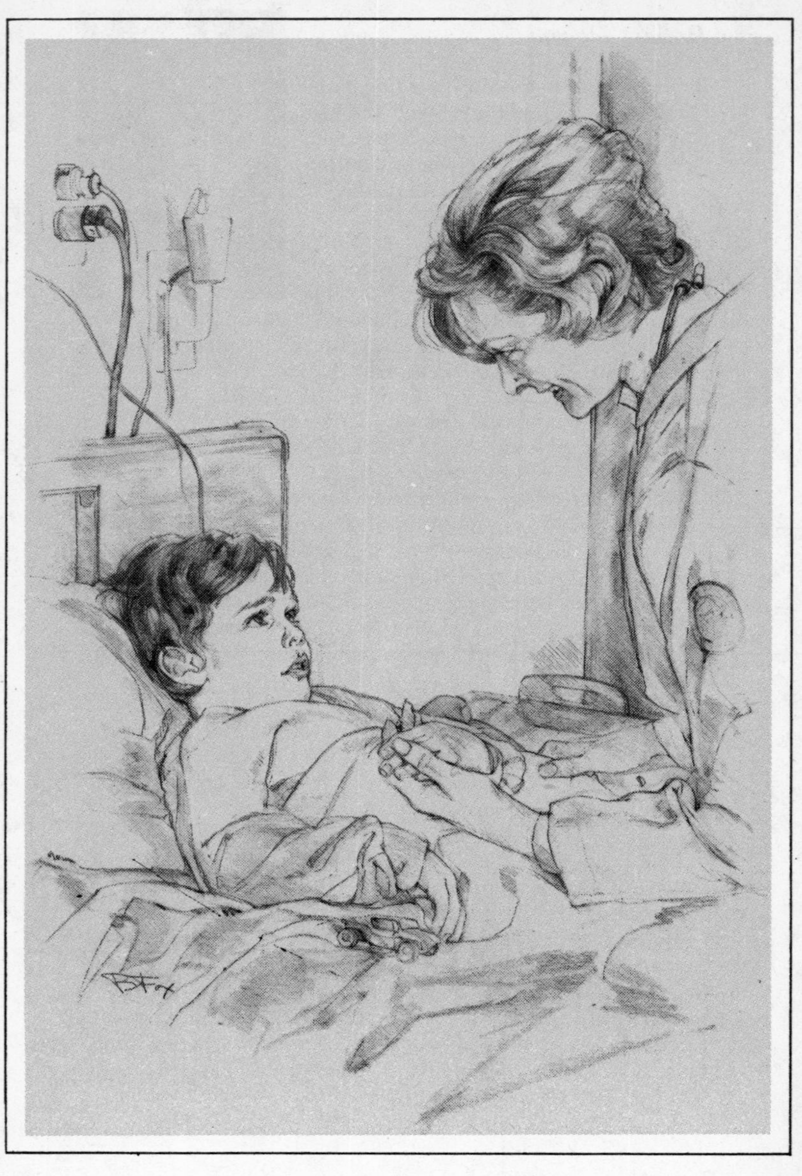

THE SCOFIELD DIAGNOSIS

A CONDENSATION OF THE BOOK BY

Henry Denker

ILLUSTRATED BY BARBARA FOX

Published by W. H. ALLEN.

The blue-eyed boy, small for his age, looked up at her as he hugged the new toy zebra to his chest in a tight, affectionate embrace. With most people he was slow to extend his affection—but he liked Dr. Jean and he had come to trust her. And Dr. Jean Scofield, moved by his faith in her, was determined to prove that her diagnosis of little Bobby's sickness was correct.

But as Jean pressed for the treatment she knew her young patient so desperately needed, she found herself dangerously at odds with the others associated with his case: there was Larry, a child specialist like herself, who loved her but thought that her judgement concerning Bobby was impaired by the tragedy in her own past; there was Cameron, the millionaire philanthropist basically opposed to women in positions of authority in the hospital; and there were Bob and Marissa Tatum, young Bobby's troubled parents, who refused categorically to accept "the Scofield diagnosis".

Chapter One

Dr. Jean Scofield, associate professor of neurology, raced down the corridor of University Hospital in answer to an urgent call from Emergency Admitting. In her late thirties, and of average height, she seemed both younger and smaller in her long, white, starched lab coat.

"Disarmingly small" was the way old Hans Benziger, chief of Neurology, liked to describe his protégée after watching her in determined confrontation with some of her male colleagues. But even in those moments her warm green eyes and auburn hair endowed her with a softness decidedly feminine and unusually attractive. So attractive that those who knew nothing of her past wondered why such a handsome woman was not married. Most assumed it was due to her total dedication to her profession.

Actually, Jean had been married once. But the marriage had ended abruptly and tragically. Whatever it had done to her personal life, it had not diminished her effectiveness as a neurologist.

She had almost reached the emergency room when the beeper in the breast pocket of her lab coat summoned her. She picked up the phone at the nurses' floor station.

"Dr. Scofield," she announced herself.

"Doctor, Administrator Carey has been trying to reach you. He would like you to come to his office."

"Sorry, I'm on my way to Emergency. I'll see Mr. Carey as soon as I'm free."

She hung up and continued on her way. Even before she reached the emergency room she heard a child crying in pain.

The admitting resident was Dr. Preston Guylay, who had once been a student in her neurology class at the university medical school. He was examining a black child who appeared to be some fourteen or fifteen months of age. In the far corner of the room, on a white metal stool, sat a young black woman. She was staring, seemingly impassive, except that she nervously twisted a tattered handkerchief.

Guylay left his anguished little patient and spoke to Jean privately. "Sorry to bother you, Professor. But I need help. Not only medically but legally. This can become messy and I don't want to make any mistakes."

"What is it?" Jean asked, staring at the whimpering child.

"Glove burn. But there may be more. I need your opinion on any neurological deficit."

Jean moved to the tiny patient. Both his hands from fingertips to wrists were red, blistery masses. Clearly second-degree burns. The fact that the affected areas ended trimly above the wrists, like a pair of short gloves, was a clear indication that the child's hands had been forcibly immersed in scalding water. No child would keep its own hands in hot water for so long.

NAI, was Dr. Scofield's immediate conclusion. Nonaccidental injury. She began her examination. "How old?"

"Twenty-two months," Guylay informed her.

"Twenty-two?" Jean was surprised. The child exhibited distinct lack of development for his age. She detected a red scar almost hidden by his eyebrow. An incisor was missing. His nose had evidently been smashed at one time, for it was flatter than the rest of his facial contour would indicate.

Softly Jean said, "Clear case of pugilistic puss. This child's been severely beaten. And frequently."

"Yes," Guylay agreed.

Jean proceeded with her neurological examination. Using her pocket flashlight, she probed the child's eyes. "Get a history?"

"Yes. The usual. She was boiling water to wash the child's dish.

The phone rang. She went into the other room to answer it. She heard a scream. When she came back she found the kid had plunged his hands into the hot water."

"Naturally," Jean said angrily. She had heard variations of that story too many times. "And what about his face?"

"She says he fell down the stairs while learning to walk."

Jean used a sterile needle to test the reflexes in the child's legs and arms. "Neurological deficit in the left leg. Do complete skeletal X rays. I'll bet you find half a dozen healed fractures, as well as evidence of a fine-line skull fracture. When you do, take the case to the Child Abuse Committee. It would be criminal to turn this child back to his parents."

"What'll I tell her?" The resident indicated the mother.

"I'll handle her," Jean said crisply. She glanced at the chart to ascertain the name, then crossed the room. "Mrs. Scott?"

The young woman looked up, staring through dazed and fearful eyes. "Yes?"

"I'm Dr. Scofield. I've examined your son. His condition is serious enough for us to keep him here for a while."

"But for how long?" the tense mother asked.

"A week. Probably longer," Jean said, knowing they would keep the child longer, for his own safety.

"I don't know. I never left him before."

"At the other hospitals?" Jean asked quickly.

The young mother realized that she had betrayed herself, and it would do no good to deny it. She admitted. "Yeah."

"It's my advice, and Dr. Guylay's, that this time you leave him. He'll be well looked after."

The mother hesitated, nodded, looked at her son, then turned and left. Once she was gone, Jean said to Guylay, "He's badly undernourished. Start intravenous feeding. Do a complete workup. Blood, electroencephalogram. I'm afraid we're going to find even more than we suspect."

"Right."

"I have to go down to Carey's office. Check with me when you get the results of those tests."

She left the emergency room, and had just reached the elevator when her beeper summoned her again.

WHILE JEAN SCOFIELD answered another urgent call, Edward Carey, director of Administration of University Hospital, was drumming his fingers on his chrome and black slate desk pad.

"Damn it, Benziger, when Dr. Scofield gets here you tell her she *has* to take that appointment!"

Hans Benziger, the elderly chief of Neurology, stared across the desk at the director. Benziger's eyes did not reveal the amusement he was enjoying. He was thinking, These days hospital administrators propose, but stubborn female doctors dispose.

Carey continued petulantly. "Did she say anything at all?"

"Aside from rejecting the appointment, no."

"Didn't you try to convince her? This is a new position. The first time that any woman has been offered a post of such importance here."

"She knows that," Benziger said.

"And she still said no?" Carey asked peevishly. "Bad. Very bad. We're supposed to have women doctors in positions of importance. And minority doctors on staff. Else no federal funding. And it doesn't matter whether they're qualified or not!"

"Well," Benziger said very deliberately, "that can't be a factor here. Dr. Scofield is extremely well qualified."

At once Carey became apologetic. "Of course. She was a student of yours. There's no doubt about her qualifications. But these days I feel like a performing seal trying to run this hospital! It's a perpetual balancing act. Get the funding. Keep the staff happy. Comply with government regulations. Please the board of trustees. Satisfy the minorities.

"Damn!" he exploded. "Isn't there *anyone* who might talk to her? Someone *not* in Neurology?"

"You mean Dr. Braham?" Benziger asked pointedly.

"Well . . . after all . . ." Carey did not complete the sentence.

"Yes. After all, Jean Scofield and Lawrence Braham are supposed to be lovers," Benziger said. "Is that it?"

"Everyone knows it. If anyone can convince her, Braham can. Talk to him," Carey half ordered, half pleaded.

"Braham is away this week," Benziger said. "A pediatrics symposium in Houston. But if he were here, I doubt even he could convince her. No, Edward, you'll have to talk to her yourself."

"I suppose you're right."

"Good." For a moment Benziger felt tempted to say something comforting to Carey, but he resisted the impulse. Jean Scofield was his most respected protégée. She was not only a highly skilled, insightful neurologist, she was a woman of great inner strength. Let Carey tangle with her, he thought. It will be good exercise for him.

In angry frustration Edward Carey threw his new organization chart down on his desk. He had had it all worked out so beautifully. And, most important, to the complete satisfaction of Horace Cameron, who was not only chairman of the board of trustees of the hospital but founder and president of InterElectronics, one of the leading multinational conglomerates in the world. Which meant that Cameron had the resources to come up with those added monies that every large, growing hospital needs periodically in these times of rising costs.

Carey had worked out his chart to meet each of Cameron's suggestions. Every piece in place. Sunderland would become chief of Neurology when Benziger resigned. And when the people from the Department of Health, Education, and Welfare asked about the progress of women at University Hospital, there would be Jean Scofield as associate chief. An empty title, but good enough to satisfy HEW and clear the way to a big fat federal grant. Now, the only crucial piece that would not fit was that woman Scofield herself. Carey lifted his phone. "Martha, where is Dr. Scofield? Dr. Benziger and I are waiting. I want her here at once! Have one of the floor nurses get to her."

"They have, sir."

"And?" Carey demanded.

"Well, sir, she sent back a message. Unless you're experiencing some neurological emergency, you'll have to wait."

Carey slammed down his phone and gave vent to a string of expletives in which he called Jean Scofield all the unflattering names he could level at any woman.

IT WAS NEITHER rudeness nor lack of concern which had caused Jean Scofield to reject Carey's summons to the impromptu meeting. It was the arrival of yet another emergency case.

A boy of five had suddenly begun to convulse. Suspecting neurological complications, the pediatrician immediately referred him to Dr. Scofield. Especially since the boy was not a regular patient of his, but one he had seen only while covering for Dr. Lawrence Braham, who was away at that symposium in Houston.

As the referring pediatrician explained to Jean on the phone, "I'm sure Larry would want you to take charge of this case personally." It was said with such studied blandness that Jean could not miss the point. While she had never made any special effort to conceal her relationship with Larry Braham, she resented those who focused on it by so meticulously pretending to ignore it.

As Jean entered the emergency room, the new patient was being transferred from the gurney—a wheeled stretcher—to a treatment table. The nurse was standing by with a catheter to apply suction to his throat so he would not gag. A middle-aged woman stood by, stunned and tearful. Jean asked, "You the mother?"

"I'm the maid. Mrs. Tatum was out when it began to happen. So I called Dr. Braham's office—"

"Wait outside!" Jean turned her about firmly. "And try to locate his mother, if you can."

"I already did," the distraught woman called back.

Jean turned to the unconscious child. "Rubber airway," she ordered. Once she had slipped it between the child's teeth—fortunately, they were not clenched—to make sure he had a clear air passage, she hooked up nasal oxygen. She was strapping on the blood-pressure cuff when he began to convulse again. Jean watched the precise manner in which the seizure proceeded, especially observing the child's head and eyes, which turned distinctly to the right. It was a significant sign, indicating an irritative adversive frontal-lobe seizure on the left side of his brain.

His entire body stiffened in the next, the tonic, phase of the seizure. It was followed by the clonic phase, a rhythmic jerking of first his right hand, then his arm. Jean cradled the boy's head in her arms to protect him from injuring himself. She ordered the nurse to affix a light restraint to prevent his slipping off the table during the spasm's most violent phase. The nurse suctioned the child's airway clear.

Eventually the boy's spasmodic movement subsided. Finally

he lay quiet, unconscious. Jean relaxed her hold. "Safety pin."

The nurse handed her a sterilized pin. Jean administered short stabs to the child's extremities. He responded with involuntary withdrawal movements of each limb. His responses were much weaker on the right side than the left.

She checked his vital signs. Respiration, blood pressure, normal. Pulse, steady. She applied her stethoscope to the boy's heart and lungs. His lungs sounded clear. She examined his head and his rib cage for contusions. None.

The boy regained consciousness. He stared at her, his blue eyes tearful. Each time she touched him he became tense, drawing back. Undoubtedly he was frightened in this strange place.

She palpated his abdomen. Aside from noting that the child was rather thin, she found nothing. No rigidity. She palpated his pelvis, spine and neck. No evidence of fracture.

That completed, Dr. Scofield was free to proceed with the more intensive neurological phase of her examination. But before she could begin, the boy's eyes and head suddenly turned to the right again. The pattern had begun to repeat. At that moment a woman's voice, high-pitched and tense, was heard outside the door.

"I have a right to see my son! You can't stop me!"

A young, beautiful, dark-haired woman burst into the room, demanding, "Where is my—" She stopped. She looked in horror at the tormented boy now being cradled by Dr. Scofield as the seizure racked his body. The mother drew back, terrified and disbelieving. Then she shrieked, "Bobby!"

Dr. Scofield ordered, "Leave this room! I'll talk to you later."

The mother hesitated, then seemed relieved to turn and escape. Jean continued to cradle the boy's head while she ordered, "Thirty milligrams phenobarb. Stat!" The nurse immediately injected the medication.

"If it recurs, give him another thirty," Scofield said, observing the seizure subside. "But watch his breathing. We don't want respiratory arrest from overmedication."

She studied the boy, who now slept normally, his eyelids sometimes flickering. Small for his age but handsome. Fortunately, when he awoke he would remember none of all this. Even during seizure, patients are totally unaware.

As quickly as possible, she knew, she had to determine the etiology of his seizures. There were endless causes to eliminate. Fever. Systemic infection. Central nervous system infection. Trauma, especially one causing a subdural hematoma—an internal hemorrhage in the protective sac that enveloped the brain. An undiscovered subdural could cause seizures as long as a year after the initial injury. If it remained untreated, it could cause paralysis, even death. Finally that most dread of all possible causes, brain tumor.

Up to now, Dr. Scofield had only one clue. The seizures started with rightward eye and head movement, indicating that the trouble probably originated on the opposite side of the boy's brain. The cause was likely to be a mass of some kind, blood clot, abscess or tumor. None of them welcome.

It was important to secure a complete history. As Jean entered the waiting room, both the boy's mother and the maid came toward her. "How is he?" the mother cried out.

"Resting," Jean was quick to reassure her. "Now, please sit down."

"I want to see the doctor!" the mother persisted.

"I'm Dr. Scofield."

"You're Dr. Scofield? I didn't realize . . ."

Jean could not decide if the woman was reacting in surprise or disapproval.

"Now, tell me how it started," Jean asked the maid. "Did you see it begin?"

The maid's lips trembled. "He came home, like every day. He goes half day to preschool, so he comes home for lunch. I made it for him. Just like Mrs. Tatum said. Only today he just wants to go to his room and lie down. I knew Mrs. Tatum would be very angry if I don't make him finish his vegetable and milk. But I let him go lie down anyway."

Dr. Scofield nodded. It was noteworthy that the child had sought to lie down. He had undoubtedly been experiencing an aura, a premonition that the seizure was coming on.

"What happened after that?" Jean continued.

"He's so quiet I get worried. So I go up to his door. I go in. I find him . . . like you saw him. It was terrible!"

The mother came forward. "Doctor, I insist on seeing my son!"

"You will. But first I need a complete history."

The mother glared at the doctor, then relented.

"We can do this better in my office," Jean said, and turned to lead the way.

AS THEY PASSED through the reception room of her suite, Jean said to her secretary, "Maggie, no calls for the next half hour."

She ushered Mrs. Tatum through her examining room. On one wall hung more than a dozen neatly framed diplomas and certifications. The other walls were devoted to glass cases, X-ray viewing boxes, and bookshelves bulging with thick volumes on all phases of neurology.

In her private consultation room were no diplomas or books. On the panelled walls hung a few works of art. The chairs were soft and comfortable, and except for the desk and a dictating machine, the office seemed in all respects like an intimate living room. Jean had designed it herself, to put at ease anxious relatives and tense patients.

As soon as she was seated, Marissa Tatum pulled a pack of cigarettes and an expensive gold lighter from her bag, asking, "Do you mind?"

Considering the tense state of the woman, Jean said, "Not at all." She began the history. "Your son's name?"

"Bobby. Robert Tatum, Jr."

"His age?"

"Five. Five years and three months."

"Has he ever had seizures before?"

"Seizures?" the mother repeated, frightened. "Never!" Her lips quivered. She stared at the doctor, suspicion and distrust evident in her eyes. "I want to see Dr. Braham!"

"Dr. Braham is out of town. And will be till late tonight," Jean informed her. "I'm sure he'd tell you your son is in capable hands. Dr. Braham refers his neurological cases to me, and instead of waiting for him to return, you can do much more for your son by answering my questions as fully as you can."

Jean Scofield continued firmly. "Now, Mrs. Tatum, is there any history of seizures in your family or your husband's?"

"Not in mine. And I never heard Bob mention any."

"Has Bobby complained of headaches lately?"

"Only on mornings when he doesn't want to go to school. He finds all sorts of excuses. Sometimes it's headaches."

"Has he had nausea? Vomiting?"

"No."

"Ever complained of double vision?"

"No. Look, Doctor, what are you getting at?"

"I promise, as soon as I know, you'll know. But if I'm to find out, you'll have to answer all my questions."

"Of course. I'm sorry." Marissa Tatum lit another cigarette.

"Any serious childhood illnesses? Surgery?"

"No."

"Does he have trouble walking? Any lack of coordination?"

"No," his mother said, glancing across at the doctor's notes.

"Ever complain of tingling or numbness?"

"No."

"Has he run any high fevers lately?"

"No."

"Has he experienced any weakness on one side of his body?"

"I never noticed any."

"Any trauma?" When Mrs. Tatum seemed puzzled, Jean explained. "Has he sustained any injury? Especially a blow on the head? Has he fallen off his bike or tripped while playing? Anything like that?"

Marissa Tatum's beautifully sculptured face turned thoughtful as she tried to recollect any events that might be of importance. After some moments, she shook her head.

"Was there anything special today? Anything he said to you that was different from other days?"

"No," the mother answered, then seemed to remember. "Yes, he did mention something early this morning about hoping his teacher wouldn't make him draw elephants again today. He wanted to draw zebras. He finds stripes more interesting."

"There's some kind of tension between him and his teacher?"

"Nothing important, I can assure you. He's not a rebellious child. He's extremely easy to get along with. And very bright."

Suddenly Mrs. Tatum burst out with the question which was at the root of her anxiety. "This won't affect his mind, will it? He won't be like those children who twitch all the time?"

"If he responds to treatment, I'm sure he'll be fine."

"*If* he responds. You mean it's possible he won't?"

Patiently Jean explained. "Before we can say anything, we have to discover the etiology—the cause. So, for the moment, please just answer my questions as fully as you can."

"I'm sorry. I'll try."

"Did anything else unusual happen today?"

"No. He went off to school. On the bus, I assume."

"Assume?"

"I had to rush off to a meeting of the Women's Guild at Mrs. Cameron's."

Jean interrupted to ask, "Mrs. *Horace* Cameron?"

"Of course," Marissa Tatum said, pretending to be casual, but quick to claim a close relationship to the wife of a man as important as the president of InterElectronics. "Whenever I have to go to one of her meetings, Esther puts Bobby on the school bus. And at noontime, when the bus drops him off, she gives him his lunch. Then he has an hour's rest before going out to play."

"Does Esther often put him on the bus instead of you?"

"Lately—I've been quite busy."

Before Jean could ask her next question her phone rang. She turned to answer it. "Yes? Please tell Mr. Carey it's impossible for me to take his call now. I'll call back later." She hung up impatiently and turned again to Mrs. Tatum.

"Has Bobby had all his immunizations?"

"Yes."

"Dr. Braham has always been his doctor?"

"No. We've only lived here for two years. Bob worked in InterElectronics' San Diego office till two years ago. That's when Mr. Cameron himself asked to have Bob transferred here to the main office."

Jean could appreciate the obvious pride the young wife took in announcing that her husband had been singled out for such a distinction by Cameron himself. Cameron's international reputation as a power in the electronics industry made such a promotion a crucial event in the career of any ambitious young executive.

Jean also realized that she was dealing with a patient in whom the chairman of the board of trustees of the hospital might have a personal interest. And Cameron had a reputation for interfering in hospital affairs beyond his duties as a trustee. She would face that problem later. For now, the patient's history was all that mattered.

"Mrs. Tatum, is Bobby allergic to anything?"

"My son is not one of those overly sensitive, allergic children," she stated with pride as well as a certain intolerance.

"Did you have any difficulty during pregnancy?"

"None," Mrs. Tatum said, reaching into her purse for another cigarette until Jean pointed out that she already had one burning.

"Now, about Bobby's birth . . ." The look on Marissa Tatum's face changed. "Was it difficult?"

"I wouldn't know. I was under anesthetic at the time. I had a cesarean. The doctor said Bobby was just fine. Everything normal. Certainly no brain damage!" The mother was determined to make that point. Then she admitted, "He was premature. He was in intensive care for several weeks, but he came out of it very well. They tested him regularly and he was fine. Fine."

Jean nodded and went on to complete a review of all the boy's systems. When she had concluded, she said, "Mrs. Tatum, what kind of games does Bobby's father play with him?"

"Games?" the mother asked, obviously puzzled.

"Does he toss him up in the air and pretend to let him fall, then catch him at the last moment?"

"You know how fathers are with sons. Yes, Bob plays games like that with him."

"Has he ever dropped him?" Jean asked.

"Of course not! Bob would cut off his right hand before he'd let anything happen to his son! Nothing in my husband's life is more dear to him than Bobby. Because . . . the doctor said I shouldn't consider having more children. Bobby is all we'll ever have. Nothing must be allowed to happen to him. Nothing!"

"Mrs. Tatum, is your husband in town?"

"No. He'll be home Friday, on the last plane from Chicago."

"I'd like to see him soon. Saturday morning?"

"Why?" Marissa Tatum leaned forward. "Because it's so bad you don't dare tell me?"

"There's nothing to tell yet. We need the whole picture. All the test results. His response to medication."

"But it could be bad," the mother ventured.

"It could," Jean was forced to admit.

"How bad?"

Jean knew that the tormented woman would be satisfied with nothing less than the complete truth, painful as that might be.

"The possibilities range all the way from seizures, which can be controlled by medication and will finally disappear, to a brain tumor—which will not disappear."

"Brain tumor," Marissa Tatum whispered. "Oh, Bobby . . ."

Jean left her desk and came around to place her arm about the mother.

"Mrs. Tatum, I did say your son may be experiencing seizures that are completely controllable by medication. Remember that."

The woman nodded slowly. "How long will he have to be here?"

"Four or five days, most likely."

"I'd like him home before Bob gets back. It will be quite a shock to find out his son is in the hospital."

Jean suggested gently, "Let's treat the boy, not his father. We'll send Bobby home when it's best for *him.*"

"Yes, of course. Can I see him now? Just for a moment?"

"He's asleep. But come with me."

As they walked down the hall, Jean suggested, "Don't you think it advisable to call your husband and tell him?"

"Oh, no," Marissa Tatum responded quickly. "He'd drop everything and fly right back. And I'm afraid Mr. Cameron might not like that."

"Nevertheless, I strongly urge that you call your husband," Jean said. The woman hesitated, then finally nodded.

Marissa Tatum approached the emergency room with obvious apprehension. She stared down at her sleeping son, then, at Dr. Scofield's gesture, slipped out of the room. Now Jean was free to proceed with her examination.

She used an otoscope to examine the boy's nose and ears for traces of blood or spinal fluid, which would indicate a recent trauma to the head. There was no evidence of either. With an ophthalmoscope she focused into his eyes, looking for any sign of elevated brain pressure or hemorrhage. She found no such sign. She repeated her earlier physical and neurological examination.

Finally she wrote up her findings on his chart and ordered extensive tests. There was no more she could do until he reacted to the medication and the results of the tests began to accumulate.

Up to the moment, seizures of unknown origin was the only diagnosis Jean could make.

She took one more look at the child before having him moved to neurological intensive care. He lay in a deep, peaceful sleep induced by two factors: the natural need for sleep that followed seizures, and the phenobarbital prescribed as an anticonvulsant. Bobby Tatum was a handsome child, with his mother's black hair and some of her striking features.

Jean was reminded of another child, one who was destined never to be born. But that belonged to another place, another life, and now was only a dull ache that she felt from time to time.

She remembered Carey's calls—he had been so persistent, she should put him off no longer.

When Jean arrived at his office, she discovered that Hans Benziger had also been invited to attend. He greeted Jean with a warm, fatherly kiss. The traces of his mellow German accent lent a disarming quality to his warning, "You know what he wants."

"I know," she responded softly, but with steel in her voice.

Carey was on his feet, positively gallant in the way he greeted her. "Well, my dear, what's that about your refusing to accept the appointment as associate chief of Neurology?" He smiled indulgently, as if not taking her refusal seriously.

Jean smiled back, just as pleasantly. "Yes, I did refuse."

"But my dear, that position was created especially for you. Do you realize that?"

"I realize that. And more," she said, abandoning her smile. "I do not wish to be treated like Daddy's little girl with phrases such as my dear. Just address me by my title. *Doctor.* And as for jobs created for me, don't bother. There's only one job I want. Chief of the Neurology Department, when Dr. Benziger retires."

"We've never had a woman—"

Jean interrupted him. "And I don't intend to be bought off with the empty title of associate chief!"

Carey glanced at Benziger for help, but he pretended to be staring out the window, oblivious. Carey had to proceed on his own. "You understand that unless you take this appointment, we'll be short of meeting our federal requirements."

"And short of federal funding."

"Exactly! After all, you should feel some gratitude toward this institution, which has done so much for you."

There was a peculiar emphasis in Carey's last phrase which made Jean Scofield wonder. Had he used it intentionally? Or was it merely a chance expression?

"If you have a competent chief of Neurology," Jean responded, "you don't need an associate."

"And the matter of federal funding?" Carey challenged.

"There's an easy way to assure yourself of that. Appoint a woman as chief. A well-qualified woman."

"Men simply do not like to work under a woman chief!" Carey declared flatly.

"There've been women chiefs in other hospitals."

"Damn few!" Carey was quick to point out. "They don't have the qualifications. They don't publish enough research papers. After all, medicine is not their primary interest. Most of them look forward to marriage. Some drop out of medicine after a while."

"As do some men!" Jean reminded sharply.

"Men don't cut down productive time with maternity leaves or to look after their children." After a slight pause, Carey added, "Of course, in your case that wouldn't be a problem."

Hans Benziger, who had been enjoying the argument until now, looked grim as he heard the second sly reference to Jean Scofield's personal life.

"What does my private life have to do with this appointment?" Jean demanded.

"I was merely citing the experience other institutions have had with female doctors on staff."

"As long as we're citing experience, Mr. Carey, let me cite some. No, women don't do as much research as men. Because the committees that dole out research grants are mainly composed of men. And they do not readily give them to women. I was lucky. I had Dr. Benziger to fight for my grants. Who knows how many great contributions women could have made to medicine if there had been other Benzigers sitting on the boards that control such decisions?"

"Don't you see, if you take this new post, you'll have advanced the cause of women in medicine," Carey replied.

"If I take this post I won't have accomplished one thing! Except give you an easy out, because you don't want a woman as chief!"

Carey shook his head sadly. "There are some men here at the hospital who think that the pressures of being chief might prove too much for you. Considering your history."

Jean Scofield glared at Carey. "Nothing about my history bears on this appointment," she said angrily, and left the room.

Hans Benziger rose from his chair. "Edward, that was unfair and unwarranted. That past episode has absolutely nothing to do with this appointment!"

"Still, there are men who feel that way."

"There are men who rob old ladies, too. That doesn't mean you have to join them!" Benziger strode out of the room.

In the hall, Benziger's own sense of guilt reproached him. From the beginning, he had feared that once he proposed Jean's name as chief of Neurology the subject of her past was bound to come up. He had assumed she was resigned to having it all aired again. Now he was not so sure. He must talk to her.

LATER IN THE DAY, Benziger invited Jean to his office. "Come, my dear, sit down." He smiled. "I trust I'm entitled to call you dear without being accused of male chauvinism."

Jean sat across from him, staring at his face, which reflected so many years of experience. It was a face any sculptor would have loved to re-create.

"Jean," he began sadly. "I wonder if I've been fair to you. Urging your appointment as chief."

"It would have been unfair *not* to nominate me."

"I didn't mean fair in that sense."

"Oh, I see."

"It was bound to come up. We both should have expected it."

"Frankly, I thought that Carey would bring Larry into it," she confessed.

"Oh, he did. He suggested that I ask Lawrence to persuade you to take that associate chiefship."

"We have it clear between us. Whatever our personal relationship, professionally we do not interfere with each other."

Benziger was always circumspect about the private lives of his staff. Yet now he asked, "Do you ever talk about marriage?"

"Larry talks about it. But I . . . I don't know if I can ever again marry. He's a good man. And yet . . ."

"He's not Cliff," Benziger said softly.

"Or else I don't dare love with the same devotion a second time."

"Jean, my dear, we have to face it. If I leave your name in nomination, they'll bring up your past. They'll turn it into proof of your unsuitability for a taxing job. I must know if you're willing to have the whole tragic thing come up again."

"Yes, I am! The future of the Neurology Department will be determined by this appointment. I think I can do the best job! I want to take the department that you built into one of the best in the country and make it even better."

Benziger couldn't argue on that score. If anyone could carry on his work and improve on it, Jean could. It was the personal conflict and hurt to her that he was trying to prevent. He was about to make one more effort, but Jean's beeper summoned her to the telephone.

She identified herself and listened, saying only, "Uh-huh. Uh-huh. I'll be right down." She hung up. "Automobile emergency. Head smashed through the windshield."

"Ah," Benziger said sadly. "Go on, my dear. We'll talk more tomorrow. Meantime, think about it."

DR. SCOFIELD leaned over the patient, a nineteen-year-old girl, and completed her examination swiftly.

"Arrange an emergency OR," she said to the nurse. "Ask Dr. Forrest to scrub. If we want to save her from becoming a paraplegic, we're going to have to relieve the pressure on her spine."

Even as she said it, she knew that the spine had most likely been irreparably damaged. Hers was a specialty that dealt with some tragic cases.

Sometimes she wondered if she had chosen to stay in neurology after Cliff's death because of the way he had died. Now she had no time to wonder, only to devote herself to this girl.

Jean scrubbed for the operation, not to assist but to verify her diagnosis. Unfortunately, she was right. The damage to the spinal cord was great. Jean went down to face the girl's mother and father. She was frank with them. The doctors would have to see what happened during the next few days. She warned them to expect no miracles.

SHE WAS CHANGING from her OR greens when she heard her beeper. She picked up the locker-room phone. "Dr. Scofield."

"One moment." The operator connected her with the caller.

"Darling?" It was Larry's voice, and very welcome and comforting after what she had just witnessed. "Busy?"

"Just packing in."

"Meet me? My plane's due in at nine fifteen."

"Okay," she promised quickly.

"You sound tired."

"Rough day. I'll tell you about it later."

"They're paging our flight. Have to go. Love you."

If she had not had so many reminders of Cliff on this hectic day, she would have responded as usual, Love you, too. Instead she said only, "I know, Larry. I know."

She sounded troubled, Lawrence Braham realized as he hung up. She works too hard, he said to himself. She needs more of a life outside the hospital. This time he would convince her.

Jean still had time, so she stopped off to look at the Tatum boy. As she walked down the deserted corridor she spied a woman on the bench outside the intensive care unit. The woman seemed terribly alone and forlorn. Jean recognized Marissa Tatum.

"Doctor, is Bobby worse? They won't let me go in and wait by his bed."

"My orders. You were to have a brief visit early in the evening and then let him rest through the night."

"Then I'll just wait," Marissa Tatum said.

"Mrs. Tatum, it would make more sense to go home. Not only for your sake but for Bobby's. It's going to be helpful if he doesn't detect tension in you. Nothing puts a child on edge more. And tension is one of the factors that can bring on seizures, if a child is prone to them."

"He's not prone!" his mother interjected defensively. "This is the first time it's happened. The very first time!"

"We must assume he will continue to have them. We treat him on that premise. Keeping him free from stress is one preventive. The worried look on your face won't help."

Marissa Tatum's eyes changed suddenly from concern to anger. "Have you ever had a child?"

Jean's first impulse was to explain. But she said only, "No, I have never had a child."

"So I thought. It's obvious you don't know how a mother feels!" With that, she turned and started down the hall. Jean watched her go. A tall young woman, lithe, Marissa Tatum displayed the high degree of beauty one sees on the covers of fashion magazines. Yet she seemed strangely insecure, Jean observed.

Chapter Two

Dr. Lawrence Braham came off the plane with Dr. Campbell and Dr. Brown. Since neither man's wife was waiting, Larry offered them a lift, but they decided to share a cab.

As Jean was pulling her car out of the parking lot she joked, "My, how considerate."

"Who?" Larry asked, puzzled.

"Campbell and Brown. If I were your wife, they'd have accepted your lift. Figuring that by now we were bored with each other and didn't particularly want to be alone. But since we're not married, they think we're desperate to seize every passionate moment we can." She laughed. "I like our being treated like clandestine lovers."

"When you talk that way, it's a sign that you're putting off the question," Larry said.

"Question?"

"I asked you to think about it while I was away," he reminded her.

"I haven't had time," she said evasively.

"That question doesn't take time. It's something you're aware of every waking moment. And if you aren't, there's something wrong with our relationship. Is there?"

"With me, perhaps. But not with our relationship."

"Then when is it going to become something more?"

"Soon."

"It's always soon. But it never gets any sooner. Why, Jeannie?"

Unable to respond, she stared ahead at the road. After a long silence, she changed the subject. "I saw a patient of yours today. Bobby Tatum."

"Bobby? With neurological difficulties? What happened?"

"Convulsive seizures."

"Bobby Tatum?"

"On cursory examination it seems to be a left frontal-lobe disturbance. Do you have a complete history on him?"

"I've been treating him for two years. For the rest I have the records of his two previous pediatricians."

"You're his third pediatrician and he's only five years old," Jean remarked. Then she said suddenly, "Can I see Bobby's records?"

"Right now?"

"Right now."

"I thought tonight you'd be a woman, not a neurologist," he reprimanded, hurt.

"I can be both," she promised. "First, those records."

A short time later they were in Larry's office. Jean examined Bobby's file. The history corroborated everything Marissa Tatum had told her. No serious illness during pregnancy, no physical trauma that might have affected the development of his nervous system. The only unusual circumstance surrounding his birth was the premature delivery by cesarean. The infant had required intensive care for several weeks. Once released, there was no indication of any difficulty that would later produce seizures.

She read through Larry's own notes on Bobby Tatum, about periodic checkups that were favorable, and an occasional cold. For a boy of five the record was uneventful.

"Well?" Larry asked.

"Nothing significant. Yet he does have those seizures. We're doing skull X rays, an echoencephalogram and an EEG first thing in the morning."

"Keep me advised."

"Of course."

"And now, what about that woman you promised me?"

Jean smiled, pulled the pins out of her hair and shook her head till her long, gleaming auburn strands fell to her shoulders. He took her in his arms and kissed her. She held him tightly.

After a long moment of closeness, she said, "I disapprove of office lovemaking." He drew back, rebuffed, until she smiled and added, "I prefer my own home."

IT WAS LONG PAST midnight, and Larry was asleep. It was comforting to hear his breathing beside her. She had lived a great part of her life alone. But she had never grown used to it.

She edged up, so that leaning against the headboard she could stare down at him. His features were strong, yet finely cut. His hair was curly, his shoulders broad and muscular. In college he had had to make a choice between going on to medical school or playing professional basketball. He had opted in favor of medical school. A good thing, Jean felt. He was an excellent pediatrician.

He had had one marriage. Unsuccessful, because his wife had refused to put up with the continuous disruption of their lives by his little patients' parents. She divorced him. It made him realize that his work was paramount in his life. Any woman from now on would have to love his profession as much as he did.

Love of their respective work was one of the bonds between Larry and Jean. They were understanding when the other's professional obligations disrupted their plans. There were no recriminations, only a quiet acceptance. Trips and vacations they planned were frequently canceled. But that only made more precious the hours they did manage together.

To Jean the most loving thing about Lawrence Braham was that he respected her as a colleague in professional situations, yet was able to treat her as a woman at all other times. He was a considerate and sensitive man.

In her mind there was a kinship between Larry and Cliff, both kind, dedicated men. Cliff had devoted himself to the diplomatic service with the same dedication that Larry gave to medicine. It had cost Cliff his life. And had changed Jean's forever.

She always thought about that more after nights she spent with Larry. She suspected a sense of guilt at being unfaithful to Cliff's memory. Yet perhaps Cliff would have approved. The memory of him both comforted and troubled her.

HOW YOUNG and eager she had been about their future in the early days of her marriage to Cliff. She had come through medical school with an enviable record, and was invited to do her residency in Neurology under Dr. Benziger. He looked forward to her moving up the academic ladder under his tutelage. For he was seeking, among his brightest students, the one who could eventually carry on when he retired.

Benziger's plan would have been fulfilled if Clifford Scofield, graduate of the Georgetown School of Foreign Service, young assistant on the Southeast Asia desk at the State Department, hadn't been notified he was being transferred out of the country.

He had not waited till she came home to tell Jean but had picked her up at the hospital. They drove to a restaurant, and finally, over the wine, he told her. He was being transferred. Away from a desk, away from living on cabled reports. At last he was going out into the field. He would have direct contact with a foreign government, responsibilities of his own. He was making his way upward in the State Department.

As she listened to him, so excited by his new opportunity, she had no desire to cast shadows upon his ambitions by mentioning what they would mean to hers. She consoled herself with the thought that any country would have a need for her science. So, over dinner, she shared his enthusiasm. She would go wherever he wanted, and she would make a good life for them, without regrets.

The next morning, first thing, she had told Benziger.

"Of course," he said. "I expected it all along." Inwardly he felt the pang a father feels when his daughter is going to marry and move to some far-off place. He was losing her. Yet he knew he had no right to influence her decision. He offered to write to a colleague, a Dr. Werner, with whom he had trained in Heidelberg, and who now headed up a small hospital in Saigon.

"But," Jean said, "Cliff won't be stationed in Saigon. He'll be out in the countryside, in the highlands, working with the peasant officials in border areas. Some kind of unification program against the Vietcong."

"Then Werner will know what medical help's needed out there among the peasants. It'll be a transition in your career, but an enlightening experience. There's a lot to learn in primitive areas. Here, secluded among our modern laboratories and huge libraries, we tend to lose sight of the patient. To go back to the basics would be good for all of us."

That is what Hans Benziger said. But with each word it became more apparent that he was trying to keep himself and Jean from feeling the disappointment too keenly.

IN SAIGON, Dr. Werner explained the medical situation in the countryside. There were a few peasant doctors, ill-trained, undersupplied. There was much work to do, but it was hardly the place for a young female physician. She would be resented by the local doctors and shunned by the natives till she proved herself. And she would be in danger always from Vietcong guerrillas.

Jean was willing to risk it. She studied sufficient native phrases to make herself understood; and, equipped with a small supply of medicines, she set out in a jeep with a guide to find one of the camps that Dr. Tom Dooley had maintained years earlier when he was in Vietnam.

Jean's first week was spent making the place habitable again. Then word began to spread. There was a new doctor, willing to help all comers, just as Dooley had done. But patients were not quick to appear. She assumed it was because she was a woman. Eventually they came. She treated young and old, surprising them with her capability. It became a source of enormous satisfaction to Jean that her work was profoundly appreciated.

She paid a price for it, though. The times she could get away to meet Cliff grew fewer and fewer. They had to snatch a day together here and there. His work required days out in the villages —in small huts in humid places with strange names like Quong Sung and My Lai.

They made the most of their rare weekends in Saigon. They ate in excellent French restaurants, walked busy streets just beginning to abound with American troops. They spent nights promising to spend more time together as soon as things let up. Secretly each knew that things were never going to let up. They lived on promises. But the rarity of their hours alone made these few nights more precious. And more desperate, somehow. It was during one of those nights when desperation was strongest that Jean decided to become pregnant. Whether out of a premonition of danger or her subconscious desire to leave her native practice in good conscience, she decided that the time had come.

She kissed Cliff good-by in Saigon that morning, and whispered in his ear what she had been hoping. He laughed, cradled her in his arms, then kissed her.

Three weeks later, the signs were favorable. By the time they met again, there was no question. Cliff made her consult a gynecologist in Saigon. She promised to spend the last two months of her pregnancy in the city, with modern medical facilities close at hand. Cliff would arrange his assignment so that he would be close to Saigon when her time came.

They parted again, as they had a dozen times in the past ten months. Cliff went back into the field. Jean returned to her primitive hospital to resume treating her patients.

In her fifth month of pregnancy Jean was awakened one night by an urgent knock on the door of her hut. She called out in Vietnamese, as she had during other nighttime emergencies, "Just a minute! The doctor is coming!"

She was drawing her cotton robe around her when a man's voice, not with the native accent she had grown used to, but clearly American, called back, "Dr. Scofield?"

Startled, she went to the door, peered into the darkness. "Yes?" The man she addressed wore the dirty combat gear of a Green Beret—a Special Forces officer.

"Doctor, there's been a Vietcong guerrilla attack. On a local village, a province capital . . . There's only one survivor, and he's in bad condition."

Jean pushed the door wider to search the officer's face. "You're trying to tell me something."

"The attack was planned to coincide with the visit to the village by an American from the State Department."

"You're saying he was there? My husband was there?"

"Yes, ma'am. They fragged his hut. Two grenades. Lots of shrapnel. He sustained a bad head wound."

"Shrapnel . . . head wound . . ." All the terrible possibilities raced through her mind. "Wait, I'll go with you!"

She drew on some clothes, trying to reassure herself that she could help him, since this was in the field of her specialty. All during the rough ride in the open jeep she kept rehearsing what she would look for, what tests she would make.

It took almost four hours to negotiate the fifty-one miles to the village. There was still smoke rising from several burned-out huts. Outside one hut two Americans in combat gear stood guard. Jean leaped from the jeep, raced past the guards and into the hut. On the earthen floor lay Cliff Scofield. Kneeling beside him was a medical officer making a desperate check of vital signs, trying to find a pulse.

Jean rushed to Cliff, pushed the doctor aside, removed the gauze pad that covered most of Cliff's head and stared at the large gaping wound. She pulled back, stunned. She turned to the officer, who confirmed her worst fears.

"No responses. In all four limbs."

"I don't believe it!" Trying to evoke some reaction, she jabbed a needle into the soles of Cliff's feet, into his thighs, his fingers, his arms. Not the slightest response. Every cell in her body was desperate to do something, anything, if only to keep him breathing, in the vain hope that something might be done at the base hospital. Yet all the while she knew it was impossible even to move him.

Finally all she could do was sit beside him, holding his hand, till long after the medical officer told her he was dead and they would take his body back to base. She was numb when she rode beside him in the ambulance. She was numb when his senior State Department officer expressed the sympathy of the entire department and the Secretary of State. She was numb until, in an American military cemetery, they lowered his body into a shallow grave and fired shots over it.

It was when they folded the flag and handed it to her that she was no longer numb, and broke down in tears. She dropped to the earth and began to talk to Cliff. No effort could pry her away. She talked in a rapid, compulsive way that led the medical officer in charge to be concerned about her. But she would not leave, nor take any sedation. At last the officer assigned a nurse to stay with her until she might talk herself out and be willing to depart.

She remained at Cliff's graveside until the rain began to fall. When she became aware of it, she covered his grave with her body. The nurse sought to restrain her. Jean pushed her aside violently. She let the rain beat down on her as she lay across his grave—her husband, the father of her unborn child.

Her pain started soon after. Her delivery was thirteen weeks premature. There was no chance of saving the child. By that time it hardly mattered. Jean Scofield was in no condition to fully appreciate the double tragedy which had overtaken her.

Once she had been brought home, Dr. Hans Benziger insisted that she be entrusted to his care. The day she was brought back to University Hospital he did a complete examination. Aside from general debilitation resulting from her refusal to take food, her physical condition was unimpaired. The trouble was not in her body.

She was given a room in the psychiatric wing. Several weeks of sedation and feeding produced no change. Visits from family and friends had not brought her out of her deep, almost catatonic depression. She sat in a corner and stared at the wall. She ate little. She grew thinner, her once lovely face drawn. She presented the classic signs of a deep, long-lasting, post-traumatic depression.

The psychiatrists whom Benziger brought in offered little real aid. The most significant factor in Jean's emotional difficulty, they felt, was that Clifford Scofield's fatal injury was to the brain. Since neurology was Jean's field, her guilt at not being able to help him was greatly magnified. It negated her entire training, making her feel doubly guilty.

The specialists theorized in that vein until Hans Benziger suddenly exploded. "Damn it, I want a cure for her! And if you can't supply one, save your theories for your students!"

They forgave his outburst, knowing how much he loved this young protégée. Eventually Benziger came under pressure from the chief of Psychiatry to consign her to a mental hospital. He stubbornly refused. He spent nights reading psychiatric literature, hoping to come across a case that would give him a clue as to how to breach the impenetrable wall Jean Scofield had erected in her tortured mind.

More weeks went by. Jean's condition did not improve, which in itself meant she had deteriorated. The longer a depression continued, the worse the prognosis.

One day Hans Benziger was sitting in an interdepartmental staff conference, half listening to Dr. Ernest Wilding, chief of Pediatrics, addressing the group on a serious problem in his department. The rate of illegitimate births was increasing. Young girls were having their babies under fictitious names, then abandoning them by slipping out of the hospital, leaving no trace of their identity. The Pediatrics Department was thus confronted with an almost insoluble problem.

There was no shortage of adoptive parents for healthy infants. But, the mothers having vanished, the adoption papers could not be completed without lengthy court procedures. During that time, damage was being inflicted on the infants. Deprived of a mother's embraces, kisses—without close physical comfort and warmth—some infants had begun to waste. They refused to eat. They developed ailments generally associated with adult emotional traumas. Skin rashes. Stomach ulcers. They failed to thrive. In severe instances, due to lack of weight gain, some even sustained brain damage. A devoted staff of pediatric nurses did what they could. Some stayed overtime to hold the infants, to rock them, feed them. Such infants fared better by far than the ones deprived of close human contact.

The problem now, Dr. Wilding was saying, seemed to be to create a program of voluntary help to replace the missing mothers. All departments were invited to make suggestions. At this stage of the discussion Hans Benziger was listening intently, since his field, neurology, spanned both the physical and psychiatric aspects of a patient's care. An idea was forming in the back of his mind.

The next day he went up to Jean Scofield's small private room. He eased the door open softly and peered in.

There she sat, on a stool, facing the wall, garbed in a plain hospital gown. Benziger looked about the room. Aside from books which he had left in the hope of enticing her to read, the room held little except the bed.

"Jean," he said softly. "How are you feeling today?"

As usual there was no answer. He moved closer to her, noticing the hollow cheeks, the deep circles under the eyes. She gave him no sign of recognition. He was always disappointed, but now no longer surprised. Something, he told himself, must be done. He patted her gently on the cheek and left.

The next morning Benziger went to see Dr. Wilding. "Ernest, about those infants you discussed yesterday at the conference—I want you to give me the sickliest one in your ward."

"What do you propose to do?"

"You said that the problem was lack of personal care. I shall attempt to supply that."

"How?"

Benziger hesitated. If he revealed his plan, Wilding would likely refuse. Yet, if he didn't reveal it he would surely refuse.

"Do you have a small private room near the infants' nursery?" he asked.

"Yes," Wilding said cautiously. "Room forty-two."

"Good. I will have a patient who is to care for the child transferred there before the day is out. Place the infant in that room, with all the equipment to feed, bathe and change it."

Wilding stared at Benziger.

"Please, Ernest. It is most important."

Wilding yielded. "Okay, Hans, bring your patient down from Neurology."

"Not Neurology," Benziger said. "Psychiatry."

"Psychiatry?" Wilding protested.

"Please. For a day or two. There's little danger. You may keep a nurse standing by so that the infant is protected from whatever it is you fear."

Finally Wilding acquiesced.

BABY SMITH, so designated since the mother had left without even naming him, was two months old. He had been healthy at birth. Since then, however, instead of a normal weight gain he actually showed a loss, exhibited a rash over most of his body and had difficulty keeping down food. He was now in a dangerous state; his discouraging prognosis justified a risk taken to ameliorate his condition. Baby Smith had been selected by Dr. Wilding as his patient most in need of personal care.

Hans Benziger had Jean Scofield brought over from the psychiatric wing. As he escorted her down the hall in Pediatrics, nurses who had known her in an earlier time were shocked at the sight of her. The happy, vivacious young woman they had known, whose green eyes sparkled so, was now frail, thin, hollow-eyed.

Benziger led her into the small room, which held only a hospital bed, a lounge chair, and a table on which had been laid out the equipment for changing and feeding an infant. In a corner of the room stood a bassinet. Benziger said, "Jean, my dear, you will be here for a while. If you want anything, tell the nurse and she will call me."

Jean did not react. It was impossible to tell if she had understood. He slipped out of the room and signaled the floor nurse. She went into the nursery and came out carrying an infant surrounded by blankets. She took that infant, Baby Smith, into room 42, came out in a few moments and nodded to Benziger.

He waited. He heard the crying of the child. Soon the plaintive sound filled the hallway. The floor nurse started for the room. Benziger intercepted her. "Wait!"

The crying continued. The nurse made no secret of her disapproval. Benziger remained steadfast.

Inside the room Jean sat staring at the blank white wall, unaware of the small, pathetic human being in the bassinet. She remained unaware even after the crying grew louder. In the only way at its command, the infant was expressing its hunger and solitude, its need for human touch.

Later, when Jean would think back over it, she would never be able to reconstruct the feelings and events which followed. But finally the sound beckoned her in a strange way, as if in a dream. Her son was crying. Cliff's son was in need of her. She rose from her chair and turned to look about the room. For the first time she saw the table, the equipment, the bassinet, the small bundle of blanket in it.

She brushed aside the blanket and stared down at the infant, crying, squirming, its arms and legs flailing. Having cried itself to the point of exhaustion, it had begun to gasp. Jean stared for a long time before she dared to reach out. She lifted it gently, as if her shocked mind were reaching into the past and guiding her. She held the pitiful little thing to her body.

Soon he ceased to gasp and fell into a light sleep. Jean sat in the lounge chair holding the child in her arms until, gaining solace from its sense of security, she herself fell asleep, for the first time since her illness without sedation. She dozed only briefly, for cries of hunger wakened her. She placed the infant on the bed and went to the table to prepare a bottle from the supplies in the warmer.

The task exceeded the skills she could summon. She was trying to cap the bottle with the nipple when it slipped from her hands and shattered on the floor. She broke down and began to weep. The cries of the infant grew louder. Soon the door opened and Hans Benziger entered.

"Jean!" he commanded.

She turned to him, tried to explain and apologize all at once, but broke down again, pointing to the mess on the floor.

"The child is hungry," Benziger said. "There is another bottle. But no one to feed him. The nurses are all busy. The child will go hungry unless *you* feed him!"

She stared at him, then surrendered to his commanding look. She took a fresh bottle from the table, filled it, and this time was able to cap it.

She lifted the infant into her arms, pressed the nipple into his mouth. The crying gave way to contented sucking. Soon it was the only sound in the room.

The vacant, distant look which had possessed Jean Scofield's eyes for so long began to diminish. She looked down at the infant with a sense of closeness and identity. Both of them had been sadly deprived.

Hans Benziger spoke in a soft but pointed way. "Jean, this infant is on the border line. If he grows worse, he will probably die. Unless we heal him. This child needs care. To make up for all the personal warmth and contact he has been denied. He needs a mother. To replace the one who abandoned him. Yes, Jean, abandoned. You know what that feels like. You were abandoned. Suddenly. Knowing what it is like, I want you to make up for it to this

infant. I will know you have succeeded if this child becomes healthy enough to be adoptable. Do you understand? Jean?"

She nodded.

SEVEN WEEKS LATER Baby Smith was selected for adoption by a family which had been approved by the hospital and the Department of Social Services. When the time came to hand Baby Smith over, Jean Scofield asked to talk to the new mother.

"He is a good baby. And he lives on affection. So whatever you do for him, do it with love. And one thing more," Jean said. "If you haven't decided on a name, I would appreciate it if you named him Clifford."

"Clifford, Cliff," the young woman said. "It's a nice name."

The seven weeks had done wonders for Jean, too. In her need to tend the infant she had refused all sedatives. She had begun to eat regularly, to keep up her strength in order to cope with the demands of foster-motherhood. Gradually she had emerged from her depression.

On the day she handed over the infant to his new parents, Jean told Hans Benziger, "I'm ready to go back to work."

Benziger smiled and nodded. "I've been waiting for you," was all he said.

The entire staff was delighted at Jean's return. She had always been respected for her ability, and loved for her kind and efficient manner. Her illness became a thing of the past.

It had not been mentioned in several years now. Not until the conflict arose over who was going to succeed Hans Benziger when he retired in six months. Then it was recalled by Dr. Ralph Sunderland, an ambitious rival for the post of chief of Neurology. He mentioned it to Edward Carey one day, citing it as proof that a woman was not up to such a demanding job. Since Carey knew that Horace Cameron favored Sunderland's appointment, he had adopted Sunderland's argument as his own.

TONIGHT, as Jean looked down at Larry Braham's handsome face, she wondered what it might do to them if she persisted in her ambition to become chief. Sunderland and Carey would make public issue of that tragic part of her past. Of course, Larry would defend her. But the trustees would impugn his motives. "He's in love with her. Why shouldn't he defend her?"

She was willing to endure her own embarrassment. She did not wish to compromise Larry. There was also another danger. If her past became an open issue, might it alter the way Larry felt about her? Sooner or later, might not some part of the slander worm its way into his mind and corrode the love they shared now? When she contemplated that, she realized how much she loved him.

Except for the memory of Cliff, she could love Larry without any reservations.

Chapter Three

Jean Scofield and Larry Braham arrived at University Hospital in separate cars and met shortly thereafter at Bobby Tatum's bedside. The youngster was having breakfast. Aside from drowsiness due to medication, he seemed healthy if withdrawn.

"Good morning, Bobby," Dr. Braham greeted him.

"Good morning, Dr. Larry. Why am I here?"

"You just fainted a few times. Dr. Scofield took care of you. You know her, don't you?"

"Yes, sir," Bobby said. Jean smiled at him. The boy did not smile back. "She did a lot of funny things to me." He pushed back his tray, staring at her suspiciously.

"We're going to do more funny things this morning, Bobby," Jean said. "And they won't hurt, I promise you."

He remained tense throughout the neurological examination, yet offered no resistance. Gently as she could, Jean repeated the tests she had done the day before. The results were the same. By the time she had finished, the portable X-ray and echoencephalogram equipment were being wheeled into the room.

The boy lay still, rigid with fear, while the X rays and the echoencephalogram—a measurement by sound waves of the internal structures of Bobby's skull—were being taken.

"I want those plates stat," Jean ordered. "I'll be down to Radiology to see them as soon as I leave here."

Another technician arrived with electroencephalogram equipment. He fixed the conductor electrodes to the boy's head and started the EEG. Both physicians watched the pen move jerkily across the graph paper, tracing the electrical impulses emitted by the little patient's brain. Jean saw the spiked focus that indicated the area from which the seizures probably emanated. As she suspected, most likely a left frontal cerebral abnormality.

As the technician removed the electrodes the boy grew even more tense. Seeking to reassure him, Jean leaned close, reaching to pat his face. He drew back from her, his dark eyes staring in fear. It was an unusual reaction, even from a five-year-old in a new environment. Jean said warmly, "Now, Bobby, we want you to rest. You'll stay with us for a few days."

Bobby was thoughtful, as if debating whether or not to trust Jean. Finally he asked, "My mommy—will she come to see me?"

"Yes, of course."

He hesitated. "She won't like it if I'm sick."

"She'll want to help you get better," Jean reassured.

For herself, far from reassured, she was suddenly disturbed by this strange and guileless remark from a frightened child. It was not the sort of remark a neurologist would set down on a patient's chart. But it was the sort of response an alert, observant physician would not be likely to forget soon.

JEAN AND LARRY went down to examine the skull plates. A radiologist stood by to interpret. "Look clean to me," he said. "Whatever the EEG picked up, it wasn't due to a fracture."

Back in Jean's examining room, she and Larry studied the EEG tape again. Helpful. But not enough. It had located irritation but did not reveal the cause.

"Of course, an X ray isn't definitive," Larry said.

"No," she admitted. "A fine-line fracture in a child could heal and leave no trace." She was thoughtful for a moment. "I hate to do an angiogram on a child. It's so uncomfortable."

"And there *is* risk," Larry added.

In the afternoon Jean stopped by to check other patients on the same floor as Bobby Tatum. Her last stop was at Bobby's bedside, in the intensive care unit. He was drowsing. She touched his arm and leg, lightly pinching the tendons to test for vestigial right-side weakness. He opened his eyes.

"Hello, Bobby," she greeted warmly.

"Hello." He was still tense, even under sedation. "Is Dr. Larry . . ." He seemed unable to find the next word.

"He was in to see you. You were asleep. Bobby, from now on I'm going to be your doctor, too."

"What's your name?" the boy asked.

"Dr. Scofield. But you can call me Dr. Jean if you like."

"Dr. Jean," he tried it out. "Why am I here?"

"You may be sick, and we want to find out why. But we won't hurt you, Bobby."

He was not relieved. Instead he groped for a small model car that lay at the edge of his bed.

"I see your mommy was here."

"I was sleeping. She brought me this." He embraced the toy.

"You'll be sleeping a lot for the next few days, Bobby. It's good for you."

He nodded. The boy was obviously frightened and withdrawn, suspicious of her attempts to befriend him. But she accounted for that—to him she was still a stranger and a doctor.

Jean came out of the intensive care unit to find Marissa Tatum waiting. "Well, Doctor?" the mother asked anxiously.

"We don't know much yet," Jean said soothingly. "But we have been able to prevent any new seizures."

"But they could come back?"

"They could," Jean admitted. "Till we find the cause, we have only one thing. Medication."

"What if that doesn't work?"

The woman was so emotional that Jean decided the truth would punish her less than her own fantasies. "Why don't we go to my office so we can discuss this in private?"

The quiet of Jean's consulting room, with its soft lighting, was a calming, more relaxing ambience in which to discuss the case with the nervous mother, who smoked incessantly.

"Even if we never discover the cause, the patient usually responds to medication," Jean began. "Then, as long as the patient is not subjected to great stresses, he can live a normal life."

The mother nodded as she tried to absorb what Jean Scofield was saying.

"Your job, once he gets home, will be to see that he takes his medication on time and in exactly the prescribed dosage. That is most important. In other respects, he's to be treated like a normal child. Except to be forbidden certain risky activities. Swimming, climbing, bicycle riding. So if a seizure does occur, he won't be thrust into sudden danger."

"What if the medication *doesn't* stop his seizures?" Marissa Tatum demanded.

It was one of those moments which doctors face too often. When a lie is eventually unwise, but the blunt truth can prove alarming. Jean Scofield always chose the carefully stated truth.

"Intransigent seizures *can* lead to damage. Brain damage."

"Intransigent?"

"When the patient continues to have seizures despite medication. But Bobby responded very well to the phenobarbital."

"Why does it happen? Brain damage from seizures, I mean."

"Some doctors believe they induce a chemical change in the brain."

"Then we must see that the seizures are controlled!"

"We'll do all *we* can," Jean said pointedly. "But you must never let Bobby detect how tense *you* are."

"I won't," the mother promised quickly.

DIRECTOR OF ADMINISTRATION Edward Carey's phone rang. Dr. Braham had arrived for their four-o'clock meeting, his secretary said.

Carey went to the door to make a ceremony of greeting him. Tired from a day of catching up on cases that had accumulated during his week away, Larry had little patience for ceremony. Still, knowing Carey's artifices, he indulged him.

"Doctor, I need your help. I needn't tell you the chairmanship of a department is the crowning achievement of every academic's career. Such rewards should go to those who have earned them." Carey smiled nervously before he continued. "Unfortunately, there's hardly a man in any department who doesn't feel that he fills that bill. The result? Each time we appoint a new chief, some malcontents leave for other institutions. It's difficult to be a colleague one day and a subordinate to the same man the next. You can imagine how much worse it would be if the person elevated to a chairmanship were a woman."

"Dr. Scofield is a most remarkable *physician!* That's the important thing, Carey!"

"Believe me, I wouldn't hesitate for an instant to recommend her as chief to the trustees. But my concern is the morale of the entire department. That's why I'm asking you to intercede. Explain to her, as only you can, that she *has* to take the new special post of associate chief."

"I'm afraid I wouldn't have much influence with her."

Carey stared at him, then smiled. A small smile, it betrayed an aura of lewdness.

"Carey, I know Dr. Scofield very well—"

"Shall we say intimately?" Carey interrupted.

Larry repeated with precise emphasis, "I know Dr. Scofield very well. But I could not convince her to do something that she doesn't choose to do. Is that clear?"

"Yes. Just as it's clear that when the infighting starts, someone is bound to mention her unfortunate depression—"

"That was years ago," Braham pointed out.

"*And* her present relationship with you. Someone is bound to bring it up."

"I'm sure you will," Braham shot back before he walked out.

Carey leaned back in his chair, defeated for the moment but not resigned to having lost. He had promised Horace Cameron that before the next meeting of the board of trustees he would resolve the matter to everyone's satisfaction. Meaning, of course, Cameron's.

A self-made success, Horace Cameron equated all women with his own dear, long-departed mother. She had cooked and washed for her large family, and raised sons and daughters of whom any woman could well be proud. She had worked hard all her married life, with no energy to think of women's rights. That was as it should be. She was Cameron's model for a good, proper woman.

The first time the name Jean Scofield had been mentioned as possible chief of Neurology, Cameron responded, "Ed, are we going to have a woman chief? In our hospital?"

Carey pointed out that the federal government, the largest single supporter of academic hospitals, insisted on women in jobs of responsibility.

"In my business, we find ways around governments every day! Find one, Carey!"

Carey thought he could. But without the help of Hans Benziger or Larry Braham, that would be difficult. There must be other ways—else Cameron might start looking for a new chief, too. A new administrative chief.

AT THE FIRST HINT on the phone that his son was ill, Bob Tatum insisted on flying home immediately. When Horace Cameron heard, he had put his private jet at Tatum's disposal. A meeting was now taking place in Jean's office with the Tatums and Larry Braham.

Jean explained in detail all that she knew about Bobby's seizures. Also all she did not know, which, unfortunately, was still a great deal.

Bob Tatum looked to Marissa but was unable to say more than, "Our poor Bobby . . . poor Bobby . . ." Then he turned to stare out the window, allowing Jean to study him closely.

He was a handsome man. Tall. Broad-shouldered. Well muscled. Jean especially noticed his powerful hands when he cracked his knuckles nervously. Undoubtedly those hands had helped to make him an all-American fullback; Larry had told her of his college career. Yet for all his physical attributes, at this moment he appeared to be only another stunned, sensitive father.

Gently Jean prodded, "Mr. Tatum? What are you thinking?"

"Thinking?" he echoed self-consciously. "Crazy, but I was thinking, at InterElectronics we make some of the complex equipment that helped put men on the moon. And here we are helpless when it comes to finding out what goes on in the head of just one little five-year-old boy."

Larry intervened: "Bob, Dr. Scofield didn't say we *couldn't* find out. She only said we haven't found out *yet*."

"Well, then, *find* out! Do something!"

"Mr. Tatum," Jean began, "we have to proceed cautiously. The fact that we have the skill to open a child's skull and explore his brain does not mean we should rush into it."

"Explore? Doctor, you're hinting at something terrible."

Jean corrected: "I haven't been hinting. I've laid out the entire case. And the facts are not as bad as you would make them seem."

"Aren't they? My son can't do any of the things a man looks forward to teaching his son as he grows up . . . can't go swimming, can't ride a bicycle—"

"Can't play football," Jean suggested, suspecting the real source of Tatum's disappointment. "Lots of boys become highly successful men without ever becoming all-Americans."

Tatum glared at her. "Nobody can forget I was all-American. But I also had a three-point-seven average for four years." He rose to his feet. "Doctor, I no more got to be what I am at InterElectronics because I played football than you got to be an expert neurologist because you happen to be such an attractive woman."

He began to pace. "I won't deny football was the way I first came to Mr. Cameron's attention. But if I didn't have the brains to make the most of that chance, I'd be what most other heroes become. A colorful conversation piece to have around for a while. Until another, newer, more colorful one comes along.

"Especially with Mr. Cameron, who likes winners. He prides himself on picking future winners. Which is okay by me. Because that's exactly the game I'm best at. I'm one of only four men eligible to succeed to Cameron's job when he's ready to quit. By which time I intend to be the only one who is his logical successor.

"Football may *open* the doors. But only brains can *keep* them open. So I want you to tell me now that my son's brain is perfect!"

"Mr. Tatum, this is what Dr. Braham and I suggest. We'll keep Bobby here to see if his seizures recur. If they don't, we'll let him go home on a regime of medication. A drug called Dilantin. When that stabilizes in his blood at the proper level, we hope he'll be seizure-free. If not, we'll make further tests."

"And operate?" Tatum asked quickly.

"That would be our last resort," Jean said cautiously, since she had not been able to rule out a brain tumor. "The main thing is, at home, don't make him self-conscious about what happened."

Tatum nodded, still visibly tormented by his son's condition. "May I see him now?"

"Of course."

The Tatums started to leave, but Jean called out, "Mr. Tatum?" He turned. "When Bobby was small, did you roughhouse with him? Throw him up in the air, make believe you were going to let him fall, then catch him?"

"Doesn't every father do that?"

"Yes. But did you ever actually drop him?"

"Of course not!" Tatum replied resentfully.

The Tatums were gone. Jean was surprised to find how tense she had become during the interview.

"Is he always like that?" she asked Larry.

"He's always been a winner. He doesn't know how to cope with defeat."

"You call having a son like Bobby a defeat?"

"He's not likely to be content with a son who is less than perfect," Larry warned. "Jean, do you suspect that the cause of Bobby's seizures is brain trauma, induced by overenthusiastic horseplay?"

"Until I make a definite diagnosis, I suspect everything," Jean said. "I'm going to keep the boy longer than four days."

"Tatum won't stand for it," Larry warned.

"He may not like it. But he'll stand for it."

BOB TATUM moved silently and cautiously to his son's bed. "Bobby?" he whispered.

The boy opened his eyes, then blinked to make sure. "Dad?"

"I heard you weren't feeling well. So I flew right back."

"I'm okay."

"They treat you well here?"

"Yes, sir. I think the nurses like me."

"Why shouldn't they? You're a terrific boy!"

"Can I go back to school? We're going to make special Indian costumes for Thanksgiving. Is it Thanksgiving yet?"

"You'll be back in school long before Thanksgiving. And you can be an Indian. Or a Pilgrim. Or anything you want, Bobby boy."

"Miss Halsted said Indians."

"Okay, then you'll be the best Indian of them all!" Tatum said, taking his son's hand. Comforted by his father's presence, Bobby closed his eyes and fell asleep.

AT THE END of eight days Dr. Scofield studied Bobby Tatum's chart carefully. There was still no clear indication of the etiology of his seizures. The results of the neurological tests were good. Were it not for his seizures, now apparently under control, he would have to be considered a perfectly healthy child.

One particular statistic had changed. The boy showed a noticeable weight gain since his admission to the hospital. She had also observed that he seemed far less tense, was much freer and friendlier than during his first few days.

She stopped by to see him. "Did they tell you? You're going home this morning, Bobby."

"Yes, Dr. Jean," the boy said. "Am I all right?"

"If you do what Mommy says, you'll be fine. Bobby, from now on, anytime you don't feel well, tell Mommy as soon as it happens. If you're in school, tell your teacher. Understand?"

The handsome dark-haired boy thought a moment, then nodded.

"Do you like it here, Bobby?"

"Oh, yes. After the first few days I liked it a lot. Neat," he said, remembering an expression he heard older boys use.

"Then you can come back and visit. Every few weeks, you can spend a day or two here. We'll be very happy to see you."

She had laid the foundation for his checkups, which would be essential. During her instructions the boy had reached out timidly toward her. She permitted him to run his small fingers gently across her hand. It was a token of affection that touched her deeply. And it was a gesture that could be revealing as well.

JEAN AND LARRY were giving final instructions to the Tatums. "He is to take his Dilantin in the prescribed doses," Jean stressed. "One pill three times a day. Every day. At home, in school, wherever—he must have his medication on schedule. As long as the Dilantin level remains stable he shouldn't have seizures."

"Good!" Tatum interjected.

"I said shouldn't, not wouldn't, Mr. Tatum," Jean pointed out. "Now, anyone in whose charge he is placed—maid, grandparent—must be made aware of what to do if a seizure does recur."

She turned to the mother. "Don't alarm his teacher. If she's frightened, it will transmit itself to your son, and eventually to his classmates. The problem of living with possible seizures is as much psychological as physical, so don't give the boy any indication of your own anxieties.

"If a seizure is about to occur, Bobby may give you a signal. He may say he's tired. He may simply lie down on his own. He may only experience a feeling of strangeness which he can't explain. It's what we call an aura. A prelude.

"If a seizure does occur, hold his head to keep him from hurting himself. If you can, insert a gauze-covered wooden tongue depressor between his teeth to keep him from biting his tongue. Do not insert anything metallic. That can cause broken teeth. Never insert your fingers. Mainly, be sure he has an open passageway to breathe. Epileptics can choke on their own mucus."

Bob Tatum stared at her hostilely. "Epileptic. You never said Bobby was an epileptic. Something's changed!"

Larry interceded. "Epileptic is a general term for anyone who has seizures. It's nothing more serious than what Dr. Scofield said before."

Tatum did not argue, but neither did he seem mollified.

Jean completed her instructions by saying, "Bring Bobby back for testing in two weeks. We'd like to keep him overnight."

Bob Tatum nodded. It was clear his cooperation was extended without any great enthusiasm.

That forced Jean to say, "Mr. Tatum, I think it would help if you understood the position of the neurologist. While we work with the patient's nervous system, we are also concerned with his mind, as distinguished from his brain. If Bobby grew up physically perfect but emotionally damaged by this experience, I would consider I'd failed him. I want to see a *completely* healthy boy. Just remember, he is not an invalid. Never let him see fear in your eyes. *Or disappointment.* Either of those could stunt him for the rest of his life."

When the Tatums were gone, the strained atmosphere Tatum left behind made Larry apologize. "He's not a bad guy. But because he's a perfectionist, he just comes on strong sometimes."

"He's a perpetual fullback," Jean commented acidly.

To change the subject, Larry asked, "Dinner tonight?"

"I'm having the Neurology residents over for a little farewell buffet. Most of them will be moving on at the end of the semester."

"I take it I'm not invited."

"There's enough talk now, Larry. Sometimes I think I ought to marry you just to protect your reputation," she said, laughing.

Before she left she glanced at Bobby Tatum's chart again. Putting aside any attitudes or prejudices formed from talking to Bob Tatum, there were provocative facts in the boy's record. He did show a weight gain while he was in the hospital. Toward the end he did become brighter, more cheerful and outgoing. Those facts could mean little. Or they could become extremely important.

Chapter Four

Two weeks had gone by quickly. Jean had to race to keep up with her own admissions to the hospital and the patients who thronged through the Neurological Clinic. Routine tests were carried out and the results passed on to Jean for diagnoses. She briefed surgeons and observed procedures. She taught her classes in the medical school. Jean always looked forward to those. She had an eager group of students.

This morning she examined her appointment log and found that the Tatum boy was due to return for a checkup today.

She had seen eight patients when Maggie announced Mrs. Tatum and Bobby. Bobby entered first, gently urged forward by his mother. He was dressed in jeans and a bright red and white striped T-shirt that set off his handsome face and his black hair. Only his blue eyes were different—less bright and yet more active.

"Good morning, Bobby," Jean greeted him.

"G'mornin', Do'tor," the boy managed, the last word almost indistinguishable.

She had noted previously that the boy spoke distinctly, was more articulate than average for his age. She turned to Mrs. Tatum. "Anything unusual during the past two weeks?"

"No, Doctor, nothing."

"No seizure? Any bed-wetting?" Which could be a sign that Bobby had had a seizure in the night.

"No."

"Good." She turned to the boy. "Come here, Bobby."

Jean watched as the boy started forward, then leaned back as if he would fall. His mother reached out to steady him.

"Bobby?" Jean invited again.

With some effort he moved toward her. She held out her arms as if to embrace him, but actually to catch him before he fell.

"There we are," she said reassuringly. She stared into his pale blue eyes, which jumped nervously. It was adding up. Slurred speech, unsteadiness, jumpy eyes. "Bobby, would you wait in the other room a little while?" Jean asked.

The boy hesitated, appeared rebuffed. Mrs. Tatum urged, "Darling, wait in there, please?"

"All right, Mommy."

His words were slurred again. He made his way toward the door, weaving and once more threatening to fall backward. Finally he reached the door safely.

"Mrs. Tatum, have you been giving Bobby his medication daily?"

"Of course!"

"How *much* do you give him?"

"What you said. One pill in the morning after breakfast. One at noon when he comes back from school. When I'm not there, Esther gives it to him. In the evening after his dinner."

"One pill . . ." Jean evaluated thoughtfully. She swung around to her phone. "Maggie, get Dr. Forrest. If he's in surgery, get a message to him that I want to see him as soon as he's free."

Marissa Tatum rose quickly. "Doctor! What is it?"

"I don't know yet. But I want a neurosurgeon to look at him. Now, I have to take Bobby down for a brain scan."

She did not want to alarm Marissa Tatum, but the boy had begun to present a set of signs that could mean one of two things: an overdose of medication, but Mrs. Tatum had ruled that out; or a tumor, a posterior fossa brain tumor involving the cerebellum.

"Mrs. Tatum, what we do is give Bobby an injection of something called technetium. It's a nuclear compound. When it gets inside the body, it moves to the brain and settles there in areas where there might be trouble. Then we put him under a scanner. The scanner tells us where there is a concentration of the technetium."

"And if there is?"

"It indicates that there's something there . . . a mass or some other difficulty. Mrs. Tatum, go down to the coffee shop or go for a walk for two hours or so. There's nothing else you can do."

Marissa Tatum nodded submissively and left the office.

IN THE DARKROOM, Jean Scofield and Walter Forrest studied the scan for concentrations of nuclear-active technetium in the boy's brain. Forrest, a tall, broad, graying man, leaned back from the viewing box that showed four films of Bobby's brain.

"I don't find anything. But we may have to go in."

"No swelling in his optic disks, no increased cranial pressure, no hot spots on the scan." Jean toted up the data.

"With all the signs he exhibits, even without confirmation on examination, a tumor could be hiding there," Forrest warned.

"Walter, would you come back to my office and talk to the boy's mother?"

"You know I'm not very diplomatic with patients' families." Forrest was known for blunt opinions and delicate surgery. "You want her to get all the gory details?"

"I have a hunch that in this case the gorier the better."

"DR. FORREST has examined Bobby," Jean began. "I've asked him to be perfectly frank with you."

"Mrs. Tatum, the signs your son exhibits are strongly indicative of a brain tumor." Marissa gasped. Forrest continued. "The tests don't reveal it. But the thing might be hiding there and we just can't pick it up. If his signs continue, we'll have to go in and take a look."

"Go in . . . take a look . . ." the mother repeated, breathless.

"If there is a tumor and it's benign, we've got a good shot at getting it all. If it's malignant, well, it depends on how far it's spread. But until we turn back a flap we won't know much."

"Turn back a flap?" Marissa Tatum mouthed the phrase.

"A flap of his skull."

She turned away, and Forrest looked to Jean. Evidently he had done it again, upset a family member by his frank, straightforward approach.

"There is another possibility," Jean suggested.

Marissa Tatum turned back, staring through tears. "Yes?"

"Bobby does show signs that might indicate a tumor. But he fails to show others. His jumpy eyes, his slurred speech, his unsteadiness could also mean an overdose of medication. I'm asking you again. How *much* Dilantin did you give the boy?"

The mother hesitated.

"It's most important that Dr. Forrest and I know. *Now.*"

Marissa Tatum was unable to answer.

Jean was sure now. She glanced at Forrest, then continued. "Mrs. Tatum, when I prescribe thirty milligrams of Dilantin three times a day, I don't mean sixty milligrams or five times a day. It's vitally important to keep the proper balance in his blood. Too little can bring back seizures. Too much might confuse the doctor into thinking she's dealing with a brain tumor."

Mrs. Tatum turned to stare off into space, her face tense.

"How much *did* you give him?"

The young woman hesitated, then admitted, "Two pills."

"Two pills three times a day?"

The mother nodded vaguely. Jean glanced at Forrest, who was annoyed, yet relieved. Jean nodded, and in order not to further embarrass the young woman, Forrest slipped out quietly.

"Why?" Jean asked pointedly.

"I thought . . . if one was good, two must be better. I didn't want that awful thing to happen again."

"Did you think *I* wanted it to happen again?"

Marissa Tatum shook her head. Tears flowed from her black eyes. They started slowly, bringing with them streaky smudges of mascara. "I . . . I didn't want Bob to see him have one of those . . ." Her words trailed off.

"I'll have to keep Bobby here five or six days. To let the effects of the overdose wear off and to do some other tests."

"I understand," Marissa Tatum agreed.

When Bobby had been settled in a bed in the neurological ward, Jean called Dr. Braham. "Larry?" she greeted crisply. "Bobby's been overmedicated. He's had double the prescribed dose."

"Marissa? Oh, no! She wouldn't do anything so foolish."

"She wouldn't. But she did. After all, she's a mother. The brightest of them can become overemotional. Would you object if I had a talk with *Mr.* Tatum? *Alone.*"

"You think Bobby's prognosis is worse than originally suspected?" Larry was concerned now.

"There's something in this situation that troubles me. But I can't put my finger on it. What about my calling Bob Tatum and having him come in?"

"No objection."

SHE WAS DICTATING case histories when her door opened briskly. She looked up. "Mr. Tatum. Come in, come in."

She pushed back from her desk to study him. He appeared full of energy. When he slipped into the chair opposite her, his shoulders seemed to loom out of it like thick branches of a huge tree.

"About Bobby," he began at once. "It's serious. That's why you wanted to talk to me alone. Good thinking. Riss . . . Marissa can be very emotional about the boy."

Jean began by telling him about Bobby's overmedication without making it seem quite so serious as it was. It was not her purpose to create friction between husband and wife. Gradually she led Tatum into describing the times he spent alone with Bobby. Then she had him talking about his own father.

"There was a man!" Tatum said with enormous admiration.

"You loved him very much?" Jean had expected a far different answer.

"Better than that, I *respected* him."

"You think a father should command or insist on respect?"

"Both!" Tatum said. "Take my father. Every break went against him. He was one hell of a halfback when he got out of high school. But just when he had scholarships to pick from, he was drafted. World War Two. When he got out it was too late.

"So he consoled himself with bringing up his sons to be athletes. I remember he used to say, 'Bobby boy, you're going to be the best there is. Every college in the country is going to knock itself out to get a fullback like you.' He kept building confidence in all three of us. My brother Steve was all-Big Ten tackle. And Grant was first-string halfback at Alabama.

"It means a lot when your dad believes in you. But it wasn't only believing. He worked with us, trained us. He made us do seven miles of roadwork every morning. He'd ride in front of us in his truck and pace us. Rain or shine. We'd run together. Steve, Grant and me. It was a competition. When I got to high school I was the youngest kid on the squad. Conditioning! How many fathers would take that much time and trouble with their sons?"

He was thoughtful for a moment. "In a way my dad was the same as Mr. Cameron. With Cameron, too, training his men is a personal thing. He doesn't leave it to others."

"Still running behind the truck, are you?"

Tatum glanced at her resentfully. "You think I didn't like that roadwork. Well, I did. And even if I didn't, I wanted to do it for *him*, because he wanted it for *me*. That's the way it should be. When I played, I played more for him than for myself. And it worked, just as he promised. It paid my way through college. Gave me the opportunity that put me where I am today."

"What do you think your father would have done if he had a son who wasn't capable of becoming a fullback?" Jean asked.

"Never could have happened! We were all big-boned and strong. Like him."

"No girls in the family?"

Tatum smiled. "We had a family joke. Dad would never have stood for girls, so Mom just didn't have any."

"Interesting," Jean said. "That's the first time you mentioned your mother."

"I know," he admitted, smiling sheepishly. "Four men in the family and not another woman, she must have been lonely."

As if he felt sentimentality was a sign of weakness, he said, "You didn't bring me here to talk about myself."

Though that had been her real motive, Jean did not contradict him. "About Bobby," Tatum said, very businesslike again. "Brief me. All the facts."

"We haven't made a definitive diagnosis yet. But part of that will involve giving him medication in the proper amounts."

"You have to understand Riss. She didn't do it out of any wrong motives. It was probably because she felt guilty."

"Guilty? About what?" Jean asked with renewed interest.

"Her delivery being premature. Bobby being born so underweight. I was afraid he'd never make it. I never dared say so. Riss was blaming herself too much already."

"Why would she blame herself?"

"Too much smoking. Too much coffee. Too active. You see, I'd been transferred again. And Riss is as fussy about houses as she is about the way she dresses. She just knocked herself out decorating that house. That meant more cigarettes, more coffee. So when Bobby was born prematurely, she blamed herself."

"And you?"

"*I* don't blame her," Tatum said loyally.

"She didn't give you a fullback," Jean pointed out.

"That boy was just born unlucky. Too soon. Too small. Never has reached what I would call good weight."

"Yes," Jean agreed, with certain thoughts of her own about that now. "He doesn't seem the type to run behind a truck, does he?"

Tatum shook his head sadly. "I'd never ask him to."

"The things you *do* ask him to do, does he do them?"

"Absolutely. He's a terrific kid. Very obedient. No back talk."

Jean nodded. "Fine, Mr. Tatum. Thank you for coming."

He did not move. "I want to know about Bobby."

"There isn't anything more to know for the time being. We'll keep him here. Get him back on his proper dosage. If you'd like to see him now, he may still be awake."

Jean went with him, ostensibly to consult Bobby's chart, mainly to observe father and son together. The boy appeared happy to see his father. Tatum leaned close, whispered to him, little things Jean could not hear but that obviously comforted him. He fell asleep holding his father's hand.

SHE RETURNED to her office and found Benziger sitting in her chair, tilted back and reading a medical paper.

"Ah, Jean," he said. "Interesting, this study on the aftereffects of cryosurgery on the brain."

"All right, Benni," she said, suspecting he was not being as direct as usual. "What now?"

Benziger smiled. "You're right. Sit down. Let's get it over with. It seems that this afternoon you called a Mr. Tatum and had him come in for a consultation."

"He's the father of a patient. There were things I had to know."

"Carey wants to know, too."

"Carey? Why?"

"Because Cameron wants to know."

"I do not discuss patients with anyone except the immediate family. You know that, Benni."

"It seems that Cameron discovered that Tatum left the office to come see you. Now Cameron wants to know the boy's condition. And what he can do about it. He does not like his executives troubled by anything that takes their minds off InterElectronics."

"What am *I* supposed to do, brief the board of trustees twice a day on the boy's condition?"

Fearing she had insulted Benziger, she apologized. "Sorry, Benni. I know you had to ask."

"That's what I'm going to welcome most when I retire. Freedom from hospital politics." He looked across at her. "Jean, my dear, are you sure you want to be chief? With all the conniving, the power struggles?"

"I'm no longer content to run behind the truck. I'm ready to come off the bench and play in the big game."

He stared at her, puzzled.

She laughed. "You would have had to be here. Okay, tell Carey no etiology has been established. When I arrive at a diagnosis, I will inform him. Or, if he would like, I'll call Cameron directly and tell him."

Benziger laughed. "If I were you, with the trustees waiting for your decision on the associate chiefship, I would avoid Mr. Cameron like the plague."

She made her notes on Tatum after Benziger left. She jotted down, "Without saying so, patient's father, like both his father and his boss, likes winners. This could be significant."

Her phone rang. An aloof British secretarial voice asked, "Dr. Scofield? One moment, please."

There was a long silence. Then a man's voice came on, soft, low and extremely confident. "Dr. Scofield? Cameron speaking."

"Oh, Mr. Cameron, yes?" Jean was on guard at once.

She realized how swiftly the word had traveled. Benziger called Carey. Carey immediately reported to Cameron. Cameron was calling. All within fifteen minutes.

There was the slightest tinge of irritation in Cameron's voice. "I made a reasonable request concerning the condition of a patient in whom I have a deep personal interest. I understand that information is not forthcoming."

"There isn't much we know. None of it definitive."

"I didn't ask for a definitive diagnosis!" Cameron was openly annoyed now. "I simply want facts. All the facts!"

"All the facts? If you wish. Clinical impression: postictal secondary to two; seizure disorder of unknown etiology, possible focus in left frontal lobe—"

Cameron exploded. "Damn it, Doctor! That's not what I want. In plain English, I insist on knowing what's wrong with that boy!"

"Mr. Cameron, that's exactly what I'd like to know, too."

There was a moment of silence before Cameron hung up briskly.

JEAN CAUGHT Larry as he was about to leave his office. "Larry? Busy this evening? I want to discuss the Tatum case."

"Of course. My office? Or dinner?"

"Dinner. But give me an hour. Something I have to do first."

"Okay."

She hesitated a moment, then dialed Radiology. When she had given specific orders, she went down to Neurology. She had an orderly roll Bobby's bed onto the elevator and up to Radiology. Within an hour she and Dr. Beecher, the resident on duty, were studying the complete set of body X rays she had ordered.

Suddenly the resident said, "You were right. There it is. Healed fine-line fracture of the fibula."

"How long ago?"

"I'd guess about two years. Maybe three."

She had confirmed one of her suspicions.

THEY WERE DAWDLING over drinks when Jean said, "Larry, Mr. Cameron called me today to inquire about Bobby Tatum."

"Cameron likes to have an electronic finger on every pulse. Get the job done, that's his motto. How did your conversation go?"

"He demanded a concise report. Maybe I was a bit sharp with him, but even if I knew what was wrong with the boy, I had no right to tell him."

"You misunderstand him," Larry defended. "He has an overpowering sense of loyalty. The men he chooses don't just work for him, he adopts them. He cares about their families, their lives. I think you should have considered that. To say nothing—" Larry stopped abruptly. "Do I have to say it?"

"As chairman of the trustees, he's going to have a lot of influence in appointing the new chief of Neurology."

"Cameron is never content to have a lot of influence. He has *all* the influence. A bad tactical mistake, Jeannie."

When he called her Jeannie, as Cliff used to do, it touched her. She wondered, Could men, too, be so affected by a single word?

She had no time to dwell on it, for Larry asked, "Now, about Bobby? Something new show up?"

She handed him the chart, TATUM, ROBERT, JR.

Puzzled, he studied it. "Well?" he asked.

"Does his weight ever trouble you?"

"He tends to be underweight. But he's not suffering from malnutrition."

"In his eight days in the hospital during his first stay he gained four pounds."

"Why not?" Larry countered. "An active child suddenly forced to undergo bed rest, being fed three meals a day, milk and cookies morning and afternoon."

"Something else changed, too. When admitted, he was withdrawn, placid—"

"Frightened," Larry interjected. "After a few days, when he got over his initial fear, he was bright and cheerful. He liked being there. And he liked *you*. What's wrong with that? I like you myself. I love you."

"He wanted to stay on," Jean said pointedly.

"He said he wanted to stay on in the hospital?"

"He didn't *say* it. He . . . communicated it. In his eyes. In his touch," she said softly.

"His touch?" Larry repeated. Then he suggested gingerly, "Jeannie, is it possible that because of her own past, the doctor might be reading something into the affection of a little boy?"

"I'm vulnerable to black-haired, blue-eyed little boys. But I'm physician enough not to let personal feelings affect my observations where a patient is concerned."

Larry covered her hand with his. "Jeannie, let's get married and have our own children. You need that. You don't owe Cliff more of your life than you've already given him."

She didn't respond. He continued. "For someone to give, there has to be someone to receive. Else giving is empty, futile."

"And sick?" she said sharply.

There was a moment of silence. Very few times in their relationship had they ever discussed her illness. He directed the conversation back to safer professional grounds.

"You said Bobby wanted to stay on. You also made a point of his weight gain. What are you getting at?"

"You're an excellent pediatrician. You ought to know."

He glanced at her, puzzled. Then his expression changed to one of surprise and disapproval. "You can't be serious!"

"What if I am?"

"*If* I didn't know his parents, *if* I hadn't examined that boy at least once every three months for two years, then maybe, possibly, I would come to the same erroneous conclusion."

"*What* conclusion?" she challenged. "I want to see if you're willing to say it."

"All right. *Child abuse.* Which is a ridiculous diagnosis! The Tatums are fine people. Socially and financially free of the pressures that lead to child abuse. You are taking a shy, sensitive boy who has a tendency to be underweight and jumping to a wild, half-baked diagnosis. Really, darling, I'm surprised at you."

"This chart states facts. His weight gain is a fact."

"But you had him under sedation. In bed. And overfed!"

"Can you explain his change in attitude? The well-adjusted, normal child becomes depressed when confined to a hospital. Conversely, a deprived or abused child thrives. Becomes happy. That boy thrived with us."

"Darling," Larry said, trying to contain his impatience, "I have observed that boy under all conditions, sick and well. I have never detected any evidence of abuse."

"Have you ever treated him for a fracture of the fibula?"

Larry stared at her, openly dubious.

"It's there. On his leg X rays."

"When did you order more X rays?" Larry demanded.

"This evening. After I talked with his father."

"I don't get the connection."

"He's a tough man, your Bob Tatum. A winner. He was brought up that way. Without realizing it, he was one type of abused child himself. His father drove him because he liked winners. So does Cameron."

"Meaning?"

"Cameron picked Bob Tatum for the same personality traits that make me suspect him of being a child abuser."

"That's a terribly serious and dangerous accusation," Larry said.

"He's strong, in personality as well as physically. No matter what he claims, he is disappointed in Bobby and might become impatient with him. He might lose his temper, resort to the thing that's always stood him in such good stead. Physical expression."

"You think he inflicted that fracture?"

"The other possibility is that he tried to toughen up the boy. Condition him, as he might say. By rough horseplay. Maybe the injury was accidental. But it was concealed nevertheless. That's almost more revealing than the injury itself."

"A fractured fibula in a child can happen without anyone knowing. And it can heal without being detected."

"Beecher, in Radiology, thinks it happened two or three years ago. Maybe it was detected, but not everything a pediatrician observes finds its way into the patient's record. Some treat nice, upper-middle-class families who abuse children and want it kept secret," Jean said firmly.

"Are you accusing his previous pediatrician? Or *me?*" he asked.

"Of course not. But don't be so intolerant of my observations."

"The Tatums are not the kind who would do anything like that," Larry defended. "They are nice, decent, intelligent people."

"If nice, decent, intelligent people could govern their emotions better than other people, there wouldn't be so many of them consulting psychiatrists! Child abuse is an emotional problem, not a cultural one."

"They're just not that kind of people," Larry insisted.

"Larry, all child abuse does not take place in the slums. The statistics show up that way only because slum families don't have the means to hide it. They are forced to go to charity clinics, which report them. Not to private practitioners, who blink at it because they don't want to lose their nice, decent, intelligent patients."

"That's a hell of an accusation to make!" Larry exploded.

Jean refused to back down. "But it *does* happen, doesn't it?"

Larry didn't answer at once. He toyed with his drink. "Yes. It happens. But what you're saying is not true of the Tatums. If I were you, I'd confine myself to treating that boy for his seizures. Let me worry about the rest of him."

Neither of them had any appetite for dessert, so Jean asked to be taken home.

After Larry dropped her off, she felt very alone. Alone in a way that reminded her of how many days and nights she had been without Cliff. There was nothing nearly so final about Larry's absence. But something had suddenly changed in their relationship. From his point of view, she had made an accusation. She hadn't intended that. She had only been determined to protect Bobby.

By the time she slipped into bed, the professional aspects of her situation paled alongside the fact that she was alone. Alone. That small two-syllable word always frightened her.

Chapter Five

Bobby Tatum was dozing lightly. "Bobby?" Jean said softly. He opened his eyes slowly. The lids fluttered, coming half open. He reached out his hand to Jean. She held it while she talked to him. She noticed that his eyes were less jumpy. He could control and focus them. "How are you feeling, Bobby?"

"Fine."

"The nurses, are they nice to you?"

"Yes, ma'am."

"Do they give you enough to eat?"

"Yes, ma'am."

Even making allowances for his overdosed condition, he was too placid and submissive. No matter what Larry said, Jean's instincts told her she was dealing with a child whose tendency to accede, to comply, to please, was not normal.

The boy slipped off to sleep again. He had pressed her hand to his cheek, so that extricating it was not easy. She did it gently, and he woke long enough to whisper, "Dr. Jean . . ." She thought he had said it affectionately. But she realized it could have been her own need that made it sound that way.

BACK IN HER OFFICE, Jean checked her schedule: "Grand rounds, 1:30." They were conducted in Cameron Hall, built with a gift from the Cameron Foundation.

Grand rounds had originated in Europe in the 1800s. In those days the professor made rounds of the wards, accompanied by his students. He would point out unique or baffling cases and ask his students to examine and diagnose them, agreeing or correcting them as part of their instruction.

These days, grand rounds were held in a meeting room. Instead of the patients themselves, usually their X rays, slides and histories were presented for opinion and discussion. The Neurology Department held its grand rounds at least once every two weeks. Today's consisted of three cases, the third of which intrigued Jean especially.

It was presented by Dr. Slake of the Department of Internal Medicine. His patient had begun to exhibit neurological signs which now made him a subject of interest for Hans Benziger's department.

A fourteen-year-old black male (no names were given during grand rounds), the patient had been admitted to the wards several months ago with a fever arising from an unknown cause. Antibiotics helped reduce his fever for a period of five days, at which time the boy was discharged. He was readmitted four days later with a fever of 104½. This time he was not released until nine fever-free days had passed. Just after his release, he ran a fever again. There had then followed a history of alternating high fevers and fever-free periods. There was no evidence of systemic infection. Two weeks ago he had begun to present signs of a neurological nature. No diagnosis had been made.

Slake admitted that his department was baffled. Considerable discussion followed. Finally Jean spoke.

"Doctor, in which ward was this patient placed?"

Slake was obviously annoyed. The question had little relevance to his problem. "The Seaton Pavilion."

"I expected that," Jean said. "I have been compiling data on Seaton. Because we've been getting an unusual number of referrals of neurological cases from Seaton, as compared with other ward buildings. I believe Psychiatric will report the same phenomenon. For some reason the cure rate in Seaton is lower than it is in other wards. That may have some bearing on your case, Dr. Slake."

"Precisely how, may I ask?"

"You said the patient is a fourteen-year-old black male. The population distribution in this city being what it is, I assume this patient comes from a slum home."

"We can assume that," Slake conceded.

"Well, so do all the Seaton cases I've investigated. I've compiled data for a report. Older ward buildings do not reflect the same rate of recurrent symptoms and readmissions. Former patients from Seaton who are readmitted to *other* wards did *not* suffer recurrences. The cause is obviously in Seaton."

"But that's our finest building," a voice protested from the rear of the auditorium. Jean recognized Edward Carey. He frequently made it a point to drop in on departmental grand rounds. "The Seaton wards are the best and newest in this city!"

"That's just the point," Jean said, turning. "Well-trained doctors, with better facilities, are curing fewer patients. And patients are having longer stays in the hospital than before."

"You are absolutely ridiculous!" Carey said vehemently.

Hans Benziger rose slowly. "Mr. Carey, grand rounds are for the exchange of information among physicians. I do not intend to have people on my service attacked."

Carey's face grew red with fury, but he did not reply.

Jean continued. "Mr. Carey has focused on the pivotal point in his phrase, best and newest. I suspect that such facilities cause these patients' recurrences. Clean, comfortable rooms. Four persons to a room, not like the older wards, where there are twelve to twenty-four. Nourishing meals. No rats. None of the pressures of slum living. Why *shouldn't* a patient prefer that to his own home?"

No one disputed her.

"We may have made living in a hospital more attractive than living in the outside world," Jean concluded.

Slake nodded thoughtfully. "Dr. Scofield, this is extremely interesting. Would you send me a copy of your data?"

"Of course, Doctor."

Carey called, "*I* certainly would like a copy. And I should prefer that anything which affects the administration of this hospital be kept absolutely confidential. I dread to speculate on what the trustees will say when they hear of this!" With that, Carey strode out of the auditorium.

IT WAS FIVE O'CLOCK. That time of day when Horace Cameron turned from the demands of his multinational empire to those activities which nourished his ego. Like a prince, Cameron held court for those seeking charitable donations, support of the arts and kindred matters. He was fond of saying of himself, "*Making* money is no great feat. Learning how to use it for the betterment of society *is*."

He repeated a number of such self-serving homilies often. He actually believed them as well. Unaware that what he was really doing was filling the void in his life created by the fact that he had no children, no heirs. Therefore his "future," as he termed it, consisted of the young men he trained to succeed him, and the number of cultural and charitable works which would bear his name.

He was a lean man, his long hands marked by prominent blue veins and mottled by brown patches. His lips were thin, and at times it was difficult to tell if he was smiling or sneering, since he wore tinted glasses which tended to obscure his eyes.

This afternoon, once drinks had been poured, Cameron lit his eighth cigar of the day, leaned back in his chair and asked, "Well, Edward?"

Edward Carey sighed, intending to convey the heavy weight of the burdens pressing upon him. "That woman again."

"Woman?" Cameron repeated, while he studied the smoke from his elegantly thin Havana cigar. "Scofield?"

Carey nodded.

"Did I ever tell you how rude she was to me when I called about the Tatum boy?" Cameron said. "And all I did was ask a simple question. Women! These days, they're always pushing to prove themselves." He took a sip of his expensive, privately bottled Scotch. "All right, now, what did she do this time?"

Carey related the confrontation which had taken place during grand rounds. Throughout, Cameron continued to sip his drink and nod grimly. When Carey finished, Cameron declared, "Such data on those new wards could be very embarrassing. Kill that report!"

"I'm afraid I don't have the power to do that."

"Who does?"

"Benziger might," Carey suggested, knowing it would be a good way to drive a wedge between the chief of the department and his protégée.

BENZIGER HAD NEVER had to confront Cameron face to face before. He was put off guard by Cameron's detailed knowledge of the events that had taken place at grand rounds only yesterday. He had no doubt as to Cameron's source.

Cameron squinted through his tinted lenses. "Now, I've been told that no doctor can publish a paper without approval of his chief. Or *her* chief."

"All the chief can do is check the material. If it's correct, he gives his approval," Benziger explained.

"Dr. Benziger, do you remember not long ago when you requested a . . . what is that equipment?"

"CAT scanner," Benziger supplied. "A computerized axial tomographic scanner—the finest diagnostic equipment available."

"That's the one. You made the request. And I raised six hundred thousand dollars—two hundred thousand of it mine. That scanner is on order and will be installed within the year."

"I don't understand," Benziger said.

"It would be embarrassing if Dr. Scofield's report were published," Cameron said.

Benziger remained silent for a moment. Finally he spoke. "Mr. Cameron, if you were asking me as a favor to donate my time, ability, medical knowledge, I would be delighted to do so. I'm aware of the many fine things you've done for the hospital. But you're asking me to depart from principle, from ethical standards. I can't do that. I'm sure you wouldn't either."

Cameron smiled. "Doctor, in the world of business there is no principle beyond succeeding. The only point now is, for important reasons, I think that report should be suppressed!" Cameron was no longer smiling.

"If Dr. Scofield's data prove to be correct," Benziger said simply, "I don't see how I can withhold my approval."

"Even though it makes fools of the entire medical and surgical staffs of our hospital?" Cameron demanded.

"I don't quite see how Dr. Scofield's paper would do that."

"Think of all the publicity we gave Seaton! As the best and newest in the state. It was designed with the advice of the chiefs of every service in our hospital. And now, along comes this woman and says it's a disaster."

"Dr. Scofield never said it was a disaster. She did say that the new building is not accomplishing what we had anticipated."

"You still don't understand!" Cameron exploded.

"What I do understand," Benziger said, "is this. We have a perfectly good building that with little alteration can be converted into a pavilion with semiprivate rooms. Which we desperately need."

"And what about the new wards that we also need?"

"It is clear that we have to rethink our approach and make plans for a new ward building."

"Make plans for a new ward building," Cameron mocked angrily. "As easy as that! I just go back to my money sources and say, 'Boys, I just made a little mistake. Now we have to build another ward. So I want each of you to come up with another million or two!' Don't you see the impossible position that woman will put me in?"

Benziger realized it was Cameron's vanity which was at stake, even more than his concern for the hospital.

Cameron ordered, "That report must never see the light of day!"

"I'm sorry, Mr. Cameron. I cannot compromise my ethical standards," Benziger said.

"Are you telling me that the only person who can withdraw or modify that report is Dr. Scofield?"

Much as he regretted having to place Jean in a position of jeopardy, Benziger had to respond, "Yes, I suppose I am saying that."

Cameron nodded, grim and thoughtful.

AN INVITATION to lunch with Cameron in his private dining room at InterElectronics would normally be considered a high honor by any member of the University Hospital medical staff. However, warned by Benziger, Jean Scofield looked upon the occasion as a command performance.

Their lunch was as spare as if Cameron were an athlete in training. His personal chef had done all he could with lean fillets of beef, greens, cottage cheese and fruit. Cameron ate little. Jean ate even less, waiting expectantly.

Over the caffein-free coffee Cameron began. "Doctor, I asked you here because I feel you're entitled to an apology."

He had intended to surprise her and he succeeded.

"I'm sorry, I don't understand."

"That day I called about the Tatum boy. Of course, ethically you had no right to discuss his case with me. And you very correctly set me straight. Though I must admit I'm not used to being talked to in quite that way." He chuckled pleasantly. "I understand the boy is doing well now."

"He's to be discharged soon. If he takes his medication, I trust he'll be fine," Jean said.

"Good, good! Nice people, the Tatums. That young man has an unlimited future. And his wife, a splendid girl! My wife has just about adopted her."

Jean wondered when he would come to the subject of the lunch.

"Yours must be fascinating work, Doctor. You not only stand astride the human brain, you explore the mind as well." He sipped his coffee. "Equally fascinating was what I heard of your findings about our new Seaton wards. In fact, I'm so interested that I'd like our computers to check out your data."

"I don't really need computers to corroborate what I've observed with my own eyes."

"Of course not. But I should think you'd want to withhold your report until your conclusions were verified by minds devoted solely to the interpretation of statistical data."

"Mr. Cameron, I think you misunderstand the reason for publishing medical papers."

"Do I?" Cameron asked.

"The purpose of my paper will be to share information among other researchers. Invite them either to refute my conclusion after their own research or else to suggest ways to reform the manner in which new hospital wards are built. Either way, the future of good medicine is served."

"I wonder, Doctor, if you realize some of the other consequences of your findings?" Cameron asked.

"I understand it might create some embarrassment for you in the raising of funds."

"Unfortunately."

"Have you considered that this might also mean spending money more wisely in the future, if we learn from our mistakes now?"

"Up to now, Doctor, you're the only one who keeps insisting that Seaton is a mistake!"

"I don't say it. The data say it," Jean pointed out.

"Say what? That patients from the ghettos don't wish to go back and live there, once they've experienced life in a fine, new, clean medical facility? Then what's your solution? To build new rundown, rat-infested hospitals?"

"Of course not!" Jean protested.

"Then may I suggest, Doctor, that you not release that paper to any medical publication?"

"And if I do release it," Jean said, "there'll be no chance at all of my being considered as chief of Neurology. Is that it?"

"Doctor, relax. I'm not in the habit of making threats. Anyone who knows me will tell you that."

Of course, Jean thought, a Cameron "suggestion" was usually enough.

Cameron rose from the table. "It's been most interesting, Doctor, most interesting."

As soon as Jean left the room, Cameron picked up the phone, dialed, and asked Miss St. John to put him on his dictating machine. He began in a cold, precise voice. "I have just completed a discussion with Dr. Scofield. I find her to be quite rigid and dogmatic. I feel she constitutes a problem for the entire board of trustees to consider. Especially since her name has been put forth as a possible successor to Dr. Benziger when he retires. Unquote.

"Miss St. John, see that copies are sent to all the trustees before the next meeting."

Chapter Six

Once the prescribed Dilantin level in Bobby Tatum's blood had stabilized, Dr. Scofield permitted his return to school. Marissa Tatum had instructed his teacher, Miss Halsted, concerning the limitations which governed her son's activity and the steps to take if by any chance Bobby suffered a seizure. She left with her several airways and padded tongue depressors. Faced with this complication, Miss Halsted greeted young Bobby with as much warmth as she could muster.

She had the class sing a welcoming song to him, as they did to all classmates who returned after an illness. At midmorning recess Miss Halsted led them out to the monkey bars in the schoolyard.

When Bobby moved to join them, Miss Halsted ordered, "You are not to climb, Bobby. You're to stay here with me!"

"Why, Miss Halsted? I'm better now," the boy pleaded.

"Your doctor said it's best for you not to."

While the other children shouted and laughed as they climbed across the iron-barred maze, Bobby and his teacher watched. At the end of twenty minutes, Miss Halsted called the children in. Bobby took his usual place between Allison Carr and Adam Wardell. Allison asked, "Bobby, you still sick?"

"I am not," he answered.

Adam intruded. "After measles I was climbing the first day. So you got to be sick."

"I am *not* sick!" he protested, tears filling his blue eyes.

"Yeah, yes you are!" Adam insisted loudly.

The rest of the morning passed without incident. But by the end of the week it was all the children talked about. Gradually they isolated Bobby. He found himself closer and closer to Miss Halsted. When the children played out in the yard, he clung to her hand and stared enviously. At night he wept silently in his bed. He knew his father did not like any display of tears.

On the last day of Bobby's second week back at school, Marissa Tatum was late picking him up. She had spent the morning with Francine Cameron working on a senior citizens' project. Though Mrs. Cameron commandeered many wives of her husband's young executives to help in her various activities, Marissa Tatum had become her favorite.

On this particular day, while waiting for his mother, Bobby slipped out into the schoolyard unobserved. He eyed the monkey bars and approached them cautiously. Rarely had he been bold enough to defy authority. Today he was tempted, in order to discover just how sick he really was.

Taking one last look around, he started to climb. He reached up with his hand, seized a bar and pulled his leg up. He lifted himself higher until he reached the top. Remembering a stunt that Adam did, Bobby wrapped his legs over the top bar and hung upside down. He felt a surge of triumph. He'd show Adam who was sick!

At that moment Marissa Tatum pulled up in front of the building and blew her horn. Miss Halsted emerged alone, surprised and puzzled. She looked about, then became frantic. "He was just here! Waiting for you!"

"Bobby!" his mother cried out desperately.

It was then Miss Halsted spied him. He hung head down, his legs wrapped over the top bar, unable to work free. Marissa Tatum leaped out of her station wagon, calling, "Bobby! Bobby!"

Her terror transmitted itself to her young son. In his effort to free himself, he slipped and fell head down on the hard rubber mat below. Marissa raced to him, gathered him in her arms. Terrified, he pressed against her. He heard her say over and over, "Don't ever do anything like that again. Do you hear me, Bobby?" She held him so close he could not even nod his head.

Across her son, she shouted to Miss Halsted, "And don't you ever leave him alone again. He's a very sick child!"

She drove directly to Lawrence Braham's office. Aside from a bruise on his head and another on his arm, Bobby appeared perfectly sound. But Larry suggested Marissa consult Dr. Scofield. He called ahead to make sure Jean would be free.

She checked the boy out, satisfied that he had not sustained any significant injury. Throughout her examination, whenever her hands were not busy, the boy held one of them, as he had that night when he fell asleep pressing her hand against his face.

While Mrs. Tatum waited outside the room, Jean asked, "Bobby, didn't Mommy tell you not to climb to high places?" The boy didn't answer. "And your teacher told you not to, didn't she?"

The boy remained stubbornly unresponsive, only gripped her hand more tightly.

"Then why did you do it, Bobby?"

The boy exploded suddenly. "I'm *not* sick! They said I was. But I'm *not!* I'm not sick."

In sympathy, Jean tousled the boy's black hair. He looked up at her, a surge of love and warmth in his eyes. That look renewed her conviction. No matter what Larry said, she felt that Bobby was abused, by emotional neglect if not by outright physical punishment. Else why this need to seek solace from strangers? But it was still only a suspicion.

IT WAS A SUNNY DAY. The sound of children's voices echoed across the schoolyard. To save Bobby the embarrassment of his restriction, Miss Halsted pretended to need his help in marking off lanes for the potato race. She did not notice that the boy appeared a bit slower today than usual.

He bent over to mark the lane as he had been instructed. Suddenly his head and eyes turned right, his small body became rigid. By the time Miss Halsted became aware, he was already entering the clonic phase of the seizure. Terrified, the young teacher raced to the classroom, found the airways and tongue depressors, raced back and tried to slip a tongue depressor between Bobby's teeth. At the same time she called out, "Someone go tell them in the office!"

She held the boy in her arms, careful to keep his head from striking the hard earth. Eventually the spasmodic movement ceased. The boy was limp and light in her arms. From both pity and fear, she began to tremble.

Marissa Tatum, off on an assignment for one of Mrs. Cameron's projects involving slum children, could not be reached. Dr. Braham's office was contacted. Larry drove out to pick up the boy. An hour after his attack, Bobby was at University Hospital. Dr. Scofield tested him for postictal weakness. She could not detect any. No signs of blood or fluid in his ears or nose. She dispatched a blood sample to be tested for Dilantin level. Then she ran a bedside EEG and a skull X ray.

When all the results came back negative, Larry Braham suggested, "Maybe he needs a higher dosage of Dilantin. Probably he hasn't stabilized yet."

"No, I don't think that's it."

"Then what? Everything came back negative."

"*Too* negative."

"You mean no postictal weakness on his right side?"

"Something else was missing," Jean said. "Every time Bobby had a seizure before, he wet himself. Not *this* time."

"Maybe it just didn't happen this time. That's possible."

"It's also possible that he didn't have a true seizure. Hysterical seizures are not as frequent in young children as in older patients. But there are reported cases."

"But why?" Larry asked.

"That school's become a traumatic place for him. Perhaps this was his way of escaping. That's one possibility. There's another. But you won't like it."

"Try me."

"Twice now he's left here a much more open child than when he was admitted. Evidently he likes it here better than in his own home. Maybe unconsciously he figured that the way to get back was to have a seizure."

Angrily Larry closed the door of her office. He spoke in a harsh whisper. "Jean, stop looking for trouble! The Tatum home is not the kind where one finds child abuse!"

"It can happen in any home. Freud himself wrote, 'The unconscious wish to beat or harm children is almost universal.'"

"Freud!" Larry dismissed him. "Very few people believe in him any longer."

"Tell that to some infant who's been beaten to death by his father!" Jean responded heatedly. "Larry, if slum patients bruised by poverty seek refuge in a hospital, why shouldn't someone bruised by neglect or even domestic friction react the same way?"

"Domestic friction? If there ever was a couple that works as a team, it's Bob and Marissa Tatum. She's the perfect corporate wife. She knocks herself out to do everything that helps Bob's career. There is absolutely no friction in that family!"

"Then why did Bobby have a hysterical seizure?" Jean demanded. "The least I can do is discuss this with the Tatums."

"I don't think that would be wise," he cautioned.

"Larry, would it make things easier for you if I withdrew from this case?" she asked bluntly.

"Bobby trusts you. I wouldn't want to shake his confidence. I want you to continue. But be careful. For your own sake."

"I'm going to have to face the Tatums with it," she said firmly.

The appointment took place the following Thursday, in the early evening.

Bob Tatum directly voiced their fears. "That last seizure means it's very serious now, isn't it? Don't try to let us down easy."

"It could become serious," Jean conceded.

Marissa Tatum turned to her husband. "I told you what she said about uncontrolled seizures."

"Brain damage? He sure doesn't act like a boy with brain damage!" Tatum protested.

"For the moment forget brain damage. There's another problem," Jean said.

"And that is?"

Jean hesitated. Child abusers, like alcoholics, were quick to turn on the very persons who tried to help them. But she had to risk that. "Your son shows signs that could be psychiatric."

Tatum rebelled instinctively, but his wife's hold on his arm kept him silent.

"In situations like that, we don't treat the boy. We treat the parents," Jean said.

"Situations like *what?*" Tatum demanded.

"A patient exhibits symptomatology that includes a number of suspicious factors. Failure to thrive. Noticeable difference in weight gain between home and hospital. Noticeable difference in attitude. Withdrawn, totally compliant, unsmiling on admission to the hospital. Then, after a few days, relaxed, outgoing and friendly. Those factors are extremely significant."

The Tatums glanced at each other, puzzled.

"This last time we admitted Bobby, I concluded that he had what we call a hysterical seizure."

"That boy has never been hysterical!" Tatum protested.

"I don't mean in the sense of becoming uncontrollably emotional. Hysteria in a medical sense means signs and symptoms that arise in the mind. Even though they may express themselves in a physical way. I believe Bobby's last seizure was of psychological, not physical, origin. In other words, he unconsciously imitated a seizure without having one."

"What does it mean?" Tatum asked.

"It's a matter of interpretation," Jean continued. "I can only give you my professional judgment. Dr. Braham does not agree with me. But I think that for some reason Bobby would rather be here in the hospital than anywhere else."

"He'd rather be here than with *us?*" Bob Tatum asked.

"I believe so," Jean said.

Tatum leaped out of his chair. "Why would any boy, with all he's got, want to be in this hospital rather than at home?"

"That's exactly what this meeting is about."

"I'm not going to take this from anyone! Certainly not from any woman doctor. Saying my son would rather be here than in his own house is ridiculous! Ridiculous! Did you hear me, Doctor?"

She not only heard him, she knew that everyone on the floor had probably heard him.

"Frankly," he went on, "if it wasn't for the way Larry Braham feels about you, I'd ask him to find another neurologist."

"What do you mean by the way Dr. Braham feels about me?"

"I did a little investigating. It became very clear why Larry recommended you so highly."

"Whatever exists between Dr. Braham and myself, in this instance we are concerned only with the welfare of your son. As I told you, Dr. Braham doesn't agree with my theory."

"And just what is your theory?" Tatum demanded.

Jean knew her next statement could be crucial to her continuance on the case and her ability to protect Bobby.

"Mr. Tatum, your son exhibits a pattern of conduct that we generally find in cases of child abuse."

"I have never laid a hand on that boy! You show me one mark on that boy's body! One!"

"X rays show a fracture of his right fibula. A bone in the leg. Now healed. But having occurred two or three years ago."

"Fracture?" Tatum disparaged at once, then recalled, "He did fall once. The day we were moving from Dayton to San Diego. Bobby was playing on the steps. One of the moving men backing down accidentally banged into him, causing him to fall down the stairs. But I never knew he broke his leg. It hurt him for a while, but then it went away."

It was not unlike stories Jean had heard before from abusing parents. Always the child had fallen accidentally and hurt himself. Had plunged its own hand into a tub of hot water and burned itself. There was one factor which did give some possible credence to Tatum's story. He had involved others in the accident. Those moving men. If true, that defeated her theory.

Tatum now asked, "Is that what you wanted to discuss with us? A leg fracture two years ago? Could that have anything to do with his seizures?"

"No," she had to admit.

"If you don't know the cause, say so. But don't go inventing theories to cover up your own professional ignorance!"

"Bob!" his wife reprimanded him in a low, guarded tone.

Of one thing Jean was sure. Tatum was an impetuous, overbearing man. Certainly the kind of father who might severely intimidate a shy young boy like Bobby.

Perhaps she was dealing with one of the more subtle forms of child abuse. Emotional and psychological abuse. Tatum could claim, and possibly with complete justification, that he had not laid a hand on the boy in anger. Yet at the same time he could have raised a son who lived terrorized all his life by this huge man. In such a situation, a boy might well seek refuge in a hysterical seizure.

Jean debated discussing that with Tatum now. He was an intelligent man. But intelligence had never proved a bar to child abuse. Nor did it provide solutions for problems that were purely emotional. The decision on whether to proceed was taken out of her hands when the phone blinked.

"Dr. Scofield," she said. "Yes, yes. How bad is it? I'll be right down." She turned to the Tatums. "I'm afraid I have to go. A case just admitted. A sixteen-year-old boy who fell off his bike and was hit by a car. It's bad. A serious head injury."

"I'm sorry," Tatum said, sincerely compassionate.

"The reason he fell off the bike," Jean explained, "was that he was having a seizure. That's why we restrict activities of seizure-prone patients. We walk a fine line between restricting a patient so he can't endanger himself and giving him enough leeway so he doesn't feel like a freak."

Tatum nodded gravely.

"Now, please?" Jean invited them to leave her office.

She reached the emergency room and examined the unconscious boy. His skull had been fractured. She ordered an operating room and called for the neurosurgical resident on duty.

She scrubbed and stood by to observe the operation. The young surgeon worked swiftly and skillfully. When he was finished and the patient had been removed to the recovery room, Jean asked, "What do you think? Can he make it?"

"I wouldn't want his chances," the surgeon said.

Jean left the hospital. She would never grow inured to sudden death among the young. Especially sudden preventable death. She stopped to get some dinner, ate only part of it, and hurried home to work on her paper about the Seaton wards.

She had been at work for more than two hours, fighting sleep, when her phone rang.

"Doctor?"

She recognized Marissa Tatum.

"Yes? What is it, Mrs. Tatum?"

"The boy on the bike. Does it happen often? That kind of thing?"

"You mean could it happen to Bobby? Not if we take the proper precautions."

"Doctor . . ." She hesitated. "One thing I want you to know. Bob was telling the truth. He has never laid a hand on our son in anger. Never!"

"That's good to know," Jean said.

"And . . ." The woman faltered.

"Yes, Mrs. Tatum? Anything else you wish to say?"

"Only that I feel sorry for the boy's parents. I know how they must feel. How I'd feel."

"I understand," Jean said, though she was puzzled. The call must have deeper implications. The woman on the other end was troubled. "Mrs. Tatum, *is* there something else?"

After a long silence Marissa Tatum said softly, "That time—the overmedication . . . Bobby did have a seizure a few days after we brought him home. I didn't want Bob to know. You said the medicine would help. I thought, The dose is wrong. I'll give him more."

"Mrs. Tatum, are you sure Bobby had only one seizure after you brought him home?"

There was a pause. "No, two. Both on the same day."

"Was anyone else there?"

"Just me. I did everything you said to do."

"Except report to me," Jean pointed out.

"I'm sorry. I tried to do what I thought best for Bobby."

"What's best for Bobby is to be truthful with me."

"Yes, Doctor. I know that now. I'm terribly sorry."

"I understand," Jean said, to comfort the distressed woman.

After she had hung up, she leaned back in her desk chair to evaluate Marissa Tatum's confession. It had clarified one thing. Bob Tatum had never physically abused his son.

The other fact had possibly greater significance. The boy had had two seizures after he returned home.

She determined she would keep Bobby Tatum in the hospital for a longer stay than she had intended.

Chapter Seven

After a difficult afternoon Jean Scofield had returned to her office. She glanced through the messages Maggie had left on her desk. Larry Braham had called to ask about Bobby Tatum's condition and why he hadn't been discharged.

She dialed his office. "Larry?"

"Jean?"

They'd been a bit distant these days, after their discussion of Tatum and child abuse.

"Before discharging Bobby, I want to run the entire series of tests again."

"That can take days."

"I don't see that it can do any harm," she said curtly.

"Oh, but it can." His answer contained a note of warning. "The Tatums are talking about signing Bobby out against advice."

"The Tatums? Or Cameron?"

Larry admitted, "Cameron called me this afternoon. He suggested flying the boy up to Boston. 'For the best opinions,' as he put it. He also managed to inquire about your paper on the Seaton wards. And what you decided."

"If I can find enough time, I hope to finish it this month," she responded angrily.

"*His* questions, not *mine*, Jeannie." Larry paused a moment. "Busy or not, you're going to have to eat dinner tonight."

"I've got some shopping to do," she evaded. "Good-by, Larry. I have to rush."

JEAN MADE THREE purchases in a toy store. A colorful jigsaw puzzle. A storybook. And a stuffed zebra. She returned to her office and unwrapped her packages, depositing their contents around the room.

The next morning, after she had cleared her schedule of the most pressing matters, she asked that Bobby Tatum be brought in. He was delivered to Jean by a pretty student nurse. Jean noticed how he clung to her hand.

Jean closed the door. "Wouldn't you like to sit down, Bobby?"

The boy hesitated, then climbed into the big leather chair opposite her. From there he could see the stuffed zebra. His delft-blue eyes widened. "Would you like that, Bobby?"

"Yes, ma'am," he said softly but eagerly.

She handed him the zebra, realizing now what had made her select it. That day of his first seizure, there had been conflict with his teacher when he was instructed to draw elephants but preferred to draw zebras. She observed him till he was thoroughly captivated by the toy.

"Bobby, do you like Miss Robinson?" Jean asked, referring to the nurse who had brought him.

"Yes, ma'am." Preoccupied with the zebra, he answered easily and, she could assume, truthfully.

Jean took down the jigsaw puzzle from the shelf. He followed her with his eyes, anxious to see, reluctant to make his curiosity obvious. Jean opened the box, and the pieces fell to her desk in disorder. She began to play with them, asking. "Are there many people you like, Bobby?"

His attention torn between the zebra, which he clutched, and the colorful puzzle on Jean's desk, he said only, "Uh-huh."

"Who?"

"Daddy. Mommy. Esther. She's our maid," he explained.

"I'm having trouble with this puzzle. Could you help me?"

Shyly the boy nodded, slipped out of his chair, still clutching the zebra. He came around to Jean's side of the desk. He reached out and touched one of the pieces. Soon he became engrossed in the puzzle. Jean leaned in close. Their heads were side by side, almost touching. His skin had the sweet smell of children. It was soft, as his silky black hair was soft.

"Has Esther ever punished you, Bobby?"

"Only sometimes," he answered, almost unaware of what he was saying. "When I won't drink my milk."

"What does she do?" Jean asked, observing that he seemed to manage the puzzle well for a child his age.

"She won't give me any treat."

"Is that all she does?"

The boy was too involved to answer at once.

"Bobby, is that all Esther does when you don't drink your milk? Does she ever spank you?"

The boy turned to her, his eyes reflecting puzzlement. "Oh, no," he said, in his childish way rising to Esther's defense.

"Bobby, does *anybody* ever hit you?"

"Yep. Ward."

"Who is Ward?"

"Ward," Bobby repeated, finding a piece and fitting it into place. Then he turned to Jean and smiled. He edged closer and pressed against her. He seemed to want as much of her to touch him as possible. She slipped her arm around him.

"Bobby, who's Ward?"

"Boy in my class."

"What does Ward do to you, Bobby?"

"Hits me."

"And do you hit him back?"

"No, ma'am."

"Why not?"

"'Cause he'll only hit me harder."

It was difficult to quarrel with his childish logic. But it was also significant. He did not dare to strike back. Typical of a child who invited abuse.

Jean turned the completed puzzle over, letting the pieces fall out. "Let's do this again." While the boy went at the pieces more surely now, she asked, "Does anyone else hit you?"

"No, ma'am."

"Daddy?"

"No, ma'am."

"Mommy?"

"No, ma'am."

Denials, but not completely unexpected. Abused children were often reluctant to admit being abused. Fear of subsequent punishment was a powerful silencer.

"Did you ever fall down and hurt yourself, real hard, Bobby?"

"No, ma'am."

"A long time ago, do you remember when you and Mommy and Daddy were moving? And the men came to take the furniture away? One of the men accidentally pushed you and you fell down the stairs? Do you remember that?"

"No, ma'am."

The boy appeared at ease, holding the zebra in one hand and working the puzzle with his other. His answers had been given free of tension. Yet they conflicted with what his mother and father said about that fine-line fracture. Could he have forgotten? Or had he deliberately blocked out the truth?

"Now we have to get you back to your room," she said. "But you'll come back again and we'll play some more."

"Promise?"

"Promise."

The boy pressed his face against hers. He kissed her. Professionally, she tried to tell herself that was unfortunate. It diminished the objectivity she strived to maintain. Personally, she was deeply touched.

She had not made the progress she hoped for in play therapy. The boy had relaxed, but not enough to open up and talk freely, and to remember. Perhaps there was nothing of importance to remember. That was always a possibility. If her intuition were not so strong, she might have accepted the results of that one session as final. But it remained a constant, nagging thing.

She sat and pondered the choices open to her. She could, on the basis of sheer suspicion, report to the Child Abuse Committee of the hospital. But with the fragmentary facts she had at hand, her suspicion might be rejected summarily. And there was that uneasy doubt that she was too deeply involved in the case and hence too inclined to exaggerate what she found.

Perhaps what was needed was another opinion. From doctors who would have no personal involvement with the patient.

She requested of Hans Benziger that she be given half an hour to present the case at grand rounds.

ON THE MORNING of grand rounds Jean arrived at her office to find her phone light blinking. Mrs. Holdrith, social-service worker on the Child Abuse Committee, was relieved to reach Jean before she became involved in her day's schedule. The committee had failed to apprise her of a group consultation concerning the disposition of the Scott case.

The Scott case. Jean remembered the little black boy, twenty-two months old, brought in several weeks ago with glove burn and a battered face. The committee wanted her opinion of the future course of action to take. Could she examine him once more, then meet with the group?

She met him in one of the examining rooms in the clinic. The first thing she noticed was that he looked more nearly normal in size for his age. While his features presented vestiges of the punishment he had suffered, his hands had cleared, leaving only slight scars from the serious burns. He clung devotedly to the nurse who accompanied him. During the weeks in the hospital he had obviously formed a strong attachment to her.

"Really a nice kid," the nurse remarked. "Very loving. Needs people. I hope nothing more happens to him."

"They told me his parents are coming along. Cooperating."

"I hope so," the nurse said fervently. "He won't let go of my hand now, but it took so long for him to let me touch him in the beginning."

Jean examined the child's eyes, ears, reflexes. She found no residual neurological deficits. The X rays had proved what she had originally suspected. Including a previous fine-line skull fracture. Fortunately, there had been no internal bleeding to create a subdural hematoma. Neurologically, at least, the little patient had a chance at normal development. She would not hazard a guess as to the psychological prognosis.

She attended the consultation. In her opinion, it would be better to return him to his family, if it was safe now, rather than consign him to institutions for the rest of his childhood. Depending on the progress his parents had made toward rehabilitation, she would concur in discharging the boy.

Within the next few months she and the committee would discover if their judgment had been correct. It was no small responsibility. Jean tried to be free of it by reminding herself she was a neurologist, not a social worker or an officer of the court. But the obligation weighed on her and she hoped she had been right.

DR. RALPH SUNDERLAND, along with Jean one of the leading contenders to succeed Hans Benziger as chief, presided over grand rounds on this afternoon. His duties were formal and limited to introducing the cases.

Just before Jean began her presentation, Hans Benziger and Larry Braham entered the auditorium and silently took seats in the last row.

Jean launched into the case of an unnamed five-year-old boy with seizures, describing in detail the symptoms the patient had exhibited on admission. She presented his echoencephalograms, his EEGs and observations as to his progress, and said that an angiogram had not been done. She noted his overdose of Dilantin, the later occurrence of what she diagnosed to be a hysterical seizure, the seizure-free period during his hospital stay, and the several seizures since his return home. She also mentioned the fine-line fracture of the right fibula.

Without expressing her suspicions, she threw the case open for questioning and suggestions.

One of the older men, an attending neurologist with a large private practice and hence sensitive to the high cost of malpractice insurance, was first to respond. "By no means would I insist on an angiogram. Though the odds of morbidity or mortality are small, one unexpected reaction in the patient can be enough to drag you into court for years, and God knows how much expense in increased insurance after that. I would advise against an angiogram unless his condition grows worse."

He missed the point of Jean's presentation, but she did not take time to correct him. One of the other men spoke up.

"I disagree. I think the neurologist should insist on an angio. There's enough here to create suspicion of a condition which, the longer it exists, the more likely it is to become a source of permanent damage."

"And what condition would you expect to find on an angio?"

"Why, a subdural hematoma."

Another doctor argued, "It's jumping to conclusions to suspect a subdural, especially with no history of trauma to the head."

The discussion moved on to the relative merits of doing an angiogram, until Hans Benziger said from the rear, "If I may . . ." As he spoke, the door of Cameron Hall opened. Edward Carey was showing a federal inspector around the hospital. The woman was to monitor compliance with Health, Education, and Welfare Department regulations that involved the employment and upgrading of minorities and women. Carey had known that Dr. Scofield was scheduled to present a case in grand rounds. That was bound to make a good impression on the inspector.

Benziger said, "Aside from the question of an angiogram, there are several interesting aspects to this case. For example, that hysterical seizure. Very unusual. In my experience I have encountered very few hysterical seizures in young children.

"And taken together with another interesting fact, a pattern begins to emerge. As I understand it, since his seizures upon his first admission the child has not suffered another while he is *in* the hospital. But once in school and twice at home. Evidently the pressures of his homelife seem to be a factor." Suddenly he asked, "Is there any evidence of physical abuse?"

"That untreated fracture, which the parents explained," Jean replied.

"Parents always have an explanation for such accidents," Benziger said. "So, it has the earmarks of a case of child abuse. If we *are* confronted with a subdural here, it would have had to be from an injury in the past six months. A year at most. Is there anything suspicious during that period?"

"Nothing I could uncover," Jean said.

"Yet it is possible. Of course, the parents would deny it. Still, that doesn't absolve the doctor from pursuing the issue. My approach would be, an angiogram is indicated. But in the meantime, as long as the issue is unresolved, safeguard the child in the hospital, under any pretext."

"That's the reason for presenting the case," Jean said. "Is there sufficient evidence on which to make a report to the Child Abuse Committee?"

Aware that Carey was now in the auditorium, Sunderland joined the discussion. "It would seem to me that Dr. Scofield is exhibiting what is, for her, remarkable reticence in this matter. I've seen her act far more decisively in other cases where she suspected abuse. Her caution in this case may be another of those interesting aspects to which Dr. Benziger referred."

Benziger responded angrily, "Grand rounds is not a place to air personal differences or to campaign for promotions."

"Where a doctor's personal interests impinge on her professional judgment, I believe it is justified," Sunderland shot back. "I think Dr. Scofield is using us. And I for one resent it."

"What do you mean, using?" Jean demanded furiously.

"It is quite transparent who your patient is. That's why you're reluctant to take the responsibility. You want us to make the decision for you."

"That's not true!" Jean said vehemently.

"It is obvious that the parents you're accusing are the Tatums," Sunderland said.

Edward Carey, embarrassed by this outbreak of personal antagonism in the presence of the federal inspector, was shocked by Sunderland's charge.

He was even more disturbed when Jean replied, "The identity of the patient has no medical significance. I regret that you felt compelled to mention it." She thereby confirmed Sunderland's identification.

Carey nudged his companion. They slipped out of the hall. "Extremely regrettable," Carey said. "That woman is so emotional. Possibly too emotional for a key job."

As soon as he could gracefully disengage himself from the inspector, Carey placed a call to Horace Cameron and reported in detail the events that had taken place at grand rounds.

Cameron listened carefully. When he hung up he gave vent to his feelings.

"Damned woman!" She was determined to have that chiefship or destroy anyone in her path. She had the audacity to persist in writing that paper about the Seaton wards. Obviously, after he exerted the least bit of pressure on her, she had sought vengeance and thought she had found it. She was determined to slander the name of InterElectronics by attributing a distasteful crime to one of his most promising young executives. This kind of scandal could attract important news coverage.

By now the story that woman had planted about the Tatums must be a juicy bit of gossip making the rounds of the hospital. That very evening doctors would be telling it to their wives and guests over the dinner table. Soon it would be all over the city.

He reached for his phone. "Get me Tatum!"

Within minutes Bob Tatum, who was en route back to the city

in one of InterElectronics' jets, was on the radiophone. "Yes, sir?"

"I want you in my library at home no later than seven thirty!" Cameron said, and cut off any response.

THE LIBRARY OF the Cameron home was a room of such dimensions that only a ceiling two stories high could give it graceful proportion. There were two huge fireplaces, each high enough for a man to stand in. A walkway ran around the room halfway up the walls to give access to volumes on the upper level. The library was kept at precisely the correct temperature and humidity to protect Cameron's collection of rare books and manuscripts.

Set against one carved-oak-paneled wall, with a wealth of luxurious antique leather bindings as background, was the desk of Horace Cameron. He was seated there when Bob Tatum entered. Tatum made the long walk across the huge Persian rugs.

"Good evening, sir."

"Tatum . . ." Cameron began.

Accustomed to being addressed more warmly, Bob Tatum knew that he was confronted by a crisis.

"Tatum, I've always been fair with you."

"Yes, sir, more than fair."

"And Francine has always been generous with your wife."

"They get along very well. Marissa worships her."

Cameron let that bit of flattery pass without comment. "Then I think I deserve honesty from you now."

"I've always been honest with you, sir," Bob Tatum said, suspecting that in his absence some corporate infighting had transpired.

"Tatum, a shocking accusation has been made against you. I hope it isn't true. But the suspicion is strong that your son has been the victim of abuse. By you."

"That's a lie!" Tatum exploded. "She tried that once before. I told her it was a lie!"

"She?" Cameron asked quickly.

"Scofield. She put me through a long examination about my family. And hinted that I might have hurt the boy while roughhousing with him. Never happened! What kind of monster do you think I am?"

Cameron stared at Tatum for a moment before he turned to the shelf behind him and drew down a volume. "I want you to put your hand on this Bible and swear that you have never abused that boy," he said.

Without hesitation Tatum placed his hand on the Bible which Cameron held. "I swear it, sir."

"Thank you, Bob."

Tatum was free to leave. Once the door closed, Cameron called Larry Braham.

"Dr. Braham, it is urgent I speak with you. This affects one of your patients. I deem it mandatory that you meet me here."

"As soon as I've covered my other calls."

At nine thirty Dr. Lawrence Braham arrived at the Cameron mansion. He was shown to the library, where Cameron was studying financial reports.

"I don't blame you for looking so puzzled, Braham. But it's essential that I receive corroboration about a matter in which I'm vitally interested."

"If it's something I'm free to discuss . . ."

"There are no ethical restrictions. The Tatum family will give you permission to speak freely. You've examined the boy?"

"Of course, many times."

"Tell me, Doctor, have you ever found on him any mark, bruise or sign that he had been beaten?"

That question put the interview into focus for Larry Braham. He knew what must have preceded Cameron's call. He was aware of the effect on Jean of his answer. Still, he had to reply frankly. "I've never detected any signs of abuse on the boy."

"Thank you!" Cameron said, as if that closed the interview.

"However," Larry persisted, "the fact that I haven't found any signs of abuse does not invalidate Dr. Scofield's conclusions. She is a physician of enormous skill and instinct, whose dedication is beyond question. . . ."

Cameron smiled knowingly. "I'm quite aware of your relationship with Dr. Scofield."

"My professional opinion of her work has nothing to do with the way I feel about her personally!" Larry answered angrily.

"Dr. Braham, I know how great a conflict my question has imposed on you. There's no need to explain or to defend her."

"If you have no further questions, I'd like to go," Larry said.

Braham left. Cameron put through a call to the Tatum house.

"Bob!" he ordered. "I want you to remove that boy from Dr. Scofield's care. I suggest you turn him over to Sunderland. An excellent man. And the next chief of the department."

He hung up and reached for his dictating machine. "Note," he began. "A letter must be circulated to all members of the board of trustees of the hospital. We are to act swiftly to demand and secure the resignation from staff of Dr. Jean Scofield."

He felt satisfied. By overreaching herself the woman had presented him with the opportunity to remove her from consideration as chief. She had also destroyed the effect of her projected paper on the Seaton wards. He would make it sound logical that, once terminated from the staff, she reacted like a disgruntled ex-employee by writing a baseless paper criticizing the new wards.

He had a perfectly logical case to present to the board.

THE NEXT MORNING Dr. Scofield found a visitor waiting at her office. Before Jean could even close the door, Marissa Tatum demanded fiercely, "What do you have against us?"

Without giving Jean a chance to answer, the beautiful young woman, obviously under enormous tension, accused: "Since the first you've had this antagonism against me. You've made no secret of it. Well, I don't intend to let you destroy my family or my husband's career. We've worked too long and sacrificed too much for the opportunity he has now. I refuse to have it jeopardized by anyone!"

"I've no wish to jeopardize your husband's career."

"Then why did you spread those vicious rumors about him?"

"Please understand, I spread no rumors. I named no names."

"You didn't have to! You only had to do what you did."

Marissa Tatum was on the verge of panic. Jean made no attempt to defend herself. Instead she said, "If I've done anything to harm you or your husband, I'm terribly sorry. Just tell me what I can do to make amends."

Her apology accomplished its purpose. The wild anger in Marissa's eyes slowly seemed to drain away. Her lips began to quiver. Jean resumed, coaxing gently.

"Tell me about it, please? For Bobby's sake. And for yours."

Now, when she resumed talking, Marissa seemed to be seeking understanding. "Do you know what Mr. Cameron made Bob do? Made him take an oath on a Bible that he didn't abuse Bobby. Do you realize what that meant?"

Before Jean could answer, Marissa continued. "Give Cameron the slightest reason to doubt you, and he'll never really trust you again. He does not promote men he doesn't trust."

The young woman turned away from Jean and began to talk in a voice strange and a bit distant.

"It isn't only Bob's career, Bob's life. It's mine, too. I've fought right along with him for us to get where we are. Because I had to. Had to," she repeated in strange mixture of determination and longing.

"I had this example before me. Of what can happen to a woman. My mother was once beautiful. I have pictures of her. Taken on the day of her wedding. And I have pictures of her later. After." Marissa Tatum's voice changed as she recalled her mother's life. "After she had become pregnant. For some reason my father couldn't face that. So the week I was born he left. Disappeared. I wondered all my life, Did he see me and was he disappointed? Did he want a son so much that he could never love a daughter? Or didn't he want a child at all? In the end you're sure of nothing except the facts of what happened. I was born. He deserted us. The connection is clear.

"The connection isn't the only thing that becomes clear. I remember my mother working in her little store all day. She'd been left penniless. An uncle lent her enough money to open a small dress shop. We lived in the back, and I remember at night she would talk me to sleep while she did alterations. She did it all. Sold the dresses. Raised the hems. I would lie there and wonder, When is she going to put aside that damned dress and hug me, kiss me? There was never enough time, never enough."

Marissa Tatum turned to face Jean Scofield. "I could see the beauty drain out of her. Until she became bitter, old before her time. She also became a shrewd, very determined mother. Bent on making sure her daughter wouldn't repeat her mistakes.

"From the beginning she taught me how to dress, how to walk. When I was fifteen she changed my name from Mary to Marissa. She had photographs made of me and got me a part-time job as a model in a department store. Then they began to use me in ads. In time I became a model in the best magazines.

"But Mother kept impressing on me that that was only a beginning. The thing for me to do was find a man, a man who had ambition. But above all, a sense of responsibility. A man with a future. 'Marissa,' she'd say, 'don't waste yourself.'

"She'd gone through her whole life feeling that the one man she loved never did love her. But it was me he never loved. When I was born he couldn't share her with me. Well, I decided that it was never going to happen to me.

"When I married Bob, I determined that his life would become my life. So when we had children he'd have no reason to be jealous of them.

"In those days I used to think it would be children. A boy, then a girl, then possibly another boy." She smiled faintly. "An ideal magazine-type family. Besides, Bob wanted sons. At least, more than one," she admitted regretfully.

"What was his reaction when he discovered there wouldn't be sons?" Jean asked.

"He'd never say anything to hurt me. But I could feel it. He was enormously disappointed."

"Disappointed enough so that he might leave you?" Jean suggested gently.

For a moment Marissa didn't answer. She turned away from Jean.

All the doctor could see was her lovely profile, which was now very determined, her head uptilted and proud.

"Bob would never leave me," she said with great conviction. Jean believed her until she added, "Never!"—evidencing her fear. "And he does love Bobby. No matter what you think."

"Mrs. Tatum, before you became pregnant, did you ever worry that Bob might react to a child in the same way as your father?"

"Never! We talked it over. We both wanted it. He loved me," the young woman said proudly. "I've made sure of that."

"Just how does a woman make sure?"

"I told you. I've made his life my life. Bob and I have come far. Together. Very far. And we're going all the way. That's what I came to tell you, Doctor. Don't do anything to hurt Bob's career. Or I'll see that you pay for it."

Marissa Tatum's eyes became fiercely protective as she concluded, "Our relationship with the Camerons has been excellent. Until *you* tried to destroy it. I warn you, don't try it again!" With that, she rose and strode out. Whatever Marissa had come to say, she had revealed infinitely more than she intended.

Chapter Eight

A copy of Horace Cameron's confidential memorandum to the board concerning the dismissal of Dr. Scofield had reached Amos Farr, a trustee and counsel to the hospital. He phoned the chairman immediately.

"Horace, you have to withdraw that memo! Recall every copy!"

"Give me one good reason!" Cameron shot back irately.

"Tenure!" Farr said. "Dr. Scofield has tenure. She can't be fired peremptorily. We'd have to prove some act of outrageous conduct on her part."

"She's made an outrageous accusation against one of my young men. She accuses him of child abuse. Why, she can be sued for that, can't she?"

"That could create more scandal than it would resolve. Besides, there's the law. In this state, and many others, a doctor can't be sued for reporting anyone for child abuse, provided the report is made in good faith."

"Damn it, Amos! I don't want a legal lecture. I just want that woman out of my hospital."

There was a brief silence, during which Farr restrained himself from reminding Cameron that it was not his personal hospital. Cameron realized it, too, for he continued in a tone somewhat chastened. "Amos, how do you suggest we go about this?"

"We can't simply remove her. If we terminated her, she could sue us," Farr explained. "This has to be done very carefully."

"Okay. How?"

"We deprive her of the right to admit patients to the hospital. That will just about kill off her practice and force her to quit."

"Good!" Cameron agreed. "How do I go about it?"

"Canvass several of the trustees individually. By phone. I don't want any letters floating around. Explain that the situation is quite delicate and get their private agreement. Later you can make it an official board matter."

"Excellent!" Cameron exulted.

By the end of the day he had recaptured every copy of his memo and had spoken to more than half the trustees. With their approval, he ordered Edward Carey to deny Jean Scofield admitting privileges. Carey was most eager to cooperate.

DR. JEAN SCOFIELD was making her usual morning rounds. She came down the corridor of the neurological wing, stopped briefly at each room where she had a patient. She had found nothing unexpected. She went on to the private room in which young Bobby Tatum had been installed at Horace Cameron's insistence.

Cameron's imperious attitude reminded Jean of the hospital anecdote about the rich mother who, on hearing that her son had been given artificial respiration, indignantly demanded, "Artificial respiration? Give him the real thing! We can afford it!"

It would be much better for the Tatum boy to be in a room with other children. He was a youngster who cried out for company, for warmth, especially for children who, themselves ill, might have compassion instead of scorn for his condition.

Jean opened the door, smiling. "Good morning, Bobby!" She discovered Marissa Tatum standing protectively at the foot of Bobby's bed. Bending over the boy was Dr. Ralph Sunderland.

Sunderland appeared self-conscious. Marissa Tatum was more aggressive. "Dr. Scofield, you've been replaced on this case. There's nothing further for you to do here."

Even Sunderland was embarrassed at the rude manner in which Mrs. Tatum handled the moment. He turned to Jean. "The family thought another opinion . . ."

"The *family* thought . . ." Jean echoed, making no secret of her suspicion that Cameron was the prime mover in the affair. "Of course," she agreed, so as not to alarm Bobby. "I'm sure it will be for the best."

"I'm sure it will," Marissa Tatum said with finality.

Jean withdrew, closing the door softly. She went directly to her office, intending to call Larry Braham. But she found him waiting. He could read her face at once.

"I guess you know," he said.

"I shouldn't have had to find out that way."

"It was done over my objection. They insisted." Larry shrugged. "Nothing was said, but Bob and Riss were both so agitated that I'm sure it was Cameron's idea."

"Larry, I don't want Bobby totally in the control of a doctor whose judgment is influenced by what Cameron wants to hear. I'm extremely worried about that boy!"

"We all are."

"No one else wants to admit the serious possibilities. I was about to demand permission to do an angiogram."

"The Tatums would have refused."

"That wouldn't have relieved me of the obligation of demanding it," Jean said angrily. Then she accepted the inevitability of the situation. "Keep me advised of how Bobby progresses?"

"Of course."

There was a knock at the door. Benziger stood in the doorway, a grim look on his face.

"Come in," Jean invited.

He handed her a single sheet of paper. She glanced at it, then passed it to Larry. He took one look and then, outraged, said, "Take away her admitting privileges? But why?"

The distressed old man dropped into a chair. "Grand rounds. The Tatum boy. Cameron considers that an act of revenge.

Because he opposed Jean as chief, she tried to even the score by slandering his protégé. His mind works that way, so he thinks everyone's does."

"I presented the case to invite opinions," Jean defended.

"It was an unfortunate mistake, my dear. But this," Benziger said, referring to the letter. "I never expected he'd get Carey to go this far. And I hear Sunderland is on the case now."

"Yes, yes he is," Jean said, taking the administrator's letter to study it carefully. . . . "For numerous reasons—including personality difficulties which have caused her to attempt to damage innocent persons and thus place this hospital in legal jeopardy, it is our considered opinion that Dr. Scofield be deprived of admitting privileges."

"I'm going to insist on a hearing," Jean said. "Let the board decide in full session, officially, that my professional conduct justifies this!"

"My dear, if you ask for a hearing there will be much gossip, much publicity. It can only make your situation more widely known and your motives more open to question."

"Don't do anything impulsive," Larry warned. "As emotional as you are about this case—"

Jean turned on him. "Just how emotional *am* I? Yes, I lost a child. Does that mean that I'm to be barred forever from having medical opinions about other children? Why not bar me from opinions about all male patients because I lost a husband? No, I refuse to have my conclusions challenged on the ground that I'm too involved or emotional. Maybe my observations are sounder *because* I'm involved!"

There was a moment of painful silence. Jean was sorry she had exploded at Larry. Benziger was upset by the fact that hospital politics were not only menacing his protégée's professional life but her private life as well.

"Don't do anything rash, my dear. But if you insist on a hearing, consider being represented by counsel," he urged.

BOBBY TATUM was permitted to take walks down the hall, accompanied by his mother. And he could see that one little girl's door was usually closed. Those who went into the room and came out did so in quiet, their faces grave. Once he saw a man dressed in black, with a white collar and not wearing any tie. He carried a long purple cloth and a small black book. Bobby stopped to stare. His mother urged him along. "Come, darling, let's go out to the solarium. It's nice and sunny."

He went, but not without looking back.

The next morning, when his mother came to take him to the solarium, he started out. But in the doorway he stopped. "Bobby?" his mother asked, puzzled.

She glanced into the corridor. The door of the little girl's room was open and a stretcher was being wheeled out. On it, wrapped in a white sheet, was a form the size of a small girl. Bobby clutched his mother's hand. "Mommy, why is she all covered up?"

"She . . . she's going away."

"Away? Why? Is she all better now?"

Marissa Tatum hesitated, wondering if a lie were permissible in such circumstances. But she decided to deal with it as best she could. "She died, Bobby."

"Like Grandma Tatum?"

"Yes, Bobby, like Grandma Tatum."

"You said only old people die."

"Sometimes . . . little children die. But only sometimes."

"Will I die too?"

"Oh, no!" she said quickly.

He remained thoughtful for a time. They went to the solarium, but he showed no interest in playing. He reached for his mother's hand and led her back to his room. He made her sit in the armchair. He crawled up in her lap. His arm around her, he pressed his head against her.

In a while he asked, "Where's Dr. Jean?"

"You have a different doctor now, Bobby. Dr. Ralph."

"I like Dr. Jean," he said, but didn't pursue it any further.

THE FOLLOWING DAY Jean carried out her duties with an unaccustomed grimness that made the other doctors and nurses remark behind her back. By late morning everyone had learned about the impending hearing.

She was dictating in her office when her door was gently eased open. She looked up. There stood a small boy in his navy-blue robe, the sash so unevenly tied that she knew he had done it by himself.

"Dr. Jean," the boy said. "Can . . . can I come in?"

"Bobby, Dr. Sunderland is your doctor now. You know that, don't you?"

"Yes, ma'am," the boy said, not daring to move toward her.

Jean hesitated, then granted: "All right, Bobby."

Timidly he started toward her, shuffling in his slippers. At her desk he stood silent. Cautiously he reached for her hand and placed it against his cheek.

"Do you have any toys?" he asked.

"Bobby," Jean said gently, "does anyone know you're here? Did you get permission to leave your room?" The boy did not answer at once. "Did you?"

"You won't send me back?" the boy pleaded. "The zebra . . . can't I have my zebra?"

There was no harm in giving him the cherished animal. She reached into the desk drawer where she had stored the toys, brought out the zebra, puzzle and storybook. She pushed the animal forward so that he could reach it. He hugged it to his chest in a tight, affectionate embrace.

"Now, Bobby, I'll take you back," she said, holding out her hand. She was determined to be firm. But the look in his eyes made her reconsider. She went to the door and locked it, then returned to her desk.

"Bobby, wouldn't you like to sit down?"

Delighted, the boy snuggled onto the armchair, still clutching his precious toy.

"Would you like to play a new game today, Bobby?" Jean began. "Instead of a puzzle, we're going to make believe."

"I make believe. Me and Esther, we do sometimes."

"Good," Jean encouraged. "We're going to make believe you're home. In your own bed. And I'm reading you to sleep."

"But it isn't dark."

"We can make it dark," Jean said, rising to draw the draperies. "Better?"

"Uh-huh," the boy said, eager for the new game.

"Now close your eyes. Make believe I'm reading you to sleep."

With her pocket flashlight focused on the first page, Jean began to read from the storybook. She could see him smile as he kept his eyes tightly clenched to play along with her. Eventually she departed from the text and began inserting words of her own. "It's nighttime, Bobby. Time for you to sleep. The better you play the game, the more asleep you are. Play that you're going into a deep sleep. You should be asleep now, Bobby. Deep asleep. With your eyes closed tight. Very tight."

She stared across at the boy, trying to determine if his breathing rhythm had changed. He seemed perfectly still until his tiny hand relaxed its grip on the toy. She turned the flashlight on his face. His eyes were closed, but no longer clenched. It was a good sign.

She reached across, lifted his free hand. It was limp and unresisting. Carefully she removed the little zebra from his grasp. He surrendered it without resistance. She knew he was under.

She began by asking simple questions about school, his days at home, his friends. Then she said, "Bobby, we are going to play birthdays."

"Birthdays?" the sleeping boy asked vaguely.

"Do you have a birthday party when you are five?"

"Uh-huh."

"Who's at your party, Bobby? Who's there right now?"

The boy's face lit up. "Gwen. Tony. Angela. Granma Pearson."

"Is it a nice party, Bobby?"

"Cake. Big chocolate cake. With white writing on it. Happy Birthday, Bobby." The boy smiled, his eyes remained closed.

"Now, Bobby, it's your four-year-old birthday party. Isn't that a nice party?"

"Uh-huh," he agreed. "White cake, with chocolate writing on. And ice cream."

"And now you're three, Bobby. Do you have a birthday party when you're three?" When he hesitated, she urged, "You remember that you're three, don't you, Bobby?"

"Uh-huh. Three years old." His speech began to take on the characteristics it possessed at that age.

"It's your three-year-old birthday party. Who's there?"

"Mommy. And Daddy."

"And your friends?"

"Don't have no friends."

"No friends at all, Bobby? Why?"

"We move to San . . . San Diego." As a three-year-old he had had trouble with the name.

But he had mentioned San Diego, one of the critical openings Jean was searching for.

"Bobby, it's just before you move to San Diego. You remember, Bobby. You live in a place called Dayton. Remember?"

"Yes, ma'am."

"You are almost three years old, Bobby. It's the day you and Mommy and Daddy are getting ready to move to San Diego. What happens, Bobby? Who comes to the house?"

"Men come. Mommy wakes me up early."

"And now the men are coming, Bobby. What are they doing?"

"Taking down. Everything down. Boxes. Big boxes."

"And what are you doing, Bobby?"

"Playing in the big room. Downstairs."

"Are you playing there all the time the men are taking down everything?" Jean asked, anxiously awaiting the boy's reply.

"No . . ."

"What do you do, Bobby? What happens?"

Suddenly he called, in imitation of his mother's angry voice and tone, "'Bobby, you stay away from those stairs. Do you hear me? Go back into the living room and stay out of the way. Unless you want to be punished.'"

"Do you go back?"

"Yes, ma'am." Then the boy confessed, "Till . . ."

"Till what, Bobby?"

"I want my teddy bear. I . . ." The boy paused, feeling the same guilt he had felt then. "I . . . I go back up the stairs."

"And?" The boy did not respond. "What happens, Bobby?"

"I go up . . ." He held out his hand as if grasping the stair rail. "One . . . two . . . three . . ." He counted up to nine and stopped.

"What happens at step nine, Bobby?"

"The man . . . mover man. Carrying the big thing down."

"And then, Bobby?" Jean asked, reconciled to hearing the same explanation the Tatums had given her.

But the boy let out a scream, just as he had when he hurtled down those stairs. He began to cry. Jean was not diverted.

"Why are you crying, Bobby?"

"Foot hurts," he said, but he pointed to the outside of his right leg, where his healed fracture had shown up on X ray.

"And Mommy?"

"She takes me in her arms and says, 'I'm sorry, darling. Mommy is very very sorry. She didn't mean to do it.'"

Jean edged closer to the boy. "Bobby, the man on the stairs, does he bang into you? Or touch you in any way?"

"No."

"But you fall down the stairs. Why, Bobby? Why?"

"Mommy is very angry. She finds me on the stairs after she told me stay away from the stairs."

"Now what does Mommy do?"

"She . . ." The boy swung out just as his furious mother must have struck out at him that day. "And I . . . I . . ." He screamed and seemed to fall backward. Then he reached out to touch his leg where the pain had been so intense moments before. He began to weep again. "Hurts. Hurts."

It was interesting to Jean how the events of that day had been altered just enough to conceal what had actually happened. There had been moving men. And the boy had been caught on the stairs. But, unlike what Bob Tatum had reported, no moving man had even touched the boy. Only his mother had. And from the boy's painful recall, she had struck him in a fury.

"Bobby, is Daddy there when it happens?"

"No, ma'am."

Jean realized that Bob Tatum's knowledge of the episode was based on what Marissa had told him. "Bobby, are there other times when Mommy gets angry with you?"

"Uh-huh," he admitted softly.

"When Mommy gets angry, what does she do?"

"Hits me."

"Does it hurt?"

"Yes, ma'am."

"Bobby, can you remember what she says and does after she hits you?"

"She . . . she cries . . . and says she's sorry. . . ." He began to imitate his mother: "'It'll never happen again, Bobby, never. So don't tell anyone. Especially Daddy. Promise, Bobby, promise.'" Then he assumed his own voice again as he pleaded with his mother, "I promise, Mommy. Only don't cry. I love you, so don't cry."

Jean was tempted to take the pathetic little boy into her arms and comfort him. But there was more she had to know.

"Bobby, we're going to remember another time. It's now. You're living in your new house. A time when you hurt your head. Do you remember that time?"

The boy's weeping subsided. He reached up and cautiously touched the left side of his head, reacting in great pain.

"Does that hurt, Bobby?"

"Yes."

"Is there a bump there?"

"Yes."

She leaned across to touch his head. Naturally she felt no bump, but the boy drew back in pain.

"When do you get that bump, Bobby?" It was important to establish the time, since it might be a vital clue to his present seizures.

"Christmas. Daddy comes home."

"Daddy is coming home for Christmas?"

"Yes."

"What happens?" She waited, then had to urge, "Bobby?"

"Mommy and me. We trim the tree. Big shiny *ormanents*."

"And then?"

His voice became apologetic as he confessed, "I break one of the *ormanents*. Big shiny red one."

Jean leaned closer. "Does Mommy punish you again, Bobby?"

"No," the boy said simply, frustrating Jean's expectations.

"And then, Bobby? After you break the *ormanent*?"

"Mommy is going out. All dressed up," the boy relived.

"And what do you do, Bobby?"

"Ask her not to go."

"And what does she say?"

"She has to go. Esther will put me to bed. Mommy kisses me."

"And then, Bobby?"

A look of bitter distaste came over his face. "I . . . I . . . I get sick," he said.

"And what does Mommy do?"

"Hits me."

"For getting sick?"

"Yes."

It was difficult to accept. She tried again. "Is that why she hits you, Bobby? Because you get sick?"

"Yes."

"How does she hit you?"

The boy swung out fiercely in imitation of an action he now remembered well.

"And then what happens?" The boy did not answer. "Bobby?"

Still the boy remained silent, but he began to tremble. Jean took him in her arms and held him close. "There's nothing to be afraid of now. Can you remember what happens after Mommy hits you?"

The boy buried his face in Jean's shoulder. Pressed close against her, he managed to shake his head.

"And is that how you get the bump on your head?"

Without relinquishing his desperate embrace, the boy nodded. She recalled now his saying to her once, "Mommy won't like it if I'm sick."

She brought him out of his hypnotic state. Awake, he stared longingly at the toy zebra. "You may have it, Bobby. To keep."

Eagerly he swooped up the animal, holding it close. Jean took his hand and led him out to the corridor. Halfway down toward the boy's room, Jean heard the voice of an angry woman behind them.

"There he is! She took him!"

It was Marissa Tatum, fiercely accusatory. "Bobby! Let go of her hand. You come right here to your mother!"

The boy looked up at Jean, tears forming in his eyes.

"Does that mean I have to give this back?" he asked simply.

"No. Bobby. It's yours. Now, go to your mother."

He went to her. Marissa dropped to one knee to embrace her son. Looking over his shoulder at Jean, she charged, "Doctor, your conduct is outrageous. And I will report it at once!"

"JEANNIE, you didn't bring that boy into your office! After being removed from the case?"

Instead of responding directly to Larry's agitation, Jean said, "Since I'm no longer on the case, it's up to *you*. Demand an immediate angio on that boy!"

"Why the sudden need for an angio?"

"I may have discovered the etiology of his seizures."

"What did you discover? How?"

She told him.

"You hypnotized that boy without parental consent?"

"There's nothing legal or medical that requires informed consent for hypnosis. Larry, insist on an angio. It's the only test that will give us a definitive diagnosis. And, if it turns out to be a subdural hematoma, he'll need surgery. Without delay!"

"At most, even if you were able to prove it, the boy only said he was hit. It won't be the first time a four-year-old has been punished by his mother."

"For getting sick?" Jean asked.

"There must have been more," Larry insisted. "It doesn't make sense. That Marissa would punish him for getting sick."

"It does. If you read the literature, Bobby's case is typical. Normally, when a child is ill, parents tend to be overly loving. But an abusing parent tends to be frustrated and angered by a child's sickness."

"So you've switched from accusing Bob to accusing Marissa? All because of a little boy's saying that his mother once punished him."

"And what about *his* version of that fine-line fracture?" Jean challenged.

"The way it happened, it *could* have been the moving man. All I know, at the time you say he received a head trauma, *I* was his pediatrician. *I* never saw any sign of it. Never heard anything about it. As far as I'm concerned, it never happened."

"There's one factor here that I won't brush aside," Jean said. "Under hypnosis, the boy couldn't remember anything that happened after his mother struck him. Whatever his head struck, he blacked out. Was unconscious. A blow like that *could* cause a subdural. Larry, insist on an angio!"

"I want to talk to Bobby first."

"He's your patient. You don't need my permission."

The conversation ended on that note. Crisp, professional, impersonal. Jean regretted it, but felt more strongly than ever that she must keep the two parts of her life separate. If, finally, this case meant losing Larry, she would have to face that.

LARRY BRAHAM tried to make his visit to the boy's room seem like the usual drop-in. "Hi, Bobby!"

"Hi, Dr. Larry." The boy was delighted to see him, though he resumed smoothing the coat of the little zebra.

"How do you feel?"

"Fine," he reported, with no particular emphasis.

"Do you like it here, Bobby?"

"Yes, fine."

"Wouldn't you rather be home and with your friends?"

"I have a friend here."

"Who?"

"Dr. Jean. She's not my doctor, so she must be my friend."

"Oh, I see. Well, the main thing now is to see that you get home for Thanksgiving. It's better to have Thanksgiving at home." He directed the conversation toward the point he wished to make: "Just like Christmas. You like Christmas at home, don't you?"

"Uh-huh," the boy said, his concentration on his zebra.

"Bobby . . . do you like trimming the tree?"

"Yep."

"Even when you break one of the *ornaments*?" Larry asked.

The boy smiled. "You said that wrong. Ornament."

"Oh. Well, did you ever break an ornament?"

"No."

Surprised by such a spontaneous contradiction, Larry felt obliged to come to the point. "Bobby, did anyone punish you last Christmas? Didn't Mommy punish you for getting sick?"

"Uh-uh," the boy denied, more deeply involved in his toy now.

"Did you ever get a bump on your head? A bump that hurt a lot? Try to remember, Bobby."

The boy gave every evidence of thinking hard. "No bump."

Larry Braham studied the boy's face. There wasn't a hint that he was speaking anything but the truth.

"JEANNIE, don't you see how impossible your situation will be? Even the boy will dispute you," Larry warned.

"What the boy recalled under hypnosis is the truth. In his conscious state he's inhibited. Afraid to remember."

"If you go before the Child Abuse Committee, or have to defend yourself at the trustees' hearing, which you insist on, what are you going to tell them? What if the trustees question the boy? And he tells them the same thing he told me? He never got sick. His mother never punished him. What then?"

She could not answer.

"Jeannie, a child of five cannot be relied upon to tell the same story twice. And you can't even prove physical abuse."

"I might, if you'd have them do an angio on that boy."

He lost patience. "Jean! Pretend you're talking to another pediatrician. A stranger. You're treating his patient, a five-year-old who has not had a seizure for days. Would you ask him to get consent to do an angio? Besides," he added, "if I ask the Tatums, I'm going to have to tell them why."

"Tell them!" she shot back.

"Now? Before your hearing? And give Cameron one more charge to make against you? Bobby was no longer your patient when you put him under hypnosis."

She realized the import of his last remark. "In fact," Larry continued, "if it's not too late, call off that hearing."

"That would be a virtual admission of Cameron's charges."

"Yes," he admitted grimly. "Yes, it would."

Larry left. Discouraged but determined, Jean sat down at her typewriter and wrote brief letters to the record departments of the twenty-nine other hospitals in the city.

Her request was simple and confidential. She would appreciate any information in their files concerning the emergency admission to the hospital of a boy named Robert Tatum, Jr., during the previous December.

If there was substance to the boy's recall under hypnosis, as she was sure there was, then he must have blacked out on being struck. His mother would have been desperate. She would have rushed him to a hospital, but not to University Hospital, because of Larry's affiliation—even more, because of Cameron's.

Jean addressed and mailed the envelopes. With records computerized, she should get responses very soon. She hoped before the day of her hearing. Within the week she received replies from all twenty-nine hospitals. There was no admission of a Robert Tatum, Jr., recorded in any of them.

The results unsettled her. Jean would have to face the trustees without any confirmation of her findings. Worse, if challenged, she would have to withdraw her suspicions of Bob Tatum in view of what she had discovered during hypnosis of his son. She had no choice but to withdraw her request for the hearing.

TWO DAYS LATER Dr. Scofield found on her desk the formal notification from Edward Carey. The board of trustees had voted officially to deprive her of admitting privileges to the hospital. The letter said nothing about continuing to teach or about tenure. But those mattered little if she could not continue to practice.

Despite the fact that she had expected the action, the finality of it shook her so severely that she closed her door, sat down at her desk and began to weep.

Her phone rang. She recovered sufficiently to answer.

"Jeannie?" It was Larry. "You got the word?"

"Yes."

"You shouldn't be alone. I'm coming to take you home."

She was relieved to agree. She needed him more now than ever. It had been years since she felt so defeated and insecure. Before she hung up, she asked, "Larry? Please, do something for me. Bring Bobby Tatum's file with you."

"Why? Jeannie, darling, don't tear yourself apart over this case. It's cost you too much already."

"Larry! Please?"

"Okay," he reluctantly agreed.

Before Larry arrived, Hans Benziger came in. He embraced her tenderly and kissed her on the cheek. "I wish there were something I could do," he said hopelessly.

To ease the old man's anguish she said, "There'll be other appointments, other hospitals."

"But it will never be the same," Benziger said. She could not disagree.

SHE EXAMINED Bobby's file while Larry mixed the drinks. She searched every entry, every lab report. Eventually she closed the file and shook her head.

"Here," Larry handed her a drink. As she sipped it he studied her. "I think you ought to get away for a while. We should go on a trip. Get away from this place."

"Is that all? Just get away?" she asked pointedly. "You're afraid I'll have another breakdown. Aren't you?"

"The trustees' action is no minor defeat. It could mean losing the most important thing in your life since Cliff. When I see how tormented you are, yes. I ask myself: Could it happen again? Being in love with you gives me the right to ask. Even Benni—" He had not meant to reveal that.

"Is it that obvious?"

Larry did not answer except to take her in his arms. After a moment she said, "So Benni is worried, too?"

"Yes."

"He shouldn't be. Psychiatrists will tell you that people who recover from breakdowns usually come out of the experience stronger than they were before."

"Usually is not enough, when you're worried about the woman you love. And we love you, Benni and I."

"I know, I know." She sounded sad as she said it.

She was not only frustrated but depressed. For the first time she realized it was not only loyalty to Cliff that stood in the way of her remarrying, but also the false island of protection she had created for herself. As long as she was not married, she had told herself, she could never again suffer that same shattering loss. Now, unmarried, she knew she had lost again. And it hurt deeply. Because this time it *was* of her own doing.

She, not Larry, had precipitated the events that would cause the two of them to be split apart. Unless she were willing to compromise her career. She could remain in the city and go into private practice. But then there would not be the satisfaction she derived from her teaching and her research. She had contributions yet to make in both fields. She was determined to make them. Despite the price in pain and loneliness that she would have to start paying again.

Chapter Nine

The next evening there were four police cars pulled up in the driveway of University Hospital, their warning lights rotating in the misty night. Several officers waited outside the entrance, talking among themselves.

Inside, in Edward Carey's office, Horace Cameron was in command. He had appropriated Carey's desk, using both phones to make and receive calls.

Marissa Tatum sat off in a corner, her eyes red from tears. Her lips trembled and she kept saying, "Bobby . . . Bobby . . ."

Larry Braham entered. "No one saw the boy. Not when he left his room. Not when he left the hospital—"

"We don't know if he left the hospital," Carey interrupted, seeking to protect his institution from the accusation that a five-year-old boy could slip out without being detected. "We're doing a search of every room, every closet, right this minute!"

Marissa suddenly cried out, "They have to find him! They have to!"

Cameron did his best to calm her. "Bob's on his way. The company jet will be here in two hours at most." He walked over to the plainclothes detective, Inspector Greer. "Ever had one like this before? A child kidnapped right out of a hospital?"

"Mr. Cameron, we don't know if he *was* kidnapped. Personally, I doubt it," the tall, lean detective said.

"It could happen," Cameron insisted.

"If some psycho nurse or nurse's aide took him, you don't have to worry. We always find them. And that type takes good care of the kid. That's why they snatch them in the first place. To have something to take care of."

"That's not the kind of kidnapping I meant."

"You mean ransom?" Greer asked. "I doubt it."

"Why not? I'd be a logical target. If there were a ransom demand, where do you think the money would come from?"

Ralph Sunderland arrived, tired and hopeless. "Can't understand. Someone must have seen him. Between his afternoon milk and cookies and the time the nurse came to bring his dinner. But nobody did. Nobody."

Inspector Greer turned to Marissa. "What's your number at home?"

There was little possibility the boy was there, but Greer knew that if a ransom call did come, it would most likely be to the Tatum home. Esther answered. No, Bobby was not there.

Greer asked, "Have there been any calls? Anything unusual?"

"Just one. From Dr. Scofield. She wanted to talk to Mrs. Tatum."

"That's all?"

"That's all."

"Thanks. Thanks a lot," the detective said. He hung up. "Only one call. From a woman who said she was Dr. Scofield."

"Of course!" Cameron said. "That explains it!"

"What?" Greer asked, eager now.

"What you said about a nurse or nurse's aide needing a child to mother. What if it were a *doctor* who had that need?"

"That's an outrageous accusation!" Larry Braham exploded.

"I'll bet right now she's off somewhere with that boy, hiding him, having him all to herself!"

To prove Cameron wrong, Larry dialed Jean's office. After the third ring, her answering service responded, and he asked that Jean call him. He hesitated a moment, then dialed her apartment. There was no answer there. By this time Cameron, Sunderland and Greer were staring at him. He made one more call.

"Benni? Larry Braham. Have you seen or talked to Jean in the last few hours? I see. I see. Left right after her clinic hours. Thanks, Benni."

He turned to face the three men. "I told her to take the afternoon off and go somewhere by herself. She was upset," he addressed Cameron, "about having her admitting privileges canceled. She's taking it very hard. I wanted her to get away from here." The more Larry Braham tried to explain, the more he gave credence to Cameron's accusation.

"Inspector," Cameron said, "shouldn't we put out an alarm for that woman?"

"If this ever gets into the papers, it could damage Dr. Scofield's career. She could sue all of you," Larry interjected.

"Let her," Cameron replied defiantly. "Inspector!"

Greer dialed a number. "Klein? Put out an APB on a doctor,

female." He relayed Jean's description. "She may be with the missing boy, Robert Tatum, Jr. Yeah, it's one of those."

The chief of hospital security arrived to report, "We've made a complete search. No sign."

Exasperated, Greer said irritably, "Let's go back over this whole thing. You're sure the kid wasn't due to have something done to him? Some examination that might scare him?"

"Inspector, we've already told you, he wasn't due for anything but to be discharged," Cameron said. "Dr. Sunderland had approved his release."

"A kid who's due to go home doesn't disappear," Greer insisted doggedly. "Is it possible that he was afraid you weren't telling him the truth?"

"But we *were* telling him the truth!" Sunderland persisted. "Tomorrow his mother was free to take him home. I told him that only this morning."

Suddenly Marissa Tatum said, "You must find him. Find him!"

Larry gripped her arms. "Marissa, please. He can't have gone far."

"What if he has a seizure? He could die. . . ."

"He probably won't have a seizure," Larry said. Actually that had been the fear uppermost in his mind from the moment he heard Bobby was missing. He went to the phone and dialed Jean's home again. There was still no answer. He found himself considering the possibility he had so vehemently denied earlier. The boy was missing. So, evidently, was Jean.

Larry tried to analyze her state of mind. This hospital was essential to her security, both professional and emotional. Deprived of it, suddenly and without justification, perhaps she would react in unpredictable fashion.

He made one more call. To Jean's answering service. Yes, Dr. Scofield had called. She had picked up his message. At least she knew that he was trying to reach her. As he hung up, the second phone rang. It was Carey's secretary to announce that Dr. Scofield was on her way in.

Marissa Tatum rose, crying out as the door opened, "What have you done with him?"

"I haven't seen him," Jean said. "But I know we have to find him. At once!"

"Damn it, woman," Cameron interceded, "what do you think we've been trying to do? We were sure he was with you."

"I wish he were." Jean looked to Larry, whose eyes admitted the speculation that had been rife in the room until she appeared.

As she turned and left, Inspector Greer called after her, "Any ideas you have, let me know. We're going to need all the help we can get to find that boy."

"We're going to need more help than that when you *do* find him!" Jean responded, and she was gone.

Cameron looked at Larry. "What did she mean by that?"

"I don't know." He started after her.

Jean stopped at the floor nurses' desk, asking the same questions that had been asked before. No one had seen the boy. Of course, there had been a change of shift since the boy was discovered missing. They had tried to reach all personnel who had been on duty at the time he had disappeared. Those they had succeeded in contacting had no information.

Jean reached her office harboring a fear that far exceeded those the others had. Larry found her at her desk.

"Jeannie?"

"It's urgent that they find him! I'm sure now. He's suffering from a subdural hematoma due to trauma to the head."

"You never received any confirmation from any hospital. You admitted that."

"I know," Jean said. "That's why I took one more look at your file on Bobby."

"Nothing there would substantiate the presence of a subdural."

"No," she agreed, "but it did provide a place to start."

"What place?"

"Pearson. Marissa Tatum's maiden name."

"Yes," he remembered vaguely. "What about it?"

"I'd been reading the pediatric literature on child abuse. There's a prevalent pattern. Middle- and upper-class abusing mothers, when confronted with an emergency, as a rule seek out a hospital or a doctor to whom their identity is not known. They pay cash, to avoid any chance of identification. *And* they almost always use other names. Very often their maiden names instead of completely fictitious ones."

Larry conjectured, "Maybe they're trying to cover up, while at the same time hoping to be caught and stopped."

"Some psychiatrists say that."

"Now what about Pearson?"

"That's where I've been all afternoon. I went back to each hospital that wrote they had no record of Robert Tatum, Jr."

"And?"

"Last December a four-year-old boy named Charles Pearson was brought to Emergency Admitting at West Side Memorial. He had suffered a trauma to the head, resulting in a marked swelling. He was kept overnight, found to have no other signs of damage. The next day his mother took him home. She paid the bill in cash."

"Back in December," Larry considered.

"Three days before Christmas," Jean said. "The mother's story was that she and the boy were trimming the tree. While she had gone to answer the phone, the boy climbed the ladder and fell off, striking his head on the floor. The admitting doctor evidently believed her, because he entered no comments on the chart."

"Almost ten months before his first seizure," Larry commented.

"Well within the time span when a subdural could begin evidencing itself in seizures," Jean agreed. "If it *is* a subdural, it could have disastrous consequences if we don't take steps at once. If *you* don't take steps," she corrected, realizing she was no longer on the case.

"I should have acted on your hunch and insisted on permission to do that angio."

"Let's hope it isn't too late. They've got to find him!"

IT WAS LONG PAST ten o'clock at night when Personnel heard from the last nurse's aide who had been on duty when Bobby Tatum disappeared. She had seen the boy in the corridor. He asked for Dr. Scofield's office. She directed him down the hall, and saw him disappear into the right office. She assumed the boy was expected and that Dr. Scofield was there. She knew nothing more till she turned on her radio late that night and heard he was missing.

Her information supplied a possible motive for the boy's leaving his room. Where he might have gone after failing to find Dr. Scofield was still unknown.

Bob Tatum had returned from his trip and was insisting on all sorts of police measures, most of which had already been tried. He took to searching the hospital neighborhood in the prowl car Inspector Greer put at his disposal.

Horace Cameron had left the hospital after giving instructions that he was to be awakened as soon as there was word about the boy. Francine Cameron arrived to comfort Marissa Tatum. However, the distressed mother had become so tense that she verged on hysteria. She was given strong sedation and put to bed.

IN THE ALL-NIGHT staff cafeteria Jean and Larry were having what seemed like their hundredth cup of coffee.

"They'll find him," Larry kept saying. He knew those were words of desperation. "Are you going to confront Marissa with what you discovered?"

"Not tonight. She doesn't need any more punishment than she's already giving herself." Jean stirred her coffee. "A woman always blames herself for any tragedy that befalls her man or her child. During those days after Cliff, I kept reliving the million little things that I might have done that would have averted his death. If I had never let him go. If I had insisted we go back to the States as soon as I was pregnant. I created endless possibilities that could have kept him alive. I did nothing wrong. Everyone knew that. *Except me*. Imagine how Marissa must feel now. How much worse it is for her."

"She doesn't know that what she did ten months ago could be what's threatening her son now," Larry said.

"She knows," Jean disputed sadly. "Intuition. Guilt. Her unconscious mind. Whatever you call it, inside her there is something that knows."

At that moment an orderly appeared in the cafeteria doorway, then approached them swiftly. "Doctor," he addressed Larry, "there's a report. Some man walking his dog found a boy lying in his driveway. A police car is bringing him in now."

They raced to Emergency Admitting. Bob Tatum and Ralph Sunderland were there, waiting. The prowl car pulled up, its lights ablaze. The car door burst open. A policeman emerged carrying a small boy, black-haired, dressed in a wrinkled, dirty blue robe, one slipper missing. He handed the boy over to his father. Bob Tatum rushed his young son into the emergency room.

He laid him on the examining table gently, leaned close and murmured into his ear, "Bobby! You're safe now. You're going to be fine. Bobby, do you hear me? Daddy is talking to you, son. Do you hear me, Bobby?"

It was obvious the boy did not hear. He was unconscious. "Undoubtedly had another seizure," Sunderland concluded. He proceeded with the routine. Blood pressure slightly on the low side. Pulse elevated. Respiratory pattern normal. All seemed to confirm his diagnosis—the boy had had another seizure.

Sunderland now noticed the condition on which Jean had been concentrating. The boy's left arm and leg moved in subtle spontaneous reactions. His right arm and leg did not. Sunderland ran his fingernails lightly across the plantar surface of the boy's left foot. The big toe went down, his other toes curled in. He turned his attention to the right foot. That large toe turned up, the others fanned out. "Positive plantar response," he observed unhappily. He drew some blood. "Electrolytes! Stat!" The nurse in charge dispatched an orderly to the lab with the blood sample. Sunderland then ordered, "Twenty-five percent glucose IV."

He picked up the phone and called Radiology. A resident was on duty. "I want a bedside echo. Stat. In Emergency. And also bedside skull and cervical-spine X rays."

Sunderland's attitude, his crisp orders, all had a mounting effect on Bob Tatum. "Damn it, Doctor, what is it?"

"The boy had another seizure. This time, however—" Sunderland turned to Jean. "Has he ever presented Todd's before?"

"Never," Jean admitted.

"What the hell is Todd's?" Tatum demanded. Larry Braham beckoned to Cameron, who had just returned from home. The older man reached out to calm Tatum with a firm hand on his shoulder.

Sunderland explained. "Todd's is a temporary one-sided paralysis that can set in after a seizure."

"How long does it last?" the suspicious father asked.

"A day. A few days at most."

"Then he'll be all right again?" Tatum demanded skeptically. "He'll be able to move? Normally?"

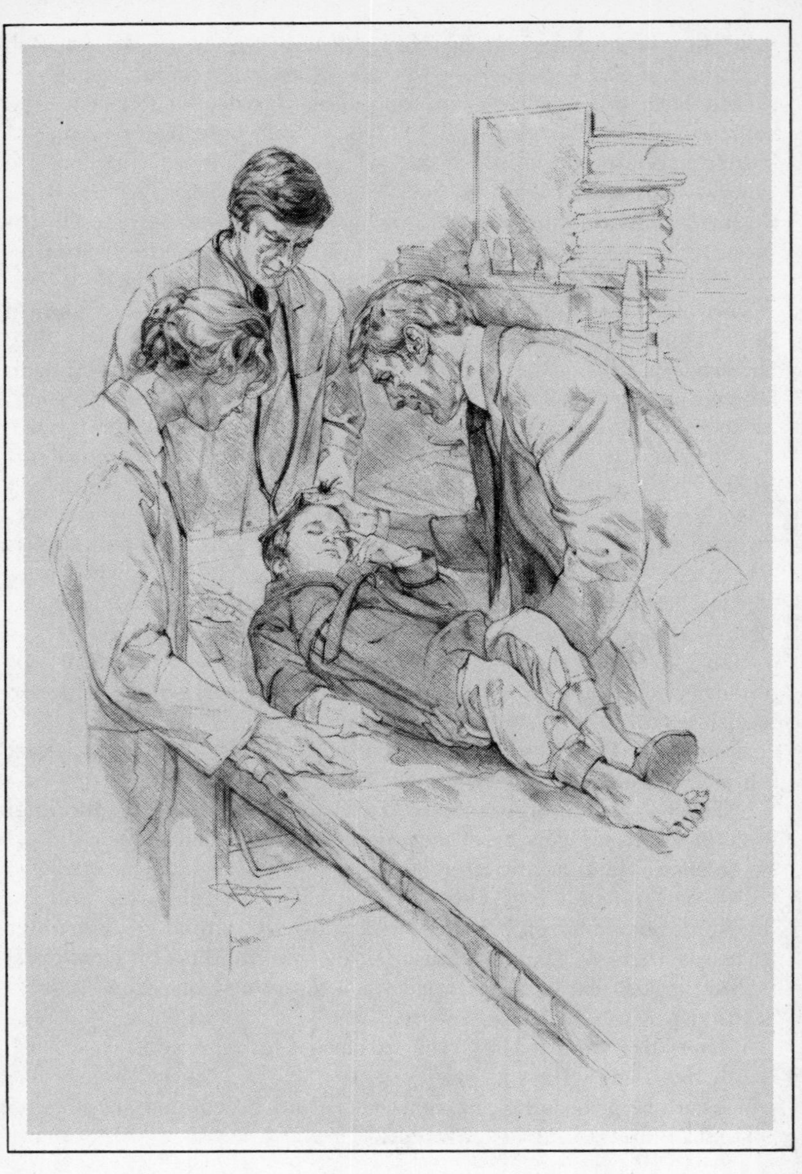

"Absolutely!"

Relieved, Bob Tatum sank down to a white metal stool and breathed deeply and swiftly. Jean watched, thinking, Whatever his shortcomings as a father, whatever his demanding nature has inflicted on the boy, Bob Tatum loves his son.

But she also wondered how much more in the way of love, kindness and indulgence this father was capable of. For she was not so sanguine as Dr. Sunderland. Todd's paralysis was the most comforting of the possible diagnoses to make.

The boy's lids flickered and opened. His blue eyes were dull. He stared up at the faces that hovered over him. Dr. Larry. Dr. Jean. Dr. Ralph. He tried to reach out to Jean, who was at his right side. He was terrified as he discovered his arm did not respond. His lips moved, but he could not formulate any words.

"Bobby?" his father said. "Bobby, can you hear me? This is Dad. Bobby?"

The boy turned to his father. Bob Tatum pressed his face against Bobby's soft cheek. At that moment a technician arrived with the X-ray equipment. The resident arrived to perform the echoencephalogram, to see if there had been any shift of the boy's brain in his skull.

As the equipment was being cleared from the room, the lab reports came back on the boy's electrolytes. His glucose and the BUN—blood urea nitrogen—were only slightly lower than normal. Sodium and potassium were both normal. There was nothing definitive in the report.

"Todd's," Sunderland reiterated. "We'll observe him for the next forty-eight hours. By then I'm sure the paralysis will clear up. Meantime, we should have the X rays and the echo in another half hour."

The boy was wheeled to his old room. Marissa Tatum had been wakened. In her drowsy, sedated state, she insisted on sitting at Bobby's bedside the rest of the night. She kept repeating, "When he wakes up, first thing he'll want to see is me."

Within the hour the X rays were delivered. The plates revealed nothing abnormal in the skull or the cervical spine. The echo, which would have been more indicative, was not at all satisfactory. The resident admitted that he could not get a good midline trace.

A new echo must wait till morning, when a more experienced man was on duty.

It was past three when Larry drove Jean home. They were both exhausted from the night of tension.

"You don't agree with Sunderland's diagnosis, do you?" Larry said. "You don't think it's Todd's?"

"Remember, I *know* something Sunderland doesn't. That emergency admission of ten months ago."

"You should have told him."

"In front of the Tatums? In front of Cameron? It could destroy that family. Unless it's handled very carefully." Jean was silent for a moment before admitting, "There's always the remote possibility that the name Pearson is a coincidence. I have to be very sure before I say anything. But when it clearly affects Bobby's prognosis, then I *am* going to speak up. My obligation is to him."

THE NEXT MORNING Bobby Tatum woke early. He found his mother smiling down at him. He tried to smile back. She held out her hand, coaxing him to reach out his right hand to her.

"Try, Bobby. Try, darling," she urged gently, though becoming desperately tense and adding to his fears.

The harder he tried, the less able he was to accomplish it. Tears ran down the sides of his cheeks, wetting his pillow. Marissa Tatum left the room, stood outside his door, frightened and weeping. A nurse led her to the empty visitors' room, then went in to see Bobby. She smiled at the tormented little patient, trying to reassure him. His lips moved, but he made no sound. She urged him on. "Try, Bobby. I think you can."

The boy mobilized all his effort and finally was able to enunciate, "Dr. Jean . . ." The nurse patted him and nodded. She went to the floor phone and told Dr. Braham of his patient's request.

One thought registered sharply on Larry Braham. Last evening, someone had said Bobby had no reason to be missing, since he'd been told he was ready to be released from the hospital. That could have been the precipitating factor in Bobby's disappearance. Deprived of Jean, fearing that he would never see her again, he might well have gone seeking her. Then through some unexplained accident he found himself out on the street and lost, wandering until he collapsed in a seizure in the driveway where he had been found.

Larry recalled reading that a doctor in New York who specialized in child abuse cases had said that physical abuse was not the sole kind. Prolonged parental deprivation could have lifelong emotional effects. Nor did it matter if the neglect was that of a drug-addicted parent or of an ambitious professional parent who did not have time to lavish love on a child.

For the first time Larry was convinced of Jean Scofield's diagnosis. All the qualities of the good executive wife that he had found so admirable in Marissa Tatum were possible destructive factors in her shy young son's condition. He knew now that it was vital to have Jean restored to the case.

Because merely dropping by to visit the boy could not be construed as a breach of ethics, Larry was able to prevail upon Jean. She had intended to visit him only briefly. But the boy held her hand tight and pressed it against his cheek desperately.

The door opened. Sunderland was staring angrily at Jean.

"Good morning, Doctor. Purely social visit," Jean said, rising.

"If you'll excuse us, Doctor, I'd like to examine my patient."

Jean had no choice but to free her hand from Bobby's grasp and leave. She had to avoid his pleading blue eyes.

Sunderland repeated his examination. He thought he detected a bit more mobility in the right leg, though the arm was no better. He was satisfied with the progress and with his diagnosis. In the corridor, he filled Larry in and said, "We'll run the echo and the EEG as a matter of routine. I'll call you once I see the results."

"Do you think an angiogram is advisable?" Larry asked.

"Last resort," Sunderland said dogmatically. "The risks are too great. The indications are not persuasive enough."

"Then you're still sure it's Todd's?"

"More certain now than I was last night. It's clearing up, isn't it?" Sunderland demanded, annoyed that a mere pediatrician would question his judgment. "Braham, this may be the first case of this kind you've had. But I've had dozens. So let me do this my way."

Larry reported his conversation to Jean.

"I'm going to insist on an angiogram at once!" Jean said.

"How?" Larry asked.

"There's only one way left."

Chapter Ten

Marissa Tatum was at her son's bedside when the nurse came in with a message asking her to call a certain extension within the hospital.

"This is Mrs. Robert Tatum. Someone at this extension asked me to call."

"I did. It's Dr. Scofield."

"You! What do you want now?"

"If you love your son, if you're concerned about his health, come see me. I'll wait in my office for fifteen minutes."

Fifteen minutes had gone by. Jean realized that she had failed. She might as well do her rounds of the last patients she had admitted before her privileges were canceled. She had just started away from her office when a voice called out, "Doctor!"

Jean turned to face Marissa Tatum. The women stared at each other for a moment. Jean opened the door, allowed Marissa to enter.

"You may smoke if you wish," Jean began.

"Thank you," Marissa said archly.

Jean had to admire the graceful way Marissa handled a habit that was essentially ungraceful.

"Mrs. Tatum, you must believe that I have only one interest in talking to you now. I think Bobby's in great danger."

"Dr. Sunderland doesn't think so!" The mother's hostile attitude reflected her rigid state of mind.

"I do not agree with Dr. Sunderland's diagnosis," Jean said flatly. "And I want you to remember what I say. If you wish, I'll write it down for you. I think your son is suffering from a subdural hematoma—"

"Subdural hematoma," Marissa Tatum repeated.

"Tell Sunderland that he should not discount a subdural hematoma. It's important. *Now.* What's going on in your son's brain at this moment can spell life or death."

The tense young mother grew pale. "You're trying to frighten me. So we'll put you back on the case. If it's that dangerous, why doesn't Sunderland know about it?" she demanded.

"Mrs. Tatum, I think I know certain facts about this case that Dr. Sunderland doesn't," Jean said with a pointed significance that forced Marissa to stare at her. "Mrs. Tatum, does the name Charles Pearson mean anything to you?"

"That was my father's name."

"Did *you* ever have occasion to use the name Charles Pearson?"

"Only on employment applications," she said bitterly. "I had to put something down where it asked, 'Father's name?'"

"I mean recently. Within the last year."

"The last year? Of course not," Marissa Tatum started to deny. She stopped, her face in a fixed pose, as if her features had suddenly lost all mobility.

Gently Jean asked, "For Bobby's sake, I must know. Did you take him to West Side Memorial last December with a head injury?"

Marissa Tatum did not respond.

"Was he released to you the next morning, this four-year-old Charles Pearson? And did you pay his bill in cash?"

Marissa Tatum answered in a breathless whisper, "It can't mean anything. I asked a number of times, and the doctor there kept saying, 'He's all right.' What difference can that make now?"

"An enormous difference. It completely changes the diagnosis and treatment of Bobby's case. And I don't think we have any time to lose."

"You're threatening me."

"Yes, I am threatening you," Jean admitted. "Unless your son has an immediate angiogram, I am very fearful about his future."

"What . . . what do you want me to do?"

"You don't have to tell anyone what happened. But you must go to Sunderland and insist he do an angiogram on Bobby!"

MARISSA TATUM called her husband at once. Within twenty minutes Bob and Marissa, accompanied by an agitated Horace Cameron, confronted Ralph Sunderland in his office. Sunderland treated Marissa's concern indulgently.

"The trouble with parents," he said, smiling at Cameron, "they see something on television or hear some gossip from some woman whose child has had a totally dissimilar ailment and they become hysterical." He turned to Marissa. "Mrs. Tatum, exactly what do you know about angiograms and why are you insisting on one?"

Unable to speak freely, she said, "Well, as I understand it, this Todd's thing can be mistaken for something else. And one can't always be sure."

"Of course one can't always be sure. That's why we make a tentative diagnosis and watch the patient's progress carefully. But we don't go rushing into an angiogram. Do you have any idea what side effects an angiogram can produce?"

"No," she admitted unsurely. "Is it dangerous?"

"Let me give you a small idea. The doctor can do everything right and still an angiogram can produce unpredictable results. Some are minor. Such as an irregular heartbeat. But there can also be cardiac arrest.

"Since it involves passing a catheter into one of the arteries, it can result in a spasm of the artery, cutting off blood to a leg or an arm, necessitating amputation. It can create an embolism by causing matter to flake off an artery wall. When that reaches the heart, that's it! Instantaneously. So, you see, we do not do angiograms whenever the whim seizes someone."

He took Marissa Tatum's hand and patted it comfortingly. "Mother, let's not get hysterical. His Todd's is clearing up."

She was torn between her fears and her need for secrecy. "What if he had some injury to his head?" she asked. "Would that change your opinion?"

"There's no record of such an injury in his file," Sunderland said. He turned to Tatum. "*Did* the boy suffer a head injury in the last year or so?"

"No," Tatum said firmly.

His wife did not have the courage to contradict him. But she did say, "I suggest that we bring Dr. Scofield back on the case."

"Marissa!" her husband exclaimed. "Why?"

"Because . . . she knows Bobby better. And he likes her. He needs all the confidence and security we can give him now."

Tatum looked to Cameron, who openly disapproved. "Marissa—" Bob Tatum began.

"Bob! Please? This one time, do it? For me? Bob, I want her to take care of my son!" Her eyes glistened with tears.

Bob Tatum decided he had to risk Cameron's disapproval. "If Marissa feels so strongly about it, I want to call Dr. Scofield back on the case."

"It would be impossible for us to work together," Sunderland threatened.

"I would still like her back on the case."

"Well!" Sunderland said, dismayed and embarrassed. "I no longer assume responsibility for the patient." With a look to Cameron, Sunderland strode out of the room.

"I wouldn't have done that, Bob," Cameron said.

"Marissa doesn't insist often. When she does, I have to respect that. Sorry, Mr. Cameron."

"I understand," Cameron replied coolly.

Bob Tatum embraced his wife. "I'll call Dr. Scofield."

BEFORE SHE EXAMINED the boy, Dr. Scofield studied the new echoencephalogram results. The fresh plate clearly showed that pressure on the left side of the boy's brain had caused it to shift from midline by four to five millimeters. She was positive now that they were not dealing with Todd's paralysis. A subdural hematoma or a brain tumor could cause such a midline shift.

When she compared for the Tatums the possible risks of doing an angiogram against the far graver risk of not doing one, Tatum agreed to sign the consent form. He asked for an explanation of what she suspected, which Jean avoided. For that vital matter would have to be handled with utmost tact, if lives were not to be disrupted or destroyed.

Jean and the assisting neuroradiologist moved into the small operating room. Bobby Tatum had already been wheeled in. Once his sedative began to take effect, Jean was ready to commence.

The procedure involved inserting a needle and a thin rubber catheter into the boy's femoral artery and gently directing it from his groin up the artery into the aortic arch. Then, from there into the left carotid artery in his neck. A wire encased in the catheter enabled the doctor to guide it. With an adult the insertion of the catheter could be made directly into the carotid. But a child's carotid was too narrow for a direct approach.

Jean would follow the catheter's course on the image intensifier, a screen that looked not much different from a television screen. It revealed the patient's entire arterial system.

Jean inserted the needle, to which the catheter was attached, into the femoral artery. She worked slowly, glancing at the image intensifier opposite her.

She stopped to monitor his pulse. A falling pulse rate in a leg or an arm could signal a spasm of the artery in that limb, which could lead to disastrous consequences. The boy's pulse had grown a bit weaker. She had to consider withdrawing the catheter. There were patients who could never be given an angiogram. Perhaps Bobby would prove to be one of those.

When his pulse rate did not fall any lower, she decided to continue. The catheter reached his aortic arch. Her eyes fixed on the screen, she maneuvered the catheter to the carotid artery. Now she had arrived at a critical moment—the injection of renographin, the dye which would allow the biplane X-ray cameras to simultaneously photograph his brain, one from the side and one from above his head.

Not all patients could tolerate the dye. Jean acted cautiously and injected only half a cubic centimeter. Now she watched not the screen but her little patient. His breathing continued shallow and regular. He evidenced no hives, blotches or other allergic reactions. She nodded to the neuroradiologist. They would inject the entire dosage.

The radiologist set both cameras in operation. They did their work swiftly. The films were removed and sent to the lab. From the developed plates they would be able to read the inside of the brain without opening the skull.

Slowly Jean withdrew the catheter. She checked his pulse again. Regular, slow, only a bit weaker than usual. He had weathered the procedure well.

Fifteen minutes later Jean, the radiologist and Larry stood before the viewing box and stared at the plates, which revealed the inside of Bobby Tatum's skull. The arteries were sharply traced on the X-ray films. The midline shift of the brain was discernible. In the left side of the boy's brain there was a cloudy gray mass.

"Middle cerebral artery depressed two to three centimeters," the radiologist observed.

"Arteries on the left side very depressed," Jean said. "No question it's a subdural hematoma."

"And an ugly one," the radiologist agreed. "Certainly could cause his paralysis."

"Surprising that a subdural like that didn't cause any—" She stopped.

"Jean?" Larry prodded.

"Now that I think of it, Marissa Tatum said he *did* have morning headaches. The first time I interviewed her. She attributed them to his not wanting to go to school. I shouldn't have missed that. The subdural's got to be removed. Today, if possible. Tomorrow at the latest."

THE TATUMS were waiting at Bobby's bedside. The boy had overcome the effects of sedation and was playing with a small sponge football his father had brought him. He almost managed to get his left hand around one end of it. But try as he did, the boy could not raise his right hand. It lay inert and useless.

"It's all right, Bobby boy," his father tried to encourage him. He realized, as did Jean and Larry, that the boy was more anguished at disappointing him than at his own paralysis. "The doctors are going to make it all right."

Tatum glanced up, and Larry indicated that they wanted to speak to him privately. "Sure. Riss, you wait here."

Jean interposed firmly, "I think she should come, too."

Marissa hesitated, glanced at Jean Scofield, whose eyes tried to assure that there would be no disclosure of secrets. Marissa kissed her son. "We'll be back in a little while, darling."

Jean conducted the consultation in her office, where a viewing box was available. In the darkened room she traced on the plate the affected area of Bobby's brain. She pointed out how pressure on the left side was causing the paralysis on his right. If allowed to continue, it must enlarge and, most likely, become fatal.

"But he recovered his ability to speak," Tatum argued.

"Temporarily, Bob," Larry said. "These things do not cure themselves. Not at this stage. They only become worse."

Tatum had to take his wife's icy-cold hand before he could ask, "What do we do?"

"Operate," Larry said. "Right away."

"I checked with Dr. Forrest," Jean added. "He can fit it into his schedule first thing in the morning."

"Fit it into his schedule," Bob Tatum repeated bitterly. "Like getting your car serviced! This is my son you're talking about! And some surgeon is going to dig into his brain, and all you can say is that he can fit him in in the morning."

"Bob, please!" His wife tried to stop him.

"No, damn it! He ought to take more time. To study the case!" Tatum turned away, disconsolate, angry, but most of all afraid.

Jean explained, "Mr. Tatum, all Dr. Forrest needs to know is on these plates. They show clearly what he has to do. Your son will be in capable hands."

Without facing them Bob Tatum asked, "Will he be cured?"

"That will depend on what Forrest finds. But Mr. Tatum, we have no time for emotionalism. We need your consent."

Tatum nodded slowly, considering. "I . . . I have to talk to Mr. Cameron first."

"Bobby is your son," Jean said.

"I know," Tatum said, "but I have to talk to Mr. Cameron."

"Then do it quickly!" She could not help saying to herself, He still needs a father, still needs a truck to run behind. For all his strength, intelligence and seeming confidence, Bob Tatum had never outgrown that need. What would happen, she wondered, when he had to face the other problem, his wife's part in all this? There were three lives at stake here, not one. And the one whom everyone assumed to be strongest might turn out to be weakest of all. She could sympathize with Marissa and the pressures with which she had to live.

Bob Tatum turned and walked out of the office. Jean signaled Larry to go after him and urge him to come to a decision. Only the two women were left in the dark, shadowed room.

Marissa Tatum moved to the viewing box, where the plate of her son's brain was so clearly displayed. Her finger traced the entire brain and finally came to rest on the gray area which was the seat of his sickness. "Did *I* do this?"

"You can answer that better than I," Jean said. "But not now. You've enough to worry you without that."

"But it was me," the woman said, in a whisper that was breathy and pained. Her beautiful face began to disintegrate in a flood of tears. Jean pushed a box of tissues toward the distressed woman. She suspected that Marissa Tatum was finally steeling herself to probe her secret wound.

Marissa began suddenly, in a spurt of words. "You'll despise me! You'll think I'm not fit to be a mother, not fit to belong to the human race!"

Jean made no attempt to console her. It was necessary for Marissa to condemn herself before she could go on.

"I never meant to do it. It just . . . just happened. No, it didn't just happen. *I did it!*"

"Exactly *what* did you do?" Jean asked softly.

"Christmas," Marissa began strangely. "I have always had this terrible feeling about Christmas. I remember the first time, in kindergarten, when the teacher said, 'Let's all tell about our Christmas.' Every child had to get up and tell what Santa Claus brought. What Mommy cooked. And what Daddy did. How Daddy took them out to play with their new sleds. How Daddy took them for hot chocolate. Every child talked about Daddy.

"When my turn came, I . . . I said my daddy had to work Christmas day, so he wasn't home. The teacher must have suspected, but she didn't say anything.

"It was like that every Christmas. I would tell myself that my father would come back. He never did. Charles Pearson deserted his only child. All he left her was his name, Pearson."

She wiped back the tears with her fingers and tried to smile. "In the end it was *his* name that trapped me. Isn't that funny?"

"You have to stop thinking of yourself as trapped," Jean said. "This could be the beginning of becoming free."

The woman shook her head. "You'll take my baby away from me. You will. Because I . . ." She faltered and could not continue.

"If you say it once, it might not be so bad. We tend to be our own worst judges."

"I always promised myself that when I had a child I would make Christmas the most wonderful day of its life. I owed it to that little girl who had to lie in kindergarten.

"You see, all my life I've been playing parts. The little girl with the father who didn't exist. The model in fine clothes. The beautiful woman. I'm not Mary but Marissa. It's a part I play so well. I have to. Otherwise I would have to face the fact that Bob could leave me, as my father deserted my mother."

"Did you feel that way before Bobby was born?" Jean asked gently.

Marissa nodded. "I was into my second month before I told him. Even though I knew how much he wanted a son, I was afraid. Behind my smile, my eyes were studying his face, to see the reaction. And as I grew big and ungainly, I kept saying to myself, He can't love me now. I'm ugly. Ugly!"

"Did you notice any change in him?"

"Yes. He became more tender, more loving. But I only suspected him more. He must be covering up, I said to myself. When he went on business trips I would check on him, make up pretexts to call him. Until it became a company joke."

She smiled wanly. "Once Mr. Cameron said to me, 'Little lady, you must be the most loving wife in the world.' He never guessed I was the most frightened and insecure. Every time Bob went on a trip while I was pregnant, I had this fear that he would never come back. Until . . . until, I think, I came to hate that baby even before it was born." She waited, expecting recrimination from Jean. "Doesn't that shock you?"

"After what you'd been through, no."

"I mean . . . from what I heard, you so much wanted to have your baby and never did. You must despise me."

The young woman was begging for judgment and condemnation. Jean did not feel it wise to give her that release.

"I always blamed Bobby's premature birth on the moving. Bob was always being transferred. To him it was exciting. He was on his way up. To me it meant setting up another home again.

"It happened just as we were moving for the third time in four years. I had Bobby. At seven and a half months. Small and so frail. Scrawny, shriveled, with black-and-blue splotches on his body. I thought, That isn't the kind you see in the baby-food ads. He won't survive. Nothing that pathetic can survive. I see, now, that was more my hope than my fear," she admitted.

"How long before you were able to hold him?"

"Six weeks. The first time was the day we brought him home from the hospital. He was still scrawny. We had him on a special weight-gaining diet for months. But he never did seem to catch up. And he never will. We're resigned to that. Bob doesn't say much about it anymore. But I disappointed him. He wanted sons. Strong sons."

"Is it his disappointment or yours?" Jean asked pointedly.

Marissa Tatum considered the question for a moment. "Does it matter? I feel it. That's bad enough."

Jean knew it was time Marissa was made to face her problem. "That Christmas, Mrs. Tatum. You must realize you will have to tell someone sometime."

Marissa's hand went to her purse, found a cigarette and her gold lighter. She had to smoke the cigarette halfway down before she could talk again.

"Mrs. Cameron . . ." she began. "You have to understand how important she is. If she takes a fancy to a man's wife, his career blossoms. The best thing that can happen is for her to take charge of your life. She took to me at once. Bob was delighted. I felt, At last I'm doing something that helps him. I can be of use to him. So I gave myself to all her charitable activities. Completely.

"I know what you're thinking. Bobby. Yes, he did suffer because of it. He was neglected. But I kept saying to myself, In the long run he'll benefit. It will ensure Bob's future. And Bobby's."

"What about Christmas?" Jean brought her back to the night she was avoiding.

"Christmas . . . three nights before . . . it was mad. I had my own party to prepare for. The Camerons would be there. It was the first time they would be coming to our new house. Bob wanted everything to be perfect. And Mrs. Cameron had her reception for the Foundling Home. One of her most cherished activities. She gives this big party for the children and the sponsors. Then, after the children are in bed, she makes her appeal for funds. Her entire budget for the year is raised that night."

"What about *you?*" Jean insisted.

"I . . . I was one of the wives she chose as hostesses. Naturally I agreed. But there were the preparations for my party. Bob was away, not due back till Christmas Eve. It was terribly hectic. I was trying to get dressed. Bobby was crying. Even though he likes Esther, he didn't want to be left alone again."

"Again?"

"I was out quite a lot, doing my own shopping and helping Mrs. Cameron on a dozen of her committees. I guess I'd been out almost every afternoon and evening for quite a spell. You have to understand!"

"I'm trying to understand," Jean said sympathetically. "It was a difficult time. Hectic."

"Yes." Marissa dropped her voice. "That night, I was so determined to make good for Bob that I became cross with Bobby. I shouted at him. Sent him to his room. I finished dressing. In a dress I had bought especially for Mrs. Cameron's party. Bob had said, 'Spend anything you like. Only, make a good impression!'

"So I bought a Halston original. Five hundred and seventy-five dollars. Bob didn't mind. He called it an investment. I was dressed and ready to leave. I could hear Bobby in his room, still sobbing. I went in to kiss him good-night, to tell him to be a good boy and go to sleep. But he kept crying. Then, when I bent over to kiss him, he—" She stopped suddenly.

"He what?"

"Whether it was nerves, or something he ate, or just sheer spite, he threw up. All over my new dress," Marissa Tatum said, then added strangely, "He destroyed everything . . . everything. . . ."

"Everything you'd worked so hard to achieve."

Marissa Tatum nodded. "The dress. Mrs. Cameron. Bob's career. My marriage. Everything that we had planned and sacrificed for was gone in one single moment. It was as if Bobby had done it deliberately."

"Of course he didn't do it deliberately."

"At that moment I couldn't think anything else," Marissa Tatum admitted softly. "So I . . . without thinking . . . I lashed out. With all my fury, I hit him. So hard that he crashed against the wall. Then he was suddenly still."

"Unconscious?" Jean asked.

"For a moment I was sure I had killed him." Marissa repeated the words in a whisper, as though she could not now believe what she had done. "Killed him.

"I was terrified! I didn't know what to do. I couldn't call Larry. Or Bob. But I had to get help for my son. Without letting anyone know. So I took him to West Side Memorial. The hospital farthest from our part of town. On the way I kept thinking of names. The name Charles Pearson came up. Yes, I decided, it would serve him right. It was the only thing he'd ever done for me. Given me a name to use at a terrible time like that.

"Bobby was still unconscious. The doctor brought him around, and said to leave him overnight. He seemed okay, but they wanted to make sure. So I gave them a fictitious name and address. And I made up a lie about his falling off the ladder while trying to trim the Christmas tree.

"Then I was suddenly standing outside this unfamiliar hospital. Alone. No husband. No son. It was the worst moment of my life."

"What about Mrs. Cameron?"

"I called. I said Bobby was ill and I couldn't leave him. She said, 'Of course, my dear, your first obligation is to your son. We'll do it again next year. Give him a kiss good-night for me.'

"It was all so easy for her. After I hung up I started to cry. I cried for hours. Why couldn't life be that simple for me? Why did I have to go on racing forever against hazards and dangers? As if life were one long obstacle course that I would never finish."

"The next day, Mrs. Tatum?"

"The doctor said Bobby was fine. No sign of any damage. I paid the bill and took Bobby home. He never said a word to anyone. Never told Bob. No one knew. No one ever had to."

"I asked you about any head traumas when he was first brought here," Jean reminded.

"I said to myself, There couldn't be any connection. It was so many months ago." Suddenly she said, "Bob mustn't know. He'll hate me! He'll leave me!"

"Still, he has to know," Jean said.

"You can't tell him!" Marissa protested.

"I didn't say I would tell him," Jean reminded her. "I only said he should know."

"You mean that I . . ." Marissa sat numb and silent, then shook her head slowly, persistently. "They'll take my baby away from me. I can't tell anyone. I can't."

"Mrs. Tatum, if you don't tell someone, I'll have to."

"But professional confidentiality—"

"Applies in all cases except child abuse. Under the law it's my duty to report it. That's why *you* have to do it. Think about telling your husband. You have till tomorrow."

"Tomorrow?"

"In the morning. Dr. Forrest. The surgery."

"Yes. The surgery. He'll come through it all right?" She begged for reassurance.

"We won't know anything until we see how his brain reacts to the surgery," was all that Jean could honestly say.

"And I did it. I did it," the distraught woman kept repeating.

She had come this far, but it was necessary to uncover the whole truth, so Jean asked, "Mrs. Tatum, that time on the stairs, Bobby's leg fracture, was it really the moving man's fault, as your husband said?"

She shook her head. "Bob was only telling you what I told him."

"Have there been other times?" There was no answer. Jean persisted. "Have there?"

Marissa nodded.

"Many times?"

"Times," was all the mother would admit. "You have to know what makes you do it. You tear yourself to bits trying to please everyone. Trying to have everyone love you. And then suddenly there are moments when it's too much to cope with. And you take out all your frustrations on the one person who really does love you. Your own child.

"That's the worst of it. Not just losing control. Not even their crying afterward. It's the look in their eyes that pleads, Mommy, why did you do that? I love you. Why did you do that to me?

"You can't explain. Not to your child. Not to anyone. But suddenly you're seeing yourself as a child. You see all your fears, all your sadness in your own child's eyes. And you hate yourself. You promise never to do it again. But you do . . . you do . . . you do. . . ."

She was silent for a moment, until she said, "They'll send me to prison. They should."

"We don't try to send parents to prison. We try to save families, Mrs. Tatum. Remember that."

AT SIX O'CLOCK THE NEXT MORNING the hospital barber was cutting away Bobby's shiny black hair. Forlorn and frightened, the boy watched it fall to the sheet tucked around him.

When the barber finished with the scissors, Bobby reached up and felt his shorn scalp. At that moment Jean Scofield opened the door. "Good morning, Bobby."

"Morning, Dr. Jean. Look what they did."

"It'll grow back, Bobby. It'll be the same as it was."

The barber said, "All right, sonny. Now we're going to give you a shave. You've watched Daddy. Well, this is the same, only we'll be shaving your head. So don't reach up no more."

The barber applied lather to the boy's scalp and began the slow and careful process. The boy held still, stiffly so, as if afraid to breathe. He reached out his left hand to Jean, but cautiously, lest he move and incur the barber's disapproval. She held his hand until the barber said, "Okay. Beautiful job!" and laughed. "You going to be okay, sonny."

They were alone. The boy. And his doctor. He still clutched her hand. She could feel how cold and damp he was. Jean could not resist. She took him in her arms and held him tight. He pressed against her breast; his tiny shaved head made him seem a pathetic waif. "You're going to be fine, Bobby!" she promised. "You'll be able to walk and run again."

"Will I be able to climb on the monkey bars?"

"Of course!"

That delighted him. She looked down and saw the smile on his face as he pressed against her. He would have been content to remain close to her, but there was a sound at the door. An orderly and a nurse had arrived with a gurney to take him up to the operating room.

The nurse realized she had intruded on an intimate moment. She joked to hide it: "Which one is the patient?"

"I am," the boy spoke up quickly. "This is Dr. Jean. She's my doctor," the boy said proudly.

"And a very good doctor, too," the nurse answered. "Now, young man, we have to go for a ride."

"I know," he said, growing tense again. He looked up at Jean, as if she could give him a dispensation at the last moment.

"Yes, Bobby, you have to go for a ride. And then I'll be with you all through the operation. Even when you're asleep and won't know it, I'll be there. And so will Dr. Larry. Watching over you every minute."

The young nurse reached out. "Up we go!" She deposited him on the gurney. The orderly folded a blanket over his body. They were halfway out the door when they heard a cry.

"Bobby! Darling!" Marissa Tatum raced toward the wheeled stretcher. She embraced the boy, half lifting him out of the blanket. Whatever had been done to calm his fears Marissa's frenetic conduct had undone. He started to cry.

"Take him up," Jean said.

Doctor and mother watched the gurney disappear into the elevator. Marissa Tatum kept saying, "I'm sorry . . . sorry . . . I couldn't help it. . . ." It was obvious the poor woman had not slept at all. "He'll be all right, won't he?"

"He's in capable hands. Why don't you wait at home? It'll take several hours."

"I'll wait in his room," Marissa insisted grimly.

As Jean turned to go, the elevator door opened. Bob Tatum emerged hurriedly. "Marissa!" He approached them, embraced his wife and held her tight. "You scared the hell out of me. You didn't sleep all night. When I woke up this morning you were gone. I didn't know what to think."

Jean tried to detect some indication of whether Marissa had told her husband of their conversation. She had to conclude that she had not.

"I have to go scrub," Jean said, excusing herself.

Marissa Tatum turned and went into Bobby's room. Bob followed Jean, overtaking her at the elevator.

"Doctor! The truth," Tatum demanded quietly.

"We've been telling you the truth all along," Jean said.

"I'm sorry," he said. "But it isn't just my son's life that's involved. If anything happens to him, it'll destroy her. You're really treating two patients. And I don't want to lose either one of them. I love them both."

Jean was sure now that Marissa had not told her husband. She would go on tormenting herself. And Tatum was right. Marissa

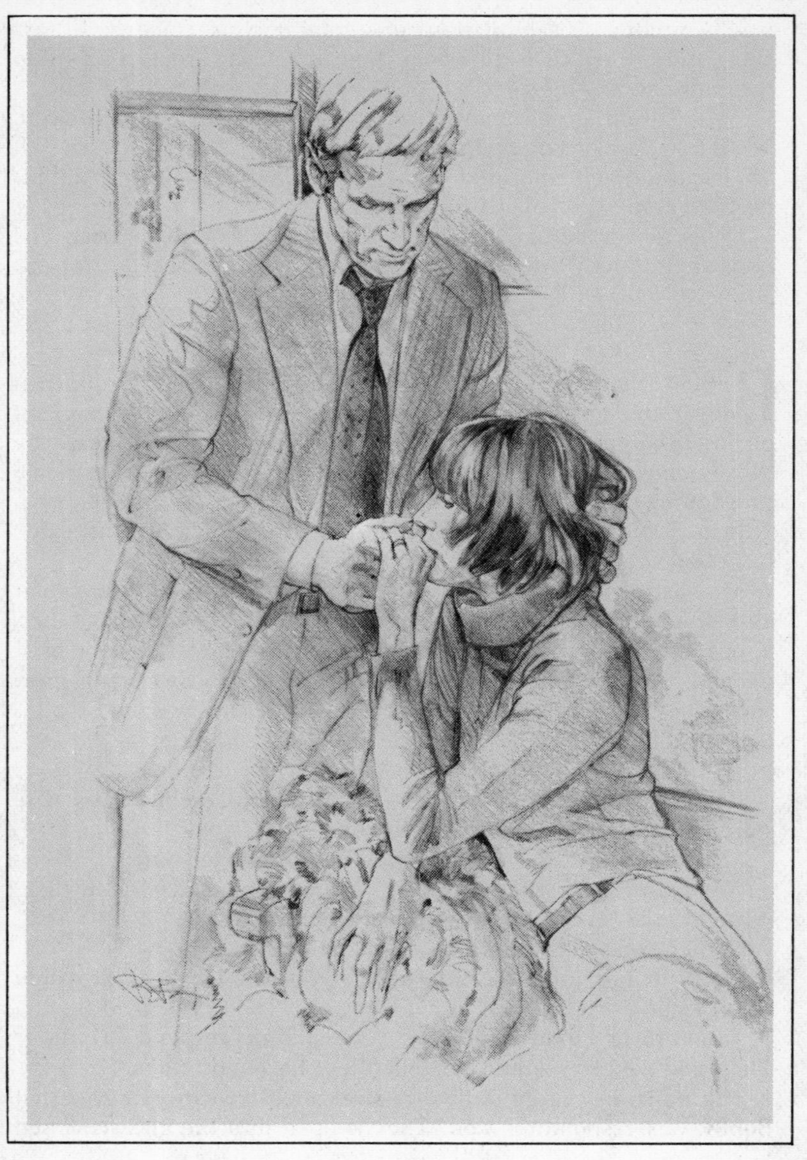

was beginning to exhibit signs of a total nervous collapse. If anything untoward took place in that operating room, it would catapult her over the edge.

"Mr. Tatum, go back and take care of your wife. She needs you. We'll take care of Bobby. We'll do our best."

"I had a coach who used to say, 'When a man claims he did his best, he's only apologizing for failure.'"

"This isn't a football game, Mr. Tatum. We *will* do our best. The odds are in Bobby's favor. I can't say any more than that."

Chapter Eleven

Patient Tatum, Robert, Jr., had been moved from the operating room to neurological intensive care and placed in a glass-enclosed cubicle from which he could be observed continually by the nursing staff. He slept, unaware of the care and the intricate procedures being employed on his behalf.

Jean Scofield and Larry Braham, still in surgical greens, came to Bobby's room to find Bob and Marissa Tatum.

The distraught mother had stopped crying, but she sat in a chair and stared, eyes hollow and fixed. Bob Tatum, watching her, appeared alarmed. He welcomed the whisper of the door as it opened. Any sound, almost any word, would be welcome now. When he saw Jean's smiling face, he had to turn away to hide his tears of relief.

"It went fine," Jean said. "Just fine."

Bob Tatum nodded, his face in his handkerchief. His wife stared, as if she had not heard the news.

"His paralysis?" Tatum asked. "Will that be okay now?"

"We can't tell until he awakes," Larry explained. "Even then, it might take several days before we can be sure."

"When can we see him?"

"He's in our intensive care unit. If you want to look, it would be all right."

Tatum turned to his wife. "Riss?" She did not respond. "Darling? They said we can see him." He held out his hand to her.

The nurse in charge of neurological intensive care reported that Bobby was responding well. They slipped into the glass-enclosed cubicle to stare down at the small sleeping patient. His head swathed in a turban of white bandages, he looked more fragile than usual. But his handsome features were more prominent.

Tatum leaned close to his son. "Bobby . . . we're here . . . Mom and Dad. You're going to be fine. Good as new."

The boy murmured softly. His mother summoned up the courage to move close, leaning over him. "Bobby . . . Bobby . . ."

The boy opened his eyes, now vague and uncertain. She reached for his right hand, clasped it, hoping to evoke some reaction. But his hand and arm were as limp as before. She looked to Jean Scofield. Jean was unable to give her any promises. Bob put his arm around his wife and led her from the room.

Outside, Marissa said, "Doctor, you told us the surgery would cure it."

"We said it *should*, not would. Besides, it's too early to tell. He's still under the influence of the anesthetic," Jean explained. "It could take hours, even days, before we know for sure."

"Are there cases where the operation doesn't work?"

"It's possible."

"Then it won't," Marissa said stolidly. "Not in a few days. Not ever."

"Riss! No!" her husband said in a low, hoarse voice. "We've got to hold on, believe. Cameron said if it didn't work here, he'd send Bobby to Boston, or New York. This isn't the end!"

"But it is." Her eyes seemed to stare beyond his, beyond Jean's. "Punishment. This is my punishment." She slumped against him. He embraced her gently and looked across at Jean. It was obvious to her that Bob Tatum had never seen his wife in this state before. She had always been the dependable, adaptable wife, up to every challenge, able to face any difficulty, a woman who always understood, who never complained. The perfect wife for a man with consuming ambition.

"Doctor, can't you give her something?" Bob pleaded.

"Medication might help. Temporarily. But it will take more than that," Jean said.

"Whatever it takes, whatever it costs. If I can't afford it, Cameron will make sure I get it."

"Cameron can't help in this situation."

"What do you mean?" When Jean didn't answer, he stared down at his wife. "Marissa?" She pressed her head against his chest.

"Give me a few minutes with her," Jean said.

Bewildered, Bob Tatum reluctantly released his wife. Jean led her down the corridor and into her office.

"Mrs. Tatum, you can't avoid this any longer."

"He'll hate me," she pleaded.

"Then I'll have to tell him. Or Dr. Braham will."

"I'll tell him," she finally agreed. "But I have to face him alone."

Jean found Tatum at Bobby's bedside. He was gently wiping perspiration from his son's cheeks with a gauze pad. When he saw Jean he came out of the glass-enclosed cubicle. "Is she all right now?"

"She's in my office. She wants to talk to you. Before you go in there, I want your word that you'll see me before you do or say anything to anyone."

"Why?"

"It's important. To you, to your wife, and to your son!"

"All right."

He started down the corridor. Jean watched until he had disappeared into her office. She went back into the tiny room where her patient lay. She stood over the boy, watching his right arm. Perhaps in his sleep he would make some involuntary movement. There was none.

IN DR. SCOFIELD'S office, Marissa Tatum held the lighter to her cigarette with an air of such determination that Bob knew she was under severe tension. Misreading the cause of her anxiety, he reassured her. "Bobby's going to be fine. Dr. Scofield thinks his paralysis will clear up."

"Does she?" Marissa evaded. There was no way to begin.

"Well, she seemed very hopeful," Bob admitted more truthfully. "Darling, he's going to be okay. You can stop worrying."

She knew she had to come to it now. "Bob . . . no matter what I tell you, I want you not to say a word. Until you've heard it all and had a chance to think about it."

"Okay!" He gave his assurance glibly.

She felt an overpowering compulsion to run from the room. But remembering she had at least one source of help in Jean Scofield, she forced herself to begin.

"Bobby . . . his seizures . . . they didn't just come on."

"I know," he said. "Dr. Scofield explained the very first time. Sometimes they never discover what they come from. Well, we're lucky. They found out and they removed the cause—"

"Bob!" Marissa interrupted, on the verge of hysteria. "Please! Just listen!" She regained control of herself. "The thing that made the operation necessary was *me*," she confessed. "I . . . I didn't mean to do it. But that night was too much . . . too much. . . ."

"What was too much? What happened?" he demanded, reaching out to take her by the arms.

"I hit him," she admitted simply.

"Hit him?" Bob asked, puzzled. "Is that all? Hell, kids get hit all the time. And most times have it coming."

"Not . . . not the way I hit him that time," she said, pressing her head against his chest, so she would not have to see his eyes. "I hit him so hard that he . . . he crashed against the wall."

"Against the wall?"

"His head . . . smashed against the wall. I'll never forget the sound. He lay there, so still. I . . . I thought he was dead."

"Riss?" he demanded, trying to hold her off and look into her eyes. But she clung so desperately he could not move her.

"You said you would listen . . . you promised," she pleaded.

"All right, I'll listen." By now his angry intolerance was quite evident. "But tell me. *Everything!*"

"Yes . . . everything." She told him of that evening, beginning with the stresses and strains of trying to please Mrs. Cameron. Up to the final details of picking up "Charles Pearson" at the hospital the next morning. Assured by the doctor that Bobby was fine, she had felt that the episode was over for all time. Submissive child that he was, Bobby had abided by her instructions never to say anything about it.

"There," she said in a painful whisper, "now you know." She paused, still clinging to him, awaiting his judgment.

He did not respond at once. Then he removed her arms from around him. He grasped her hands in a punishing grip as he held her off and stared into her eyes.

"You're not a mother, you're a monster! How could you do that to my son? You could have killed him! You were only a step away from being a murderer. A murderer of your own son!"

She made no effort to defend herself. She broke down and wept, slipping into a chair.

"You know what this means, don't you?" he asked coldly.

She nodded. But he had to say it.

"You are never going to see that boy again!"

"Bob . . ."

"You are never going to see him again. Or me neither. And if you fight the divorce, I'll tell the whole world what you really are!"

"Bob, no! Please, please, I beg you. . . . Don't."

He slammed the door with such force that the sound echoed down the corridor. People turned to stare.

The sound of that door alerted Jean. She emerged from the intensive care unit to see Bob Tatum striding down the corridor alone. She raced to her office.

She could hear the pathetic sound of Marissa Tatum, whimpering like a small child, perhaps the child who in her early years had wept secretly. Jean reached out to console her. Marissa drew back, staring at her venomously.

"Tell him, you said. He has to know. Now I have no husband and no son."

"It was a momentary reaction. He'll think it over. He'll—"

"You don't know him. Once he makes up his mind . . ." She didn't have to complete the thought.

The defeated young woman, no longer beautiful, nor controlled and regal in her bearing, turned and slowly walked to the door.

"Did you explain about Mrs. Cameron . . . about how important that evening was for his career?"

"My husband is the wrong man to explain to. His father used to tell him, 'Bob, the perfect play doesn't need explanations.' To him everything that happens is like a football play. If it works, no explanations are necessary. If it doesn't, no explanation will suffice."

A thin, bitter smile crossed her tearstained face. "Well, I'm no longer on the team. I fumbled on a crucial play. There is no place for losers in his scheme of things."

FOR THE NEXT FEW HOURS Jean Scofield was immersed in her duties in the clinic. She examined twenty-eight patients, made nineteen diagnoses, referred a number of patients to Neurosurgery, and discovered four cases which she suspected were psychiatric, not neurological, in origin. It had been a routine afternoon.

The only event that brightened her day was a call from the *Journal of Clinical Medicine.* The editorial staff had accepted her paper on the patient return rate in the Seaton wards.

But nothing she had experienced in this crowded, eventful day had made any deep personal impression on her. In mind and spirit Jean was still with Marissa Tatum, who had lost both her husband and her son.

There was an affinity between them now. Jean, too, had suffered such a double loss long ago. Marissa Tatum had no dear and devoted Hans Benziger to care for her. No one to depend on. She had made her whole life Bob Tatum's life. Without him, she was the deserted, insecure little girl again.

Jean dialed Bob Tatum's office. "Mr. Tatum!" she demanded.

"I'm sorry, he's not in his office."

"Then get him."

"I can't do that. He's in a meeting with Mr. Cameron."

"Then switch me to Mr. Cameron's office."

"Oh, I couldn't interrupt them," Tatum's secretary said, aghast. "We never interrupt Mr. Cameron in conference."

"Tell him Dr. Scofield is calling. That it is urgent that I talk to Mr. Tatum at once!"

"Well, that's different. One moment, Doctor."

The voice of Horace Cameron came on the phone. "Doctor? What's the word about the young man? How is he now?"

"The boy's condition is stable and hopeful. But that is not what I want to discuss with Mr. Tatum. Put him on, please."

"There's nothing you have to say that you can't say to me."

"I'm afraid there is," Jean said. "I insist."

After a moment of resentful hesitation, Cameron turned the phone over to Bob Tatum. "Yes?" Tatum demanded brusquely.

"Mr. Tatum, it is vital that I talk to you at once. In private."

"About what?"

"I think you know."

"I refuse to discuss that with anyone."

"Even with Mr. Cameron?" Jean challenged. "Or have you told him already?" Tatum's silence was answer enough.

"Mr. Tatum, your wife's life is at stake. Unless we help her. The first step is your understanding. If it's necessary to convince Mr. Cameron, I will convince him. Put him back on the phone!"

She heard a click and then silence. She sat drumming her fingers on the desk top, then came to a decision. She grabbed her coat from the rack and stopped at Maggie's desk to say, "I will be out for the rest of the afternoon. I can't be reached."

WHEN JEAN PRESENTED herself at Cameron's office twenty minutes later, his receptionist was protectively hostile. No one dared come to this office without an appointment. She was finally persuaded to call Cameron's officious executive secretary, Miss St. John. Tall, thin, efficient, she wore severe black-framed spectacles.

In her clipped British manner she explained that Mr. Cameron had a visitor. It would be impossible to see him today. Perhaps a time could be set, say, next week. Better still, next month.

"What I have to say won't keep till next month, next week. I insist on seeing him now. While Mr. Tatum is in his office."

That Jean knew who Cameron's visitor was changed Miss St. John's attitude markedly. "One moment," she said. She disappeared into her office. She returned to say, "Mr. Cameron will see you. But briefly. He's under great pressure of time."

"So am I," Jean said, brushing by the woman.

Horace Cameron was behind his desk in the posture of a reigning monarch. At his side stood Bob Tatum, hostile and defiant. Jean knew it would not be easy to do what she had to.

"I assume Mr. Tatum has told you everything his wife told him," she said. Cameron did not deny it. "This is nasty business. Certainly not the kind of thing that nice, refined, upper-class people are used to discussing."

Cameron's face flushed with anger as Jean continued.

"The abuse of a child is not a class matter. It is, Mr. Tatum, a *family* matter. And before you judge your wife, a little self-examination is in order."

"If you came here to defend Marissa by accusing me, it won't work!" Tatum shot back.

"I'm not here to defend or accuse. Only to get you to take a good look at yourself. And at what you've done to the two people in this world whom I'm sure you love most."

"That's all past. She is not fit to take care of my son. Or to be my wife. Both things will be arranged legally."

Cameron nodded sharply. It was clear he and Bob Tatum had agreed on this course of action. They had decided to fire Marissa as they would an unworthy employee. And do it in such a way as to prevent any scandal from besmirching the name InterElectronics. If need be, blackmail Marissa into silence.

"Gentlemen, you're not taking into account *my* position in this case. I am bound by law to do something about this."

"What do you mean, bound by law?" Cameron demanded.

"A doctor who discovers clinical evidence of child abuse is obligated to report it. But these matters can be handled confidentially. Because the intent of the law is not to disgrace the parents but to protect the child. So *you* make the choice. If you victimize this woman, *I* will make the matter public. But if you want to help her, I will see that she gets help."

Tatum turned to Cameron, seeking his advice. The old man stared straight ahead.

Image, Cameron was thinking. How would such a public scandal affect the image of InterElectronics? Distasteful business, child abuse. Shocking. Even if, as a last resort, he rid himself of Tatum, it would not ensure that scandal could be avoided. Scofield was blackmailing him as he had intended to blackmail Marissa Tatum. Damn this woman, he had resented her from the first. She was tough. As tough as any man he had ever dealt with. Necessity forced him to affect the appearance of reasonableness. "Bob, I think we should listen to the doctor."

Surprised at first, Bob Tatum acceded to his boss. He slipped into a chair but sat forward, ready to combat her every step of the way.

Jean began. "Child abuse doesn't only mean striking a child. It can also mean the *failure* to do something. Depriving a child. Both forms of abuse can be equally destructive. Your wife is a victim,

Mr. Tatum. She was deprived. Severely deprived during her entire childhood—of a father."

"Yes, I know," Tatum replied, but with no great tolerance. "Times that's all she talked about. Finding him. Making him face up to his desertion."

"She must have talked about him almost as much as *you* talk about *your* father," Jean said.

"There was one hell of a difference! My dad devoted himself to us. He trained us, brought us up to be what we are."

"So you could run behind the truck forever. Only this time it's Mr. Cameron's truck," Jean pointed out.

Cameron's face grew more flushed. Jean was not deterred.

"I'm sure your father thought he was doing the right thing. But the price, Mr. Tatum. The price of that ambition is where it crosses the line from constructive ambition to abuse. I told you this is a family matter. Somehow, for reasons we don't yet understand, individuals who have been abused in childhood have a way of finding each other. They marry. And their children tend to be abused. Somehow they feed on one another. Provoke one another. You did that to your wife."

"No man has worked harder to give his wife everything she could want!" Tatum defended. "Security. A good home. Position in life."

"And made her run behind the truck at the same time."

"I never asked *anything* of her."

"You didn't have to. She asked *everything* of herself. Don't you see, Mr. Tatum, that poor girl was hanging on to your marriage, your life-style, your career, hanging on by her fingernails in a desperate effort to keep the one thing she had never had before. A complete family. Mother, father and child."

"But she had it!" Tatum protested.

"Did she? What security was there in picking up stakes every time you received a promotion? For a girl whose life was a search for roots, it was a rootless existence. And those endless days and nights when you were traveling. Each time you left, there was the fear, Would you come back?"

"I always did."

"That wasn't the only pressure on her. She had *all* the cards stacked against her. Premature deliveries lead to isolation in intensive care. In Bobby's case, for weeks. Well, mother love isn't born fully developed as the infant emerges. It comes with physical closeness. With caring for the child. Feeding it. For some reason, mothers deprived of closeness tend to become abusers. As do women who have difficult deliveries. Maybe because during the delivery the mother feels the child is endangering her own life. In your wife's case, fear of losing you complicated her difficult delivery more. The pressures were too great. And under enough pressure almost any mother can abuse her child."

Somber and thoughtful, Tatum looked away from Jean. For the first time he began to understand the forces at work in the mind of the tormented woman whom he had loved.

Jean turned to Horace Cameron. "You played a part in it, too, Mr. Cameron," she accused.

Cameron bristled. He was not used to being rebuked, not by employees, associates, politicians. Certainly not by a woman.

"Your price is too high," Jean said. "The loyalty you demand exceeds the rewards you offer. Not that Marissa Tatum wasn't willing to pay the price. She would do anything for her husband. But there was also the need to please your wife, to further Bob's career.

"What precipitated this tragedy had to do with Mrs. Cameron. Bobby needed his mother that night. Just as those orphans needed their Christmas party. How do children express their needs? By asking. By crying. By pretending to be sick. At any other time Marissa Tatum would have done what any other mother would do. She would have cleaned up her little boy, comforted him, read him to sleep. And that would have been the end of it.

"But that night it wasn't just mother and child. It was mother, husband, career, Cameron, Mrs. Cameron, and then, finally, child. It was the honor, plus the obligation, to assist Mrs. Cameron. All the plans and expectations. All the care focused on that new dress to make just the right impression. When that dress was ruined, it seemed that her marriage was ruined. She had missed a fateful rung on the corporate ladder. She stood in danger of losing, of being deserted again.

"Each of us has limits. I discovered that I had mine. I don't judge Marissa Tatum. She'll judge herself—which is worse. She needs help. She needs it now."

She turned to Bob Tatum. "Most of all she needs you. *And* her son. She will never make it alone."

"What she did to Bobby—" he protested.

"Think of what *you* did to him," Jean reminded. "It's one thing for a father to *try* to be kind and loving. It's another to actually *be* kind and loving. He is never going to be a fullback, Mr. Tatum. But he is a bright, intelligent, sensitive human being of unlimited potential. If you can truly love that, you'll have yourself quite a son. Believe me."

"His right arm and leg . . ."

"You have to love that boy whatever way he is. If you can't, *you've* failed, not *he*. He loves you despite your disappointment in him. He never stops trying to please you. Give him a chance. Give her a chance, too," Jean urged.

"Do you know where she is now?"

"At the hospital."

"I'll find her," Tatum said. He looked at Cameron for permission to be excused.

"Just go!" Jean said vehemently. "You don't need permission. You don't need anything but to know your wife and son need you!"

Tatum started for the door. Cameron edged forward in his chair, as if to forbid him. Then he eased back slowly as Bob Tatum left.

"If you report this, there's bound to be a scandal," Cameron began. "Surely there must be some diplomatic way to handle it."

"Mr. Cameron, I assure you it will be handled with complete confidentiality. Not out of concern for your corporate image, but because I have no desire to punish Marissa Tatum."

"The chiefship of Neurology is still open," Cameron reminded.

"I will still make my report. And I might as well tell you that my paper on the Seaton wards has been accepted by the *Journal of Clinical Medicine*."

Cameron exploded. "Damn it, what is it about you? Any man would realize the advantages he could derive from a situation like this. That's why I like to deal with men. They're realists. But women . . ." He dismissed them without another word.

"*Any* man? Don't you mean the kind of man you select?"

Cameron did not answer. Eventually he conceded: "Sunderland would have known how to handle this. No fuss. No scandal."

He took off his tinted glasses and rubbed his eyes. Without those forbidding lenses his eyes were revealed as a tired brown. Wrinkles around them showed his age clearly. He was silent for a moment before he admitted grudgingly, "But then Sunderland missed the diagnosis on the Tatum boy, didn't he?"

"It happens. To all of us," Jean explained.

"All I know, the Scofield diagnosis was right."

"Yes. I know. You like winners," Jean said wryly, not accepting his judgment as praise.

Cameron smiled, then confessed, "Despite you, I managed to get a copy of your data on the Seaton wards."

"Of course."

"How did you know?" Cameron asked, surprised.

"I didn't," Jean said, herself smiling now. "I just assumed you would. You had to prove me wrong. After all, who defies Horace Cameron and gets away with it?"

Cameron's tired face relaxed in a smile. "I'm glad I don't have to deal with you every day." Then he admitted, "My man agrees with your conclusions. The Seaton wards present us with a new problem. I already have a staff working on it. I didn't want to tell you or Benziger. Vanity, I suppose."

It was the most profuse apology Horace Cameron had made to anyone in years.

The sharp trader in him could not surrender without one last try. "Look, if I myself nominated you for chief—" He stopped, shook his head. "No," he concluded, "you wouldn't agree not to report the Tatum matter if I made you chief, would you?"

"No, I would not."

HORACE CAMERON sat back in his huge chair, very thoughtful. Finally he instructed Miss St. John to reach Hans Benziger at once, no matter where he was.

"Cameron?" Benziger said. "What can I do for you?"

"I want a report on the Tatum boy. On whether his paralysis is clearing."

"I'm not the doctor on the case," Benziger reminded him.

"Please, Benziger! Don't make me humiliate myself to that woman. I'm anxious about the boy. But I don't want to ask her."

"If the Tatums give their permission, I'm sure she'd be willing to keep you advised of the boy's condition."

"It isn't that," Cameron confessed. "But if I ask her and she does tell me, she's going to be sure that's why I've changed my mind about the chiefship."

"Do I understand you correctly?" Benziger asked.

"I'm going to put that woman's name before the board myself!" Cameron blurted out. "Much as I hate to admit it, she's a winner. So find out, please? About the boy?"

"Of course."

"Thanks, thanks very much." Before Cameron hung up, he asked, "As chief, she's not going to be a continuous pain in the neck to the trustees, is she?"

"She will be," Benziger said. "That's why she's going to make such a good head of the department."

JEAN SCOFIELD, in white lab coat, was about to enter the intensive care unit. She changed her mind and headed for the visitors' lounge.

In the far corner sat Marissa Tatum, her husband at her side. She was turned away from him. When he caught sight of Jean he left his wife's side.

In a discouraged whisper he said, "I can't reach her. No matter what I promise, she won't listen."

"Does she say anything at all?"

"Just 'Bobby . . . Bobby . . . Bobby.'"

Jean glanced at the clock on the lounge wall. It was seven hours since the boy had come out of surgery. The anesthetic should have worn off. If he was going to recover the use of his right arm and leg, some signs should become apparent soon. The question in Jean's mind was what dangerous effect there would be on Marissa Tatum if her son did not recover. It could be the final, shattering blow.

Jean had to take a calculated risk. She approached Marissa, put her arm around her. "We have to go see Bobby," she said.

The distraught woman brushed aside Jean's help, rose and started for the door. She rushed past her husband's outstretched hand. She had to face this truth by herself. She made her way to the intensive care unit and the small glass-enclosed cubicle.

Bob Tatum followed until Jean beckoned to him not to enter. They could see all they had to through the glass wall.

The boy lay still, his eyes closed. Finally he sensed a presence in the room. He opened his eyes, saw his mother and smiled. Marissa reached for his left hand. She pressed it to her lips and kissed it. Her closeness and devotion made Bobby reach out with his right hand to stroke her cheek.

"You're the prettiest one, Mommy. The prettiest one," he said.

She began to weep, not at his words but at the touch of his right hand.

Jean said to Bob Tatum, "It's okay to go in now."

"Then what happens?"

"We find the right kind of help. I think she'll be fine. Fine."

SHE RETURNED TO her office to find three messages there. One from Dr. Benziger, the word urgent underscored. One from Larry Braham. One from Emergency Admitting. An eighteen-month-old child had been brought in with a fracture of the skull. The mother's story was suspicious. Jean ignored the other messages and rushed down to Emergency.

She had just completed her examination when Larry Braham found her. Before she would speak to him she completed her consultation with the resident, advised immediate surgery and demanded a complete history from the mother of the newly admitted victim. She would see that this child remained in the hospital long after it recovered.

Finally she had time for Larry. A situation he was never happy with, but to which he was resigned.

"Don't you ever return calls?" he asked.

"There was an emergency."

"There'll always be an emergency," Larry conceded. "You never called Benni back either."

"I told you—"

Larry interrupted. "Yes. *I* know. An emergency. But what *you* don't know—Cameron is proposing your name before the trustees as the new chief of Neurology."

"What does he want in exchange?"

"Not a thing, from what Benni told me."

"Cameron?" Jean asked, openly dubious.

"Benni warned me not to tell you the reason. But I will. Cameron thinks you're a winner." Larry laughed. "You'll accept anyhow, won't you?"

"That depends," Jean said thoughtfully.

"Depends?" he asked, puzzled.

"On how you feel about winners."

"Are you saying if you take the chiefship, that's the end of any possibility of marriage?"

"It'll mean more work, less time together," she pointed out.

"I realize that," he agreed.

"It won't be fair. And I've been too unfair to you as it is."

"Have I ever accused you of being unfair?"

"No," she conceded.

"Then?" he demanded.

She hesitated. "I've always compared you to Cliff. I kept trying to discover what special quality he had that I couldn't find in you."

"I wanted to know the same thing. I even asked Benni," Larry confessed. "He said Cliff was an unusual man, a very terrific guy. Well, there's nothing I can do about that, Jeannie. I'm what I am. But evidently I'm just not up to Cliff."

"Don't ever say that!" she protested quickly. "Because these past days I discovered the only difference between Cliff and you. I had lost him so I wanted him back. Desperately. When I faced losing you, I realized I felt the same way. I wanted you back."

She stopped, then confided softly, "I want your arm around me at night. Every night. So, darling, if you're not averse to marrying a woman chief . . ."

"I wouldn't marry any other kind," Larry said. "*When?*"

"Just as soon as I let Cameron know that I accept his offer. If he accepts my terms."

"You're going to lay down terms to Cameron?" Larry asked.

"Damn right! I want it very clear. He runs InterElectronics. I run the Neurology Department!"

Henry Denker

Henry Denker holds strong opinions on the subject of his latest novel: "The purpose of *The Scofield Diagnosis* is to reveal the existence of the problem of child abuse—an area that we gentlefolk have tended to cover up. When I told friends the book's subject, they all made the common assumption that it must be about a slum family. But once I told them it wasn't, that it was about 'nice, comfortable people', there would be a lull in the conversation, which was often followed by a confidential revelation of a case within their own family or within the family of close friends."

Mr. Denker is pleased that there is, finally, public recognition of this serious problem. He feels that if people realize "that the object of the law is not to take children away from their parents but to keep families together by helping abusers, there would be less fear in dealing with the realities."

A disciplined writer, Henry Denker works every morning, seven days a week. His usual procedure is to research one book while writing another, "so that research becomes a hobby and a relaxation from the hard work of writing."

THE LANTERN NETWORK

a condensation of the book by

Ted Allbeury

Illustrated by Cecil Vieweg
Published by Peter Davies

The quiet, unassuming man who lives alone in the flat upstairs—have we not all at some time known of such a man and wondered what might have happened in his past to make him so strangely friendless?

James Walters was just such a man. And perhaps the couple downstairs did indeed wonder about him. And when he met a violent death they wondered again. . . . But not for long. Walters was so nondescript. So totally forgettable.

Chief Superintendent Bailey of Special Branch, however, was different. It was his job to wonder. And besides, there was something about Walters that worried him. The man was just *too* forgettable, *too* nondescript. . . .

In *The Lantern Network*, Ted Allbeury looks back down the years, and unravels a moving story of loyalty and courage, and ill-fated love. Himself an officer in British Intelligence during the last war, he writes with rare authenticity of the men—and the women—of the French Resistance; and of the bitter legacy of suffering that one brave man continued to endure, even when the war was over.

PART ONE: SPRING 1967

It was Lovegrove, the Foreign Office liaison man, who had raised the issue at the weekly meeting.

"This little fellow at the embassy reception: Walters. We wondered if he shouldn't be questioned."

Paynter, the MI5 man, slowly blew out cigarette smoke with his eyes half closed before he spoke. "We haven't got much cause to question him. Why don't we just keep it on file and leave it at that?"

Lovegrove fidgeted with his files and then looked up at Paynter. "My masters have a feeling that he might be worth pursuing. You saw the MI6 report? Two incidents in ten days is a bit much."

Paynter tried to hide his irritation: "O.K., Lovegrove, we'll have a look if it doesn't take too much time."

CHIEF SUPERINTENDENT NICHOLAS BAILEY was thirty-seven. He had had seven years in Special Branch, four years in the CID and a year with Special Patrol Group which had given him the kind of qualifications that Special Branch set store by. His knowledge of French and German had been valued too.

Paynter read the last few paragraphs of a report before pushing a thin file to Bailey.

"This is it, Nick. There's not much to it. A man of ours was at a routine reception at the Polish Embassy for one of their trade missions. A chap called James Walters was there as a subcontractor for one of their engineering suppliers. He chatted to Petrov for about ten minutes and our man got the impression that they had met before, that they weren't just having cocktail-party words.

"The other bit is from the MI6 man in Paris. Walters was noticed last Saturday at a small gallery in Paris. It's known as a place the KGB use as a dead-letter drop. The FO want us to pursue it."

"Have we got any grounds to pull him in and have a chat?"

"I wouldn't think so, there's nothing more than I've told you. You can find some excuse I'm sure, but you'll have to tread carefully or we'll get complaints. It's all yours, but I shouldn't spend too much time on him. Anyway, let me know if I can help."

BAILEY CALLED for information from the police at Putney where Walters lived in one of the quiet streets off the Lower Richmond Road. Their records showed that on two occasions in the previous four years they had had to contact Walters because of break-ins at his small factory at Wandsworth. He owned the whole house in which he lived and rented the ground floor to a middle-aged couple named Palmer. Local inquiries indicated that he lived a very secluded life: he had few visitors and very little post. Nobody came in to clean or cook. He appeared to have no hobbies.

BAILEY PRESSED the bell-push that carried the card with Walters's name. It was a Saturday morning and Bailey stood watching the children playing in the road as he waited. Then the catch on the door opened with a buzz and he pushed the door open and walked up the stairs.

Walters stood at the top of the stairs. Bailey recognized him from the photographs in the file.

"Mr. Walters? I wonder if I could have a word with you."

"Who are you?"

"My name's Bailey. Sergeant Bailey. I'm a crime prevention officer at the local nick. I wanted to talk about your place at Wandsworth."

Walters looked intently at Bailey's face as if he might have to describe it some time. He waved Bailey into the sitting room.

Bailey stood until Walters pointed to a chair at a round walnut table. "Sit down, Sergeant."

"Thank you, sir. I was checking through our records and I saw that your factory had been broken into a couple of times in the past. We didn't have a crime prevention bloke then and I wondered if you had had any more trouble recently."

Walters stroked his hand slowly across the pile of the old-fashioned table cloth as he looked at Bailey. "We do get break-ins about once or twice a year, but there's no cash there, no valuables, and the machinery's too solid to damage."

"Is it all insured, sir?"

"Yes, it is."

Bailey looked slowly round the room. All his instincts were roused. There *was* something about the man. He was closed in. And the way he looked at Bailey's face made Bailey feel that his own professionally casual approach was being observed, equally professionally.

"You're the owner, sir, are you?"

"Yes. It's a private limited company. My accountant is the other director. He owns two shares, I own the rest. A cup of tea before you go? I'll just put the kettle on."

"I wouldn't say no, sir." Bailey had not missed the broad hint. But he had decided he was going to dig just an inch or two deeper.

When Walters came back from the kitchen, Bailey asked, "What do you make at the works, Mr. Walters?"

"We fabricate steel. Pipes, ducting, that sort of thing."

"Is it export stuff or the home market?"

"Mainly this country. Some of what we make goes to contractors who assemble it overseas."

"D'you have to travel abroad much?"

"Very seldom."

Bailey noticed the tightening of the mouth. For a moment he hesitated and then he said: "I understand that you went to Paris recently, Mr. Walters."

Walters looked at him. "You're not from the local police are you?"

"Not all the time, sir. Would you like to see my ID card?"

Walters shook his head but stayed silent.

"We thought you might be able to help us in our inquiries."

"What about?"

"One or two things, sir. There is an art gallery in Paris, sir. *Galerie d'aujourd'hui* I think it's called. What d'you know about that, sir?"

"What do you want to know?"

"Not much, sir. Do you go to France very often?"

"Ah. I see." Walters stood up slowly. "Excuse me a moment. The tea should be ready. Back in a second."

There was just the slightest hesitation as Walters turned to go but it registered in Bailey's subconscious. He heard the slow footsteps as Walters walked out to the landing. Something metallic was dropped and footsteps stopped as the something was picked up. A door handle rattled and a door was closed.

Through the net curtains at the window Bailey could see the tops of trees. There was an odd sort of silence.

And years of professional training clicked together and he ran to the kitchen and put his foot against the door. It swung open easily and Bailey saw Walters falling to the floor. His crêpe soles skidded in blood as he shoved Walters up to a sitting position. He felt for his heart with one hand and for his wrist with the other. There was an old-fashioned razor on the floor between Walters's feet. But Walters was dead and the bright arterial blood from his throat was everywhere. Bailey left bloody footprints on the linoleum and carpet as he searched for the phone. He dialled New Scotland Yard, and he was breathing heavily as he waited for a reply.

"Duty Officer, Special Branch."

"Chief Superintendent Bailey here. I want Deputy Assistant Commissioner Murphy, quickly."

Then Murphy was on the line. "Murphy here. What is it?"

"You remember that chap Walters?"

"No. Who is he . . . oh yes. The Foreign Office thing."

"I came to his flat to suss him out a bit and he's cut his throat."

There was a long pause. "Right. You stay there and I'll send a team. Don't contact the local police or doctors. When you've finished there come and see me at my flat."

NESCAFE

While he waited Bailey went over his words to Walters again and again but there was nothing that warranted the man's action. Apart from a guilty conscience.

The doctor took charge of the body and the others cleaned up the mess as far as they could. The driver went off with Bailey's keys to bring him clean clothes and then took him to Murphy's flat.

Murphy was not best pleased and his big body moved restlessly in the creaking wicker chair. "But for God's sake, Nick. He wouldn't kill himself over questions like that, not if he's innocent. And if he's guilty then he has a cover story and tries it out. If he's an agent he doesn't give up at a couple of questions, he bluffs it out—then, maybe, he kills himself."

"So what d'you think? Tax frauds, perhaps? Or sex, maybe combined with blackmail?"

"God knows." Murphy went to the phone, dialled a number and talked for ten minutes. When he came back he sat down heavily and leaned forward.

"You'd better stay with this. Find out all you can about him, though it doesn't sound as though there's much." He put his hand on Bailey's knee. "But don't take too long, my boy. We've got too much real stuff to be chasing will-o'-the-wisps."

THE AUTOPSY on Walters's body was unrevealing. There were bone fractures that were at least twenty years old and an enlarged spleen that would have given trouble if the man had lived a few more years. The age of the dead man was estimated as between forty-five and fifty and the examiners considered he had been healthy, but at some time had been involved in either a serious road or industrial accident.

Bailey went first to see Walters's accountant, a Mr. Slansky, a man in his early thirties, fresh-faced and cheerful.

"Any idea of why he did it, Mr. Bailey?"

"I was hoping you might be able to tell me something."

Slansky pursed his lips and leaned back in his chair. "I've known him for several years, but I knew very little about him."

"What about the business itself?"

"It makes money. He draws about five thousand a year as salary and a couple of thousand out of the net profits."

"And who will own the business now?"

"I suppose the Public Trustees Office will take over until they find a will. It's a miracle how claimants appear in these cases."

"How did you meet him?"

Slansky closed his eyes in concentration. "He knew my old man, they met at a chess club somewhere. But I don't think they were more than acquaintances."

"What about women?"

Slansky shrugged. "He never spoke of any women friends. He didn't have friends, you know. He just didn't need people. Didn't need to talk either. Just got on with things."

"Who's in charge at the works now?"

"I've made the foreman temporary manager. He's a good chap. Very loyal."

ARTHUR MCGUINESS had one of those smooth raw Scots faces that go with long service in the regular army and shaving in cold water. He stood in his brown overalls in the tiny office at the works.

"No, I wouldn't say we were friends. It was master and man and no' the worse for that. He was O.K."

"Did he understand the manufacturing side?"

"Och aye, there was no job in the workshop that he couldna do better himself."

"What were his interests outside the business?"

McGuiness looked at Bailey with surprise. "He was ma boss, man, I didna' mind his business, and he didna' mind mine."

"Did he ever talk politics?"

McGuiness laughed. "He didna' talk, mister. He was a doer not a clacker."

"Any regular visitors?"

"Just the usual. Salesmen and suppliers."

Bailey looked across the shop floor. "Any foreigners work here?"

"Two Pakistanis."

He made a note of McGuiness's home address and then left, going next to the contractor who had invited Walters to the reception at the Polish Embassy.

Mr. Silver was helpful, but he didn't add much. "We'd sent him invitations before but he didn't go. He wasn't that kind of man."

"You invite all your sub-contractors to these things?"

"Usually. Depends on what the embassies say. It's their party, not ours."

"And this time they suggested that sub-contractors should be invited?"

"I expect so. We shouldn't have asked him otherwise."

BAILEY SEARCHED Walters's flat carefully and professionally. Not only was there nothing to connect its late owner with the KGB, there was nothing that connected him with anything. Bailey heaped the few personal things on the dining-table.

There was a current British passport nearing the end of its validity. It gave his name as James Fuller Walters. Born Hazel Grove, Cheshire, 1 August 1917. There were three books on chess, with a cheap miniature chess set. A thick machinery handbook, and a small set of drawing and tracing instruments in a velvet-lined case that was well-made and fairly ancient. There was a large brown envelope with a couple of dozen cuttings from newspapers. Most of them were small classified advertisements by individuals offering things like pianos or watches for sale. There were two large cuttings of photographs, both faded. The first was of a group of people standing at a war memorial and the second was a small item from a newspaper about Wandsworth Metal Fabrications, a local firm which was contributing to the export drive. It was Walters's company.

There was a bundle of cashed cheques with a current account that showed a credit balance of £1,401 15s. The cheques seemed to be routine payments but the Special Branch accountancy experts could check these over.

The place was neutral, like a superior prison cell or a monk's retreat. Everything clean and in place, and no hint of the personality who had lived there. There had also been very little in the clothes that Walters was wearing when he died. The appointments in the diary had been checked. They were all business appointments.

Bailey had left the Palmers, who lived in the flat below Walters, until last. Palmer was a middle-grade official, working in the local housing department. His wife was a typist.

Bailey was offered, and accepted, the ritual cup of tea, and when they had all had a sip or two he got going.

"You know about the tragedy upstairs?"

"We saw what it said in the local paper. I gather you found his body and it looked like he might have killed himself."

"We're pretty sure he did commit suicide and that means we have to make a few routine inquiries."

"Of course." Palmer pulled down his maroon sweater as if preparing for anything that might happen.

"Did he have any visitors, any friends?"

Palmer looked quizzically at his wife and then at Bailey.

"Apart from people delivering things or reading meters nobody ever came. We often talked about it. We invited him down frequently. He only came two or three times."

"What sort of man was he?"

"He was a nice quiet man, very quiet, very gentle." Mrs. Palmer held her husband's hand as she spoke. And her husband took up her statement. "We sometimes wondered if he'd got some problem. We used to hear him walking up and down late at night. It wasn't a nuisance or anything like that, not noisy, but it made the light swing a bit." Palmer leaned forward as if he were gaining confidence from talking. He turned to his wife. "D'you remember the gramophone-record time?"

She nodded and looked at Bailey. "The first time he came down here we'd just had a new record player and I played him some records. And there was one that he asked us to play twice." She smiled. "I always said that he'd had tears in his eyes when he heard it. John says I imagined it. But I didn't."

"What was the record?"

"It was a song. In French. Josephine Baker singing *J'ai deux amours.*"

There was nothing more to be learned from the Palmers but he left them a phone number where they could contact him.

THERE HAD BEEN other things he had to do and it was three months later that he was asked to the weekly liaison meeting of the various security agencies.

It was Paynter's turn to chair the meeting and when they

reached the point in the agenda headed "Walters, J. F.—security investigation", he nodded in Bailey's direction.

"Chief Superintendent Bailey has been doing the check on the chap. As you know he cut his throat and that's about the only indication we have had that he might have been doing something naughty. I think we may have frightened him into it. He was a quiet little nonentity and he must have panicked. If he had been in 'the business' he wouldn't have been so frightened or so stupid. I think we can close the file, but let's hear what Bailey's got to say."

Bailey opened his file and looked briefly round the table. "Gentlemen, I've been able to produce very little on this man. I was on the case exclusively for five weeks and I've spent time on it sporadically for a further three months. All the information I've gathered merely supports my own opinion that Walters was an inoffensive man who lived a quiet life running his business. No visitors, no friends, a self-contained man. He had only been to the one embassy reception." He leaned back in his seat, pushing the file to one side: "Here was a man of forty-nine or whatever he was. He didn't do anything. Just went to work and came back again. I suppose it's the nothingness that challenges me, that makes me suspicious."

"Suspicious of what?"

"I really don't know."

Paynter waited to see if any of the others wanted to speak, but there were no takers. "Can I take it, gentlemen, that we agree to close the file?"

Lovegrove, the Foreign Office liaison man, fiddled with a pencil. He looked at Paynter then at Bailey. "Maybe we don't close it. Let's see if anything else comes up sometime."

Paynter looked at Bailey: "Agreed, Nick?"

"Agreed, sir."

It was nearly five o'clock when Bailey got back to Kensington. He'd parked his car and taken a taxi to St. James's Park. He got out at the Buckingham Palace circle and walked to the bridge and then down to the Passport Office in Petty France. A Russian from the Trade Mission had defected that morning and he was to do the preliminary interview.

PART TWO: WINTER 1943

Charles Parker sat in the hedge with the others, looking up to where the full, white moon hung in an almost cloudless sky. The lights which made an inverted "L" were in place but unlit, and his thumb lay across the button on his torch that would give the identification signal to the plane.

He tried not to think of all the loose ends he was leaving at Brive. Local legend said that the village had got its name of Brive-la-Gaillarde from putting on a brave face over centuries of sieges. But the present community of smallholders and fruit-growers, after three years of harassment by the Germans, were now very near the end of their tether. He closed his eyes and bent his head in the direction of a faint sound. Then he flashed his torch twice and as the men moved to the lights their figures cast long shadows on the moonlit grass. As the lights went on they could see the dark shape of the Lysander, its wings wagging as the pilot fought the cross-wind. He pressed the torch button—dot dash dot dash. Then the small plane was lost below the blackness of the trees, and moments later it was bumping across the field.

Parker ran forward and took the short ladder that was already halfway down to the ground. There were two passengers—he could see that one was Fredericks and the other was a dark man, the replacement radio operator for a network in Paris. Parker helped him down with the two heavy cases of radio equipment and then went up the ladder and pulled it up behind him, ducking as the pilot closed the canopy. The engine revved and he barely had time to sit beside Fredericks behind the pilot before they were moving. Then they were airborne and banking in a wide turn.

He was asleep when they touched down at Tangmere and Fredericks shook him awake. He remembered being shoved into a big black Humber and then he slept again until they were going through Streatham. It was just getting light and there were hoses across the main road. They were diverted round the common and he saw the still-smoking ruins of several houses and a pub. There were buildings still burning at Clapham.

The sun was out as they crossed Westminster Bridge. Ten minutes later he was at Orchard House.

Fredericks carried Parker's kit up the stairs where Foster was waiting for them. He held out his hand.

"Glad to see you back, Charles. Freddie's fixed you a bed at his place for today and when you've rested we'll talk." His hand brushed at his hair diffidently. "There are just a couple of quickies, Charles."

Parker nodded. "One's Bordeaux, yes?"

"Yes. What d'you think?"

Parker noticed the tired eyes. "I think it was penetrated by the Germans months ago. Take it from me that it's insecure."

"Feeling, Charles, or a fact or two?"

Parker took a deep breath. "Facts, yes. From Bordeaux to La Rochelle the Germans are thick on the ground. SD, Gestapo, Feldgendarmerie, Milice—the lot. They picked up Grandclement and held him for four days. When he came out the story was that he'd fooled them. But since then they've picked up seven caches of arms and explosives. In my opinion he did a deal, and my people have been told to break off all contact with his group." He closed his eyes. "What was the other question?"

"Would you trust Devereux?"

"With my life."

"O.K., Charles, we'll talk again when you've had a sleep."

Parker had almost forgotten that he was back in safety. As he undressed he looked out of the window. All he could see were pots of geraniums at the sides of the basement steps. Devereux would be preparing the explosive about now for the raid on the railway sheds at Tulle. If they got the roundhouse it would stop supplies to the car-engine factory for at least four weeks, but even a couple of shunting locos would be a worthwhile prize.

As he settled under the blankets he realized that he stank. He hadn't had a bath for a month. He wondered what Foster and Fredericks had brought him back from France to discuss.

CHARLES DU PUY PARKER had been born in Birmingham on the last day of October 1918. His father, a sergeant in the regular army, died when the boy was scarcely one. His mother was

French and she had met the man who was to be her husband when they had brought him, badly gassed, into the hospital in Bruges where she was a nurse. Her parents had liked him although they regretted that he was English. As he had joined the army from an orphanage there were no English relatives to please, and they had married when he was honourably discharged, with a pension of seven shillings a week.

He had gone back to his old job in England as a toolmaker, but after six months it was clear that he would not survive in the dirt and stench of a factory, and he had taken on hourly work as a jobbing gardener. But the fogs of the next winter had kindled again the terrible fires in his lungs. He was not a man to complain, but the pale, drawn face and the blue round the mouth and eyes told the story clearly enough for those who cared to notice. He died in the spring of 1919.

At home Charles's mother spoke only in French, and from time to time relatives from Paris and Lyons came to visit, and she was complimented on Charles's accent and fluency. When World War II began he was an engineer with an agricultural engineering company and by February 1940 he had been called up. Four months later he was interviewed in a tatty little office in a ministry block in Westminster. The thin man whose eyes were always half closed against the smoke of his cigarette asked him questions, and did not seem over-impressed with his answers. That the interview had been in French had been its own small clue.

A week later he was posted to Wanborough Manor just outside Guildford, and there he learned the basics of the arts and crafts that the Special Operations Executive required. By the time Parker had finished his parachute training SOE was ensconced in Baker Street and it was there that he had his final briefing. Their only worry was that he had never lived in France. His French would pass but language alone doesn't make a Frenchman, and on that score they cautioned him against taking unnecessary risks.

They dropped him and Devereux, his second-in-command, south of Clermont-Ferrand. They moved down to the Corrèze the next day and in the months that followed Charles du Puy Parker successfully held together a *réseau*, or network, of men and women who came to control the whole area of the Corrèze.

Parker was a loner, but a loner who cared for his men. If they died, it was because, with largely improvised equipment and inadequate resources, risks had to be taken. They were calculated risks and sometimes the calculations were wrong. But Parker's men were Frenchmen, and they knew the risks.

Parker had become something of a legend for his ability to harass the Germans and yet keep his men alive, and SOE in Baker Street thought that he could be better used. In addition, it was their experience that legendary leaders became prime targets for the Germans' security organizations.

ON THE DAY following Parker's return to England, Foster and Fredericks hinted at a new assignment. But they sent him first on a refresher course at Beaulieu, and amongst other things he learned a new way of killing a man without making a noise.

Foster and Fredericks came down at the end of the first week, and on the Sunday evening told him about his new task.

It was Foster who led off, and Charles Parker listened carefully.

"We want you to go back again—not to the Corrèze but to the adjoining Dordogne. We'll be sending a radio operator in with you. There's the nucleus of a réseau in the area already. We want you to do what you've done in the Corrèze—sabotage, post us on troop movements. You'll still be in overall charge of the réseau of Corrèze and of the group at Limoges. The network will be code named LANTERN. We want a good solid controlled area so that when the time comes there will be an army across the main roads that can harry even major German units when they start moving them about. You'll be in this country for at least a month and we've planned a series of refresher sessions for you. There are new weapons and new explosives techniques that will be useful for you. Any queries?"

"Who's my radio operator?"

"She'll be down tomorrow. If you don't approve you'll have to give us your views by this time next week. Good radio operators are pretty thin on the ground at the moment."

The weeks went by and Parker absorbed the new training, and in the evenings he pored over the maps of his new area and read the reports on the SOE groups there.

2

It was Parker's last night in England before they dropped him back in France. He and the girl had sat drinking beer in an almost empty pub and she had tried to hide her tension. On the way back he stopped his small MG. The moon was almost full and there was the sparkle of frost on the road ahead. He turned to look at her. Antoinette Dupont was very pretty. She was a Seychelloise from Mahé and the brown eyes and light brown skin glowed with health.

"Are you scared, 'Toinette?"

Her head turned quickly and the brown eyes looked carefully at his face. "I'm afraid so."

"The drop, or what comes after?"

She laughed softly. "Just this minute I'm scared of everything. What was my report like?"

"The radio part was exceptionally good. I think they wanted to hold you as an instructor."

"And the rest?"

"Not bad. A suggestion that you were over-emotional."

The big eyes looked at him quickly. "And you disagreed?"

He half laughed. "No, I agreed. Most of my good people are emotional. I insisted that you were ideal for my operation and Baker Street agreed too."

She looked at the stolid face. "How old are you, Charles?"

"Twenty-five."

"You remind me of my father."

"How old's he?"

"Fifty something."

"Thanks pal," he said. And started the car.

Fredericks was waiting for them. "They've put forward your drop, it's tonight. Are you both ready?"

They nodded and Parker said, "You take 'Toinette to get her kit and I'll join you in five minutes."

He felt no regrets at leaving England again. He didn't really belong anywhere, the war had come too early in his life for any roots to be disturbed. And he had no fear of either the drop or what might await him at the other end.

THE DAKOTA was already on the runway as their car pulled up, and they walked with Fredericks to the main hut. The Field Security sergeant handed them their clothes in cardboard boxes and left them to change. When Fredericks came back the girl was wearing a thick jersey and a tweed skirt with a coat slung over her arm. Parker wore a well-mended brown woollen suit and a fisherman's heavy jersey.

"Have they checked you both?"

"Yes," said Parker. "They checked us first."

A whole section of SOE spent its time on collecting genuine clothing from countries where agents were dropped. And there was a group of elderly ladies in a basement in Margaret Street who sewed and patched in French, German, Dutch and Belgian styles.

Fredericks led the way to the Dakota, where their gear was spread along the narrow seat. They clambered into their overalls and thick parachute assemblies. Parker peered out of the door and raised his hand to Fredericks just as the door was closing.

Inside the aircraft the light was dim and the atmosphere freezing. As they sat side by side on the slatted seat the girl was shaking, and Parker put out his hand to cover hers. The roar of the engines was too loud for them to speak to one another. He stood up and beckoned the girl to stand too. He carefully checked all the straps on her parachute harness and then checked over the small suitcase that housed her radio, and his own two canvas bags.

An hour and a half after they had sat down again the co-pilot walked back from the cockpit. He bent down to shout in Parker's ear. "The sheet says the girl goes first, is that O.K.?"

Parker nodded, and the RAF man bent down to shout again. "About another ten minutes, sir."

There was a little flak shortly afterwards and Parker guessed it was the defences guarding the German submarine base at Bordeaux. From then on the plane was dropping fast and the co-pilot was standing by the door checking the parachute clips. Then he beckoned them to the white line. Parker attached the girl's cord to the clip and stood behind her as the door swung open. They were at about 4,000 feet and Parker could see a river below them shining in the moonlight. Then the airman's hand went up and Parker tapped the girl's shoulder. She didn't hesitate but Parker noticed that her legs were sprawled apart as she fell. He hooked up his own cord and nodded to the airman and jumped.

The air was cold as steel and when the main canopy cracked open he felt no pull because of the numbness of his body. He could see a large field coming up fast, hit the ground and was rolling, tugging at his 'chute to spill the air. There was a torch a long way away, flashing. He headed for the small dim light, his parachute clutched like a bundle of washing under his arm, his two bags slung across his shoulders. The earth was hard as rock and he stumbled unsteadily in the furrows.

He was almost in the blackness of the hedge before he realized it was there. And then Devereux's tall frame loomed up. "Welcome back, Chaland. The girl's O.K. How about I take the 'chute?"

"Yeah, I know, and half the girls in the Corrèze will be wearing white silk knickers."

"No, chief. They dye 'em now. You've been away a long time."

"For Christ's sake what's that light?"

"Ah, that's my surprise. It's a car."

"You must be crazy, what about the curfew?"

Devereux laughed softly. "It's the doctor's car, there was a false alarm from a pregnant lady who's overdue."

"You cheeky bastard. Is the doctor in the car?"

"Sure he is."

They stumbled with the girl to the car. The driver was a thin elderly man with a vinegary expression, and he launched the car into gear the moment they had swung the doors to.

Seven kilometres outside Brantôme they stopped. Parker could see the dim outline of straggling farm buildings.

"Here we are, chief. The de Baissac farm. It's a lousy dump but we daren't go into Brantôme after curfew."

Parker squeezed the doctor's shoulder in thanks, and they all scrambled out. Devereux led them to a wooden building. "There's straw and sacks of seed," he whispered. "Let's get settled down. I've got sausage, bread and some brandy."

They piled the bales of straw so that there was an area like a small room. Devereux shone his torch over the girl and Parker.

"Let me introduce you," Parker said. "'Toinette, this is Jean-Luc. He's got his own radio operator but sometimes you may have to take his traffic. Same applies with them as with me. On radio things you're the boss. Nobody, including me, can override you on length of transmissions or timing. They can suggest, but it's your decision." He turned to Devereux, "You understand that, Jean-Luc?"

"O.K. chief." He waved a bottle and a package. "Let's have the feast, eh?"

They slept fitfully until about six o'clock when they washed their faces in a cattle trough. Devereux and Parker walked across two fields and burned the parachutes and buried the metal buckles in a ditch. It was still pitch black at eight o'clock when they piled into the back of a rusty Fiat van half full of sacks of grain for the mill. There were few people moving in Brantôme as they trundled through and twenty minutes later they were on a narrow dirt road leading up to a farm at Puy Henry. Halfway up the steep hill the road stopped and there was just a narrow path up to the farm.

Devereux led the way to a cottage joined to the main farm building by a stone barn. The old door opened with a massive key. It was a typical Dordogne farm cottage, two up, two down, and walls at least a metre thick. They opened the shutters and the wintry light barely illuminated the whitewashed rooms. Parker told the girl to fetch their kit from the van, and as she left he turned to Devereux.

"How secure is this place?"

"You can see anyone approaching for at least ten minutes before they get here, so it's physically well placed. You've rented it for two hundred francs a week. The farmer's son was taken by the Germans a year ago. They hate the Boche. It's isolated and there's only the one pathway up. There's electricity and a telephone."

Parker nodded, "How many people know I'm here?"

"Me. The farmer and his family and, I suspect, Frenez at Limoges and the Communist Bonnier know."

"How the hell do they know?"

"I don't *know* that they do, but there was a rumour from the Commies that you were on your way back."

"Is there any food here?"

"Some, not much. Have you got coupons?"

"Sure."

As the girl returned Parker moved to the rough kitchen chairs. "Let's talk for a few minutes and then you'd better go. How're things in Brive?"

"We've had orders from London that we still come under you. I've lost Martin and du Champs but we've done a lot of sabotage operations."

"And everybody has moved?"

"It's been difficult." Devereux looked embarrassed.

"For God's sake, Jean-Luc, you know the rules—if anybody gets caught—everybody in a réseau gets the hell out of it. You too."

"Nobody's been tailing us, I'm sure of that."

"Devereux, you leave me now, and by midnight I want everybody to have left the district or to have moved their quarters. Bring them into this area if you like, but move them fast."

"O.K., chief."

Parker turned to the girl.

"When's your first radio schedule, 'Toinette?"

"It's up to me in the next forty-eight hours. They'll be listening on the hour every hour."

He walked to the door. "Set it up in the small bedroom for now. We'll find a permanent place tonight. Tell them we've arrived and that we are safe. By the way, what's your security check word?"

She blushed as she looked at him. "I'm not allowed to tell you."

He grinned. "Good girl, but get moving."

He went next door and talked to the farmer and his wife and was satisfied that they wouldn't talk. On the way back he explored the barn. Except for three calves and a few chickens the place was just storage for hay and straw and a few farm implements. There was a boarded area up near the roof that carried another layer of straw bales and he decided that that was the place for the radio.

It was ten o'clock that night before they had it in place and the aerial laid along the rafters. When they got back to the cottage Devereux had arrived, dishevelled and sweating despite the cold, from the long walk up the steep hill. Parker stood aggressively, hands on hips, in front of the door.

"Are they dispersed?" he asked.

"You were right, chief. They've picked up Lachaise. I've dispersed the others."

"Did they get her radio, too?"

"I'm afraid so."

Parker swung round to face the girl. "I'll need to tell London immediately. Can you transmit again tonight?"

She nodded. "Yes."

Parker ushered them inside and sat at the kitchen table as he wrote out his new message to London, crossing out words as he went along to reduce the air time. He shoved it across to the girl. "Can you manage on your own?"

She nodded, took his pencil and torch, and closed the cottage door behind her as she left.

Parker turned swiftly on Devereux and spoke through his teeth in anger.

"Now you go back to the road, my friend, and check whether you've been followed." Then he turned away from the other man as if he were no longer there.

He sat at the table consumed by his anger and frustration. He had come back full of plans for building up the new réseau in the Dordogne, and now, on his first full day he had to report back that his old réseau from the Corrèze had been dispersed and its highly efficient and experienced girl radio operator was in the hands of the Gestapo, complete with radio and maybe codes as well. There would be nothing constructive for weeks, just that slow, grinding build-up again. The work of many months destroyed by the ignoring of elementary security precautions. It was a bad start but it was to deal with this kind of situation that they had put him in charge.

When Devereux came back he was shivering with cold and reported that there had been no watchers and no vehicles and it was beginning to snow. Parker told him to bed down in the barn.

PARKER WAS UP at six the next morning, moving around the area of the buildings slowly and cautiously in the dark. Puy Henry was one of those conical hills typical of the area. And as Devereux had said, it was not only isolated, but there was no dead ground to provide cover for anyone approaching from either the road or the fields below.

He went into the barn and shook Devereux awake.

"Tell me what you know about the Germans in Périgueux."

Devereux shook his head like a dog coming out of water. "There are two SD men. The senior is Heinz Bode and the other is Otto Lange. There's a Gestapo man who covers this area from Bordeaux."

"What do we know about them?"

"Bode is young, about twenty-six, a real Nazi lout. Cunning but not intelligent. Very active. Lange is about forty, speaks good French, keeps a fantastic card index, moves around the area a lot. The Gestapo man is Gustav Nolke. A professional. Was something senior in the Kriminalpolizei in Germany. He came down here from Paris, and reports direct to them."

"What are the locals like?"

Devereux shrugged. "About average. There's a big màquis around Junilac, more around Nontron and Coussac."

"Who oversees them?"

"The Commies. They're spread everywhere, wanting to take over. They want a meeting with you to get more arms. Michel Bonnier—the one I mentioned, a very shrewd operator—had training in Moscow before the war."

Parker looked at Devereux, aware of the signs of strain on the gaunt face. Devereux was tall and thin, a gangling sort of man, brave and loyal. Parker had in mind to send him back to England for more training. But from the hints in London the invasion couldn't be more than six or seven months away and he was going to need every good body he could lay hands on.

"You chose this place well, Jean-Luc," and he put his hand on the other man's bent knee. "Let's get something to eat."

That evening Parker, Devereux and the girl went to Brantôme. They sat in the warmth of a small restaurant over bowls of potato soup. The German soldiers there disturbed the girl so much that she left half her meal untouched. Parker noticed a group of three Waffen SS with the sleeve bands of the 2nd SS Panzer division *Das Reich*. Most of the *Das Reich* division were down in the Toulouse area but when the invasion came they would be the ones he would have to harass as they were called up to the north to help repulse any attack on the Channel ports or maybe the Atlantic coast.

Parker had automatically taken the seat facing the door. When two SD men came in he would have recognized them even without Devereux's description. He leaned forward towards the girl and said, "Two Germans have just come in. They're SD. Don't look round. Just go on talking. They'll check our papers. If they question you, just charm them. Listen to me and let me give my papers up first."

The tall one, Bode, had fair wavy hair and blue eyes, and he stood against the closed door with both hands stuck in his leather belt while Lange carefully checked the papers. The patron moved among his customers trying to make things seem normal. Even the German soldiers had fallen silent.

Both Parker and Devereux had put their papers on the table and gone on eating. Lange came to their table last and Parker handed up his identity card and his German pass.

Lange was whistling softly to himself as he looked at the identity card. "Your name?"

"Chaland—Charles."

"Occupation?"

"Agricultural engineer."

Lange put down the identity card and examined the German pass. "Why do you need this?"

Parker laughed. "Tractors break down, my friend, both sides of the zone borders."

Lange was tapping the pass against his chin as he looked at Parker. "What was the name of the German officer who signed your pass?"

"I've no idea. I'm a Frenchman. I don't read German script."

Lange nodded and then put down the pass on the table. When he came to the girl Bode walked over from the door, looking the girl over with a supercilious smile. He stood while Lange checked her card and watched her as Lange put his questions. Then he turned to the girl. "And what are you doing here?"

"I'm with Monsieur Chaland. I am his assistant."

"What's your occupation?"

"I'm a botanist. I deal with pests."

There was a laugh from one of the soldiers who obviously understood French, and Bode turned round slowly. The men were still smiling and the provocation was too much. He walked over to their table and asked for their documents and Lange joined him. Five minutes later they left.

Parker poured another drink for them all. "Don't get up, 'Toinette. They'll wait outside to see who goes first. You did well, girl. If you stand up to the bastards they generally back down if they aren't really suspicious."

All the next day Parker called on local farmers offering his services. He was welcomed, and given enough offers of work to last him for months. While he was in Périgueux he rented a room and paid six months' rent in advance. It was in one of the small streets between the cathedral and the river, and the most desirable feature of the house was that it had separate entrances back and front. He said nothing to the girl or Devereux about the room, or the radio he had left in the dusty attic.

They were eating their evening meal in the cottage when there was a knock on the door—the morse V-sign. When Parker opened the door he saw a girl; there were snowflakes on her eyelashes and around the edge of the hood she wore. She said, "I bring a message from Michel Bonnier to Monsieur Chaland."

He stood back from the door and signalled to her to step inside. He saw her take in the room and the others at the table, and nodded to 'Toinette. "Get her some coffee and cheese with bread." Then he turned to the girl. "We'll go upstairs."

She followed him up to the bedroom. He waved her to the low bed and sat on a box facing her. She was dark-skinned and her big eyes were almost black. Her mouth was full and sensuous but she had no air of sexuality and her face had only the beauty of calmness. She was attractive as a child or a timid animal is attractive.

"What was the message from Michel?" he said.

"He would like to meet you and wishes to co-operate with your organization."

"Can I see your identity card?"

She reached in the pocket of her coat and pulled out an old

leather wallet held together with a broad elastic band. She pulled out the card and handed it to him, and he looked at it carefully. The photograph matched, the physical description was accurate and the card was valid until 28.12.53. The Germans were looking that far ahead for the Thousand Year Reich! Parker looked across at her as he handed back the card. Her name was Sabine Patou.

"Tell Michel that I will meet him one week from today at the museum in Périgueux at eleven. Tell him to be looking at the Sèvres porcelain. The password will be 'Champs Élysées'. Then we walk outside separately and cross the road to the park."

3

The only person looking at the Sèvres exhibits was a man, aged about thirty with dark curly hair, a broken nose set in a round face, barrel-chested and wearing workmen's overalls. He had turned as Parker stood alongside him and without any pause he had said, "The Champs Élysées is German territory these days." And he grinned as he held out his hand. Parker took it briefly then turned and walked away.

They sat on a park bench while young mothers wheeled tattered prams along the paths and children played with hoops and blew on cold fingers.

"Your courier told me you needed help."

"Then she misinformed you, Chaland. I said we could co-operate that is all. We need things that you can supply and we will help you in any way you ask."

Parker looked at the round face. "You mean if your masters in Moscow say that you can."

The grey eyes and the thin mouth showed their anger. "We take orders from nobody. I give the orders."

"What is it you need?"

"Arms and ammunition. Rifles, machine-guns, mortars, grenades, flares and medical supplies."

Parker stood up. "Let's walk, we'll look odd sitting here in the freezing cold. How did you know where I was, Bonnier?"

"I heard talk from one of Devereux's men that you were coming back," Bonnier said.

"Who was the talker?"

"The one the Germans picked up, I've forgotten his name."

"How many men have you got?"

Bonnier's grey eyes were on Parker's face, working something out. "Are you on my side, Chaland?"

"I'm on the side of anyone who'll fight the Germans."

"I've got over two thousand maquisards but very few arms."

"And if you get the arms you'll go rampaging around the countryside shooting the Boche and they'll take civilian reprisals."

"What would you have us do?" And the anger was no longer concealed.

"You could train with your arms, you could plan ambushes and tactics and be ready to operate when it really mattered."

Bonnier's eyes half closed: "Are your people really going to come?"

"They're going to come all right."

"When?"

Parker smiled. "If I knew I couldn't tell you. But I haven't come back here for a quiet life. I'm an Englishman remember, not a Frenchman."

Bonnier smiled. "When it's all over and I'm mayor of Périgueux we'll make you a Frenchman."

"Maybe we'll do that, Michel."

Bonnier noted the Christian name, and Parker noted what he had always suspected; that when it was all over the Communists expected to be running the country.

"If I get you a first drop of supplies it will be on three conditions. First, that you accept a British officer to train your people. Second, that you control your people until we give you the word. A few small jobs maybe, but you don't start stirring up the Germans until we're ready. And third, that the drop is organized by me. We've got the experience, you haven't."

Bonnier shrugged. "Beggars can't be choosers."

"That's not good enough, my friend. Beggars can make a bloody nuisance of themselves once they've got the material. This is going to be one part of France where we all work together. No politics, no post-war vote catching."

Bonnier put his hand out palm upwards. "Agreed, my friend.

My men's morale will go sky-high with supplies; they'll do what I say."

As Parker put his hand on Bonnier's open hand, Bonnier's eyes glistened with tears. "Will they come, Charles, will it ever come right again?"

"They'll come. It won't be long."

Bonnier was silent. As Parker stood up Bonnier looked at him. "Do you want help to get your radio girl, Lachaise, out of jail?"

"My God, yes!"

"I've heard from my contacts that she hasn't talked and they've burnt her feet and her hands. She's in a bad way. She won't live long. They're taking her to a doctor at Brive early tomorrow morning. He's a physician who does a lot for the Germans on the side. Abortions and the like."

"Any idea what they're going to get him to do?"

"No idea. Death certificate, make her fit enough to send to Paris. God knows."

"Could you get me a van, an ambulance and a taxi by this afternoon?" Parker paused thoughtfully. "We'll have to get them in place before the curfew tonight. I'm thinking of an ambush."

Bonnier said softly, "Leave it to me."

A VAN, an ambulance and a taxi were parked at the end of the road up the hill to the cottage at Puy Henry by the time Parker had cycled back. There was a message for him with 'Toinette.

"Michel Bonnier came with the vehicles and he's waiting with his men down in the bottom field. If you flash him on your torch he'll come up."

Devereux was inside the cottage.

"I need a doctor," Parker said.

"There's old Pignon in the village. He'd be very safe. Or there's Renard in Périgueux."

Parker looked at the man's face. "It's for serious burns and probably broken bones. Lachaise."

Devereux nodded. "It's old Pignon then. I'll phone him. How long has he got?"

Parker shrugged. "We want him as soon as possible. But he doesn't have to come. It's voluntary."

Devereux shook his head. "It's not. But he'll love it."

Parker walked away from the cottage and flashed his torch into the darkness. He flashed just once, and despite the cold he stood waiting. It was nearly twenty minutes before he saw Bonnier's breath as he came up the last few metres.

"Thanks for the vehicles," Parker said. "Where'd you get them?"

"The van is from the priest at Agonac, the ambulance we have had for two months and the taxi was stolen from Bordeaux a year ago. We've changed all the numbers for tonight."

"Let's go inside. How are your men down there?"

"O.K., Chaland."

Once inside the cottage they spread the maps across the table. Parker pushed his finger at the map. "We'll ambush them at the scrapyard at la Garde. It's about three kilometres short of Thenon. There're no telephones, no police." He looked up at Bonnier. "I've got a feeling they'll have an escort of some kind. Are you prepared to take them on?"

Bonnier grinned. "You give the orders and we'll see to them."

Parker looked at his watch. "What weapons have you got?"

"Two Lugers, a Lee-Enfield .303 and a submachine-gun."

"Do you want to leave Sabine here? 'Toinette will be staying."

"No. Better she's with my people."

"How many torches have we got?"

"We've got four."

"I've got one. There's a bend in the road. Put one of your men at the start of the bend and he signals just after they pass. The taxi is waiting and he starts the engine at the signal. The engine's got to be warm. He'll get about two minutes to start the engine, move across onto the road and make impact with their ambulance or the escort. Your lookout has the machine-gun and he covers the road behind so they can't back away the rear vehicle if there are two. Tyres first, then escort. We don't want any survivors. You and I can deal with them. The road's not wide enough for them to turn a vehicle on one lock. When we've dealt with the Germans you send a runner back to bring up our ambulance with the doctor and we transfer the girl."

Parker looked at Devereux. "Jean-Luc, you'll drive the girl down to Toulouse. I'll give you the address. Understood?"

Devereux nodded. Parker looked back at Bonnier. "Michel, when the ambulance has gone, remove their vehicles, whatever they are. Smash the cylinder heads and pistons if you've got time. We'll have to dump your taxi as well. A pity."

Bonnier shrugged. "I'll take my men off as soon as we've cleared the vehicles." The grey eyes looked at Parker's face. "Do we get our arms drop then?"

"You'd have got it without this, Michel. You go and give your men their instructions. I gather we are to expect the Germans any time after eleven."

'Toinette was leaning against the wall and after Parker had closed the door he said, "Send a signal to Baker Street. We want medical help near Toulouse by tomorrow afternoon. Tell them that it will be fractures, burns and the usual Gestapo stuff. Tell them what we're doing. Mention Bonnier's help. And pass on my request for an arms drop. And make it short."

PARKER AND BONNIER walked together to the corner of the main road. Parker asked, "Shall I check your weapon, Michel?"

Bonnier handed over his gun and Parker turned it to take advantage of the faint light of the moon.

"D'you realize what this is, Michel?"

"One of my fellows said it was a Schmeisser machine-gun."

Parker looked at Bonnier in disbelief. "That means you've never fired it?"

"There's only thirty rounds."

Parker handed over his Luger. "This is the thumb safety catch. Up. for the firing position. You can have your weapon back afterwards. It isn't a machine-gun, it's an assault rifle. I won't ask where you got it, but it's only been German army issue for about nine months. I'll show you how to use it next week."

They heard the taxi's engine churn and then catch. It was switched off quickly and then started again. The second time it caught immediately. It was only twenty metres away but it was quite invisible.

The two men leaned on the low stone wall over a culvert. They were silent for several minutes and then Bonnier said, "Have you contacted your people about a drop for me?"

"Yes."

"Any reply?"

"Not yet. Have you got any suitable places in mind for the drop?"

"My base is at Bournaud and there are big areas under our control there—look, my God, there's the torch."

They both ran to the crossroads and Parker banged on the side of the taxi as he ran. It started easily and rolled past them to the edge of the main road. They saw the headlights of two army motor-cyclists. He shouted to Bonnier, "Let them pass."

Then they could see the lights of the ambulance, even its white paint. The taxi lurched forward into the main road. It hit the ambulance and slewed sideways across the road, and then there was a burst of firing and single shots. There was another pair of motor-cyclists covering the rear of the ambulance, and as Parker wrenched open the driving door of the ambulance he was conscious of a headlight from a bike lying on its side on the road, and then a shower of orange sparks as the second bike ground along on its side, its foot-pedal gouging up the road surface.

Parker reached up, grabbed the ambulance driver's collar and dragged him to the road. Parker hit him behind the ear with the Schmeisser and raced to the rear doors. They were not locked and he pulled down the mobile steps and jumped in. He shone his torch on the figure strapped to the leather bed. There were two thin grey hospital blankets over the girl, covering half her face as well as her body. He pulled back the blankets and shone the torch on her face. He thought at first that she was dead but there was a nerve fibrillating in her cheek. Her face was a waxy yellow with bruises along her jaw and small circular burns from cigarettes on both her cheeks.

Then Bonnier, grinning in triumph, climbed aboard. "All four cyclists finished. We stripped them. Fantastic. Uniforms and documents and four almost new BMWs." Then he saw Parker's face. "Christ, how's the girl?"

"She must be almost finished. Get our ambulance and the doctor. I'll stay here."

Devereux, the doctor and Sabine were there in less than three minutes. The doctor bent over the girl, his hand holding her wrist, and he pulled back the lid of one eye as Parker shone his torch. Then he stood up. "If God cares I can keep her alive for about thirty-six hours. She needs hospital care, and drugs I could never get."

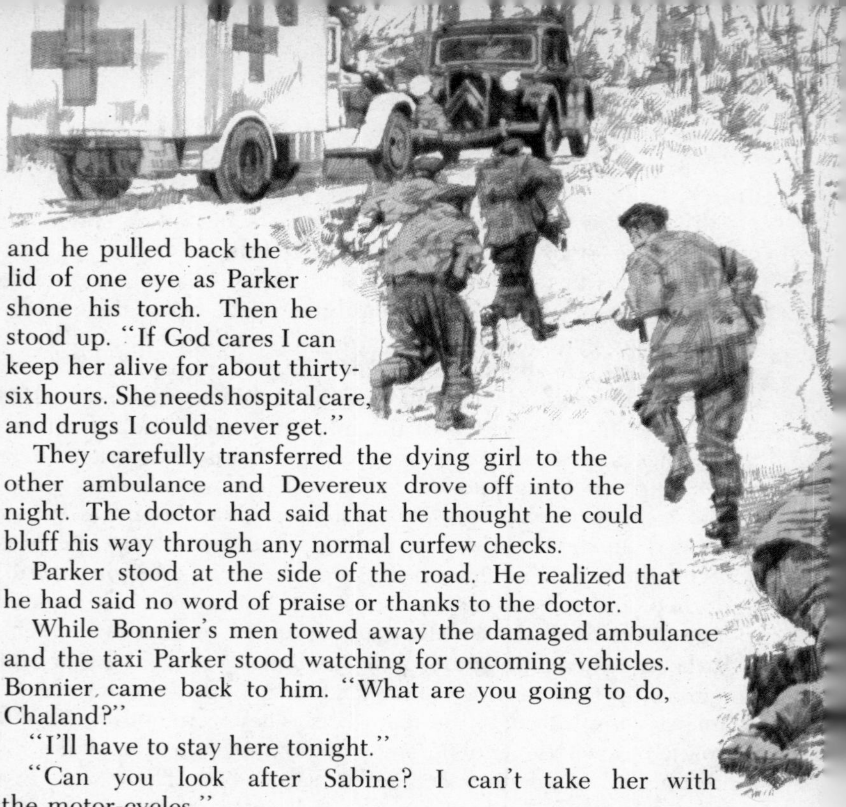

They carefully transferred the dying girl to the other ambulance and Devereux drove off into the night. The doctor had said that he thought he could bluff his way through any normal curfew checks.

Parker stood at the side of the road. He realized that he had said no word of praise or thanks to the doctor.

While Bonnier's men towed away the damaged ambulance and the taxi Parker stood watching for oncoming vehicles. Bonnier came back to him. "What are you going to do, Chaland?"

"I'll have to stay here tonight."

"Can you look after Sabine? I can't take her with the motor-cycles."

"Yes. Send her back to the scrapyard and tell her to wait for me."

Parker heard the motor-cycles head off up the side-road and then he was alone. Everywhere was silent, and despite the cold he could feel trickles of sweat running down his back. The sky was clear now, and he could see a few stars. And in the stillness and the silence he wondered if he were mad. He shivered and then set off for the scrapyard.

The girl was huddled against a pile of rusty cylinder blocks. He found a piece of tarpaulin and made a roof over their heads. He sat close to the girl and a line of pale moonlight washed her face. She turned to look at him.

"Are the Germans on the motor-cycles all right?"

Parker looked to see if she were smiling. She wasn't. "They're fine, Sabine. Dead as pigs."

"You don't mind that they're dead."

"I'm glad that they're dead."

"But they're men. Fathers, husbands, sons. There are people who love them, who think they are still alive."

"How old are you, Sabine?"

"Eighteen."

"Where were you when the Germans smashed France?"

"In Paris."

"Well, out on the country roads there were tens of thousands of people, women and children, and those bastard Germans machine-gunned them down. Those refugees were loved by people too."

He turned towards her almost violently, his fist slamming into his open palm. "Those pigs kill people like they were animals. They smash their way round France as if we were scum."

The girl put her head on one side to see him more clearly, and she said softly. "But you're not French."

"Who says so?"

"Your words. You use old-fashioned words like my mother."

He looked at her face. "Where is your mother?"

"She's dead. She was one of the refugees they killed."

"What happened to you?"

"Some soldiers gave me a lift in a truck. Then they raped me and threw me out into a ditch."

"And now you feel soft for Germans, girl?"

"They were French soldiers, Monsieur Chaland."

He closed his eyes. "God Almighty, what a world."

"And what about you? Your mother, your father?"

"My father died years ago. My mother's still alive."

"And why do you risk your life here in France?"

It was a long time before he answered. "When I was a small boy my mother talked all the time about France. She was French. Everything that was good was French. I grew up to believe the skies were bluer in France, the marigolds more golden. I know now that it isn't true, but that makes no difference. This country is where the world begins for me. And that's why I'm here."

She leaned back against the metal blocks and patted her shoulder. "Put your head here and sleep. You must be very tired."

She could see either confusion or indignation on his face that she should think he needed any such comfort. She smiled and put her arm through his. "Let's both sleep."

4

By the time the New Year came in, Parker had crossed and re-crossed a dozen times the vast triangle of his territory. At Limoges he had found André Frenez and his réseau with a dozen operations waiting for his approval but with a desperate need for a radio operator and explosives.

In February there had been a three-plane arms drop for Bonnier and a Lysander operation bringing a team to train Bonnier's men.

He had transferred Devereux to command the Périgueux réseau despite his shortcomings. But only after he had recruited Lemaire, who ran the garage at the edge of the town.

They had found a lodging for 'Toinette near the garage, and her radio was housed in the side wall of the deep servicing pit in the workshop and she used an abandoned storeroom for her transmissions. When she was transmitting, Lemaire and his men kept an eye out for the Germans.

In the first week in April the three réseaux had been given a trial run on a joint operation. They had blown railway tracks at La Rochefoucauld, a power line at Nontron, and had completely destroyed the telephone exchange at Dignac. There had been thirty-two men in the groups and only one minor casualty.

As Parker sat eating bread and cheese in the cottage at Puy Henry he heard the sound of a car. Then silence. He waited for the knock.

It was 'Toinette. Lemaire had stayed with the car. She pulled out several sheets of message pad. He took them from her and handed her a three-page message for encoding. "Don't wait, 'Toinette. I'll bring my stuff down to you this evening."

He bent down to read the messages on the table and he was aware that the girl was still there. There were three messages.

The third message expressed regret at informing him of his mother's death from pneumonia. Did he have instructions?

He sat at the table and wrote out his replies and several more requests and reports to London. He looked up at 'Toinette. She was leaning forward, her eyes on his face.

"I've put them in order of urgency, 'Toinette. How are things down at the garage?"

"I was sad about your mother, Charles."

He stood up. "Be sad for those who are still alive. How are things down at the garage?"

"The Germans came yesterday. They found nothing and I wasn't there. They questioned Lemaire about the vehicles in the garage."

She stood with his messages in her hand. "Is it all right if I move my place?"

"Who is he?"

She laughed. "How the hell did you know?"

"Who is he?"

"It's Victor, the schoolmaster."

Victor had been in the French army. He was a member of the réseau and lived in a small apartment in Périgueux. Parker looked intently at the girl. "Have you been sleeping with him at your place?"

"Yes. But we'd like to be together."

"Remember what they told you. No emotional involvements."

"I'd be O.K., Charles. Really."

He shook his head: "You'd be a danger if you move to Victor's place. I'd have to send you back to England."

"But why? Why only me? Everybody in the réseau sleeps with somebody."

"It would be safer if they didn't. But sleeping is one thing, an emotional relationship is something else. If Victor is picked up it's a pressure point on you. Or it could be the other way round. You both need to be single-minded for this work. It's not just your lives, it's everybody in the group."

He could see the anger and frustration on her face. "Don't you ever think of anything except this bloody game?"

He smiled. "It won't be long 'Toinette, and then it'll all be over."

She looked at his face, shaking her head in mystification.

HE CYCLED down to Périgueux and left his cycle at the garage and then walked to his room on the other side of the town. It was just as he had left it, neat and tidy, quiet and calm. He sat for over an hour encoding his report to London. When he had finished he stood looking out of the window as the light faded.

There seemed to be more Germans in the town than a week ago, and more military vehicles. Shopkeepers were putting up the shutters for the night and the café opposite was quite full. And then in the light from the *pâtisserie* he saw Sabine, and a few metres behind her was the Gestapo man, Nolke. In a few strides Nolke caught up with the girl and she stood still as he spoke to her. She shook her head and walked on but Nolke caught her shoulder and spun her round to face him. Parker looked at his watch. He had an hour before his transmission schedule came up. He locked the door behind him and raced down the stairs. Across the road he could see Nolke gripping the girl's arm. Nolke was not in uniform, he was wearing a black leather coat and a beret.

When Parker got up to them he stopped and said to Sabine, "Hello, darling," then turned to look at Nolke, puzzled but amiable. "I don't think I know you, monsieur."

Nolke's eyes went over Parker's face. "Your papers."

"Who the hell are you to ask for my papers?"

"Gestapo, my friend. Let's have your papers."

Parker kept his eyes away from the girl. "I've never heard of Gestapo people in Périgueux. Let's go to the police station." And he slid his arm into the girl's and stood waiting, looking at Nolke, who hesitated and then stepped into the road and waved down an army lorry.

"You," he said to Sabine, "you can go, but I'll be seeing you again." He opened the lorry door, shoved Parker in and then squeezed alongside him and told the driver to go to the Gestapo Headquarters.

"NOW, MY FRIEND, I'll have your papers." Nolke stood over Parker as he sat in the chair alongside the table. Parker gave him the papers and sat silent. Nolke laid them on the table, bending over to examine them carefully. After a few minutes he walked over to the door and locked it.

"These are forged, my friend. You're really in the shit." He stared at Parker's impassive face and his fist came out so suddenly that Parker flinched even before the knuckles split his cheek. He could feel blood running down to his jaw but he didn't take his eyes off Nolke. If Nolke had been sure that his papers were forged he wouldn't have needed to use the rough stuff.

"What's your name?"

"Chaland. Charles Chaland."

"What's your work?"

"I service and repair agricultural machinery."

"What's the girl's name?"

And Parker knew that Nolke had just been trying a pick-up. He gave no answer and Nolke's big fist blinded him as it crashed between his eyes.

"Who is she?"

"Go to hell." Nolke's boot got him expertly under his knee-cap and he fought against unconsciousness. The chair fell backwards and his head struck the floor. He tried to struggle up but the room tilted and he blacked out.

When he came to Nolke was sitting at the desk drinking coffee. He barely glanced at Parker as he slowly stood up. Then as if he had just noticed Parker the German threw his identity card and his travel pass on the floor.

"In future don't interfere when a German officer is talking to a lady. I'll be looking out for you, my friend." He nodded his dismissal.

The cold air gripped Parker as he stood outside the building. It was just before curfew and the streets were almost empty. He steadied himself with one arm on a wall as he moved off slowly. At the corner he halted, it seemed impossible to take another step and when a car stopped the noise of its brakes made him groan. He saw the cobbles coming up at his face and then it was all over.

WHEN HE AWOKE he could see the moon through the tops of bare-branched trees, one eye was closed and the other quivered without stopping. Sabine's shadow fell across his face and a cold wet cloth touched his forehead. He turned his head slightly, saw Bonnier crouching beside him, his breath clouding in the cold air.

"How d'you feel, chief?"

"Fine."

Bonnier gave a grunting laugh. "You don't look it. Can you eat? We've got a chicken, special donation from the locals. Try some chicken soup, chef's recommendation."

Parker turned his head slowly and saw Sabine's serious face. The dark eyes watched him, and he realized that her arm was under his head, supporting him gently. He sighed with pain as he took a breath and blood came from his nose and mouth when he struggled to sit up.

When Bonnier and the girl lifted him so that he could drink the soup he saw that there were tears on Sabine's cheeks. He lay back and the girl's soft fingers stroked his face. "Look at the stars, Charles. The same stars are over England." When, involuntarily, he shivered, she took off her thick jacket and covered his body as best she could.

5

André Frenez was waiting for him outside the station at Limoges. Neither man acknowledged the other, but Parker kept Frenez in sight as they walked towards the river. At Pont St. Étienne, Frenez turned left and waited for Parker to catch up.

Parker had only met Frenez a few times before he had been recalled to Baker Street, and in those days Frenez was the leader of an independent réseau. He was one of those men whom Parker instinctively disliked. He was a lawyer in Limoges and moved among the bourgeoisie and the aristocrats with an ease that annoyed them as much as it annoyed Parker. Frenez's pale blue eyes missed nothing and the half smile that seemed permanently on his lips was all too frequently openly amused with a cynicism that was typical of the man. Frenez was always sure of himself.

"Who fixed your face, Chaland?"

"Nolke."

"He was up here last week. We're going now to the water-bailiff's cottage. There are a lot of people for you to meet and I want to talk with you first."

The water-bailiff was obviously impressed by his visitor. He tactfully said that he needed to check the river levels and left them alone in the old cottage.

Frenez sat in his chair leaning forward, his whole body indicating his energy and impatience. "The messages I've had from you seem to want to hold us back."

"That's partly true. I don't want to stir up the Germans too early. Apart from the reprisals I don't want them to see a pattern of targets."

Frenez nodded. "Any idea when it's going to be—the landings?"

"No, André, and I've got to say the same to everybody—if I did know I couldn't say. But we'll fix an internal radio net quite soon. Late evening. No traffic if there's no news."

"I hear you got Lachaise away from the Germans. Any news of her?"

"We got her to Algiers alive. I've heard nothing since and I don't expect to."

"How d'you get on with Bonnier?"

"O.K."

"I wouldn't trust those bastards, they're getting set to take over when it's all over."

"So is de Gaulle."

Frenez smiled a cold smile. "By the way, I've got a communications problem."

"What's that?"

"I've got twenty-three people I need to keep contact with in the réseau and they're spread all round the countryside. I need three, maybe four, letter boxes and I haven't got one."

"You'd better do what we do, use beehives. You stick the messages down the side of the tray. Nobody fiddles about with beehives."

Frenez grinned. "I like that, Chaland. Let's go back into town. You'll be staying out of town tonight at Chalus. The butcher there is one of ours. He'll be doing guard all night with his son. Your visit is the next best thing to having Charles de Gaulle in the parlour."

"And how are things with you, André?"

Frenez looked up quickly, surprised. He was silent for a moment before he answered.

"I get tired of being the omniscient boss. The guy who has all the answers. You must feel the same, Chaland." Frenez sighed. "And I don't like this patient, waiting game. I'd like to walk into an SS officers' mess and just spray them with a machine-gun and call it a day."

"Would you like a week's relaxation in London?"

Frenez leaned back, shaking his head. "No, I'll just see it out, Chaland. But thanks for asking. London never does."

"It's my job to ask, not theirs. What are you going to do after the war. Politics?"

"You're crazy, Chaland." Frenez leaned forward again, his eyes alight. "When it's over I'm going to Saigon and I'll have a villa covered with bougainvillaea. Sunshine all day, every day, and I'll show the rich locals how to avoid income tax for large fees and I shall live happy ever after." And as he stood up smiling, Parker realized that he might actually mean what he said.

Back at the cottage at Puy Henry, Parker spent the evening reading his copies of the signals traffic from the three réseaux and two things were clear. The Germans were stepping up their action in the area and Parker's groups were losing morale because of his instructions to hold back.

Sabine brought a message from Bonnier. His maquisards were growing in number and they needed still more arms and ammunition urgently. The Germans were mounting patrols against them now so that they had to keep on the move all the time. He looked up from the paper to the girl. "I need a night's sleep, Sabine. We'll cycle over to Bonnier's tomorrow. You'd better stay."

The girl dusted the rooms while Parker sat with maps and his notebook. She got them a meal and tuned the old-fashioned bakelite radio to the BBC French service. Almost at the end of the messages was the coded clearance for a drop for the réseau in the Corrèze. The girl was watching his face. Apart from the twitching muscles under the bruising around his eye she saw the tell-tale white streaks at his mouth that signalled his exhaustion.

"Why not sleep long tomorrow, Charles? You need rest if you're to carry on."

He turned his head slowly to look at her. "There was a message for us on the radio. There's to be a drop tomorrow night for my old réseau at Brive. I'll have to organize it."

"Well, go to bed now."

"I need to sit up until curfew time in case anyone comes."

"I could do that."

He smiled. "You'd never be able to wake me."

"We'll see."

He stood up slowly and wearily. "You're going to make somebody a wonderful mother."

She blushed and went out to the primitive kitchen, and after a few minutes he followed her and sat on a stool as she bent over

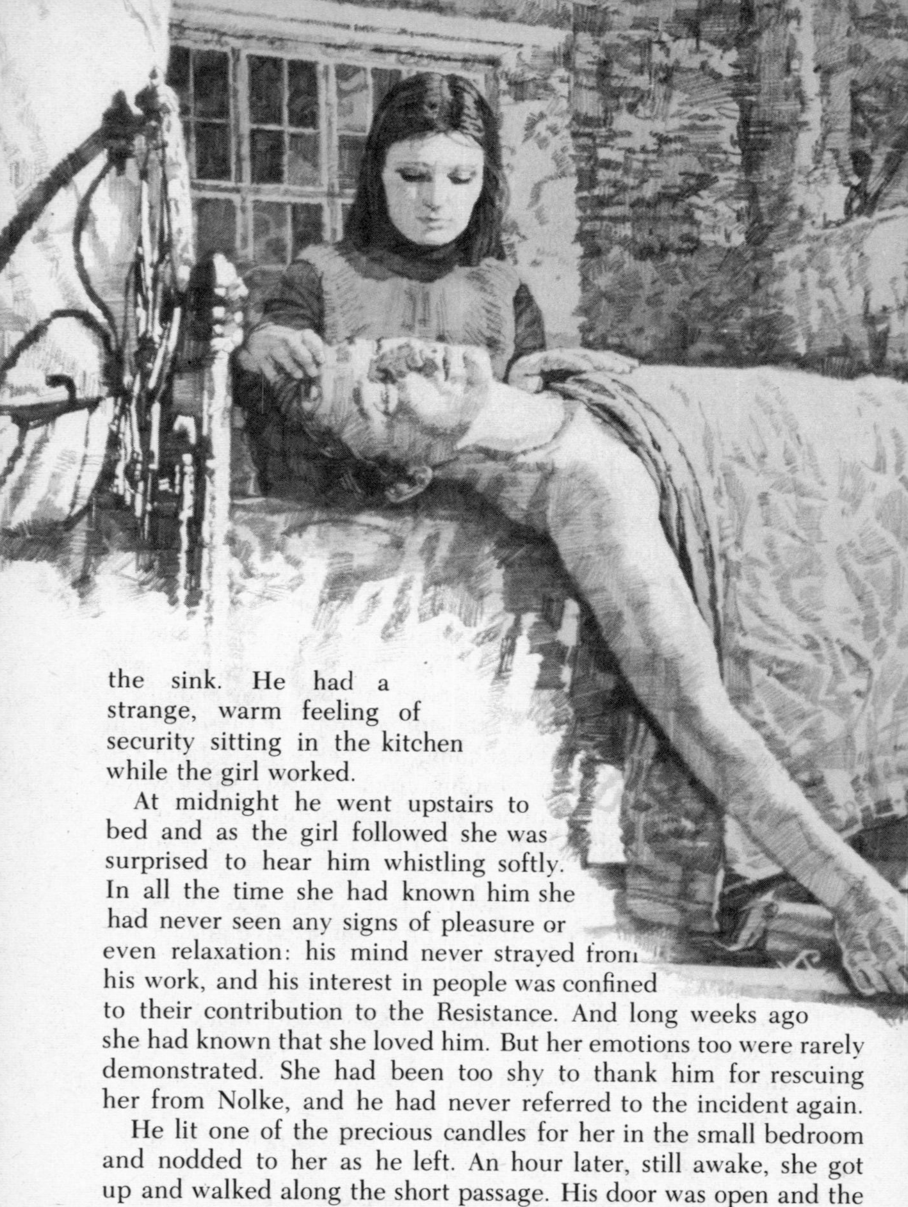

the sink. He had a strange, warm feeling of security sitting in the kitchen while the girl worked.

At midnight he went upstairs to bed and as the girl followed she was surprised to hear him whistling softly. In all the time she had known him she had never seen any signs of pleasure or even relaxation: his mind never strayed from his work, and his interest in people was confined to their contribution to the Resistance. And long weeks ago she had known that she loved him. But her emotions too were rarely demonstrated. She had been too shy to thank him for rescuing her from Nolke, and he had never referred to the incident again.

He lit one of the precious candles for her in the small bedroom and nodded to her as he left. An hour later, still awake, she got up and walked along the short passage. His door was open and the moonlight splashed across his face. He looked an old man, his eyes black sockets in the deep shadow from the moonlight, his cheeks hollow and the skin over his nose drawn tight. One naked arm hung down to trail on the floor. Despite the coolness of the night there was sweat on his forehead and along the edge of his jaw.

She sat beside him for an hour. Everything was still and silent in the night until far away a church clock struck two and she went back to her bed.

THEY CYCLED together the next morning to meet Bonnier at Nontron. The meeting was in the private office of a small shoe factory. Its owner, Langlois, was a mild, gentle man with the air of a schoolmaster, but appearance belied the facts. Langlois had led six-man teams on fifteen sabotage missions and his men were efficient and disciplined.

Parker, Bonnier, Langlois and the girl sat around the old-fashioned desk and Bonnier started in straightaway. "How long do we have to wait, Chaland? London keeps you in the picture but nobody tells us anything. When will the landings be?"

Parker looked across at him. "I'll arrange a big arms drop. We'll be able to do that next moon, just another four weeks. And that will be the last drop of arms you get before you use them."

The others sat silent, aware of the significance of what Parker had said. Finally Bonnier spoke. "I'll believe it when it happens."

Parker's eyes half closed in momentary anger. "You and your men would still be running round with a few pitchforks if it hadn't been for London. No doubt you get your marching orders from Moscow but if it was left to them you'd rot."

Langlois had seen the resentment on Bonnier's face and he leaned forward. "Michel, in a short while we shall all have much to do. We must spend the time in between preparing. The landings will only be the start, our part in harassing the Germans will be vital."

Bonnier stood up, and beckoning to Sabine, he left.

PARKER HAD A rendezvous in Périgueux with Devereux that evening, and as he walked down the street he saw a man on the opposite side of the road watching the café. He was wearing a raincoat although the skies were pale blue and the sun was strong.

Only German security men wore raincoats on a warm spring evening. Parker walked past the café. Devereux was sitting at one of the tables reading a paper. They had frequently met at the café and it looked as if someone had tipped off the Germans. The net was closing in on him, or on Devereux.

He walked back past the café so that he could make certain that Devereux had seen him. The watcher was still there. He walked back to the centre of the town. He left a message for Devereux with the woman at the cash desk of the cinema, and he left a second message that would give the garage address with the porter at the Hotel Domino.

It was two hours before Devereux arrived at the garage. And he had changed his clothes in the meantime to workmen's overalls.

"You're sure you've not been tailed?"

"I was tailed all right. There were two of them but I gave them the slip at the cathedral. I went back to my place and changed."

"Any idea who they were?".

"They were Nolke's men."

"Who were they looking for?"

"Must be you. If they knew me they'd have picked me up."

Parker put both hands flat on the table and looked up at Devereux. "Somebody's keeping the Germans informed. Any idea who it could be?"

Devereux leaned back in his chair. "Has Frenez lost any men to the Germans recently?"

"Yes, four, but they were all killed."

"Did they all die immediately?"

"I don't know."

Devereux sighed. "I find it impossible to see anyone in the Resistance as a traitor. Maybe someone could talk too much. But a traitor—no."

Parker pursed his lips. "You're too nice a man, Devereux. For me anyone could be a traitor. All it needs is the right pressure—a wife, a pretty daughter." He looked at his watch. "We haven't got long until curfew. How are your group?"

"We've done two locomotives with that grease they dropped," Devereux said. "They did about ten kilometres and then ground to a standstill. Repairs will take six months."

"How's 'Toinette?"

"She's O.K."

Parker sensed the second's hesitation. "Except for what?"

"She's moved in with her fellow."

"Did you give her permission?"

"Yes."

"You knew I had forbidden it?"

"Yes, chief, but she's desperate for some security. There have been three raids by the Germans in this district in the last two weeks. The fellow helps where we can't."

Parker's voice was cold. "You'd better get on your way, Jean-Luc. I'll contact you the day after tomorrow."

6

It had taken two weeks to arrange the latest dropping zone for Bonnier's maquisards and it was the end of April before the moon and the weather were suitable.

By mid May the training had begun to pay off. The three réseaux had laid down good communications between them and detailed plans had been made for the sabotage of hundreds of targets. There was talk everywhere of an Allied invasion and there were rumours of landings on the Mediterranean coast and at Bordeaux. Parker had warned all concerned that the talk of landings was being put around by the Germans in the hope of the Resistance showing its hand prematurely.

On 20 May a group of Bonnier's maquis disobeyed orders and attacked a German column in the steep hills just north of St. Pardoux. They caught the Germans in what looked like a perfect ambush, a narrow road flanked by deeply wooded steep hills on each side with tree trunks across the road to halt the vehicles. But they learned their first expensive lesson. The Germans accepted the challenge and had carried out a ruthless, angry, destruction patrol that left twenty-five of Bonnier's men dead and seven badly wounded before the Germans went on their way north. The Germans lost ten men and a burnt out scout car. The lesson was that if you want to take pot shots at an armoured column you must expect to pay a high price for your bravery or stupidity.

Politics were intruding into the fabric of the Resistance, and London ordered Parker to use extreme caution with Bonnier. It was now the official line of the French Communist Party to denigrate all Resistance operations controlled from London. But Bonnier still accepted Parker's orders. There was no reluctance in his co-operation and he had transferred Sabine to Parker's small headquarters staff to act as courier to his maquis and to the leaders of the three réseaux under Parker's command.

On the evening of 3 June Parker had been sitting with Bonnier, Sabine, Devereux and Frenez in the farm cottage at Puy Henry, listening to the BBC French service. Parker had a feeling that that day would be the start, and he listened intently to the coded messages.

When the announcer had finished it was more than he could do to hold back the news. He stood up, turned off the radio and held up his hand.

"My friends, the waiting is over. Some time in the next ten days we shall receive our order to attack. I must emphasize that nothing will be done beyond last-minute reconnaissance until I tell you. If that order is disobeyed the invasion could fail. The Germans will know that the landings are imminent. I want to say now that London relies on this circuit to play its part in fighting the Germans in the way we know best. Sabotage and harassment. There will be room for a thousand heroes and they will have my every support, but we are fighting a grim battle. The Germans will have no mercy, and they will no longer need to pretend. Bonnier, Devereux, go back to your men—Frenez, you will stay here tonight." He turned to Sabine. "Sabine—a bottle."

And they had drunk their toasts and thought their own thoughts, and gone. Their excitement was barely contained. Only Parker seemed unaffected by the news. He had sat in the garden with Frenez and Sabine, watching the sun go down across the valley. He felt a great peace in his mind that the time of real action was so near. He wondered when he would get the message from England ordering him to direct the special operations of his réseaux that must follow the Allied landings. There would be a special BBC message and the next radio signal that they would receive would be in a code for him alone.

NEXT MORNING, as if to bring all concerned a cautionary tale, Baker Street sent a signal listing the nine SOE agents in Paris and the Occupied Zone who had been captured in the previous month. There circuits were no longer to be considered secure. Parker had never contacted any of them but he had heard of them during training and they were rated as highly experienced people.

He and Sabine sat listening that night to the BBC broadcast. There were long lists of messages but none was for him. It was the next evening when his release message was broadcast, and as he heard it he knew that one kind of war was over and a new one was about to begin.

Later, he and Sabine played chess on a pocket set until midnight. She won every game although she doubted if he noticed:

PARKER CYCLED to Périgueux on June 5 and used Devereux's courier to pass on his orders. The objectives now were to help take some of the pressure from the Allied troops and to harass the German troops who would be drawn up as reinforcements. The Germans would be fighting on French soil, but from now on they would be fighting for their survival and the survival of Germany. It would be a bitter struggle.

Parker had monitored all the BBC programmes on June 5 but on the morning of the 6th he missed Eisenhower's statement about the Allied landings. It was mid-morning before he learned that the landings had started, twenty-four hours later than expected. That afternoon two SS divisions moved into his area and the public exhilaration quickly turned to fear. The civilian population were treated with open hostility now, and French traitors were denouncing as members of the Resistance all those whom they hated or envied.

Baker Street ordered a special concentration on the crack SS division *Das Reich* which was moving up from the south to Normandy. Parker specified the targets and the attack plan with the group at Brive and headed north to Limoges to get Frenez's men alerted for their part against the SS division. He sent a courier to Bonnier ordering him to cut the N21 and the N20 roads at as many places as the maquis could cover. For two days and nights Parker moved around the Limoges area planning the sabotage patrols and the snipers. When the *Das Reich* division got thirty kilometres outside Limoges they would be out of Parker's area and others would carry the load, but he intended to show what could be done by determined men.

Frenez had shaken him awake mid-morning of June 8.

"Chaland. There's a courier from Devereux."

Parker sat on the side of his bed as the young man spoke.

"Monsieur Devereux sent me up to tell you that the Germans have come to a complete halt at Souillac. They won't be up here for another twenty-four hours."

"How did you hold them?"

"We mined the roads in ten places at hundred-metre intervals. They've got armoured vehicles stuck down the holes and they can't get their recovery teams up the road to them. They're having to dismantle them."

"What about the rest of the programme?"

"All the pylons are down except those at Brive. They're guarded by SS. The railway line is out at Sarlat and Gourdon."

Parker sat naked at the rough table and scribbled a note to Devereux. His depression was lifting and he was beginning to catch the feeling of elation that the others had had for days.

At Chalus, the next day, they watched the SS *Das Reich* columns cross the village square and halt for breakfast just outside the town. Parker and Frenez took their men three kilometres north of the town, and assembled them along the crest of the hill on the south side of the road. There were twenty men in the party but Parker had sent most of them off to blow the culvert just north of Oradour.

It was a hot morning, and as they looked across the landscape there was a mist coming up from the fields where the cattle stood knee deep in the small streams lined with poplars. The slope of the hill was thick with buttercups and in the shallow dip where they lay the white heads of cow parsley gave them cover. Parker pulled his Bren gun back gently against the springs of the bipod and put his eye to the sight. There was no wind and the range was set for five-hundred metres. The road was a little farther away but there would be a fall in the trajectory to allow for. And then they came.

A squadron of eight motor-cyclists followed by four scout cars. Then came the troop carriers and trucks, their canvas covers down and machine-guns mounted on the metal framework. Parker watched carefully. The troops sat with rifles at the ready, and as he looked down the road he could see the dust from the long column as it spread over three kilometres down the road.

Parker waited for a suitable target. He didn't want to attack until at least a third of the SS division was past their ambush. Then he saw what he wanted. A fresh-faced blond German with the insignia of a Sturmbannführer. He was talking to his driver as he sat back in his open car. He had a Luger in his right hand and his left hand held the windscreen frame to steady his ride. Parker said: "The blond pig in the car in two minutes. I'll fire first. Just one magazine each and we scatter. I'll see you in Limoges at six."

Parker pressed the long grass back on each side of the gun barrel and lifted the stock to his shoulder, slid the catch up to continuous fire, lined up the blond German in the sights and squeezed the trigger. The car's windscreen went white and the black-uniformed officer half stood and fell back, and the car hit the ditch and went on its side. Parker swung the gun to the left and traversed it along two troop lorries then back to the halted vehicles behind the car. A tanker went up in a burst of black smoke and he saw men jumping from the carriers. Then, crouching, he scrambled back down the slope, the gun bouncing against his right leg as he ran. He fell again and again in his headlong rush. The van was there and he threw the gun into the back and started the engine. An hour later he was in Rochechouart heading due east for Limoges. He left the Bren in the van at the laundry near the cathedral.

DEVEREUX PICKED him up at six and they drove straight back to Périgueux. There were two road-blocks on the way but the chain-harrow in the back of the van had seen him through both of them.

He was back at Puy Henry at ten o'clock, and after they had eaten he walked along the ridge of the hill with Sabine and they sat in the dusk looking across the valley. There was the scent of clover in the evening air and it was tempting to imagine that the war was a figment of a tired mind.

He turned to the girl. "Did you pass the messages to Bonnier today?"

She nodded. "Yes. His news was not good. They attacked a German column near Thiviers. The Germans went after them and used artillery. Bonnier lost almost a hundred dead and fifty wounded."

He saw the girl shiver.

"Anything else?"

"I'm afraid there is. The Gestapo man saw me in Périgueux. He stopped me and asked for my papers."

"So?"

"He wants to sleep with me."

"What did you do?"

"I said I would see him tomorrow evening."

"Did he ask where you live?"

"Yes. I said I lived at Lemaire's garage. It was stupid but I was frightened. He walked back with me there to check, and Lemaire backed up my story. He's picking me up there at nine tomorrow."

"And what are you going to do?"

She shrugged. "I'll sleep with him. If I don't he'll arrest everybody at the garage. He's had other girls the same way. One girl left the town and went to Paris and he arrested her parents and had them deported. They're in Belsen now."

He looked at the soft brown eyes and the full mouth, and saw them for the first time as other men saw them. She was wearing a silk blouse and he could see the fullness of her breasts and the brown skirt emphasized her long shapely legs. The girl was no longer the girl who washed up in the kitchen, but a girl desired by men. Parker stood up and held out his hand to her to help her stand up. Her hand was small and firm and warm, and he held it all the way back to the cottage.

Next morning Parker had trouble starting the van but they were in Périgueux by midday. He phoned Lemaire at the garage from a call-box and for the first time he gave him the address of his room in the town.

When Lemaire came Parker looked at him intently before he spoke. "There's a farm just outside Brantôme where Devereux took me and 'Toinette the night I came back. D'you know it?"

"Yes, it's the de Baissac farm."

"I want a hole dug there for tonight. A deep one."

Lemaire nodded and smiled. "About two metres long and one metre wide, eh?"

"Bring back a piece of his farm equipment as cover for me."

"O.K. I'll be back in time to join in the fun."

"You'll close the garage at six. There'll be nobody there but me. Understood?"

Lemaire shrugged. "Why leave it to chance, Chaland? Two can make it easier than one. Why give away an advantage?"

"He won't have a chance."

PARKER HAD drawn the curtains on the office window at Lemaire's garage and left a chink of light showing. He sat in the open door of a ramshackle Citroën that was hidden by a lorry. The Luger lay heavy in the pocket of his overalls, its butt free of the pocket. He could hear evening noises from the direction of the town. His eyes never left the open gates of the yard.

It was nine thirty when Nolke came through the big gates and he was carrying a box of chocolates. He walked quite slowly, looking to both sides of the yard. It was dusk now and the light from the window was a thin bar along the concrete.

Nolke paused at the door and listened, his hand poised to knock and his head bent in concentration. His hand hesitated and he moved aside to the window and bent to look through the gap in the curtains. As he stood up the butt of the Luger smashed behind his ear. The box of chocolates fell from his hand as his knees crumpled, and Parker's hands went under his arms, catching him before he fell. Parker straddled the German and his thumbs went up behind Nolke's ear. The German shuddered violently as Parker's body weight came through his thumbs on the pressure point.

Parker lifted the body onto the back of the van and covered it with sacks and the cultivator frame. Lemaire was waiting for him at the farm outside Brantôme and he wondered in silence why Parker had thrown a box of chocolates in with the corpse. Boxes of chocolates were hard to come by.

They went back to Périgueux together and checked the office

at the garage. There was nothing there to connect the place with Nolke. Parker walked back to his room, where the girl was waiting. It was too near curfew to go back to Puy Henry.

There was only one bed and he switched out the lights as he and the girl undressed. He arranged his clothes on the floor as a pillow for his head and spread his jacket over his body. As he lay there his mind was on a treadmill of the events of the last two days but as his eyes closed he was aware only of the smell of dust from the threadbare carpet. . . .

It seemed only minutes before the knocking on the door, but it was, in fact, almost two hours later. The knocking came again. Urgent, almost frantic.

"Who is that?"

"Frenez. Let me in, Chaland, quickly."

Parker opened the door and Frenez's face was white and strained. His coolness and elegance might never have existed. Parker led him to a chair by the table. He saw the girl sitting up in bed watching them.

"It's the SS, Chaland. Two hundred of them this morning." Frenez was shaking, his whole body racked as if by an ague. "It was a reprisal for our attack yesterday." He groaned and put his head in his hands. "They wiped out Oradour. They came at two o'clock and killed them all. Men, women and children. They machine-gunned the men in the square. Just mowed them down. They put the women and children in the church and set fire to it and machine-gunned those who tried to get out."

He laid his head on the table and sobbed. "And they killed the wrong people, by God. We were at Oradour-sur-Vayres, and they went to Oradour-sur-Glaue instead. . . . Six hundred innocent people dead, Chaland, because of what we did."

Parker was pulling on his trousers as he looked at Frenez. The man was ill, near collapse. Parker crept down the stairs and phoned for the doctor. When he came, half an hour later, he took the still distraught Frenez away in his car.

The girl was sitting up in bed as Parker closed the door behind him, and she saw the grim cast of his face as he leaned back against the door. She pushed aside the thin blanket and walked over to him. She slid off the dirty jacket, unfastened the belt at his waist and as his trousers fell to his feet she lifted each foot free of the coarse cloth. He walked with her like a child to the bed. As he lay with his eyes closed she could feel him shivering and her arms went round him. His head cradled against her shoulder, his face against her breasts. She touched his cheek gently and said: "Try to sleep, Charles. Try to sleep."

He shook his head. "I don't think I'll ever sleep again," he said.

"You will, my love." She pulled him to her and lay with her eyes open as he took her, urgently and fiercely. When it was over he lay alongside her and he was almost instantly asleep. All through the night she lay beside him looking at his face, touching his hair. The nightmare of the last two days had been more than even he could take.

When Parker awoke, the sleep and the new day seemed to have restored his confidence. She had saved a fresh egg for his breakfast and as they sat together at the small table he seemed to have a need to talk. He had told her about his mother and father, and the house in Birmingham, as if it were something she was entitled to know. She realized that he was telling her more than he told the others. Their relationship had changed.

He had to leave at two o'clock to meet Bonnier, but before he left he arranged for Lemaire to take her back to Puy Henry.

7

During the next six weeks there were nine arms drops. In early August, 'Toinette was to return on the next Lysander operation, due in ten days' time.

Early in the month, Parker spent two days with Frenez and some of his group leaders. Frenez had settled back into his old role, helped by the knowledge that the German atrocities at Oradour and elsewhere had not frightened the population, but angered and embittered them enough to attack openly the known traitors and collaborators and to support the Resistance groups.

On Parker's return from seeing Frenez in Limoges, Devereux had bad news for him. The Abwehr had put top priority on the capture of Parker. There were posters going up in the area offering 100,000 francs for information leading to Parker's arrest.

'TOINETTE USED the old garage store room for her transmissions. There were old charts showing tyre pressures for different cars hanging askew on the back of the door, and a calendar for 1940 that had been treasured for the half-naked girl advertising tyres.

There was a small table which stank of oil with a metal vice clamped to one edge, and the radio was inside a concealing framework of cardboard boxes with the aerial slung up over one of the angle irons supporting the tin roof. 'Toinette sat at the table to transmit and receive, and one of Lemaire's men always stood outside the window with another at the gates watching for Germans.

She was taking down a long signal from London confirming priority targets, and she had one earpiece of the headphones tucked in her hair so that she could hear a shouted warning. There was no ventilation in the store and sweat had dripped onto her pad. She wiped her mouth with the back of her hand and went on working. Ten minutes later the transmission closed and London signed off.

'Toinette pulled off the headphones from the tangle of her hair and leaned back in her chair. As always she looked at the window to see which of Lemaire's men would help her put away the radio. But the man who was looking through the window was a stranger and he was pointing a Luger at her. As she stood up the gun jabbed at the glass and the window pane shattered.

"Don't move, mam'selle. Just stay quite still." As he walked round the shack to the door she raced for the window and her knee was on the sill when his hand grabbed her hair and she fell back screaming.

The German stood looking down at her as she sprawled on the floor and he turned briefly as another man came through the door. He stood alongside the man with the gun and looked down at her.

"This is her, Gunther. Let's take her back." He reached down and grabbed the neck of her blouse and jerked her to her feet.

As they took her through the garage she saw Lemaire and four of his men. They were manacled and there was blood on their faces and clothes. Nobody moved or spoke as they led her past the little group. She stumbled as they pushed her ahead of them to the black car that was parked in the yard. She was shoved into the back seat with the Gestapo men on each side of her. The driver let in the clutch and the car moved off quickly. As they left Périgueux she knew they were taking her to the Gestapo house on the far side of the bridge.

The big iron gates were open as the car swung into the driveway and pulled up in front of the big house. The poplars cast long shadows across the lawns as the sun went down behind the low hills.

The hallway was empty except for a big switchboard and two operators. The two men took the girl up the wide curving stairway to the first floor. They pushed her to the farthest office and the hand-painted lettering on the door said "Gunther Heine". The man with the gun pushed her inside and waved her to the chair by the desk. The other man said something in German, laughed, and walked away. The man she assumed was Heine sat down at the desk and laid the Luger on it. Then he leaned back and looked at the girl.

"What's your name?"

"Dupont. Antoinette Dupont."

"Where do you live?"

"At the garage."

"There's no living accommodation there. Where do you live?"

The girl was silent. He turned to look out of the window. After a few minutes he turned back to her. "It's stupid, my dear, to play the heroine. It's a lovely summer evening. You should be out with some young man, not sitting here. These people don't care about you, you know. You've been arrested, so they'll replace you, and they'll commit more stupidities and the innocent population will suffer. What do they achieve? The armies will decide the war, not these schoolboys playing games."

He pulled out a drawer and pushed across a packet of Gauloises. "Have a cigarette."

"I don't smoke."

He smiled. "You do, my dear. Just look at the nicotine on your right-hand fingers."

He stood up. "What times are your radio schedules?"

She shook her head. "I am an officer in the British Army. I will give you my name, rank and number."

His harsh laugh startled her. "My dear young woman, you are in civilian clothes, you were caught working an illegal radio transmitter—you are a spy and we are entitled to treat you as such unless you co-operate, and I'm afraid that won't be very nice." He walked round the desk to stand in front of her. "Well, my dear, what is it to be? A sensible discussion in private between you and me or. . . ."

The girl said nothing but he could see that she was trembling.

"It will be your choice, mam'selle. Not mine."

He watched her face and then walked back to his desk and pressed a bell. She could hear it ringing far across the building. There was the clatter of boots along the landing and an officer in SS uniform came in with four SS men. Heine waved to the girl and said in French, "Persuade her." And he turned at the door and said to the girl, "I'll see you in half an hour." And the door closed.

The SS officer was a big man, his hair cut short almost to his scalp. There were heavy pock-marks on his cheeks and neck and he stood with hands on his hips. He stood in front of the girl and said in bad French. "What time you go on air, Fräulein?"

She made no answer. She remembered what they had said when she was training—"Hold out for forty-eight hours to let the others disperse and then talk as little as you have to. Be unconscious as soon as you can. That uses up time."

His hand roughly lifted her chin so that she was forced to look at him. "One more chance, Fräulein. Only one."

His thumb pressed into her chin and she closed her eyes, hunching her shoulders to take the blow.

But his hand was at the collar of her blouse and it pulled sharply. He wrenched at her clothes until the blouse hung in tatters and she fell backwards off the chair as he loosened the leather belt of her skirt. His fingers dug deep in her long hair and pulled her to her feet. She could smell his stale breath as his hand grabbed the thin strip of her panties across her hips and with two sharp tugs it was broken. As she struggled his other fist smashed in a blinding explosion on her nose. Then her feet were off the floor as he flung her on the desk. The edge caught her spine a sickening blow and then he was on her. They took turns having her and she was faintly aware of voices raised in anger before she lost consciousness.

Heine stood watching the girl come back to consciousness. She was still naked, her hands handcuffed behind her, her arms over the back of the chair. There was blood caked on her mouth and breasts from her broken nose, and blood still trickled from her swollen lips.

As Heine watched, the girl lifted her head. One eye was completely closed and she turned her sound eye away from the light of the window and saw him.

"Are you going to co-operate now, mam'selle?"

The girl didn't answer.

"The boys are still enthusiastic, my dear. It's them or me."

She lifted her blood-caked face: "When it's all over it will be your turn. The others will still find you wherever you are."

Heine pulled up another chair and sat in front of her. "I am not asking you to betray your friends, my dear. Just your schedules and your security check words. Nobody will ever know."

A vision of the gardens at Wanborough came into her mind. Trees and lawns and geraniums in pots, and the man had said: "If you talk at all, you'll go on talking. So you don't talk. Don't try and be clever with lies. They'll break you down."

"When we've had a chat you can be released. I give you my word of honour."

She slowly lifted her head. "Is all this," and she nodded at her body, "part of your honour?"

Heine's hand lifted her head roughly by her hair and she could see the anger on his face. "I really can't wait much longer, Antoinette. I shall have to call them back again." Her teeth clamped on his hand and she felt them grate on his bones as he snatched his hand away.

She was alone for a few moments and then the black-shirted hooligans were back.

PARKER HAD been with Bonnier in the hills when Sabine brought the news of 'Toinette's capture.

He went straight back to Périgueux to find Devereux. Already the réseau had moved houses and meeting places. They met late in the afternoon in the vestry at the cathedral. One of Devereux's men stood guard at the door.

"What do they know, Jean-Luc?"

"I don't think they know anything beyond the garage set-up."

"Did they get the radio?"

"Yes, and the code pads and the messages she had taken down from London."

"Where is she?"

"We're not sure. She's probably in the Gestapo house over the river."

"And Lemaire and his men?"

"The Germans shot them at the prison this morning."

"And who betrayed them?"

Devereux sighed. "The girl's lover. They had quarrelled. She wanted to leave him. She preferred one of Lemaire's men."

"That's a reason. Where's the proof?"

Devereux shrugged. "You know that proof is not possible, Chaland. Since the arrests the man has cracked up. He's receiving treatment in the German army field-hospital at Ribérac."

For a moment Parker closed his eyes. When he opened them he said, "Contact Bonnier. I want him to raid the place tomorrow. Send a man who knows the traitor well. I want him killed."

There was knocking at the vestry door. The guard peered in. "There's a messenger for you, chief," and he looked towards Devereux.

"Send him in."

The young boy carried an envelope and stood while Devereux read it. "You can go," he said to the boy, and he handed the paper to Parker.

It just said: "Mademoiselle Dupont died at noon today."

Parker handed back the note in silence. Then he said quietly, "Find out how 'Toinette died so that I can tell London."

SABINE WAS OUT when he got back to the room in Périgueux and the place seemed too empty, too quiet. He walked across to the window and looked out at the street. He wondered which direction she would come from. He missed her.

He leaned against the drab velvet curtains, his head resting against the window frame. He thought of 'Toinette. He remembered seeing her crouched in a small circle on the lawn around an instructor, her fingers connecting and strapping the detonators to some "plastique", the brown eyes looking up for approval. And sometimes he had walked with her to the place where she was billeted, and he had tested her Morse with dit-dah-dit-dah's as they walked.

Parker grew more agitated as the evening wore on and Sabine had not returned. She arrived pale-faced and dishevelled just after ten. There was a bruise on her cheek and blood on her mouth.

"What happened, Sabine?"

"I went to Puy Henry."

"But why?"

There were tears in her eyes. "I was foolish, Charles. I first saw you at that cottage. I wanted a little peace."

"So what happened?"

"The Gestapo were waiting. They checked my papers and I said I had nothing to do with the cottage. I was walking on the hill and I was curious."

"So why the bruises on your mouth?"

"One of the men tried to have sex with me in the barn. I shouted and screamed and a Gestapo officer came. I told him I was pregnant and he took me back to the cottage."

"He could have called a doctor to check if he suspected you. Positive grounds for arrest on suspicion."

The white face looked young and defenceless. "I *am* pregnant, Charles. The doctor told me yesterday."

She saw the astonishment on his face. This was going to be one more load on his back and she wondered what his reaction would be.

Her heart melted as he smiled and held out his arms. She clung to him with her head on his shoulder and he gently stroked her pliant back.

"We'll ask the good Devereux to find a priest to marry us, my love."

He made love to her, gently and tenderly. She felt part of summer, part of the normal world again. And for the first time for months Parker slept soundly, unmoving beside her.

LAWS, STATUTES AND REGULATIONS had been pushed aside and Devereux's men mounted guard inside and outside the small church as the priest performed the ceremony. The organist wove a strand of the "Marseillaise" into the softly played psalm as the priest signed the documents. And down the path to the lych-gate Devereux's men had laid out the traditional bridal path of moss and flowers. They all went back, a quiet, happy group to the room in Périgueux.

There they toasted the groom and his bride. Then they left with the farm van and only Devereux stayed. Parker was giving Devereux new orders when a transmission came through from London. The message was quite short, and when Parker had decoded it he passed it across the table to Devereux. It read: "To LANTERN stop Operation Ratweek stop All groups authorized herewith to eliminate all local personnel of Abwehr, SD and Gestapo stop message ends acknowledge."

Devereux shrugged. "Maybe those boys are waking up at last."

"How many men have you got to spare, Jean-Luc. Tough ones?"

"Three, maybe four."

"That's not enough. I need at least twelve." He stood up. "Send a messenger up to Bonnier and tell him what I want."

"And if his Commie friends object?"

"Then tell Bonnier there will be no more drops. Moscow can send their supplies."

Devereux nodded and left.

PARKER HAD WALKED with the girl down to the bank of the river. They sat on the shallow slope. The river was glassy and slow-moving, blue from the sky with reflections of the yellow irises that flanked its edges. Kingfishers darted and swooped and fish rose to make silent circles on the smooth surface of the water. He laced his fingers in hers and turned to look at her. "I thought I was so observant but I never saw how beautiful you are. I was stupid."

"You'll never be stupid, my love. You had work to do. Too many other things to occupy your mind."

"I think we should find a small cottage near Brantôme."

"Are you sure you want to stay in France? What about England?"

He shrugged. "There's nothing there for me. I belong here."

"And what will you do?"

He smiled. "I'll do what I'm supposed to be doing now. Repair farm machinery. There's going to be money in farming when it's over." He put his arm round her tightly. "What do you want, a boy or a girl?"

"We'll have a boy first and then a girl."

There was a breeze now across the river, bending the rushes and brushing the surface that shimmered in the fading light. For Parker it was a new world. A world in which, like other men, he had a stake. A wife, and a child to be born. They would have a cottage and they would walk to meet him from his work. And those two would be his to care for. An easy, light load compared to what he now had. It was like being unlocked, set free, born again.

8

They sat round the long dining-table at the back of the inn. There were three cars, two trucks and two motor-cycles parked at the edge of the orchard behind the inn. The table was covered with large-scale maps which Devereux had long ago "borrowed" from the Town Hall.

Only Bonnier, Devereux and Parker sat at the table. The others were posted around the inn and checking weapons and ammunition in the stables. Parker sensed the tension between him and Bonnier. He was only chief in name now. Bonnier questioned London's motives and talked of referring the operation to Paris. He was pointing at one of the maps, looking up at Parker as he spoke.

"I'd like to have those boys if you've no objection." His thick finger was pointing at the Gestapo HQ. It was an ideal target for Bonnier and his men, but Parker suspected that the Communist was looking for the applause that came from attacking the best known of the three German counter-intelligence organizations.

He shrugged. "How many men will you need?"

"A driver and eight men."

"There are only fifteen of us all told. And there are four targets."

"I know of three. What's the fourth?"

"There's the Gestapo house across the river."

Bonnier smiled grimly up at Parker. "The place they took that stupid bitch of a radio operator."

"She's dead, Bonnier."

"I know, my friend. I had two men killed finishing off the traitor in the hospital. Remember?"

"You take four men, Bonnier." He turned to Devereux. "You take four men too, Jean-Luc. I'll take the others to cover the Gestapo place and the Abwehr people."

They shared out the vehicles and the weapons, and Parker took the men whom Bonnier and Devereux had left behind. They had synchronized their watches and assembled their own groups in separate rooms.

Bonnier and his men had left just before midnight and Devereux had left at ten minutes past midnight. Parker's was the nearest target.

There was nothing on the road. No people. No vehicles. The curfew was still the law, but even the usual German troops and Feldgendarmerie were not on the streets.

At the house across the river there were two Gestapo officers, four sergeants and three civilian clerks on the premises and Parker had found a servant of the previous owners who had sketched out a rough layout of the house.

The house was set well back from the road. Lights from the windows shone yellow across the drive and the lawns. The wide entrance to the driveway was open, with wrought iron gates fixed back by blocks of stone.

Parker took two men with him over the wall, leaving the others to follow as soon as they heard firing in the house. There was a clump of tall cypresses about halfway across the lawns and Parker crawled there with his men. They lay watching the big entrance door. It was half open and light flowed out and they could hear music from a radio. He was to go in first and the other two would give him covering fire. He wanted to get up to the first floor if possible before he opened fire.

They ran crouching across the driveway and Parker stood flattened against the stone frame of the door as he slowly moved his head to look inside the hall. A civilian sat at a field telephone-exchange in the middle of the hall, reading a book and smoking. No telephone wires had been cut as yet, so that the Germans would not be given any prior warning by dead lines. Parker pointed silently and the others understood and nodded. He grinned as they handed him the sock with wet sand.

As he stood inside the entrance the radio was loud enough to drown any slight sound he might make and he walked firmly to the back of the man at the telephone board. The heavy sock took him behind the ear and Parker caught him before he fell. He laid the inert body on the floor and had made two strides up the broad staircase when he heard the shouts and the clattering of boots and as he turned he saw that the hall was full of Germans in field grey, and as he went to turn again a strong arm crooked across his throat and something metallic struck his hand and the Tommy-gun clattered to the tiled floor. His arms were thrust behind his back and handcuffs snapped. The arm left his throat and as he was released he saw a tall man, elegant in his SS uniform, standing watching him. His lean handsome face showed no emotion and his pale grey eyes watched without blinking. He waved towards the open office and Parker was hustled inside and thrown clumsily onto the chair. The officer walked in slowly and sat on the edge of the desk, one long leg swinging easily.

"Well, m'sieur, you really are in trouble." He lit a cigarette. "We caught your Communist friend at long last, Monsieur Chaland. And we were waiting for you." He smiled a sour half smile. "We've wanted you for a long time."

Parker looked up at the handsome face. "There's no need for us to play games. I'll give you name, rank and number. Nothing else. Just call your thugs."

"Not so much hurry, my hero." He held up his hand. "Where's your radio?"

But before Parker could have spoken the door burst open and two men stood holding up Bonnier. His eyes were closed and his head lolled sideways. Blood covered his face. The SS officer shouted. "Take him away, you fools, take him away." He stamped his foot and his pale face was reddening with anger. "For Christ's sake," he said to no one in particular.

Again he stood in front of Parker. "Are you sure you want the rough stuff, my friend? A pity. You'll talk in the end. They always do."

THREE HOURS LATER he came to. He was naked and his body felt as if it was on fire. He could smell burnt hair but his arms were too heavy with pain to move to find what hair was burnt. A shadow came across his face and he saw the SS man looking at him. He heard him order somebody to fetch the doctor and a few minutes later he heard him say, "For Christ's sake, how can he talk with a dislocated jaw. Fix it. Quickly."

Inside his head he heard the bones grating as the doctor hooked back his jaw. He felt the sweat burst out of him with the pain.

"Chaland, can you hear me?"

Parker made no answer and he closed his eyes.

"Chaland, I know about the girl. The girl named Sabine. I'm checking the church records now for her address."

Parker's eyes opened and there was nothing he could do to stop the tears that slowly ran scalding down his face.

LATER THAT DAY, August 24, General de Gaulle entered Paris. In Warsaw the Poles rose against their German oppressors and the Russians halted their troops the other side of the Vistula and waited until the rising had been ruthlessly crushed by the Germans. The people who organized risings could do the same again some day against their new masters. It was better if their deaths were chalked up to the Germans.

In September SOE operations in France were wound up by London with what some said was indecent haste. There were extraordinarily few medals, and dozens of agents were unaccounted for, slaughtered in one concentration camp or another. In the world outside the Germans were fighting their last battles while their SS compatriots did their best to eliminate the victims who could testify to their crimes.

Sabine Chaland *née* Patou was given two widow's pensions. One from the British and one from the French. And eighteen months later she stood in the rain while an officer from Paris pinned the posthumous Croix de Guerre onto the black dress she wore. The name of Charles Chaland was carved with the other names on the plaque on the north side of the war memorial in Périgueux. The south side was already full of names from World War I.

The baby was a girl and she was baptized Chantal Marie. For almost five years several decent men who knew Sabine's background made tentative advances regarding marriage towards the pretty widow but after that time they gave up.

When the little girl was three they moved to a house in Brantôme to be nearer the school. Those who didn't know wondered why the young widow so frequently toiled up the steep hill at Puy Henry, to sit while the small girl picked wild flowers in the summer, or to stand in winter winds with her dark hair blowing across her cold rosy cheeks.

PART THREE: AUTUMN 1967

1

Bailey was shaving when the memory came flooding back. He could see a picture, a photograph, and there was something wrong. It was six months ago, and the picture was one of the press cuttings in Walters's flat. There were soldiers at the war memorial: he had assumed that they were English, but he realized now that their helmets were French; there was a ridge down the centre. The song on the Palmers' record had been French. And Walters had been seen by the MI6 man at an art gallery in Paris a couple of weeks before he died. And Bailey had forgotten to check Walters's birth certificate.

It would not be possible to check it until the following morning, so he looked along the bookshelves for something to take his mind off Walters. Bailey wasn't an efficient bachelor and that was why he had chosen the two-room flat. His cooking leaned towards tins and fish fingers, and the furniture was accidental, but comfortable.

He took down the still unread Thomson's *Europe Since Napoleon* and put it on the low table beside his chair. He sipped slowly and absent-mindedly at a glass of claret. Thoughts about Walters seeped through. Maybe he was like Walters. They were both holed up in their small sanctuaries. Half hidden from the rest of the world. . . .

Next morning, he waited impatiently in his office for the brown envelope to come up, then emptied the newspaper cuttings onto his desk and sorted through to find the picture of the war memorial. It was brown at the edges and the main area was yellow with age. He walked down the corridor to the laboratory. The assistant laid the photograph under a plastic lens and slowly adjusted the height of the frame. Then he stood aside.

Bailey looked through the flat lens. There were twenty or so men in civilian clothes but wearing decorations—and in the centre a woman holding the hand of a small girl who had a medal pinned to her blouse. Four soldiers had rifles at the present, and a bugler had his bugle to his lips. The monument itself was on the right-hand side of the picture and the editorial cropping had cut off most of the flag that filled the top left corner. It was quite impossible to make out the identity of anybody in the picture.

He slid the cutting from under the lens and turned it over. The text was in French and there were snippets about the harvest and a new bridge at somewhere called Périgueux. He looked at the assistant: "Is it possible to get a ten-by-eight enlargement of the magnified picture?"

"Sure. I'll let you have it by tomorrow midday."

"That'll be fine." He left the cutting with the assistant and went back to his own office.

He looked at the cuttings of the classified advertisements. There were nine of them, all roughly two inches long and he laid them side by side. There was secondhand furniture for sale, offers for landscape gardening, musical instruments, second mortgages, loans up to £5,000 without security, tax advice, and a number of household services. Some advertisements only appeared once and others were repeated in every issue. He saw it straight away. A two-line advertisement that just said "French polishing by skilled men 01-059 6048". The same advertisement appeared on every cutting but each time the telephone number was different. He wrote out a list of the numbers for the Post Office to check for him. Then he drove home.

DEPUTY ASSISTANT COMMISSIONER MURPHY reached for the phone and asked for Paynter. He turned to Bailey. "They'll get him."

Murphy put the receiver back to his ear and pressed the scrambler button. "Paynter? D'you remember the case of the man Walters? The one who killed himself . . . yes, that's the one . . . your chap saw him at the embassy and an SIS man saw him in Paris. . . . No, we didn't close the file. . . . Nick Bailey was on it and he's unearthed a bit more . . . nothing exciting but Walters had some telephone numbers . . . two at the Soviet Embassy, two of Polish Embassy staff, and the Hungarian Press attaché's private number. . . . D'you want him to follow up? . . . I think so . . . fine, leave it with me. Cheers."

Murphy hung up and looked across at Bailey. "Much as I expected. Agrees that you should take the inquiry a bit farther. We can't ignore those bloody telephone numbers."

FROM THE BIRTH certificate all Bailey had got was details of the place of birth. A street in South Croydon, Mason Road. Number 57.

An old man answered the door. He stood with his head askew because one eye was obviously blind.

"Who's that?"

"My name's Bailey, and I wondered if you could help me."

"What about?"

"I'm trying to trace Mr. and Mrs. Walters who used to live here."

The good blue eye looked him over and the old man held the door-frame to maintain his balance. "What d'you want 'em for?"

"I wanted to speak to them about their son."

"Which son would that be?"

"James Fuller Walters."

"You'd better come in, mister, you'd better come in."

The old man turned and shuffled into the dimness of the small house, leaving Bailey to close the door behind him. It was a neat little parlour and the black and white TV flickered in the corner without sound. The old man stood behind the tall armchair, his hands holding its back for support.

"Are you from the social security?"

"No. I just wanted some details."

The old man shook his head slowly. "There ain't no details. He's dead."

"When was this?"

"October. The twenty-first of October, 1944." His lips trembled. "He were just coming up to twenty-two. A good lad, no trouble to me or his ma."

"What happened?"

"He were on leave. He went up to town with his girl. They were hit by the V2 at Marble Arch."

Bailey reached inside his jacket pocket and pulled out his wallet. He handed the photograph of Walters to the old man.

"Have you ever seen that man before, Mr. Walters? Have a good look."

"Oh ah. I've seen 'im lots of times on the telly. Used to be always goin' on about the blacks. Funny name 'e 'ad. Old-fashioned. Now what was it." He snapped his thin fingers. "I know. It was Enoch."

He handed the picture back to Bailey who glanced at it as he slid it into his wallet. There was a resemblance to Enoch Powell. The watching eyes. The square jaw and the quiff of dark hair.

MURPHY HAD Lovegrove with him when Bailey was shown into his office. The Foreign Office man had been brought from the Oval Test Match and was suitably annoyed. Murphy swept his protests aside. "It was you who insisted that we kept it open, Lovegrove. And you were right. So let's hear the story." He waved at Bailey.

"Whoever the dead man is, he isn't James Fuller Walters. The real Walters died in October, 1944."

"There was a phoney application for a passport in the dead man's name, yes?"

"Yes, sir."

Murphy lifted his eyebrows at the FO man. "You really must sort out your people at Petty France. Somebody will have signed the bloody photograph—a so-called doctor or a JP."

Lovegrove's face flushed with anger. "We've got every reasonable check you could have. If we went any further we should have complaints about delays in issuing passports."

Murphy was too professional and too interested in the new information to play politics with the FO man, and he leaned forward towards Bailey. "O.K. You've made the point. A faked passport application off the details of a dead man. Typical KGB. Now find out who Walters really was, and what he was up to."

BAILEY CAUGHT the Paris plane and the MI6 man met him. They sat in a restaurant.

"It's a legitimate gallery. Small. Mainly drawings and water-colours. It's owned and run by a woman, Monique Fleury. Just about makes a living. She's rather nice."

"And it's just a letter box?"

"As far as I know. The French don't take it too seriously."

"What's the name of her KGB contact?"

"He's a low grade. A KGB lieutenant working as the Third Secretary's secretary. It's a Polish name, Andrei Siwecki."

"Old, young, or what?"

"Early thirties."

"And the woman?"

"She's thirty-five, but looks younger."

BAILEY WATCHED the gallery for two days armed with a poor photograph of Siwecki. He had actually seen him twice before he recognized him the third time.

On the third day Bailey wandered into the gallery. He rather liked the water-colour landscapes, which were beautifully evocative of Provence. A young woman offered him a catalogue. "Did any of them appeal to you, m'sieur?"

He smiled at her. "They're all too expensive for me."

Her shoulders went up in a Gallic shrug. "But you don't know the prices."

"They would be too dear."

She looked at him smiling, her head on one side. "You've got an English accent. It's very attractive."

He smiled back at her. "In that case I'll ask you to have dinner with me tonight."

"Tonight the gallery has a little party for the artist." She smiled as she saw his disappointment. "But of course you could come. There will be about thirty all told. Nothing very special."

"Maybe I should be in the way."

The fine eyebrows went up. "We start at eight. Try and come." And she turned away dismissively to straighten a small pile of catalogues on the teak table.

He arrived at eight thirty and there was music playing over the hubbub of conversation and laughter. Siwecki was there, smiling, his arm round the girl's slim waist.

The young man who had let him in took him over to the girl,

and she led him to the table of drinks. "I don't even know your name."

"Nick. Nicholas Bailey. And yours?"

"Monique Fleury."

And with a glass of white wine she took him back to her circle. He bowed and smiled round the group and the conversation went on. He left about ten and the girl held his hand as she walked him to the door. As he stood there he said, "How about I call for you about midday and take you to lunch?"

She nodded. "I'll look forward to that."

AS THEY ATE he quizzed her about the problems of running a small gallery.

Finally she asked him: "And what do you do, Nick?"

"Guess."

She half closed the blue eyes: "Something to do with power. A politician or a lawyer. Or maybe a policeman."

He laughed. "I'm an insurance assessor."

"What on earth is that?"

"If people claim on a loss I check to see that what we pay is a fair amount."

She shrugged smiling. "Exactly. Policeman, judge and jury all rolled into one."

"Can you come out for dinner tonight?"

She shook her head. "Andrei is taking me to dinner."

"Is he your lover?"

She looked at him speculatively. "Andrei is married. His wife is in Moscow; she is the hostage so that he doesn't defect. He is charming, intelligent and good company. And he makes love to me like a wild animal."

She smiled as she saw his face. "And now I've spoilt it all."

He put his hand on the table and instantly her hand turned up to his, her fingers spread to lace through his.

"What sort of man is he?"

She moved glasses around on the table as she considered her reply. "Quite civilized, intelligent, ambitious, a liar." She smiled. "Just a normal, slightly selfish man."

"Siwecki—it's a Polish name, isn't it?"

"I think his father was Polish. He's Russian himself."

"What does he do?"

"God knows. He's a secretary to some embassy official. You never know with Soviet officials what they're up to."

His hand slid up to hold her slim waist. "I'm leaving Paris tomorrow. Can I call you when I come back?"

She smiled warmly. "Of course. I shall look forward to it."

IT WAS EARLY evening when the train pulled into Périgueux and Bailey inquired the way to the Hotel Domino. After eating he checked the address of the local paper and walked around the town. He was asleep well before midnight.

Next morning at the newspaper offices he asked to see the editor, and three minutes later he was shown in. The editor was a man in his middle thirties and he waved Bailey to a leather chair. "Jean Prévert, editor-in-chief. Can I help you, M'sieur Bailey?"

Bailey pulled out the envelope and slid the cutting across the desk. "Could you tell me if that is from your journal, Monsieur Prévert?"

The young man smiled as he looked at the picture. "Yes, but we've improved our quality of newsprint since then. It's very old." His eyebrows rose quizzically. "What else do you want to know?"

"I wonder if you could help me identify any of the people in the photograph."

Prévert looked down at the cutting. "Michaux could. I expect he took the photograph." He pressed one of the buttons on his desk and leaned back. "Is it important?"

"Not really. But it's important to me."

Then the door opened and an elderly man with a mass of yellow-white hair came in, his spectacles up on his forehead. Prévert pointed at the cutting. "Is this one of yours, André?"

The old man pulled down his spectacles and examined the picture. "Yes, chief. It must have been fifty-two or fifty-three."

"Do you recognize any of the people?"

The old man nodded. "Some of them." He pointed at one of the fuzzy, indistinct faces. "That's Devereux, Michel, the brother of Jean-Luc and . . ." he stood upright, turned to Bailey. "This was a commemorative service. We've stopped having them now, but we used to have them every year until about sixty or sixty-one . . ." He pointed at the picture. "They had the Resistance people in the first few rows and then the old soldiers." He paused, caught up in his thoughts, and Bailey looked across at Prévert.

"Maybe I could take M'sieur Michaux for a coffee and have a chat about the people who are in the photograph."

Prévert nodded, smiling. "An excellent idea."

THE OLD MAN leaned on the table, looking at the photograph, and Bailey opened his writing-pad and waited.

"Going from left to right—the front row. First there's old Frenez. He's a lawyer. Pots of money and a great big house. Then there's Servagnat—he's dead now. Next to him there's Devereux, he's there representing his brother Jean-Luc who was executed by the Germans, in forty-four.

"Then we've got the widow Chaland and her daughter. Then there's Mangeul the chemist, he was one of Devereux's men. And then we've got that bastard Bonnier. He's in the top brass of the Communists in Paris. At the back we've got the local worthies, and this little bunch are the ex-soldiers of both wars. I can't make out any of their faces."

"Did the Resistance do much in this area?"

"*Mon Dieu*, they did. They really harassed the Germans. But the Boches got their own back in the end. Most of the Resistance people were caught eventually and executed. Those who survived never really settled down. Frenez and Bonnier are the exceptions."

"Who was the local leader of the Resistance?"

"Oh, that was Chaland. No doubt about that. A young fellow, not local. He'd had training in England for the work. There were rumours that he was English, but I don't think so."

"What's he doing now?"

"He's dead, my friend. That's his widow and daughter in the photograph. He was killed by the Germans. They picked him up during a Resistance raid on a Gestapo HQ. He was shipped off to Natzweiler and he was executed there like the rest of them. He's the real local hero. His widow has a state pension. She was something to do with the Resistance. She's much respected in these parts."

"Where does she live?"

"In Brantôme. I don't know the actual address but any of the locals can tell you."

"Were there any Englishmen in these groups?"

"Oh, yes. Three or four. They were mainly with Bonnier's maquis. He could tell you all about them."

THE WHITE WALLS were high, and swept down to the tall gate where wrought-iron ivy leaves supported a Cross of Lorraine. There was a paved area instead of a garden, with tubs of geraniums and lobelia. The blue house door was standing ajar, and Bailey pushed the brass bell button and waited.

The girl who came to the door was breathtakingly beautiful. Long black hair and hazel eyes, a neat nose and a full mouth that revealed white, even teeth.

"I wonder if I could speak to Madame Chaland?"

"Maman is not here. Why do you want to speak to her?"

"I wanted her help."

"You are English?"

"Yes."

She hesitated. "My mother will be back tomorrow. Can it wait until then?"

"It could, but I'm only here for two days, and there are other people I would like to talk to after I've talked to your mother."

She looked at him for a moment and then stood aside. "You'd better come in for a moment and I will telephone Maman."

The room was dark, but soothing rather than gloomy. The highly polished parquet floor had a patina that rivalled the polish of the grand piano. The young woman waved him to a chair and walked through to the next room. He could hear her voice on the telephone but it wasn't loud enough for him to hear what she was saying.

He was looking at the music that lay open on the piano as she came back into the room. She stood looking at him, her eyes alight. "You play the piano?"

He shook his head and the light faded from her eyes. "Are *you* a musician?" he said.

She laughed. "I am a professional musician." She lifted a linen handbag from an armchair and slid a key ring onto her finger. "Maman says to go over with you now. She's at the cottage."

"It's very kind of you."

AS THE SMALL FIAT turned out onto the main road he said: "How far is the cottage?"

"Oh, not far, it's at Puy Henry. We shall be there in a quarter of an hour. You'd better hold on to something, it's a bumpy ride up to the farm."

She brought the small car to a sweeping stop that threw up a cloud of dust. They were outside a whitewashed farm cottage. She said, "You may find my mother a little aloof. When my father was killed it was really the end of her life. She made another life for my sake but it's not the same."

The woman inside had laid out cards on the rough table. She was playing patience. She stood up as they came in, her face solemn and composed. "Chantal said you had not introduced yourself." She made it sound like a discourtesy.

"I'm sorry. My name is Nicholas Bailey. It was very good of you to see me."

She stood still, her hands clasped in front of her, her eyes guarded. "What is it you wanted to talk about?"

"They told me at the *Courier Français* that your late husband was the head of the Resistance in this area. I wondered if you remembered any of the Englishmen who were here with the Resistance."

"It's a long time ago, m'sieur."

"I know. It was just a hope."

The woman looked at her daughter. "There is some wine in the kitchen. Bring us some glasses, darling."

She waved Bailey to a chair, and sat opposite to him. "There were two or three officers dropped in this area. They were military instructors and I don't remember their names. Maybe SOE could help you."

"I see. Maybe they could."

There was a silence that was broken by the girl returning with the wine and the glasses. He looked across at the woman. "They told me at the newspaper that you worked in the Resistance."

"I worked with my husband. I was not important."

"I understand your husband was a great hero in these parts?"

"He still is. He was a brave man." There was a tension in the silence as they sipped the wine. Bailey felt a compelling burden to break the silence.

"Was he English?"

"Of course." She leaned forward slightly. "But his mother was French and it had come from her, his love of France."

Bailey pushed back his chair. "It was good of you to see me, Madame."

She stood up as if to ensure that he would go. "Not at all, m'sieur. I hope you find the help you want from others."

She held out her hand, and it was warm and dry to the touch. She didn't come out to see them off but she had kissed her daughter affectionately.

The girl drove him back to his hotel and politely declined his invitation to dinner.

FRENEZ HAD BEEN offhand on the phone but he agreed to see Bailey immediately after lunch. The small waiting-room at his office was well appointed. None of the gloom of most country lawyers' offices.

Frenez had white hair, but it only enhanced his good looks. He waved with his long cigarette holder for Bailey to sit in the chair opposite. "What's the trouble, m'sieur?"

"There's no trouble. You said you would see me. My name's Bailey."

"Of course. What can I do for you?" Frenez had the resigned air that he presumably used when listening to importunate litigants.

"I wanted to ask if you could remember the names of the Englishmen who worked in the Resistance in this area."

"With the Resistance or the maquis?"

"Weren't they the same?"

Frenez screwed up his eyes. "Far from it."

"But they both had Englishmen serving with them?"

"The maquis certainly did. Two lieutenants and a captain. But you'd have to talk to Bonnier about them."

"You don't remember their names?"

Frenez shook his head. "I may have heard their names but they were of no interest to me. I was in Chaland's command. And Chaland himself was more French than the French themselves."

"But Chaland wasn't French."

Frenez leaned back in his chair, looking at Bailey through the cloud of cigarette smoke. It was several seconds before he replied. "What are you anyway? Why all the questions?"

"I'm trying to trace what happened to an Englishman who might have been in the Resistance in this area."

"So why not do your checking in London? That's where the records will be."

"When I came out here I wasn't sure that he was anything to do with the Resistance. And I'm still not sure."

"What was his name?"

"I don't know. What sort of man was Chaland?"

Frenez held out his hands: "Brave, dedicated, tough, ruthless—a leader. And a hero—no doubt about that."

"What happened to him?"

"He led a raid on a Gestapo HQ and they were waiting for him. They shipped him off to Germany. He was executed in Natzweiler."

"What date was this?"

"He was captured the day de Gaulle marched into Paris."

"What did he look like?"

"Stocky, average height, dark hair, an ordinary sort of face."

"You knew him well?"

"Yes, my réseau came under his control."

"Did he have any enemies?"

The lawyer sighed quietly. "Everybody had enemies in those days. Germans. Frenchmen. But it's obvious that *someone* must have tipped off the Gestapo."

"Any idea who the traitor was?"

Frenez leaned forward. "I'd deny it if you repeated it, but I'd say it was Bonnier."

"He was in command of the maquis?"

"Yes. Another brave one, but a Commie, and always grinding their political axe. Waiting for the big take-over when the Germans left."

"*Did* he take over?"

Frenez stood up, a broad smile on his face. "No, there were others who also made plans for the future. Now I must get on with my work, M'sieur Bailey."

2

In England the remaining records of SOE occupied ten metal filing cabinets in a Nissen hut at the Intelligence Corps depot. All that remained of the records of the SOE operation in the Dordogne was twenty files bound together with pink tape.

Bailey had read halfway through the file marked "Parker" before he realized that Parker was Chaland. A bundle of Part I.I Orders recorded promotions from Lieutenant to Captain and then Major. And there were records of pay passed to an account at Coutts Bank. There were brown-edged signal forms with over a hundred signals from the OC of operation LANTERN. There was a recommendation for a DSO and the confirmation from the War Office dated September 1944. A letter from the French Ministry of Defence notified the award of a Croix de Guerre. Held together with a paperclip were two pieces of paper. The top one was a decoded signal from LANTERN reporting that Chaland had been arrested by the Gestapo in Périgueux and mentioning the possibility that he was either dead or in a German camp. The second paper was badly typed and said simply: "Charles du Puy Parker not traced during V.A.'s investigation. Assumed dead."

BAILEY PARKED the hired car just past the gate to the garden. It had taken him an hour from Hanover and twenty minutes to find the cottage just outside Hildesheim. The cottage was cosy looking, like an illustration from a children's book. Bailey walked through the small white gate to the front door. When there was no answer to his knock he walked slowly round to the back of the house.

A man was lying on a canvas-shaded settee, his hand reaching for a glass beside him on the lawn. At Bailey's cough he turned his head and the long legs swung to the ground.

"Herr Schmidt?"

Schmidt stood up, stretching lazily. "What is it you want?"

"I wanted some information about an Englishman who was in Natzweiler while you were Commandant."

The deep lines beside the leathery lips set in anger. "I've made all the statements to journalists that I'm going to make so get the hell out of here."

The big man came menacingly forward but Bailey stood his ground. When the man was two feet away he said. "I'm not a journalist. I'm a British official and I require some information about a British officer who may have been murdered in Natzweiler concentration camp."

Bubbles of saliva on his lips marked the man's anger. "Read the record of my trial. It's all there. You bastards jailed me for fifteen years. Now Germans don't kiss British arses any longer."

"Herr Schmidt, I had better explain. If I suspect you are not co-operating with me I shall apply to the War Crimes Commission for their assistance. I don't mind which way we do it."

Schmidt stood, hands on hips, head aggressively thrust forward. Then suddenly he relaxed, and pointing to a white chair he sat back on the swinging garden seat and reached for his drink.

"What was the man's name?"

"Chaland. Charles Chaland."

Schmidt's arm stopped with the glass halfway to his mouth. "But he wasn't English. He was French. And he wasn't executed."

"Tell me about him."

Schmidt stood up. "Come inside. We'll go in my study." The two men walked through the hall. Schmidt pushed open a door and pointed to a leather armchair and opened a metal filing cabinet. After a few minutes searching he brought out a tattered old-fashioned ledger. He sat down at the desk and slowly turned the pages, his fingers tracing down lists of names.

"Yes, here it is. He was brought to the camp on 9 September 1944. Arrested as an Allied agent in Périgueux, France, responsible for murder of unnamed German officers. To await disposal instructions from Berlin. On 3 November, hospitalized. No further entries. Is he the man you wanted to check on?"

"I think so. What was he treated for in hospital?"

Schmidt leaned back. "He'd been in Gestapo hands and he was in bad shape."

"What happened after he came out of hospital?"

"He didn't come out."

"You mean he died?"

"No." Schmidt looked towards the window where the sun shone through the pale green leaves of virginia creeper that clung to the glass. Then he looked back at Bailey. "You won't believe it but the really brutal people were the 'kapos'—the prisoners who were in charge of the other prisoners. And in most camps the 'kapos' were Commies. They ran the camp. They administered rations, discipline in the huts and medical supplies. It was the Commies who took over Chaland. They fixed the hospital treatment for him and he dropped out of sight. But I can tell you he was not executed."

There was a long silence as both men looked at each other. It now seemed to Bailey more than possible that the man who had cut his throat had been Chaland. He broke the silence: "What do you think happened to Chaland?" he said.

Schmidt shook his head. "The camp was in chaos long before the Americans got there. I would have thought Chaland would have been repatriated by the French."

"Were there many French Resistance people in Natzweiler?"

"Yes, several. And British."

"What happened to the British?"

"They were executed on Gestapo orders, and most of the French were too."

"Can you give me the names of those who were not executed?"

Schmidt turned the pages of the ledger. "Not executed—Scavron, Toulet, Bonnier and Gautier."

"Do you remember Bonnier?"

"Vaguely. He was one of the 'kapos'."

THE BROWN autumn leaves swirled along the pavements in front of the shops in the Champs Élysées, and although it was only six thirty the lights were on in shop windows and cafés. Then he saw her, picking her way through the tables towards him. She sat down breathlessly, loosened her scarf and pushed back her hair over her shoulders.

"So the wandering boy is back. I thought we had lost you."

"It took me longer than I expected. I'm glad you could come. What'll you have?"

"Just a coffee."

When the coffee had been brought, Bailey said: "How are things with you and the gallery?"

"I'm fine. The gallery just keeps its head above water."

"And how's lover boy?"

She smiled: "Andrei? He's O.K."

"Would you do me a favour?"

Her head tilted on one side. "A lot of troubles start with a question like that."

"No trouble. I promise."

Her smile faded slowly. "What are you, Nicholas?" she said softly. "You're not an insurance man are you?"

"In a kind of a way I am. It was a half-truth."

"The other half of a half-truth must be a half-lie."

"I'm afraid so."

She looked absent-mindedly round the restaurant and sighed.

He said, "You get letters and packages left at your gallery which you give to Siwecki. Yes?"

"Yes. Just paperbacks."

"They'll have coded messages in them, Monique. That's a standard KGB device."

"I don't believe it."

"You do, my love, though you'd rather not. Your gallery is a dead-letter box for the KGB in Paris."

"How do you know this?"

"The French Security people, the SDECE, know about it and told their opposite numbers in London. When the paperbacks come in future I want you to take them. You don't tell Siwecki they've come for twenty-four hours, then you just hand 'em over to him as you usually do."

"Why the delay?"

"So that SDECE can have a look at them first."

"But they'll be in my office at the gallery."

"That's O.K."

There were tears in her eyes. "It's a horrible world, isn't it?"

"Not really. Not if we don't ask too much of our friends."

"But Andrei must have known it could make trouble for me."

"He doesn't think for a moment that he's been spotted, I expect. The Russians live in a world of their own. And I'll make clear to SDECE that you had no idea what's been going on. They wouldn't want you to stop, it would make the Russians suspicious."

"And how do I treat Andrei?"

"The same as ever. If you like him, O.K. If not, downgrade him, or give him the chop altogether."

"When I was coming here tonight I was happy. I was looking forward to seeing you again. And afterwards there was Andrei. And now two people I liked aren't what they seemed."

His index finger stroked the back of her hand. "Nobody's what they seem, my love."

She looked at her watch. "I'll have to go, Nick. I'll phone you later tonight or early tomorrow."

THE MEETING with Bonnier had been arranged for four o'clock and Bailey stood in the reception area looking at the photographs of Soviet dignitaries. Then a large man stood half out of one of the office doors and waved him inside.

It would have been impossible to visualize Bonnier as a Resistance fighter were it not for a photograph on the wall showing him in a line of men facing de Gaulle, ready to receive one of the medals held on a cushion by an aide. Now his face was unhealthily red, the colour that overweight men get from high blood pressure. He breathed heavily as he sat with one big paw cradled in the other.

"Well, my friend, you wanted to speak to me." The piggy eyes held all the left-over residue from a hundred negotiations with powerful opponents.

"I wanted to ask you about a man who was in the Resistance with you. Charles Chaland. Could you tell me about him?"

Bonnier swivelled his chair so that he was sideways on to the desk. "He was a brave man. And a good leader."

"Was he a Communist?"

Bonnier swung round to look at Bailey. "No. He had no interest in politics at all. He was only interested in fighting the Boche."

"What happened to him?"

"He was caught by the Gestapo and they almost killed him. They sent him to a camp. I looked after him on the journey. So did Devereux. They shot Devereux a month after we got there."

"What had they done to Chaland?"

"His arms were broken and there were bones sticking out of his feet. I'd been arrested too but they didn't bother with the likes of me when they'd got him. I got the cold bath treatment but they were all working on Chaland. I saw him later when we were put on the railway wagons for Germany. After we got there he was a sick man but we got him some medical treatment."

"What happened to him?"

Bonnier carefully moved a pile of papers to make room for his arm on the desk. "I don't know, the camp was in turmoil in the last few weeks. It was every man for himself."

"Do you know M'sieur Frenez?"

"I knew him, but not well. He was part of Chaland's SOE units."

"He told me that somebody tipped off the Germans. Have you any idea who that could have been?"

"Could have been anybody. The Germans paid informants well."

"But you've no idea of who it could be?"

Bonnier slowly stood up, wheezing as he did so. "God knows. Have a look at Frenez himself."

"If I needed to talk again would you be willing?"

Bonnier spread his arms, shrugging. "Of course. Just telephone."

THE VIEW from the train was of autumn. In a few days summer had suddenly ended and the leaves had turned from their dusty summer greens to the colours of sunsets and hot metal. Bailey wondered whether his journey to Périgueux was really necessary. He had telephoned Madame Chaland and she had reluctantly agreed to see him.

When he finally stood outside the blue-painted door it was Madame Chaland herself who opened it and her mien was not unfriendly. She walked with him to a small study at the side of the house and waved him to one of the chairs.

"I've spoken with Monsieur Frenez and Monsieur Bonnier, and I wondered if you could help me on something?"

"I'll try."

"Frenez told me that somebody had tipped off the Germans to your husband. He suggested in confidence that it might have been Bonnier who was the traitor."

She looked at him in silence for long moments and then said, "There were dozens of people who could have felt that to get rid of my husband would be advantageous."

"But he wasn't political."

"Agreed. But he was a man of immense influence in this area. If he had lived people would have taken great notice of what he said. He was seen as a brave and honest man. If you go down to Périgueux you will find a small square named after him—Place Chaland. People still put flowers around the little fountain."

"How did you meet him, Madame?"

She smiled. "I was the courier between Bonnier and my husband and eventually I stayed with him. But it was for a very short time. He was captured very soon after we were married."

"Your husband never spoke of a possible traitor?"

"It's hard to explain now, but his life was too occupied to think of such things. Action was what he set store by. Could his men do what he planned? That was the only thing. But he would have been a very gentle man in peacetime. He would have been a good husband, and a good father."

He looked at her. "I'm sorry I have to talk about these things."

"It is all a long time ago. In a way I like to talk about him. I live here with Chantal but part of me belongs in that cottage at Puy Henry." She shrugged. "Of course if you really wanted to find out about my husband's capture it would be easy enough. The police in Limoges still have the Gestapo records. In the week that Charles was captured the SOE in this area made a concerted attack on the German counter-intelligence groups. Their records were taken in Limoges and Angoulême."

Bailey looked at the pretty woman who had been part of all this history and he found it hard to imagine her as a Resistance worker. She turned to look at him.

"What are you really trying to find out, M'sieur Bailey?"

A variety of lies leapt into his mind but he couldn't bring himself to use them. She deserved better than that.

"I can't tell you, Madame. It sounds silly but I don't really know what I'm looking for. I'm trying to trace the background of a man. When I've done my checking I'll be happy to explain."

She nodded and stood up. "Chantal and I will be taking lunch in half an hour. Would you like to join us?"

"I should really like that, Madame."

IN LIMOGES Bailey parked the hired car near to the Préfecture. Despite his credentials the police had checked with Paris before they would co-operate. And even then they had left an inspector with him as he sat in a small office looking at the Gestapo records for 1944. It took him an hour to find it. There was a pencilled number in the top right-hand corner and he asked the inspector if it had any significance. He leaned forward to look, and then said, "Yes, it means that the document has been microfilmed for SDECE and Deuxième Bureau records in Paris."

The paper was typed:

Abwehr Aussenstelle, Limoges
7 August 1944

The information concerning CHALAND, CHARLES (See file 3491) received yesterday 6 August from BONNIER, MICHEL has been evaluated as follows:

It is now considered that motive of informant is internal conflicts of Resistance groups in this area. Informant is longtime member of Communist Party and information is that all Communist-influenced Resistance groups have been instructed to establish with local population that they are sole active Resistance to German troops.

We now suspect that rivalry between CHALAND and BONNIER is sufficiently intense to cause BONNIER to seek elimination of CHALAND.

The information was passed to Milice sergeant at Brantôme by informant personally. Informant and Milice sergeant at same school.

Action will be taken by Gestapo against CHALAND but surveillance will be organized by Abwehr and SD.

Signed Otto Paulsen (Hptn)

HE HAD phoned Bonnier's office three times. He could imagine no reason why Parker should have deserted the woman he loved and her unborn child. And why had he lived that strange, solitary life when he could have been with his family? He was sure that the answer lay with Bonnier.

Bonnier was out until early evening. At six thirty he was put through. "M'sieur Bonnier, this is Nicholas Bailey. I spoke with you a few days ago about Charles Chaland. Could I see you again?"

"I'm sorry, my friend. I cannot help you any further."

There was a pause and Bailey said slowly. "I've seen the Gestapo records at Limoges."

"For Christ's sake. . . ." Bonnier stopped and there was a long silence. Then, "Where are you, Bailey?"

"Hotel Normandie, Rue des Capucines."

"I'll come round and see you in an hour."

BONNIER SEEMED huge in the small bedroom and he walked in as if he owned the place. He threw his wet raincoat across Bailey's suitcase and turned to the porter. "Bring some whisky. Scotch. A bottle." And as the man closed the door Bonnier sat on the bed glaring at Bailey.

"Right, say what you've got to say."

"I checked the Gestapo records at Limoges for 1944."

"And?"

"And I saw the report that you had tipped them off about Chaland."

"That doesn't mean a thing, comrade. Could have been planted by the Germans."

"I don't think that photocopies for SDECE would have been sent if the authorities had any doubts."

"Those bastards would do anything to embarrass the Party." Bonnier's big hands were gripping the bedclothes as if he would tear the room to pieces. "What is it you want?"

"The truth about Chaland."

"I've told you all I know."

Bailey shook his head: "Not by a long way, Bonnier. I want the whole story."

The big man turned as a waiter came in with the whisky and glasses, and then he waited until the barman had left. "I hear you've been in Périgueux sniffing around his family. Those two aren't going to like what comes out of this inquiry."

"Just tell me what happened. I already know part of the story."

Bonnier reached forward and poured himself a whisky. He looked over his glass at Bailey as he sipped. "Don't bluff me, Bailey. I've been calling bluffs all my life. You tell me your bit and if you're right I'll tell you the rest."

"I'll tell you part. Enough for you to know that I'm not bluffing. Your little friend Siwecki has been using an art gallery on the Left Bank as a dead-letter drop. And he makes contact with an Englishman there. But he hasn't seen the Englishman for nearly seven months now."

Bonnier had listened intently with his big head on one side like a blackbird listening for worms in a lawn. When Bailey stopped talking Bonnier said quietly: "O.K. Let's talk."

He moved over to one of the armchairs and Bailey sat opposite. Bonnier leaned his head back against the top of the chair and closed his eyes. His massive chest rose and fell with his breathing and Bailey waited in silence. Finally Bonnier started talking.

"Chaland and I were caught on the same night. We killed a lot of Germans before they got us. Chaland was taken at the Gestapo house on the other side of the river. They had been after him for months and they knew who he was as soon as they got him. The Allies were driving across France and the Germans were desperate to keep the Resistance off the backs of their troops. So they were in a hurry to round up everyone in Chaland's group.

"We heard Chaland screaming all through the night and the next day. Devereux and I were given the cold bath treatment but their hearts weren't in it. We didn't know much and they knew it. Chaland was the one. The screams stopped in the middle of the second night and we knew he was either dead or unconscious and they couldn't revive him.

"After a couple of days we were all rounded up and taken on trucks to the railway station to be shipped to Germany. Chaland was on a stretcher, and the rest of us had shackles on our feet and handcuffs. And a chain round our necks attached to the handcuffs and the shackles. Chaland was in a coma all the time. He looked dead already.

"We were in the wagons for two nights and three days. On the second night Chaland was delirious. Talking in English to an imaginary guy he called Fredericks, telling him that the Germans had found out he was married to Sabine and that she was pregnant. And they'd threatened to bring her in and rape her in front of him, and then they'd cut her open. So he told them what they wanted to know, names and code-names, addresses, arms caches, everything. And he was begging Fredericks to warn his people.

"He was still alive when we got to the camp at Natzweiler. It was a miracle. The party members fixed for me to become a 'kapo' and as soon as I could I got Chaland transferred to the hospital. By spring it was nearly over. The Americans and the British were across the Rhine and the Party was sending orders to our people at the camp to get Chaland out.

"By then he was on his feet for a few hours every day and I got him out of the camp to a Party member's house. I stayed with him until the surrender and somebody came from the Party HQ at Dresden and took over. When he was fit they told him they knew what he had done and he tried to kill himself. They told him he would be exposed if he didn't work for the Party.

"They sent me to talk to him a few weeks after that. It was like talking to a ghost. He looked an old man. I told him he was the local hero in Périgueux and that his wife was being well looked after and that if he went back we would make public what had happened. At least forty people were killed by the Germans because he talked.

"In the end he was sent back to England by the Russians. They fixed false documents and the money to set up a small business. I was out of the picture by then. They used him as a courier."

The room seemed dark and cold to Bailey as he sat there. The details were too terrible to contemplate.

He looked over at Bonnier. "Not a nice story, Bonnier."

"They were not nice times, comrade."

"They still aren't."

Bonnier sat in silence looking across at Bailey. Waiting for him to react.

Bailey said at last: "Does anyone else know Chaland's background? Does Siwecki know?"

"Siwecki's just a messenger boy. It was all a long time ago, my friend, though it may still be on some dusty KGB file in Moscow."

"D'you regret any of this, Bonnier?"

The big man shifted in the chair, shrugging. "He talked, comrade, he was a traitor. Forty people died so that a woman could stay alive and have a child."

Bailey looked at him: "So we both keep our little secrets. Is that how it should be?"

Bonnier stood up, smiling: "A good British compromise. That's what your people say, isn't it?"

He reached for his raincoat and walked to the door. But as he left Bailey realized that it wasn't all over yet.

SIWECKI WAS SITTING with Monique in the gallery as Bailey walked in. The girl seemed pleased to see him, and he leaned back against the wall between two big paintings, sipping white wine with them.

"What's happened to Walters, Andrei?"

Siwecki's head came up fast, his mouth open. "Walters? Who the devil is Walters?"

"The Englishman. The KGB courier from London."

Siwecki glanced quickly at the girl. "I'll see you later, Monique. I'll call you."

Bailey's foot came down on Siwecki's. "Don't go, Andrei. Just answer one question."

Siwecki hesitated. "What is it?"

"All I want to know is how many times a year did he come to France?"

"Every month."

"Did he ever go elsewhere in France other than Paris?"

"Sometimes. I had him followed once and he drove down to a small place called Brantôme. He parked the car opposite a house. Two women came out and walked to a restaurant but he didn't follow. He drove back to Paris."

"Any idea why he did this?"

"No idea at all. Seemed crazy to me."

Bailey looked at the girl's shocked face. "Don't worry, Monique, there's no problem."

And he turned and left the gallery without looking back.

BONNIER'S OFFICE had said that he was not there. At his home number there was no reply. And Bailey knew by instinct where Bonnier would be.

Bailey paid his plane fare in dollars to get quick service. An hour and a half later the plane put down at Bordeaux and Bailey booked a hire car at the airport. An hour and a half later he was on the bridge at Brantôme. He parked the car fifty yards from the house and walked to the big iron gate. There was one light on in the house. He was breathing heavily as he pressed the bell.

The girl answered the door and he said, "Where's your mother, Chantal?"

"She went to the cottage about five minutes ago."

"Why?"

"There was a phone call. She didn't say who it was but she seemed upset. I said I would go with her but she begged me not to interfere. I'm so frightened. What's going on?"

"Get your coat quickly. We must get up there at once."

At the crest of the hill he saw two cars. One was Madame Chaland's Fiat. He pulled his car into the side. As he got out he said: "Stay here, Chantal. I'll be back soon."

He ran up the path and to the side of the cottage. He could hear the woman's sobs over Bonnier's angry voice.

". . . And I promise you, Madame, that if he talks I shall talk too and your life in Brantôme will be finished. . . ."

Bailey shoved open the door of the cottage. Bonnier was standing at the end of the table, his face red with anger. As he saw Bailey his anger was diverted and he walked round the table to stand, hands on hips, and his head thrust forward aggressively.

"What do you want, sonny boy?"

"I want you to leave, Bonnier. Now."

The blood-shot eyes glared and Bailey saw the big right fist swinging for his face. He caught it with both hands as Bonnier's left fist took him in the ribs. He swung Bonnier round and put his shoulder to his massive chest. The impact sent the sixteen-stone man back against the wall, but his free arm came round and his strong fingers scrabbled to find the pressure point behind Bailey's ear. But Bonnier was too old, too out of condition. Bailey released Bonnier's right hand and reaching for his throat sent Bonnier back against the wall. There was a sickening noise like a coconut cracking and Bonnier's large body collapsed and slid down the wall, his feet tangling in a chair as he fell.

Bailey's fingers searched the big hairy wrist for a pulse but there was none. Bonnier was dead. Bailey turned to look at the woman, her face distraught. He leaned against the table to recover his breath. When he could speak he said, "I want you to go to your car, Madame. Just down the hill is my car. Chantal is there, and I want you to take her back to your house. Tell her nothing at all about what has happened here. Anything Bonnier told you was lies to protect himself from me."

The woman's face looked grey and old, and her hands trembled. But she slowly recovered, and walked slowly to the door. A little later he heard her car start.

It took him half an hour to get Bonnier to his car and twenty minutes to get him in place on the right-hand front seat. Bailey had seen some hose looped across two pegs on the kitchen wall and he carried it to the back seat.

He had done fifteen kilometres before he turned up a lane on the left-hand side of the road. He drove the car slowly into the ditch, so that it leaned almost at its point of balance. Bonnier's body slid like a huge carnival figure behind the wheel and when Bailey had stuffed the hose up the exhaust pipe, twisting it to drive it right home, he trailed the hose to the front of the car. He leaned over and started the engine. He pushed the hose in through the window, and closed the glass on it.

AT BRIVE-LA-GAILLARDE, Bailey found a telephone kiosk and dialled the Brantôme number. Madame Chaland answered and he described where he was and asked her to pick him up. She sounded back in control of herself and she said she could be there in half an hour.

Bailey sat in the shelter of a hedge while he waited. He tried to recall every word that he had said to Walters. He remembered the comparatively mild pressure that he had applied by asking the purpose of the visit to France. The man must have decided in a few seconds to kill himself to prevent an exposure that he felt could have destroyed the security of his wife and child. He had shown every kind of courage there was until his wife was threatened. And because of that single hostage to fate the hero became a traitor. The choice would have driven the bravest man to the edge of treachery, and, beaten to a pulp, his resistance must have been minimal.

He saw the car lights approaching slowly and he stepped out into the road. As he slid into the seat he said. "Turn here, don't go into Brive."

He waited as she criss-crossed the road and then said: "How is Chantal?"

"I think she is confused and a little worried, but I have told her absolutely nothing."

"I want to ask you to forget everything that happened tonight. You never saw Bonnier."

"He may have told others that he was seeing me."

"No, he won't have. He had good reason not to. I know something from his past which scared him."

"Was it true what he said about Charles, that he was a traitor?"

"You must know that it wasn't true. He must have risked his life dozens of times for the sake of other people."

"Bonnier said it was to save me."

"I told you. Bonnier was scared. Frightened men can be desperate. It was a crude attempt at blackmail."

"Where is he now?"

"He's dead, and I want you to forget tonight."

He was silent till they entered Brantôme. Then he said: "Will you take me up to Puy Henry? My hire car is still up there. I must stay here for a few days to see what happens about Bonnier. If it all dies down I shall go back to London. If there are problems I shall stay on and deal with them. I don't want you or Chantal to be involved in any way. Can I stay up there to sleep?"

"Yes, of course."

She stopped at his car and he drove it on up the hill.

IN THE EVENING paper there was a brief report.

PROMINENT COMMUNIST FOUND DEAD

Périgueux: Early this morning the body was found of Michel Bonnier, a member of the Communist Party's main committee. It was discovered by farmer Georges Yves Bilbaud, in a car on a minor road off the Brive–Périgueux road.

Inspecteur Tassy at police HQ in Périgueux stated that the authorities are investigating all possibilities, including murder. Michel Bonnier was a leader of the maquisards in the area during the war and it is being suggested that there may be political aspects to this crime.

Maître Frenez of Limoges who knew Bonnier well during Resistance days told our reporter:

"Michel Bonnier was a fine leader of men, and his record in the wartime Resistance was second to none. Although I did not share his political ideology I respected the man."

Agence France—Presse

THERE HAD BEEN nothing to connect Bonnier's death with any particular person in the area and over the next seven days the news items were briefer and indicated that a verdict would be brought in at the inquest of murder by persons unknown. Bailey's SDECE contact told him the autopsy had indicated that Bonnier had not died from carbon-monoxide poisoning as was first suspected but from cerebral lesions from a blow to the head. There were a hundred theories but no suspects, and neither SDECE nor the police were in mourning.

TO: DEPUTY ASSISTANT COMMISSIONER MURPHY—SPECIAL BRANCH
From: Chief Superintendent Bailey, N.
Subject: *Walters, J. F.—Security Suspect*

Following the request from FO liaison I have investigated the background of the above.

Despite intensive investigations in the UK and overseas I have been unable to establish the true identity of the subject, or find any connection with any foreign intelligence service beyond the original information (See P File/49731).

Ted Allbeury

Brought up in Birmingham, Ted Allbeury left school when he was fourteen and went to work in a local iron foundry. By the time World War II broke out he had progressed to the firm's drawing office. Although as a jig-and-tool draughtsman he was technically in a Reserved Occupation, he joined the army at once. He desperately wanted to play the most active role he possibly could in a war that he passionately believed to be just and necessary.

Helped by his facility for languages—he had taught himself French and German in the evenings after work—he was accepted into the Intelligence Corps. By the end of the war he was a lieutenant-colonel, working in counter-intelligence.

After the war he worked in advertising, public relations, and as a highly successful farmer. For a time he even ran a pirate commercial radio station on a fort in the Thames estuary.

He was fifty-four years of age before, on the brink of a nervous breakdown, the result of a profound personal tragedy, he turned to writing as a form of self-healing. He wrote of what he knew, drawing on his experience as a young man in the world of spies and counter-spies. He completed three or four chapters, then felt he had run out of steam and put the work on one side. It was his business partner at that time who saw those chapters, and asked his permission to take them away and show them to a London publisher. . . .

The rest, as the saying goes, is history. That first book, *A Choice of Enemies,* once finished, was chosen by the *New York Times* as one of the ten best espionage stories of 1973. And since then Ted Allbeury has gone on from strength to strength. His books sell right round the world, translated into innumerable languages.

And yet, for all his books' success, Ted Allbeury remains an active partner in his own public relations firm, writing only in his spare time. He still doesn't believe it, he says. His fame might all quite easily turn out to be some horrible mistake. And even if we don't take these words wholly seriously, it's clear enough that he's a man of boundless energy and enthusiasm. And, as long as his readers can look forward to many more "spare time" books from Ted Allbeury, who's complaining?

THE GOLD OF TROY. Picture credits: Pages 182/183: National Gallery, London. Page 184: Staatsbibliothek Berlin. Page 235: Top: Photo: Sipahioglu, Instanbul. Bottom right: Interfoto-Archiv, Munich. Page 236: Museum of Archaeology, Instanbul; photos: Sipahioglu-Ozkan Sahin. Page 237: Top left, top right, bottom: Museum of Archaeology, Instanbul; photos Sipahioglu-Ozkan Sahin. Page 251: Top: Robert Descharnes, Paris. Centre: Photo Deutsches Archäologisches Institut, Athens. Bottom: Plan of the Acropolis of Mycenae by Schliemann; photo: Douglas R. G. Sellick, London. Page 252: Top left, bottom left and right: National Archaeological Museum, Athens; photos: Harissiadis. Top right: National Archaeological Museum; photo: Hirmer, Munich. Page 253: Top left: National Archaeological Museum; photo: Emile. Top right and centre: National Archaeological Museum. Bottom right: National Archaeological Museum, Athens; photo: Harissiadis. Bottom left: National Archaeological Museum; photo: Hirmer, Munich.

Photograph of Robert Payne on p. 267 by Jerry Bauer.

Photograph of Ted Allbeury on p. 511 by Granville Davies.

THE LANTERN NETWORK. Title page photograph by Michael St. Maur Shiel.

PP97